PENGUIN CLASSICS

EVELINA

FRANCES BURNEY (1752–1840), the daughter of Dr Burney, spent her youth in the midst of the London society which included Dr Johnson, Edmund Burke, Sir Joshua Reynolds, David Garrick, the Blue Stocking Circle and many members of the aristocracy. When she published her first novel, *Evelina*, anonymously in 1778, the revelation of its authorship brought her immediate fame. In 1786 she was appointed second keeper of the robes to Queen Charlotte and in 1793 married General d'Arblay, a French refugee in England. She and her husband were interned by Napoleon and lived in France from 1802 to 1812. Her other major novels are *Cecilia* (1782) and *Camilla* (1796). Like *Evelina*, they take as their theme the entry into the world of a young girl of beauty and understanding but no experience, and expose her to circumstances and events that develop her character. Her novels were admired by Jane Austen. She also wrote *The Wanderer*, published in 1814, but it was not a success. In 1832 she edited the *Memoirs* of her father. She was also a prodigious writer of lively letters and journals; her *Early Diary 1768–1778* includes sketches of Johnson, Garrick and many others, and her later *Diary and Letters 1778–1840* gives a vivid account of her life at court.

MARGARET ANNE DOODY is John and Barbara Glynn Family Professor of Literature at the University of Notre Dame, where she is currently Director of the Ph.D. Program in Literature. She is the author of many critical works, including *Frances Burney: The Life in the Works* (1998) and *The True Story of the Novel* (1996), as well as of several novels, most recently *Aristotle and the Secrets of Life* (2003).

FRANCES BURNEY

Evelina

Edited with an Introduction and Notes by
MARGARET ANNE DOODY

PENGUIN BOOKS

PENGUIN BOOKS

Published by the Penguin Group
Penguin Books Ltd, 80 Strand, London WC2R ORL, England
Penguin Group (USA) Inc. 375 Hudson Street, New York, New York 10014, USA
Penguin Books Australia Ltd, 250 Camberwell Road, Camberwell, Victoria 3124, Australia
Penguin Books Canada Ltd, 10 Alcorn Avenue, Toronto, Ontario, Canada M4V 3B2
Penguin Books India (P) Ltd, 11 Community Centre, Panchsheel Park, New Delhi – 110 017, India
Penguin Books (NZ) Ltd, Cnr Rosedale and Airborne Roads, Albany, Auckland, New Zealand
Penguin Books (South Africa) (Pty) Ltd, 24 Sturdee Avenue, Rosebank 2196, South Africa

Penguin Books Ltd, Registered Offices: 80 Strand, London WC2R ORL, England

www.penguin.com

Published in Penguin Classics 1994
Reprinted with new Chronology and revised Further Reading 2004

17

Introduction, Chronology and notes copyright © Margaret Anne Doody, 1990, 2004
All rights reserved

Set in Garamond Monotype
Typeset by Datix International Ltd, Bungay, Suffolk
Printed in England by Clays Ltd, St Ives plc

ISBN-13: 978-0-14-043347-0

www.greenpenguin.co.uk

Penguin Books is committed to a sustainable future
for our business, our readers and our planet.
The book in your hands is made from paper
certified by the Forest Stewardship Council.

CONTENTS

INTRODUCTION

Evelina is actually a sequel. Behind it lies another novel, a vanished work. On or around her fifteenth birthday in June 1767, Frances Burney made a bonfire of all of her writings, including a complete work of prose fiction, 'The History of Caroline Evelyn'. Burney has left us two accounts of this strange conflagration, one written in the dedicatory preface 'To Doctor Burney' of her last novel *The Wanderer* (1814), another in the account of herself in the biography of her father, *The Memoirs of Doctor Burney* (1832). In both of these accounts, one written when she was nearly sixty-two, the other when she was almost eighty, she shows what a vivid impression this incident made upon her. In both, she asserts that she burned her writings in a laudable attempt to conquer her tendency to scribble fiction, her 'writing passion':

From the time, however, that she attained her fifteenth year, she considered it her duty to combat this writing passion as illaudable, because fruitless. Seizing, therefore, an opportunity . . . she made over to a bonfire, in a paved play-court, her whole stock of prose goods and chattels; with the sincere intention to extinguish for ever in their ashes her scribbling propensity . . . This grand feat . . . which consumed her productions, extirpated neither the invention nor the inclination that had given them birth; and, in defiance of all the projected heroism of the sacrifice, the last of the little works that was immolated, which was the History of Caroline Evelyn, the Mother of Evelina, left, upon the mind of the writer, so animated an impression of the singular situations to which that Caroline's infant daughter,—from the unequal birth by which she hung suspended between the elegant connexions of her mother, and the vulgar ones of her grandmother,—might be exposed; and presented contrasts and mixtures of society so unusual, yet, thus circumstanced, so natural, that irresistibly and almost unconsciously, the whole of *A Young Lady's Entrance into the World*, was pent up in the inventor's memory, ere a paragraph was committed to paper. (*Memoirs*, II, pp. 125–6)

The older Frances Burney, in her accounts of the matter, dramatizes the girl's response to the suppression of female writing. Writing by women is viewed as at best mere 'scribbling', some unhealthy taint is seen to cling to it, as to other solitary self-gratifications – 'I struggled against the propensity .. and on my fifteenth birth-day I made so resolute a conquest over an inclination at which I blushed' ('To Doctor Burney', *The Wanderer*, p. 8). Burney's account also tells the reader that the view of female writing as something shameful, something to be conquered, as the girl grows into maturity, is a wrong view. The writer subtly endorses the idea of her own – and other women writers' – creativity. For by 1814 (or by 1832) the world had long known *Evelina*, and the popularity of the work was beyond dispute.

Burney thus shows herself as vindicated, and presents her writings as a 'passion' of her nature, something ineluctable, not 'illaudable, because fruitless' but fruitful. She is an inventor, she has the force of genius, which is a force of nature. One novel was destroyed – a sacrifice known only to Frances's sister Susanna, who 'witnessed the conflagration; and—well I remember!—wept, with tender partiality, over the imaginary ashes of Caroline Evelyn, the mother of Evelina' ('To Doctor Burney', *The Wanderer*, p. 8). The mother was offered up, a victim on the altar of female respectability, just as the character Caroline Evelyn, seduced and abandoned, had died. Yet the daughter born of her mother's fall and death became the daughter-novel and succeeded where the mother-novel had failed to live.

The story of the writing of *Evelina* is (for Burney makes it so) an allegory of women's writing, and a story about female persistence. The mind of the 'inventor' imagined the whole story of *Evelina*, 'ere a paragraph was committed to paper'. Or, as Burney says in the preface to *The Wanderer*, 'The passion, however, though resisted, was not annihilated: my bureau was cleared; but my head was not emptied; and, in defiance of every self-effort, Evelina struggled herself into life' (p. 8). This is a slightly more painful account; the passion for writing is treated as something dutifully resisted, but overwhelmingly powerful, like the sexual instinct, and the Evelina who 'struggled herself into life' is an entity including both novel and character, a living being like a foetus to which the novelist is impelled to give birth. Frances Burney certainly wished to emphasize her own compulsion to write, and to make a plea for the passion for writing as a justifiable passion in a woman. All of her accounts of or references to the writing of *Evelina* treat the process as a heroic struggle, as an enabling act of both personal and general importance.

There were many real and prosaic obstacles in the way of writing the novel. Burney might imagine the plot and characters in her head while doing other things, but the space and leisure for actual writing were difficult to obtain. As Burney puts it, 'Writing, indeed, was far more difficult to her than composing; for that demanded what she rarely found attainable—secret opportunity. . .' (*Memoirs*, II, p. 126). It is perhaps hard for us to imagine the steady pressure of the need for *secrecy*. Frances Burney knew not only that scribbling on the part of a woman with any pretensions to being called a 'young lady' was reprehensible, but that her case was also complicated by the advent of a hated stepmother who could act as a powerful forbidder. The bonfire of Frances's fifteenth birthday coincides with the period of the courtship of Doctor Charles Burney and the widowed Mrs. Allen, a friend from a former time spent in King's Lynn, Norfolk, where Frances had been born. The couple married in October 1767. Mrs. Allen was in love with Charles Burney, but not with his children, and his children by his first marriage were not fond of her. They regarded her as capricious, bossy and ill-tempered, while the second Mrs. Burney could complain with some truth that the children caballed against her. Hester Burney, Frances's elder sister, married her cousin, the musician Charles Rousseau Burney, in September 1770, evidently largely in order to escape from the changed home, so Frances lost (in part) the sister who had been another mother to her. The Burney children left at home carried on an intermittent secret war against the unwanted stepmother, mimicking her and referring to her by various satirical code names: 'Mrs. Precious', 'the Lady'. Talking against her (which they often did) was referred to as 'talking treason'. There was enough 'treason' to make Mrs. Burney uncomfortable. Some other accounts of the family by outsiders tend to endorse the Burney children's opinions of Elizabeth Allen Burney's erratic manners and bad temper, but it is hard not to feel a little pity for 'the Lady'. We may feel especially sorry for her when we realize that she is represented and caricatured in that unwanted maternal (grand) parent, Madame Duval.

Yet, just as Madame Duval could lay a claim to Evelina which the girl is not allowed to shrug off, so too Mrs. Burney could utter commands and injunctions which her stepdaughters could not readily disobey. Hence the intensified need for cunning and secrecy. Looking at the family papers from this period, one sometimes has the impression that the Burney family members hardly took their tea without a stratagem. A letter from Frances Burney to her sister Hester, dated October 1777, illustrates the amount of political effort and family manoeuvring that went into simple events:

Sister Charles Burney,
  Please to send me an Invitation to spend the Day with you to-morrow. When I come, I will give you sufficient Reason to rejoice & make glad.
  The excuse to be *fudged* up for this purpose, I leave to your own ingenuity.
  Write a Note that I may make public.
  Provide a very genteel Dinner, but don't get more than 2 Courses & a Dessert, as I hate a fuss. — Specify in your Note that I must not get away early.—If you fail, you will be ready to break your Heart when you know more.
                                        Yrs. F. B.

  (*Early Journals and Letters*, ed. L. E. Troide (Oxford, 1990), II, p. 287.)

In order to go and see her sister, Frances has to have a written invitation, and something that will pass muster with the step-mother, something that can be made 'public'. The Burney children are busy 'fudging' things up, covering matters up by secret conclave and arrangements of their self-representations. To say as much is not to accuse Frances and Hester of immoral conduct, simply to recognize their reaction to a situation. The lives of women depend upon the strategies of gaining *permission*. Frances Burney, although twenty-five years old, is not able to voice a determination to visit her sister; she and the married sister must contrive an occasion. The inevitable chicane of such contrivances is in some contrast to the buoyant tone of this note, with its joke about the dinner ('2 Courses & a Dessert' would have made a rather fine dinner for people living as modestly as Charles and Hester Burney). Burney teases her sister joyfully with the promise (hyperbolically expressed) of important and joyful news – we may speculate that the news thus alluded to has to do with the prospect of publishing *Evelina*. She had been carrying on negotiations for the publication of her novel since the previous year. Her brother Charles, disguised to look both grown-up and vulgar in 'an old great coat, and a large old hat' (*Memoirs*, II, pp. 128–9), had taken two manuscript volumes to the bookseller Thomas Lowndes. In December 1776, Lowndes provisionally accepted the book, but wanted to see all three volumes, and in 1777 Frances had made great progress in completing the last volume and (presumably) revising the rest. The book was to be published in January 1778.

Publication was anonymous. The title page was not even to say 'By a Lady'. Burney steadfastly resists any form of identification. She went to great trouble in copying out her manuscript to disguise her own handwriting. As she herself explains, 'She now copied the manuscript in a feigned hand; for as she was the Doctor's principal amanuensis, she feared her common writing might accidentally be seen by some compositor of the History of Music, and lead to detection' (*Memoirs*, II, pp. 126–7). This remark reminds us that Burney was not really a genteel unemployed young lady during the years of writing *Evelina*. She had found a way to become close to her father (and to escape her stepmother) by becoming her father's active assistant in his writing projects. Doctor Burney had gone on tours of the Continent in undertaking researches for a history of music, and had published two important literary works as preliminaries: *The Present State of Music in France and Italy* (1771) and *The Present State of Music in Germany* (1773). The first volume of the great and extensive *A General History of Music* had appeared in 1776. Frances Burney was closely involved in day-to-day work on these projects, apparently collecting material and collating notes as well as acting as amanuensis, or copyist. Her labour and commitment are taken for granted by Charles Burney's own biographers; those interested in Frances should realize that she had something like the equivalent of a full-time job. This kind of work gave her a valued place in her father's eyes, and served as a justifying occupation, which also conveniently made it less likely that her family would think of marrying her off. The desire to see *Evelina* in print may have been stimulated by so much publication on her father's part. Although she was putting in many hours of work on her father's projects, the occupation provided her with a retreat in Charles Burney's study, and we may presume that she had some moments of leisure to steal for writing down parts of *Evelina* during intervals spent in the study while the Doctor was out giving music lessons. But most of her time in that study was devoted to the Doctor's projects, and Frances thought that her own handwriting was by now so well known and identifiable in various printing houses as to put her in danger of discovery. We find it hard to imagine copying out a full-length work by hand – how much harder to imagine copying out a work in a hand *artificially* assumed for the occasion. That Frances did so in copying *Evelina* is a sure sign that she truly desired to publish in secret. Some of the manuscript in this assumed hand remains to us. In the Pierpont Morgan Library, New York City, there is a sheet of *Evelina* manuscript labelled (later) by the author 'Specimen of the Feign'd hand in which Evelina was written for disguise to Mr. Lownds [*sic*]'. This 'specimen' is a fragment of the account of the visit to Cox's

Museum (see p. 85). It differs slightly from the printed version, permitting us to see Burney at work, revising even in the late stages of preparing the manuscript. Presumably this sheet got thrown out of the packet sent to Lowndes because in making some of her revisions, and writing over deletions, Burney had begun to write in what was too much like her ordinary hand. The 'Feign'd hand' is clear, spiky, much more up-and-down than Frances Burney's ordinary cursive style. The effect striven for is more authoritative, more 'masculine' perhaps, less rounded and flowing.

Enough of the manuscript of *Evelina* remains for us to form some idea of the processes of its writing. As well as the fragment in the 'Feign'd hand' we have a bundle of less finished papers amongst the manuscripts in the Berg Library. These are evidently not yet ready for the printer's eye, the writing huddled together on the paper in an economical way, new paragraphs indicated only by the letter X in order to save space. In these earlier manuscript versions, Burney's writing is fast and fluent, although she makes numerous corrections. In the section in which Mrs. Selwyn and Evelina encounter the three rude gentlemen by the banks of the Avon, for instance (see p. 303), Mrs. Selwyn first says, 'I sh^d be sorry to give my servants the trouble of teaching you how to Walk.' The laughing gentleman 'wished they wd. begin their Lesson, that he might have the pleasure of rolling them into the Avon'. Burney then changes Mrs. Selwyn's 'servants' to the singular, and the gentleman wishes 'the Man would begin his Lesson'. Evidently Burney saw the awkwardness of the threat against multiple servants. In a later revision, which must have taken place between the time this manuscript was written and actual publication, Mrs. Selwyn is made to sound less harsh and vulgar. Her servant is no longer to be given the trouble of teaching the gentleman 'how to Walk' but is merely to teach him 'better Manners'. A number of the corrections are designed to elevate the characters' language slightly, removing some colloquialisms. In the Berg manuscript, Lady Louisa makes her first full entrance into the book thus:

Mean time the young lady, hobbling, rather than walking, into the Room; passed Mrs. Beaumont, saying, 'How do do?' & with an air of languour, flung herself on a Sofa, protesting, in a most affected voice, & speaking so low, she cd. not be heard, that she was fatigued to Death.

On this manuscript page Burney alters this sentence; it is of course absurd to say Lady Louisa could not be heard, as her sentence is recorded, and Burney (immediately, as I believe) changes the 'not' to a 'hardly'. More interesting is the excision of the rude (and low) 'How do do?' which is altered on the page to 'How are you, Ma'am?' Lady Louisa is thus given somewhat more passable manners. Between the manuscript page that we have and the copy the printer cast off, another set of changes has taken place (see pp. 309–10). Lady Louisa's youth is given more emphasis (her youth acting as a partial excuse for her behaviour) and she is made still less rude: we are now told that she 'made a passing courtsie to Mrs. Beaumont', which is what she should do, instead of merely passing the lady who is her senior and her hostess in the manner earlier recorded.

Part of the subject of *Evelina* is obviously 'manners' in the very extensive meanings of that word, from minute points of etiquette to the codes or mores that govern entire groups. There is an interesting cancelled introduction to the novel in the Berg manuscript. On one side of the page we have a flat statement:

The plan of the following Letters is to display the Manners of the Times. The characters are attempted from *Nature*, tho' not from *Life*;—however rough the Sketches, faint the outlines, & unequal the Colouring.

The other side of the page is a fragment of a more ambitious style of preface:

The light of reason, though it's [*sic*] rays emit a lustre w$^{ch.}$ illuminates the earthly Fabrick with a refulgence that seems big with Immortality, is of a Nature too subtle & delicate for common use, & though it opens the Mind, refines the Ideas, & enlarges the Soul, those who in a peculiar degree are irradiated by this *heavenly Fire*, are such as, in the common purposes of Life, conduct themselves with less propriety & Utility, than those of more ordinary Understand^g, & meaner Capacity [.] The former *think*, the latter *act*—& while the one meditates on the Means the other profits by the occasion.

The language here is too entangled and artificial to be pleasing, but there are glimmerings of a guiding idea more interesting in some ways than the conventional and relatively safe objective of supplying 'Manners' and 'Nature'. Burney seems to be saying that Reason (which here shares some of the qualities of the Romantics' Imagination) is neither common nor narrowly useful. She is thus arguing against the prevailing doctrines of the Enlightenment, especially as such doctrines came filtered through Whig beliefs.

Far from conducing to happiness and utility, too much reason is, ironically, a handicap. We may take it that the author means us to see that the characters who experience intellectual light (Villars, Orville, Macartney and, above all, Evelina) are handicapped in making progress through the world. Certainly, at the end of the novel, although the novelist rewards the 'good' characters with all the prizes that novelistic convention can supply, she steadfastly refuses to punish most of the faulty characters. Those who have been pursuing worldly ambitions and success are free to continue their progress, and few of these have failed to take what they want. The Branghtons are continuing to rise in the world; Lord Merton will still make the financially based marriage with Lady Louisa. In all of Burney's novels she is interested in displaying the success of the vulgar and bad – a success relative to their own ideas. On the appearance of Burney's second novel, *Cecilia* (1782), readers were to be exercised by the muted ending, and by the success of an unamiable family in gaining the heroine's lost estate; some of the reviewers tried to point out to the author that she should have done otherwise. Burney did not believe that those with open minds and enlarged souls are particularly equipped to gain fortune and place. But here in her first published novel the comic plot works itself out so pleasantly that few readers are going to question its resolution, or examine its ironies.

In the version of the preface finally used (see p. 7) the author rewords her claim: 'To draw characters from nature, though not from life, and to mark the manners of the times'. Here she is on safe ground, for she repeats the substance of much novel criticism and theory since at least the time of Henry Fielding's *Tom Jones* (1749). By disclaiming characters 'from life' Burney is merely saying that her characters are not based, lampoon-like, on particular individuals. Such a statement serves the purposes of the disclaimer customarily prefixed to modern novels, telling us 'any resemblance to actual persons, living or dead, is purely coincidental' – and, like such a disclaimer, may be taken with a grain of salt. Like Fielding, Burney offers us general truth, 'Human Nature', and she too emphasizes her role as a current historian, recording contemporary behaviour. The alterations made in the manuscript show us that Burney was meticulous in recording the behaviour of her characters. In particular, she had to be careful as she was dealing with some characters from the upper classes of society, whose register of manners was above that of the circle she usually frequented, as well as with a number of personages whose behaviour was much rougher and more ungracious than that of her middle-class world.

Yet it is unjust to speak of Frances Burney's 'middle-class world'. The fact is, Frances Burney, like her own Evelina, had a very dubious social status and was living on a cusp between social classes. It was her father's ambition to prove that a musician could be a gentleman. Roger Lonsdale, Doctor Burney's biographer, has given us a record of Doctor Burney's struggle and noted his acute desire to re-create himself as a gentleman of letters.[1] But, of course, in the eyes of the gentry of eighteenth-century England, no mere fiddler or music-teacher could have any claim to gentility. The Burney family really belonged to the world of 'Bohemia', as we were later to term that fascinating but unclassed realm of artists and performers. Frances Burney thus had a much better education for a novelist than most real 'young ladies' could have achieved. Opera singers, dancers, musicians, speaking various languages, came regularly to the house – and so too did actors like Garrick, or Christopher Smart, a friend of Charles Burney because of Smart's transvestite show of the 1750s rather than for his poetry. Frances Burney saw much more of the world than nice young ladies could do. Her sense of solidarity with the musicians and performers of all kinds can be seen in her novels from *Evelina* to *The Wanderer*, and she speaks for the performers who should be listened to and appreciated – and, as the last novel points out, appropriately paid. All sorts of people came for music and conversation at the Burney house – first the house in Poland Street, then, after 1774, the house in Leicester Square formerly belonging to Isaac Newton. (The house was torn down in 1925 in one of London's fits of vandalism.) Doctor Burney did try to maintain a certain middle-class protocol, treating his daughters as ladies whose presence should not be affronted by grossness. The traveller Richard Twiss embarrassed the family by improper conversation (which included high praise of a lewd book called *The Dictionary of Love*). After Twiss left, Frances Burney wrote in her Diary, 'Even my gentle & candid Father says that *he has quite mistaken the Thing*, & that he shall never see a *Table Cloth* in his House again' (*Early Journals and Letters*, ed. L. E. Troide, II, p. 24). But this was a rare outburst. Usually the whole family was happy to participate in conversations that ranged over all sorts of topics, such as the Amazons' lack of a left breast. Frances was certainly acquainted with the talk of the town in all its vulgarity, as, for instance, in the jokes about the unfortunate Italian soprano, Lucrezia Agujari, known as 'La Bastardella':

[Y]ou have doubtless heard the story of the Pig's Eating half her side, & of its being repaired by a silver kind of machine. You may be sure that she has not Escaped the witticisms of our *Wags* upon this score: it is too fair a subject for Ridicule to have been suffered to pass untouched. Mr. Bromfield has given her the Nick name of *Argentine* . . . & my Lord Sandwich has made a Catch, in Italian, & in Dialogue between her & the Pig . . . beginning with *Caro Mio Porco*—the Pig answers by a Grunt;—& it Ends by his exclaiming *ah che bel mangiare*! (March 1775; *Early Journals and Letters*, II, p. 98)

Frances Burney needed no special instruction as to the crudity of male humour against women; in her diaries as in her novels she is an acute recorder of various brutalities.

Life at the Burneys' home did more to encourage wit and curiosity than pious illusions about the prettiness of human behaviour. Doctor Burney might maintain the decencies but he could not afford to be prudish in his professional life, and many of the visitors who came to sing, play and talk were engaged in illicit liaisons which the Burney young people knew about. There was amusement at Susanna Burney's blunder in supposing Agujari and her partner Giuseppe Colla were actually and legally husband and wife (*Early Journals and Letters*, II, pp. 75–6). Frances Burney also knew about other scandals, including a story about one of the clergymen who came to call while Agujari was there, 'the famous Mr Penneck, that worthy & gentle, & pious Parson, who knocked down Mr Colman upon suspecting his having a *Penchant* for a Miss Miller, an Actress' (*Early Journals and Letters*, II, p. 75). Frances Burney's education, as far as books went, was self-education; she read widely and voraciously under her own direction. Her reading was also, happily, uncensored; she read and enjoyed Sterne's novels (and her early Diary shows their influence), at a time when most girls of any gentility would have been strictly prohibited from touching *Tristram Shandy*. Her general education in her father's house not only gave her a wide knowledge of literature, history, music and the arts; she was also allowed to know more about the real 'manners' of her times than well-bred and sheltered young ladies could know.

Frances Burney also gained a very thorough knowledge of the entertainments of London. Evelina visits all the places of public entertainment as a visitor, a tourist, usually as a genteel visitor, paid for by Lady Howard or the Mirvans. Frances Burney often did not have to pay, and was taken behind the scenes, or by people who were behind the scenes. She had knowledge of the opera and theatre, not because the Burney family were wealthy enough to keep going out, but because Charles Burney's work gave him a special relationship to managers, actors and singers. Few young women can have seen as much of the London entertainment world as Frances Burney did, and *Evelina*'s accounts of public places and entertainments gave the book added appeal for provincial contemporaries. Yet the pleasure offered the reader, of vicarious participation in fashionable amusements, does not exhaust the significance of the novel's emphasis on such amusements. In the first part of *Evelina* especially, we can see an incessant return to the problems of representation, and to the problematic nature of spectacle. The heroine and her party are perpetually to be present at mimetic performances. The heroine encounters her grandmother after seeing 'the performance of a little comedy, in French and Italian, by puppets, so admirably managed, that they both astonished and diverted us all' (see p. 54). Immediately afterwards, Madame Duval and Captain Mirvan start quarrelling, in mixed languages, a little comedy that diverts most of their neighbours, and the reader. But the situation raises the disturbing possibility that the Captain and Madame Duval are but puppets. Of course, on one level they obviously are the author's playthings, supplying an image very like that used by Thackeray for all the personages in his *Vanity Fair*, mere puppets to be put back in the box. (Indeed Thackeray himself may have been influenced by Burney.) The novel itself is a contrived representation. But our discomfort arises from the apprehension (which was also Thackeray's apprehension) that the characters, insofar as they represent human beings, show us that human beings are but puppets. We all respond to circumstances, to the artifices imposed by nationality, gender, age, marital status, profession. This artificial response greatly concerns Burney, for she has a strong and modern interest in the idea of individual development, and of the independent self. She is always sympathetic to the views expressed by the romantic Belfield in *Cecilia*: 'If man dared act for himself . . . how noble indeed would he be!' (*Cecilia*, p. 15). The central characters in all of Burney's novels try to learn to think and act for themselves, to get away from the restrictions of prejudice that create false identity (the phrase 'Pride and Prejudice' used in Austen's famous title is Burney's own invention in *Cecilia*).

Evelina has to think and act for herself at an important point, where she finds herself tempted to reveal young Macartney's secrets to Lord Orville. In order to clear herself of the embarrassing implications of Macartney's secret visit to her, she could tell his story to Lord Orville, and at first she thinks she will do precisely that to get rid of the 'mystery' and earn the attractive nobleman's good opinion. But when she does try to think for herself she determines against telling her half-brother's tale, becoming 'sensible ... of the utter impropriety, nay, treachery, of revealing the story, and publishing the misfortunes and poverty of Mr. Macartney ... I ought not to betray Mr. Macartney' (see p. 335). In deciding against being a 'good girl' and a sweet thing she runs counter to the implicit definition of her created by Lord Orville in their previous conversation: '"The sweetness of Miss Anville's disposition," said he, in a softened voice, "I have long admired ..."' In refusing to become such a perfect puppet of a young lady, succumbing to her role of sweetness and dependence, Evelina reaches for a term usually used by men; she alludes to Macartney's 'reliance upon my honour which I should blush to find myself unworthy of'. Evelina determines to have *honour*, not in the feminine sense (where it means only chastity) but in the larger sense which includes an integrity not usually convenient to accord to women. This moment of consideration, this resistance to becoming the doll that Orville would make of her, seems very important in Burney's own scheme of the novel, and shows Evelina triumphant, despite the forces not just arrayed against her but exerted upon her to shape her. Having acquired something worthy of being considered a 'self', she is eligible for all the rewards a novel can offer.

The strongest lines of the novel, however, emphasize the determined and artificial elements of our lives, which are much more accessible to view here than any exhibitions of moral individuality. The more we look at literal exhibitions within the novel, the more we recognize the power of representation. People are like characters on the stage, in plays by Foote or Congreve. Everyone works at self-representation. Madame Duval (mis)represents herself as French and as young and beautiful – with the help of a certain quantity of rouge and a great deal of assurance. Captain Mirvan, with even more assurance and grosser effect, represents himself as Englishman and as authority. Both of these characters are vulgar failures compared to such serious and elegant practioners of the subtleties of social control as Sir Clement Willoughby, but both Madame Duval and the Captain have a certain force because they truly believe in their representations of themselves. Indeed, at one point Sir Clement collides with Madame Duval in a situation in which he has the worst of it, because Madame Duval and the Branghtons do not consider themselves bound by the conventions he assumed must bind them. Madame Duval screams abuse and the Branghtons steadily lose their awe of him, first relaxing into their chairs and then beginning to laugh at him. It is amusing to us to see Sir Clement's upper-class aplomb deserting him. Sir Clement is suddenly in a theatre where he cannot be properly represented according to his own concept of his persona, and he begins to erode. The more he loses social power, the more social power the Branghtons gain:

The ha, ha, ha's, and he, he, he's, grew more and more uncontroulable, as if the restraint from which they had burst, had added to their violence. Sir Clement could no longer endure being the object who excited them, and, having no answer ready for Madame Duval, he hastily stalked towards Mr. Smith and young Branghton, and sternly demanded what they laughed at? (see p. 236)

Willoughby wins back some power temporarily, but at the loss of his social persona; he has descended to the Branghtons level in being the angry man instead of the smooth aristocrat controlling plebeians loftily from above. Madame Duval appropriately rewards him here for his earlier participation in literally stripping her of her social persona – when he and Captain Mirvan had her coach held up and caused Madame Duval to be thrown into a ditch, her wig torn off and her silk dress ruined. Loss of costume and appearance only temporarily discomfited her; here, without physical violence being offered, Sir Clement suffers from an assault on his social being which is felt as a violent attack. Well may Madame Duval exalt, 'you shall see I'm as cunning as you, so you may go and find somebody else to use in that manner, and to put your mask on, and to make a fool of' (see p. 235). Madame Duval's mangled locution offers interesting possibilities: 'find somebody else . . . to put your mask on'. Her primary meaning seems to be 'find somebody else to deceive with the mask you put on', the mask being Willoughby's assumed politeness and *délicatesse*. But the other meaning seems to insist upon coming through also: 'find somebody else upon whom to affix the mask you wish that person to wear'. The masking of thoroughly polished and socially consistent self-representation is achieved through placing masks on others as well as on oneself. Interlocutors and companions are assigned roles, behaviour and aspects. This is particularly true of the women, for they are always objects to be observed, and as objects they are also to be interpreted and instructed. Ladies are not supposed to wear rouge, to paint themselves as Madame Duval does – but the assigned role of a 'lady' allows others to try to paint the woman by making her blush. The role of woman as spectacle is made clear in the theatre scene, in which (in the intervals of watching Congreve's *Love for Love*) Mr. Lovel entertains himself with making Evelina blush, partly by discoursing on her change in colour:

I presumed not to infer that *rouge* was the only succedaneum for health; but, really, I have known so many different causes for a lady's colour, such as flushing,—anger,—*mauvaise honte*,—and so forth, that I never dare decide to which it may be owing. (see p. 88)

The blush is valued as a sincere and unfeigned sign of exquisite inner emotion, made publicly accessible – yet the blush induced, the colour affixed to a young lady's face, itself partakes the character of a mask imposed. That it is an imposition is underlined by the nature and effect of the verses that Macartney writes on 'The Beauties of the Wells'. He apparently pays Evelina back for her generosity to him by public compliment, but his supposed compliment is an act of power, although it wears the mask of a tribute. It is an embarrassment and an indignity; Evelina finds herself pointed at by impudent young men who quote the verses at her without even speaking to her:

'Yes,' cried one, "'tis certainly she!—mark but her *blushing cheek*!'

'And then her *eye*,—her *downcast eye*!' cried another.

. . .

'But then,' said the first, 'her *mind*,—now the difficulty is, to find out the truth of *that*, for she will not say a word.'

'She is *timid*,' answered another; 'mark but her *timid air*.' (see p. 362)

Evelina at this point does not even know the verses (her script), but she finds her walk with Mrs. Selwyn turned into an imputed performance, and herself given the category of spectacle. To the young men she has become a piece of theatre. Indeed, young men of this type like to boast that they go to the theatre to observe members of the audience, not to watch the actors in the production already prepared for them – a piece of affectation that arouses the derision of Captain Mirvan, who yet is himself most cruelly interested in turning other people into unwilling performers in his own productions.

In the uncomfortable walk pursued by her tormentors, Evelina finds that any natural gesture to try to escape or shrug off this rudeness is incorporated into a representation – her downcast eye, her timid air only fulfil the expectations created by her persona as it has appeared in print. Anything she does is merely representation. She is in a sense turned into the puppet of Macartney and the young men. Such moments, which might be described as 'being puppeted', are exquisitely painful. The pain is brought out in the last such moment in the novel, the cruel joke against Lovel when he is shown the monkey as his similar and brother. The reader is an accomplice in this trick of Captain Mirvan's, as we have disliked Lovel and would like to see him requited for the pain he gave Evelina. He punished Evelina for laughing at him when she first met him; now he is to be laughed at by all. Yet his punishment is disproportionate, as are all Mirvan's cruel jokes, and the reader is made uncomfortable about the degree of complicity originally offered. The monkey not only mimics Lovel, but bites him, in an astonishing turn, as if a figure of speech should draw blood. The imposed mask shows itself as cruel. Mr. Lovel's altered countenance is turned jokingly into another set of signs, indications of a new (and entirely unwanted) social persona:

'What argufies so many words?' said the unfeeling Captain, 'it is but a slit of the ear; it only looks as if you had been in the pillory.'

'Very true,' added Mrs. Selwyn, 'and who knows but it may acquire you the credit of being an anti-ministerial writer?'

. . .

'Ha, ha, ha!' cried the Captain; 'see what comes of studying for an hour what you shall put on.' (see p. 446)

The pillory is an archetype of undesired theatrical performance that wrecks the personality. Almost the only thing that could support one in such an ordeal would be the strong political convictions that could give one credit in some quarters, and an assurance of inner worth. But Lovel has in effect been in the pillory without the consolation of political martyrdom or belief. He has no persona to wear for this representation of himself, and his usual self-representation, the cause and effect of his 'studying for an hour' what to 'put on' is shot to pieces. Yet Lovel, like Madame Duval in a similar fix, gathers the shreds of his dignity together by starting a discussion of what he *will* wear in future – in particular what he should do about his head. Unlike Madame Duval, he shuns the idea of a wig: '*I* wear a wig?—no, not if you would give me a thousand pounds an hour!' (see p. 446). This statement, with a hyperbole that reminds us of Lewis Carroll, comically restores Lovel's vision of his own self-love, his belief that he has a 'natural' beauty, which would be ruined by an old-fashioned artifice.

Lovel may be harshly used, but most of the characters go largely unpunished for the outrageous and aggressive modes of self-representation in which they engage. Unrepentant, despite his experience with Madame Duval and the Branghtons, Sir Clement Willoughby boasts to Evelina about his powers of social dissimulation. She is amazed to hear him articulate his unflattering opinions of the women with whom she is staying:

'I am quite amazed,' said I, 'that, with such opinions, you can behave to them all with so much attention and civility.'

'Civility! my angel,—why I could worship, could adore them, only
to procure myself a moment of your conversation? Have you not seen
me pay my court to the gross Captain Mirvan, and the virago Madame
Duval? Were it possible that a creature so horrid could be formed, as to
partake of the worst qualities of all these characters . . . even to such a
monster as that, I would pay homage, and pour forth adulation . . . (see
p. 381)

Sir Clement Willoughby boasts of the extent of his hypocrisy.
He is quite right; such hypocrisy is most effective. A being like
Captain Mirvan arouses disgust and fear, and must be shut out
of the higher circles of society. Such calculated and elegant self-
representation as Sir Clement possesses allows him to obtain all
the satisfactions and pleasures he requires (from supper to sex)
without the inconvenience of arousing antagonism. The sophisticated members of society understand that one can get one's own
way more certainly by observing a code of manners, which
others will also have to observe – that is, that the entire social
arena is one large complex theatre. The more others are also
fettered by conventions, the better off the clever and nimble
will be.

The Branghtons and their circle show us characters who are
just beginning to understand the meaning of the power of
manners. Mr. Branghton is bluff and limited, but his children are
on the move. The younger of the Branghton girls, Polly, is
beginning to acquire the sophistication necessary for true dissimulation. She is ready (unlike her parent) to pretend to like the
opera, for she has taken in that representation's value in establish-
ing the position and taste of the members of the audience.
Opera, above all representations, rubs off, as it were, gives a
social role and status to the spectator. Much more than the
theatre, the opera (in eighteenth-century London as in present-
day London or New York) operates as a social signifier. The
bastard among mimetic arts, it unites theatricality (the outer
world, and the word) with music (the inner world, the supposed
spiritual or emotional self expressed). The social status of opera,
its role as a shibboleth, a test of 'culture' and 'taste', must be
well understood if a reader is properly to appreciate the high

comedy of the Branghtons' visit to the Opera-house. They are entirely out of their element (intellectual and musical as well as social) but they respond in different ways to their perplexity. They are correct in noticing that the opera is highly artificial. They are not unused to theatrical representation, but they object to telling a story through song:

'But pray, Miss,' said the son, 'what makes that fellow look so doleful while he's singing?'

'Probably because the character he performs is in distress.'

'Why then I think he might as well let alone singing till he's in better cue: it's out of all nature for a man to be piping when he's in distress.' (see p. 104)

Mr. Branghton decides the opera is nonsense: 'I can't like nonsense, let it be never so much the taste' (see p. 104); 'there isn't one ounce of sense in the whole Opera, nothing but one continued squeaking and squalling from beginning to end' (ibid). In a sense, the Branghton judgement is justifiable. A number of eminent Augustan writers had anxiously pondered the potential loss of English language, English thought, English poetry and drama under the onslaught of the opera. The opera had been a favourite target of satirists of an earlier generation. The note supplied by Pope to his personification of the opera as the 'Harlot form' who appears in Book IV of *The Dunciad* (first published 1742) provides a succinct summary of the charges:

The Attitude given to this Phantom represents the nature and genius of the *Italian* Opera; its affected airs, its effeminate sounds, and the practice of patching up these Operas with favourite Songs, incoherently put together. These things were supported by the subscriptions of the Nobility.

Opera is an import, and an imposition of the upper classes; it is not manly, it is *effeminate* – there is something about it that feminizes the spectator as well as the *castrato* singer. It is feminine in that it is anti-intellectual, offering sound without sense, and in its hybrid nature and capacity to please rich men it is a bastard and a harlot.

Frances Burney, who had read *The Dunciad* by 1773, understands this view, though she certainly does not share it. She turns the tables on the earlier Augustan satirists, by making the bluff Englishmen who ridicule opera the objects of her own satire. Frances Burney, of course, had a musical background, came from an environment in which musical productions, including operas, are considered of importance, and she was a personal acquaintance and admirer of many of the Italian singers, including the 'Signor Millico' who is referred to in this scene in *Evelina*. In this novel, as in other of Burney's novels, a parade of 'Englishness' is deeply suspect. Herself of Scottish and French descent, Burney regards patriotic pretensions, displays of 'Englishness', with a cold and quizzical eye. Captain Mirvan constantly flaunts his 'Englishness' as a leading feature of his self-representation – it is being English, and being male, that gives him his authority. Maleness and Englishness are again reflected in the sturdy philistinism of Mr. Branghton at the opera.

In creating the Branghtons, Frances Burney allowed herself the luxury of aiming at a rather easy and common butt of satire. Since the Restoration, it had been good safe fun for dramatists and novelists to mock the attitudes, habits and pretensions of the 'Cits' – descendants of the Puritans, the new money-grubbing class who lived in the City of London, as distinct from its fashionable (and growing) West End. Evelina, who is between social classes, samples both aspects of London. She visits the Mirvans and Lady Howard at the house in Queen Ann Street, but she is forced to go with her grandmother to stay in lodgings above a hosier's in High Holborn, and to visit the Branghton establishment further east in Snow Hill. The Branghtons offer a disarmingly accessible object of criticism. Yet Burney escapes the mere repetition of convention by the uses to which she puts the City family (who are, when all is said and done, Evelina's undeniable cousins). Burney leads the reader to recognize that the upper levels of society merely play, as it were, the Branghtons' tunes in another key.

The satire makes us see at last not how *un*like the Branghtons are to the fashionable folk (though Evelina herself wishes, at first, to emphasize the difference) but how *like*. Mr. Smith offers a very important middle term. He has social aspirations and insights beyond the view of the Branghton men, and he represents just the level of stylishness and sophistication that both male and female Branghtons can grasp. Mr. Smith was Doctor Johnson's favourite character in the novel, 'such a struggle to appear a gentleman' Johnson said of him. Mr. Smith does *struggle* – he opens our eyes to the complication of deliberations and self-representations that being 'a gentleman' involves. His pretensions take him only as far as his judgement reaches, but within that comically limited area his performance is very good – he can't realize that the better instructed, used to a wider reference and a more educated 'gentility', can see through his performance. But that only means their performance is better calculated, more informed – not that there is any natural gentility of 'blood'. Smith fails when he thinks he is succeeding. But his performance is an exact parallel to the performance of Sir Clement Willoughby in the upper ranks of society. If the Branghton men are bluff, selfish and cruel, so are the men in the upper ranks, like Lord Merton and Jack Coverley. What might be called 'Branghtonianism' is universal. Burney made up the last name of her citizen characters; she is fond of inventing names for her favourite satiric butts, and the name 'Branghton' is based on 'brangle', a dialect word meaning 'to brawl' and 'to wrangle'. Quarrelling and contentiousness are signified by the Branghtons' name, and their style of quarrelling, contentiousness and self-aggrandizement at the expense of others is found throughout the society depicted in *Evelina*.

The Branghtons, as we have seen, find fault with the opera for being unnatural: 'it's out of all nature for a man to be piping when he's in distress'. The representation is, in young Branghton's view, invalid. Tom Branghton is in philosophical difficulties here, for 'nature' means only what he would do himself in certain imaginary circumstances, and such a standard would preclude almost all dramatic representation of any interest – we would be left with the fireworks and conjurors, the non-mimetic shows in which such as Tom delight. The Branghtons are also poorly placed to offer argument against the artificial. They actually like the artificial very much – fireworks being arguably much more artificial than sad songs. The Branghtons make their living because their talent for artifice meets a public demand for it. Mr. Branghton is a silversmith. His business could not succeed without a communal taste for luxury and artifice. The Branghtons' lives are just as 'unnatural' as the lives of the aristocrats.

The novel makes us question what is or might be 'natural'. The natural is that which can be imitated by man – imitated, and in a sense overgone. We are shown this in the scene of the visit to Cox's Museum, where the party look at the elaborate and richly wrought simulacra of life. Sir Clement asks the heroine what she thinks 'of this brilliant *spectacle*?' She replies that although it is 'very fine, and very ingenious . . . I seem to *miss something*' (see p. 85). What Evelina hesitatingly misses is life itself, common breath, which is done away with, even surpassed, by the automata. The artificer can offer sights that nature cannot: 'our attention was attracted by a pine-apple, which, suddenly opening, discovered a nest of birds, who immediately began to sing' (ibid). Is not that a dainty dish to set before a heroine? Captain Mirvan stoutly prefers biological life, declaring a preference for a pineapple that is edible, while Madame Duval denies the necessity of use, and opts for the perfection of the artificial. Her own affectation is then shown up by the forced application of smelling-salts which painfully afflict her biological and unredeemably physical nostrils. But the questions raised by the brilliant automata blend in with other disturbing suggestions within the novel. The show in Cox's Museum offers an extreme degree of representation, of figuring and feigning without human form or emotion, or the need of meaning – it offers a kind of zero degree of artifice. There is a hint that the world is tending towards that inhuman perfection of bland artificiality – or, at the other extreme, to the mire of the ditch into which Madame Duval is hurled. In being covered with humiliating blood at the end in the monkey scene, Lovel is at least rescued from the state to which he aspires, the state of the elegant and shining automaton.

Madame Duval, the painted woman, the Jezebel, is never able to assimilate to the artifice she admires. A deal of self-construction has gone into her self-representation: she has pretended to be French for so long that she reacts with patriotic indignation to any slurs upon her adoptive country – but she is really in origin an English barmaid, and uses her pseudo-Frenchness as a cover for her slips in English pronunciation, diction and grammar. At the age of fifty she is properly considered an 'elderly woman' (see p. 54), although 'she really looks to be less than fifty'. Madame Duval 'dresses very gaily, paints very high, and the traces of former beauty are still very visible in her face' (see p. 59). To Madame Duval herself, the beauty is still present. She has defied society's strictures and all the contemporary formulae that decree that a woman past childbearing years has no value, and must have neither sexual desires nor satisfaction. Madame Duval drags Monsieur Du Bois about with her, her companion, escort, *cicisbeo* and presumably her lover – just as Agujari had her Signor Colla. That the relationship is sexual is fully indicated when Madame Duval flies into a rage at Monsieur Du Bois's flirtation with Evelina. Madame Duval has broken through a lot of prohibitions and regulations, in the process forfeiting all claims to recognition in English society. Yet there is not much she could do to win any recognition in English society anyway, as she has no distinction of birth to compensate for the atrocious fact of her age.

Madame Duval is at once a highly comic and a highly sinister character. She is Evelina's real grandmother, and she represents the maternal inheritance – which is no inheritance. To discover that one is Woman is a terrible blow. In the novel *Evelina* that discovery is signalled by the advent of Madame Duval. Finding the Mother, viewing the inevitable female fate, is bad news for Evelina. In the published version of the novel, Evelina's reaction to Madame Duval's annunciation of her identity as the grandmother is emphatic enough. The heroine, 'amazed, frightened, and unspeakably shocked' falls back into the arms of Mrs. Mirvan, 'more dead than alive'. The Berg manuscript version of the scene indicates even greater disturbance: 'I heard no more—

seized with unspeakable horror,—my Blood chill'd—my Heart sunk—I gasp'd for Breath—& more *Dead* than alive, I fell into Mrs Mirvan's arms.' The plot level of the story offers as a justification for all this turmoil the fact that the grandmother was the cause of the ill fate of the mother, a rather feeble justification for a degree of horrific response, which Burney toned down in the published account. But on the figurative level Evelina's reaction of 'unspeakable horror' is entirely justified. The revelation of the Mother, the buried figure of the maternal, the author of one's being who should always be buried but yet will not stay dead – that is a Gothic moment. For a woman to recognize the Mother is to recognize the female fate – which is perpetually to give birth and be killed, to be declared officially dead even while living, because of the untoward and unsightly advance of Age, like a Cranach picture of an ancient Eve. Evelina, Eve's daughter, Eve-in-a-veil, can hardly bear to acknowledge the terrible and ridiculous female destiny – which is, as always, female anatomy. In creating this representation of the female, Burney drew upon conventions of ridicule; Madame Duval in many respects resembles the female roles created by transvestite artists like Smart or Foote, the 'pantomime dame', mock-women born of mockery and mimesis. That Madame Duval represents something deeply important to Burney, how-ever, and is not to be shrugged off as merely participating in theatrical tradition, may be gathered from the fact that the author's own beloved grandmother Sleepe was born a Dubois, and was genuinely the French or half-French woman the hero-ine's grandmother pretends to be. A deal of family material goes into the 'family romance' of the novel's story. Mr. Macartney, the heroine's half-brother, turns out to be the true bastard whereas Evelina at last reclaims her legitimacy. This substitute and sibling bears an important name. Macartney was the maiden name of Frances Burney's own godmother, Frances Greville, after whom she was named. Frances Greville's own daughter, Mrs. Crewe, née Greville, was another Frances. Macartney's sister's name thus 'should' be 'Frances' – a hidden sign of the author's own investment in her Evelina.

Using Madame Duval as at once both a scapegoat and an explorer of feminine roles, the novel investigates the lot of Woman, which a Young Lady entering the World must learn to bear. Evelina is born a second time in entering society and learning its rules, which is to say she must learn to restrain her own inclinations and her desires, must understand that women are not supposed to have wants, desires or powers. In her first social occasions she acts too naturally – laughing, crying, running away when she feels like it. Such reactions as those will never do. She must learn the artifice, which means she has to accept the masks that are imposed on women. She must endure being a spectacle, as when, at her first ball, she finds the men feel free to look the girls over while they are denied almost all power of choice. Evelina herself had not noticed how her social situation costumed her anatomy and her destiny. The appropriate destiny for someone in Evelina's position, a well-educated, pretty bastard with no money, is to be the kept mistress of some gentleman. Evelina did not catch that definition of herself, but it was clear enough to Sir Clement Willoughby, and presumably to M. Du Bois. She is perpetually puppeted, and, in order to evade the destinies and definitions she does not want, she inevitably develops a certain slyness, of which some modern critics like Julia Epstein and Kristina Straub have complained.[2] As she is not expected to offer any resistance to masculine operations, she becomes an unwilling accomplice in the Captain's brutal jokes against her grandmother. When she does nerve herself up to object, she meets severe threats, and no support from the other women – she has already had to learn that Mrs. Mirvan is powerless against her husband, and keeps him happy by colluding with him. The young Frances Burney, watching a wedding in King's Lynn in 1768, had thought marriage a rather dreadful thing: 'how short a time does it take to put an eternal end to a Woman's liberty!' (*Early Journals and Letters*, ed. L. E. Troide (Toronto, 1989), I, p. 17). Although the novel ends with the wedding by which we wish to be gratified and consoled, there are a number of indications that most marriages would not be like marriage with Lord Orville. Lord Merton unconsciously fingers his riding-whip while talking of his forthcoming marriage to the unloved Louisa. The novel keeps reminding us that women are valued only when young and pretty (and not valued much even then). A woman is not expected to learn, mature and develop – her development is an unwelcome phenomenon. Lord Merton says to Evelina, 'I don't know what the devil a woman lives for after thirty: she is only in other folks' way' (see p. 305). What Merton says is enacted by Captain Mirvan and Sir Clement when they have Madame Duval thrown into the ditch – thrown away, as rubbish, out of other folks' way.

The episode of the old women's race illustrates the same set of attitudes to women. The two poor women, both over eighty, are chosen to make a spectacle of themselves so that the young aristocratic men will have something to gamble upon – and the occasion of the sporting bet will be a *comic* event. It is not a comic event to Evelina, yet again she is made an accomplice, forbidden to touch or help the poor old women as they 'hobbled along . . . yet frequently, and to the inexpressible diversion of the company, they stumbled and tottered' (see p. 346). Part of the 'fun' lies in the hope that one of these cruelly abused old women will die on the spot. As Kristina Straub notes, even Lord Orville does not share Evelina's anguished disapproval of this hideous spectacle; he merely disapproves of the gentlemen's thriftless gambling, and takes no note of the deeper sin of cruelty to women and to the poor, which is apparently invisible to all but Evelina.

Evelina visibly develops in perceptiveness and capacities of judgement. The novel can thus be seen as a story of an individual's development, a *Bildungsroman*. Lord Merton's remark that a woman over thirty is only in other folks' way is extremely ironic within the context of a *Bildungsroman*, since it tells us that the *Bildung* in question is neither interesting nor necessary. It would be preferable for a woman to die after her bloom – as Caroline Evelyn had done. And when Frances Burney burned her novel, perhaps in a fit of self-destructive rage at her father and at the woman soon to be her stepmother, she had colluded in the destruction of the unwanted woman, killing off poor

Caroline Evelyn for good. But *Evelina* struggled herself into life. And Madame Duval returned, gigantic, monstrous and curiously inviting, like a return of the repressed.

That Frances Burney associated some kind of curious guilt with her novel can be apprehended from some equally effusive and cryptic verses 'To —— ——' prefixed to the novel. On the reverse side of what appears to be the first manuscript version of this 'Ode', Burney pencilled '4 in the Mon^g'; evidently she wrote it in the middle of one sleepless night. The first line, originally 'Friend of my Soul, & Parent of my Heart', was changed to the more weighty 'author of my being!' The poem is a kind of riddle; its addressee is never to read it, it seems, never to know that he is the addressee. The un-named 'author' of the author's being is of course her father, Doctor Charles Burney, who is curiously related to this offspring of her brain, which is illicitly going forth without his knowledge. The poem can be read as a plea that expects to go unanswered, like the heroine Evelina's plea for recognition by her father. The plot of *Evelina* is driven by the heroine's need to be restored to her rightful position by her father's recognition of her. As long as Sir John Belmont denies that Evelina is his daughter, she is a bastard with no fortune and no inheritance – and no name. The Father's recognition is the primary social construction. Without the Father, we have no last name, which is to say no social or tribal position. A Mother's province is only the first name – and Evelina's first name is made into an anagram to serve as a false or artificial last name, Anville. Yet this maternal fiction is very close to the name of the man who will claim Evelina in marriage, and Lord Orville's decision to marry Evelina in a sense does away with her need for the last name of Belmont, which she is never to bear. Evelina is restored to her father, but in this case, unlike that of the Prodigal Son, it is not the child but the father who must acknowledge precedent guilt, which cut him off from his own offspring.

While the plot seems to be driven by the story of the need for paternal name and recognition, Burney seems more interested in the girl's relation with her mother and with the mother figures, amiable and otherwise, who stand in for the absent Mother. The Mother too is 'author' of one's being, and Caroline Evelyn is an 'author' of Evelina, as well as an 'author' by right of the letter she has penned, as Susan C. Greenfield has emphasized in her essay on 'Female Authorship in *Evelina*'.[3] Most major eighteenth-century novels in England and elsewhere deal, with some seriousness, with a problem of identity. 'Who are you?' is an interesting question to pose to a number of central characters of novels, including Defoe's Roxana, Fielding's Tom Jones, Richardson's Clarissa – or Sterne's Tristram Shandy. In her first novel Burney shapes the identity of her heroine by making her the centre of an epistolary fiction. Supposedly object of the gaze, passive and costumed spectacle, the girl is really subject, always recording, judging, thinking. If those around her do not care what is going on in her pretty little head – the more fools they. Evelina as subject becomes, that is, her own author, and the more she proceeds as a writer, the more confidence she acquires, the less she really needs the external authorizing of the Father. She has come of age without him.

Burney's own concept of all authority and authorship has its subversive side – look at her ironic dedication addressed 'To the Authors of the Monthly and Critical Reviews'. She knows all the little chicaneries of authorship, the deceits and petty stratagems of the world of letters. The more authority is claimed, the less, perhaps, it exists. The writing of real importance may be the 'hidden writing' of journals or letters – such as Evelina is supposed to write. Or it may be the hidden private text of the Mother to the Daughter.

Burney's story has, like every good novel, long tap-roots in the tradition. Heliodorus' *Aithiopika* (c. AD 250–380), a novel perpetually translated and imitated from the Renaissance through to the Enlightenment, gives us a lost and displaced heroine, rejected by her father, who bears about with her the mother's text, a silken girdle embroidered with Ethiopian royal script that few can decipher. The mother's text is a communication dedicated in uncertainty:

perhaps my writing may remain mute and useless, or perhaps it will be of real advantage to you, for the secrets of Fate are hidden from mankind. This writing will be to you ... if you are spared, a token of recognition and if not, it will serve as my funerary inscription for you, and a mother's tears and funeral dirge at your tomb.[4]

The Mother may try to transmit an identity through writing to the absent, separated, and in some sense orphaned, Daughter. There is an additional fear on this mother's part, even as she writes, that her writing may be silenced, that her utterance will remain *kōpha*, mute, dumb. That anxiety is re-used by Mary Wollstonecraft, whose heroine in her unfinished *The Wrongs of Woman, or Maria* cannot tell if what she is writing for her daughter will ever reach her. In the Greek novel it is evident that the relation between mother and daughter is partly modelled on the mythical relation between Demeter and Persephone. In traditional myth it is the Daughter, the *Kōre*, who is doomed to descend to the underworld before returning to unite with the Mother and bring life and light. In Burney's novel, the *Kōre* Evelina descends to the underworld of the Branghtons and the Plutonic despotism of Mirvan before she can ascend. Yet in Burney's version of the myth it is the Mother, the Demeter figure, who has truly descended to the shades and the Maiden who must carry out her bidding, clearing her name and finding a spiritual union with her. The union, even the fusion, of the two is recognized by the sorrowing father, Sir John, who sees in his long-lost daughter the 'dear resemblance of thy murdered mother!' (see p. 428). The daughter is the semblance of the departed wife, rather as Perdita, the Lost One, resembles her mother in Shakespeare's *A Winter's Tale* (another story with roots in Greek fiction). The horror of this fact has already been got over in the unwanted reunion with Madame Duval – for there is a horror in resembling, that is, representing, one who is dead. Such a task of representation is an unwelcome reminder that one will oneself die. Men may pretend that they each manufacture a strong and eternally durable individual identity; they tend towards the hardness of the goldsmith's artifice. But women must accept the existence of identity in relationship, and the fact of biological incarnation and transitory life. In her novel Burney makes us accept that biological and transitory existence as a bearable existence, through the comedy that goes beyond, though it includes, the mockery of social affectations and stupidities. She harmonizes the two visions, though not really very sweetly. She reminds us that as soon as we know our own biological selves as individual entities, we are ripe for the social artifices and conscious representations that are seldom as beautiful as the surprising birds that sing in an artificial pineapple of politeness.

NOTE ON BURNEY'S DRAMAS

The turn of the century has seen major developments in Frances Burney's reputation. At last she has received a memorial in Westminster Abbey (though alas, to 'Fanny Burney'). More importantly, her dramas are receiving new attention, a developement which owes something to biographers (first Joyce Hemlow and then, I think, myself) but even more to those who were pioneers in setting out texts of the comedies in readable and actable form, editors such as Tara Ghosal Wallace and Katharine Rogers. Since 1995 all of Burney's plays have been available in an extremely well researched scholarly and readable edition by Peter Sabor. The presence of the plays in print has enabled a new treatment of Burney as a dramatic writer, first visible in Barbara Darby's study, appearing at a point just after some stage production had been attempted. Both *The Witlings* and *A Busy Day* have now been performed professionally; it appears likely that sooner rather than later we shall have competing performance texts of these two comedies.

A Busy Day appears so far to have been more successful (at least in making it to a major venue, such as London's West End) than *The Witlings*. This is partly because a connection could be manufactured between this drama of 1800 and the work of Jane Austen, whose works were so popular in film and TV versions in the mid and late 1990s. Advertising for the London production of *A Busy Day* carried phrases such as 'this glorious slice of Regency life' – although 1800 is not (strictly speaking) 'the Regency'. Productions of *A Busy Day* from 1994 on were made possible by Tara Ghosal Wallace's edition of the text, though I have not seen this debt acknowledged in any programme or advertising material for these productions; the closest to it was a reference by production company Show of Strength to having found the play in a bookstore bin – as if they had discovered a manuscript text in that situation! Tara Ghosal Wallace should have been awarded a glass of champagne and a front-row seat at the London opening of *A Busy Day*, because her edition made the play available for the first time, put that particular play to the fore of Burney's comedies and paved the way for informed discussion of Burney's comedies.

The London production of *A Busy Day* in 2000, although not perfect (some patches of modern interpolation came over awkwardly), proved that this is a really funny and significant play; it probably will remain in the repertoire. Future productions of other comedies seems likely. *Love and Fashion* was sold originally to a professional theatre for production in 1800, and would be stageable, while many of us would love to see *The Woman-Hater*. New critical interpretations of Burney make these plays more comprehensible, their depths and nuances more accessible. While it is unlikely that the tragedies will be professionally produced, reading performances and amateur productions may give a more complete idea of Burney's depth and versatility. It is predictable that the interest in dramatic Burney will soon induce a theatre director or a film or TV company to produce a dramatized *Evelina* – seeing in this novel the dramatic qualities that stimulated Sheridan and Murphy to urge Burney to write for the stage in the first place.

Margaret Anne Doody

NOTES

1. See Roger Lonsdale, *Dr. Charles Burney: A Literary Biography* (Oxford: Clarendon Press, 1965).
2. See Julia L. Epstein, 'Fanny Burney's Epistolary Voice', *The Eighteenth Century: Theory and Interpretation*, 27 (1986), pp. 162–79 and *The Iron Pen: Frances Burney and the Politics of Women's Writing* (Madison, WI: University of Wisconsin Press, 1989); see also Kristina Straub, *Divided Fictions: Fanny Burney and the Feminine Strategy* (Lexington, KY: University of Kentucky Press, 1987).

3. Susan C. Greenfield, "'Oh Dear Resemblance of Thy Murdered Mother': Female Authorship in *Evelina*', *Eighteenth-century Fiction*, 3 (1991), pp. 301–20.

4. Taken from Heliodorus' *Aithiopika*, Bk. IV, as *Les Ethiopiques*, Greek-French edn., ed., R. M. Rattenbury, T. W. Lumb and J. Maillon, 3 vols. (Paris: *Les Belles Lettres*, 1960), II, p. 17. My essay 'Beyond *Evelina*: The Individual Novel and the Community of Literature', in *Eighteenth-century Fiction*, 3 (1991), pp. 359–71, develops the connections between Heliodorus' story and Burney's, while examining *Evelina*'s relationship to a number of other works.

ACKNOWLEDGEMENTS

I am pleased to acknowledge my gratitude to the Henry W. and Albert A. Berg Collection of the New York Public Library and to the Pierpont Morgan Library (both in New York City), which house original Burney manuscripts quoted in the Introduction.

I also wish to express my thanks to Roger Lonsdale, Robert Mack, Douglas Murray, Peter Sabor and Lars Troide for advice and encouragement while this edition was being prepared.

FURTHER READING

BIOGRAPHY AND AUTOBIOGRAPHY

Burney, Frances, *Diary and Letters of Madame D'Arblay*, ed. Charlotte Barrett, 7 vols. (London: Henry Colburn, 1842–6).

—*Early Journals and Letters*, ed. Lars Troide, I and II (Oxford: Oxford University Press, 1988, 1990).

—*The Journals and Letters of Fanny Burney* [Madame D'Arblay], ed. Joyce Hemlow et al, 12 vols. (Oxford: Oxford University Press, 1972–84).

—*Memoirs of Dr Burney* by Madame D'Arblay (Frances Burney), 3 vols. (London: Edward Moxon, 1832).

Crump, Janice, ed., *Known Scribbler: Frances Burney on Literary Life* (Peterborough, Ont: Broadview, 2002).

Doody, Margaret Anne, *Frances Burney: The Life in the Works* (New Brunswick, NJ: Rutgers University Press; and Cambridge, Cambridge University Press, 1988).

Harman, Claire, *Fanny Burney: A Biography* (London: HarperCollins, 2000).

Hemlow, Joyce, *The History of Fanny Burney* (Oxford: Clarendon Press, 1958).

Rogers, Katharine M., *Frances Burney: The World of Female Difficulties* (Lanham, MD: Rowman & Littlefield, 1991).

Thaddeus, Janice Farrar, *Frances Burney: A Literary Life* (New York: Palgrave, 2000).

CRITICAL WORKS

Bilger, Audrey, *Laughing Feminism: Subversive Comedy in Frances Burney, Maria Edgeworth and Jane Austen* (Detroit, MI: Wayne State University Press, 2002).

Cook, Elizabeth Heckendorn, *Epistolary Bodies: Gender and Genre in the*

Eighteenth-Century Republic of Letters (Stanford, CA: Stanford University Press, 1996).

Copeland, Edward W., 'Money in the Novels of Fanny Burney', *Studies in the Novel*, 8 (1976), pp. 24–37.

Darby, Barbara, *Frances Burney, Dramatist: Gender, Performance, and the Late Eighteenth-Century Stage* (Lexington, KY: University Press of Kentucky, 1997).

Doody, Margaret Anne, 'George Eliot and the Eighteenth-century Novel', *Nineteenth-century Fiction*, 35 (1980), pp. 260–91.

Eighteenth-century Fiction, Special *Evelina* Issue, 3 (1991).

Epstein, Julia L., 'Fanny Burney's Epistolary Voice', *The Eighteenth Century: Theory and Interpretation*, 27 (1986), pp. 162–79.

—*The Iron Pen: Frances Burney and the Politics of Women's Writing* (Madison, WI: University of Wisconsin Press, 1989).

Goldstein, Lauren, 'Move Over Austen', *Time Europe*, vol 15, no. 19 (2000).

Greenfield, Susan C., *Mothering Daughters: Novels and the Politics of Family Romance, Frances Burney to Jane Austen* (Detroit, MI: Wayne State University Press, 2003).

Newton, Judith Lowder, *Women, Power and Subversion: Social Strategies in British Fiction 1778–1860* (Athens, GA: University of Georgia Press, 1981).

Sabor, Peter, General Introduction to *The Compete Plays of Frances Burney*, 3 vols., I (London: Pickering and Chatto, 1995).

Schellenberg, Betty A., 'From Propensity to Profession: Female Authorship and the Early Career of Frances Burney', *Eighteenth-century Fiction*, 14 (2002).

Spacks, Patricia M., 'Dynamics of Fear: Fanny Burney', in *Imagining a Self: Autobiography and Novel in Eighteenth-century England* (Cambridge, MA: Harvard University Press, 1976), pp. 158–92.

—'Privacy, Dissimulation and Propriety: Frances Burney and Jane Austen', *Eighteenth-century Fiction*, 12 (2000).

Straub, Kristina, *Divided Fictions: Fanny Burney and the Feminine Strategy* (Lexington, KY: University of Kentucky Press, 1987).

Waddell, J. N., 'Fanny Burney's Contribution to English Vocabulary', *Neuphilologische Mitteilungen*, 81 (1980), pp. 260–63.

—'Additions to *OED* from the Writings of Fanny Burney', *Notes and Queries*, 225 (1980), pp. 27–32.

DRAMA

EDITIONS

Coveney, Alan, *A Busy Day* by Fanny Burney (London: Theatre Communications Group, 2002).

Delery, Clayton, ed. *The Witlings*, Early Women Writers 1650–1800, no. 3 (East Lansing MI: Colleagues Press, 1995).

Rogers, Katharine M., *The Witlings*, in *The Meridian Anthology of Restoration and Eighteenth-Century Plays by Women* (Collingdale, PA: DIANE Publishing Co, 1994).

Sabor, Peter, Geoffrey Sill, Stewart Cooke, eds., *The Complete Plays of Frances Burney*. 3 vols. (London: Pickering and Chatto, 1995).

Sabor, Peter, and Geoffrey Sill, *The Witlings and The Woman-Hater* (Peterborough, Ont.: Broadview Press, 2002).

PRODUCTIONS

A Busy Day by Show of Strength production company, Hen and Chicken Theatre, Bedminster, Bristol, Sept–Oct. 1993; revival by Show of Strength production company at King's Head Theatre, London, June–July 1994.

The Witlings, directed by Rebecca Greene Uddon, World Première, Main Street Theatre, Houston, TX, Feb–Mar. 1998.

BBC Radio 4, reading of Burney's Journal and Letters, summer 2000.

A Busy Day, directed by Jonathan Church, text adapted by Alan Coveney; with Stephanie Beacham, Sara Crewe, John McCallum, Ben Moor. Opening in Bristol Theatre Royal, spring 2000; summer 2000 at Lyric Theatre (London's West End) June–Sept. 2000.

A Busy Day, directed by Stuart Gelzer, text adapted by Stuart Gelzer and Marie E. McAllister, North American Première, Chancellor High School, Spotsylvania County, West Virginia,

A NOTE ON THE TEXT

This text is based on the third edition of *Evelina*, which appeared in 1779 after the second edition earlier that same year. The first edition of 1778 had many errors, as Frances Burney noted when she submitted a list of corrections to Thomas Lowndes. These changes were not all incorporated until the third edition. Some substantial emendations to the first edition appear in the second and subsequent editions. As other publishers have produced copies of the first edition, it seemed right to offer a corrected and slightly amplified version that was still close to the first sprightly running. Changes to the text have been checked against the 'New Edition' of 1784, a more regularized text, and our sparing alterations are often in line with that. In general, the editorial principle has been to preserve the freshness of the eighteenth-century writing, including idiom, punctuation and spelling, as far as possible. Changes have been made in order to ensure regularity, principally in punctuation, especially around speech; we have supplied a consistency as to use of capital letters (in names of streets, for instance). We have also standardized spellings according to Burney's own common usage. Where the text most commonly uses an eighteenth-century spelling (for example, 'chear', 'ideot') we have supplied that spelling in all instances, even when it is occasionally replaced in the original printing by the more modern spelling. Penguin house style has prevailed in the spelling of 'judgement', but we have sustained, for example, 'head-ach'. We have, however, been particularly attentive to keeping the idiom and energy of Burney's writing, not tampering with locutions (for example, 'stayed supper'), and remembering that the narrator here is also a character.

Notes have been supplied fully, in the consciousness that

Penguin editions are read around the world and not just in Britain, and that neither eighteenth-century manners nor English place-names are necessarily matters of course for readers in Japan or Kenya or, for that matter, Canada and the United States.

Volume One

TO ——— ———[1]

Oh author of my being!—far more dear
   To me than light, than nourishment, or rest,
Hygieia's[2] blessings, Rapture's burning tear,
   Or the life blood that mantles in my breast!

If in my heart the love of Virtue glows,
   'T was planted there by an unerring rule;
From thy example the pure flame arose,
   Thy life, my precept—thy good works, my school.

Could my weak pow'rs thy num'rous virtues trace,
   By filial love each fear should be repress'd;
The blush of Incapacity I'd chace,
   And stand, recorder of thy worth, confess'd:

But since my niggard[3] stars that gift refuse,
   Concealment is the only boon I claim;
Obscure be still the unsuccessful Muse,
   Who cannot raise, but would not sink, thy fame.

Oh! of my life at once the source and joy!
   If e'er thy eyes these feeble lines survey,
Let not their folly their intent destroy;
   Accept the tribute – but forget the lay.

TO THE

AUTHORS

OF THE

MONTHLY and CRITICAL
REVIEWS [4]

GENTLEMEN,

The liberty which I take in addressing to You the trifling
production of a few idle hours, will, doubtless, move your
wonder, and, probably, your contempt. I will not, however,
with the futility of apologies, intrude upon your time, but briefly
acknowledge the motives of my temerity: lest, by a premature
exercise of that patience which I hope will befriend me, I should
lessen its benevolence, and be accessary to my own condemnation.

Without name, without recommendation, and unknown alike
to success and disgrace, to whom can I so properly apply
for patronage, as to those who publicly profess themselves
Inspectors of all literary performances?

The extensive plan of your critical observations,—which, not
confined to works of utility or ingenuity, is equally open to
those of frivolous amusement,—and yet worse than frivolous
dullness,—encourages me to seek for your protection, since,—
perhaps for my sins!—it entitles me to your annotations. [5] To
resent, therefore, this offering, however insignificant, would ill

become the universality of your undertaking, though not to despise it may, alas! be out of your power.

The language of adulation, and the incense of flattery, though the natural inheritance, and constant resource, from time immemorial, of the Dedicator, to me offer nothing but the wistful regret that I dare not invoke their aid. Sinister views would be imputed to all I could say; since, thus situated, to extol your judgement, would seem the effect of art, and to celebrate your impartiality, be attributed to suspecting it.

As Magistrates of the press, and Censors[6] for the public,—to which you are bound by the sacred ties of integrity to exert the most spirited impartiality,[7] and to which your suffrages should carry the marks of pure, dauntless, irrefragable truth—to appeal for your MERCY, were to solicit your dishonour; and therefore,—though 'tis sweeter than frankincense,—more grateful to the senses than all the odorous perfumes of Arabia,[8]—and though

> It droppeth like the gentle rain from heaven
> Upon the place beneath, ————[9]

I court it not! to your justice alone I am entitled, and by that I must abide. Your engagements are not to the supplicating author, but to the candid public, which will not fail to crave

> The penalty and forfeit of your bond.[10]

No hackneyed writer, inured to abuse, and callous to criticism, here braves your severity;—neither does a half-starv'd garretteer,[11]

> Oblig'd by hunger—and request of friends, ——[12]

implore your lenity: your examination will be alike unbiassed by partiality and prejudice:—no refractory murmuring will follow your censure, no private interest be gratified by your praise.

Let not the anxious solicitude with which I recommend myself to your notice, expose me to your derision. Remember, Gentlemen, you were all young writers once, and the most experienced veteran of your corps, may, by recollecting his first publication, renovate his first terrors, and learn to allow for mine. For, though Courage is one of the noblest virtues of this nether sphere, and, though scarcely more requisite in the field of battle, to guard the fighting hero from disgrace, than in the private commerce of the world, to ward off that littleness of soul which leads, by steps imperceptible, to all the base train of the inferior passions, and by which the too timid mind is betrayed into a servility derogatory to the dignity of human nature; yet is it a virtue of no necessity in a situation such as mine; a situation which removes, even from cowardice itself, the sting of ignominy;—for surely that courage may easily be dispensed with, which would rather excite disgust than admiration! Indeed, it is the peculiar privilege of an author, to rob terror of contempt, and pusillanimity of reproach.

Here let me rest,—and snatch myself, while I yet am able, from the fascination of EGOTISM,[13]—a monster[14] who has more votaries than ever did homage to the most popular deity of antiquity; and whose singular quality is, that while he excites a blind and involuntary adoration in almost every individual, his influence is universally disallowed, his power universally contemned, and his worship, even by his followers, never mentioned but with abhorrence.

In addressing you jointly, I mean but to mark the generous sentiments by which liberal criticism, to the utter annihilation of envy, jealousy, and all selfish views, ought to be distinguished.

I have the honour to be,

GENTLEMEN,

Your most obedient

Humble servant,

*** ****

PREFACE

1   *In the republic of letters, there is no member of such inferior rank, or who is so much disdained by his brethren of the quill, as the humble Novelist: nor is his fate less hard in the world at large, since, among the whole class of writers, perhaps not one can be named of which the votaries are more numerous but less respectable.*

2   *Yet, while in the annals of those few of our predecessors, to whom this species of writing is indebted for being saved from contempt, and rescued from depravity, we can trace such names as Rousseau,[15] Johnson,*[16] Marivaux,[17] Fielding,[18] Richardson,[19] and Smollet,[20] no man need blush at starting from the same post, though many, nay, most men, may sigh at finding themselves distanced.*

3   *The following letters are presented to the public*—for such, by novel writers, novel readers will be called,—with a very singular mixture of *timidity and confidence, resulting from the peculiar situation of the editor; who, though trembling for their success from a consciousness of their imperfections, yet fears not being involved in their disgrace, while happily wrapped up in a mantle of impenetrable obscurity.*

4   *To draw characters from nature, though not from life, and to mark the manners of the times,[21] is the attempted plan of the following letters. For this purpose, a young female, educated in the most secluded retirement, makes, at the age of seventeen, her first appearance upon the great and busy stage of life; with a virtuous mind, a cultivated understanding, and a feeling heart, her ignorance of the forms, and inexperience in the manners, of the world, occasion all the little incidents which these volumes record, and which form the natural progression of the life of a young woman of*

---

* However superior the capacities in which these great writers deserve to be considered, they must pardon me that, for the dignity of my subject, I here rank the authors of Rasselas and Eloîse as Novelists.

obscure birth, but conspicuous beauty, for the first six months after her
Entrance into the world.

    Perhaps were it possible to effect the total extirpation of novels, our
young ladies in general, and boarding-school damsels in particular, might
profit from their annihilation: but since the distemper they have spread
seems incurable, since their contagion bids defiance to the medicine of
advice or reprehension, and since they are found to baffle all the mental
art of physic, save what is prescribed by the slow regimen of Time, and
bitter diet of Experience, surely all attempts to contribute to the number
of those which may be read, if not with advantage, at least without injury,
ought rather to be encouraged than contemned.

    Let me, therefore, prepare for disappointment those who, in the
perusal of these sheets, entertain the gentle expectation of being transported
to the fantastic regions of Romance, where Fiction is coloured by all the
gay tints of luxurious Imagination, where Reason is an outcast, and where
the sublimity of the Marvellous, rejects all aid from sober Probability.
The heroine of these memoirs, young, artless, and inexperienced, is

No faultless Monster, that the world ne'er saw,[22]

but the offspring of Nature, and of Nature in her simplest attire.

    In all the Arts, the value of copies can only be proportioned to the
scarceness of originals: among sculptors and painters, a fine statue, or a
beautiful picture, of some great master, may deservedly employ the
imitative talents of younger and inferior artists, that their appropriation
to one spot, may not wholly prevent the more general expansion of their
excellence; but, among authors, the reverse is the case, since the noblest
productions of literature, are almost equally attainable with the meanest.
In books, therefore, imitation cannot be shunned too sedulously; for the
very perfection of a model which is frequently seen, serves but more
forcibly to mark the inferiority of a copy.

    To avoid what is common, without adopting what is unnatural, must
limit the ambition of the vulgar herd of authors: however zealous,
therefore, my veneration of the great writers I have mentioned, however I
may feel myself enlightened by the knowledge of Johnson, charmed with the
eloquence of Rousseau, softened by the pathetic powers of Richardson, and
exhilarated by the wit of Fielding, and humour of Smollet; I yet presume
not to attempt pursuing the same ground which they have tracked;

whence, though they may have cleared the weeds, they have also culled the flowers, and though they have rendered the path plain, they have left it barren.

The candour of my readers, I have not the impertinence to doubt, and to their indulgence, I am sensible I have no claim: I have, therefore, only to entreat, that my own words may not pronounce my condemnation, and that what I have here ventured to say in regard to imitation, may be understood, as it is meant, in a general sense, and not be imputed to an opinion of my own originality, which I have not the vanity, the folly, or the blindness, to entertain.

Whatever may be the fate of these letters, the editor is satisfied they will meet with justice; and commits them to the press, though hopeless of fame, yet not regardless of censure.

LETTER I

Howard Grove, Kent

Can any thing, my good Sir, be more painful to a friendly mind, than a necessity of communicating disagreeable intelligence? Indeed, it is sometimes difficult to determine, whether the relator or the receiver of evil tidings is most to be pitied.

I have just had a letter from Madame Duval;[23] she is totally at a loss in what manner to behave; she seems desirous to repair the wrongs she has done, yet wishes the world to believe her blameless. She would fain cast upon another the odium of those misfortunes for which she alone is answerable. Her letter is violent, sometimes abusive, and that of *you!*—*you*, to whom she is under obligations which are greater even than her faults, but to whose advice she wickedly imputes all the sufferings of her much-injured daughter, the late Lady Belmont. The chief purport of her writing I will acquaint you with; the letter itself is not worthy your notice.

She tells me that she has, for many years past, been in continual expectation of making a journey to England, which prevented her writing for information concerning this melancholy subject, by giving her hopes of making personal enquiries; but family occurrences have still detained her in France, which country she now sees no prospect of quitting. She has, therefore, lately used her utmost endeavours to obtain a faithful account of whatever related to her *ill-advised* daughter; the result of which giving her *some reason* to apprehend that, upon her death-bed, she bequeathed an infant orphan to the world, she most graciously says, that if *you*, with whom *she understands* the child is placed, will procure authentic proofs of its relationship to her, you may send it to Paris, where she will properly provide for it.

This woman is, undoubtedly, at length, self-convicted of her most unnatural behaviour: it is evident, from her writing, that she is still as vulgar and illiterate as when her first husband, Mr. Evelyn, had the weakness to marry her; nor does she at all apologize for addressing herself to me, though I was only once in her company.

Her letter has excited in my daughter Mirvan, a strong desire to be informed of the motives which induced Madame Duval to abandon the unfortunate Lady Belmont, at a time when a mother's protection was peculiarly necessary for her peace and her reputation. Notwithstanding I was personally acquainted with all the parties concerned in that affair, the subject always appeared of too delicate a nature to be spoken of with the principals; I cannot, therefore, satisfy Mrs. Mirvan otherwise than by applying to you.

By saying that you *may* send the child, Madame Duval aims at *conferring*, where she most *owes* obligation. I pretend not to give you advice; you, to whose generous protection this helpless orphan is indebted for every thing, are the best and only judge of what she ought to do; but I am much concerned at the trouble and uneasiness which this unworthy woman may occasion you.

My daughter and my grand-child join with me in desiring to be most kindly remembered to the amiable girl; and they bid me remind you, that the annual visit to Howard Grove, which we were formerly promised, has been discontinued for more than four years.

I am, dear Sir,
with great regard,
Your most obedient friend and servant,
M. HOWARD

LETTER II

Mr. Villars to Lady Howard

Berry Hill, Dorsetshire

Your Ladyship did but too well foresee the perplexity and uneasiness of which Madame Duval's letter has been productive. However, I ought rather to be thankful that I have so many years remained unmolested, than repine at my present embarrassment; since it proves, at least, that this wretched woman is at length awakened to remorse.

In regard to my answer, I must humbly request your Ladyship to write to this effect: 'That I would not, upon any account, intentionally offend Madame Duval, but that I have weighty, nay unanswerable reasons for detaining her grand-daughter at present in England; the principal of which is, that it was the earnest desire of one to whose Will she owes implicit duty. Madame Duval may be assured that she meets with the utmost attention and tenderness; that her education, however short of my wishes, almost exceeds my abilities; and I flatter myself, when the time arrives that she shall pay her duty to her grandmother, Madame Duval will find no reason to be dissatisfied with what has been done for her.'

Your Ladyship will not, I am sure, be surprised at this answer. Madame Duval is by no means a proper companion or guardian for a young woman: she is at once uneducated and unprincipled; ungentle in her temper, and unamiable in her manners. I have long known that she has persuaded herself to harbour an aversion for me—Unhappy woman! I can only regard her as an object of pity!

I dare not hesitate at a request from Mrs. Mirvan, yet, in complying with it, I shall, for her own sake, be as concise as I possibly can; since the cruel transactions which preceded the birth of my ward, can afford no entertainment to a mind so humane as hers.

Your Ladyship may probably have heard, that I had the honour to accompany Mr. Evelyn, the grand-father of my young charge, when upon his travels, in the capacity of a tutor.[24] His unhappy marriage, immediately upon his return to England, with Madame Duval, then a waiting-girl at a tavern, contrary to the advice and entreaties of all his friends, among whom I was myself the most urgent, induced him to abandon his native land, and fix his abode in France. Thither he was followed by shame and repentance; feelings which his heart was not framed to support: for, notwithstanding he had been too weak to resist the allurements of beauty, which nature, though a niggard to her of every other boon, had with a lavish hand bestowed on his wife; yet he was a young man of excellent character, and, till thus unaccountably infatuated, of unblemished conduct. He survived this ill-judged marriage but two years. Upon his death-bed, with an unsteady hand, he wrote me the following note:

'My friend! forget your resentment, in favour of your humanity;—a father, trembling for the welfare of his child, bequeaths her to your care.—O Villars! hear! pity! and relieve me!'

Had my circumstances permitted me, I should have answered these words by an immediate journey to Paris; but I was obliged to act by the agency of a friend, who was upon the spot, and present at the opening of the will.

Mr. Evelyn left to me a legacy of a thousand pounds, and the sole guardianship of his daughter's person till her eighteenth year, conjuring me, in the most affecting terms, to take the charge of her education till she was able to act with propriety for herself; but in regard to fortune, he left her wholly dependent on her mother, to whose tenderness he earnestly recommended her.

Thus, though he would not, to a woman low-bred and illiberal as Mrs. Evelyn, trust the conduct and morals of his daughter, he nevertheless thought proper to secure to her the respect and duty which, from her own child, were certainly her due; but, unhappily, it never occurred to him that the mother, on her part, could fail in affection or justice.

Miss Evelyn, Madam, from the second to the eighteenth year of her life, was brought up under my care, and, except when at school, under my roof. I need not speak to your Ladyship of the virtues of that excellent young creature. She loved me as her father; nor was Mrs. Villars less valued by her; while to me she became so dear, that her loss was little less afflicting than that which I have since sustained of Mrs. Villars herself.

At that period of her life we parted; her mother, then married to Monsieur Duval, sent for her to Paris. How often have I since regretted that I did not accompany her thither! protected and supported by me, the misery and disgrace which awaited her, might, perhaps, have been avoided. But, to be brief—Madame Duval, at the instigation of her husband, earnestly, or rather tyrannically, endeavoured to effect a union between Miss Evelyn and one of his nephews. And, when she found her power inadequate to her attempt, enraged at her non-compliance, she treated her with the grossest unkindness, and threatened her with poverty and ruin.

Miss Evelyn, to whom wrath and violence had hitherto been strangers, soon grew weary of such usage; and rashly, and without a witness, consented to a private marriage with Sir John Belmont, a very profligate young man, who had but too successfully found means to insinuate himself into her favour. He promised to conduct her to England—he did.——O, Madam, you know the rest!— Disappointed of the fortune he expected, by the inexorable rancour of the Duvals, he infamously burned the certificate of their marriage,[25] and denied that they had ever been united!

She flew to me for protection. With what mixed transports of joy and anguish did I again see her! By my advice she endeavoured to procure proofs of her marriage;—but in vain: her credulity had been no match for his art.

Every body believed her innocent, from the guiltless tenor of her unspotted youth, and from the known libertinism of her barbarous betrayer. Yet her sufferings were too acute for her tender frame, and the same moment that gave birth to her infant, put an end at once to the sorrows and the life of its mother.

The rage of Madame Duval at her elopement, abated not while this injured victim of cruelty yet drew breath. She probably intended, in time, to have pardoned her, but time was not allowed. When she was informed of her death, I have been told, that the agonies of grief and remorse, with which she was seized, occasioned her a severe fit of illness. But, from the time of her recovery to the date of her letter to your Ladyship, I had never heard that she manifested any desire to be made acquainted with the circumstances which attended the death of Lady Belmont, and the birth of her helpless child.

That child, Madam, shall never, while life is lent me, know the loss she has sustained. I have cherished, succoured, and supported her, from her earliest infancy to her sixteenth year; and so amply has she repaid my care and affection, that my fondest wish is now circumscribed by the desire of bestowing her on one who may be sensible of her worth, and then sinking to eternal rest in her arms.

Thus it has happened that the education of the father, daughter, and grand-daughter, has devolved on me. What infinite misery have the two first caused me! Should the fate of the dear survivor be equally adverse, how wretched will be the end of my cares—the end of my days!

Even had Madame Duval merited the charge she claims, I fear my fortitude would have been unequal to such a parting; but, being such as she is, not only my affection, but my humanity recoils, at the barbarous idea of deserting the sacred trust reposed in me. Indeed, I could but ill support her former yearly visits to the respectable mansion at Howard Grove; pardon me, dear Madam, and do not think me insensible of the honour which your Ladyship's condescension confers upon us both; but so deep is the impression which the misfortunes of her mother have made on my heart, that she does not, even for a moment, quit my sight, without exciting apprehensions and terrors which almost overpower me. Such, Madam, is my tenderness, and such my weakness!—But she is the only tie I have upon earth, and I trust to your Ladyship's goodness not to judge of my feelings with severity.

I beg leave to present my humble respects to Mrs. and Miss Mirvan; and have the honour to be,

Madam,

Your Ladyship's most obedient

and most humble servant,

ARTHUR VILLARS

LETTER III

[Written some months after the last]

Lady Howard to the Rev. Mr. Villars

Howard Grove, March 8

Dear and Rev. Sir,

Your last letter gave me infinite pleasure: after so long and tedious an illness, how grateful to yourself and to your friends must be your returning health! You have the hearty wishes of every individual of this place for its continuance and increase.

Will you not think I take advantage of your acknowledged recovery, if I once more venture to mention your pupil and Howard Grove together? Yet you must remember the patience with which we submitted to your desire of not parting with her during the bad state of your health, though it was with much reluctance we forbore to solicit her company. My granddaughter, in particular, has scarce been able to repress her eagerness to again meet the friend of her infancy; and for my own part, it is very strongly my wish to manifest the regard I had for the unfortunate Lady Belmont, by proving serviceable to her child; which seems to me the best respect that can be paid to her memory. Permit me, therefore, to lay before you a plan which Mrs. Mirvan and I have formed, in consequence of your restoration to health.

I would not frighten you;—but do you think you could bear to part with your young companion for two or three months?

Mrs. Mirvan proposes to spend the ensuing spring in London, whither, for the first time, my grand-child will accompany her: Now, my good friend, it is very earnestly their wish to enlarge and enliven their party by the addition of your amiable ward, who would share, equally with her own daughter, the care and attention of Mrs. Mirvan. Do not start at this proposal; it is time that she should see something of the world. When young people are too rigidly sequestered from it, their lively and romantic imaginations paint it to them as a paradise of which they have been beguiled; but when they are shewn it properly, and in due time, they see it such as it really is, equally shared by pain and pleasure, hope and disappointment.

You have nothing to apprehend from her meeting with Sir John Belmont, as that abandoned man is now abroad, and not expected home this year.

Well, my good Sir, what say you to our scheme? I hope it will meet with your approbation; but if it should not, be assured I can never object to any decision of one who is so much respected and esteemed as Mr. Villars, by

His most faithful humble servant,

M. HOWARD

LETTER IV

Mr. Villars to Lady Howard

Berry Hill, March 12

I am grieved, Madam, to appear obstinate, and I blush to incur the imputation of selfishness. In detaining my young charge thus long with myself in the country, I consulted not solely my own inclination. Destined, in all probability, to possess a very moderate fortune, I wished to contract her views to something within it. The mind is but too naturally prone to pleasure, but too easily yielded to dissipation: it has been my study to guard her against their delusions, by preparing her to expect,—and to despise them. But the time draws on for experience and observation to take place of instruction: if I have, in some measure, rendered her capable of using one with discretion, and making the other with improvement, I shall rejoice myself with the assurance of having largely contributed to her welfare. She is now of an age that happiness is eager to attend,—let her then enjoy it! I commit her to the protection of your Ladyship, and only hope she may be found worthy half the goodness I am satisfied she will meet with at your hospitable mansion.

Thus far, Madam, I chearfully submit to your desire. In confiding my ward to the care of Lady Howard, I can feel no uneasiness from her absence, but what will arise from the loss of her company, since I shall be as well convinced of her safety as if she were under my own roof;—but, can your Ladyship be serious in proposing to introduce her to the gaieties of a London life? Permit me to ask, for what end, or what purpose? A youthful mind is seldom totally free from ambition; to curb that, is the first step to contentment, since to diminish expectation, is to increase enjoyment. I apprehend nothing more than too much raising her hopes and her views, which the natural vivacity of her disposition would render but too easy to effect. The town-acquaintance of Mrs. Mirvan are all in the circle of high life; this artless young creature, with too much beauty to escape notice, has too much sensibility to be indifferent to it; but she has too little wealth to be sought with propriety by men of the fashionable world.

Consider, Madam, the peculiar cruelty of her situation; only child of a wealthy Baronet, whose person she has never seen, whose character she has reason to abhor, and whose name she is forbidden to claim; entitled as she is to lawfully inherit his fortune and estate, is there any probability that he will *properly* own her? And while he continues to persevere in disavowing his marriage with Miss Evelyn, she shall never, at the expence of her mother's honour, receive a part of her right, as the donation of his bounty.

And as to Mr. Evelyn's estate, I have no doubt but that Madame Duval and her relations will dispose of it among themselves.

It seems, therefore, as if this deserted child, though legally heiress of two large fortunes, must owe all her rational expectations to adoption and friendship. Yet her income will be such as may make her happy, if she is disposed to be so in private life; though it will by no means allow her to enjoy the luxury of a London fine lady.

Let Miss Mirvan, then, Madam, shine in all the splendor of high life; but suffer my child still to enjoy the pleasures of humble retirement, with a mind to which greater views are unknown.

I hope this reasoning will be honoured with your approbation; and I have yet another motive which has some weight with me; I would not willingly give offence to any human being, and surely Madame Duval might accuse me of injustice, if, while I refuse to let her grand-daughter wait upon her, I consent that she should join a party of pleasure to London.

In sending her to Howard Grove, not one of these scruples arise; and therefore Mrs. Clinton, a most worthy woman, formerly her nurse, and now my housekeeper, shall attend her thither next week.

Though I have always called her by the name of Anville,[26] and reported in this neighbourhood that her father, my intimate friend, left her to my guardianship, yet I have thought it necessary she should herself be acquainted with the melancholy circumstances attending her birth; for, though I am very desirous of guarding her from curiosity and impertinence, by concealing her name, family, and story, yet I would not leave it in the power of chance, to shock her gentle nature with a tale of so much sorrow.

You must not, Madam, expect too much from my pupil. She is quite a little rustic,[27] and knows nothing of the world, and though her education has been the best I could bestow in this retired place, to which Dorchester,[28] the nearest town, is seven miles distant, yet I shall not be surprised if you should discover in her a thousand deficiencies of which I have never dreamed. She must be very much altered since she was last at Howard Grove,—but I will say nothing of her; I leave her to your Ladyship's own observations, of which I beg a faithful relation; and am,

Dear Madam, with great respect,
Your obedient and most humble servant,
ARTHUR VILLARS

LETTER V

Mr. Villars to Lady Howard

March 18

Dear Madam,

This letter will be delivered to you by my child,—the child of my adoption,—my affection! Unblessed with one natural friend, she merits a thousand. I send her to you, innocent as an angel, and artless as purity itself: and I send you with her the heart of your friend, the only hope he has on earth, the subject of his tenderest thoughts, and the object of his latest cares. She is one, Madam, for whom alone I have lately wished to live; and she is one whom to serve I would with transport die! Restore her but to me all innocence as you receive her, and the fondest hope of my heart will be amply gratified.

A. VILLARS

LETTER VI

Lady Howard to the Rev. Mr. Villars

Howard Grove

Dear and Rev. Sir,

The solemn manner in which you have committed your child to my care, has in some measure damped the pleasure which I receive from the trust, as it makes me fear that you suffer from your compliance, in which case I shall very sincerely blame myself for the earnestness with which I have requested this favour; but remember, my good Sir, she is within a few days' summons, and be assured I will not detain her a moment longer than you wish.

You desire my opinion of her.

She is a little angel! I cannot wonder that you sought to monopolize her. Neither ought you, at finding it impossible.

Her face and person answer my most refined ideas of complete beauty: and this, though a subject of praise less important to you, or to me, than any other, is yet so striking, it is not possible to pass it unnoticed. Had I not known from whom she received her education, I should, at first sight of so perfect a face, have been in pain for her understanding; since it has been long and justly remarked, that folly has ever sought alliance with beauty.

She has the same gentleness in her manners, the same natural grace in her motions, that I formerly so much admired in her mother. Her character seems truly ingenuous and simple; and, at the same time that nature has blessed her with an excellent understanding, and great quickness of parts, she has a certain air of inexperience and innocency that is extremely interesting.

You have no reason to regret the retirement in which she has lived; since that politeness which is acquired by an acquaintance with high life, is in her so well supplied by a natural desire of obliging, joined to a deportment infinitely engaging.

I observe with great satisfaction a growing affection between this amiable girl and my grand-daughter, whose heart is as free from selfishness or conceit, as that of her young friend is from all guile. Their regard may be mutually useful, since much is to be expected from emulation, where nothing is to be feared from envy. I would have them love each other as sisters, and reciprocally supply the place of that tender and happy relationship, to which neither of them have a natural claim.

Be satisfied, my good Sir, that your child shall meet with the same attention as our own. We all join in most hearty wishes for your health and happiness, and in returning our sincere thanks for the favour you have conferred on us.

I am, Dear Sir,

Your most faithful servant,

M. HOWARD

LETTER VII

Lady Howard to the Rev. Mr. Villars

Howard Grove, March 26

Be not alarmed, my worthy friend, at my so speedily troubling you again; I seldom use the ceremony of waiting for answers, or writing with any regularity, and I have at present immediate occasion for begging your patience.

Mrs. Mirvan has just received a letter from her long-absent husband, containing the welcome news of his hoping to reach London by the beginning of next week. My daughter and the Captain have been separated almost seven years, and it would therefore be needless to say what joy, surprise, and consequently confusion, his, at present, unexpected return has caused at Howard Grove. Mrs. Mirvan, you cannot doubt, will go instantly to town to meet him; her daughter is under a thousand obligations to attend her; I grieve that her mother cannot.

And now, my good Sir, I almost blush to proceed;—but, tell me, may I ask—will you permit—that your child may accompany them? Do not think us unreasonable, but consider the many inducements which conspire to make London the happiest place at present she can be in. The joyful occasion of the journey; the gaiety of the whole party; opposed to the dull life she must lead if left here, with a solitary old woman for her sole companion, while she so well knows the chearfulness and felicity enjoyed by the rest of the family,—are circumstances that seem to merit your consideration. Mrs. Mirvan desires me to assure you, that one week is all she asks, as she is certain that the Captain, who hates London, will be eager to revisit Howard Grove: and Maria is so very earnest in wishing to have the company of her friend, that, if you are inexorable, she will be deprived of half the pleasure she otherwise hopes to receive.

However, I will not, my good Sir, deceive you into an opinion that they intend to live in a retired manner, as that cannot be fairly expected. But you have no reason to be uneasy concerning Madame Duval; she has not any correspondent in England, and obtains no intelligence but by common report.[29] She must be a stranger to the name your child bears; and, even should she hear of this excursion, so short a time as a week, or less, spent in town upon so particular an occasion, though previous to their meeting, cannot be construed into disrespect to herself.

Mrs. Mirvan desires me to assure you, that if you will oblige her, her *two* children shall equally share her time and her attention. She has sent a commission to a friend in town to take a house for her, and while she waits for an answer concerning it, I shall for one from you to our petition. However, your child is writing herself, and that, I doubt not, will more avail than all we can possibly urge.

My daughter desires her best compliments to you, *if*, she says, you will grant her request, but *not else*.

Adieu, my dear Sir,—we all hope every thing from your goodness.

                                        M. Howard

LETTER VIII

Evelina to the Rev. Mr. Villars

Howard Grove, March 26

This house seems to be the house of joy; every face wears a smile, and a laugh is at every body's service. It is quite amusing to walk about, and see the general confusion; a room leading to the garden is fitting up for Captain Mirvan's study. Lady Howard does not sit a moment in a place; Miss Mirvan is making caps;[30] every body so busy!—such flying from room to room!—so many orders given, and retracted, and given again!—nothing but hurry and perturbation.

Well but, my dear Sir, I am desired to make a request to you. I hope you will not think me an encroacher; Lady Howard insists upon my writing!—yet I hardly know how to go on; a petition implies a want,—and have you left me one? No, indeed.

I am half ashamed of myself for beginning this letter. But these dear ladies are so pressing—I cannot, for my life, resist wishing for the pleasures they offer me,—provided you do not disapprove them.

They are to make a very short stay in town. The Captain will meet them in a day or two. Mrs. Mirvan and her sweet daughter both go;—what a happy party! Yet I am not *very* eager to accompany them: at least, I shall be contented to remain where I am, if you desire that I should.

Assured, my dearest Sir, of your goodness, your bounty, and your indulgent kindness, ought I to form a wish that has not your sanction? Decide for me, therefore, without the least apprehension that I shall be uneasy, or discontented. While I am yet in suspense, perhaps I may *hope*, but I am most certain, that when you have once determined, I shall not repine.

They tell me that London is now in full splendour. Two Playhouses are open,[31]—the Opera-House,[32]—Ranelagh,[33]—and the Pantheon.[34]—You see I have learned all their names. However, pray don't suppose that I make any point of going, for I shall hardly sigh to see them depart without me; though I shall probably never meet with such another opportunity. And, indeed, their domestic happiness will be so great,—it is natural to wish to partake of it.

I believe I am bewitched! I made a resolution when I began, that I would not be urgent;[35] but my pen—or rather my thoughts, will not suffer me to keep it—for I acknowledge, I must acknowledge, I cannot help wishing for your permission.

I almost repent already that I have made this confession; pray forget that you have read it, if this journey is displeasing to you. But I will not write any longer; for the more I think of this affair, the less indifferent to it I find myself.

Adieu, my most honoured, most reverenced, most beloved father! for by what other name can I call you? I have no happiness or sorrow, no hope or fear, but what your kindness bestows, or your displeasure may cause. You will not, I am sure, send a refusal, without reasons unanswerable, and therefore I shall chearfully acquiesce. Yet I hope—I hope you will be able to permit me to go!   I am,

With the utmost affection,

gratitude, and duty,

Your

EVELINA ———

I cannot to *you* sign *Anville*, and what other name may I claim?[36]

LETTER IX

Mr. Villars to Evelina

Berry Hill, March 28

To resist the urgency of entreaty, is a power which I have not yet acquired: I aim not at an authority which deprives you of liberty, yet I would fain guide myself by a prudence which should save me the pangs of repentance. Your impatience to fly to a place which your imagination has painted to you in colours so attractive, surprises me not; I have only to hope that the liveliness of your fancy may not deceive you: to refuse, would be raising it still higher. To see my Evelina happy, is to see myself without a wish: go then, my child, and may that Heaven which alone can, direct, preserve, and strengthen you! To That, my love, will I daily offer prayers for your felicity; O may it guard, watch over you! defend you from danger, save you from distress, and keep vice as distant from your person as from your heart! And to Me, may it grant the ultimate blessing of closing these aged eyes in the arms of one so dear—so deservedly beloved!

ARTHUR VILLARS

LETTER X

Evelina to the Rev. Mr. Villars

Queen-Ann-Street,[37] London, Saturday April 2

This moment arrived. Just going to Drury-Lane Theatre. The celebrated Mr. Garrick[38] performs Ranger.[39] I am quite in extacy. So is Miss Mirvan. How fortunate, that he should happen to play! We would not let Mrs. Mirvan rest till she consented to go;

her chief objection was to our dress, for we have had no time to *Londonize*[40] ourselves; but we teazed her into compliance, and so we are to sit in some obscure place, that she may not be seen. As to me, I should be alike unknown in the most conspicuous or most private part of the house.

I can write no more now. I have hardly time to breathe—only just this, the houses and streets are not quite so superb as I expected. However, I have seen nothing yet, so I ought not to judge.

Well, adieu, my dearest Sir, for the present; I could not forbear writing a few words instantly on my arrival; though I suppose my letter of thanks for your consent is still on the road.

Saturday Night

O my dear Sir, in what raptures am I returned! Well may Mr. Garrick be so celebrated, so universally admired—I had not any idea of so great a performer.

Such ease! such vivacity in his manner! such grace in his motions! such fire and meaning in his eyes!—I could hardly believe he had studied a written part, for every word seemed to be uttered from the impulse of the moment.

His action—at once so graceful and so free!—his voice—so clear, so melodious, yet so wonderfully various in its tones—such animation!—every look *speaks*!

I would have given the world to have had the whole play acted over again. And when he danced—O how I envied Clarinda![41] I almost wished to have jumped on the stage and joined them.

I am afraid you will think me mad, so I won't say any more; yet I really believe Mr. Garrick would make you mad too, if you could see him. I intend to ask Mrs. Mirvan to go to the play every night while we stay in town. She is extremely kind to me, and Maria, her charming daughter, is the sweetest girl in the world.

I shall write to you every evening all that passes in the day, and that in the same manner as, if I could see, I should tell you.

Sunday

This morning we went to Portland Chapel,[42] and afterwards we walked in the Mall of St. James's Park,[43] which by no means answered my expectations: it is a long straight walk, of dirty gravel, very uneasy to the feet; and at each end, instead of an open prospect, nothing is to be seen but houses built of brick. When Mrs. Mirvan pointed out the *Palace* to me—I think I was never much more surprised.

However, the walk was very agreeable to us; every body looked gay, and seemed pleased, and the ladies were so much dressed, that Miss Mirvan and I could do nothing but look at them. Mrs. Mirvan met several of her friends. No wonder, for I never saw so many people assembled together before. I looked about for some of my acquaintance, but in vain, for I saw not one person that I knew, which is very odd, for all the world seemed there.

Mrs. Mirvan says we are not to walk in the Park again next Sunday, even if we should be in town, because there is better company in Kensington Gardens.[44] But really if you had seen how much every body was dressed, you would not think that possible.

Monday

We are to go this evening to a private ball, given by Mrs. Stanley, a very fashionable lady of Mrs. Mirvan's acquaintance.

We have been *a-shopping*,[45] as Mrs. Mirvan calls it, all this morning, to buy silks, caps, gauzes,[46] and so forth.

The shops are really very entertaining, especially the mercers,[47] there seem to be six or seven men belonging to each shop, and every one took care, by bowing and smirking, to be noticed; we were conducted from one to another, and carried from room to room, with so much ceremony, that at first I was almost afraid to go on.

I thought I should never have chosen a silk, for they produced so many I knew not which to fix upon, and they recommended them all so strongly, that I fancy they thought I only wanted persuasion to buy every thing they shewed me. And, indeed, they took so much trouble, that I was almost ashamed I could not.

At the milliners,[48] the ladies we met were so much dressed, that I should rather have imagined they were making visits than purchases. But what most diverted me was, that we were more frequently served by men than by women;[49] and such men! so finical, so affected! they seemed to understand every part of a woman's dress better than we do ourselves; and they recommended caps and ribbands with an air of so much importance, that I wished to ask them how long they had left off wearing them.

The dispatch with which they work in these great shops is amazing, for they have promised me a compleat suit of linen[50] against the evening.

I have just had my hair dressed.[51] You can't think how oddly my head feels; full of powder and black pins, and a great *cushion* on the top of it. I believe you would hardly know me, for my face looks quite different to what it did before my hair was dressed. When I shall be able to make use of a comb for myself I cannot tell for my hair is so much entangled, *frizzled* they call it, that I fear it will be very difficult.

I am half afraid of this ball to-night, for you know, I have never danced but at school,[52] however, Miss Mirvan says there is nothing in it. Yet I wish it was over.

Adieu, my dear Sir; pray excuse the wretched stuff I write, perhaps I may improve by being in this town, and then my letters will be less unworthy your reading.

Mean time I am,

> Your dutiful and affectionate,
>
> though unpolished,
>
> EVELINA

Poor Miss Mirvan cannot wear one of the caps she made, because they dress her hair too large for them.

LETTER XI

Evelina in continuation

Queen-Ann-Street, April 5, Tuesday Morning

I have a vast deal to say, and shall give all this morning to my pen. As to my plan of writing every evening the adventures of the day, I find it impracticable; for the diversions here are so very late, that if I begin my letters after them, I could not go to bed at all.

We passed a most extraordinary evening. A *private* ball[53] this was called, so I expected to have seen about four or five couple; but Lord! my dear Sir, I believe I saw half the world! Two very large rooms were full of company; in one, were cards for the elderly ladies,[54] and in the other, were the dancers. My mamma Mirvan, for she always calls me her child, said she would sit with Maria and me till we were provided with partners, and then join the card-players.

The gentlemen, as they passed and repassed, looked as if they thought we were quite at their disposal, and only waiting for the honour of their commands; and they sauntered about, in a careless indolent manner, as if with a view to keep us in suspense. I don't speak of this in regard to Miss Mirvan and myself only, but to the ladies in general; and I thought it so provoking, that I determined, in my own mind, that, far from humouring such airs, I would rather not dance at all, than with any one who should seem to think me ready to accept the first partner who would condescend to take me.

Not long after, a young man, who had for some time looked at us with a kind of negligent impertinence, advanced, on tip-toe, towards me; he had a set smile on his face, and his dress was so foppish,[55] that I really believe he even wished to be stared at; and yet he was very ugly.

Bowing almost to the ground, with a sort of swing, and waving his hand with the greatest conceit, after a short and silly pause, he said, 'Madam—may I presume?'—and stopped, offering to take my hand. I drew it back, but could scarce forbear laughing. 'Allow me, Madam,' continued he, affectedly breaking off every half moment, 'the honour and happiness—if I am not so unhappy as to address you too late—to have the happiness and honour——'

Again he would have taken my hand, but, bowing my head, I begged to be excused, and turned to Miss Mirvan to conceal my laughter. He then desired to know if I had already engaged myself to some more fortunate man? I said No, and that I believed I should not dance at all. He would keep himself, he told me, disengaged, in hopes I should relent; and then, uttering some ridiculous speeches of sorrow and disappointment, though his face still wore the same invariable smile, he retreated.

It so happened, as we have since recollected, that during this little dialogue, Mrs. Mirvan was conversing with the lady of the house. And very soon after another gentleman, who seemed about six-and-twenty years old, gayly, but not foppishly, dressed, and indeed extremely handsome, with an air of mixed politeness and gallantry, desired to know if I was engaged, or would honour him with my hand. So he was pleased to say, though I am sure I know not what honour he could receive from me; but these sort of expressions, I find, are used as words of course,[56] without any distinction of persons, or study of propriety.

Well, I bowed, and I am sure I coloured; for indeed I was frightened at the thoughts of dancing before so many people, all strangers, and, which was worse, *with* a stranger; however, that was unavoidable, for though I looked round the room several times, I could not see one person that I knew. And so, he took my hand, and led me to join in the dance.

The minuets were over before we arrived, for we were kept late by the milliner's making us wait for our things.

He seemed very desirous of entering into conversation with me; but I was seized with such a panic, that I could hardly speak a word, and nothing but the shame of so soon changing my mind, prevented my returning to my seat, and declining to dance at all.

He appeared to be surprised at my terror, which I believe was but too apparent: however, he asked no questions, though I fear he must think it very strange; for I did not chuse to tell him it was owing to my never before dancing but with a school-girl.

His conversation was sensible and spirited; his air and address were open and noble; his manners gentle, attentive, and infinitely engaging; his person is all elegance, and his countenance, the most animated and expressive I have ever seen.

In a short time we were joined by Miss Mirvan, who stood next couple to us. But how was I startled, when she whispered me that my partner was a nobleman! This gave me a new alarm; how will he be provoked, thought I, when he finds what a simple rustic he has honoured with his choice! one whose ignorance of the world makes her perpetually fear doing something wrong!

That he should be so much my superior every way, quite disconcerted me; and you will suppose my spirits were not much raised, when I heard a lady, in passing us, say, 'This is the most difficult dance[57] I ever saw.'

'O dear, then,' cried Maria to her partner, 'with your leave, I'll sit down till the next.'

'So will I too, then,' cried I, 'for I am sure I can hardly stand.'

'But you must speak to your partner first,' answered she; for he had turned aside to talk with some gentlemen. However, I had not sufficient courage to address him, and so away we all three tripped, and seated ourselves at another end of the room.

But, unfortunately for me, Miss Mirvan soon after suffered herself to be prevailed upon to attempt the dance; and just as she rose to go, she cried, 'My dear, yonder is your partner, Lord Orville, walking about the room in search of you.'

'Don't leave me then, dear girl!' cried I; but she was obliged to go. And now I was more uneasy than ever; I would have given the world to have seen Mrs. Mirvan, and begged of her to make my apologies; for what, thought I, can I possibly say to him in excuse for running away? he must either conclude me a fool, or half mad; for any one brought up in the great world, and accustomed to its ways, can have no idea of such sort of fears as mine.

My confusion increased when I observed that he was every where seeking me, with apparent perplexity and surprise; but when, at last, I saw him move towards the place where I sat, I was ready to sink with shame and distress. I found it absolutely impossible to keep my seat, because I could not think of a word to say for myself, and so I rose, and walked hastily towards the card-room, resolving to stay with Mrs. Mirvan the rest of the evening, and not to dance at all. But before I could find her, Lord Orville saw and approached me.

He begged to know if I was not well? You may easily imagine how much I was embarrassed. I made no answer, but hung my head, like a fool, and looked on my fan.

He then, with an air the most respectfully serious, asked if he had been so unhappy as to offend me?

'No, indeed!' cried I: and, in hopes of changing the discourse, and preventing his further enquiries, I desired to know if he had seen the young lady who had been conversing with me?

No;—but would I honour him with any commands to her?

'O by no means!'

Was there any other person with whom I wished to speak?

I said *no*, before I knew I had answered at all.

Should he have the pleasure of bringing me any refreshment?

I bowed, almost involuntarily. And away he flew.

I was quite ashamed of being so troublesome, and so much *above* myself as these seeming airs made me appear; but indeed I was too much confused to think or act with any consistency.

If he had not been swift as lightning, I don't know whether I should not have stolen away again; but he returned in a moment. When I had drunk a glass of lemonade, he hoped, he said, that I would again honour him with my hand, as a new dance was just begun. I had not the presence of mind to say a single word, and so I let him once more lead me to the place I had left.

Shocked to find how silly, how childish a part I had acted, my former fears of dancing before such a company, and with such a partner, returned more forcibly than ever. I suppose he perceived my uneasiness, for he entreated me to sit down again, if dancing was disagreeable to me. But I was quite satisfied with the folly I had already shewn, and therefore declined his offer, tho' I was really scarce able to stand.

Under such conscious disadvantages, you may easily imagine, my dear Sir, how ill I acquitted myself. But, though I both expected and deserved to find him very much mortified and displeased at his ill fortune in the choice he had made, yet, to my very great relief, he appeared to be even contented, and very much assisted and encouraged me. These people in high life have too much presence of mind, I believe, to *seem* disconcerted, or out of humour, however they may feel: for had I been the person of the most consequence in the room, I could not have met with more attention and respect.

When the dance was over, seeing me still very much flurried, he led me to a seat saying that he would not suffer me to fatigue myself from politeness.

And then, if my capacity, or even if my spirits had been better, in how animated a conversation might I have been engaged! It was then I saw that the rank of Lord Orville was his least recommendation, his understanding and his manners being far more distinguished. His remarks upon the company in general were so apt, so just, so lively, I am almost surprised myself that they did not re-animate me; but indeed I was too well convinced of the ridiculous part I had myself played before so nice[58] an observer, to be able to enjoy his pleasantry: so self-compassion gave me feeling for others. Yet I had not the courage to attempt either to defend them, or to rally[59] in my turn, but listened to him in silent embarrassment.

When he found this, he changed the subject, and talked of public places, and public performers; but he soon discovered that I was totally ignorant of them.

He then, very ingeniously, turned the discourse to the amusements and occupations of the country.

It now struck me, that he was resolved to try whether or not I was capable of talking upon *any* subject. This put so great a constraint upon my thoughts, that I was unable to go further than a monosyllable, and not even so far, when I could possibly avoid it.

We were sitting in this manner, he conversing with all gaiety, I looking down with all foolishness, when that fop who had first asked me to dance, with a most ridiculous solemnity, approached, and after a profound bow or two, said, 'I humbly beg pardon, Madam,—and of you too, my Lord,—for breaking in upon such agreeable conversation—which must, doubtless, be much more delectable—than what I have the honour to offer—but—'

I interrupted him—I blush for my folly,—with laughing; yet I could not help it, for, added to the man's stately foppishness, (and he actually took snuff between every three words), when I looked round at Lord Orville, I saw such extreme surprise in his face,—the cause of which appeared so absurd, that I could not for my life preserve my gravity.

I had not laughed before from the time I had left Miss Mirvan, and I had much better have cried then; Lord Orville actually stared at me; the beau,[60] I know not his name, looked quite enraged. 'Refrain—Madam,' said he, with an important air, 'a few moments refrain!—I have but a sentence to trouble you with,—May I know to what accident I must attribute not having the honour of your hand?'

'Accident, Sir!' repeated I, much astonished.

'Yes, accident, Madam—for surely,—I must take the liberty to observe—pardon me, Madam,—it ought to be no common one—that should tempt a lady—so young a one too,—to be guilty of ill manners.'

A confused idea now for the first time entered my head, of something I had heard of the rules of an assembly,[61] but I was never at one before,—I have only danced at school,—and so giddy and heedless I was, that I had not once considered the impropriety of refusing one partner, and afterwards accepting another. I was thunderstruck at the recollection: but, while these thoughts were rushing into my head. Lord Orville, with some warmth, said, 'This lady, Sir, is incapable of meriting such an accusation!'

The creature—for I am very angry with him—made a low bow, and, with a grin the most malicious I ever saw, 'My Lord,' said he, 'far be it from me to *accuse* the lady, for having the discernment to distinguish and prefer—the superior attractions of your Lordship.'

Again he bowed, and walked off.

Was ever any thing so provoking? I was ready to die with shame. 'What a coxcomb!'[62] exclaimed Lord Orville; while I, without knowing what I did, rose hastily, and moving off, 'I can't imagine,' cried I, 'where Mrs. Mirvan has hid herself!'

'Give me leave to see,' answered he. I bowed and sat down again, not daring to meet his eyes; for what must he think of me, between my blunder, and the supposed preference?

He returned in a moment, and told me that Mrs. Mirvan was at cards, but would be glad to see me; and I went immediately. There was but one chair vacant, so, to my great relief, Lord Orville presently left us. I then told Mrs. Mirvan my disasters, and she good-naturedly blamed herself for not having better instructed me, but said she had taken it for granted that I must know such common customs. However, the man may, I think, be satisfied with his pretty speech, and carry his resentment no farther.

In a short time, Lord Orville returned. I consented, with the best grace I could, to go down another dance, for I had had time to recollect myself, and therefore resolved to use some exertion, and, if possible, appear less a fool than I had hitherto done; for it occurred to me that, insignificant as I was, compared to a man of his rank and figure, yet, since he had been so unfortunate as to make choice of me for a partner, why I should endeavour to make the best of it.

The dance, however, was short, and he spoke very little; so I had no opportunity of putting my resolution in practice. He was satisfied, I suppose, with his former successless efforts to draw me out: or, rather, I fancied, he had been enquiring *who I was*. This again disconcerted me, and the spirits I had determined to exert, again failed me. Tired, ashamed, and mortified, I begged to sit down till we returned home, which I did soon after. Lord Orville did me the honour to hand me to the coach, talking all the way of the honour I had done *him*! O these fashionable people!

Well, my dear Sir, was it not a strange evening? I could not help being thus particular, because, to me, every thing is so new. But it is now time to conclude. I am, with all love and duty,

Your

EVELINA

LETTER XII

Evelina in continuation

Tuesday, April 5

There is to be no end to the troubles of last night. I have this moment, between persuasion and laughter, gathered from Maria the most curious dialogue that ever I heard. You will, at first, be startled at my vanity; but, my dear Sir, have patience!

It must have passed while I was sitting with Mrs. Mirvan in the card-room. Maria was taking some refreshment, and saw Lord Orville advancing for the same purpose himself; but he did not know her, though she immediately recollected him. Presently after, a very gay-looking man, stepping hastily up to him, cried, 'Why, my Lord, what have you done with your lovely partner?'

'*Nothing!*' answered Lord Orville, with a smile and a shrug.

'By Jove,' cried the man, 'she is the most beautiful creature I ever saw in my life!'

Lord Orville, as he well might, laughed, but answered, 'Yes, a pretty modest-looking girl.'

'O my Lord!' cried the madman, 'she is an angel!'

'A *silent* one,' returned he.

'Why ay, my Lord, how stands she as to that? She looks all intelligence and expression.'

'A poor weak girl!' answered Lord Orville, shaking his head.

'By Jove,' cried the other, 'I am glad to hear it!'

At that moment, the same odious creature who had been my

former tormentor, joined them. Addressing Lord Orville with great respect, he said, 'I beg pardon, my Lord,—if I was—as I fear might be the case—rather too severe in my censure of the lady who is honoured with your protection—but, my Lord, ill-breeding is apt to provoke a man.'

'Ill-breeding!' cried my unknown champion, 'impossible! that elegant face can never be so vile a mask!'

'O Sir, as to that,' answered he, 'you must allow *me* to judge; for though I pay all deference to your opinion—in other things,—yet I hope you will grant—and I appeal to your Lord-ship also—that I am not totally despicable as a judge of good or ill manners.'

'I was so wholly ignorant,' said Lord Orville gravely, 'of the provocation you might have had, that I could not but be surprised at your singular resentment.'

'It was far from my intention,' answered he, 'to offend your Lordship; but really, for a person who is nobody, to give herself such airs,—I own I could not command my passions. For, my Lord, though I have made diligent enquiry—I cannot learn who she is.'

'By what I can make out,' cried my defender, 'she must be a country parson's daughter.'

'He! he! he! very good, 'pon honour!' cried the fop,—'well, so I could have sworn by her manners.'

And then, delighted at his own wit, he laughed, and went away, as I suppose, to repeat it.

'But what the deuce is all this?' demanded the other.

'Why a very foolish affair,' answered Lord Orville; 'your Helen[63] first refused this coxcomb, and then—danced with me. This is all I can gather of it.'

'O Orville,' returned he, 'you are a happy man! But, *ill-bred?*—I can never believe it! And she looks too sensible to be *ignorant.*'

'Whether ignorant or mischievous, I will not pretend to determine, but certain it is, she attended to all *I* could say to her, though I have really fatigued myself with fruitless endeavours to entertain her, with the most immoveable gravity; but no sooner did Lovel[64] begin his complaint, than she was seized with a fit of laughing, first affronting the poor beau, and then enjoying his mortification.'

'Ha! ha! ha! why there's some *genius* in that, my Lord, though perhaps rather—*rustick.*'

Here Maria was called to dance, and so heard no more.

Now tell me, my dear Sir, did you ever know any thing more provoking? '*A poor weak girl!*' '*ignorant or mischievous!*'. What mortifying words! I am resolved, however, that I will never again be tempted to go to an assembly. I wish I had been in Dorsetshire.

Well, after this, you will not be surprised that Lord Orville contented himself with an enquiry after our healths this morning, by his servant, without troubling himself to call,[65] as Miss Mirvan had told me he would: but perhaps it may be only a country custom.

I would not live here for the world. I care not how soon we leave town. London soon grows tiresome. I wish the Captain would come. Mrs. Mirvan talks of the opera for this evening; however, I am very indifferent about it.

Wednesday morning

Well, my dear Sir, I have been pleased against my will, I could almost say, for I must own I went out in very ill-humour, which I think you cannot wonder at: but the music and the singing were charming; they soothed me into a pleasure the most grateful, the best suited to my present disposition in the world. I hope to persuade Mrs. Mirvan to go again on Saturday. I wish the opera was every night. It is, of all entertainments, the sweetest, and most delightful. Some of the songs seemed to melt my very soul. It was what they call a *serious* opera,[66] as the *comic* first singer was ill.

To-night we go to Ranelagh. If any of those three gentlemen who conversed so freely about me should be there——but I won't think of it.

Thursday morning

Well, my dear Sir, we went to Ranelagh. It is a charming place, and the brilliancy of the lights, on my first entrance, made me almost think I was in some enchanted castle, or fairy palace, for all looked like magic to me.

The very first person I saw was Lord Orville. I felt so confused!—but he did not see me. After tea, Mrs. Mirvan being tired, Maria and I walked round the room alone. Then again we saw him, standing by the orchestra. We, too, stopped to hear a singer. He bowed to me; I courtsied, and I am sure I coloured. We soon walked on, not liking our situation: however, he did not follow us; and when we passed by the orchestra again, he was gone. Afterwards, in the course of the evening, we met him several times; but he was always with some party, and never spoke to us, tho' whenever he chanced to meet my eyes, he condescended to bow.

I cannot but be hurt at the opinion he entertains of me. It is true, my own behaviour incurred it—yet he is himself the most agreeable and, seemingly, the most amiable man in the world, and therefore it is, that I am grieved to be thought ill of by him: for of whose esteem ought we to be ambitious, if not of those who most merit our own?—But it is too late to reflect upon this now. Well, I can't help it;—However, I think I have done with assemblies!

This morning was destined for *seeing sights*,[67] auctions,[68] curious shops, and so forth; but my head ached, and I was not in a humour to be amused, and so I made them go without me, though very unwillingly. They are all kindness.

And now I am sorry I did not accompany them, for I know not what to do with myself. I had resolved not to go to the play to-night; but I believe I shall. In short, I hardly care whether I do or not.

*   *   *   *   *

I thought I had done wrong! Mrs. Mirvan and Maria have been half the town over, and so entertained!—while I, like a fool, stayed at home to do nothing. And, at an auction in Pall-mall, who should they meet but Lord Orville! He sat next to Mrs. Mirvan, and they talked a great deal together: but she gave me no account of the conversation.

I may never have such another opportunity of seeing London; I am quite sorry that I was not of the party; but I deserve this mortification, for having indulged my ill-humour.

Thursday night

We are just returned from the play, which was King Lear, and has made me very sad.[69] We did not see any body we knew.

Well, adieu, it is too late to write more.

Friday

Captain Mirvan is arrived. I have not spirits to give an account of his introduction, for he has really shocked me. I do not like him. He seems to be surly, vulgar, and disagreeable.

Almost the same moment that Maria was presented to him, he began some rude jests upon the bad shape of her nose, and called her a tall, ill-formed thing. She bore it with the utmost good humour; but that kind and sweet-tempered woman, Mrs. Mirvan, deserved a better lot. I am amazed she would marry him.

For my own part, I have been so shy, that I have hardly spoken to him, or he to me. I cannot imagine why the family was so rejoiced at his return. If he had spent his whole life abroad, I should have supposed they might rather have been thankful than sorrowful. However, I hope they do not think so ill of him as I do. At least, I am sure they have too much prudence to make it known.

Saturday night

We have been to the opera, and I am still more pleased than I was on Tuesday. I could have thought myself in paradise, but for the continual talking of the company around me. We sat in the pit,[70] where every body was dressed in so high a style, that, if I had been less delighted with the performance, my eyes would have found me sufficient entertainment from looking at the ladies.

I was very glad I did not sit next the Captain, for he could not bear the music, or singers, and was extremely gross in his observations on both. When the opera was over, we went into a place called the coffee-room, where ladies as well as gentlemen assemble. There are all sorts of refreshments, and the company walk about, and *chat*[71] with the same ease and freedom as in a private room.

On Monday we go to a ridotto,[72] and on Wednesday we return to Howard Grove. The Captain says he won't stay here to be *smoked with filth*[73] any longer; but, having been seven years *smoked with a burning sun*,[74] he will retire to the country, and sink into a *fair-weather chap*.[75]

Adieu, my dear Sir.

LETTER XIII

Evelina in continuation

Tuesday, April 12

My dear Sir,

We came home from the ridotto so late, or rather, so early, that it was not possible for me to write. Indeed we did not *go*, you will be frightened to hear it,—till past eleven o'clock: but nobody does. A terrible reverse of the order of nature! We sleep with the sun, and wake with the moon.

The room was very magnificent, the lights and decorations were brilliant, and the company gay and splendid. But I should have told you, that I made many objections to being of the party,[76] according to the resolution I had formed. However, Maria laughed me out of my scruples, and so once again—I went to an assembly.

Miss Mirvan danced a minuet, but I had not the courage to follow her example. In our walks I saw Lord Orville. He was quite alone, but did not observe us. Yet, as he seemed of no

party, I thought it was not impossible that he might join us; and
tho' I did not wish much to dance at all,—yet, as I was more
acquainted with him than with any other person in the room, I
must own I could not help thinking it would be infinitely more
desirable to dance again with him, than with an entire stranger.
To be sure, after all that had passed, it was very ridiculous to
suppose it even probable, that Lord Orville would again honour
me with his choice; yet I am compelled to confess my absurdity,
by way of explaining what follows.

Miss Mirvan was soon engaged; and, presently after, a very
fashionable, gay-looking man, who seemed about 30 years of
age, addressed himself to me, and begged to have the honour of
dancing with me. Now Maria's partner was a gentleman of Mrs.
Mirvan's acquaintance; for she had told us it was highly improper
for young women to dance with strangers, at any public assembly. Indeed it was by no means my wish so to do; yet I did not
like to confine myself from dancing at all; neither did I dare
refuse this gentleman, as I had done Mr. Lovel, and then, if any
acquaintance should offer, accept him: and so, all these reasons
combining, induced me to tell him—yet I blush to write it to
you!—that I was *already engaged*;[77] by which I meant to keep
myself at liberty to dance or not, as matters should fall out.

I suppose my consciousness betrayed my artifice, for he looked
at me as if incredulous; and, instead of being satisfied with my
answer, and leaving me, according to my expectation, he walked
at my side, and, with the greatest ease imaginable, began a
conversation, in the free style which only belongs to old and
intimate acquaintance. But, what was most provoking, he asked
me a thousand questions concerning *the partner to whom I was
engaged*. And, at last, he said, 'Is it really possible that a man
whom you have honoured with your acceptance, can fail to be at
hand to profit from your goodness?'

I felt extremely foolish, and begged Mrs. Mirvan to lead to a
seat, which she very obligingly did. The Captain sat next her,
and, to my great surprise, this gentleman thought proper to
follow, and seat himself next to me.

'What an insensible!' continued he, 'why, Madam, you are

missing the most delightful dance in the world! The man must be either mad, or a fool—Which do you incline to think him yourself?'

'Neither, Sir,' answered I in some confusion.

He begged my pardon for the freedom of his supposition, saying, 'I really was off my guard, from astonishment that any man can be so much and so unaccountably his own enemy. But where, Madam, can he possibly be?—has he left the room?—or has not he been in it?'

'Indeed, Sir,' said I peevishly, 'I know nothing of him.'

'I don't wonder that you are disconcerted, Madam, it is really very provoking. The best part of the evening will be absolutely lost. He deserves not that you should wait for him.'

'I do not, Sir,' said I, 'and I beg you not to——'

'Mortifying, indeed, Madam,' interrupted he, 'a lady to wait for a gentleman:—O fie!—careless fellow!—what can detain him?—Will you give me leave to seek him?'

'If you please, Sir,' answered I, quite terrified lest Mrs. Mirvan should attend to him, for she looked very much surprised at seeing me enter into conversation with a stranger.

'With all my heart,' cried he; 'pray what coat has he on?'

'Indeed I never looked at it.'

'Out upon him!' cried he; 'What! did he address you in a coat not worth looking at?—What a shabby wretch!'

How ridiculous! I really could not help laughing, which, I fear, encouraged him, for he went on.

'Charming creature!—and can you really bear ill usage with so much sweetness?—Can you, *like patience on a monument*,[78] smile in the midst of disappointment?—For my part, though I am not the offended person, my indignation is so great, that I long to kick the fellow round the room!—unless, indeed,—' (hesitating and looking earnestly at me) 'unless, indeed—it is a partner of your own *creating*?'

I was dreadfully abashed, and could not make any answer.

'But no!' cried he (again, and with warmth), 'it cannot be that you are so cruel! Softness itself is painted in your eyes:—You could not, surely, have the barbarity so wantonly to trifle with my misery.'

I turned away from this nonsense, with real disgust. Mrs. Mirvan saw my confusion, but was perplexed what to think of it, and I could not explain to her the cause, lest the Captain should hear me. I therefore proposed to walk, she consented, and we all rose; but, would you believe it? this man had the assurance to rise too, and walk close by my side, as if of my party!

'Now,' cried he, 'I hope we shall see this ingrate.—Is that he?'—pointing to an old man, who was lame, 'or that?' And in this manner he asked me of whoever was old or ugly in the room. I made no sort of answer; and when he found that I was resolutely silent, and walked on, as much as I could, without observing him, he suddenly stamped his foot, and cried out, in a passion, 'Fool! ideot! booby!'[79]

I turned hastily toward him: 'O Madam,' continued he, 'forgive my vehemence, but I am distracted to think there should exist a wretch who can slight a blessing for which I would forfeit my life!—O! that I could but meet him!—I would soon ——But I grow angry: pardon me, Madam, my passions are violent, and your injuries affect me!'

I began to apprehend he was a madman, and stared at him with the utmost astonishment. 'I see you are moved, Madam,' said he, 'generous creature!—but don't be alarmed, I am cool again, I am indeed,—upon my soul I am,—I entreat you, most lovely of mortals! I entreat you to be easy.'

'Indeed, Sir,' said I very seriously, 'I must insist upon your leaving me; you are quite a stranger to me, and I am both unused, and averse to your language and your manners.'

This seemed to have some effect on him. He made me a low bow, begged my pardon, and vowed he would not for the world offend me.

'Then, Sir, you must leave me,' cried I.

'I am gone, Madam, I am gone!' with a most tragical air; and he marched away, a quick pace, out of sight in a moment; but before I had time to congratulate myself, he was again at my elbow.

'And could you really let me go, and not be sorry?—Can you

see me suffer torments inexpressible, and yet retain all your favour for that miscreant who flies you?—Ungrateful puppy!—I could bastinado[80] him!'

'For Heaven's sake, my dear,' cried Mrs. Mirvan, 'who is he talking of?'

'Indeed—I do not know, Madam,' said I, 'but I wish he would leave me.'

'What's all that there?' cried the Captain.

The man made a low bow, and said, 'Only, Sir, a slight objection which this young lady makes to dancing with me, and which I am endeavouring to obviate. I shall think myself greatly honoured, if you will intercede for me.'

'That lady, Sir,' said the Captain coldly, 'is her own mistress.' And he walked sullenly on.

'You, Madam,' said the man, who looked delighted, to Mrs. Mirvan, 'you, I hope, will have the goodness to speak for me.'

'Sir,' answered she gravely, 'I have not the pleasure of being acquainted with you.'

'I hope when you have, Ma'am,' cried he, undaunted, 'you will honour me with your approbation; but, while I am yet unknown to you, it would be truly generous in you to countenance me; and, I flatter myself, Madam, that you will not have cause to repent it.'

Mrs. Mirvan, with an embarrassed air, replied, 'I do not at all mean, Sir, to doubt your being a gentleman,—but,—'

'But *what*, Madam?—that doubt removed, why a *but*?'

'Well, Sir,' said Mrs. Mirvan (with a good-humoured smile), 'I will even treat you with your own plainness, and try what effect that will have on you: I must therefore tell you, once for all,——'

'O pardon me Madam!' interrupted he eagerly, 'you must not proceed with those words, *once for all*; no, if *I* have been too *plain*, and though a *man*, deserve a rebuke, remember, dear ladies, that if you *copy*, you ought, in justice, to *excuse* me.'

We both stared at the man's strange behaviour.

'Be nobler than your sex,' continued he, turning to me, 'honour me with one dance, and give up the ingrate who has merited so ill your patience.'

Mrs. Mirvan looked with astonishment at us both. 'Who does he speak of, my dear?—you never mentioned——'

'O Madam!' exclaimed he, 'he was not worth mentioning—it is pity he was ever thought of; but let us forget his existence. One dance is all I solicit; permit me, Madam, the honour of this young lady's hand; it will be a favour I shall ever most gratefully acknowledge.'

'Sir,' answered she, 'favours and strangers have with me no connection.'

'If you have hitherto,' said he, 'confined your benevolence to your intimate friends, suffer me to be the first for whom your charity is enlarged.'

'Well, Sir, I know not what to say to you,—but—'

He stopped her *but* with so many urgent entreaties, that she at last told me, I must either go down one dance, or avoid his importunities by returning home. I hesitated which alternative to chuse; but this impetuous man at length prevailed, and I was obliged to consent to dance with him.

And thus was my deviation from truth punished; and thus did this man's determined boldness conquer.

During the dance, before we were too much engaged in it for conversation, he was extremely provoking about *my partner*, and tried every means in his power to make me own that I had deceived him; which, though I would not so far humble myself as to acknowledge, was, indeed, but too obvious.

Lord Orville, I fancy, did not dance at all; he seemed to have a large acquaintance, and joined several different parties: but you will easily suppose I was not much pleased to see him, in a few minutes after I was gone, walk towards the place I had just left, and bow to, and join Mrs. Mirvan!

How unlucky I thought myself, that I had not longer withstood this stranger's importunities! The moment we had gone down the dance, I was hastening away from him, but he stopped me, and said that I could by no means return to my party, without giving offence, before we had *done our duty of walking up the dance.*[81] As I know nothing at all of these rules and customs, I was obliged to submit to his directions; but I fancy I looked rather uneasy, for he took notice of my inattention, saying, in his free way, 'Whence that anxiety?—Why are those lovely eyes perpetually averted?'

'I wish you would say no more to me, Sir,' cried I peevishly, 'you have already destroyed all my happiness for this evening.'

'Good Heaven! what is it I have done?—How have I merited this scorn?'

'You have tormented me to death; you have forced me from my friends, and intruded yourself upon me, against my will, for a partner.'

'Surely, my dear Madam, we ought to be better friends, since there seems to be something of sympathy in the frankness of our dispositions.—And yet, were you not an angel—how do you think I could brook such contempt?'

'If I have offended you,' cried I, 'you have but to leave me—and O how I wish you would!'

'My dear creature,' said he, half laughing, 'why, where could you be educated?'[82]

'Where I most sincerely wish I now was!'

'How conscious you must be, all beautiful that you are, that those charming airs serve only to heighten the bloom of your complexion!'

'Your freedom, Sir, where you are more acquainted, may perhaps be less disagreeable; but to *me*——'

'You do me justice,' cried he, interrupting me, 'yes, I do indeed improve upon acquaintance; you will hereafter be quite charmed with me.'

'Hereafter, Sir, I hope I shall never——'

'O hush!—hush!—have you forgot the situation in which I found you?—Have you forgot, that when deserted, I pursued you,—when betrayed, I adored you?—but for me——'

'But for you, Sir, I might, perhaps, have been happy.'

'What then, am I to conclude that, *but for me*, your *partner* would have appeared?—poor fellow!—and did my presence awe him?'

'I wish *his* presence, Sir, could awe *you*!'

'His presence!— perhaps then you see him?'

'Perhaps, Sir, I do,' cried I, quite wearied of his raillery.

'Where?—where?—for Heaven's sake shew me the wretch!'

'Wretch, Sir?'

'O, a very savage!—a sneaking, shamefaced, despicable puppy!'

I know not what bewitched me—but my pride was hurt, and my spirits were tired, and—in short—I had the folly, looking at Lord Orville, to repeat, '*Despicable*, you think?'

His eyes instantly followed mine; 'Why is *that* the gentleman?'

I made no answer; I could not affirm, and I would not deny;—for I hoped to be relieved from his teazing, by his mistake.

The very moment we had done what he called our duty, I eagerly desired to return to Mrs. Mirvan.

'To your *partner* I presume, Madam?' said he, very gravely.

This quite confounded me; I dreaded lest this mischievous man, ignorant of his rank, should address himself to Lord Orville, and say something which might expose my artifice. Fool! to involve myself in such difficulties! I now feared what I had before wished, and, therefore, to *avoid* Lord Orville, I was obliged myself to *propose* going down another dance, though I was ready to sink with shame while I spoke.

'But your *partner*, Ma'am?' said he, affecting a very solemn air, 'perhaps he may resent my detaining you: if you will give me leave to ask his consent—'

'Not for the universe.'

'Who is he, Madam?'

I wished myself a hundred miles off. He repeated his question, 'What is his name?'

'Nothing—nobody—I don't know.—'

He assumed a most important solemnity; 'How!—not know? —Give me leave, my dear Madam, to recommend this caution to you; Never dance in public with a stranger,—with one whose name you are unacquainted with,—who may be a mere adventurer,—a man of no character,—consider to what impertinence you may expose yourself.'

Was ever any thing so ridiculous? I could not help laughing, in spite of my vexation.

At this instant, Mrs. Mirvan, followed by Lord Orville, walked up to us. You will easily believe it was not difficult for me to recover my gravity; but what was my consternation, when this strange man, destined to be the scourge of my artifice, exclaimed, 'Ha! my Lord Orville!—I protest I did not know your Lordship. What can I say for my usurpation?—Yet, faith, my Lord, such a prize was not to be neglected.'

My shame and confusion were unspeakable. Who could have supposed or foreseen that this man knew Lord Orville! But falsehood is not more unjustifiable than unsafe.

Lord Orville—well he might,—looked all amazement.

'The philosophic coldness of your Lordship,' continued this odious creature, 'every man is not endowed with. I have used my utmost endeavours to entertain this lady, though I fear without success; and your Lordship will not be a little flattered, if acquainted with the difficulty which attended my procuring the honour of only one dance.' Then, turning to me, who was sinking with shame, while Lord Orville stood motionless, and Mrs. Mirvan astonished,—he suddenly seized my hand, saying, 'Think, my Lord, what must be my reluctance to resign this fair hand to your Lordship!'

In the same instant, Lord Orville took it of him; I coloured violently, and made an effort to recover it. 'You do me too much honour, Sir,' cried he (with an air of gallantry, pressing it to his lips before he let it go), 'however, I shall be happy to profit by it, if this lady' (turning to Mrs. Mirvan) 'will permit me to seek for her party.'

To compel him thus to dance, I could not endure, and eagerly called out, 'By no means,—not for the world!—I must beg——'

'Will you honour *me*, Madam, with your commands,' cried my tormentor, 'may *I* seek the lady's party?'

'No Sir,' answered I, turning from him.

'What *shall* be done, my dear?' said Mrs. Mirvan.

'Nothing, Ma'am;—any thing, I mean——'

'But do you dance, or not? you see his Lordship waits.'

'I hope not,—I beg that—I would not for the world—I am sure I ought to—to—'

I could not speak; but that confident man, determined to discover whether or not I had deceived him, said to Lord Orville, who stood suspended, 'My Lord, this affair, which, at present, seems perplexed, I will briefly explain;—this lady proposed to me another dance,—nothing could have made me more happy—I only wished for your Lordship's permission, which, if now granted, will, I am persuaded, set every thing right.'

I glowed with indignation. 'No, Sir—It is your absence, and that alone, can set every thing right.'

'For Heaven's sake, my dear,' cried Mrs. Mirvan, who could no longer contain her surprise, 'what does all this mean?—were you pre-engaged?—had Lord Orville——'

'No, Madam,' cried I, '—only—only I did not know that gentleman,—and so,—and so I thought—I intended—I—'

Overpowered by all that had passed, I had not strength to make my mortifying explanation; – my spirits quite failed me, and I burst into tears.

They all seemed shocked and amazed.

'What is the matter, my dearest love?' cried Mrs. Mirvan, with the kindest concern.

'What have I done?' exclaimed my evil genius, and ran officiously for a glass of water.

However, a hint was sufficient for Lord Orville, who comprehended all I would have explained. He immediately led me to a seat, and said, in a low voice, 'Be not distressed, I beseech you; I shall ever think my name honoured by your making use of it.'

This politeness relieved me. A general murmur had alarmed Miss Mirvan, who flew instantly to me; while Lord Orville, the moment Mrs. Mirvan had taken the water, led my tormenter away.

'For Heaven's sake, dear Madam,' cried I, 'let me go home—indeed, I cannot stay here any longer.'

'Let us all go,' cried my kind Maria.

'But the Captain—what will he say—I had better go home in a chair.'

Mrs. Mirvan consented, and I rose to depart. Lord Orville and that man both came to me. The first, with an attention I had but ill merited from him, led me to a chair, while the other followed, pestering me with apologies. I wished to have made mine to Lord Orville, but was too much ashamed.

It was about one o'clock. Mrs. Mirvan's servants saw me home.

And now,—what again shall ever tempt me to an assembly? I dread to hear what you will think of me, my most dear and honoured Sir: you will need your utmost partiality, to receive me without displeasure.

This morning Lord Orville has sent to enquire after our healths: and Sir Clement Willoughby, for that, I find, is the name of my persecutor, has called: but I would not go down stairs till he was gone.

And now, my dear Sir, I can somewhat account for the strange, provoking, and ridiculous conduct of this Sir Clement last night; for Miss Mirvan says, he is the very man with whom she heard Lord Orville conversing at Mrs. Stanley's, when I was spoken of in so mortifying a manner. He was pleased to say he was glad to hear I was a fool, and therefore, I suppose, he concluded he might talk as much nonsense as he pleased to me: however, I am very indifferent as to his opinion;—but for Lord Orville,—if then he thought me an ideot, now, I am sure, he must suppose me both bold and presuming. Make use of his name!—what impertinence!—he can never know how it happened,—he can only imagine it was from an excess of vanity:—well, however, I shall leave this bad city to-morrow, and never again will I enter it!

The Captain intends to take us to-night to the Fantocini.[83] I cannot bear that Captain; I can give you no idea how gross he is. I heartily rejoice that he was not present at the disagreeable conclusion of yesterday's adventure, for I am sure he would have contributed to my confusion; which might perhaps have diverted him, as he seldom or never smiles but at some other person's expence.

And here I conclude my London letters,—and without any regret, for I am too inexperienced and ignorant to conduct myself with propriety in this town, where every thing is new to me, and many things are unaccountable and perplexing.

Adieu, my dear Sir; Heaven restore me safely to you! I wish I was to go immediately to Berry Hill; yet the wish is ungrateful to Mrs. Mirvan, and therefore I will repress it. I shall write an account of the Fantocini from Howard Grove. We have not been to half the public places that are now open, though I dare say you will think we have been to all. But they are almost as innumerable as the persons who fill them.

LETTER XIV

Evelina in continuation

Queen-Ann-Street, April 13

How much will you be surprised, my dearest Sir, at receiving another letter from London of your Evelina's writing! But, believe me, it was not my fault, neither is it my happiness, that I am still here: our journey has been postponed by an accident equally unexpected and disagreeable.

We went last night to see the Fantocini, where we had infinite entertainment from the performance of a little comedy, in French and Italian, by puppets, so admirably managed, that they both astonished and diverted us all, except the Captain, who has a fixed and most prejudiced hatred of whatever is not English.

When it was over, while we waited for the coach, a tall elderly woman brushed quickly past us, calling out, 'My God! what shall I do?'

'Why what *would* you do?' cried the Captain.

'*Ma foi, Monsieur*,'[84] answered she, 'I have lost my company, and in this place I don't know nobody.'

There was something foreign in her accent, though it was difficult to discover whether she was an English or a French woman. She was very well dressed, and seemed so entirely at a loss what to do, that Mrs. Mirvan proposed to the Captain to assist her.

'Assist her!' cried he, 'ay, with all my heart;—let a link-boy call her a coach.'

There was not one to be had, and it rained very fast.

'*Mon Dieu*,' exclaimed the stranger, 'what shall become of me? *Je suis au désespoir!*'[85]

'Dear Sir,' cried Miss Mirvan, 'pray let us take the poor lady into our coach. She is quite alone, and a foreigner—.'

'She's never the better for that,' answered he, 'she may be a woman of the town,[86] for any thing you know.'

'She does not appear such,' said Mrs. Mirvan, 'and indeed she seems so much distressed, that we shall but follow the golden rule[87] if we carry her to her lodgings.'

'You are mighty fond of new acquaintance,' returned he, 'but first let us know if she be going our way.'

Upon enquiry, we found that she lived in Oxford Road, and, after some disputing, the Captain, surlily, and with a very bad grace, consented to admit her into his coach; though he soon convinced us, that he was determined she should not be too much obliged to him, for he seemed absolutely bent upon quarrelling with her: for which strange inhospitality, I can assign no other reason, than that she appeared to be a foreigner.

The conversation began, by her telling us, that she had been in England only two days; that the gentlemen belonging to her were Parisians, and had left her, to see for a hackney-coach,[88] as her own carriage was abroad; and that she had waited for them till she was quite frightened, and concluded that they had lost themselves.

'And pray,' said the Captain, 'why did you go to a public place without an Englishman?'

'*Ma foi*, Sir,' answered she, 'because none of my acquaintance is in town.'

'Why then,' said he, 'I'll tell you what; your best way is to go out of it yourself.'

'*Pardi*,[89] *Monsieur*,' returned she, 'and so I shall; for, I promise you, I think the English a parcel of brutes; and I'll go back to France as fast as I can, for I would not live among none of you.'

'Who wants you?' cried the Captain; 'do you suppose, Madam

French, we have not enough of other nations to pick our pockets already?[90] I'll warrant you, there's no need for you for to put in your oar.'

'Pick your pockets, Sir! I wish nobody wanted to pick your pockets no more than I do; and I'll promise you, you'd be safe enough. But there's no nation under the sun can beat the English for ill-politeness; for my part, I hate the very sight of them, and so I shall only just visit a person of quality or two, of my particular acquaintance, and then I shall go back again to France.'

'Ay, do,' cried he, 'and then go to the devil together, for that's the fittest voyage for the French and the quality.'[91]

'We'll take care, however,' cried the stranger, with great vehemence, 'not to admit none of your vulgar, unmannered English among us.'

'O never fear,' returned he coolly, 'we sha'n't dispute the point with you; you and the quality may have the devil all to your-selves.'

Desirous of changing the subject of a conversation which now became very alarming, Miss Mirvan called out, 'Lord, how slow the man drives!'

'Never mind, Moll,' said her father, 'I'll warrant you he'll drive fast enough to-morrow, when you're going to Howard Grove.'

'To Howard Grove!' exclaimed the stranger; 'why *mon Dieu*, do you know Lady Howard?'

'Why, what if we do?' answered he, 'that's nothing to you; she's none of *your* quality, I'll promise you.'

'Who told you that,' cried she, 'you don't know nothing about the matter; besides, you're the ill-bredest person ever I see; and as to your knowing Lady Howard, I don't believe no such a thing; unless, indeed, you are her steward.'

The Captain, swearing terribly, said, with great fury, '*You* would much sooner be taken for her wash-woman.'[92]

'Her wash-woman, indeed!—Ha, ha, ha!—why you ha'n't no eyes; did you ever see a wash-woman in such a gown as this?— besides, I'm no such mean person, for I'm as good as Lady

Howard, and as rich too; and besides, I'm now come to England
to visit her.'

'You may spare yourself that there trouble,' said the Captain,
'she has paupers enough about her already.'

'Paupers, Mr.!—no more a pauper than yourself, nor so much
neither;—but you are a low, dirty fellow, and I shan't stoop to
take no more notice of you.'

'Dirty fellow!' (exclaimed the Captain, seizing both her wrists),
'hark you, Mrs. Frog,[93] you'd best hold your tongue, for I must
make bold to tell you, if you don't, that I shall make no
ceremony of tripping you out of the window; and there you may
lie in the mud till some of your *Monseers* come to help you out of
it.'

Their increasing passion quite terrified us; and Mrs. Mirvan
was beginning to remonstrate with the Captain, when we were
all silenced by what follows.

'Let me go, villain that you are, let me go, or I'll promise you
I'll get you put to prison for this usage; I'm no common person,
I assure you, and, *ma foi*, I'll go to Justice Fielding[94] about you;
for I'm a person of fashion, and I'll make you know it, or my
name i'n't Duval.'

I heard no more: amazed, frightened, and unspeakably
shocked, an involuntary exclamation of *Gracious Heaven!* escaped
me, and, more dead than alive, I sunk into Mrs. Mirvan's arms.
But let me draw a veil over a scene too cruel for a heart so
compassionately tender as yours; it is sufficient that you know
this supposed foreigner proved to be Madame Duval,—the
grand-mother of your Evelina!

O, Sir, to discover so near a relation in a woman who had
thus introduced herself!—what would become of me, were it not
for you, my protector, my friend, and my refuge?

My extreme concern, and Mrs. Mirvan's surprise, immediately
betrayed me. But I will not shock you with the manner of her
acknowledging me, or the bitterness, the *grossness*—I cannot
otherwise express myself,—with which she spoke of those unhappy past transactions you have so pathetically related to me.
All the misery of a much-injured parent, dear, though never

seen, regretted, though never known, crowded so forcibly upon my memory, that they rendered this interview—one only excepted—the most afflicting I can ever know.

When we stopped at her lodgings, she desired me to accompany her into the house, and said she could easily procure a room for me to sleep in. Alarmed and trembling, I turned to Mrs. Mirvan. 'My daughter, Madam,' said that sweet woman, 'cannot so abruptly part with her young friend; you must allow a little time to wean them from each other.'

'Pardon me, Ma'am' answered Madame Duval, (who, from the time of her being known, somewhat softened her manners), 'Miss can't possibly be so nearly connected to this child as I am.'

'No matter for that,' cried the Captain, (who espoused my cause to satisfy his own pique, though an awkward apology had passed between them), 'she was sent to us, and so, d'ye see, we don't chuse for to part with her.'

I promised to wait upon her at what time she pleased the next day, and, after a short debate, she desired me to breakfast with her, and we proceeded to Queen-Ann-Street.

What an unfortunate adventure! I could not close my eyes the whole night. A thousand times I wished I had never left Berry Hill; however, my return thither shall be accelerated to the utmost of my power; and, once more in that abode of tranquil happiness, I will suffer no temptation to allure me elsewhere.

Mrs. Mirvan was so kind as to accompany me to Madame Duval's house this morning. The Captain too, offered his service, which I declined, from a fear she should suppose I meant to insult her.

She frowned most terribly upon Mrs. Mirvan, but she received me with as much tenderness as I believe she is capable of feeling. Indeed, our meeting seems really to have affected her; for when, overcome by the variety of emotions which the sight of her occasioned, I almost fainted in her arms, she burst into tears, and said, 'Let me not lose my poor daughter a second time!' This unexpected humanity softened me extremely; but she very soon excited my warmest indignation, by the ungrateful mention she made of the best of men, my dear, and most generous benefactor.

However, grief and anger mutually gave way to terror, upon her avowing the intention of her visiting England was to make me return with her to France. This, she said, was a plan she had formed from the instant she had heard of my birth, which, she protested, did not reach her ears till I must have been twelve years of age; but Monsieur Duval, who, she declared, was the worst husband in the world, would not permit her to do any thing she wished: he had been dead but three months, which had been employed in arranging certain affairs, that were no sooner settled, than she set off for England. She was already out of mourning, for she said nobody here could tell how long she had been a widow.

She must have been married very early in life; what her age is, I do not know, but she really looks to be less than fifty. She dresses very gaily, paints very high, and the traces of former beauty are still very visible in her face.

I know not when, or how, this visit would have ended, had not the Captain called for Mrs. Mirvan, and absolutely insisted upon my attending her. He is become, very suddenly, so warmly my friend, that I quite dread his officiousness. Mrs. Mirvan, however, whose principal study seems to be healing those wounds which her husband inflicts, appeased Madame Duval's wrath, by a very polite invitation to drink tea and spend the evening here. Not without great difficulty was the Captain prevailed upon to defer his journey some time longer; but what could be done? it would have been indecent for me to have quitted town the very instant I discovered that Madame Duval was in it; and to have stayed here solely under her protection—Mrs. Mirvan, thank Heaven, was too kind for such a thought. That she should follow us to Howard Grove, I almost equally dreaded; it is, therefore, determined that we remain in London for some days, or a week: though the Captain has declared that the *old French hag,* as he is pleased to call her, shall fare never the better for it.

My only hope, is to get safe to Berry Hill; where, counselled and sheltered by you, I shall have nothing more to fear. Adieu, my ever dear and most honoured Sir! I shall have no happiness till I am again with you!

LETTER XV

Mr. Villars to Evelina

Berry Hill, April 16

In the belief and hope that my Evelina would ere now have bid
adieu to London, I had intended to have deferred writing, till I
heard of her return to Howard Grove; but the letter I have this
moment received, with intelligence of Madame Duval's arrival in
England, demands an immediate answer.

Her journey hither equally grieves and alarms me: how much
did I pity my child, when I read of a discovery at once so
unexpected and unwished! I have long dreaded this meeting and
its consequence; to claim you, seems naturally to follow acknowledging you: I am well acquainted with her disposition, and have
for many years foreseen the contest which now threatens us.

Cruel as are the circumstances of this affair, you must not, my
love, suffer it to depress your spirits; remember, that while life is
lent me, I will devote it to your service; and, for future time, I
will make such provision as shall seem to me most conducive to
your future happiness. Secure of my protection, and relying on
my tenderness, let no apprehensions of Madame Duval disturb
your peace; conduct yourself towards her with all the respect
and deference due to so near a relation, remembering always,
that the failure of duty on her part, can by no means justify any
neglect on yours: indeed, the more forcibly you are struck with
improprieties and misconduct in another, the greater should be
your observance and diligence to avoid even the shadow of
similar errors. Be careful, therefore, that no remissness of attention, no indifference of obliging, make known to her the independence I assure you of; but when she fixes the time for her
leaving England, trust to me the task of refusing your attending
her: disagreeable to myself I own it will be, yet to you, it would
be improper, if not impossible.

In regard to her opinion of me, I am more sorry than

surprised at her determined blindness; the palliation which she feels the want of, for her own conduct, leads her to seek for failings in all who were concerned in those unhappy transactions which she has so much reason to lament. And this, as it is the cause, so we must, in some measure, consider it as the excuse of her inveteracy.

How grateful to me are your wishes to return to Berry Hill! your lengthened stay in London, and the dissipation in which I find you are involved, fill me with uneasiness: I mean not however that I would have you sequester yourself from the party to which you belong, since Mrs. Mirvan might thence infer a reproof which your youth and her kindness would render inexcusable. I will not, therefore, enlarge upon this subject, but content myself with telling you, that I shall heartily rejoice when I hear of your safe arrival at Howard Grove, for which place I hope you will be preparing at the time you receive this letter.

I cannot too much thank you, my best Evelina, for the minuteness of your communications; continue to me this indulgence, for I should be miserable if in ignorance of your proceedings.

How new to you is the scene of life in which you are now engaged,—balls—plays—operas—ridottos—Ah, my child! at your return hither, how will you bear the change? My heart trembles for your future tranquillity.—Yet I will hope every thing from the unsullied whiteness of your soul, and the native liveliness of your disposition.

I am sure I need not say, how much more I was pleased with the mistakes of your inexperience at the private ball, than with the attempted adoption of more fashionable manners at the ridotto. But your confusion and mortifications were such as to entirely silence all reproofs on my part.

I hope you will see no more of Sir Clement Willoughby, whose conversation and boldness are extremely disgustful to me. I was gratified by the good-nature of Lord Orville, upon your making use of his name, but I hope you will never again put it to such a trial.

Heaven bless thee, my dear child, and grant that neither

misfortune nor vice may ever rob thee of that gaiety of heart
which, resulting from innocence, while it constitutes your own,
contributes also to the felicity of all who know you!

ARTHUR VILLARS

LETTER XVI

Evelina to the Rev. Mr. Villars

Queen-Ann-Street, Thursday morning, April 14

Before our dinner was over yesterday, Madame Duval came to
tea: though it will lessen your surprise, to hear that it was near
five o'clock, for we never dine till the day is almost over.[95] She
was asked into another room, while the table was cleared, and
then was invited to partake of the desert.[96]

She was attended by a French gentleman, whom she introduced by the name of Monsieur Du Bois: Mrs. Mirvan received
them both with her usual politeness; but the Captain looked very
much displeased, and after a short silence, very sternly said to
Madame Duval, 'Pray who asked you to bring that there spark[97]
with you.'

'O,' cried she, 'I never go no-where without him.'

Another short silence ensued, which was terminated by the
Captain's turning roughly to the foreigner, and saying, 'Do you
know, *Monseer*,[98] that you're the first Frenchman I ever let come
into my house?'

Monsieur Du Bois made a profound bow. He speaks no
English, and understands it so imperfectly, that he might, possibly, imagine he had received a compliment.

Mrs. Mirvan endeavoured to divert the Captain's ill-humour,
by starting new subjects; but he left to her all the trouble of
supporting them, and leaned back in his chair in gloomy silence,
except when any opportunity offered of uttering some sarcasm

upon the French. Finding her efforts to render the evening agreeable were fruitless, Mrs. Mirvan proposed a party to Ranelagh. Madame Duval joyfully consented to it, and the Captain, though he railed against the dissipation of the women, did not oppose it, and therefore Maria and I ran upstairs to dress ourselves.

Before we were ready, word was brought us, that Sir Clement Willoughby was in the drawing-room. He introduced himself under the pretence of enquiring after all our healths, and entered the room with the easy air of an old acquaintance; though Mrs. Mirvan confesses that he seemed embarrassed, when he found how coldly he was received, not only by the Captain, but by herself.

I was extremely disconcerted at the thoughts of seeing this man again, and did not go down stairs till I was called to tea. He was then deeply engaged in a discourse upon French manners with Madame Duval and the Captain, and the subject seemed so entirely to engross him, that he did not, at first, observe my entrance into the room. Their conversation was supported with great vehemence; the Captain roughly maintaining the superiority of the English in every particular, and Madame Duval warmly refusing to allow of it in any; while Sir Clement exerted all his powers of argument and of ridicule to second and strengthen whatever was advanced by the Captain: for he had the sagacity to discover, that he could take no method so effectual for making the master of the house his friend, as to make Madame Duval his enemy: and indeed, in a very short time, he had reason to congratulate himself upon his successful discernment.

As soon as he saw me, he made a most respectful bow, and hoped I had not suffered from the fatigue of the ridotto: I made no other answer than a slight inclination of the head, for I was very much ashamed of that whole affair. He then returned to the disputants, where he managed the argument so skillfully, at once provoking Madame Duval, and delighting the Captain, that I could not forbear admiring his address, though I condemned his subtlety. Mrs. Mirvan, dreading such violent antagonists, attempted frequently to change the subject; and she might have

succeeded, but for the interposition of Sir Clement, who would
not suffer it to be given up, and supported it with such humour
and satire, that he seems to have won the Captain's heart; though
their united forces so enraged and overpowered Madame Duval,
that she really trembled with passion.

I was very glad when Mrs. Mirvan said it was time to be
gone. Sir Clement arose to take leave; but the Captain very
cordially invited him to join our party: he *had* an engagement, he
said, but would give it up to have that pleasure.

Some little confusion ensued in regard to our manner of
setting off: Mrs. Mirvan offered Madame Duval a place in her
coach, and proposed that we four females should go all together:
however, this she rejected, declaring she would by no means go
so far without a gentleman, and wondering so polite a lady
could make *so English* a proposal. Sir Clement Willoughby said
his chariot was waiting at the door, and begged to know if it
could be of any use. It was, at last, decided, that a hackney-coach
should be called for Monsieur Du Bois and Madame Duval, in
which the Captain, and, at his request, Sir Clement, went also;
Mrs. and Miss Mirvan and I had a peaceful and comfortable ride
by ourselves.

I doubt not but they quarrelled all the way; for when we met
at Ranelagh, every one seemed out of humour: and, though we
joined parties, poor Madame Duval was avoided as much as
possible by all but me.

The room was so very much crowded, that, but for the
uncommon assiduity of Sir Clement Willoughby, we should not
have been able to procure a box (which is the name given to the
arched recesses that are appropriated for tea-parties) till half the
company had retired. As we were taking possession of our
places, some ladies of Mrs. Mirvan's acquaintance stopped to
speak to her, and persuaded her to *take a round*[99] with them.
When she returned to us, what was my surprise, to see that Lord
Orville had joined her party! The ladies walked on; Mrs. Mirvan
seated herself, and made a slight, though respectful, invitation to
Lord Orville to drink his tea with us, which, to my no small
consternation, he accepted.

I felt a confusion unspeakable at again seeing him, from the recollection of the ridotto adventure: nor did my situation lessen it, for I was seated between Madame Duval and Sir Clement, who seemed as little as myself to desire Lord Orville's presence. Indeed, the continual wrangling and ill-breeding of Captain Mirvan and Madame Duval, made me blush that I belonged to them. And poor Mrs. Mirvan and her amiable daughter had still less reason to be satisfied.

A general silence ensued after he was seated: his appearance, from different motives, gave a universal restraint to every body. What his own reasons were for honouring us with his company, I cannot imagine, unless, indeed, he had a curiosity to know whether I should invent any new impertinence concerning him.

The first speech was made by Madame Duval, who said, 'It's quite a shocking thing to see ladies come to so genteel a place as Ranelagh with hats on;[100] it has a monstrous vulgar look: I can't think what they wear them for. There's no such a thing to be seen in Paris.'

'Indeed,' cried Sir Clement, 'I must own myself no advocate for hats; I am sorry the ladies ever invented or adopted so tantalizing a fashion; for, where there is beauty, they only serve to shade it, and where there is none, to excite a most unavailing curiosity. I fancy they were originally worn by some young and whimsical coquet.'

'More likely,' answered the Captain, 'they were invented by some wrinkled old hag, who'd a mind for to keep the young fellows in chace, let them be never so weary.'

'I don't know what you may do in England,' cried Madame Duval, 'but I know in Paris no woman need n't be at such a trouble as that, to be taken very genteel notice of.'

'Why, will you pretend for to say,' returned the Captain, 'that they don't distinguish the old from the young there as well as here?'

'They don't make no distinguishments at all,' said she; 'they're vastly too polite.'

'More fools they!' cried the Captain, sneeringly.

'Would to Heaven,' cried Sir Clement, 'that, for our own

sakes, we Englishmen too were blessed with so accommodating a blindness!'

'Why the devil do you make such a prayer as that?' demanded the Captain: 'them are the first foolish words I've heard you speak; but I suppose you're not much used to that sort of work. Did you ever make a prayer before, since you were a sniveler?'

'Ay, now,' cried Madame Duval, 'that's another of the unpolitenesses of you English, to go to talking of such things as that: now in Paris, nobody never says nothing about religion, no more than about politics.'

'Why then,' answered he, 'it's a sign they take no more care of their souls than of their country, and so both one and t'other go to old Nick.'[101]

'Well, if they do,' said she, 'who's the worse, so long as they don't say nothing about it? it's the tiresomest thing in the world to be always talking of them sort of things, and nobody that's ever been abroad troubles their heads about them.'

'Pray then,' cried the Captain, 'since you know so much of the matter, be so good as to tell us what they *do* trouble their heads about?—hay, Sir Clement! ha'n't we a right to know that much?'

'A very comprehensive question,' said Sir Clement, 'and I expect much instruction from the lady's answer.'

'Come, Madam,' continued the Captain, 'never flinch; speak at once; don't stop for thinking.'

'I assure you I am not going,' answered she, 'for as to what they *do* do, why they've enough to do, I promise you, what with one thing or another.'

'But *what*, *what* do they do, these famous *Monseers*?' demanded the Captain; 'can't you tell us? do they game?—or drink?—or fiddle?—or are they jockies?—or do they spend all their time in flummering[102] old women?'

'As to that, Sir,—but indeed I sha'n't trouble myself to answer such a parcel of low questions, so don't ask me no more about it.' And then, to my great vexation, turning to Lord Orville, she said, 'Pray, Sir, was you ever in Paris?'

He only bowed.

'And pray, Sir, how did you like it?'

This *comprehensive*[103] question, as Sir Clement would have called it, though it made him smile, also made him hesitate; however, his answer was expressive of his approbation.

'I thought you would like it, Sir, because you look so like a gentleman. As to the Captain, and as to that other gentleman, why they may very well not like what they don't know: for I suppose, Sir, you was never abroad?'

'Only three years, Ma'am,' answered Sir Clement, drily.

'Well, that's very surprising! I should never have thought it: however, I dare say you only kept company with the English.'

'Why pray, who *should* he keep company with?' cried the Captain: 'what, I suppose you'd have him ashamed of his own nation, like some other people not a thousand miles off, on purpose to make his own nation ashamed of him?'

'I'm sure it wou'd be a very good thing if you'd go abroad yourself.'

'How will you make out that, hay, Madam? come, please to tell me, where wou'd be the good of that?'

'Where! why a great deal. They'd make quite another person of you.'

'What, I suppose you'd have me learn to cut capers?—and dress like a monkey?—and palaver[104] in French gibberish?—hay, would you?—And powder, and daub, and make myself up, like some other folks?'

'I would have you learn to be more politer, Sir, and not to talk to ladies in such a rude, old-fashion way as this. You, Sir, as have been in Paris' (again addressing herself to Lord Orville) 'can tell this English gentleman how he'd be despised, if he was to talk in such an ungenteel manner as this, before any foreigners. Why there is n't a hair-dresser, nor a shoe-maker, nor nobody, that would n't blush to be in your company.'

'Why look ye, Madam,' answered the Captain, 'as to your hair-pinchers and shoe-blacks,[105] you may puff off their manners, and welcome; and I am heartily glad you like 'em so well; but as to me, since you must needs make so free of your advice, I must e'en tell you, I never kept company with any such gentry.'

'Come, ladies and gentlemen,' said Mrs. Mirvan, 'as many of

you as have done tea, I invite to walk with me.' Maria and I
started up instantly; Lord Orville followed; and I question
whether we were not half round the room ere the angry disputants knew that we had left the box.

As the husband of Mrs. Mirvan had borne so large a share in
this disagreeable altercation, Lord Orville forbore to make any
comments upon it; so that the subject was immediately dropped,
and the conversation became calmly sociable, and politely chearful, and, to every body but me, must have been highly
agreeable:—but, as to myself, I was so eagerly desirous of
making some apology to Lord Orville for the impertinence of
which he must have thought me guilty at the ridotto, and yet so
utterly unable to assume sufficient courage to speak to him
concerning an affair in which I had so terribly exposed myself,
that I hardly ventured to say a word all the time we were
walking. Besides, the knowledge of his contemptuous opinion,
haunted and dispirited me, and made me fear he might possibly
misconstrue whatever I should say. So that, far from enjoying a
conversation which might, at any other time, have delighted me,
I continued silent, uncomfortable, and ashamed. O Sir, shall I
ever again involve myself in so foolish an embarrassment? I am
sure that if I do, I shall deserve yet greater mortification.

We were not joined by the rest of the party till we had taken
three or four turns round the room, and then, they were so
quarrelsome, that Mrs. Mirvan complained of being fatigued,
and proposed going home. No one dissented. Lord Orville
joined another party, having first made an offer of his services,
which the gentlemen declined, and we proceeded to an outward
room, where we waited for the carriages. It was settled that we
should return to town in the same manner we came to Ranelagh
and, accordingly, Monsieur Du Bois handed Madame Duval into
a hackney-coach, and was just preparing to follow her, when she
screamed, and jumped hastily out, declaring she was wet through
all her clothes. Indeed, upon examination, the coach was found
to be in a dismal condition; for the weather proved very bad,
and the rain had, though I know not how, made its way into the
carriage.

Mrs. and Miss Mirvan, and myself, were already disposed of
as before; but no sooner did the Captain hear this account, than,
without any ceremony, he was so civil as to immediately take
possession of the vacant seat in his own coach, leaving Madame
Duval and Monsieur Du Bois to take care of themselves. As to
Sir Clement Willoughby, his own chariot was in waiting.

I instantly begged permission to offer Madame Duval my own
place, and made a motion to get out; but Mrs. Mirvan stopped
me, saying that I should then be obliged to return to town with
only the foreigner, or Sir Clement.

'O never mind the old Beldame,'[106] cried the Captain, 'she's
weather-proof, I'll answer for her; and besides as we are all, I
hope, *English*, why she'll meet with no worse than she expects
from us.'

'I do not mean to defend her,' said Mrs. Mirvan; 'but indeed,
as she belongs to our party, we cannot, with any decency, leave
the place, till she is, by some means, accommodated.'

'Lord, my dear,' cried the Captain, whom the distress of
Madame Duval had put into very good humour, 'why she'll
break her heart, if she meets with any civility from a filthy
Englishman.'

Mrs. Mirvan, however, prevailed, and we all got out of the
coach, to wait till Madame Duval could meet with some better
carriage. We found her, attended by Monsieur Du Bois, standing
amongst the servants, and very busy in wiping her negligee,[107]
and endeavouring to save it from being stained by the wet, as
she said it was a new Lyons silk.[108] Sir Clement Willoughby
offered her the use of his chariot,[109] but she had been too much
piqued by his raillery to accept it. We waited some time, but in
vain, for no hackney-coach could be procured. The Captain, at
last, was persuaded to accompany Sir Clement himself, and we
four females were handed into Mrs. Mirvan's carriage, though
not before Madame Duval had insisted upon our making room
for Monsieur Du Bois, to which the Captain only consented in
preference to being incommoded by him in Sir Clement's
chariot.

Our party drove off first. We were silent and unsociable; for the difficulties attending this arrangement had made every one languid and fatigued. Unsociable, I must own, we continued; but very short was the duration of our silence, as we had not proceeded thirty yards, before every voice was heard at once,— for the coach broke down! I suppose we concluded of course, that we were all half killed, by the violent shrieks that seemed to come from every mouth. The chariot was stopped, the servants came to our assistance, and we were taken out of the carriage, without having been at all hurt. The night was dark and wet; but I had scarce touched the ground, when I was lifted suddenly from it, by Sir Clement Willoughby, who begged permission to assist me, though he did not wait to have it granted, but carried me in his arms back to Ranelagh.

He enquired very earnestly if I was not hurt by the accident? I assured him I was perfectly safe, and free from injury, and desired he would leave me, and return to the rest of the party, for I was very uneasy to know whether they had been equally fortunate. He told me he was happy in being honoured with my commands, and would joyfully execute them; but insisted upon first conducting me to a warm room, as I had not wholly escaped being wet. He did not regard my objections, but made me follow him to an apartment, where we found an excellent fire, and some company waiting for carriages. I readily accepted a seat, and then begged he would go.

And go, indeed, he did; but he returned in a moment, telling me that the rain was more violent than ever, and that he had sent his servants to offer their assistance, and acquaint *the Mirvans* of my situation. I was very mad[110] that he would not go himself; but as my acquaintance with him was so very slight, I did not think proper to urge him contrary to his inclination.

Well, he drew a chair close to mine, and, after again enquiring how I did, said, in a low voice, 'You will pardon me, Miss Anville, if the eagerness I feel to vindicate myself, induces me to snatch this opportunity of making sincere acknowledgements for the impertinence with which I tormented you at the last ridotto. I can assure you, Madam, I have been a true and sorrowful penitent ever since; but—shall I tell you honestly what encouraged me to——'

He stopped; but I said nothing, for I thought instantly of the conversation Miss Mirvan had overheard, and supposed he was going to tell me himself what part Lord Orville had borne in it; and really I did not wish to hear it repeated. Indeed, the rest of his speech convinces me that such was his intention; with what view, I know not, except to make a merit of his defending me.

'And yet,' he continued, 'my excuse may only expose my own credulity, and want of judgement and penetration. I will, therefore, merely beseech your pardon, and hope that some future time——'

Just then, the door was opened by Sir Clement's servant, and I had the pleasure of seeing the Captain, Mrs. and Miss Mirvan, enter the room.

'O ho,' cried the former, 'you have got a good warm birth[111] here; but we shall beat up your quarters.[112] Here, Lucy, Moll, come to the fire, and dry your trumpery.[113] But, hey-day,—why where's old Madam French?'

'Good God,' cried I, 'is not Madame Duval then with you?'

'With me! No,—thank God.'

I was very uneasy to know what might have become of her, and, if they would have suffered me, I should have gone out in search of her myself; but all the servants were dispatched to find her, and the Captain said we might be very sure her *French beau* would take care of her.

We waited some time without any tidings, and were soon the only party in the room. My uneasiness increased so much, that Sir Clement now made a voluntary offer of seeking her. However, the same moment that he opened the door with this design, she presented herself at it, attended by Monsieur Du Bois.

'I was this instant, Madam,' said he, 'coming to see for you.'

'You are mighty good, truly,' cried she, 'to come when all the mischief's over.'

She then entered,—in such a condition!—entirely covered with mud, and in so great a rage, it was with difficulty she could speak. We all expressed our concern, and offered our assistance,—except the Captain; who no sooner beheld her, than he burst into a loud laugh.

We endeavoured, by our enquiries and condolements, to prevent her attending to him; and she was, for some time, so wholly engrossed by her anger and her distress, that we succeeded without much trouble. We begged her to inform us how this accident had happened. 'How!' repeated she,—'why it was all along of your all going away,—and there poor Monsieur Du Bois—but it was n't his fault,—for he's as bad off as me.'

All eyes were then turned to Monsieur Du Bois, whose clothes were in the same miserable plight with those of Madame Duval, and who, wet, shivering, and disconsolate, had crept to the fire.

The Captain laughed yet more heartily; while Mrs. Mirvan, ashamed of his rudeness, repeated her enquiries to Madame Duval; who answered, 'Why, as we were a-coming along, all in the rain, Monsieur Du Bois was so obliging, though I'm sure it was an unlucky obligingness for me, as to lift me up in his arms, to carry me over a place that was ancle-deep in mud; but instead of my being ever the better for it, just as we were in the worst part,—I'm sure I wish we had been fifty miles off,—for, somehow or other, his foot slipped,—at least, I suppose so,—though I can't think how it happened, for I'm no such great weight,—but, however that was, down we both came together, all in the mud; and the more we tried to get up, the more deeper we got covered with the nastiness[114]—and my new Lyons negligee, too, quite spoilt!— however, it's well we got up at all, for we might have laid there till now, for aught you all cared; for nobody never came near us.'

This recital put the Captain into an extacy; he went from the lady to the gentleman, and from the gentleman to the lady, to enjoy alternately the sight of their distress. He really shouted with pleasure; and, shaking Monsieur Du Bois strenuously by the hand, wished him joy of having *touched English Ground*,[115] and then he held a candle to Madame Duval, that he might have a more complete view of her disaster, declaring repeatedly, that he had never been better pleased in his life.

The rage of poor Madame Duval was unspeakable; she dashed the candle out of his hand, stamped upon the floor, and, at last spat in his face.

This action seemed immediately to calm them both, as the joy of the Captain was converted into resentment, and the wrath of Madame Duval into fear; for he put his hands upon her shoulders, and gave her so violent a shake, that she screamed out for help; assuring her, at the same time, that if she had been one ounce less old, or less ugly, she should have had it all returned on her own face.

Monsieur Du Bois, who had seated himself very quietly at the fire, approached them, and expostulated very warmly with the Captain; but he was neither understood nor regarded, and Madame Duval was not released, till she quite sobbed with passion.

When they were parted, I entreated her to permit the woman who has the charge of the ladies' cloaks to assist in drying her cloaths; she consented, and we did what was possible to save her from catching cold. We were obliged to wait in this disagreeable situation near an hour, before a hackney-coach could be found; and then we were disposed in the same manner as before our accident.

I am going this morning to see poor Madame Duval, and to enquire after her health, which I think must have suffered by her last night's misfortunes; though, indeed, she seems to be naturally strong and hearty.

Adieu, my dear Sir, till to-morrow.

LETTER XVII

Evelina in continuation

Friday morning, April 15

Sir Clement Willoughby called here yesterday at noon, and Captain Mirvan invited him to dinner. For my part, I spent the day in a manner the most uncomfortable imaginable.

I found Madame Duval at breakfast in bed, though Monsieur Du Bois was in the chamber; which so much astonished me, that I was, involuntarily, retiring, without considering how odd an appearance my retreat would have, when Madame Duval called me back, and laughed very heartily at my ignorance of foreign customs.[116]

The conversation, however, very soon took a more serious turn; for she began, with great bitterness, to inveigh against the *barbarous brutality of that fellow the Captain*, and the horrible ill-breeding of the English in general, declaring she should make her escape with all expedition from so *beastly a nation*. But nothing can be more strangely absurd, than to hear politeness recommended in language so repugnant to it as that of Madame Duval.

She lamented, very mournfully, the fate of her Lyons silk, and protested she had rather have parted with all the rest of her wardrobe, because it was the first gown she had bought to wear upon leaving off her weeds.[117] She has a very bad cold, and Monsieur Du Bois is so hoarse, he can hardly speak.

She insisted upon my staying with her all day, as she intended, she said, to introduce me to some of my own relations. I would very fain have excused myself, but she did not allow me any choice.

Till the arrival of these relations, one continued series of questions on her side, and of answers on mine, filled up all the time we passed together. Her curiosity was insatiable; she enquired into every action of my life, and every particular that had fallen under my observation, in the lives of all I knew. Again, she was so cruel as to avow the most inveterate rancour against the sole benefactor her deserted child and grand-child have met with; and such was the indignation her ingratitude raised, that I would actually have quitted her presence and house, had she not, in a manner the most peremptory, absolutely forbid me. But what, good Heaven! can induce her to such shocking injustice? O my friend and father! I have no command of myself when this subject is started.

She talked very much of taking me to Paris, and said I greatly wanted the polish of a French education. She lamented that I had been brought up in the country, which, she observed, had given me a very *bumpkinish air*. However, she bid me not despair, for she had known many girls, much worse than me, who had become very fine ladies after a few years residence abroad; and she particularly instanced a Miss Polly Moore, daughter of a chandler's-shop woman,[118] who, by an accident not worth relating, happened to be sent to Paris, where, from an aukward, ill-bred girl, she so much improved, that she has since been taken for a woman of quality.

The relations to whom she was pleased to introduce me, consisted of a Mr. Branghton, who is her nephew, and three of his children, the eldest of which is a son, and the two younger are daughters.

Mr. Branghton appears about forty years of age. He does not seem to want a common understanding, though he is very contracted and prejudiced: he has spent his whole time in the city,[119] and I believe feels a great contempt for all who reside else-where.

His son seems weaker in his understanding, and more gay in his temper; but his gaiety is that of a foolish, over-grown school-boy, whose mirth consists in noise and disturbance. He disdains his father for his close attention to business, and love of money, though he seems himself to have no talents, spirit, or generosity, to make him superior to either. His chief delight appears to be tormenting and ridiculing his sisters, who, in return, most heartily despise him.

Miss Branghton, the eldest daughter, is by no means ugly, but looks proud, ill-tempered, and conceited. She hates the city, though without knowing why; for it is easy to discover she has lived no-where else.

Miss Polly Branghton is rather pretty, very foolish, very ignorant, very giddy, and, I believe, very good-natured.

The first half hour was allotted to *making themselves comfortable*, for they complained of having had a very dirty walk, as they came on foot from Snow Hill,[120] where Mr. Branghton keeps a silver-smith's shop; and the young ladies had not only their coats

to brush, and shoes to dry, but to adjust their head-dress, which
their bonnets had totally discomposed.

The manner in which Madame Duval was pleased to introduce
me to this family, extremely shocked me. 'Here, my dears,' said
she, 'here's a relation you little thought of: but you must know
my poor daughter Caroline had this child after she run away
from me,—though I never knew nothing of it, not I, for a long
while after; for they took care to keep it a secret from me,
though the poor child has never a friend in the world besides.'

'Miss seems very tender-hearted, Aunt,' said Miss Polly, 'and
to be sure she's not to blame for her mama's undutifulness, for
she could n't help it.'

'Lord no,' answered she, 'and I never took no notice of it to
her; for indeed, as to that, my own poor daughter was n't so
much to blame as you may think, for she'd never have gone
astray, if it had not been for that meddling old parson I told
you of.'

'If Aunt pleases,' said young Mr. Branghton, 'we'll talk o'
somewhat else, for Miss looks very uneasy-like.'

The next subject that was chosen, was the age of the three
young Branghtons and myself. The son is twenty; the daughters,
upon hearing that I was seventeen, said that was just the age of
Miss Polly; but their brother, after a long dispute, proved that
she was two years older, to the great anger of both sisters, who
agreed that he was very ill-natured and spiteful.

When this point was settled, the question was put, Which was
tallest?—We were desired to measure, as the Branghtons were all
of different opinions. None of them, however, disputed my
being the tallest in the company, but, in regard to one another
they were extremely quarrelsome: the brother insisted upon their
measuring *fair*, and not with *heads* and *heels*; but they would by
no means consent to lose those privileges of our sex, and
therefore the young man was *cast*,[121] as shortest; though he
appealed to all present upon the injustice of the decree.

This ceremony over, the young ladies began, very freely, to
examine my dress, and to interrogate me concerning it. 'This
apron's[122] your own work, I suppose, Miss? but these sprigs[123]

a'n't in fashion now. Pray, if it is not impertinent, what might you give a yard for this lutestring?[124]—Do you make your own caps, Miss?—' and many other questions equally interesting and well-bred.

They then asked me *how I liked London?* and whether I should not think the country a very *dull place*, when I returned thither? 'Miss must try if she can't get a good husband,' said Mr. Branghton, 'and then she may stay and live here.'

The next topic was public places, or rather the theatres, for they knew of no other; and the merits and defects of all the actors and actresses were discussed: the young man here took the lead, and seemed to be very conversant on the subject. But during this time, what was my concern, and, suffer me to add, my indignation, when I found, by some words I occasionally heard, that Madame Duval was entertaining Mr. Branghton with all the most secret and cruel particulars of my situation! The eldest daughter was soon drawn to them by the recital; the youngest and the son still kept their places, intending, I believe, to divert me, though the conversation was all their own.

In a few minutes, Miss Branghton, coming suddenly up to her sister, exclaimed, 'Lord, Polly, only think! Miss never saw her papa!'

'Lord, how odd!' cried the other; 'why then, Miss, I suppose you would n't know him?'

This was quite too much for me; I rose hastily, and ran out of the room: but I soon regretted I had so little command of myself, for the two sisters both followed, and insisted upon comforting me, notwithstanding my earnest entreaties to be left alone.

As soon as I returned to the company, Madame Duval said, 'Why, my dear, what was the matter with you? why did you run away so?'

This question almost made me run again, for I knew not how to answer it. But, is it not very extraordinary, that she can put me in situations so shocking, and then wonder to find me sensible of any concern?

Mr. Branghton junior now enquired of me, whether I had

seen the Tower,[125] or St. Paul's Church?[126] and upon my answering in the negative, they proposed making a party to shew them to me. Among other questions, they also asked if I had ever seen *such a thing as an Opera*? I told them I had. 'Well,' said Mr. Branghton, 'I never saw one in my life, so long as I've lived in London, and I never desire to see one, if I live here as much longer.'

'Lord, Papa,' cried Miss Polly, 'why not? you might as well for once, for the curiosity of the thing: besides, Miss Pomfret saw one, and she says it was very pretty.'

'Miss will think us very vulgar,' said Miss Branghton, 'to live in London, and never have been to an Opera; but it's no fault of mine, I assure you Miss, only Papa don't like to go.'

The result was, that a party was proposed, and agreed to, for some early opportunity. I did not dare contradict them; but I said that my time, while I remained in town, was at the disposal of Mrs. Mirvan. However, I am sure I will not attend them, if I can possibly avoid so doing.

When we parted, Madame Duval desired to see me the next day; and the Branghtons told me, that the first time I went towards Snow Hill, they should be very glad if I would call upon them.

I wish we may not meet again till that time arrives.

I am sure I shall not be very ambitious of being known to any more of my relations, if they have any resemblance to those whose acquaintance I have been introduced to already.

LETTER XVIII

Evelina in continuation

I had just finished my letter to you this morning, when a violent rapping at the door made me run down stairs; and who should I see in the drawing-room, but—Lord Orville!

He was quite alone, for the family had not assembled to breakfast. He enquired, first of mine, then of the health of Mrs. and Miss Mirvan, with a degree of concern that rather surprised me, till he said that he had just been informed of the accident we had met with at Ranelagh. He expressed his sorrow upon the occasion with the utmost politeness, and lamented that he had not been so fortunate as to hear of it in time to offer his services. 'But, I think,' he added, 'Sir Clement Willoughby had the honour of assisting you?'

'He was with Captain Mirvan, my Lord.'

'I had heard of his being of your party.'

I hope that flighty man has not been telling Lord Orville he only assisted *me*! however, he did not pursue the subject, but said, 'This accident, though extremely unfortunate, will not, I hope, be the means of frightening you from gracing Ranelagh with your presence in future?'

'Our time, my Lord, for London, is almost expired already.'

'Indeed! do you leave town so very soon?'

'O yes, my Lord, our stay has already exceeded our intentions.'

'Are you, then, so particularly partial to the country?'

'We merely came to town, my Lord, to meet Captain Mirvan.'

'And does Miss Anville feel no concern at the idea of the many mourners her absence will occasion?'

'O, my Lord,—I'm sure you don't think—' I stopped there, for, indeed, I hardly knew what I was going to say. My foolish embarrassment, I suppose was the cause of what followed;—for he came to me, and took my hand, saying, 'I *do* think, that whoever has once seen Miss Anville, must receive an impression never to be forgotten.'

This compliment,—from Lord Orville,—so surprised me, that I could not speak; but felt myself change colour, and stood, for some moments, silent, and looking down: however, the instant I recollected my situation, I withdrew my hand, and told him that I would see if Mrs. Mirvan was not dressed. He did not oppose me, so away I went.

I met them all on the stairs, and returned with them to breakfast.

I have since been extremely angry with myself for neglecting so excellent an opportunity of apologizing for my behaviour at the ridotto: but, to own the truth, that affair never once occurred to me during the short *tête-à-tête*[127] which we had together. But, if ever we should happen to be so situated again, I will certainly mention it; for I am inexpressibly concerned at the thought of his harbouring an opinion that I am bold or impertinent, and I could almost kill myself for having given him the shadow of a reason for so shocking an idea.

But was it not very odd that he should make me such a compliment? I expected it not from him;—but gallantry, I believe, is common to all men, whatever other qualities they may have in particular.

Our breakfast was the most agreeable meal, if it may be called a *meal*, that we have had since we came to town. Indeed, but for Madame Duval I should like London extremely.

The conversation of Lord Orville is really delightful. His manners are so elegant, so gentle, so unassuming, that they at once engage esteem, and diffuse complacence. Far from being indolently satisfied with his own accomplishments, as I have already observed many men here are, though without any pretentions to his merit, he is most assiduously attentive to please and to serve all who are in his company; and, though his success is invariable, he never manifests the smallest degree of consciousness.

I could wish that *you*, my dearest Sir, knew Lord Orville, because I am sure you would love him; and I have felt that wish for no other person I have seen since I came to London. I sometimes imagine, that, when his youth is flown, his vivacity abated, and his life is devoted to retirement, he will, perhaps, resemble him whom I most love and honour. His present sweetness, politeness, and diffidence, seem to promise in future the same benevolence, dignity, and goodness. But I must not expatiate upon this subject.

When Lord Orville was gone,—and he made but a very short visit,—I was preparing, most reluctantly, to wait upon Madame Duval; but Mrs. Mirvan proposed to the Captain, that she should be invited to dinner in Queen-Ann-Street, and he readily consented, for he said he wished to ask after her Lyons negligee.

The invitation is accepted, and we expect her every moment, But to me, it is very strange, that a woman, who is the uncontrolled mistress of her time, fortune, and actions, should chuse to expose herself voluntarily to the rudeness of a man who is openly determined to make her his sport. But she has very few acquaintance, and, I fancy, scarce knows how to employ herself.

How great is my obligation to Mrs. Mirvan, for bestowing her time in a manner so disagreeable to herself, merely to promote my happiness! every dispute in which her undeserving husband engages, is productive of pain, and uneasiness to herself; of this I am so sensible, that I even besought her not to send to Madame Duval, but she declared she could not bear to have me pass all my time, while in town, with her only. Indeed she could not be more kind to me, were she your daughter.

LETTER XIX

Evelina in continuation

Saturday morning, April 16

Madame Duval was accompanied by Monsieur Du Bois. I am surprised that she should chuse to introduce him where he is so unwelcome; and, indeed, it is strange that they should be so constantly together: though I believe I should not have taken notice of it, but that Captain Mirvan is perpetually rallying me upon my *grand-mama's beau*.

They were both received by Mrs. Mirvan with her usual good-breeding; but the Captain, most provokingly, attacked her immediately, saying, 'Now, Madam, you that have lived abroad, please to tell me this here; Which did you like best, the *warm room* at Ranelagh, or the *cold bath*[128] you went into afterwards? though, I assure you, you look so well that I should advise you to take another dip.'

'*Ma foi*, Sir,' cried she, 'nobody asked for your advice, so you may as well keep it to yourself: besides, it's no such great joke to be splashed, and to catch cold, and spoil all one's things, whatever you may think of it.'

'*Splashed*, quoth-a!—why I thought you were soused[129] all over.—Come, come, don't mince the matter, never spoil a good story; you know you had n't a dry thread about you—'Fore George. I shall never think on't without hallowing![130] such a poor, forlorn, draggle-tailed[131]—*gentlewoman*! and poor *Monseer* French, here, like a drowned rat, by your side!—'

'Well, the worse pickle we was in, so much the worser in you not to help us, for you knowed where we were fast enough, because, while I laid in the mud, I'm pretty sure I heard you snigger; so it's like enough you jostled us down yourself, for Monsieur Du Bois says, that he is sure he had a great jolt given him, or he should n't have fell.'

The Captain laughed so immoderately, that he really gave me also a suspicion that he was not entirely innocent of the charge; however, he disclaimed it very peremptorily.

'Why then,' continued she, 'if you did n't do that, why did n't you come to help us?'

'Who, I?—what, do you suppose I had forgot I was an *Englishman*, a filthy, beastly *Englishman*?'

'Very well, Sir, very well; but I was a fool to expect any better, for it's all of a piece with the rest; you know you wanted to fling me out of the coach-window, the very first time ever I see you: but I'll never go to Ranelagh with you no more, that I'm resolved; for I dare say, if the horses had runn'd over me, as I laid in that nastiness, you'd never have stirred a step to save me.'

'Lord, no, to be sure, Ma'am, not for the world! I know your opinion of our nation too well, to affront you by supposing a *Frenchman* would want *my* assistance to protect you. Did you think that *Monseer* here, and I, had changed characters, and that he should pop you into the mud, and I help you out of it? Ha, ha, ha!'

'O, very well, Sir, laugh on, it's like your manners; however, if poor Monsieur Du Bois had n't met with that unlucky accident himself, I should n't have wanted nobody's help.'

'O, I promise you, Madam, you'd never have had mine; I knew my distance better; and as to your being a little ducked, or so, why, to be sure, *Monseer* and you settled that between yourselves; so it was no business of mine.'

'What, then, I suppose, you want to make me believe as Monsieur Du Bois served me that trick o' purpose?'

'O' purpose! ay, certainly, who ever doubted that? Do you think a *Frenchman* ever made a blunder? If he had been some clumsy-footed *English* fellow, indeed, it might have been accidental: but what the devil signifies all your hopping and capering with your dancing-masters, if you can't balance yourselves upright?'

In the midst of this dialogue, Sir Clement Willoughby made his appearance. He affects to enter the house with the freedom of an old acquaintance, and this very *easiness*, which, to me, is astonishing, is what most particularly recommends him to the Captain. Indeed, he seems very successfully to study all the humours of that gentleman.

After having heartily welcomed him, 'You are just come in time, my boy,' said he, 'to settle a little matter of a dispute between this here gentlewoman and I; do you know, she has been trying to persuade me, that she did not above half like the ducking *Monseer* gave her t'other night?'

'I should have hoped,' said Sir Clement, with the utmost gravity, 'that the friendship subsisting between that lady and gentleman, would have guarded them against any actions professedly disagreeable to each other; but, probably, they might not have discussed the matter previously; in which case, the gentleman, I must own, seems to have been guilty of inattention, since, in my humble opinion, it was his business first to have enquired whether the lady preferred soft, or hard ground, before he dropped her.'

'O very fine, Gentlemen, very fine,' cried Madame Duval, 'you may try to set us together by the ears as much as you will; but I'm not such an ignorant person as to be made a fool of so easily; so you need n't talk no more about it, for I sees into your designs.'

Monsieur Du Bois, who was just able to discover the subject upon which the conversation turned, made his defence, in French, with great solemnity: he hoped, he said, that the company would at least acknowledge, he did not come from a nation of brutes, and consequently, that to wilfully offend any lady, was, to him, utterly impossible; but that, on the contrary, in endeavouring, as was his duty, to save and guard her, he had himself suffered, in a manner which he would forbear to relate, but which, he greatly apprehended, he should feel the ill effects of for many months; and then, with a countenance exceedingly lengthened, he added, that he hoped it would not be attributed to him as national prejudice, when he owned that he must, to the best of his memory, aver, that his unfortunate fall was owing to a sudden, but violent push, which, he was shocked to say, some malevolent person, with a design to his injury, must certainly have given him; but whether with a view to mortify him, by making him let the lady fall, or whether merely to spoil his clothes, he could not pretend to determine.

This disputation was, at last, concluded by Mrs. Mirvan's proposing that we should all go to Cox's Museum.[132] Nobody objected, and carriages were immediately ordered.

In our way down stairs, Madame Duval, in a very passionate manner, said, '*Ma foi*, if I would n't give fifty guineas only to know who gave us that shove!'

This Museum is very astonishing, and very superb; yet, it afforded me but little pleasure, for it is a mere shew, though a wonderful one.

Sir Clement Willoughby, in our walk round the room, asked me what my opinion was of this brilliant *spectacle*?

'It is very fine, and very ingenious,' answered I, 'and yet—I don't know how it is,—but I seem to *miss something*.'

'Excellently answered!' cried he, 'you have exactly defined my own feelings, though in a manner I should never have arrived at. But I was certain your taste was too well formed, to be pleased at the expence of your understanding.'

'*Pardi*,' cried Madame Duval, 'I hope you two is difficult enough! I'm sure if you don't like this, you like nothing; for it's the grandest, prettiest, finest sight that ever I see, in England.'

'What,' cried the Captain with a sneer, 'I suppose this may be in your French taste? it's like enough, for it's all *kickshaw*[133] work. But, pr'ythee, friend,' (turning to the person who explained the devices) 'will you tell me the *use* of all this? for I'm not enough of a conjurer[134] to find it out.'

'Use, indeed!' repeated Madame Duval disdainfully, 'Lord, if every thing's to be useful!—'

'Why, Sir, as to that, Sir,' said our conductor, 'the ingenuity of the mechanism,—the beauty of the workmanship,—the—undoubtedly, Sir, any person of taste may easily discern the utility of such extraordinary performances.'

'Why then, Sir,' answered the Captain, 'your person of taste must be either a coxcomb, or a Frenchman; though, for the matter of that, 'tis the same thing.'

Just then, our attention was attracted by a pine-apple, which, suddenly opening, discovered a nest of birds, who immediately began to sing. 'Well,' cried Madame Duval, 'this is prettier than all the rest! I declare, in all my travels, I never see nothing eleganter.'

'Hark ye, friend,' said the Captain, 'hast never another pine-apple?'

'Sir?—'

'Because, if thou hast, pr'ythee give it us without the birds; for, d'ye see, I'm no Frenchman, and should relish something more substantial.'

This entertainment concluded with a concert of mechanical music: I cannot explain how it was produced, but the effect was pleasing. Madame Duval was in extacies; and the Captain flung himself into so many ridiculous distortions, by way of mimicking her, that he engaged the attention of all the company; and, in the midst of the performance of the Coronation Anthem,[135] while Madame Duval was affecting to beat time, and uttering many expressions of delight, he called suddenly for salts,[136] which a lady, apprehending some distress, politely handed to him, and which, instantly applying to the nostrils of poor Madame Duval, she involuntarily snuffed up such a quantity, that the pain and surprise made her scream aloud. When she recovered, she reproached him, with her usual vehemence; but he protested he had taken that measure out of pure friendship, as he concluded, from her raptures, that she was going into hysterics. This excuse by no means appeased her, and they had a violent quarrel; but the only effect her anger had on the Captain, was to increase his diversion. Indeed, he laughs and talks so terribly loud in public, that he frequently makes us ashamed of belonging to him.

Madame Duval, notwithstanding her wrath, made no scruple of returning to dine in Queen-Ann-Street. Mrs. Mirvan had secured places for the play at Drury-Lane Theatre, and, though ever uneasy in her company, she very politely invited Madame Duval to be of our party; however, she had a bad cold, and chose to nurse it. I was sorry for her indisposition, but I knew not how to be sorry she did not accompany us, for she is—I must not say what, but very unlike other people.

LETTER XX

Evelina in continuation

Our places were in the front row of a side-box.[137] Sir Clement Willoughby, who knew our intention, was at the door of the Theatre, and handed us from the carriage.

We had not been seated five minutes, before Lord Orville, who we saw in the stage-box,[138] came to us; and he honoured us with his company all the evening. Miss Mirvan and I both rejoiced that Madame Duval was absent, as we hoped for the enjoyment of some conversation, uninterrupted by her quarrels with the Captain: but I soon found that her presence would have made very little alteration, for so far was I from daring to speak, that I knew not where even to look.

The play was Love for Love,[139] and though it is fraught with wit and entertainment, I hope I shall never see it represented again; for it is so extremely indelicate,—to use the softest word I can,—that Miss Mirvan and I were perpetually out of countenance, and could neither make any observations ourselves, nor venture to listen to those of others. This was the more provoking, as Lord Orville was in excellent spirits, and exceedingly entertaining.

When the Play was over, I flattered myself I should be able to look about me with less restraint, as we intended to stay the Farce,[140] but the curtain had hardly dropped, when the box-door opened, and in came Mr. Lovel, the man by whose foppery and impertinence I was so much teazed at the ball where I first saw Lord Orville.

I turned away my head, and began talking to Miss Mirvan, for I was desirous to avoid speaking to him;—but in vain, for as soon as he had made his compliments to Lord Orville and Sir Clement Willoughby, who returned them very coldly, he bent his head forward, and said to me, 'I hope, Ma'am, you have enjoyed your health since I had the honour—I beg ten thousand pardons, but I protest I was going to say the honour of *dancing* with you—however, I mean the honour of *seeing* you dance?'

He spoke with a self-complacency that convinced me he had studied this address, by way of making reprisals for my conduct at the ball: I therefore bowed slightly, but made no answer.

After a short silence, he again called my attention, by saying, in an easy, negligent way, 'I think, Ma'am, you was never in town before?'

'No, Sir.'

'So I did presume. Doubtless, Ma'am, every thing must be infinitely novel to you. Our customs, our manners, and *les etiquettes de nous autres*,[141] can have very little resemblance to those you have been used to. I imagine, Ma'am, your retirement is at no very small distance from the capital?'

I was so much disconcerted at this sneering speech, that I said not a word; though I have since thought my vexation both stimulated and delighted him.

'The air we breathe here, however, Ma'am,' continued he, very conceitedly, 'though foreign to that you have been accustomed to, has not, I hope, been at varience with your health?'

'Mr. Lovel,' said Lord Orville, 'could not your *eye* have spared that question?'

'O, my Lord,' answered he, 'if *health* were the only cause of a lady's bloom, my eye, I grant, had been infallible from the first glance; but—'

'Come, come' cried Mrs. Mirvan, 'I must beg no insinuations of that sort; Miss Anville's colour, as you have successfully tried, may, you see, be heightened;—but I assure you, it would be past your skill to lessen it.'

''Pon honour, Madam,' returned he, 'you wrong me; I presumed not to infer that *rouge* was the only succedaneum for health; but, really, I have known so many different causes for a lady's colour, such as flushing,—anger,—*mauvaise honte*[142]—and so forth, that I never dare decide to which it may be owing.'

'As to such causes as them there,' cried the Captain, 'they must belong to those that they keep company with.'

'Very true, Captain,' said Sir Clement; 'the natural complexion has nothing to do with occasional sallies of the passions, or any accidental causes.'

'No, truly,' returned the Captain, 'for now here's me, why I look like any other man just now; and yet, if you were to put me in a passion, 'fore George you'd soon see me have as fine a high colour as any painted Jezabel[143] in all this place, be she never so bedaubed.'

'But,' said Lord Orville, 'the difference of natural and of artificial colour, seems to me very easily discerned; that of Nature is mottled, and varying; that of art, *set*, and *too* smooth; it wants that animation, that glow, that *indescribable something* which, even now that I see it, wholly surpasses all my powers of expression.'

'Your Lordship,' said Sir Clement, 'is universally acknowledged to be a *connoisseur* in beauty.'

'And you Sir Clement,' returned he, 'an *enthusiast*.'[144]

'I am proud to own it,' cried Sir Clement; 'in such a cause, and before such objects, enthusiasm is simply the consequence of not being blind.'

'Pr'ythee a truce with all this palavering,' cried the Captain, 'the women are vain enough already; no need for to puff 'em up more.'

'We must all submit to the commanding officer,' said Sir Clement, 'therefore let us call another subject. Pray, Ladies, how have you been entertained with the play?'

'Want of entertainment,' said Mrs. Mirvan, 'is its least fault; but I own there are objections to it, which I should be glad to see removed.'

'I could have ventured to answer for the Ladies,' said Lord Orville, 'since I am sure this is not a play that can be honoured with their approbation.'

'What, I suppose it is not sentimental enough!' cried the Captain, 'or else it's too good for them; for I'll maintain it's one of the best comedies in the language, and has more wit in one scene, than there is in all the new plays put together.'

'For my part,' said my Lovel, 'I confess I seldom listen to the players: one has so much to do, in looking about, and finding out one's acquaintance, that, really, one has no time to mind the stage. Pray,'—(most affectionately fixing his eyes upon a diamond-ring on his little finger) 'pray—what was the play to-night?'

'Why, what the D—l,' cried the Captain, 'do you come to the play, without knowing what it is?'

'O yes, Sir, yes, very frequently: I have no time to read play-bills;[145] one merely comes to meet one's friends, and shew that one's alive.'

'Ha, ha, ha!—and so,' cried the Captain, 'it costs you five shillings a night, just to shew that you're alive! Well, faith, my friends should all think me dead and under ground, before I'd be at that expence for 'em. Howsomever, this here you may take from me;—they'll find you out fast enough, if you've any thing to give 'em.—And so you've been here all this time, and don't know what the play was?'

'Why, really, Sir, a play requires so much attention,—it is scarce possible to keep awake, if one listens;—for, indeed, by the time it is evening, one has been so fatigued, with dining,—or wine,—or the house,[146]—or studying,—that it is—it is perfectly an impossibility. But, now I think of it, I believe I have a bill in my pocket; O, ay, here it is—Love for Love, ay,—true,—ha, ha,—how could I be so stupid!'

'O, easily enough, as to that, I warrant you,' said the Captain, 'but, by my soul, this is one of the best jokes I ever heard! Come to a play, and not know what it is!—Why, I suppose you wouldn't have found it out, if they had fobbed you off with a scraping of fiddlers, or an opera?—Ha! ha! ha!—why now, I should have thought you might have taken some notice of one Mr. *Tattle*[147] that is in this play!'

This sarcasm, which caused a general smile, made him colour: but, turning to the Captain with a look of conceit, which implied that he had a retort ready, he said, 'Pray, Sir, give me leave to ask,—what do *you* think of *one Mr. Ben,*[148] who is also in this play?'

The Captain, regarding him with the utmost contempt, answered in a loud voice, 'Think of him!—why I think he's a *man!*' And then, staring full in his face, he struck his cane on the ground, with a violence that made him start. He did not, however, chuse to take any notice of this; but, having bit his nails some time, in manifest confusion, he turned very quick to me, and, in a sneering tone of voice, said, 'For my part, I was most struck with the *country* young lady, Miss Prue;[149] pray what do *you* think of her, Ma'am?'

'Indeed, Sir,' cried I, very much provoked, 'I think—that is, I do not think any thing about her.'

'Well, really, Ma'am, you prodigiously surprise me!—*mais apparemment ce n'est qu'un façon de parler?*[150]—though I should beg your pardon, for probably you do not understand French?'

I made no answer, for I thought his rudeness intolerable; but Sir Clement, with great warmth, said, 'I am surprised that you can suppose such an object as Miss Prue would engage the attention of Miss Anville even for a moment.'

'O Sir,' returned this fop, ''tis the first character in the piece!—so well drawn,—so much the thing!—such true country-breeding,—such rural ignorance!—ha! ha! ha!—'tis most admirably hit off, 'pon honour!'

I could almost have cried, that such impertinence should be levelled at me; and yet, chagrined as I was, I could never behold Lord Orville and this man at the same time, and feel any regret for the cause I had given of displeasure.

'The only female in the play,' said Lord Orville, 'worthy of being mentioned to these ladies, is Angelica.'[151]

'Angelica,' cried Sir Clement, 'is a noble girl; she tries her lover severely, but she rewards him generously.'

'Yet, in a trial so long,' said Mrs. Mirvan, 'there seems rather too much consciousness of her power.'

'Since my opinion has the sanction of Mrs. Mirvan's,' added Lord Orville, 'I will venture to say, that Angelica bestows her hand rather with the air of a benefactress, than with the tenderness of a mistress. Generosity without delicacy, like wit without judgement, generally give as much pain as pleasure. The uncertainty in which she keeps Valentine, and her manner of trifling with his temper, give no very favourable idea of her own.'

'Well, my Lord,' said Mr. Lovel, 'it must, however, be owned, that uncertainty is not the *ton* among our ladies at present; nay, indeed, I think they say, though, faith,' taking a pinch of snuff, 'I hope it is not true—but they say, that *we* now are most shy and backward.'

The curtain then drew up, and our conversation ceased. Mr. Lovel, finding we chose to attend to the players, left the box. How strange it is, Sir, that this man, not contented with the large share of foppery and nonsense which he has from nature, should think proper to affect yet more! for what he said of Tattle and of Miss Prue, convinced me that he really had listened to the play, though he was so ridiculous and foolish as to pretend ignorance.

But how malicious and impertinent in this creature to talk to me in such a manner! I am sure I hope I shall never see him again. I should have despised him heartily as a fop, had he never spoken to me at all; but now, that he thinks proper to resent his supposed ill-usage, I am really quite afraid of him.

The entertainment was, The Deuce is in him,[152] which Lord Orville observed to be the most finished and elegant *petite piece* that was ever written in English.

In our way home, Mrs. Mirvan put me into some consternation, by saying it was evident, from the resentment which this Mr. Lovel harbours of my conduct, that he would think it a provocation sufficiently important for a duel, if his courage equalled his wrath.

I am terrified at the very idea. Good Heaven! that a man so weak and frivolous should be so revengeful! However, if bravery would have excited him to affront Lord Orville, how much reason have I to rejoice, that cowardice makes him contented with venting his spleen upon me! But we shall leave town soon, and, I hope, see him no more.

It was some consolation to me, to hear, from Miss Mirvan, that, while he was speaking to me so cavalierly, Lord Orville regarded him with great indignation.

But, really, I think there ought to be a book, of the laws and customs *à-la-mode*,[153] presented to all young people upon their first introduction into public company.

To-night we go to the opera, where I expect very great pleasure. We shall have the same party as at the play; for Lord Orville said he should be there, and would look for us.

LETTER XXI

Evelina in continuation

I have a volume to write of the adventures of yesterday.

In the afternoon,—at Berry Hill, I should have said the *evening*, for it was almost six o'clock,[154]—while Miss Mirvan and I were dressing for the opera, and in high spirits, from the expectation of great entertainment and pleasure, we heard a carriage stop at the door, and concluded that Sir Clement Willoughby, with his usual assiduity, was come to attend us to the Haymarket;[155] but, in a few moments, what was our surprise, to see our chamber-door flung open, and the two Miss Branghtons enter the room! They advanced to me with great familiarity, saying, 'How do you do, cousin?—so we've caught you at the glass!—well, I'm determined I'll tell my brother of that!'

Miss Mirvan, who had never before seen them, and could not, at first, imagine who they were, looked so much astonished, that I was ready to laugh myself, till the eldest said, 'We're come to take you to the opera, Miss; papa and my brother are below, and we are to call for your grand-mama as we go along.'

'I am very sorry,' answered I, 'that you should have taken so much trouble, as I am engaged already.'

'Engaged! Lord, Miss, never mind that,' cried the youngest, 'this young lady will make your excuses, I dare say; it's only doing as one would be done by, you know.'

'Indeed, Ma'am,' said Miss Mirvan, 'I shall myself be very sorry to be deprived of Miss Anville's company this evening.'

'Well, Miss, that is not so very good-natured in you,' said Miss Branghton, 'considering we only come to give our cousin pleasure; it's no good to us; it's all upon her account; for we came, I don't know how much round about to take her up.'

'I am extremely obliged to you,' said I, 'and very sorry you have lost so much time; but I cannot possibly help it, for I engaged myself without knowing you would call.'

'Lord, what signifies that?' said Miss Polly, 'you're no old maid, and so you need n't be so very formal: besides, I dare say those you are engaged to, a'n't half so near related to you as we are.'

'I must beg you not to press me any further, for I assure you it is not in my power to attend you.'

'Why we came all out of the city on purpose: besides, your grand-mama expects you;—and pray, what are we to say to her?'

'Tell her, if you please, that I am much concerned,—but that I am pre-engaged.'

'And who to?' demanded the abrupt Miss Branghton.

'To Mrs. Mirvan,—and a large party.'

'And, pray, what are you all going to do, that it would be such a mighty matter for you to come along with us?'

'We are all going to—to the opera.'

'O dear, if that be all, why can't we go all together?'

I was extremely disconcerted at this forward and ignorant behaviour, and yet their rudeness very much lessened my concern at refusing them. Indeed, their dress was such as would have rendered their scheme of accompanying our party impracticable,[156] even if I had desired it; and this, as they did not themselves find out, I was obliged, in terms the least mortifying I could think of, to tell them.

They were very much chagrined, and asked where I should sit?

'In the pit,' answered I.

'In the pit!' repeated Miss Branghton, 'well, really, I must own I should never have supposed that my gown was not good enough for the pit: but come, Polly, let's go; if Miss does not think us fine enough for her, why to be sure she may chuse.'

Surprised at this ignorance, I would have explained to them that the pit at the opera required the same dress as the boxes; but they were so much affronted, they would not hear me, and, in great displeasure, left the room, saying they would not have troubled me, only they thought I should not be so proud with my own relations, and that they had at least as good a right to my company as strangers.

I endeavoured to apologize, and would have sent a long message to Madame Duval; but they hastened away without listening to me; and I could not follow them down stairs, because I was not dressed. The last words I heard them say, were, 'Well, her grand-mama will be in a fine passion, that's one good thing.'

Though I was extremely mad at this visit, yet I so heartily rejoiced at their going, that I would not suffer myself to think gravely about it.

Soon after, Sir Clement actually came, and we all went down stairs. Mrs. Mirvan ordered tea; and we were engaged in a very lively conversation, when the servant announced Madame Duval, who instantly followed him into the room.

Her face was the colour of scarlet, and her eyes sparkled with fury. She came up to me with a hasty step, saying, 'So, Miss, you refuses to come to me, do you? And pray who are you, to dare to disobey me?'

I was quite frightened;—I made no answer;—I even attempted to rise, and could not, but sat still, mute and motionless.

Every body, but Miss Mirvan, seemed in the utmost astonishment; and the Captain, rising and approaching Madame Duval, with a voice of authority, said, 'Why how now, Mrs. Turkey Cock, what's put you into this here fluster?'

'It's nothing to you,' answered she, 'so you may as well hold your tongue, for I sha'n't be called to no account by you, I assure you.'

'There you're out, Madam Fury,' returned he, 'for you must know I never suffer any body to be in a passion in my house, but myself.'

'But you *shall*,' cried she, in a great rage, 'for I'll be in as great a passion as ever I please, without asking your leave, so don't give yourself no more airs about it. And as for you, Miss,' again advancing to me, 'I order you to follow me this moment, or else I'll make you repent it all your life.' And, with these words, she flung out of the room.

I was in such extreme terror, at being addressed and threatened in a manner to which I am so wholly unused, that I almost thought I should have fainted.

'Don't be alarmed, my love,' cried Mrs. Mirvan, 'but stay where you are, and I will follow Madame Duval, and try to bring her to reason.'

Miss Mirvan took my hand, and most kindly endeavoured to raise my spirits: Sir Clement, too, approached me, with an air so interested in my distress, that I could not but feel myself obliged to him; and, taking my other hand, said, 'For Heaven's sake, my dear Madam, compose yourself; surely the violence of such a wretch ought merely to move your contempt; she can have no right, I imagine, to lay her commands upon you, and I only wish that you would allow *me* to speak to her.'

'O no! not for the world!—indeed, I believe,—I am afraid—I had better follow her.'

'Follow her! Good God, my dear Miss Anville, would you trust yourself with a mad woman? for what else can you call a creature whose passions are so insolent? No, no; send her word at once to leave the house, and tell her you desire that she will never see you again.'

'O Sir! you don't know who you talk of!—it would ill become me to send Madame Duval such a message.'

'But *why*,' cried he, (looking very inquisitive), '*why* should you scruple to treat her as she deserves?'

I then found that his aim was to discover the nature of her connection with me; but I felt so much ashamed of my near relationship to her, that I could not persuade myself to answer him, and only entreated that he would leave her to Mrs. Mirvan, who just then entered the room.

Before she could speak to me, the Captain called out, 'Well, Goody,[157] what have you done with Madame French? is she cooled a little? 'cause if she be n't, I've just thought of a most excellent device to bring her to.'

'My dear Evelina,' said Mrs. Mirvan, 'I have been vainly endeavouring to appease her; I pleaded your engagement, and promised your future attendance: but I am sorry to say, my love, that I fear her rage will end in a total breach (which I think you had better avoid) if she is any further opposed.'

'Then I will go to her, Madam,' cried I, 'and, indeed, it is now no matter, for I should not be able to recover my spirits sufficiently to enjoy much pleasure *any* where this evening.'

Sir Clement began a very warm expostulation, and entreaty, that I would not go; but I begged him to desist, and told him, very honestly, that, if my compliance were not indispensably necessary, I should require no persuasion to stay. He then took my hand, to lead me down stairs; but the Captain desired him to be quiet, saying he would 'squire me himself, 'because,' he added (exultingly rubbing his hands), 'I have a wipe[158] ready for the old lady, which may serve her to *chew* as she goes along.'

We found her in the parlour. 'O, you're come at last, Miss, are you?—fine airs you give yourself, indeed!—*ma foi*,[159] if you had n't come, you might have stayed, I assure you, and have been a beggar for your pains.'

'Hey-day, Madam,' cried the Captain (prancing forward, with a look of great glee), 'what, a'n't you got out of that there passion yet? why then, I'll tell you what to do to cool yourself; call upon your old friend, *Monseer* Slippery, who was with you at Ranelagh, and give my service to him, and tell him, if he sets any store by your health, that I desire he'll give you such another souse as he did before: he'll know what I mean, and I'll warrant you he'll do't for my sake.'

'Let him, if he dares!' cried Madame Duval; 'but I sha'n't stay to answer you no more; you are a vulgar fellow,—and so, child, let us leave him to himself.'

'Hark ye, Madam,' cried the Captain 'you'd best not call names, because, d'ye see, if you do, I shall make bold to shew you the door.'

She changed colour, and saying, '*Pardi*, I can shew it myself,' hurried out of the room, and I followed her into a hackney-coach. But before we drove off, the Captain, looking out of the parlour window, called out, 'D'ye hear, Madam,—don't forget my message to *Monseer*.'

You will believe our ride was not the most agreeable in the world; indeed, it would be difficult to say which was least pleased, Madame Duval or me, though the reasons of our discontent were so different: however, Madame Duval soon got the start of me; for we had hardly turned out of Queen-Ann-Street, when a man, running full speed, stopped the coach. He came up to the window, and I saw he was the Captain's servant. He had a broad grin on his face, and panted for breath. Madame Duval demanded his business; 'Madam,' answered he, 'my master desires his compliments to you, and—and—and he says he wishes it well over with you. He! he! he!—'

Madame Duval instantly darted forward, and gave him a violent blow on the face; 'Take that back for your answer, sirrah,' cried she, 'and learn to grin at your betters another time. Coachman, drive on!'

The servant was in a violent passion, and swore terribly; but we were soon out of hearing.

The rage of Madame Duval was greater than ever, and she inveighed against the Captain with such fury, that I was even apprehensive she would have returned to his house, purposely to reproach him, which she repeatedly threatened to do; nor would she, I believe have hesitated a moment, but that, notwithstanding her violence, he has really made her afraid of him.

When we came to her lodgings, we found all the Branghtons in the passage, impatiently waiting for us, with the door open.

'Only see, here's Miss!' cried the brother.

'Well, I declare I thought as much!' said the younger sister.

'Why, Miss,' said Mr. Branghton, 'I think you might as well have come with your cousins at once; it's throwing money in the dirt, to pay two coaches for one fare.'

'Lord, father,' cried the son, 'make no words about that; for I'll pay for the coach that Miss had.'

'O, I know very well,' answered Mr. Branghton, 'that you're always more ready to spend than to earn.'

I then interfered, and begged that I might myself be allowed to pay the fare, as the expence was incurred upon my account; they all said *no*, and proposed that the same coach should carry us on to the opera.

While this passed, the Miss Branghtons were examining my dress, which, indeed, was very improper for my company; and as I was extremely unwilling to be so conspicuous amongst them, I requested Madame Duval to borrow a hat or bonnet[160] for me of the people of the house. But she never wears either herself, and thinks them very *English* and barbarous; therefore she insisted that I should go full dressed, as I had prepared myself for the pit, though I made many objections.

We were then all crowded into the same carriage; but when we arrived at the Opera-house, I contrived to pay the coachman. They made a great many speeches; but Mr. Branghton's reflection had determined me not to be indebted to him.

If I had not been too much chagrined to laugh, I should have been extremely diverted at their ignorance of whatever belongs to an opera. In the first place, they could not tell at what door we ought to enter, and we wandered about for some time, without knowing which way to turn: they did not chuse to apply to me, though I was the only person of the party who had ever before been at an opera; because they were unwilling to suppose that their *country cousin*, as they were pleased to call me, should be better acquainted with any London public place than themselves. I was very indifferent and careless upon this subject, but not a little uneasy at finding that my dress, so different from that of the company to which I belonged, attracted general notice and observation.

In a short time, however, we arrived at one of the door keeper's *bars*.[161] Mr. Branghton demanded for what part of the house they took money? They answered the pit, and regarded us all with great earnestness. The son then advancing, said, 'Sir, if you please, I beg that I may treat Miss.'

'We'll settle that another time,' answered Mr. Branghton, and put down a guinea.

Two tickets of admission were given to him.

Mr. Branghton, in his turn, now stared at the door-keeper, and demanded what he meant by giving him only two tickets for a guinea?

'Only two, Sir!' said the man, 'why don't you know that the tickets are half a guinea[162] each?'

'Half a guinea each!' repeated Mr. Branghton, 'why I never heard of such a thing in my life! And pray, Sir, how many will they admit?'

'Just as usual, Sir, one person each.'

'But one person for half a guinea!—why I only want to sit in the pit, friend.'

'Had not the Ladies better sit in the gallery,[163] Sir; for they'll hardly chuse to go into the pit with their hats on?'

'O, as to that,' cried Miss Branghton, 'if our hats are too high, we'll take them off when we get in. I sha'n't mind it, for I did my hair on purpose.'

Another party then approaching, the door-keeper could no longer attend to Mr. Branghton, who, taking up the guinea, told him it should be long enough before he'd see it again, and walked away.

The young ladies, in some confusion, expressed their surprise, that their *papa* should not know the Opera prices, which, for their parts, they had read in the papers a thousand times.

'The price of stocks,' said he, 'is enough for me to see after; and I took it for granted it was the same thing here as at the Play-house.'

'I knew well enough what the price was,' said the son, 'but I would not speak, because I thought perhaps they'd take less, as we're such a large party.'

The sisters both laughed very contemptuously at this idea, and asked him if he ever heard of *people's abating*[164] any thing at a public place?

'I don't know whether I have or no,' answered he, 'but I'm sure if they would, you'd like it so much the worse.'

'Very true, Tom,' cried Mr. Branghton; 'tell a woman that any thing is reasonable, and she'll be sure to hate it.'

'Well,' said Miss Polly, 'I hope that Aunt and Miss will be of our side, for Papa always takes part with Tom.'

'Come, come,' cried Madame Duval, 'if you stand talking here, we sha'n't get no place at all.'

Mr. Branghton then enquired the way to the gallery, and, when we came to the door-keeper, demanded what was to pay.

'The usual price, Sir,' said the man.

'Then give me change,' cried Mr. Branghton, again putting down his guinea.

'For how many, Sir?'

'Why—let's see,—for six.'

'For six, Sir? why you've given me but a guinea.'

'*But* a guinea! why how much would you have? I suppose it i'n't half a guinea apiece here too?'

'No, Sir, only five shillings.'

Mr. Branghton again took up his unfortunate guinea, and protested he would submit to no such imposition. I then proposed that we should return home, but Madame Duval would not consent, and we were conducted by a woman who sells books of the Opera,[165] to another gallery-door, where, after some disputing, Mr. Branghton at last paid, and we all went up stairs.

Madame Duval complained very much of the trouble of going so high, but Mr. Branghton desired her not to hold the place too cheap, 'for, whatever you may think,' cried he, 'I assure you I paid pit price;[166] so don't suppose I come here to save my money.'

'Well, to be sure,' said Miss Branghton, 'there's no judging of a place by the outside, else, I must needs say, there's nothing very extraordinary in the staircase.'

But, when we entered the gallery, their amazement and disappointment became general. For a few instants, they looked at one another without speaking, and then they all broke silence at once.

'Lord, Papa,' exclaimed Miss Polly, 'why you have brought us to the one-shilling gallery!'[167]

'I'll be glad to give you two shillings, though,' answered he, 'to pay. I was never so fooled out of my money before, since the hour of my birth. Either the door-keeper's a knave, or this is the greatest imposition that ever was put upon the public.'

'*Ma foi*,' cried Madame Duval, 'I never sat in such a mean place in all my life;—why it's as high!—we sha'n't see nothing.'

'I thought at the time,' said Mr. Branghton, 'that three shillings was an exorbitant price for a place in the gallery, but as we'd been asked so much more at the other doors, why I paid it without many words; but then, to be sure, thinks I, it can never be like any other gallery,—we shall see some *crinkum-crankum*[168] or other for our money;—but I find it's as arrant a take-in as ever I met with.'

'Why it's as like the twelvepenny gallery at Drury-Lane,' cried the son, 'as two peas are one to another. I never knew father so bit before.'

'Lord,' said Miss Branghton, 'I thought it would have been quite a fine place,—all over I don't know what,—and done quite in taste.'

In this manner they continued to express their dissatisfaction till the curtain drew up; after which, their observations were very curious. They made no allowance for the customs, or even for the language of another country[169] but formed all their remarks upon comparisons with the English theatre.

Notwithstanding my vexation at having been forced into a party so very disagreeable, and that, too, from one so much— so very much the contrary—yet, would they have suffered me to listen, I should have forgotten every thing unpleasant, and felt nothing but delight in hearing the sweet voice of Signor Millico,[170] the first singer; but they tormented me with continual talking.

'What a jabbering they make!' cried Mr. Branghton; 'there's no knowing a word they say. Pray what's the reason they can't as well sing in English?—but I suppose the fine folks would not like it, if they could understand it.'

'How unnatural their action is!' said the son; 'why now who ever saw an Englishman put himself in such out-of-the-way postures?'

'For my part,' said Miss Polly, 'I think it's very pretty, only I don't know what it means.'

'Lord, what does that signify?' cried her sister; 'mayn't one like a thing without being so very particular?—You may see that Miss likes it, and I don't suppose she knows more of the matter than we do.'

A gentleman, soon after, was so obliging as to make room in the front row for Miss Branghton and me. We had no sooner seated ourselves, than Miss Branghton exclaimed, 'Good gracious! only see!—why, Polly, all the people in the pit are without hats, dressed like any thing!'

'Lord, so they are,' cried Miss Polly, 'well, I never saw the like!—it's worth coming to the Opera if one saw nothing else.'

I was then able to distinguish the happy party I had left; and I saw that Lord Orville had seated himself next to Mrs. Mirvan. Sir Clement had his eyes perpetually cast towards the five-shilling gallery, where I suppose he concluded that we were seated; however, before the Opera was over, I have reason to believe that he had discovered me, high and distant as I was from him. Probably he distinguished me by my head-dress.

At the end of the first act, as the green curtain dropped, to prepare for the dance,[171] they imagined that the Opera was done, and Mr. Branghton expressed great indignation that he had been *tricked* out of his money with so little trouble. 'Now if any Englishman was to do such an impudent thing as this,' said he, 'why he'd be pelted;—but here, one of these outlandish gentry may do just what he pleases, and come on, and squeak out a song or two, and then pocket your money without further ceremony.'

However, so determined he was to be dissatisfied, that, before the conclusion of the third act, he found still more fault with the Opera for being too long, and wondered whether they thought their singing good enough to serve us for supper.

During the symphony[172] of a song of Signor Millico's, in the second act, young Mr. Branghton said, 'It's my belief that that fellow's going to sing another song!—why there's nothing but singing!—I wonder when they'll speak.'

This song, which was slow and pathetic, caught all my attention, and I lean'd my head forward to avoid hearing their observations, that I might listen without interruption; but, upon turning round, when the song was over, I found that I was the object of general diversion to the whole party; for the Miss Branghtons were tittering, and the two gentlemen making signs and faces at me, implying their contempt of my affectation.

This discovery determined me to appear as inattentive as themselves; but I was very much provoked at being thus prevented enjoying the only pleasure, which, in such a party, was within my power.

'So, Miss,' said Mr. Branghton, 'you're quite in the fashion, I see;—so you like Operas? well, I'm not so polite; I can't like nonsense, let it be never so much the taste.'

'But pray, Miss,' said the son, 'what makes that fellow look so doleful while he's singing?'

'Probably because the character he performs is in distress.'

'Why then I think he might as well let alone singing till he's in better cue: it's out of all nature for a man to be piping when he's in distress. For my part, I never sing but when I'm merry; yet I love a song as well as most people.'

When the curtain dropped, they all rejoiced.

'How do *you* like it?—and how do *you* like it?' passed from one to another with looks of the utmost contempt. 'As for me,' said Mr. Branghton, 'they've caught me once, but if ever they do again, I'll give 'em leave to sing me to Bedlam[173] for my pains: for such a heap of stuff never did I hear; there is n't one ounce of sense in the whole Opera, nothing but one continued squeaking and squalling from beginning to end.'

'If I had been in the pit,' said Madame Duval, 'I should have liked it vastly, for music is my passion; but sitting in such a place as this, is quite unbearable.'

Miss Branghton, looking at me, declared, that she was not *genteel* enough to admire it.

Miss Polly confessed, that, if they would but sing *English* she should like it *very well*.

The brother wished he could raise a riot in the house,[174] because then he might get his money again.

And, finally, they all agreed, that it was *monstrous dear*.

During the last dance, I perceived, standing near the gallery-door, Sir Clement Willoughby. I was extremely vexed, and would have given the world to have avoided being seen by him: my chief objection was, from the apprehension that he wou'd hear Miss Branghton call me *cousin*.—I fear you will think this London journey has made me grow very proud, but indeed this family is so low-bred and vulgar, that I should be equally ashamed of such a connection in the country, or any where. And really I had already been so much chagrined that Sir Clement had been a witness of Madame Duval's power over me, that I could not bear to be exposed to any further mortification.

As the seats cleared, by parties going away, Sir Clement approached nearer to us; the Miss Branghtons observed with surprise, what a fine gentleman was come into the gallery, and they gave me great reason to expect, that they would endeavour to attract his notice, by familiarity with me, whenever he should join us; and so I formed a sort of plan, to prevent any conversation. I am afraid you will think it wrong; and so I do myself now,—but, at the time, I only considered how I might avoid immediate humiliation.

As soon as he was within two seats of us, he spoke to me; 'I am very happy, Miss Anville, to have found you, for the Ladies below have each an humble attendant, and therefore I am come to offer my services here.'

'Why then,' cried I (not without hesitating), 'if you please,—I will join them.'

'Will you allow me the honour of conducting you?' cried he eagerly; and, instantly taking my hand, he would have marched away with me: but I turned to Madame Duval, and said, 'As our party is so large, Madam, if you will give me leave, I will go down to Mrs. Mirvan, that I may not crowd you in the coach.'

And then, without waiting for an answer, I suffered Sir Clement to hand me out of the gallery.

Madame Duval, I doubt not, will be very angry, and so I am with myself, now, and therefore I cannot be surprised: but Mr. Branghton, I am sure, will easily comfort himself, in having escaped the additional coach expence of carrying me to Queen-Ann-Street: as to his daughters, they had no time to speak, but I saw they were in utter amazement.

My intention was to join Mrs. Mirvan, and accompany her home. Sir Clement was in high spirits and good humour; and, all the way we went, I was fool enough to rejoice in secret at the success of my plan; nor was it till I got down stairs, and amidst the servants, that any difficulty occurred to me of meeting with my friends.

I then asked Sir Clement how I should contrive to acquaint Mrs. Mirvan that I had left Madame Duval?

'I fear it will be almost impossible to find her,' answered he; 'but you can have no objection to permitting me to see you safe home.'

He then desired his servant, who was waiting, to order his chariot to draw up.

This quite startled me; I turned to him hastily, and said that I could not think of going away without Mrs. Mirvan.

'But how can we meet with her?' cried he; 'you will not chuse to go into the pit yourself,[175] I cannot send a servant there; and it is impossible for *me* to go and leave you alone.'

The truth of this was indisputable, and totally silenced me. Yet, as soon as I could recollect myself, I determined not to go in his chariot, and told him I believed I had best return to my party up stairs.

He would not hear of this; and earnestly entreated me not to withdraw the trust I had reposed in him.

While he was speaking, I saw Lord Orville, with several ladies and gentlemen, coming from the pit passage: unfortunately, he saw me too, and, leaving his company, advanced instantly towards me, and, with an air and voice of surprise, said, 'Good God, do I see Miss Anville!'

I now most severely felt the folly of my plan, and the awkwardness of my situation; however, I hastened to tell him, though in a hesitating manner, that I was waiting for Mrs. Mirvan: but what was my disappointment, when he acquainted me that she was already gone home!

I was inexpressibly distressed; to suffer Lord Orville to think me satisfied with the single protection of Sir Clement Willoughby, I could not bear; yet I was more than ever averse to returning to a party which I dreaded his seeing: I stood some moments in suspense, and could not help exclaiming, 'Good Heaven, what can I do!'

'Why, my dear Madam,' cried Sir Clement, 'should you be thus uneasy?—you will reach Queen-Ann-Street almost as soon as Mrs. Mirvan, and I am sure you cannot doubt being as safe.'

I made no answer, and Lord Orville then said, 'My coach is here; and my servants are ready to take any commands Miss Anville will honour me with for them. I shall myself go home in a chair,[176] and therefore—'

How grateful did I feel for a proposal so considerate, and made with so much delicacy! I should gladly have accepted it, had I been permitted, but Sir Clement would not let him even finish his speech; he interrupted him with evident displeasure, and said, 'My Lord, my own chariot is now at the door.'

And just then the servant came, and told him the carriage was ready. He begged to have the honour of conducting me to it, and would have taken my hand, but I drew it back, saying, 'I can't—I can't indeed! pray go by yourself—and as to me, let me have a chair.'

'Impossible!' cried he with vehemence, 'I cannot think of trusting you with strange chairmen,[177]—I cannot answer it to Mrs. Mirvan,—come, dear Madam, we shall be home in five minutes.'

Again I stood suspended. With what joy would I then have compromised with my pride, to have been once more with Madame Duval and the Branghtons, provided I had not met with Lord Orville! However, I flatter myself that he not only saw, but pitied my embarrassment, for he said, in a tone of voice unusually softened, 'To offer my services in the presence of Sir Clement Willoughby would be superfluous; but I hope I need not assure Miss Anville, how happy it would make me to be of the least use to her.'

I courtsied my thanks. Sir Clement, with great earnestness, pressed me to go; and while I was thus uneasily deliberating what to do, the dance, I suppose, finished, for the people crowded down stairs. Had Lord Orville then repeated his offer, I would have accepted it, notwithstanding Sir Clement's repugnance; but I fancy he thought it would be impertinent. In a very few minutes I heard Madame Duval's voice, as she descended from the gallery; 'Well,' cried I, hastily, 'if I must go—' I stopped, but Sir Clement immediately handed me into his chariot, called out 'Queen-Ann-Street,' and then jumped in himself. Lord Orville, with a bow and a half smile, wished me good night.

My concern was so great, at being seen and left by Lord Orville in so strange a situation, that I should have been best pleased to have remained wholly silent during our ride home: but Sir Clement took care to prevent that.

He began by making many complaints of my unwillingness to trust myself with him, and begged to know what could be the reason? This question so much embarrassed me, that I could not tell what to answer, but only said, that I was sorry to have taken up so much of his time.

'O Miss Anville,' cried he, taking my hand, 'If you knew with what transport I would dedicate to you not only the present but all the future time allotted to me, you would not injure me by making such an apology.'

I could not think of a word to say to this, nor to a great many other equally fine speeches with which he ran on, though I would fain have withdrawn my hand, and made almost continual attempts; but in vain, for he actually grasped it between both his, without any regard to my resistance.

Soon after, he said that he believed the coachman was going the wrong way, and he called to his servant, and gave him directions. Then again addressing himself to me, 'How often, how assiduously have I sought an opportunity of speaking to you, without the presence of that brute, Captain Mirvan! Fortune has now kindly favoured me with one, and permit me' (again seizing my hand) 'permit me to use it, in telling you that I adore you.'

I was quite thunderstruck at this abrupt and unexpected declaration. For some moments I was silent, but, when I recovered from my surprise, I said, 'Indeed, Sir, if you were determined to make me repent leaving my own party so foolishly, you have very well succeeded.'

'My dearest life,' cried he, 'is it possible you can be so cruel? Can your nature and your countenance be so totally opposite? Can the sweet bloom upon those charming cheeks, which appears as much the result of good-humour as of beauty—'

'O, Sir,' cried I, interrupting him, 'this is very fine; but I had hoped we had had enough of this sort of conversation at the Ridotto, and I did not expect you would so soon resume it.'

'What I then said, my sweet reproacher, was the effect of a mistaken, a prophane idea, that your understanding held no competition with your beauty; but now, now that I find you equally incomparable in both, all words, all powers of speech, are too feeble to express the admiration I feel of your excellencies.'

'Indeed,' cried I, 'if your thoughts had any connection with your language, you would never suppose that I could give credit to praise so very much above my desert.'

This speech, which I made very gravely, occasioned still stronger protestations, which he continued to pour forth, and I continued to disclaim, till I began to wonder that we were not in Queen-Ann-Street, and begged he would desire the coachman to drive faster.

'And does this little moment,' cried he, 'which is the first of happiness I have ever known, does it already appear so very long to you?'

'I am afraid the man has mistaken the way,' answered I, 'or else we should ere now have been at our journey's end. I must beg you will speak to him.'

'And can you think me so much my own enemy?—if my good genius has inspired the man with a desire of prolonging my happiness, can you expect that I should counteract its indulgence?'

I now began to apprehend that he had himself ordered the man to go a wrong way, and I was so much alarmed at the idea, that, the very instant it occurred to me, I let down the glass, and made a sudden effort to open the chariot-door myself, with a view of jumping into the street; but he caught hold of me, exclaiming, 'For Heaven's sake, what is the matter?'

'I—I don't know,' cried I (quite out of breath), 'but I am sure the man goes wrong, and, if you will not speak to him, I am determined I will get out myself.'

'You amaze me,' answered he (still holding me), 'I cannot imagine what you apprehend. Surely you can have no doubts of my honour?'

He drew me towards him as he spoke. I was frightened

dreadfully, and could hardly say, 'No, Sir, no,—none at all,—
only Mrs. Mirvan,—I think she will be uneasy.'

'Whence this alarm, my dearest angel?—What can you fear?—
my life is at your devotion, and can you, then, doubt my
protection?'

And so saying he passionately kissed my hand.

Never, in my whole life, have I been so terrified. I broke
forcibly from him, and, putting my head out of the window,
called aloud to the man to stop.[178] Where we then were I know
not, but I saw not a human being, or I should have called for
help.

Sir Clement, with great earnestness, endeavoured to appease
and compose me; 'If you do not intend to murder me,' cried I,
'for mercy's, for pity's sake, let me get out!'

'Compose your spirits, my dearest life,' cried he, 'and I will do
every thing you would have me.' And then he called to the man
himself, and bid him make haste to Queen-Ann-Street. 'This
stupid fellow,' continued he, 'has certainly mistaken my orders;
but I hope you are now fully satisfied.'

I made no answer, but kept my head at the window, watching
which way he drove, but without any comfort to myself, as I
was quite unacquainted with either the right or the wrong.

Sir Clement now poured forth abundant protestations of
honour, and assurances of respect, entreating my pardon for
having offended me, and beseeching my good opinion: but I was
quite silent, having too much apprehension to make reproaches,
and too much anger to speak without.

In this manner we went through several streets, till at last, to
my great terror, he suddenly ordered the man to stop, and said,
'Miss Anville, we are now within twenty yards of your house;
but I cannot bear to part with you, till you generously forgive
me for the offence you have taken, and promise not to make it
known to the Mirvans.'

I hesitated between fear and indignation.

'Your reluctance to speak, redoubles my contrition for having
displeased you, since it shews the reliance I might have on a
promise which you will not give without consideration.'

'I am very, very much distressed,' cried I, 'you ask a promise which you must be sensible I ought not to grant, and yet dare not refuse.'

'Drive on!' cried he to the coachman;—'Miss Anville, I will not compel you; I will exact no promise, but trust wholly to your generosity.'

This rather softened me; which advantage he no sooner perceived, than he determined to avail himself of, for he flung himself on his knees, and pleaded with so much submission, that I was really obliged to forgive him, because his humiliation made me quite ashamed: and, after that, he would not let me rest till I gave him my word that I would not complain of him to Mrs. Mirvan.

My own folly and pride, which had put me in his power, were pleas which I could not but attend to in his favour. However, I shall take very particular care never to be again alone with him.

When, at last, we arrived at our house, I was so overjoyed, that I should certainly have pardoned him then, if I had not before. As he handed me up stairs, he scolded his servant aloud, and very angrily, for having gone so much out of the way. Miss Mirvan ran out to meet me,—and who should I see behind her, but—Lord Orville!

All my joy now vanished, and gave place to shame and confusion; for I could not endure that he should know how long a time Sir Clement and I had been together, since I was not at liberty to assign any reason for it.

They all expressed great satisfaction at seeing me, and said they had been extremely uneasy and surprised that I was so long coming home, as they had heard from Lord Orville that I was not with Madame Duval. Sir Clement, in an affected passion, said that his booby of a servant had misunderstood his orders, and was driving us to the upper end of Piccadilly.[179] For my part, I only coloured, for though I would not forfeit my word, I yet disdained to confirm a tale in which I had myself no belief.

Lord Orville, with great politeness, congratulated me, that the troubles of the evening had so happily ended, and said, that he had found it impossible to return home, before he enquired after my safety.

In a very short time he took leave, and Sir Clement followed him. As soon as they were gone, Mrs. Mirvan, though with great softness, blamed me for having quitted Madame Duval. I assured her, and with truth, that for the future I would be more prudent.

The adventures of the evening so much disconcerted me, that I could not sleep all night. I am under the most cruel apprehensions, lest Lord Orville should suppose my being on the gallery-stairs with Sir Clement was a concerted scheme,[180] and even that our continuing so long together in his chariot, was with my approbation, since I did not say a word on the subject, nor express any dissatisfaction at the coachman's pretended blunder.

Yet his coming hither to wait our arrival, though it seems to imply some doubt, shews also some anxiety. Indeed Miss Mirvan says, that he appeared *extremely* anxious, nay uneasy and impatient for my return. If I did not fear to flatter myself, I should think it not impossible but that he had a suspicion of Sir Clement's design, and was therefore concerned for my safety.

What a long letter is this! however, I shall not write many more from London, for the Captain said this morning, that he would leave town on Tuesday next. Madame Duval will dine here to-day, and then she is to be told his intention.

I am very much amazed that she accepted Mrs. Mirvan's invitation, as she was in such wrath yesterday. I fear that to-day I shall myself be the principal object of her displeasure; but I must submit patiently, for I cannot defend myself.

Adieu, my dearest Sir. Should this letter be productive of any uneasiness to you, more than ever shall I repent the heedless imprudence which it recites.

LETTER XXII

Evelina in continuation

Monday morning, April 18

Mrs. Mirvan has just communicated to me an anecdote concerning Lord Orville, which has much surprised, half pleased, and half pained me.

While they were sitting together during the opera, he told her that he had been greatly concerned at the impertinence which the young lady under her protection had suffered from Mr. Lovel; but that he had the pleasure of assuring her, she had no future disturbance to apprehend from him.

Mrs. Mirvan, with great eagerness, begged he would explain himself, and said she hoped he had not thought so insignificant an affair worthy his serious attention.

'There is nothing,' answered he, ' which requires more immediate notice than impertinence, for it ever encroaches when it is tolerated.' He then added, that he believed he ought to apologize for the liberty he had taken of interfering, but that, as he regarded himself in the light of a *party concerned*, from having had the honour of dancing with Miss Anville, he could not possibly reconcile to himself a patient neutrality.

He then proceeded to tell her, that he had waited upon[181] Mr. Lovel the morning after the play; that the visit had proved an amicable one, but the particulars were neither entertaining nor necessary; he only assured her, Miss Anville might be perfectly easy, since Mr. Lovel had engaged his honour never more to mention, or even to hint at what had passed at Mrs. Stanley's assembly.

Mrs. Mirvan expressed her satisfaction at this conclusion, and thanked him for his polite attention to her young friend.

'It would be needless,' said he, 'to request that this affair may never transpire, since Mrs. Mirvan cannot but see the necessity of keeping it inviolably secret; but I thought it incumbent upon

me, as the young lady is under your protection, to assure both
you and her of Mr. Lovel's future respect.'

Had I known of this visit previous to Lord Orville's making
it, what dreadful uneasiness would it have cost me! Yet that he
should so much interest himself in securing me from offence,
gives me, I must own, an internal pleasure greater than I can
express; for I feared he had too contemptuous an opinion of me,
to take any trouble upon my account. Though, after all, this
interference might rather be to satisfy his own delicacy, than
from thinking well of me.

But how cool, how quiet is true courage![182] Who, from
seeing Lord Orville at the play, would have imagined his resentment would have hazarded his life? yet his displeasure was
evident, though his real bravery and his politeness equally
guarded him from entering into any discussion in our presence.

Madame Duval, as I expected, was most terribly angry yesterday; she scolded me for I believe two hours, on account of
having left her, and protested she had been so much surprised at
my going, without giving her time to answer, that she hardly
knew whether she was awake or asleep. But she assured me, that
if ever I did so again, she would never more take me into public.
And she expressed an equal degree of displeasure against Sir
Clement, because he had not even spoken to her, and because he
was always of the Captain's side in an argument. The Captain, as
bound in honour, warmly defended him, and then followed a
dispute in the usual style.

After dinner, Mrs. Mirvan introduced the subject of our
leaving London. Madame Duval said she should stay a month or
two longer. The Captain told her she was welcome, but that he
and his family should go into the country on Tuesday morning.

A most disagreeable scene followed; Madame Duval insisted
upon keeping me with her; but Mrs. Mirvan said, that as I was
actually engaged on a visit to Lady Howard, who had only
consented to my leaving her for a few days, she could not think
of returning without me.

Perhaps if the Captain had not interfered, the good-breeding
and mildness of Mrs. Mirvan might have had some effect upon

Madame Duval; but he passes no opportunity of provoking her, and therefore made so many gross and rude speeches, all of which she retorted, that, in conclusion, she vowed she would sooner go to law, in right of her relationship,[183] than that I should be taken away from her.

I heard this account from Mrs. Mirvan, who was so kindly considerate as to give me a pretence for quitting the room, as soon as this dispute began, lest Madame Duval should refer to me, and insist on my obedience.

The final result of the conversation was, that, to soften matters for the present, Madame Duval should make one in the party for Howard Grove, whither we are positively to go next Wednesday. And though we are none of us satisfied with this plan, we know not how to form a better.

Mrs. Mirvan is now writing to Lady Howard, to excuse bringing this unexpected guest, and to prevent the disagreeable surprise, which must, otherwise, attend her reception. This dear lady seems eternally studying my happiness and advantage.

To-night we go to the Pantheon, which is the last diversion we shall partake of in London, for to-morrow——

*   *   *   *   *

This moment, my dearest Sir, I have received your kind letter.

If you thought us too dissipated the first week, I almost fear to know what you will think of us this second,—however, the Pantheon this evening will probably be the last public place which I shall ever see.

The assurance of your support and protection in regard to Madame Duval, though what I never doubted, excites my utmost gratitude: how, indeed, cherished under your roof, the happy object of your constant indulgence, how could I have borne to become the slave of her tyrannical humours?—pardon me that I speak so hardly of her, but, whenever the idea of passing my days with her occurs to me, the comparison which naturally follows, takes from me all that forbearance, which, I believe, I owe her.

You are already displeased with Sir Clement: to be sure, then, his behaviour after the Opera will not make peace with you.

Indeed, the more I reflect upon it, the more angry I am. I was entirely in his power, and it was cruel in him to cause me so much terror.

O my dearest Sir, were I but worthy the prayers and the wishes you offer for me, the utmost ambition of my heart would be fully satisfied! but I greatly fear you will find me, now that I am out of the reach of your assisting prudence, more weak and imperfect than you could have expected.

I have not now time to write another word, for I must immediately hasten to dress for the evening.

LETTER XXIII

Evelina in continuation

Queen-Ann-Street, Tuesday, April, 19

There is something to me half melancholy in writing an account of our last adventures in London; however, as this day is merely appropriated to packing, and preparations for our journey, and as I shall shortly have no more adventures to write, I think I may as well complete my town journal at once. And, when you have it all together, I hope, my dear Sir, you will send me your observations and thoughts upon it to Howard Grove.

About eight o'clock we went to the Pantheon. I was extremely struck with the beauty of the building, which greatly surpassed whatever I could have expected or imagined. Yet, it has more the appearance of a chapel, than of a place of diversion; and, though I was quite charmed with the magnificence of the room, I felt that I could not be as gay and thoughtless there as at Ranelagh, for there is something in it which rather inspires awe and solemnity, than mirth and pleasure. However, perhaps it may only have this effect upon such a novice as myself.

I should have said, that our party consisted only of Captain,

Mrs. and Miss Mirvan, as Madame Duval spent the day in the city:—which I own I could not lament.

There was a great deal of company; but the first person we saw was Sir Clement Willoughby. He addressed us with his usual ease, and joined us for the whole evening. I felt myself very uneasy in his presence; for I could not look at him, nor hear him speak, without recollecting the chariot adventure; but to my great amazement, I observed that he looked at *me* without the least apparent discomposure, though certainly he ought not to think of his behaviour without blushing. I really wish I had not forgiven him, and then he could not have ventured to speak to me any more.

There was an exceeding good concert, but too much talking to hear it well. Indeed I am quite astonished to find how little music is attended to in silence; for though every body seems to admire, hardly any body listens.

We did not see Lord Orville, till we went into the tea-room, which is large, low, and under ground, and serves merely as a foil to the apartments above; he then sat next to us; he seemed to belong to a large party, chiefly of ladies; but, among the gentlemen attending them, I perceived Mr. Lovel.

I was extremely irresolute whether or not I ought to make any acknowledgements to Lord Orville for his generous conduct in securing me from the future impertinence of that man; and I thought, that as he had seemed to allow Mrs. Mirvan to acquaint me, though no one else, of the measures which he had taken, he might, perhaps, suppose me ungrateful if silent: however, I might have spared myself the trouble of deliberating, as I never once had the shadow of an opportunity of speaking unheard by Sir Clement. On the contrary, he was so exceedingly officious and forward, that I could not say a word to any body, but instantly he bent his head forward, with an air of profound attention, as if I had addressed myself wholly to him: and yet, I never once looked at him, and would not have spoken to him on any account.

Indeed, Mrs. Mirvan, herself, though unacquainted with the behaviour of Sir Clement after the opera, says it is not right for a

young woman to be seen so frequently in public with the same
gentleman; and, if our stay in town was to be lengthened, she
would endeavour to represent to the Captain the impropriety of
allowing his constant attendance; for Sir Clement, with all his
easiness,[184] could not be so eternally of our parties, if the Captain
was less fond of his company.

At the same table with Lord Orville, sat a gentleman,—I call
him so only because he *was* at the same table,—who, almost
from the moment I was seated, fixed his eyes steadfastly on my
face, and never once removed them to any other object during
tea-time, notwithstanding my dislike of his staring, must, I am
sure, have been very evident. I was quite surprised, that a man
whose boldness was so offensive, could have gained admission
into a party of which Lord Orville made one; for I naturally
concluded him to be some low-bred, and uneducated man; and I
thought my idea was indubitably confirmed, when I heard him
say to Sir Clement Willoughby, in an *audible whisper*,—which
is a mode of speech very distressing and disagreeable to by-
standers,—'For Heaven's sake, Willoughby, who is that lovely
creature?'

But what was my amazement, when, listening attentively for
the answer, though my head was turned another way, I heard Sir
Clement say, 'I am sorry I cannot inform your Lordship, but I
am ignorant myself.'

Lordship!—how extraordinary! that a *nobleman*, accustomed, in
all probability, to the first rank of company in the kingdom,
from his earliest infancy, can possibly be deficient in *good manners*,
however faulty in morals and principles! Even Sir Clement
Willoughby appeared modest in comparison with this person.

During tea, a conversation was commenced upon the times,
fashions, and public places, in which the company of both tables
joined. It began by Sir Clement's enquiring of Miss Mirvan, and
of me, if the Pantheon had answered our expectations.

We both readily agreed that it had greatly exceeded them.

'Ay, to be sure,' said the Captain, 'why you don't suppose
they'd confess they did n't like it, do you? Whatever's the fashion,
they must like of course;—or else I'd be bound for it they'd

own, that there never was such a dull place as this here invented.'

'And has, then, this building,' said Lord Orville, 'no merit that may serve to lessen your censure? Will not your eye, Sir, speak something in its favour?'

'Eye!' cried the Lord (I don't know his name), 'and is there any eye here, that can find pleasure in looking at dead walls or statues, when such heavenly living objects as I now see demand all their admiration?'

'O, certainly,' said Lord Orville, 'the lifeless symmetry of architecture, however beautiful the design and proportion, no man would be so mad as to put in competition with the animated charms of nature: but when, as to-night, the eye may be regaled at the same time, and in one view, with all the excellence of art, and all the perfection of nature, I cannot think that either suffer by being seen together.'

'I grant, my Lord,' said Sir Clement, 'that the cool eye of unimpassioned philosophy may view both with equal attention, and equal safety; but, where the heart is not so well guarded, it is apt to interfere, and render, even to the eye, all objects but one insipid and uninteresting.'

'Aye, aye,' cried the Captain, 'you may talk what you will of your eye here, and your eye there, and, for the matter of that, to be sure you have two,—but we all know they both squint one way.'

'Far be it from me,' said Lord Orville, 'to dispute the *magnetic* power of beauty, which irresistably draws and attracts whatever has soul and sympathy: and I am happy to acknowledge, that though we have now no *gods* to occupy a mansion professedly built for them,[185] yet we have secured their *better halves*, for we have *goddesses* to whom we all most willingly bow down.' And then, with a very droll air, he made a profound reverence to the ladies.

'They'd need be goddesses with a vengeance,' said the Captain, 'for they're mortal dear to look at. Howsomever, I should be glad to know what you can see in e'er a face among them that's worth half a guinea for a sight.'

'Half a guinea!' exclaimed that same Lord, 'I would give half I am worth, for a sight of only *one*, provided I make my own choice. And, prithee, how can money be better employed than in the service of fine women?'

'If the ladies of his own party can pardon the Captain's speech,' said Sir Clement, 'I think he has a fair claim to the forgiveness of all.'

'Then you depend very much, as I doubt not but you may,' said Lord Orville, 'upon the general sweetness of the sex;—but, as to the ladies of the Captain's party, they may easily pardon, for they cannot be hurt.'

'But they must have a devilish good conceit of themselves, though,' said the Captain, 'to believe all that. Howsomever, whether or no, I should be glad to be told, by some of you, who seem to be knowing in them things, what kind of diversion can be found in such a place as this here, for one who has had, long ago, his full of face-hunting?'

Every body laughed, but nobody spoke.

'Why look you there, now,' continued the Captain, 'you're all at a dead stand!¹⁸⁶—not a man among you can answer that there question. Why, then, I must make bold to conclude, that you all come here for no manner of purpose but to stare at one another's pretty faces;—though, for the matter of that, half of 'em are plaguy ugly,—and, as to t'other half,—I believe it's none of God's manufactory.'

'What the ladies may come hither for, Sir,' said Mr. Lovel (stroking his ruffles, and looking down), 'it would ill become *us* to determine; but as to we men, doubtless we can have no other view, than to admire them.'

'If I be n't mistaken,' cried the Captain (looking earnestly in his face), 'you are that same person we saw at Love for Love t'other night; be n't you?'

Mr. Lovel bowed.

'Why, then, Gentlemen,' continued he, with a loud laugh, 'I must tell you a most excellent good joke;—when all was over, as sure as you're alive, he asked what the play was! Ha, ha, ha!'

'Sir,' said Mr. Lovel, colouring, 'if you were as much used to

a town life as I am,—which, I presume, is not precisely the
case,—I fancy you would not find so much diversion from a
circumstance so common.'

'Common! what, is it common?' repeated the Captain; 'why
then, 'fore George, such chaps are more fit to be sent to school,
and well disciplined with a cat o' nine tails,[187] than to poke their
heads into a play-house. Why, a play is the only thing left, now-
a-days, that has a grain of sense in it; for as to all the rest of your
public places, d'ye see, if they were all put together, I would n't
give *that* for 'em!' snapping his fingers. 'And now we're talking
of them sort of things, there's your operas,—I should like to
know, now, what any of you can find to say for them.'

Lord Orville, who was most able to have answered, seemed
by no means to think the Captain worthy an argument, upon a
subject concerning which he had neither knowledge nor feeling:
but, turning to us, he said, 'The ladies are silent, and we seem to
have engrossed the conversation to ourselves, in which we are
much more our own enemies than theirs. But,' addressing himself
to Miss Mirvan and me, 'I am most desirous to hear the opinions
of these young ladies, to whom all public places must, as yet, be
new.'

We both, and with eagerness, declared that we had received as
much, if not more pleasure, at the opera than any where: but we
had better have been silent; for the Captain, quite displeased,
said, 'What signifies asking them girls? Do you think they know
their own minds yet? Ask 'em after any thing that's called
diversion, and you're sure they'll say it's vastly fine;—they are a
set of parrots, and speak by rote, for they all say the same thing:
but ask 'em how they like making puddings and pies,[188] and I'll
warrant you'll pose 'em. As to them operas, I desire I may hear
no more of their liking such nonsense; and for you, Moll,' to his
daughter, 'I charge you, as you value my favour, that you'll
never again be so impertinent as to have a taste of your own
before my face. There are fools enough in the world, without
your adding to their number. I'll have no daughter of mine
affect them sort of megrims.[189] It is a shame they a'n't put down;
and if I'd my will, there's not a magistrate in this town, but

should be knocked of the head for suffering them.[190] If you've a
mind to praise any thing, why you may praise a play, and
welcome, for I like it myself.'

This reproof effectually silenced us both for the rest of the
evening. Nay, indeed, for some minutes it seemed to silence
every body else; till Mr. Lovel, not willing to lose an opportunity
of returning the Captain's sarcasm, said, 'Why, really Sir, it is
but natural to be most pleased with what is most familiar, and, I
think, of all our diversions, there is not one so much in common
between us and the country, as a play. Not a village but has its
barns and comedians;[191] and as for the stage business, why it
may be pretty equally done any where; and even in regard to *us*,
and the *canaille*,[192] confined as we all are within the semi-circle of
a theatre, there is no place where the distinction is less obvious.'

While the Captain seemed considering for Mr. Lovel's meaning, Lord Orville, probably with a view to prevent his finding it,
changed the subject to Cox's Museum, and asked what he
thought of it?

'Think!—' said he, 'why I think as how it i'n't worth thinking
about. I like no such *jem cracks*.[193] It is only fit, in my mind, for
monkeys,—though, for ought I know, they too might turn up
their noses at it.'

'May we ask your Lordship's own opinion?' said Mrs.
Mirvan.

'The mechanism,' answered he, 'is wonderfully ingenious: I
am sorry it is turned to no better account; but its purport is so
frivolous, so very remote from all aim at instruction or utility,
that the sight of so fine a shew only leaves a regret on the mind,
that so much work, and so much ingenuity, should not be better
bestowed.'

'The truth is,' said the Captain, 'that in all this huge town, so
full as it is of folks of all sorts, there i'n't so much as one public
place, besides the play-house, where a man, that's to say, a man
who *is* a man, ought not to be ashamed to shew his face. T'other
day they got me to a ridotto; but I believe it will be long enough
before they get me to another. I knew no more what to do with
myself, than if my ship's company had been metamorphosed into

Frenchmen. Then, again, there's your famous Ranelagh, that you make such a fuss about,—why what a dull place is that!—it's the worst of all.'

'Ranelagh dull!'—'Ranelagh dull!' was echoed from mouth to mouth, and all the ladies, as if of one accord, regarded the Captain with looks of the most ironical contempt.

'As to Ranelagh,' said Mr. Lovel, 'most indubitably, though the price is plebeian,[194] it is by no means adapted to the plebeian taste. It requires a certain acquaintance with high life, and—and—and something of—of—something *d'un vrai goût*, to be really sensible of its merit. Those whose—whose connections, and so forth, are not among *les gens comme il faut*, can feel nothing but *ennui*[195] at such a place as Ranelagh.'

'Ranelagh!' cried Lord ——, 'O, 'tis the divinest place under heaven,—or, indeed,—for aught I know——'

'O you creature!' cried a pretty, but affected young lady, patting him with her fan, 'you sha'n't talk so; I know what you are going to say; but, positively, I won't sit by you, if you're so wicked.'

'And how can one sit by you, and be good?' said he, 'when only to look at you is enough to make one wicked—or wish to be so?'

'Fie, my Lord!' returned she, 'you are really insufferable. I don't think I shall speak to you again these seven years.'

'What a metamorphosis,' cried Lord Orville, 'should you make a patriarch[196] of his Lordship!'

'Seven years!' said he, 'dear Madam, be contented with telling me you will not speak to me *after* seven years, and I will endeavour to submit.'

'O, very well, my Lord,' answered she, 'pray date the end of our speaking to each other as early as you please, I'll promise to agree to your time.'

'You know, dear Madam,' said he, sipping his tea, 'you know I only live in your sight.'

'O yes, my Lord, I have long known that. But I begin to fear we shall be too late for Ranelagh this evening.'

'O no, Madam,' said Mr. Lovel, looking at his watch, 'it is but just past ten.'

'No more!' cried she, 'O then we shall do very well.'

All the ladies now started up, and declared they had no time to lose.

'Why what the D—l,' cried the Captain, leaning forward with both his arms on the table, 'are you going to Ranelagh at this time of night?'

The ladies looked at one another, and smiled.

'To Ranelagh?' cried Lord ——, 'Yes, and I hope you are going too; for we cannot possibly excuse these ladies.'

'I go to Ranelagh?—if I do, I'll be——.'

Every body now stood up, and the stranger Lord, coming round to me, said, '*You* go, I hope?'

'No, my Lord, I believe not.'

'O you cannot, must not be so barbarous.' And he took my hand, and ran on saying such fine speeches and compliments, that I might almost have supposed myself a goddess, and him a pagan, paying me adoration. As soon as I possibly could, I drew back my hand; but he frequently, in the course of conversation, contrived to take it again, though it was extremely disagreeable to me; and the more so, as I saw that Lord Orville had his eyes fixed upon us, with a gravity of attention that made me uneasy.

And, surely, my dear Sir, it was a great liberty in this Lord, notwithstanding his rank, to treat me so freely. As to Sir Clement, he seemed in misery.

They all endeavoured to prevail with the Captain to join the Ranelagh party; and this Lord told me, in a low voice, that *it was tearing his heart out* to go without me.

During this conversation, Mr. Lovel came forward, and assuming a look of surprise, made me a bow, and enquired how I did, protesting, upon his honour, that he had not seen me before, or would sooner have paid his respects to me.

Though his politeness was evidently constrained, yet I was very glad to be thus assured of having nothing more to fear from him.

The Captain, far from listening to their persuasions of accompanying them to Ranelagh, was quite in a passion at the proposal, and vowed he would sooner go to the *Black-hole in Calcutta*.[197]

'But,' said Lord ———, 'if the *ladies* will take their tea at Ranelagh, you may depend upon our seeing them safe home, for we shall all be proud of the honour of attending them.'

'May be so,' said the Captain; 'but I'll tell you what, if one of these places be n't enough for them to-night, why to-morrow they shall go to ne'er a one.'

We instantly declared ourselves very ready to go home.

'It is not for yourselves that we petition,' said Lord ———, 'but for *us*; if you have any charity, you will not be so cruel as to deny us; we only beg you to prolong our happiness for a few minutes,—the favour is but a small one for you to grant, though so great a one for us to receive.'

'To tell you a piece of my mind,' said the Captain, surlily, 'I think you might as well not give the girls so much of this palaver: they'll take it all for gospel. As to Moll, why she's well enough, but nothing extraordinary, though, perhaps, you may persuade her that her pug-nose is all the fashion: and as to the other, why she's good white and red to be sure; but what of that?—I'll warrant she'll moulder away as fast as her neighbours.'

'Is there,' cried Lord ———, 'another man in this place, who, seeing such objects, could make such a speech?'

'As to that there,' returned the Captain, 'I don't know whether there be or no, and, to make free, I don't care; for I sha'n't go for to model myself by any of these fair-weather chaps, who dare not so much as say their souls are their own,—and, for aught I know, no more they ben't. I'm almost as much ashamed of my countrymen, as if I was a Frenchman, and I believe in my heart there i'n't a pin to chuse between them; and, before long, we shall hear the very sailors talking that lingo, and see never a swabber without a bag and a sword.'[198]

'He, he, he!— well, 'pon honour,' cried Mr. Lovel, 'you gentlemen of the ocean have a most severe way of judging.'

'Severe! 'fore George, that is impossible; for, to cut the matter short, the men, as they call themselves, are no better than monkeys; and as to the women, why they are mere dolls. So, now you've got my opinion of this subject; and so I wish you good night.'

The ladies, who were very impatient to be gone, made their courtsies, and tripped away, followed by all the gentlemen of their party, except the Lord I have before mentioned, and Lord Orville, who stayed to make enquiries of Mrs. Mirvan concerning our leaving town; and then saying, with his usual politeness, something civil to each of us, with a very grave air, he quitted us.

Lord —— remained some minutes longer, which he spent in making a profusion of compliments to me, by which he prevented my hearing distinctly what Lord Orville said, to my great vexation, especially as he looked—I thought so, at least,—as if displeased at his particularity of behaviour to me.

In going to an outward room, to wait for the carriage, I walked, and could not possibly avoid it, between this nobleman and Sir Clement Willoughby; and, when the servant said the coach stopped the way, though the latter offered me his hand, which I should much have preferred, this same Lord, without any ceremony, took mine himself; and Sir Clement, with a look extremely provoked, conducted Mrs. Mirvan.

In all ranks and all stations of life, how strangely do characters and manners differ! Lord Orville, with a politeness which knows no intermission, and makes no distinction, is as unassuming and modest, as if he had never mixed with the great, and was totally ignorant of every qualification he possesses; this other Lord, though lavish of compliments and fine speeches, seems to me an entire stranger to real good-breeding; whoever strikes his fancy, engrosses his whole attention. He is forward and bold, has an air of haughtiness towards men, and a look of libertinism towards women, and his conscious quality[199] seems to have given him a freedom in his way of speaking to either sex, that is very little short of rudeness.

When we returned home, we were all low-spirited; the evening's entertainment had displeased the Captain, and his displeasure, I believe, disconcerted us all.

And here I thought to have concluded my letter; but, to my great surprise, just now we had a visit from Lord Orville. He called, he said, to pay his respects to us before we left town, and made many enquiries concerning our return; and, when Mrs.

Mirvan told him we were going into the country without any view of again quitting it, he expressed his concern in such terms—so polite, so flattering, so serious—that I could hardly forbear being sorry myself. Were I to go immediately to Berry Hill, I am sure I should feel nothing but joy;—but, now we are joined by this Captain, and by Madame Duval, I must own I expect very little pleasure at Howard Grove.

Before Lord Orville went, Sir Clement Willoughby called. He was more grave than I had ever seen him, and made several attempts to speak to me in a low voice, and to assure me that his regret upon the occasion of our journey, was entirely upon my account. But I was not in spirits, and could not bear to be teazed by him. However, he has so well paid his court to Captain Mirvan, that he gave him a very hearty invitation to the Grove. At this, he brightened,—and, just then, Lord Orville took leave.

No doubt but he was disgusted at this ill-timed, ill-bred partiality; for surely it was very wrong to make an invitation before Lord Orville, in which he was not included! I was so much chagrined, that, as soon as he went, I left the room; and I shall not go down stairs till Sir Clement is gone.

Lord Orville cannot but observe his assiduous endeavours to ingratiate himself into my favour; and does not this extravagant civility of Captain Mirvan, give him reason to suppose, that it meets with our general approbation? I cannot think upon this subject, without inexpressible uneasiness;—and yet, I can think of nothing else.

Adieu, my dearest Sir. Pray write to me immediately. How many long letters has this one short fortnight produced! More than I may, probably, ever write again: I fear I shall have tired you with reading them; but you will now have time to rest, for I shall find but little to say in future.

And now, most honoured Sir, with all the follies and imperfections which I have thus faithfully recounted, can you, and with unabated kindness, suffer me to sign myself

> Your dutiful,
> and most affectionate
> EVELINA?

LETTER XXIV

Mr. Villars to Evelina

Berry Hill, April 22

How much do I rejoice that I can again address my letters to
Howard Grove! My Evelina would have grieved had she known
the anxiety of my mind, during her residence in the great world.
My apprehensions have been inexpressibly alarming; and your
journal, at once exciting and relieving my fears, has almost
wholly occupied me, since the time of your dating it from
London.

Sir Clement Willoughby must be an artful designing man; I
am extremely irritated at his conduct. The passion he pretends
for you has neither sincerity nor honour; the manner and the
opportunities he has chosen to declare it, are bordering upon
insult.

His unworthy behaviour after the opera, convinces me, that,
had not your vehemence frightened him, Queen-Ann-Street
would have been the last place whither he would have ordered
his chariot. O my child, how thankful am I for your escape! I
need not now, I am sure, enlarge upon your indiscretion and
want of thought, in so hastily trusting yourself with a man so
little known to you, and whose gaiety and flightiness should
have put you on your guard.

The nobleman you met at the Pantheon, bold and forward as
you describe him to be, gives me no apprehension; a man who
appears so openly licentious, and who makes his attack with so
little regard to decorum, is one who, to a mind such as my
Evelina's, can never be seen but with the disgust which his
manners ought to excite.

But Sir Clement, though he seeks occasion to give real offence,
contrives to avoid all appearance of intentional evil. He is far
more dangerous, because more artful; but I am happy to observe,
that he seems to have made no impression upon your heart, and

therefore a very little care and prudence may secure you from those designs which I fear he has formed.

Lord Orville appears to be of a better order of beings. His spirited conduct to the meanly impertinent Lovel, and his anxiety for you after the opera, prove him to be a man of sense and of feeling. Doubtless, he thought there was much reason to tremble for your safety, while exposed to the power of Sir Clement; and he acted with a regard to real honour, that will always incline me to think well of him, in so immediately acquainting the Mirvan family with your situation. Many men of this age, from a false and pretended delicacy to a friend, would have quietly pursued their own affairs, and thought it more honourable to leave an unsuspecting young creature to the mercy of a libertine, than to risk his displeasure by taking measures for her security.

Your evident concern at leaving London, is very natural; and yet it afflicts me. I ever dreaded your being too much pleased with a life of dissipation, which youth and vivacity render but too alluring; and I almost regret the consent for your journey, which I had not the resolution to withhold.

Alas, my child, the artlessness of your nature, and the simplicity of your education, alike unfit you for the thorny paths[200] of the great and busy world. The supposed obscurity of your birth and situation, makes you liable to a thousand disagreeable adventures. Not only my views, but my hopes for your future life, have ever centered in the country. Shall I own to you, that, however I may differ from Captain Mirvan in other respects, yet my opinion of the town, its manners, inhabitants, and diversions, is much upon a level with his own? Indeed it is the general harbour of fraud and of folly, of duplicity and of impertinence; and I wish few things more fervently, than that you may have taken a lasting leave of it.

Remember, however, that I only speak in regard to a public and dissipated life; in private families, we may doubtless find as much goodness, honesty, and virtue, in London as in the country.

If contented with a retired station, I still hope I shall live to see my Evelina the ornament of her neighbourhood, and the pride and delight of her family: giving and receiving joy from such society as may best deserve her affection, and employing herself in such useful and innocent occupations as may secure and merit the tenderest love of her friends, and the worthiest satisfaction of her own heart.

Such are my hopes, and such have been my expectations. Disappoint them not, my beloved child, but chear me with a few lines, that may assure me, this one short fortnight spent in town, has not undone the work of seventeen years spent in the country.

ARTHUR VILLARS

LETTER XXV

Evelina to the Rev. Mr. Villars

Howard Grove, April 25

No, my dear Sir, no; *the work of seventeen years* remains such as it was, ever unworthy your time and your labour, but not more so now,—at least I hope not,—than before that fortnight which has so much alarmed you.

And yet, I must confess, that I am not half so happy here at present, as I was ere I went to town: but the change is in the place, not in me. Captain Mirvan and Madame Duval have ruined Howard Grove. The harmony that reigned here is disturbed, our schemes are broken, our way of life is altered, and our comfort is destroyed. But do not suppose *London* to be the source of these evils; for, had our excursion been any where else, so disagreeable an addition to our household, must have caused the same change at our return.

I was sure you would be displeased with Sir Clement Willoughby, and therefore I am by no means surprised at what you say of him: but for Lord Orville—I must own I had greatly feared, that my weak and imperfect account would not have procured him the good opinion which he so well deserves, and which I am delighted to find you seem to have of him. O Sir, could I have done justice to the merit of which I believe him possessed;—could I have painted him to *you* such as he appeared to *me*,—then, indeed, you would have had some idea of the claim which he has to your approbation!

After the last letter which I wrote in town, nothing more passed previous to our journey hither, except a very violent quarrel between Captain Mirvan and Madame Duval. As the Captain intended to travel on horseback, he had settled that we four females should make use of his coach. Madame Duval did not come to Queen-Ann-Street, till the carriage had waited some time at the door, and then, attended by Monsieur Du Bois, she made her appearance.

The Captain, impatient to be gone, would not suffer them to enter the house, but insisted that we should immediately get into the coach. We obeyed; but were no sooner seated, than Madame Duval said, 'Come, Monsieur Du Bois, these girls can make very good room for you; sit closer, children.'

Mrs. Mirvan looked quite confounded, and M. Du Bois, after making some apologies about crowding us, actually got into the coach, on the side with Miss Mirvan and me. But no sooner was he seated, than the Captain, who had observed this transaction very quietly, walked up to the coach-door, saying, 'What, neither with your leave, nor by your leave?'

M. Du Bois seemed rather shocked, and began to make abundance of excuses; but the Captain neither understood nor regarded him, and, very roughly, said, 'Look'ee, *Monseer*, this here may be a French fashion, for aught I know;—but Give and Take is fair in all nations; and so now, d'ye see, I'll make bold to shew you an English one.'

And then, seizing his wrist, he made him jump out of the coach.

M. Du Bois instantly put his hand upon his sword, and threatened to resent this indignity. The Captain, holding up his stick, bid him draw at his peril. Mrs. Mirvan, greatly alarmed, got out of the coach, and, standing between them, entreated her husband to re-enter the house.

'None of your clack!' cried he, angrily, 'what the D—l, do you suppose I can't manage a Frenchman?'

Mean time, Madame Duval called out to M. Du Bois, '*Eh, laissez-le, mon ami, ne le corrigez pas; c'est un vilain bête qui n'en vaut pas la peine.*'[201]

'*Monsieur le Capitaine,*' cried M. Du Bois, '*voulez-vous bien me demander pardon?*'[202]

'O ho, you demand pardon; do you?' said the Captain, 'I thought as much; I thought you'd come to;—so you have lost your relish for an English salutation, have you?' strutting up to him with looks of defiance.

A crowd was now gathering, and Mrs. Mirvan again besought her husband to go into the house.

'Why what a plague is the woman afraid of?—did you ever know a Frenchman that could not take an affront?—I warrant, *Monseer* knows what he is about;—don't you, *Monseer?*'

M. Du Bois, not understanding him, only said, '*Plaît-il, Monsieur?*'[203]

'No, nor *dish*[204] me, neither,' answered the Captain; 'but be that as it may, what signifies our parleying here? If you've any thing to propose, speak at once; if not, why let us go on our journey without more ado.'

'*Parbleu, je n'entends rien, moi!*' cried M. Du Bois, shrugging his shoulders, and looking very dismal.

Mrs. Mirvan then advanced to him, and said, in French, that she was sure the Captain had not any intention to affront him, and begged he would desist from a dispute which could only be productive of mutual misunderstanding, as neither of them knew the language of the other.

This sensible remonstrance had the desired effect, and M. Du Bois, making a bow to every one, except the Captain, very wisely gave up the point, and took leave.

We then hoped to proceed quietly on our journey; but the turbulent Captain would not yet permit us: he approached

Madame Duval with an exulting air, and said, 'Why how's this, Madam? what, has your champion deserted you? why I thought you told me, that you old gentlewomen had it all your own way, among them French sparks?'

'As to that, Sir,' answered she, 'it's not of no consequence what you thought; for a person who can behave in such a low way, may think what he pleases for me, for I sha'n't mind.

'Why, then, Mistress, since you must needs make so free,' cried he, 'please to tell me the reason why you took the liberty for to ask any of your followers into my coach, without my leave? Answer me to that.'

'Why then, pray, Sir,' returned she, 'tell me the reason why you took the liberty to treat the gentleman in such a unpolite way, as to take and pull him neck and heels out? I'm sure he had n't done nothing to affront you, nor nobody else; and I don't know what great hurt he would have done you, by just sitting still in the coach; he would not have eat it.'

'What, do you think, then, that my horses have nothing to do, but to carry about your snivelling Frenchmen? If you do, Madam, I must make bold to tell you, you are out, for I'll see 'em hanged first.'

'More brute you, then! for they've never carried nobody half so good.'

'Why, look'ee, Madam, if you must needs provoke me, I'll tell you a piece of my mind; you must know, I can see as far into a mill-stone as another man,[205] and so, if you thought for to fobb me off with one of your smirking French puppies for a son-in-law, why you'll find yourself in a hobble,[206]—that's all.'

'Sir, you're a —— but I won't say, what;—but, I protest, I had n't no such a thought, no more had n't Monsieur Du Bois.'

'My dear,' said Mrs. Mirvan, 'we shall be very late.'

'Well, well,' answered he, 'get away then; off with you, as fast as you can, it's high time. As to Molly, she's fine lady enough in all conscience; I want none of your French chaps to make her worse.'

And so saying, he mounted his horse, and we drove off. And I could not but think with regret of the different feelings we experienced upon leaving London, to what had belonged to our entering it!

During the journey Madame Duval was so very violent against the Captain, that she obliged Mrs. Mirvan to tell her, that, when in her presence, she must beg her to chuse some other subject of discourse.

We had a most affectionate reception from Lady Howard, whose kindness and hospitality cannot fail of making every body happy, who is disposed so to be.

Adieu, my dearest Sir. I hope, though I have hitherto neglected to mention it, that you have always remembered me to whoever has made any enquiry concerning me.

LETTER XXVI

Evelina to the Rev. Mr. Villars

Howard Grove, April 27

O my dear Sir, I now write in the greatest uneasiness! Madame Duval has made a proposal which terrifies me to death, and which was as unexpected, as it is shocking.

She had been employed for some hours this afternoon in reading letters from London, and, just about tea-time, she sent for me into her room, and said, with a look of great satisfaction, 'Come here, child, I've got some very good news to tell you: something that will surprise you, I'll give you my word, for you ha'n't no notion of it.'

I begged her to explain herself; and then, in terms which I cannot repeat, she said she had been considering what a shame it was, to see me such a poor country, shame-faced thing, when I ought to be a fine lady; and that she had long, and upon several occasions, blushed for me, though she must own the fault was none of mine: for nothing better could be expected from a girl who had been so immured. However, she assured me she had, at length, hit upon a plan, which would make quite another creature of me.

I waited, without much impatience, to hear what this preface led to; but I was soon awakened to more lively sensations, when she acquainted me, that her intention was to prove my birthright, and to claim, by law, the inheritance of my real family!

It would be impossible for me to express my extreme consternation, when she thus unfolded her scheme. My surprise and terror were equally great. I could say nothing; I heard her with a silence which I had not the power to break.

She then expatiated very warmly upon the advantages I should reap from her plan; talked in a high style of my future grandeur; assured me how heartily I should despise almost every body and every thing I had hitherto seen; predicted my marrying into some family of the first rank in the kingdom; and, finally, said I should spend a few months in Paris, where my education and manners might receive their last polish.

She enlarged also upon the delight she should have, in common with myself, from mortifying the pride of certain people, and shewing them, that she was not to be slighted with impunity.

In the midst of this discourse, I was relieved by a summons to tea. Madame Duval was in great spirits; but my emotion was too painful for concealment, and every body enquired into the cause. I would fain have waved the subject, but Madame Duval was determined to make it public. She told them, that she had it in her head to *make something* of me, and that they should soon call me by another name than that of Anville, and yet that she was not going to have the child married, neither.

I could not endure to hear her proceed, and was going to leave the room; which, when Lady Howard perceived, she begged Madame Duval would defer her intelligence to some other opportunity; but she was so eager to communicate her scheme, that she could bear no delay, and therefore they suffered me to go, without opposition. Indeed, whenever my situation or affairs are mentioned by Madame Duval, she speaks of them with such bluntness and severity, that I cannot be enjoined a task more cruel than to hear her.

I was afterwards acquainted with some particulars of the conversation by Miss Mirvan, who told me that Madame Duval informed them of her plan with the utmost complacency, and seemed to think herself very fortunate in having suggested it; but soon after, she accidentally betrayed, that she had been instigated to the scheme by her relations the Branghtons, whose letters, which she received to-day, first mentioned the proposal. She declared that she would have nothing to do with any *round-about ways*, but go openly and instantly to law, in order to prove my birth, real name, and title to the estate of my ancestors.

How impertinent and officious, in these Branghtons, to interfere thus in my concerns! You can hardly imagine what a disturbance this plan has made in the family. The Captain, without enquiring into any particulars of the affair, has peremptorily declared himself against it, merely because it has been proposed by Madame Duval, and they have battled the point together with great violence. Mrs. Mirvan says she will not even *think*, till she hears your opinion. But Lady Howard, to my great surprise, openly avows her approbation of Madame Duval's intention: however, she will write her reasons and sentiments upon the subject to you herself.

As to Miss Mirvan, she is my second self, and neither hopes nor fears but as I do. And as to *me*,—I know not what to say, nor even what to wish; I have often thought my fate peculiarly cruel, to have but one parent, and from that one to be banished for ever;—while, on the other side, I have but too well known and felt the propriety of the separation. And yet, you may much better imagine than I can express, the internal anguish which sometimes oppresses my heart, when I reflect upon the strange indifferency, that must occasion a father never to make the least enquiry after the health, the welfare, or even the life of his child!

O Sir, to *me*, the loss is nothing!—greatly, sweetly, and most benevolently have you guarded me from feeling it;—but for *him*,

I grieve indeed!—I must be divested, not merely of all filial piety, but of all humanity, could I ever think upon this subject, and not be wounded to the soul.

Again I must repeat, I know not what to *wish*: think for me, therefore, my dearest Sir, and suffer my doubting mind, that knows not which way to direct its hopes, to be guided by your wisdom and unerring counsel.

EVELINA

LETTER XXVII

Lady Howard to the Rev. Mr. Villars

Howard Grove

Dear Sir,

I cannot give a greater proof of the high opinion I have of your candour, than by the liberty I am now going to take, of presuming to offer you advice, upon a subject concerning which you have so just a claim to act for yourself: but I know you have too unaffected a love of justice, to be partially tenacious of your own judgement.

Madame Duval has been proposing a scheme which has put us all in commotion, and against which, at first, in common with the rest of my family, I exclaimed; but upon more mature consideration, I own my objections have almost wholly vanished.

This scheme is no other than to commence a law-suit with Sir John Belmont, to prove the validity of his marriage with Miss Evelyn, the necessary consequence of which proof, will be securing his fortune and estate to his daughter.

And why, my dear Sir, should not this be? I know that, upon first hearing, such a plan conveys ideas that must shock you; but I know, too, that your mind is superior to being governed by

prejudices, or to opposing any important cause on account of a
few disagreeable attendant circumstances.

Your lovely charge, now first entering into life, has merit
which ought not to be buried in obscurity. She seems born for an
ornament to the world. Nature has been bountiful to her of whatever she had to bestow; and the peculiar attention you have given
to her education, has formed her mind to a degree of excellence,
that, in one so young, I have scarce ever seen equalled. Fortune, alone, has hitherto been sparing of her gifts; and she, too,
now opens the way which leads to all that is left to wish for her.

What your reasons may have been, my good Sir, for so
carefully concealing the birth, name, and pretensions of this
amiable girl, and forbearing to make any claim upon Sir John
Belmont, I am totally a stranger to; but, without knowing, I
respect them, from the high opinion I have of your character
and judgement: but I hope they are not insuperable; for I cannot
but think, that it was never designed, for one who seems meant
to grace the world, to have her life devoted to retirement.

Surely Sir John Belmont, wretch as he has shewn himself,
could never see his accomplished daughter, and not be proud to
own her, and eager to secure her the inheritance of his fortune.
The admiration she met with in town, though merely the effect
of her external attractions, was such, that Mrs. Mirvan assures
me, she would have had the most splendid offers, had there not
seemed to be some mystery in regard to her birth, which, she
was well informed, was assiduously, though vainly, endeavoured
to be discovered.

Can it be right, my dear Sir, that this promising young
creature should be deprived of the fortune, and rank of life, to
which she is lawfully entitled, and which you have prepared her
to support and to use so nobly? To despise riches, may, indeed,
be philosophic, but to dispense them worthily, must, surely, be
more beneficial to mankind.

Perhaps a few years, or, indeed, a much shorter time, may
make this scheme impracticable: Sir John, though yet young,
leads a life too dissipated for long duration; and, when too late,
we may regret that something was not sooner done; for it will be

next to impossible, after he is gone, to settle or prove any thing with his heirs and executors.

Pardon the earnestness with which I write my defense of this affair; but your charming ward has made me so warmly her friend, that I cannot be indifferent upon a subject of such importance to her future life.

Adieu, my dear Sir;—send me speedily an answer to this remonstrance, and believe me to be, &c.

M. HOWARD

LETTER XXVIII

Mr. Villars to Lady Howard

Berry Hill, May 2

Your letter, Madam, has opened a source of anxiety to which I look forward with dread, and which to see closed, I scarcely dare expect. I am unwilling to oppose my opinion to that of your Ladyship, nor indeed, can I, but by arguments which, I believe, will rather rank me as a hermit, ignorant of the world, and fit only for my cell, than as a proper guardian, in an age such as this, for an accomplished young woman. Yet, thus called upon, it behoves me to explain, and endeavour to vindicate, the reasons by which I have been hitherto guided.

The mother of this dear child,—who was led to destruction by her own imprudence, the hardness of heart of Madame Duval, and the villainy of Sir John Belmont,—was once, what her daughter is now, the best beloved of my heart; and her memory, so long as my own holds, I shall love, mourn, and honour! On the fatal day that her gentle soul left its mansion, and not many hours ere she ceased to breathe, I solemnly plighted my faith, *That her child, if it lived, should know no father, but myself, or her acknowledged husband.*

You cannot, Madam, suppose that I found much difficulty in adhering to this promise, and forbearing to make any *claim* upon Sir John Belmont. Could I feel an affection the most paternal for this poor sufferer, and not abominate her destroyer? Could I wish to deliver to *him*, who had so basely betrayed the mother, the helpless and innocent offspring, who, born in so much sorrow, seemed entitled to all the compassionate tenderness of pity?

For many years, the *name* alone of that man, accidentally spoken in my hearing, almost divested me of my christianity, and scarce could I forbear to execrate him. Yet I sought not, neither did I desire, to deprive him of his child, had he, with any appearance of contrition, or, indeed, of humanity, endeavoured to become less unworthy such a blessing;—but he is a stranger to all parental feelings, and has, with a savage insensibility, forborne to enquire even into the existence of this sweet orphan, though the situation of his injured wife was but too well known to him.

You wish to be acquainted with my intentions.—I must acknowledge, they were such as I now perceive would not be honoured with your Ladyship's approbation: for though I have sometimes thought of presenting Evelina to her father, and demanding the justice which is her due, yet, at other times, I have both disdained and feared the application; disdained, lest it should be refused, and feared, lest it should be accepted!

Lady Belmont, who was firmly persuaded of her approaching dissolution, frequently and earnestly besought me, that if her infant was a female, I would not abandon her to the direction of a man so wholly unfit to take the charge of her education; but, should she be importunately demanded, that I would retire with her abroad, and carefully conceal her from Sir John, till some apparent change in his sentiments and conduct should announce him less improper for such a trust. And often would she say, 'Should the poor babe have any feelings correspondent with its mother's, it will have no want, while under your protection.' Alas! she had no sooner quitted it herself, than she was plunged into a gulph of misery, that swallowed up her peace, reputation, and life.

During the childhood of Evelina I suggested a thousand plans for the security of her birth-right;—but I as oftentimes rejected them. I was in a perpetual conflict, between the desire that she should have justice done her, and the apprehension that, while I improved her fortune, I should endanger her mind. However, as her character began to be formed, and her disposition to be displayed, my perplexity abated; the road before me seemed less thorny and intricate, and I thought I could perceive the right path from the wrong: for, when I observed the artless openness, the ingenuous simplicity of her nature; when I saw that her guileless and innocent soul fancied all the world to be pure and disinterested as herself, and that her heart was open to every impression with which love, pity, or art might assail it;—then did I flatter myself, that to follow my own inclination, and to secure her welfare, was the same thing; since, to expose her to the snares and dangers inevitably encircling a house of which the master is dissipated and unprincipled, without the guidance of a mother, or any prudent and sensible female, seemed to me no less than suffering her to stumble into some dreadful pit, when the sun was in its meridian. My plan, therefore, was not merely to educate and to cherish her as my own, but to adopt her the heiress of my small fortune, and to bestow her upon some worthy man, with whom she might spend her days in tranquillity, chearfulness, and good-humour, untainted by vice, folly, or ambition.

So much for the time past. Such have been the motives by which I have been governed; and I hope they will be allowed not merely to account for, but also to justify, the conduct which has resulted from them. It now remains to speak of the time to come.

And here, indeed, I am sensible of difficulties which I almost despair of surmounting according to my wishes. I pay the highest deference to your Ladyship's opinion, which it is extremely painful to me not to concur with; yet, I am so well acquainted with your goodness, that I presume to hope it would not be absolutely impossible for me to offer such arguments as might lead you to think with me, that this young creature's chance of happiness seems less doubtful in retirement, than it would be in the gay and dissipated world: but why should I perplex your Ladyship with reasoning that can turn to so little account? for, alas! what arguments, what persuasions can I make use of, with any prospect of success, to such a woman as Madame Duval? Her character, and the violence of her disposition, intimidate me from making the attempt: she is too ignorant for instruction, too obstinate for entreaty, and too weak for reason.

I will not, therefore, enter into a contest from which I have nothing to expect but altercation and impertinence. As soon would I discuss the effect of sound with the deaf, or the nature of colours with the blind,[207] as aim at illuminating with conviction a mind so warped by prejudice, so much the slave of unruly and illiberal passions. Unused as she is to controul, persuasion would but harden, and opposition incense her. I yield, therefore, to the necessity which compels my reluctant acquiescence, and shall now turn all my thoughts upon considering of such methods for the conducting this enterprize, as may be most conducive to the happiness of my child, and least liable to wound her sensibility.

The law-suit, therefore, I wholly and absolutely disapprove.

Will you, my dear Madam, forgive the freedom of an old man, if I own myself greatly surprised, that you could, even for a moment, listen to a plan so violent, so public, so totally repugnant to all female delicacy? I am satisfied your Ladyship has not weighed this project. There was a time, indeed, when, to assert the innocence of Lady Belmont, and to blazon[208] to the world the *wrongs*, not *guilt*, by which she suffered, I proposed, nay attempted, a similar plan: but then, all assistance and encouragement was denied. How cruel to the remembrance I bear of her woes, is this tardy resentment of Madame Duval! She was deaf to the voice of Nature, though she has hearkened to that of Ambition.

Never can I consent to have this dear and timid girl brought forward to the notice of the world by such a method; a method, which will subject her to all the impertinence of curiosity, the

sneers of conjecture, and the stings of ridicule. And for what?—
the attainment of wealth, which she does not want, and the
gratification of vanity, which she does not feel.—A child to
appear against a father!—no, Madam, old and infirm as I am, I
would even yet sooner convey her myself to some remote part of
the world, though I were sure of dying in the expedition.

Far different had been the motives which would have stimulated her unhappy mother to such a proceeding; all her felicity in
this world was irretrievably lost; her life was become a burthen
to her, and her fair fame, which she had early been taught to
prize above all other things, had received a mortal wound:
therefore, to clear her own honour, and to secure from blemish
the birth of her child, was all the good which Fortune had
reserved herself the *power* of bestowing. But even this last
consolation was withheld from her!

Let milder measures be adopted; and—since it must be so,—
let application be made to Sir John Belmont; but as to a law-
suit, I hope, upon this subject, never more to hear it mentioned.

With Madame Duval, all pleas of delicacy would be ineffectual;
her scheme must be opposed by arguments better suited to her
understanding. I will not, therefore, talk of its impropriety, but
endeavour to prove its inutility. Have the goodness, then, to tell
her, that her own intentions would be frustrated by her plan,
since, should the law-suit be commenced, and even should the
cause be gained, Sir John Belmont would still have it in his
power, and, if irritated, no doubt in his inclination, to cut off her
grand-daughter with a shilling.[209]

She cannot do better, herself, than to remain quiet and inactive
in the affair: the long and mutual animosity between her and Sir
John, will make her interference merely productive of debates
and ill will. Neither would I have Evelina appear till summoned.
And as to myself, I must wholly decline *acting,* though I will,
with unwearied zeal, devote all my thoughts to giving counsel:
but, in truth, I have neither inclination nor spirits adequate to
engaging personally with this man.

My opinion is, that he would pay more respect to a letter from
your Ladyship upon this subject, than from any other person. I

therefore advise and hope, that you will yourself take the trouble of writing to him, in order to open the affair. When he shall be inclined to see Evelina, I have for him a posthumous letter, which his much-injured lady left to be presented to him, if ever such a meeting should take place.

The views of the Branghtons, in suggesting this scheme, are obviously interested; they hope, by securing to Evelina the fortune of her father, to induce Madame Duval to settle her own upon themselves. In this, however, they would probably be mistaken; for little minds have ever a propensity to bestow their wealth upon those who are already in affluence, and, therefore, the less her grand-child requires her assistance, the more gladly she will give it.

I have but one thing more to add, from which, however, I can by no means recede: my word so solemnly given to Lady Belmont, that her child should never be owned but with herself, must be inviolably adhered to.

I am dear Madam, with great respect,
Your Ladyship's most obedient servant,
ARTHUR VILLARS

LETTER XXIX

Mr. Villars to Evelina

Berry Hill, May 2

How sincerely do I sympathize in the uneasiness and concern which my beloved Evelina has so much reason to feel! The cruel scheme in agitation is equally repugnant to my judgement and my inclination,—yet to oppose it, seems impracticable. To follow the dictates of my own heart, I should instantly recall you to myself, and never more consent to your being separated from me; but the manners and opinion of the world demand a different conduct. Hope, however, for the best, and be satisfied you shall meet with no indignity; if you are not received into your own family as you ought to be, and with the distinction that is your due, you shall leave it for ever; and, once again restored to my protection, secure your own tranquillity, and make, as you have hitherto done, all the happiness of my life!

LETTER XXX

Evelina to the Rev. Mr. Villars

Howard Grove, May 6

The die is thrown,[210] and I attend the event in trembling! Lady Howard has written to Paris, and sent her letter to town, to be forwarded in the ambassador's packet,[211] and in less than a fortnight, therefore, she expects an answer. O Sir, with what anxious impatience shall I wait its arrival! upon it seems to depend the fate of my future life. My solicitude is so great, and my suspense so painful, that I cannot rest a moment in peace, or turn my thoughts into any other channel.

Deeply interested as I now am in the event, most sincerely do I regret that the plan was ever proposed: methinks it *cannot* end to my satisfaction; for either I must be torn from the arms of my *more* than father,—or I must have the misery of being finally convinced, that I am cruelly rejected by him who has the natural claim to that dear title; a title, which, to write, mention, or think of, fills my whole soul with filial tenderness.

The subject is discussed here eternally. Captain Mirvan and Madame Duval, as usual, quarrel whenever it is started: but I am so wholly engrossed by my own reflections, that I cannot even listen to them. My imagination changes the scene perpetually; one moment, I am embraced by a kind and relenting parent, who takes me to that heart from which I have hitherto been banished, and supplicates, through me, peace and forgiveness from the ashes of my mother!—at another, he regards me with detestation, considers me as the living image of an injured saint, and repulses me with horror!—But I will not afflict you with the melancholy phantasms of my brain, I will endeavour to compose my mind to a more tranquil state, and forbear to write again, till I have, in some measure, succeeded.

May Heaven bless you, my dearest Sir! and long, long may it continue you on earth, to bless

Your grateful
EVELINA

LETTER XXXI

Lady Howard to Sir John Belmont, Bart.

Howard Grove, May 5

Sir,

You will, doubtless, be surprised at receiving a letter from one who had for so short a period the honour of your acquaintance, and that at so great a distance of time; but the motive which has induced me to take this liberty, is of so delicate a nature, that were I to commence making apologies for my officiousness, I fear my letter would be too long for your patience.

You have, probably, already conjectured the subject upon which I mean to treat. My regard for Mr. Evelyn and his amiable daughter was well known to you: nor can I ever cease to be interested in whatever belongs to their memory or family.

I must own myself somewhat distressed in what manner to introduce the purport of my writing; yet, as I think that, in affairs of this kind, frankness is the first requisite to a good understanding between the parties concerned, I will neither torment you nor myself with punctilious ceremonies, but proceed instantly and openly to the business which occasions my giving you this trouble.

I presume, Sir, it would be superfluous to tell you, that your child resides still in Dorsetshire, and is still under the protection of the Reverend Mr. Villars, in whose house she was born: for, though no enquiries concerning her have reached his ears, or mine, I can never suppose it possible you have forborne to make them. It only remains, therefore, to tell you, that your daughter is now grown up; that she has been educated with the utmost care, and the utmost success; and that she is now a most deserving, accomplished, and amiable young woman.

Whatever may be your view for her future destination in life, it seems time to declare it. She is greatly admired, and, I doubt not, will be very much sought after: it is proper, therefore, that her future expectations, and your pleasure concerning her, should be made known.

Believe me, Sir, she merits your utmost attention and regard. You could not see and know her, and remain unmoved by those sensations of affection which belong to so near and tender a relationship. She is the lovely resemblance of her lovely mother;—pardon, Sir, the liberty I take in mentioning that unfortunate lady, but I think it behoves me, upon this occasion, to shew the esteem I felt for her; allow me, therefore, to say, and be not offended at my freedom, that the memory of that excellent lady has but too long remained under the aspersions of calumny; surely it is time to vindicate her fame!—and how can that be done in a manner more eligible, more grateful to her friends, or more honourable to yourself, than by openly receiving as your child, *the daughter of the late Lady Belmont*?

The venerable man who has had the care of her education, deserves your warmest acknowledgements, for the unremitting pains he has taken, and attention he has shewn, in the discharge of his trust. Indeed she has been peculiarly fortunate in meeting with such a friend and guardian: a more worthy man, or one whose character seems nearer to perfection, does not exist.

Permit me to assure you, Sir, she will amply repay whatever

regard and favour you may hereafter shew her, by the comfort and happiness you cannot fail to find in her affection and duty. To be owned *properly* by you, is the first wish of her heart; and I am sure, that to merit your approbation will be the first study of her life.

I fear that you will think this address impertinent; but I must rest upon the goodness of my intention to plead my excuse.

I am, Sir,

Your most obedient humble servant,

M. Howard

END OF THE FIRST VOLUME

Volume Two

LETTER I

Evelina to the Rev. Mr. Villars

Howard Grove, Kent, May 10

Our house has been enlivened today, by the arrival of a London visitor; and the necessity I have been under of concealing the uneasiness of my mind, has made me exert myself so effectually, that I even think it is really diminished; or, at least, my thoughts are not so totally, so very anxiously occupied by one only subject, as they lately were.

I was strolling this morning with Miss Mirvan, down a lane about a mile from the grove, when we heard the trampling of horses; and, fearing the narrowness of the passage, we were turning hastily back, but stopped upon hearing a voice call out, 'Pray, Ladies, don't be frightened, for I will walk my horse.' We turned again, and then saw Sir Clement Willoughby. He dismounted, and approaching us, with the reins in his hand, presently recollected us. 'Good Heaven,' cried he, with his usual quickness, 'do I see Miss Anville?—and you too, Miss Mirvan?'

He immediately ordered his servant to take charge of his horse, and then, advancing to us, took a hand of each, which he pressed to his lips, and said a thousand fine things concerning his good fortune, our improved looks, and the charms of the country, when inhabited by such rural deities. 'The town, Ladies, has languished since your absence,—or, at least, I have so much languished myself, as to be absolutely insensible to all it had to offer. One refreshing breeze, such as I now enjoy, awakens me to new vigour, life, and spirit. But I never before had the good luck to see the country in such perfection.'

'Has not almost every body left town, Sir?' said Miss Mirvan.

'I am ashamed to answer you, Madam—but indeed it is as full as ever, and will continue so, till after the birth-day.[1] However, you Ladies were so little seen, that there are but few who know what it has lost. For my own part, I felt it too sensibly, to be able to endure the place any longer.'

'Is there any body remaining there, that we were acquainted with!' cried I.

'O yes, Ma'am.' And then he named two or three persons we have seen when with him; but he did not mention Lord Orville, and I would not ask him, lest he should think me curious. Perhaps, if he stays here some time, he may speak of him by accident.

He was proceeding in this complimentary style, when we were met by the Captain; who no sooner perceived Sir Clement, than he hastened up to him, gave him a hearty shake of the hand, a cordial slap on the back, and some other equally gentle tokens of satisfaction, assuring him of his great joy at his visit, and declaring he was as glad to see him as if he had been a messenger who brought news that a French ship was sunk. Sir Clement, on the other side, expressed himself with equal warmth, and protested he had been so eager to pay his respects to Captain Mirvan, that he had left London in its full lustre, and a thousand engagements unanswered, merely to give himself that pleasure.

'We shall have rare sport,' said the Captain, 'for do you know the old Frenchwoman is among us? 'Fore George, I have scarce made any use of her yet, by reason I have had nobody with me that could enjoy a joke: howsomever, it shall go hard but we'll have some diversion now.'

Sir Clement very much approved of the proposal; and we then went into the house, where he had a very grave reception from Mrs. Mirvan, who is by no means pleased with his visit, and a look of much discontent from Madame Duval, who said to me, in a low voice, 'I'd as soon have seen Old Nick as that man, for he's the most impertinent person in the world, and is n't never of my side.'

The Captain is now actually occupied in contriving some scheme which, he says, is *to play the old Dowager off*,[2] and so eager and delighted is he at the idea, that he can scarcely constrain his raptures sufficiently to conceal his design, even from herself.

I wish, however, since I do not dare put Madame Duval upon her guard, that he had the delicacy not to acquaint me with his intention.

LETTER II

Evelina in continuation

May 13th

The Captain's operations are begun,—and, I hope, ended; for indeed, poor Madame Duval has already but too much reason to regret Sir Clement's visit to Howard Grove.

Yesterday morning, during breakfast, as the Captain was reading the news-paper, Sir Clement suddenly begged to look at it, saying he wanted to know if there was any account of a transaction, at which he had been present the evening before his journey hither, concerning a poor Frenchman, who had got into a scrape which might cost him his life.

The Captain demanded particulars; and then Sir Clement told a long story, of being with a party of country friends, at the Tower,[3] and hearing a man call out for mercy in French; and that when he enquired into the occasion of his distress, he was informed, that he had been taken up upon suspicion of treasonable practices against the government.[4] 'The poor fellow,' continued he, 'no sooner found that I spoke French, than he besought me to hear him, protesting that he had no evil designs; that he had been but a short time in England, and only waited the return of a Lady from the country, to quit it for ever.'

Madame Duval changed colour, and listened with the utmost attention.

'Now, though I by no means approve of so many foreigners continually flocking into our country,' added he, addressing himself to the Captain, 'yet I could not help pitying the poor

wretch, because he did not know enough of English to make his
defence: however, I found it impossible to assist him, for the
mob would not suffer me to interfere. In truth, I am afraid he
was but roughly handled.'

'Why, did they duck him?' said the Captain.

'Something of that sort,' answered he.

'So much the better! so much the better!' cried the Captain,
'an impudent French puppy!—I'll bet you what you will he was
a rascal. I only wish all his countrymen were served the same.'

'I wish you had been in his place, with all my soul!' cried
Madame Duval, warmly;—'but pray, Sir, did n't nobody know
who this poor gentleman was?'

'Why, I did hear his name,' answered Sir Clement, 'but I
cannot recollect it.'

'It was n't,—it was n't—Du Bois?' stammered out Madame
Duval.

'The very name!' answered he, 'yes, Du Bois, I remember it
now.'

Madame Duval's cup fell from her hand, as she repeated 'Du
Bois! Monsieur Du Bois, did you say?'

'Du Bois! why that's *my* friend,' cried the Captain, 'that's
Monseer Slippery, i'n't it?—Why he's plaguy fond of sousing
work; howsomever, I'll be sworn they gave him his fill of it.'

'And I'll be sworn,' cried Madame Duval, 'that you're a—but
I don't believe nothing about it, so you need n't be so overjoyed,
for I dare say it was no more Monsieur Du Bois than I am.'

'I thought at the time,' said Sir Clement, very gravely, 'that I
had seen the gentleman before, and now I recollect, I think it
was in company with you, Madam.'

'With *me*, Sir!' cried Madame Duval.

'Say you so!' said the Captain, 'why then, it must be he, as
sure as you're alive!—Well but, my good friend, what will they
do with poor *Monseer*?'

'It is difficult to say,' answered Sir Clement, very thoughtfully,
'but I should suppose, that if he has not good friends to appear
for him, he will be in a very unpleasant situation; for these are
serious sort of affairs.'

'Why, do you think they'll hang him?' demanded the Captain.

Sir Clement shook his head, but made no answer.

Madame Duval could no longer contain her agitation; she started from her chair, repeating, with a voice half choaked, 'Hang him!—they can't,—they shan't,—let them at their peril!—however, it's all false, and I won't believe a word of it;—but I'll go to town this very moment, and see M. Du Bois myself;—I won't wait for nothing.'

Mrs. Mirvan begged her not to be alarmed; but she flew out of the room, and up stairs into her own apartment. Lady Howard blamed both the gentlemen for having been so abrupt, and followed her. I would have accompanied her, but the Captain stopped me; and, having first laughed very heartily, said he was going to read his commission to his ship's company.[5]

'Now, do you see,' said he, 'as to Lady Howard, I sha'n't pretend for to enlist her into my service, and so I shall e'en leave her to make it out as well as she can; but as to all you, I expect obedience and submission to orders; I am now upon a hazardous expedition, having undertaken to convoy a crazy vessel[6] to the shore of Mortification; so, d'ye see, if any of you have any thing to propose, that will forward the enterprize,—why speak and welcome; but if any of you, that are of my chosen crew, capitulate, or enter into any treaty with the enemy,—I shall look upon you as mutinying, and turn you adrift.'[7]

Having finished this harangue, which was interlarded with many expressions, and sea-phrases, that I cannot recollect, he gave Sir Clement a wink of intelligence, and left us to ourselves.

Indeed, notwithstanding the attempts I so frequently make of writing some of the Captain's conversation, I can only give you a faint idea of his language; for almost every other word he utters, is accompanied by an oath, which, I am sure, would be as unpleasant for you to read, as for me to write. And, besides, he makes use of a thousand sea-terms, which are to me quite unintelligible.

Poor Madame Duval sent to enquire at all probable places, whether she could be conveyed to town in any stage-coach: but the Captain's servant brought her for answer, that no London stage would pass near Howard Grove till to-day. She then sent to order a chaise; but was soon assured, that no horses could be procured. She was so much inflamed by these disappointments, that she threatened to set out for town on foot, and it was with difficulty that Lady Howard dissuaded her from this mad scheme.

The whole morning was filled up with these enquiries. But, when we were all assembled to dinner, she endeavoured to appear perfectly unconcerned, and repeatedly protested that she gave not any credit to the report, as far as it regarded M. Du Bois, being very certain that he was not the person in question.

The Captain used the most provoking efforts to convince her that she deceived herself; while Sir Clement, with more art, though not less malice, affected to be of her opinion; but, at the same time that he pretended to relieve her uneasiness, by saying that he doubted not having mistaken the name, he took care to enlarge upon the danger to which the *unknown gentleman* was exposed, and expressed great concern at his perilous situation.

Dinner was hardly removed, when a letter was delivered to Madame Duval. The moment she had read it, she hastily demanded from whom it came? 'A country boy brought it,' answered the servant, 'but he would not wait.'

'Run after him this instant!' cried she, 'and be sure you bring him back. *Mon Dieu! quel avanture! que ferai-je?*'[8]

'What's the matter? what's the matter?' said the Captain.

'Why nothing,—nothing's the matter. *O mon Dieu?*'

And she rose, and walked about the room.

'Why, what—has *Monseer* sent to you?' continued the Captain: 'is that there letter from him?'

'No,—it i'n't;—besides, if it is, it's nothing to you.'

'O then, I'm sure it is! Pray now, Madame, don't be so close; come, tell us all about it,—what does he say? how did he relish the horse-pond?—which did he find best, sousing *single* or *double*?'[9]—'Fore George, 'twas plaguy unlucky you was not with him!'

'It's no such a thing, Sir,' cried she, very angrily, 'and if you're so very fond of a horse-pond, I wish you'd put yourself into one, and not be always a-thinking about other people's being served so.'

The man then came in, to acquaint her they could not overtake the boy. She scolded violently, and was in such perturbation, that Lady Howard interfered, and begged to know the cause of her uneasiness, and whether she could assist her?

Madame Duval cast her eyes upon the Captain and Sir Clement, and said she should be glad to speak to her Ladyship, without so many witnesses.

'Well, then, Miss Anville,' said the Captain, turning to me, 'do you and Molly go into another room, and stay there till Mrs. Duval has opened her mind to us.'

'So you may think, Sir,' cried she, 'but who's fool then? no, no, you need n't trouble yourself to make a ninny[10] of me, neither, for I'm not so easily taken in, I'll assure you.'

Lady Howard then invited her into the dressing-room, and I was desired to attend her.

As soon as we had shut the door, 'O my Lady,' exclaimed Madame Duval, 'here's the most cruellest thing in the world has happened!—but that Captain is such a beast, I can't say nothing before him,—but it's all true! poor M. Du Bois is tooked up!'

Lady Howard begged her to be comforted, saying that, as M. Du Bois was certainly innocent, there could be no doubt of his ability to clear himself.

'To be sure, my Lady,' answered she, 'I know he is innocent; and to be sure they'll never be so wicked as to hang him for nothing?'

'Certainly not,' replied Lady Howard, 'you have no reason to be uneasy. This is not a country where punishment is inflicted without proof.'[11]

'Very true, my Lady; but the worst thing is this; I cannot bear that that fellow, the Captain, should know about it; for if he does, I sha'n't never hear the last of it;—no more won't poor M. Du Bois.'

'Well, well,' said Lady Howard, 'shew me the letter, and I will endeavour to advise you.'

The letter was then produced. It was signed by the clerk of a country justice; who acquainted her, that a prisoner, then upon

trial for suspicion of treasonable practices against the government, was just upon the point of being committed to jail, but
having declared that he was known to her, this clerk had been
prevailed upon to write, in order to enquire if she really could
speak to the character and family of a Frenchman who called
himself Pierre Du Bois.

When I heard the letter, I was quite amazed at its success. So
improbable did it seem, that a foreigner should be taken before a
country justice of peace,[12] for a crime of so dangerous a nature,
that I cannot imagine how Madame Duval could be alarmed,
even for a moment. But, with all her violence of temper, I see
that she is easily frightened, and, in fact, more cowardly than
many who have not half her spirit; and so little does she reflect
upon circumstances, or probability, that she is continually the
dupe of her own—I ought not to say *ignorance*, but yet, I can
think of no other word.

I believe that Lady Howard, from the beginning of the
transaction, suspected some contrivance of the Captain, and this
letter, I am sure, must confirm her suspicion: however, though
she is not at all pleased with his frolick, yet she would not
hazard the consequence of discovering his designs: her looks,
her manner, and her character, made me draw this conclusion
from her apparent perplexity; for not a word did she say, that
implied any doubt of the authenticity of the letter. Indeed there
seems to be a sort of tacit agreement between her and the
Captain, that she should not appear to be acquainted with his
schemes; by which means she at once avoids quarrels, and
supports her dignity.

While she was considering what to propose, Madame Duval
begged to have the use of her Ladyship's chariot, that she might
go immediately to the assistance of her friend. Lady Howard
politely assured her, that it would be extremely at her service;
and then Madame Duval besought her not to own to the Captain
what had happened, protesting that she could not endure he
should know poor M. Du Bois had met with so unfortunate an
accident. Lady Howard could not help smiling, though she
readily promised not to *inform* the Captain of the affair. As to

me, she desired my attendance; which I was by no means rejoiced at, as I was certain she was going upon a fruitless errand.

I was then commissioned to order the chariot.

At the foot of the stairs I met the Captain, who was most impatiently waiting the result of the conference. In an instant we were joined by Sir Clement. A thousand enquiries were then made concerning Madame Duval's opinion of the letter, and her intentions upon it: and when I would have left them, Sir Clement, pretending equal eagerness with the Captain, caught my hand, and repeatedly detained me, to ask some frivolous question, to the answer of which he must be totally indifferent. At length, however, I broke from them; they retired into the parlour, and I executed my commission.

The carriage was soon ready, and Madame Duval having begged Lady Howard to say she was not well, stole softly down stairs, desiring me to follow her. The chariot was ordered at the garden-door; and when we were seated, she told the man, according to the clerk's directions, to drive to Mr. Justice Tyrell's, asking, at the same time, how many miles off he lived?

I expected he would have answered that he knew of no such person; but, to my great surprise, he said, 'Why 'Squire Tyrell lives about nine miles beyond the park.'

'Drive fast, then,' cried she, 'and you sha'n't be no worse for it.'

During our ride, which was extremely tedious, she tormented herself with a thousand fears for M. Du Bois' safety; and piqued herself very much upon having escaped unseen by the Captain, not only that she avoided his triumph, but because she knew him to be so much M. Du Bois' enemy, that she was sure he would prejudice the Justice against him, and endeavour to take away his life. For my part, I was quite ashamed of being engaged in so ridiculous an affair, and could only think of the absurd appearance we should make upon our arrival at Mr. Tyrell's.

When we had been out near two hours, and expected every moment to stop at the place of our destination, I observed that Lady Howard's servant, who attended us on horseback, rode on forward till he was out of sight, and soon after returning, came up to the chariot-window, and delivering a note to Madame Duval, said he had met a boy, who was just coming with it to Howard Grove, from the Clerk of Mr. Tyrell.

While she was reading it, he rode round to the other window, and, making a sign for secrecy, put into my hand a slip of paper, on which was written, 'Whatever happens, be not alarmed,—for *you* are safe,—though you endanger all mankind!'

I readily imagined that Sir Clement must be the author of this note, which prepared me to expect some disagreeable adventure: but I had no time to ponder upon it, for Madame Duval had no sooner read her own letter, than in an angry tone of voice, she exclaimed, 'Why now what a thing is this! here we're come all this way for nothing!'

She then gave me the note, which informed her, that she need not trouble herself to go to Mr. Tyrell's as the prisoner had had the address to escape. I congratulated her upon this fortunate incident; but she was so much concerned at having rode so far in vain, that she seemed less pleased than provoked. However, she ordered the man to make what haste he could home, as she hoped, at least, to return before the Captain should suspect what had passed.

The carriage turned about, and we journeyed so quietly for near an hour, that I began to flatter myself we should be suffered to proceed to Howard Grove without further molestation, when suddenly, the footman called out, 'John, are we going right?'

'Why, I a'n't sure,' said the coachman, 'but I'm afraid we turned wrong.'

'What do you mean by that, Sirrah?' said Madame Duval, 'why if you lose your way, we shall be all in the dark.'

'I think we should turn to the left,' said the footman.

'To the left!' answered the other, 'no, no, I'm partly sure we should turn to the right.'

'You had better make some enquiry,' said I.

'*Ma foi,*' cried Madame Duval, 'we're in a fine hole, here!— they neither of them know no more than the post. However, I'll tell my Lady, as sure as you're born, so you'd better find the way.'

'Let's try this lane,' said the footman.

'No,' said the coachman, 'that's the road to Canterbury; we had best go straight on.'

'Why that's the direct London road,' returned the footman, 'and will lead us twenty miles about.'

'*Pardi*,' cried Madame Duval, 'why they won't go one way nor t'other! and, now we're come all this jaunt for nothing, I suppose we shan't get home to-night!'

'Let's go back to the public-house,' said the footman, 'and ask for a guide.'

'No, no,' said the other, 'if we stay here a few minutes, somebody or other will pass by: and the horses are almost knocked up already.'

'Well, I protest,' cried Madame Duval, 'I'd give a guinea to see them sots both horse-whipped! As sure as I'm alive, they're drunk! Ten to one but they'll overturn us next!'

After much debating, they, at length, agreed to go on, till we came to some inn, or met with a passenger who could direct us. We soon arrived at a small farm-house, and the footman alighted, and went into it.

In a few minutes he returned, and told us we might proceed, for that he had procured a direction; 'But,' added he, 'it seems there are some thieves hereabouts; and so the best way will be for you to leave your watches and purses with the farmer, who I know very well, and who is an honest man, and a tenant of my Lady's.'

'Thieves!' cried Madame Duval, looking aghast, 'the Lord help us!—I've no doubt but we shall be all murdered!'

The farmer came up to us, and we gave him all we were worth, and the servants followed our example. We then proceeded, and Madame Duval's anger so entirely subsided, that, in the mildest manner imaginable, she entreated them to make haste, and promised to tell their Lady how diligent and obliging they had been. She perpetually stopped them, to ask if they apprehended any danger; and was, at length, so much overpowered by her fears, that she made the footman fasten his horse to the back of the carriage, and then come and seat himself within it. My endeavours to encourage her were fruitless; she sat in the middle, held the man by the arm, and protested that if he did but save her life, she would make his fortune. Her uneasiness gave me much concern, and it was with the utmost difficulty I forbore to acquaint her that she was imposed upon; but the mutual fear of the Captain's resentment to me, and of her own to him, neither of which would have any moderation, deterred me. As to the footman, he was evidently in torture from restraining his laughter, and I observed that he was frequently obliged to make most horrid grimaces, from pretended fear, in order to conceal his risibility.

Very soon after, 'The robbers are coming!' cried the coach-man.

The footman opened the door, and jumped out of the chariot.

Madame Duval gave a loud scream.

I could no longer preserve my silence.

'For Heaven's sake, my dear Madam,' said I, 'don't be alarmed,—you are in no danger—you are quite safe,—there is nothing but—'

Here the chariot was stopped, by two men, in masks, who, at each side, put in their hands, as if for our purses. Madame Duval sunk to the bottom of the chariot, and implored their mercy. I shrieked involuntarily, although prepared for the attack: one of them held me fast, while the other tore poor Madame Duval out of the carriage, in spite of her cries, threats, and resistance.

I was really frightened, and trembled exceedingly. 'My angel!' cried the man who held me, 'you cannot surely be alarmed,—do you not know me?—I shall hold myself in eternal abhorrence, if I have really terrified you.'

'Indeed, Sir Clement, you have,' cried I,—'but, for Heaven's sake, where is Madame Duval?—why is she forced away?'

'She is perfectly safe; the Captain has her in charge: but suffer me now, my adored Miss Anville, to take the only opportunity that is allowed me, to speak upon another, a much dearer, much sweeter subject.'

And then he hastily came into the chariot, and seated himself next to me. I would fain have disengaged myself from him, but he would not let me; 'Deny me not, most charming of women,' cried he, 'deny me not this only moment that is lent me, to pour forth my soul into your gentle ears,—to tell you how much I suffer from your absence,—how much I dread your displeasure,—and how cruelly I am affected by your coldness!'

'O Sir, this is no time for such language,—pray leave me, pray go to the relief of Madame Duval,—I cannot bear that she should be treated with such indignity.'

'And will you,—can you command my absence?—When may I speak to you, if not now?—does the Captain suffer me to breathe a moment out of his sight?—and are not a thousand impertinent people for ever at your elbow.'

'Indeed, Sir Clement, you must change your style, or I will not hear you. The *impertinent people* you mean, are among my best friends,[13] and you would not, if you really wished me well, speak of them so disrespectfully.'

'Wish you well!—O Miss Anville, point but out to me how, in what manner I may convince you of the fervour of my passion,—tell me but what services you will accept from me,—and you shall find my life, my fortune, my whole soul at your devotion.'

'I want *nothing*, Sir, that you can offer;—I beg you not to talk to me so—so strangely. Pray leave me, and pray assure yourself, you cannot take any method so successless to shew any regard for me, as entering into schemes so frightful to Madame Duval, and so disagreeable to myself.'

'The scheme was the Captain's; I even opposed it: though, I own, I could not refuse myself the so-long-wished-for happiness, of speaking to you once more, without so many of—your *friends* to watch me. And I had flattered myself, that the note I charged the footman to give you would have prevented the alarm you have received.'

'Well, Sir, you have now, I hope, said enough; and, if you will not go yourself to see for Madame Duval, at least suffer *me* to enquire what is become of her.'

'And when may I speak to you again?'

'No matter when,—I don't know,—perhaps—'

'Perhaps what, my angel?'

'Perhaps *never*, Sir,—if you torment me thus.'

'Never! O Miss Anville, how cruel, how piercing to my soul is that icy word!—Indeed, I cannot endure such displeasure.'

'Then, Sir, you must not provoke it. Pray leave me directly.'

'I will, Madam: but let me, at least, make a merit of my obedience,—allow me to hope that you will, in future, be less averse to trusting yourself for a few moments alone with me.'

I was surprised at the freedom of this request; but, while I hesitated how to answer it, the other mask came up to the chariot-door, and, in a voice almost stifled with laughter, said, 'I've done for her!—the old buck[14] is safe;—but we must sheer off directly, or we shall be all aground.'[15]

Sir Clement instantly left me, mounted his horse, and rode off. The Captain, having given some directions to the servants, followed him.

I was both uneasy and impatient to know the fate of Madame Duval, and immediately got out of the chariot to seek her. I desired the footman to shew me which way she was gone; he pointed with his finger, by way of answer, and I saw that he dared not trust his voice to make any other. I walked on, a very quick pace, and soon, to my great consternation, perceived the poor lady, seated upright in a ditch. I flew to her, with unfeigned concern at her situation. She was sobbing, nay, almost roaring, and in the utmost agony of rage and terror. As soon as she saw me, she redoubled her cries, but her voice was so broken, I could not understand a word she said. I was so much shocked, that it was with difficulty I forbore exclaiming against the cruelty of the Captain, for thus wantonly ill-treating her; and I could not forgive myself for having passively suffered the deception. I used my utmost endeavours to comfort her, assuring her of our present safety, and begging her to rise, and return to the chariot.

Almost bursting with passion, she pointed to her feet, and with frightful violence, she actually beat the ground with her hands.

I then saw, that her feet were tied together with a strong rope, which was fastened to the upper branch of a tree, even with an hedge which ran along the ditch where she sat. I endeavoured to untie the knot, but soon found it was infinitely beyond my strength. I was, therefore, obliged to apply to the footman; but being very unwilling to add to his mirth, by the sight of Madame Duval's situation, I desired him to lend me a knife; I returned with it, and cut the rope. Her feet were soon disentangled, and then, though with great difficulty, I assisted her to rise. But what was my astonishment, when, the moment she was up, she hit me a violent slap on the face! I retreated from her with precipitation and dread, and she then loaded me with reproaches, which, though almost unintelligible, convinced me that she imagined I had voluntarily deserted her; but she seemed not to have the slightest suspicion that she had not been attacked by real robbers.

I was so much surprised and confounded at the blow, that, for some time, I suffered her to rave without making any answer; but her extreme agitation, and real suffering, soon dispelled my anger, which all turned into compassion. I then told her, that I had been forcibly detained from following her, and assured her of my real sorrow at her ill usage.

She began to be somewhat appeased; and I again entreated her to return to the carriage, or give me leave to order that it should draw up to the place where we stood. She made no answer, till I told her, that the longer we remained still, the greater would be the danger of our ride home. Struck with this hint, she suddenly, and with hasty steps, moved forward.

Her dress was in such disorder, that I was quite sorry to have her figure exposed to the servants, who all of them, in imitation of their master, hold her in derision: however, the disgrace was unavoidable.

The ditch, happily, was almost quite dry, or she must have suffered still more seriously; yet, so forlorn, so miserable a figure, I never before saw. Her head-dress had fallen off; her linen was torn; her negligee had not a pin left in it; her petticoats she was obliged to hold on; and her shoes were perpetually slipping off. She was covered with dirt, weeds, and filth, and her face was really horrible, for the pomatum and powder from her head,[16] and the dust from the road, were quite *pasted* on her skin by her tears, which, with her *rouge*, made so frightful a mixture, that she hardly looked human.

The servants were ready to die with laughter, the moment they saw her; but not all my remonstrances could prevail upon her to get into the carriage, till she had most vehemently reproached them both, for not rescuing her. The footman, fixing his eyes on the ground, as if fearful of again trusting himself to look at her, protested that the robbers had vowed they would shoot him, if he moved an inch, and that one of them had stayed to watch the chariot; while the other carried her off; adding, that the reason of their behaving so barbarously, was to revenge our having secured our purses. Notwithstanding her anger, she gave immediate credit to what he said, and really imagined that her want of money had irritated the pretended robbers to treat her with such cruelty. I determined, therefore, to be carefully upon my guard, not to betray the imposition, which could now answer no other purpose, than occasioning an irreparable breach between her and the Captain.

Just as we were seated in the chariot, she discovered the loss which her head had sustained, and called out, 'My God! what is becomed of my hair?—why the villain has stole all my curls!'[17]

She then ordered the man to run and see if he could find any of them in the ditch. He went, and presently returning, produced a great quantity of hair, in such a nasty condition, that I was amazed she would take it; and the man, as he delivered it to her, found it impossible to keep his countenance; which she no sooner observed, than all her stormy passions were again raised. She flung the battered curls in his face, saying, 'Sirrah, what do you grin for? I wish you'd been served so yourself, and you would n't have found it no such joke: you are the impudentest fellow ever I see, and if I find you dare grin at me any more, I shall make no ceremony of boxing your ears.'

Satisfied with the threat, the man hastily retired, and we drove on.

Her anger now subsiding into grief, she began most sorrowfully to lament her case.

'I believe,' she cried, 'never nobody was so unlucky as I am! and so here, because I ha'n't had misfortunes enough already, that puppy has made me lose my curls!—Why, I can't see nobody without them:—only look at me,—I was never so bad off in my life before. *Pardi*, if I'd know'd as much, I'd have brought two or three sets with me: but I'd never a thought of such a thing as this.'

Finding her now somewhat pacified, I ventured to ask an account of her adventure, which I will endeavour to write in her own words.

'Why, child, all this misfortune comes of that puppy's making us leave our money behind us; for as soon as the robber see I did not put nothing in his hands, he lugged me out of the chariot by main force, and I verily thought he'd have murdered me. He was as strong as a lion; I was no more in his hands than a child. But I believe never nobody was so abused before, for he dragged me down the road, pulling and hawling me all the way, as if I'd no more feeling than a horse. I'm sure I wish I could see that man cut up and quartered alive![18] however, he'll come to the gallows; that's one good thing. So, as soon as we'd got out of sight of the chariot,—though he need n't have been afraid, for, if he'd beat me to a mummy,[19] those cowardly fellows would n't have said nothing to it.—So, when I was got there, what does he do, but, all of a sudden, he takes me by both the shoulders, and he gives me such a shake! *Mon Dieu!* I shall never forget it, if I live to be an hundred. I'm sure I dare say I'm out of joint all over. And, though I made as much noise as ever I could, he took no more notice of it than nothing at all, but there he stood, shaking me in that manner, as if he was doing it for a wager. I'm determined, if it costs me all my fortune, I'll see that villain hanged. He shall be found out, if there's e'er a justice in England. So when he had shook me till he was tired, and I felt all over like a jelly, without saying never a word, he takes and pops me into the ditch! I'm sure I thought he'd have murdered me, as much as I ever thought any thing in my life, for he kept bumping me about, as if he thought nothing too bad for me. However, I'm resolved I'll never leave my purse behind me again, the longest day I have to live. So when he couldn't stand over me no longer, he holds out his hands again for my money; but he was as cunning as could be, for he would n't speak a word, because I should n't swear to his voice; however, that sha'n't save him, for I'll swear to him any day in the year, if I can but catch him. So, when I told him I had no money, he fell to jerking me again, just as if he had but that moment begun! And, after that, he got me close by a tree, and out of his pocket he pulls a great cord!—It's a wonder I did not swoon away, for as sure as you're alive, he was going to hang me to that tree. I screamed like any thing mad, and told him if he would but spare my life, I'd never prosecute him, nor tell nobody what he'd done to me: so he stood some time, quite in a brown study, a-thinking what he should do. And so, after that, he forced me to sit down in the ditch, and he tied my feet together, just as you see them, and then, as if he had not done enough, he twitched off my cap, and, without saying nothing, got on his horse, and left me in that condition, thinking, I suppose, that I might lie there and perish.'

Though this narrative almost compelled me to laugh, yet I was really irritated with the Captain, for carrying his love of tormenting,—*sport*, he calls it,—to such barbarous and unjustifiable extremes. I consoled and soothed her as well as I was able, and told her that, since M. Du Bois had escaped, I hoped when she recovered from her fright, all would end well.

'Fright, child!' repeated she, 'why that's not half;—I promise you, I wish it was; but here I'm bruised from top to toe, and it's well if ever I have the right use of my limbs again. However, I'm glad the villain got nothing but his trouble for his pains. But here the worst is to come, for I can't go out, because I've got no curls, and so he'll be escaped, before I can get to the Justice to stop him. I'm resolved I'll tell Lady Howard how her man served me, for if he had n't made me fling 'em away, I dare say I could have pinned them up well enough for the country.'

'Perhaps Lady Howard may be able to lend you a cap that will wear without them.'

'Lady Howard, indeed! why, do you think I'd wear one of her dowdies?[20] No, I'll promise you, I sha'n't put on no such disguisement. It's the unluckiest thing in the world that I did not make the man pick up the curls again; but he put me in such a passion, I could not think of nothing. I know I can't get none at Howard Grove for love nor money, for of all the stupid places ever I see, that Howard Grove is the worst! there's never no getting nothing one wants.'

This sort of conversation lasted till we arrived at our journey's end; and then, a new distress occurred; Madame Duval was eager to speak to Lady Howard and Mrs. Mirvan, and to relate her misfortunes, but she could not endure that Sir Clement or the Captain should see her in such disorder, for she said they were so ill-natured, that instead of pitying her, they would only make a jest of her disasters. She therefore sent me first into the house, to wait for an opportunity of their being out of the way, that she might steal up stairs unobserved. In this I succeeded, as the gentlemen thought it most prudent not to seem watching for her; though they both contrived to divert themselves with peeping at her as she passed.

She went immediately to bed, where she had her supper. Lady Howard and Mrs. Mirvan both of them very kindly sat with her, and listened to her tale with compassionate attention; while Miss Mirvan and I retired to our own room, where I was very glad to end the troubles of the day in a comfortable conversation.

The Captain's raptures, during supper, at the success of his plan, were boundless. I spoke, afterwards, to Mrs. Mirvan, with the openness which her kindness encourages, and begged her to remonstrate with him upon the cruelty of tormenting Madame Duval so causelessly. She promised to take the first opportunity of starting the subject, but said he was, at present, so much elated that he would not listen to her with any patience. However, should he make any new efforts to molest her, I can by no means consent to be passive. Had I imagined he would have been so violent, I would have risked his anger in her defence much sooner.

She has kept her bed all day, and declares she is almost bruised to death.

Adieu, dear Sir. What a long letter have I written! I could almost fancy I sent it you from London!

LETTER III

Evelina in continuation

Howard Grove, May 15th

This insatiable Captain, if left to himself, would not, I believe, rest, till he had tormented Madame Duval into a fever. He seems to have no delight but in terrifying or provoking her, and all his thoughts apparently turn upon inventing such methods as may do it most effectually.

She had her breakfast again in bed yesterday morning; but during ours, the Captain, with a very significant look at Sir Clement, gave us to understand, that he thought she had now rested long enough to bear the hardships of a fresh campaign.[21]

His meaning was obvious, and, therefore, I resolved to endeavour immediately to put a stop to his intended exploits. When breakfast was over, I followed Mrs. Mirvan out of the parlour, and begged her to lose no time in pleading the cause of Madame Duval with the Captain. 'My love,' answered she, 'I have already expostulated with him; but all I can say is fruitless, while his favourite Sir Clement contrives to urge him on.'

'Then I will go and speak to Sir Clement,' said I, 'for I know he will desist, if I request him.'

'Have a care, my dear!' said she, smiling, 'it is sometimes dangerous to make requests to men, who are too desirous of receiving them.'

'Well then, my dear Madam, will you give me leave to speak myself to the Captain?'

'Willingly; nay, I will accompany you to him.'

I thanked her, and we went to seek him. He was walking in the garden with Sir Clement. Mrs. Mirvan most obligingly made an opening for my purpose, by saying, 'Mr. Mirvan, I have brought a petitioner with me.'

'Why what's the matter now?' cried he.

I was fearful of making him angry, and stammered very much,

when I told him, I hoped he had no new plan for alarming Madame Duval.

'*New* plan!' cried he, 'why, you don't suppose the *old* one would do again, do you? Not but what it was a very good one, only I doubt she would n't bite.'

Indeed, Sir,' said I, 'she has already suffered too much, and I hope you will pardon me, if I take the liberty of telling you, that I think it my duty to do all in my power to prevent her being again so much terrified.'

A sullen gloominess instantly clouded his face, and, turning short from me, he said, I might do as I pleased, but that I should much sooner repent than repair my officiousness.

I was too much disconcerted at this rebuff, to attempt making any answer, and, finding that Sir Clement warmly espoused my cause, I walked away, and left them to discuss the point together.

Mrs. Mirvan, who never speaks to the Captain when he is out of humour, was glad to follow me, and with her usual sweetness, made a thousand apologies for her husband's ill manners.

When I left her, I went to Madame Duval, who was just risen, and employed in examining the cloaths she had on the day of her ill usage.

'Here's a sight!' cried she. 'Come here, child,—only look— *Pardi*, so long as I've lived, I never see so much before! Why, all my things are spoilt, and, what's worse, my sacque[22] was as good as new. Here's the second negligee I've had used in this manner!—I am sure I was a fool to put it on, in such a lonesome[23] place as this; however, if I stay here these ten years, I'll never put on another good gown, that I'm resolved.'

'Will you let the maid try if she can iron it out, or clean it, Ma'am?'

'No, she'll only make bad worse.—But look here, now, here's a cloak! *Mon Dieu!* why, it looks like a dish-clout![24] Of all the unluckinesses, that ever I met, this is the worst! for, do you know, I bought it but the day before I left Paris?—Besides, into the bargain, my cap's quite gone; where the villain twitched it, I don't know, but I never see no more of it, from that time to this. Now you must know this was the becomingest cap I had in the world, for I've never another with pink ribbon in it; and, to tell you the truth, if I had n't thought to have seen M. Du Bois, I'd no more have put it on than I'd have flown; for as to what one wears in such a stupid place as this, it signifies no more than nothing at all.'

She then told me, that she had been thinking all night of a contrivance to hinder the Captain from finding out her loss of curls; which was, having a large gauze handkerchief pinned on her head as a hood, and saying she had the tooth-ach.

'To tell you the truth,' added she, 'I believe that Captain is one of the worst men in the world; he's always making a joke of me; and as to his being a gentleman, he has no more manners than a bear, for he's always upon the grin when one's in distress; and, I declare, I'd rather be done any thing to than laugh'd at, for, to my mind, it's one or other the disagreeablest thing in the world.'

Mrs. Mirvan, I found, had been endeavouring to dissuade her from the design she had formed, of having recourse to the law, in order to find out the supposed robbers; for she dreads a discovery of the Captain, during Madame Duval's stay at Howard Grove, as it could not fail being productive of infinite commotion. She has, therefore, taken great pains to shew the inutility of applying to justice, unless she were more able to describe the offenders against whom she would appear, and has assured her, that as she neither heard their voices, nor saw their faces, she cannot possibly swear to their persons, or obtain any redress.

Madame Duval, in telling me this, extremely lamented her hard fate, that she was thus prevented from revenging her injuries; which, however, she vowed she would not be persuaded to *pocket tamely*,[25] 'because,' added she, 'if such villains as these are let to have their own way, and nobody takes no notice of their impudence, they'll make no more ado than nothing at all of tying people in ditches, and such things as that: however, I shall consult with M. Du Bois, as soon as I can ferret out where he's hid himself. I'm sure I've a right to his advice, for it's all along of his gaping about at the Tower that I've met with these misfortunes.'

'M. Du Bois,' said I, 'will, I am sure, be very sorry when he hears what has happened.'

'And what good will that do now?—that won't unspoil all my cloaths; I can tell him, I a'n't much obliged to him, though it's no fault of his—yet it i'n't the less provokinger for that. I'm sure, if he had been there, to have seen me served in that manner, and put neck and heels into a ditch, he'd no more have thought it was me, than the Pope of Rome. I'll promise you, whatever you may think of it, I sha'n't have no rest, night nor day, till I find out that rogue.'

'I have no doubt, Madam, but you will soon discover him.'

'*Pardi*, if I do, I'll hang him, as sure as fate!—but what's the oddest, is that he should take such a 'special spite against *me*, above all the rest! it was as much for nothing, as could be, for I don't know what I had done, so particular bad, to be used in that manner: I'm sure, I had n't given him no offence, as I know of, for I never see his face all the time; and as to screaming a little, I think it's very hard if one must n't do such a thing as that, when one's put in fear of one's life.'

During this conversation, she endeavoured to adjust her head-dress, but could not at all please herself. Indeed, had I not been present, I should have thought it impossible for a woman at her time of life to be so very difficult in regard to dress. What she may have in view, I cannot imagine, but the labour of the toilette seems the chief business of her life.

When I left her, in my way down stairs, I met Sir Clement, who, with great earnestness, said he must not be denied the honour of a moment's conversation with me; and then, without waiting for an answer, he led me to the garden, at the door of which, however, I absolutely insisted upon stopping.

He seemed very serious, and said, in a grave tone of voice, 'At length, Miss Anville, I flatter myself I have hit upon an expedient that will oblige you, and therefore, though it is death to myself, I will put it in practice.'

I begged him to explain himself.

'I saw your desire of saving Madame Duval, and scarce could I refrain giving the brutal Captain my real opinion of his savage

conduct; but I am unwilling to quarrel with him, lest I should be
denied entrance into a house which you inhabit: I have been
endeavouring to prevail with him to give up his absurd new
scheme, but I find him impenetrable:—I have therefore determined to make a pretence for suddenly leaving this place, dear as
it is to me, and containing all I most admire and adore;—and I
will stay in town till the violence of this boobyish humour is
abated.'

He stopped; but I was silent, for I knew not what I ought to
say. He took my hand, which he pressed to his lips, saying, 'And
must I, then, Miss Anville, must I quit you—sacrifice voluntarily
my greatest felicity,—and yet not be honoured with one word,
one look of approbation?'

I withdrew my hand, and said, with a half laugh, 'You know
so well, Sir Clement, the value of the favours you confer, that it
would be superfluous for me to point it out.'

'Charming, charming girl! how does your wit, your understanding rise upon me daily! and must I, can I part with you?—will
no other method—'

'O Sir, do you so soon repent the good office you had
planned for Madame Duval?'

'For Madame Duval!—cruel creature, and will you not even
suffer me to place to your account the sacrifice I am about to
make?'

'You must place it, Sir, to what account you please; but I am
too much in haste now to stay here any longer.'

And then I would have left him, but he held me, and, rather
impatiently, said, 'If, then, I cannot be so happy as to oblige *you*,
Miss Anville, you must not be surprised, should I seek to oblige
myself. If my scheme is not honoured with your approbation,
for which alone it was formed, why should I, to my own
infinite dissatisfaction, pursue it?'

We were then, for a few minutes, both silent; I was really
unwilling he should give up a plan which would so effectually
break into the Captain's designs, and, at the same time, save me
the pain of disobliging him; and I should instantly and thankfully
have accepted his offered civility, had not Mrs. Mirvan's caution

made me fearful. However, when he pressed me to speak, I said, in an ironical voice, 'I had thought, Sir, that the very strong sense you have yourself of the favour you propose to me, would sufficiently have repaid you, but, as I was mistaken, I must thank you myself.' And now, making a low court'sy, 'I hope, Sir, you are satisfied.'

'Loveliest of thy sex—' he began, but I forced myself from him, and ran up stairs.

Soon after, Miss Mirvan told me that Sir Clement had just received a letter, which obliged him instantly to leave the Grove, and that he had actually ordered a chaise. I then acquainted her with the real state of the affair. Indeed, I conceal nothing from her, she is so gentle and sweet-tempered, that it gives me great pleasure to place an entire confidence in her.

At dinner, I must own, we all missed him; for though the flightiness of his behaviour to me, when we are by ourselves, is very distressing, yet, in large companies, and general conversation, he is extremely entertaining and agreeable. As to the Captain, he has been so much chagrined at his departure, that he has scarce spoken a word since he went: but Madame Duval, who made her first public appearance since her accident, was quite in raptures that she escaped seeing him.

The money which we left at the farm-house, has been returned to us. What pains the Captain must have taken to arrange and manage the adventures which he chose we should meet with! Yet he must certainly be discovered, for Madame Duval is already very much perplexed, at having received a letter this morning from M. Du Bois, in which he makes no mention of his imprisonment. However, she has so little suspicion, that she imputes his silence upon the subject, to his fears that the letter might be intercepted.

Not one opportunity could I meet with, while Sir Clement was here, to enquire after his friend Lord Orville: but I think it was strange he should never mention him unasked. Indeed, I rather wonder that Mrs. Mirvan herself did not introduce the subject, for she always seemed particularly attentive to him.

And now, once more, all my thoughts involuntarily turn upon

the letter I so soon expect from Paris. This visit of Sir Clement has, however, somewhat diverted my fears, and therefore I am very glad he made it at this time. Adieu, my dear Sir.

LETTER IV

Sir John Belmont to Lady Howard

Paris, May 11

Madam,

I have this moment the honour of your Ladyship's letter, and I will not wait another, before I return an answer.

It seldom happens that a man, though extolled as a saint, is really without blemish; or that another, though reviled as a devil, is really without humanity. Perhaps the time is not very distant, when I may have the honour to convince your Ladyship of this truth, in regard to Mr. Villars and myself.

As to the young lady, whom Mr. Villars so obligingly proposes presenting to me, I wish her all the happiness to which, by your Ladyship's account, she seems entitled; and, if she has a third part of the merit of *her* to whom you compare her, I doubt not but Mr. Villars will be more successful in every other application he may make for her advantage, than he can ever be in any with which he may be pleased to favour me.

I have the honour to be,

Madam,

your Ladyship's most humble

and most obedient servant

JOHN BELMONT

LETTER V

Evelina to the Rev. Mr. Villars

Howard Grove, May 18

Well, my dear Sir, all is now over! the letter so anxiously expected, is at length arrived, and my doom is fixed. The various feelings which oppress me, I have not language to describe; nor need I,—you know my heart, you have yourself formed it,—and its sensations upon this occasion, you may but too readily imagine.

Outcast as I am, and rejected for ever by him to whom I of right belong,—shall I now implore *your* continued protection?— no, no,—I will not offend your generous heart, which, open to distress, has no wish but to relieve it, with an application that would seem to imply a doubt. I am more secure than ever of your kindness, since you now know upon that is my sole dependence.

I endeavour to bear this stroke with composure, and in such a manner as if I had already received your counsel and consolation. Yet, at times, my emotions are almost too much for me. O Sir, what a letter for a parent to write! must I not myself be deaf to the voice of Nature, if I could endure to be thus absolutely abandoned, without regret? I dare not even to you, nor would I, could I help it, to myself, acknowledge all that I think; for, indeed, I have, sometimes, sentiments upon this rejection, which my strongest sense of duty can scarcely correct. Yet, suffer me to ask,—might not this answer have been softened?—was it not enough to disclaim me for ever, without treating me with contempt, and wounding me with derision?

But, while I am thus thinking of myself, I forget how much more he is the object of sorrow, than I am! Alas, what amends can he make himself, for the anguish he is hoarding up for time to come! My heart bleeds for him, whenever this reflection occurs to me.

What is said of *you*, my protector, my friend, my benefactor!—
I dare not trust myself to comment upon. Gracious Heaven!
what a return for goodness so unparalleled!

I would fain endeavour to divert my thoughts from this
subject, but even that is not in my power; for, afflicting as this
letter is to me, I find that it will not be allowed to conclude the
affair, though it does all my expectations: for Madame Duval has
determined not to let it rest here. She heard the letter in great
wrath, and protested she would not be so easily answered; she
regretted her facility in having been prevailed upon to yield the
direction of this affair to those who knew not how to manage it,
and vowed she would herself undertake and conduct it in future.

It is in vain that I have pleaded against her resolution, and
besought her to forbear an attack, where she has nothing to
expect but resentment; especially as there seems to be a hint, that
Lady Howard will one day be more openly dealt with: she will
not hear me; she is furiously bent upon a project which is
terrible to think of,—for she means to go herself to Paris, take
me with her, and there, *face to face*, demand justice!

How to appease or to persuade her, I know not; but for the
universe would I not be dragged, in such a manner, to an
interview so awful, with a parent I have never yet beheld!

Lady Howard and Mrs. Mirvan are both of them infinitely
shocked at the present situation of affairs, and they seem to be
even more kind to me than ever; and my dear Maria, who is the
friend of my heart, uses her utmost efforts to console me, and,
when she fails in her design, with still greater kindness, she
sympathizes in my sorrow.

I very much rejoice, however, that Sir Clement Willoughby
had left us before this letter arrived. I am sure the general
confusion of the house would, otherwise, have betrayed to him
the whole of a tale which I now, more than ever, wish to have
buried in oblivion.

Lady Howard thinks I ought not to disoblige Madame Duval,
yet she acknowledges the impropriety of my accompanying her
abroad upon such an enterprise. Indeed I would rather die, than
force myself into his presence. But so vehement is Madame

Duval, that she would instantly have compelled me to attend her to town, in her way to Paris, had not Lady Howard so far exerted herself, as to declare she could by no means consent to my quitting her house, till she gave me up to you, by whose permission I had entered it.

She was extremely angry at this denial; and the Captain, by his sneers and raillery, so much increased her rage, that she has positively declared, should your next letter dispute her authority to guide me by her own pleasure, she will, without hesitation, make a journey to Berry Hill, and *teach you to know who she is*.

Should she put this threat in execution, nothing could give me greater uneasiness, for her violence and volubility would almost distract you.

Unable as I am to act for myself, or to judge what conduct I ought to pursue, how grateful do I feel myself, that I have such a guide and director to counsel and instruct me as yourself!

Adieu, my dearest Sir! Heaven, I trust, will never let me live to be repulsed and derided by *you*, to whom I may now sign myself

Wholly your
EVELINA

LETTER VI

Mr. Villars to Evelina

Berry Hill, May 21

Let not my Evelina be depressed by a stroke of fortune for which she is not responsible. No breach of duty on your part, has incurred the unkindness which has been shewn you; nor have you, by any act of imprudence, provoked either censure or reproach. Let me entreat you, therefore, my dearest child, to support yourself with that courage which your innocency ought to inspire; and let all the affliction you allow yourself, be for him only, who, not having that support, must one day be but too severely sensible how much he wants it.

The hint thrown out concerning myself, is wholly unintelligible to me: my heart, I dare own, fully acquits me of vice, but *without blemish*, I have never ventured to pronounce myself. However, it seems his intention to be hereafter more explicit, and *then*,—should any thing appear, that has on *my* part, contributed to those misfortunes we lament, let me, at least, say, that the most partial of my friends cannot be so much astonished as I shall myself be, at such a discovery.

The mention, also, of any *future applications* I may make, is equally beyond my comprehension. But I will not dwell upon a subject which almost compels from me reflections that cannot but be wounding to a heart so formed for filial tenderness as my Evelina's. There is an air of mystery throughout the letter, the explanation of which I will await in silence.

The scheme of Madame Duval is such as might be reasonably expected from a woman so little inured to disappointment, and so totally incapable of considering the delicacy of your situation. Your averseness to her plan gives me pleasure, for it exactly corresponds with my own. Why will she not make the journey she projects by herself? She would not have even the wish of an opposition to encounter. And then, once more, might my child and myself be left to the quiet enjoyment of that peaceful happiness, which she alone has interrupted. As to her coming hither, I could, indeed, dispense with such a visit; but, if she will not be satisfied with my refusal by letter, I must submit to the task of giving it her in person.

My impatience for your return is increased by your account of Sir Clement Willoughby's visit to Howard Grove. I am but little surprised at the perseverance of his assiduities to interest you in his favour; but I am very much hurt that you should be exposed to addresses, which, by their privacy, have an air that shocks me. You cannot, my love, be too circumspect; the slightest carelessness on your part, will be taken advantage of, by a man of his disposition. It is not sufficient for you to be reserved; his conduct even calls for your resentment: and should he again, as will doubtless be his endeavour, contrive to solicit your favour in private, let your disdain and displeasure be so marked, as to constrain a change in his behaviour. Though, indeed, should his visit be repeated while you remain at the Grove, Lady Howard must pardon me if I shorten your's.

Adieu, my child. You will always make my respects to the hospitable family to which we are so much obliged.

LETTER VII

Mr. Villars to Lady Howard

Berry Hill, May 27

Dear Madam,

I believe your Ladyship will not be surprised at hearing I have had a visit from Madame Duval, as I doubt not her having made known her intention before she left Howard Grove. I would gladly have excused myself this meeting, could I have avoided it decently; but, after so long a journey, it was not possible to refuse her admittance.

She told me, that she came to Berry Hill, in consequence of a letter I had sent to her grand-daughter, in which I had forbid her going to Paris. Very roughly, she then called me to account for the authority which I assumed; and, had I been disposed to have argued with her, she would very angrily have disputed the right by which I used it. But I declined all debating. I therefore listened very quietly, till she had so much fatigued herself with talking, that she was glad, in her turn, to be silent. And then, I begged to know the purport of her visit.

She answered, that she came to make me relinquish the power I had usurped over her grand-daughter, and assured me she would not quit the place till she succeeded.

But I will not trouble your Ladyship with the particulars of this disagreeable conversation; nor should I, but on account of the result, have chosen so unpleasant a subject for your perusal. However, I will be as concise as I possibly can, that the better occupations of your Ladyship's time may be the less impeded.

When she found me inexorable in refusing Evelina's attending her to Paris, she peremptorily insisted, that she should, at least live with her in London, till Sir John Belmont's return. I remonstrated against this scheme with all the energy in my power; but the contest was vain; she lost her patience, and I my time. She declared that if I was resolute in opposing her, she would instantly make a will, in which she would leave all her fortune to strangers, though, otherwise, she intended her grand-daughter for her sole heiress.

To me, I own, this threat seemed of little consequence; I have long accustomed myself to think, that, with a competency,[26] of which she is sure, my child might be as happy as in the possession of millions: but the incertitude of her future fate, deters me from following implicitly the dictates of my present judgement. The connections she may hereafter form, the style of life for which she may be destined, and the future family to which she may belong, are considerations which give but too much weight to the menaces of Madame Duval. In short, Madam, after a discourse infinitely tedious, I was obliged, though very reluctantly, to compromise with this ungovernable woman, by consenting that Evelina should pass one month with her.

I never made a concession with so bad a grace, or so much regret. The violence and vulgarity of this woman, her total ignorance of propriety, the family to which she is related, and the company she is likely to keep, are objections so forcible to her having the charge of this dear child, that nothing less than my diffidence of the right I have of depriving her of so large a fortune, would have induced me to listen to her proposal. Indeed we parted, at last, equally discontented, she, at what I had refused, I, at what I had granted.

It now only remains for me to return your Ladyship my humble acknowledgements for the kindness which you have so liberally shewn to my ward: and to beg you would have the goodness to part with her, when Madame Duval thinks proper to claim the promise which she has extorted from me. I am,

Dear Madam, &c.

ARTHUR VILLARS

LETTER VIII

Mr. Villars to Evelina

Berry Hill, May 28

With a reluctance which occasions me inexpressible uneasiness, I have been almost compelled to consent that my Evelina should quit the protection of the hospitable and respectable Lady Howard, and accompany Madame Duval to a city which I had hoped she would never again have entered. But alas, my dear child, we are the slaves of custom, the dupes of prejudice, and dare not stem the torrent of an opposing world, even though our judgements condemn our compliance! however, since the die is cast,[27] we must endeavour to make the best of it.

You will have occasion, in the course of the month you are to pass with Madame Duval, for all the circumspection and prudence you can call to your aid: she will not, I know, propose any thing to you which she thinks wrong herself; but you must learn not only to *judge* but to *act* for yourself: if any schemes are started, any engagements made, which your understanding represents to you as improper, exert yourself resolutely in avoiding them, and do not, by a too passive facility, risk the censure of the world, or your own future regret.

You cannot too assiduously attend to Madame Duval herself; but I would wish you to mix as little as possible with her associates, who are not likely to be among those whose acquaintance would reflect credit upon you. Remember, my dear Evelina, nothing is so delicate as the reputation of a woman: it is, at once, the most beautiful and most brittle of all human things.[28]

Adieu, my beloved child; I shall be but ill at ease till this month is elapsed.

                                                                              A. V.

LETTER IX

Evelina to the Rev. Mr. Villars

London, June 6

Once more, my dearest Sir, I write to you from this great city. Yesterday morning, with the truest concern, I quitted the dear inhabitants of Howard Grove, and most impatiently shall I count the days till I see them again. Lady Howard and Mrs. Mirvan took leave of me with the most flattering kindness; but indeed I knew not how to part with Maria, whose own apparent sorrow redoubled mine. She made me promise to send her a letter every post. And I shall write to her with the same freedom, and almost the same confidence, you allow me to make use of to yourself.

The Captain was very civil to me, but he wrangled with poor Madame Duval to the last moment; and, taking me aside, just before we got into the chaise, he said, 'Hark'ee, Miss Anville, I've a favour for to ask of you, which is this; that you will write us word how the old gentlewoman finds herself, when she sees it was all a trick: and what the French lubber[29] says to it, and all about it.'

I answered that I would obey him, though I was very little pleased with the commission, which, to me, was highly improper; but he will either treat me as an *informer*, or make me a party in his frolic.

As soon as we drove away, Madame Duval, with much

satisfaction, exclaimed '*Dieu Merci*, we've got off at last! I'm sure I never desire to see that place again. It's a wonder I've got away alive; for I believe I've had the worst luck ever was known, from the time I set my foot upon the threshold. I know I wish I'd never a gone. Besides, into the bargain, it's the most dullest place in all Christendom: there's never no diversions, nor nothing at all.'

Then she bewailed M. Du Bois, concerning whose adventures she continued to make various conjectures during the rest of our journey.

When I asked her what part of London she should reside in, she told me that Mr. Branghton was to meet us at an inn, and would conduct us to a lodging. Accordingly, we proceeded to a house in Bishopsgate-Street,[30] and were led by a waiter into a room where we found Mr. Branghton.

He received us very civilly, but seemed rather surprised at seeing me, saying 'Why I did n't think of your bringing Miss; however she's very welcome.'

'I'll tell you how it was,' said Madame Duval; 'you must know I've a mind to take the girl to Paris, that she may see something of the world, and improve herself a little; besides, I've another reason, that you and I will talk more about; but do you know, that meddling old parson as I told you of, would not let her go: however, I'm resolved I'll be even with him, for I shall take her on with me, without saying never a word more to nobody.'

I started at this intimation, which very much surprised me. But I am very glad she has discovered her intention, as I shall be carefully upon my guard not to venture from town with her.

Mr. Branghton then hoped we had passed our time agreeably in the country.

'O Lord, Cousin,' cried she, 'I've been the miserablest creature in the world! I'm sure all the horses in London sha'n't drag me into the country again of one while: why how do you think I've been served?—only guess.'

'Indeed Cousin, I can't pretend to do that.'

'Why then I'll tell you. Do you know, I've been robbed!—that

is, the villain would have robbed me if he could, only I'd
secured all my money.'

'Why then, Cousin, I think your loss can't have been very
great.'

'O Lord, you don't know what you're a-saying; you're talking
in the unthinkingest manner in the world: why it was all along
of not having no money, that I met with that misfortune.'

'How's that, Cousin? I don't see what great misfortune you
can have met with, if you'd secured all your money.'

'That's because you don't know nothing of the matter; for
there the villain came to the chaise, and because we had n't got
nothing to give him, though he'd no more right to our money
than the man in the moon, yet, do you know, he fell into the
greatest passion ever you see, and abused me in such a manner,
and put me in a ditch, and got a rope, o' purpose to hang me,—
and I'm sure, if that was n't misfortune enough, why I don't
know what is.'

'This is a hard case indeed, Cousin. But why don't you go to
Justice Fielding?'[31]

'O, as to that, I'm a-going to him directly; but only I want
first to see poor M. Du Bois, for the oddest thing of all is, that
he has wrote to me, and never said nothing of where he is, nor
what's become of him, nor nothing else.'

'M. Du Bois! why he's at my house at this very time.'

'M. Du Bois at your house! well, I declare this is the surpris-
ingest part of all! however, I assure you, I think he might have
comed for me, as well as you, considering what I have gone
through on his account; for, to tell you the truth, it was all along
of him that I met with that accident; so I don't take it very kind
of him, I promise you.'

'Well but, Cousin, tell me some of the particulars of this
affair.'

'As to the particulars, I'm sure they'd make your hair stand an
end to hear them; however, the beginning of it all was through
the fault of M. Du Bois: but I'll assure you, he may take care of
himself in future, since he don't so much as come to see if I'm
dead or alive;—but there I went for him to a justice of peace,

and rode all out of the way, and did every thing in the world, and was used worser than a dog, and all for the sake of serving of him, and now, you see, he don't so much—well, I was a fool for my pains,—however, he may get somebody else to be treated so another time, for if he's taken up every day in the week, I'll never go after him no more.'

This occasioned an explanation, in the course of which, Madame Duval, to her utter amazement, heard that M. Du Bois had never left London during her absence! nor did Mr. Branghton believe that he had ever been to the Tower, or met with any kind of accident.

Almost instantly, the whole truth of the transaction seemed to *rush upon her mind*,[32] and her wrath was inconceivably violent. She asked me a thousand questions in a breath, but, fortunately, was too vehement to attend to my embarrassment, which must, otherwise, have betrayed my knowledge of the deceit. Revenge was her first wish, and she vowed she would go the next morning to Justice Fielding, and enquire what punishment she might lawfully inflict upon the Captain for his assault.

I believe we were an hour in Bishopsgate-Street, before poor Madame Duval could allow any thing to be mentioned but her own story; at length, however, Mr. Branghton told her, that M. Du Bois, and all his own family, were waiting for her at his house. A hackney-coach was then called, and we proceeded to Snow Hill.

Mr. Branghton's house is small and inconvenient, though his shop, which takes in all the ground floor, is large and commodious. I believe I told you before that he is a silver-smith.

We were conducted up two pair of stairs,[33] for the dining-room, Mr. Branghton told us, was *let*. His two daughters, their brother, M. Du Bois, and a young man, were at tea. They had waited some time for Madame Duval, but I found they had not any expectation that I should accompany her; and the young ladies, I believe, were rather more surprised than pleased when I made my appearance; for they seemed hurt that I should see their apartment. Indeed I would willingly have saved them that pain, had it been in my power.

The first person who saw me was M. Du Bois: '*Ah, mon Dieu!*' exclaimed he, '*voilà Mademoiselle!*'[34]

'Goodness,' cried young Branghton, 'if there is n't Miss!'

'Lord, so there is,' said Miss Polly; 'well, I'm sure I should never have dreamed of Miss's coming.'

'Nor I neither, I'm sure,' cried Miss Branghton, 'or else I would not have been in this room to see her; I'm quite ashamed about it,—only not thinking of seeing any body but my aunt—however, Tom, it's all your fault, for you know very well I wanted to borrow Mr. Smith's room, only you were so *grumpy*[35] you would not let me.'

'Lord, what signifies?' said the brother, 'I dare be sworn Miss has been up two pair of stairs before now;—Ha'n't you, Miss?'

I begged that I might not give them the least disturbance, and assured them that I had not any choice in regard to what room we sat in.

'Well,' said Miss Polly, 'when you come next, Miss, we'll have Mr. Smith's room; and it's a very pretty one, and only up one pair of stairs, and nicely furnished, and every thing.'

'To say the truth,' said Miss Branghton, 'I thought that my cousin would not, upon any account, have come to town in the summer-time; for it's not at all the *fashion*,—so, to be sure, thinks I, she'll stay till September, when the play-houses open.'

This was my reception, which I believe you will not call a very *cordial* one. Madame Duval, who, after having severely reprimanded M. Du Bois for his negligence, was just entering upon the story of her misfortunes, now wholly engaged the company.

M. Du Bois listened to her with a look of the utmost horror, repeatedly lifting up his eyes and hands, and exclaiming, '*O ciel! quel barbare!*'[36] The young ladies gave her the most earnest attention; but their brother, and the young man, kept a broad grin upon their faces during the whole recital. She was, however, too much engaged to observe them: but, when she mentioned having been tied in a ditch, young Branghton, no longer able to constrain himself, burst into a loud laugh, declaring that he had never heard any thing so *funny*[37] in his life! His laugh was heartily re-echoed by his friend; the Miss Branghtons could not resist the example; and poor Madame Duval, to her extreme amazement, was absolutely overpowered and stopped by the violence of their mirth.

For some minutes the room seemed quite in an uproar; the rage of Madame Duval, the astonishment of M. Du Bois, and the angry interrogatories of Mr. Branghton, on one side; the convulsive tittering of the sisters, and the loud laughs of the young men, on the other, occasioned such noise, passion, and confusion, that had any one stopped an instant on the stairs, he must have concluded himself in Bedlam. At length, however, the father brought them to order; and, half laughing, half frightened, they made Madame Duval some very awkward apologies. But she would not be prevailed upon to continue her narrative, till they had protested they were laughing at the Captain, and not at her. Appeased by this, she resumed her story; which, by the help of stuffing handkerchiefs into their mouths, the young people heard with tolerable decency.

Every body agreed, that the ill usage the Captain had given her was *actionable*,[38] and Mr. Branghton said he was sure she might recover what damages she pleased, since she had been put in fear of her life.

She then, with great delight, declared, that she would lose no time in satisfying her revenge, and vowed she would not be contented with less than half his fortune: 'For though,' said she, 'I don't put no value upon the money, because, *Dieu merci*,[39] I ha'n't no want of it, yet I don't wish for nothing so much as to punish that fellow; for, I'm sure, whatever's the cause of it, he owes me a great *grudge*,[40] and I know no more what it's for than you do, but he's always been doing me one spite or other, ever since I knew him.'

Soon after tea, Miss Branghton took an opportunity to tell me, in a whisper, that the young man I saw was a lover of her sister's, that his name was Brown, and that he was a haber-dasher,[41] with many other particulars of his circumstances and family; and then she declared her utter aversion to the thoughts of such a match; but added, that her sister had no manner of spirit or ambition, though, for her part, she would ten times rather die an old maid, than marry any person but a gentleman. 'And, for that matter,' added she, 'I believe Polly herself don't care much for him, only she's in such a hurry, because, I suppose, she's a mind to be married before me; however, she's very welcome, for, I'm sure, I don't care a pin's point whether I ever marry at all;—it's all one to me.'

Some time after this, Miss Polly contrived to tell *her* story. She assured me, with much tittering, that her sister was in a great fright, lest she should be married first, 'So I make her believe that I will,' continued she, 'for I love dearly to plague her a little; though, I declare, I don't intend to have Mr. Brown in reality; I'm sure I don't like him half well enough,—do you, Miss?'

'It is not possible for me to judge of his merits,' said I, 'as I am entirely a stranger to him.'

'But, what do you think of him, Miss?'

'Why, really, I—I don't know—'

'But do you think him handsome? Some people reckon him to have a good pretty person,—but, I'm sure, for my part, I think he's monstrous ugly:—don't *you*, Miss?'

'I am no judge,—but I think his person is very—very well.'

'*Very well!*—Why, pray, Miss,' in a tone of vexation, 'what fault can you find with it?'

'O, none at all!'

'I'm sure you must be very ill-natured if you could. Now there's Biddy says she thinks nothing of him,—but I know it's all out of spite. You must know, Miss, it makes her as mad as can be, that I should have a lover before her, but she's so proud that nobody will court her, and I often tell her she'll die an old maid. But, the thing is, she has taken it into her head, to have a liking for Mr. Smith, as lodges on the first floor; but, Lord, he'll never have her, for he's quite a fine gentleman; and besides, Mr. Brown heard him say, one day, that he'd never marry as long as he lived, for he'd no opinion of matrimony.'

'And did you tell your sister this?'

'O, to be sure, I told her directly; but she did not mind me; however, if she will be a fool, she must.'

This extreme want of affection, and good-nature, increased the distaste I already felt for these unamiable sisters; and a confidence so entirely unsolicited and unnecessary, manifested equally their folly and their want of decency.

I was very glad when the time for our departing arrived. Mr. Branghton said our lodgings were in Holborn,[42] that we might be near his house, and neighbourly. He accompanied us to them himself.

Our rooms are large, and not inconvenient; our landlord is a hosier.[43] I am sure I have a thousand reasons to rejoice that I am so little known; for my present situation is, in every respect, very unenviable; and I would not, for the world, be seen by any acquaintance of Mrs. Mirvan.

This morning Madame Duval, attended by all the Branghtons, actually went to a Justice in the neighbourhood, to report the Captain's ill usage of her. I had great difficulty in excusing myself from being of the party, which would have given me very serious concern. Indeed, I was extremely anxious, though at home, till I heard the result of the application; for I dread to think of the uneasiness which such an affair would occasion the amiable Mrs. Mirvan. But, fortunately, Madame Duval has received very little encouragement to proceed in her design, for she has been informed that, as she neither heard the voice, nor saw the face of the person suspected, she will find it difficult to cast him upon *conjecture*, and will have but little probability of gaining her cause, unless she can procure witnesses of the transaction. Mr. Branghton, therefore, who has considered all the circumstances of the affair, is of opinion, that the law-suit will not only be expensive, but tedious and hazardous, and has advised against it. Madame Duval, though very unwillingly, has acquiesced in his decision; but vows that if ever she is so affronted again, she will be revenged, even if she ruins herself. I am extremely glad that this ridiculous adventure seems now likely to end without more serious consequences.

Adieu, my dearest Sir. My direction is at Mr. Dawkins's, a hosier in High Holborn.

LETTER X

Evelina to Miss Mirvan

June 7th

I have no words, my sweet friend, to express the thankfulness I feel for the unbounded kindness which you, your dear mother, and the much-honoured Lady Howard, have shewn me; and still less can I find language to tell you with what reluctance I parted from such dear and generous friends, whose goodness reflects, at once, so much honour on their own hearts, and on her to whom it has been so liberally bestowed. But I will not repeat what I have already written to the kind Mrs. Mirvan; I will remember your admonitions, and confine to my own breast that gratitude with which you have filled it, and teach my pen to dwell upon subjects less painful to my generous correspondent.

O Maria, London now seems no longer the same place where I lately enjoyed so much happiness; every thing is new and strange to me; even the town itself has not the same aspect:—my situation so altered! my home so different!—my companions so changed!—But you well know my averseness to this journey.

Indeed, to me, London now seems a desart; that gay and busy appearance it so lately wore, is now succeeded by a look of gloom, fatigue, and lassitude; the air seems stagnant, the heat is intense, the dust intolerable, and the inhabitants illiterate and under-bred. At least, such is the face of things in the part of the town where I at present reside.

Tell me, my dear Maria, do you never re-trace in your memory the time we passed here when together? to mine, it recurs for ever! And yet, I think I rather recollect a dream, or some visionary fancy, than a reality.—That I should ever have been known to Lord Orville,—that I should have spoken to—have danced with him,—seems now a romantic illusion: and that elegant politeness, that flattering attention, that high-bred delicacy, which so much distinguished him above all other men, and which struck us with such admiration, I now re-trace the remembrance of, rather as belonging to an object of ideal perfection, formed by my own imagination, than to a being of the same race and nature as those with whom I at present converse.

I have no news for you, my dear Miss Mirvan; for all that I could venture to say of Madame Duval, I have already written to your sweet mother; and as to adventures, I have none to record. Situated as I now am, I heartily hope I shall not meet with any; my wish is to remain quiet and unnoticed.

Adieu! excuse the gravity of this letter, and believe me,

Your most sincerely
affectionate and obliged
EVELINA ANVILLE

LETTER XI

Evelina to the Rev. Mr. Villars

Holborn, June 9

Yesterday morning, we received an invitation to dine and spend the day at Mr. Branghton's; and M. Du Bois, who was also invited, called to conduct us to Snow Hill.

Young Branghton received us at the door, and the first words he spoke were, 'Do you know, Sisters a'n't dressed yet?'

Then, hurrying us into the house, he said to me, 'Come, Miss, you shall go up stairs and catch 'em,—I dare say they're at the glass.'

He would have taken my hand, but I declined this civility, and begged to follow Madame Duval. Mr. Branghton then appeared, and led the way himself. We went, as before, up two pair of stairs; but the moment the father opened the door, the daughters both gave a loud scream. We all stopped, and then Miss Branghton called out, 'Lord, Papa, what do you bring the company up here for? why, Polly and I a'n't half dressed.'

'More shame for you,' answered he, 'here's your aunt, and cousin, and M. Du Bois, all waiting, and ne'er a room to take them to.'

'Who'd have thought of their coming so soon?' cried she: 'I'm sure for my part I thought Miss was used to nothing but quality hours.'[44]

'Why, I sha'n't be ready this half-hour yet,' said Miss Polly; 'can't they stay in the shop, till we're dressed?'

Mr. Branghton was very angry, and scolded them violently; however, we were obliged to descend, and stools were procured for us in the shop, where we found the brother, who was highly delighted, he said, that his sisters had been *catched*; and he thought proper to entertain me with a long account of their tediousness, and the many quarrels they all had together.

When, at length, these ladies were equipped to their satisfaction, they made their appearance; but before any conversation was suffered to pass between them and us, they had a long and most disagreeable dialogue with their father, to whose reprimands, though so justly incurred, they replied with the utmost pertness and rudeness, while their brother, all the time, laughed aloud.

The moment they perceived this, they were so much provoked, that, instead of making any apologies to Madame Duval, they next began a quarrel with him. 'Tom, what do you laugh for? I wonder what business you have to be always a-laughing when Papa scolds us.'

'Then what business have you to be such a while getting on your cloaths? You're never ready, you know well enough.'

'Lord, Sir, I wonder what that's to you! I wish you'd mind your own affairs, and not trouble yourself about ours. How should a boy like you know any thing?'

'A boy, indeed! not such a boy, neither; I'll warrant you'll be glad to be as young, when you come to be old maids.'

This sort of dialogue we were amused with till dinner was ready, when we again mounted up two pair of stairs.

In our way, Miss Polly told me that her sister had asked Mr. Smith for his room to dine in, but he had refused to lend it;

'because,' she said, 'one day it happened to be a little greased: however, we shall have it to drink tea in, and then, perhaps, you may see him, and I assure you he's quite like one of the quality, and dresses as fine, and goes to balls and dances, and every thing quite in taste;—and besides, Miss, he keeps a foot-boy of his own, too.'

The dinner was ill-served, ill-cooked, and ill-managed. The maid who waited had so often to go down stairs for something that was forgotten, that the Branghtons were perpetually obliged to rise from table themselves, to get plates, knives and forks, bread or beer. Had they been without *pretensions*, all this would have seemed of no consequence; but they aimed at appearing to advantage, and even fancied they succeeded.[45] However, the most disagreeable part of our fare was, that the whole family continually disputed whose turn it was to rise, and whose to be allowed to sit still.

When this meal was over, Madame Duval, ever eager to discourse upon *her travels*, entered into an argument with Mr. Branghton, and in broken English, M. Du Bois, concerning the French nation: and Miss Polly, then addressing herself to me, said, 'Don't you think, Miss, it's very dull sitting up stairs here? we'd better go down *to shop*, and then we shall see the people go by.'

'Lord, Poll,' said the brother, 'you're always wanting to be staring and gaping; and I'm sure you need n't be so fond of shewing yourself, for you're ugly enough to frighten a horse.'

'Ugly, indeed! I wonder which is best, you or me. But, I tell you what, Tom, you've no need to give yourself such airs, for if you do, I'll tell Miss of you know what—'

'Who cares if you do? you may tell what you will; I don't mind—'

'Indeed,' cried I, 'I do not desire to hear any secrets.'

'O, but I'm resolved I'll tell you, because Tom's so very spiteful. You must know, Miss, t'other night—'

'Poll,' cried the brother, 'if you tell of that, Miss shall know all about your meeting young Brown,—you know when!—So I'll be quits with you, one way or another.'

Miss Polly coloured, and again proposed our going down stairs till Mr. Smith's room was ready for our reception.

'Aye, so we will,' said Miss Branghton; 'I'll assure you, Cousin, we have some very genteel people pass by our shop sometimes. Polly and I always go and sit there, when we've cleaned ourselves.'

'Yes, Miss,' cried the brother, 'they do nothing else all day long, when father don't scold them. But the best fun is, when they've got all their dirty things on, and all their hair about their ears, sometimes I send young Brown up stairs to them; and then, there's such a fuss!—there they hide themselves, and run away, and squeel and squall like any thing mad: and so then I puts the two cats into the room, and I gives 'em a good whipping, and so that sets them a squalling too; so there's such a noise, and such an uproar!—Lord, you can't think, Miss, what fun it is!'

This occasioned a fresh quarrel with the sisters; at the end of which, it was, at length, decided that we should go to the shop.

In our way down stairs, Miss Branghton said aloud, 'I wonder when Mr. Smith's room will be ready.'

'So do I,' answered Polly; 'I'm sure we should not do any harm to it now.'

This hint had not the desired effect; for we were suffered to proceed very quietly.

As we entered the shop, I observed a young man, in deep mourning, leaning against the wall, with his arms folded, and his eyes fixed on the ground, apparently in profound and melancholy meditation: but the moment he perceived us, he started, and, making a passing bow, very abruptly retired. As I found he was permitted to go quite unnoticed, I could not forbear enquiring who he was.

'Lord!' answered Miss Branghton, 'he's nothing but a poor Scotch poet.'

'For my part,' said Miss Polly, 'I believe he's just starved, for I don't find he has any thing to live upon.'

'Live upon!' cried the brother, 'why he's a poet, you know, so he may live upon learning.'

'Aye, and good enough for him too,' said Miss Branghton, 'for he's as proud as he's poor.'

'Like enough,' replied the brother, 'but, for all that, you won't find he will live without meat and drink: no, no, catch a Scotchman at that if you can! why, they only come here for what they can get.'⁴⁶

'I'm sure,' said Miss Branghton, 'I wonder Papa 'll be such a fool as to let him stay in the house, for I dare say he'll never pay for his lodging.'

'Why, no more he would if he could get another Lodger: you know the bill's been put up this fortnight. Miss, if you should hear of a person that wants a room, I assure you it is a very good one, for all it's up three pair of stairs.'

I answered that as I had no acquaintance in London, I had not any chance of assisting them: but both my compassion and my curiosity were excited for this poor young man; and I asked them some further particulars concerning him.

They then acquainted me, that they had only known him three months. When he first lodged with them, he agreed to board also; but had lately told them, he would eat by himself, though they all believed he had hardly ever tasted a morsel of meat since he left their table. They said, that he had always appeared very low-spirited, but, for the last month, he had been *duller* than ever, and, all of a sudden, had put himself into mourning, though they knew not for whom, nor for what, but they supposed it was only for convenience, as no person had ever been to see or enquire for him since his residence amongst them: and they were sure he was very poor, as he had not paid for his lodgings the last three weeks: and finally, they concluded he was a poet, or else half-crazy, because they had, at different times, found scraps of poetry in his room.

They then produced some unfinished verses, written on small pieces of paper unconnected, and of a most melancholy cast. Among them was the fragment of an ode, which, at my request, they lent me to copy; and, as you may perhaps like to see it, I will write it now.

O LIFE! thou lingering dream of grief, of pain,
And every ill that Nature can sustain,
 Strange, mutable, and wild!

Now flattering with Hope most fair,
Depressing now with fell Despair,
 The nurse of Guilt, the slave of Pride,
  That, like a wayward child,
  Who, to himself a foe,
Sees joy alone in what's denied,
 In what is granted, woe!

———

O thou poor, feeble, fleeting pow'r,
By Vice seduc'd, by Folly woo'd,
By Mis'ry, Shame, Remorse, pursu'd;
And as thy toilsome steps proceed,
Seeming to Youth the fairest flow'r,
Proving to Age the rankest weed,
 A gilded, but a bitter pill,
 Of varied, great, and complicated ill!

These lines are harsh, but they indicate an internal wretchedness which, I own, affects me. Surely this young man must be involved in misfortunes of no common nature: but I cannot imagine what can induce him to remain with this unfeeling family, where he is, most unworthily, despised for being poor, and, most illiberally, detested for being a Scotchman. He may, indeed, have motives which he cannot surmount, for submitting to such a situation. Whatever they are, I most heartily pity him, and cannot but wish it were in my power to afford him some relief.

During this conversation, Mr. Smith's foot-boy came to Miss Branghton, and informed her, that his master said she might have the room now when she liked it, for that he was presently going out.

This very genteel message,[47] though it perfectly satisfied the Miss Branghtons, by no means added to my desire of being introduced to this gentleman: and upon their rising, with intention to accept his offer, I begged they would excuse my attending them, and said I would sit with Madame Duval till the tea was ready.

I therefore once more went up two pair of stairs, with young Branghton, who insisted upon accompanying me; and there we remained, till Mr. Smith's foot-boy summoned us to tea, when I followed Madame Duval into the dining-room.

The Miss Branghtons were seated at one window, and Mr. Smith was lolling indolently out of the other. They all approached us at our entrance, and Mr. Smith, probably to shew he was master of the apartment, most officiously handed me to a great chair, at the upper end of the room, without taking any notice of Madame Duval, till I rose, and offered her my own seat.

Leaving the rest of the company to entertain themselves, he, very abruptly, began to address himself to me, in a style of gallantry equally new and disagreeable to me. It is true, no man can possibly pay me greater compliments, or make more fine speeches, than Sir Clement Willoughby, yet his language, though too flowery, is always that of a gentleman, and his address and manners are so very superior to those of the inhabitants of this house, that to make any comparison between him and Mr. Smith would be extremely unjust. This latter seems very desirous of appearing a man of gaiety and spirit; but his vivacity is so low-bred, and his whole behaviour so forward and disagreeable, that I should prefer the company of *dullness* itself, even as that goddess is described by Pope,[48] to that of this *sprightly* young man.

He made many apologies that he had not lent his room for our dinner, which, he said, he should certainly have done, had he seen me first; and he assured me, that when I came again, he should be very glad to oblige me.

I told him, and with sincerity, that every part of the house was equally indifferent to me.

'Why, Ma'am, the truth is, Miss Biddy and Polly take no care of any thing, else, I'm sure, they should be always welcome to my room; for I'm never so happy as in obliging the ladies,— that's my character, Ma'am;—but, really, the last time they had it, every thing was made so greasy and so nasty, that, upon my word, to a man who wishes to have things a little genteel, it was quite cruel. Now, as to you, Ma'am, it's quite another thing; for I should not mind if every thing I had was spoilt, for the sake of having the pleasure to oblige you; and, I assure you, Ma'am, it makes me quite happy, that I have a room good enough to receive you.'

This elegant speech was followed by many others, so much in the same style, that to write them would be superfluous; and, as he did not allow me a moment to speak to any other person, the rest of the evening was consumed in a painful attention to this irksome young man, who seemed to intend appearing before me to the utmost advantage.

Adieu, my dear Sir. I fear you will be sick of reading about this family; yet I must write of them, or not of any, since I mix with no other. Happy shall I be, when I quit them all, and again return to Berry Hill!

LETTER XII

Evelina in continuation

June 10th

This morning, Mr. Smith called, *on purpose*, he said, to offer me a ticket for the next Hampstead assembly.[49] I thanked him, but desired to be excused accepting it; he would not, however, be denied, nor answered, and, in a manner both vehement and free, pressed and urged his offer till I was wearied to death: but, when he found me resolute, he seemed thunderstruck with amazement, and thought proper to desire I would tell him my reasons.[50]

Obvious as they must, surely, have been to any other person, they were such as I knew not how to repeat to him; and, when he found I hesitated, he said, 'Indeed, Ma'am, you are too modest; I assure you the ticket is quite at your service, and I shall be very happy to dance with you; so pray don't be so coy.'

'Indeed, Sir,' returned I, 'you are mistaken; I never supposed you would offer a ticket, without wishing it should be accepted; but it would answer no purpose to mention the reasons which make me decline it, since they cannot possibly be removed.'

This speech seemed very much to mortify him, which I could not be concerned at, as I did not chuse to be treated by him with so much freedom. When he was, at last, convinced that his application to me was ineffectual, he addressed himself to Madame Duval, and begged she would interfere in his favour, offering, at the same time, to procure another ticket for herself.

'*Ma foi*, Sir,' answered she, angrily, 'you might as well have had the complaisance to ask me before, for, I assure you, I don't approve of no such rudeness: however, you may keep your tickets to yourself, for we don't want none of 'em.'

This rebuke almost overset him; he made many apologies, and said that he should certainly have first applied to her, but that he had no notion the *young* lady would have refused him, and, on the contrary, had concluded that she would have assisted him to persuade Madame Duval herself.

This excuse appeased her; and he pleaded his cause so successfully, that, to my great chagrin, he gained it: and Madame Duval promised that she would go herself, and take me to the Hampstead assembly whenever he pleased.

Mr. Smith then, approaching me with an air of triumph, said, 'Well, Ma'am, now, I think, you can't possibly keep to your denial.'

I made no answer, and he soon took leave, though not till he had so wonderfully gained the favour of Madame Duval, that she declared, when he was gone, he was the prettiest young man she had seen since she came to England.

As soon as I could find an opportunity, I ventured, in the most humble manner, to entreat Madame Duval would not insist upon my attending her to this ball; and represented to her, as well as I was able, the impropriety of my accepting any present from a young man so entirely unknown to me: but she laughed at my scruples, called me a foolish, ignorant country girl, and said she should make it her business to teach me something of the world.

This ball is to be next week. I am sure it is not more improper for, than unpleasant to me, and I will use every possible endeavour to avoid it. Perhaps I may apply to Miss Branghton for advice, as I believe she will be willing to assist me, from disliking, equally with myself, that I should dance with Mr. Smith.

July 11th

O, my dear Sir! I have been shocked to death!—and yet, at the same time, delighted beyond expression, in the hope that I have happily been the instrument of saving a human creature from destruction!

This morning, Madame Duval said she would invite the Branghton family to return our visit to-morrow; and, not chusing to rise herself,—for she generally spends the morning in bed,—she desired me to wait upon them with her message. M. Du Bois, who just then called, insisted upon attending me.

Mr. Branghton was in the shop, and told us that his son and daughters were out; but desired me to step up stairs, as he very soon expected them home. This I did, leaving M. Du Bois below. I went into the room where we had dined the day before, and, by a wonderful chance, I happened so to seat myself, that I had a view of the stairs, and yet could not be seen from them.

In about ten minutes time, I saw, passing by the door, with a look perturbed and affrighted, the same young man I mentioned in my last letter. Not heeding, as I suppose, how he went, in turning the corner of the stairs, which are narrow and winding, his foot slipped, and he fell, but almost instantly rising, I plainly perceived the end of a pistol, which started from his pocket, by hitting against the stairs.

I was inexpressibly shocked. All that I had heard of his misery occurring to my memory, made me conclude, that he was at that very moment, meditating suicide! Struck with the dreadful idea, all my strength seemed to fail me. He moved on slowly, yet I soon lost sight of him; I sat motionless with terror; all power of action forsook me; and I grew almost stiff with horror: till recollecting that it was yet possible to prevent the fatal deed, all my faculties seemed to return, with the hope of saving him.

My first thought was to fly to Mr Branghton, but I feared that an instant of time lost, might for ever be rued; and therefore, guided by the impulse of my apprehensions, as well as I was able, I followed him up stairs, stepping very softly, and obliged to support myself by the banisters.

When I came within a few stairs of the landing-place, I stopped, for I could then see into his room, as he had not yet shut the door.

He had put the pistol upon a table, and had his hand in his pocket, whence, in a few moments, he took out another. He then emptied something on the table from a small leather bag; [51] after which, taking up both the pistols, one in each hand, he dropped hastily upon his knees, and called out 'O God!—forgive me!'

In a moment, strength, and courage seemed lent me as by inspiration: I started, and rushing precipitately into the room, just caught his arm, and then, overcome by my own fears, I fell down at his side, breathless and senseless. My recovery, however, was, I believe, almost instantaneous; and then the sight of this unhappy man, regarding me with a look of unutterable astonishment, mixed with concern, presently restored to me my recollection. I arose, though with difficulty; he did the same; the pistols, as I soon saw, were both on the floor.

Unwilling to leave them, and, indeed, too weak to move, I leaned one hand on the table, and then stood perfectly still; while he, his eyes cast wildly towards me, seemed too infinitely amazed to be capable of either speech or action.

I believe we were some minutes in this extraordinary situation; but as my strength returned, I felt myself both ashamed and awkward, and moved towards the door. Pale, and motionless, he suffered me to pass, without changing his posture, or uttering a syllable; and, indeed,

He looked a bloodless image of despair!*[52]

When I reached the door, I turned round; I looked fearfully at

* Pope's Iliad

the pistols, and, impelled by an emotion I could not repress, I hastily stepped back, with an intention of carrying them away: but their wretched owner, perceiving my design, and recovering from his astonishment, darting suddenly down, seized them both himself.

Wild with fright, and scarce knowing what I did, I caught, almost involuntarily hold of both his arms, and exclaimed, 'O Sir! have mercy on yourself!'

The guilty pistols fell from his hands, which, disengaging from me, he fervently clasped, and cried, 'Sweet Heaven! is this thy angel?'

Encouraged by such gentleness, I again attempted to take the pistols, but, with a look half frantic, he again prevented me, saying, 'What would you do?'

'Awaken you,' I cried, with a courage I now wonder at, 'to worthier thoughts, and rescue you from perdition.'

I then seized the pistols; he said not a word,—he made no effort to stop me;—I glided quick by him, and tottered down stairs, ere he had recovered from the extremest amazement.

The moment I reached again the room I had so fearfully left, I threw away the pistols, and flinging myself on the first chair, gave free vent to the feelings I had most painfully stifled, in a violent burst of tears, which, indeed, proved a happy relief to me.

In this situation I remained some time; but when, at length, I lifted up my head, the first object I saw was the poor man who had occasioned my terror, standing, as if petrified, at the door, and gazing at me with eyes of wild wonder.

I started from the chair, but trembled so excessively, that I almost instantly sunk again into it. He then, though without advancing, and in a faltering voice, said, 'Whoever or whatever you are, relieve me, I pray you, from the suspense under which my soul labours—and tell me if indeed I do not dream!'

To this address, so singular and so solemn, I had not then the presence of mind to frame any answer: but, as I presently perceived that his eyes turned from me to the pistols, and that he seemed to intend regaining them, I exerted all my strength, and saying 'O for Heaven's sake forbear!' I rose and took them myself.

'Do my senses deceive me!' cried he, 'do *I* live—? and do *you*?'

As he spoke, he advanced towards me! and I, still guarding the pistols, retreated, saying 'No, no—you must not—must not have them!'—

'Why—for what purpose, tell me!—do you withhold them?'—

'To give you time to *think*,—to save you from eternal misery,—and, I hope, to reserve you for mercy,—and forgiveness.'

'Wonderful!' cried he, with uplifted hands and eyes, 'most wonderful!'

For some time, he seemed wrapped in deep thought, till a sudden noise of tongues below, announcing the approach of the Branghtons, made him start from his reverie: he sprung hastily forward,—dropped on one knee,—caught hold of my gown, which he pressed to his lips, and then, quick as lightning, he rose, and flew up stairs to his own room.

There was something in the whole of this extraordinary and shocking adventure, really too affecting to be borne; and so entirely had I spent my spirits and exhausted my courage, that, before the Branghtons reached me, I had sunk on the ground, without sense or motion.

I believe I must have been a very horrid sight to them, on their entrance into the room; for, to all appearance, I seemed to have suffered a violent death, either by my own rashness, or the cruelty of some murderer; as the pistols had fallen close by my side.

How soon I recovered, I know not, but probably, I was more indebted to the loudness of their cries, than to their assistance; for they all concluded that I was dead, and, for some time, did not make any effort to revive me.

Scarcely could I recollect *where*, or, indeed, *what* I was, ere they poured upon me such a torrent of questions and enquiries, that I was almost stunned with their vociferation. However, as soon and as well as I was able, I endeavoured to satisfy their curiosity, by recounting what had happened as clearly as was in my power. They all looked aghast at the recital, but, not being well enough to enter into any discussions, I begged to have a chair called, and to return instantly home.

Before I left them, I recommended, with great earnestness, a vigilant observance of their unhappy lodger, and that they would take care to keep from him, if possible, all means of self-destruction.

M. Du Bois, who seemed extremely concerned at my indisposition, walked by the side of the chair, and saw me safe to my own apartment.

The rashness and the misery of this ill-fated young man, engross all my thoughts. If, indeed, he is bent upon destroying himself, all efforts to save him will be fruitless. How much do I wish it were in my power to discover the nature of the malady which thus maddens him, and to offer or to procure alleviation to his sufferings! I am sure, my dearest Sir, you will be much concerned for this poor man; and, were you here, I doubt not but you would find some method of awakening him from the error which blinds him, and of pouring the balm of peace and comfort into his afflicted soul!

LETTER XIII

Evelina in continuation.

Holborn, June 13th

Yesterday all the Branghtons dined here.

Our conversation was almost wholly concerning the adventure of the day before. Mr. Branghton said, that his first thought was instantly to turn his lodger out of doors, 'Lest,' continued he, 'his killing himself in my house, should bring me into any trouble; but then, I was afraid I should never get the money he owes me, whereas, if he dies in my house, I have a right to all he leaves behind him, if he goes off in my debt. Indeed, I would put him in prison,—but what should I get by that?[53] he could not earn any thing there to pay me. So I considered about it some time, and then I determined to ask him, point-blank, for my money out of hand. And so I did, but he told me he'd pay me next week: however, I gave him to understand, that, though I was no Scotchman, yet I did not like to be over-reached[54] any more than he; so then he gave me a ring, which, to my certain knowledge, must be worth ten guineas, and told me he would not part with it for his life, and a good deal more such sort of stuff, but that I might keep it till he could pay me.'

'It is ten to one, Father,' said young Branghton, 'if he came fairly by it.'

'Very likely not,' answered he, 'but that will make no great difference; for I shall be able to prove my right to it all one.'[55]

What principles! I could hardly stay in the room.

'I'm determined,' said the son, 'I'll take some opportunity to affront him soon, now I know how poor he is, because of the airs he gave himself to me when he first came.'

'And pray how was that, child?' said Madame Duval.

'Why you never knew such a fuss[56] in your life as he made, because, one day at dinner, I only happened to say, that I supposed he had never got such a good meal in his life, before he came to England: there he fell in such a passion as you can't think; but, for my part, I took no notice of it, for to be sure, thinks I, he must needs be a gentleman, or he'd never go to be so angry about it. However, he won't put his tricks upon me again, in a hurry.'

'Well,' said Miss Polly, 'he's grown quite another creature to what he was, and he does n't run away from us, nor hide himself, nor any thing; and he's as civil as can be, and he's always in the shop, and he saunters about the stairs, and he looks at every body as comes in.'

'Why you may see what he's after plain enough,' said Mr. Branghton; 'he wants to see Miss again.'

'Ha, ha, ha! Lord, how I should laugh,' said the son, 'if he should have fell in love with Miss!'

'I'm sure,' said Miss Branghton, 'Miss is welcome; but, for my part, I should be quite ashamed of such a beggarly conquest.'

Such was the conversation till tea-time, when the appearance of Mr. Smith gave a new turn to the discourse.

Miss Branghton desired me to remark with what a *smart air*, he entered the room, and asked me if he had not very much a *quality look*?

'Come,' cried he, advancing to us, 'you ladies must not sit together; wherever I go, I always make it a rule to part the ladies.'

And then, handing Miss Branghton to the next chair, he seated himself between us.

'Well, now ladies, I think we sit very well. What say you? for my part, I think it was a very good motion.'

'If my Cousin likes it,' said Miss Branghton, 'I'm sure I've no objection.'

'O,' cried he, 'I always study what the ladies like,—that's my first thought. And, indeed, it is but natural that you should like best to sit by the gentlemen, for what can you find to say to one another?'

'Say?' cried young Branghton, 'O, never you think of that, they'll find enough to say, I'll be sworn. You know the women are never tired of talking.'

'Come, come, Tom,' said Mr. Smith, 'don't be severe upon the ladies; when I'm by, you know I always take their part.'

Soon after, when Miss Branghton offered me some cake, this man of gallantry said, 'Well, if I was that lady, I'd never take any thing from a woman.'

'Why not, Sir?'

'Because I should be afraid of being poisoned for being so handsome.'

'Who is severe upon the ladies *now*?' said I.

'Why, really, Ma'am, it was a slip of the tongue; I did not intend to say such a thing; but one can't always be on one's guard.'

Soon after, the conversation turning upon public places, young Branghton asked if I had ever been to *George's* at Hampstead?[57]

'Indeed I never heard the place mentioned.'

'Did n't you, Miss?' cried he, eagerly, 'why then you've a deal of fun to come, I'll promise you; and, I tell you what, I'll treat you there some Sunday soon. So now, Bid and Poll, be sure you don't tell Miss about the chairs, and all that, for I've a mind to surprise her; and if I pay, I think I've a right to have it my own way.'

'George's at Hampstead!' repeated Mr Smith, contemptuously, 'how came you to think the young Lady would like to go to such a low place as that! But, pray Ma'am, have you ever been to Don Saltero's at Chelsea?'[58]

'No, Sir.'

'No!—nay, then, I must insist on having the pleasure of conducting you there before long. I assure, you, Ma'am, many genteel people go, or else, I give you my word, *I* should not recommend it.'

'Pray, Cousin,' said Mr Branghton, 'have you been at Sadler's Wells,[59] yet?'

'No, Sir.'

'No! why then you've seen nothing!'

'Pray, Miss,' said the Son, 'how do you like the Tower of London.'

'I have never been to it, Sir.'

'Goodness!' exclaimed he, 'not seen the Tower!—why may be you ha' n't been o' top of the Monument,[60] neither?'

'No, indeed, I have not.'

'Why then you might as well not have come to London, for aught I see, for you've been no where.'

'Pray, Miss,' said Polly, 'have you been all over Paul's Church,[61] yet?'

'No, Ma'am.'

'Well, but, Ma'am,' said Mr. Smith, 'how do you like Vaux-hall[62] and Marybone?'[63]

'I never saw either, Sir.'

'No—God bless me!—you really surprise me,—why Vauxhall is the first pleasure in life!—I know nothing like it.—Well, Ma'am, you must have been with strange people, indeed, not to have taken you to Vauxhall. Why you have seen nothing of London yet.—However, we must try if *we* can't make you amends.'

In the course of this *catechism*, many other places were mentioned, of which I have forgotten the names; but the looks of surprise and contempt that my repeated negatives incurred, were very diverting.

'Come,' said Mr. Smith, after tea, 'as this Lady has been with such a queer set of people, let's shew her the difference; suppose we go somewhere to-night!—I love to do things with spirit!— Come, Ladies, where shall we go? For my part, I should like Foote's,[64]—but the Ladies must chuse; I never speak myself.'

'Well, Mr. Smith is always in such spirits!' said Miss Branghton.

'Why yes, Ma'am, yes, thank God, pretty good spirits;—I have not yet the cares of the world upon me,—I am not *married*,—ha, ha, ha,—you'll excuse me, Ladies,—but I can't help laughing!—'

No objection being made, to my great relief, we all proceeded to the little theatre in the Haymarket, where I was extremely entertained by the performance of the Minor[65] and the Commissary.[66]

They all returned hither to supper.[67]

LETTER XIV

Evelina in continuation

June 15

Yesterday morning, Madame Duval again sent me to Mr. Branghton's attended by M. Du Bois, to make some party for the evening; because she had had the vapours[68] the preceeding day, from staying at home.

As I entered the shop, I perceived the unfortunate North Briton,[69] seated in a corner, with a book in his hand. He cast his melancholy eyes up, as we came in, and, I believe, immediately recollected my face, for he started and changed colour. I delivered Madame Duval's message to Mr. Branghton; who told me I should find Polly up stairs, but that the others were gone out.

Up stairs, therefore, I went; and seated on a window, with Mr. Brown at her side, sat Miss Polly. I felt a little awkward at disturbing them, and much more so, at their behaviour afterwards: for, as soon as the common enquiries were over, Mr. Brown grew so fond,[70] and so foolish, that I was extremely disgusted. Polly, all the time, only rebuked him with, 'La now, Mr. Brown, do be quiet, can't you?—you should not behave so before company.—Why now what will Miss think of me?'— while her looks plainly shewed not merely the pleasure, but the pride which she took in his caresses.

I did not, by any means, think it necessary to punish myself by witnessing their tenderness, and, therefore, telling them I would see if Miss Branghton were returned home, I soon left them, and again descended into the shop.

'So, Miss, you've come again,' said Mr. Branghton, 'what, I suppose, you've a mind to sit a little in the shop, and see how the world goes, hay, Miss?'

I made no answer; and M. Du Bois instantly brought me a chair.

The unhappy stranger, who had risen at my entrance, again seated himself; and, though his head leaned towards his book, I could not help observing, that his eyes were most intently and earnestly turned towards me.

M. Du Bois, as well as his broken English would allow him, endeavoured to entertain us, till the return of Miss Branghton and her brother.

'Lord, how tired I am!' cried the former, 'I have not a foot to stand upon.' And then, without any ceremony, she flung herself into the chair from which I had risen to receive her.[71]

'You tired!' said the brother, 'why then what must I be, that have walked twice as far?' And with equal politeness, he paid the same compliment to M. Du Bois which his sister had done to me.

Two chairs and three stools compleated the furniture of the shop, and Mr. Branghton, who chose to keep his own seat himself, desired M. Du Bois to take another; and then, seeing that I was without any, called out to the stranger, 'Come, Mr. Macartney, lend us your stool.'

Shocked at their rudeness, I declined the offer, and approaching Miss Branghton, said, 'If you will be so good as to make room for me on your chair, there will be no occasion to disturb that gentleman.'

'Lord, what signifies that?' cried the brother, 'he has had his share of sitting, I'll be sworn.'

'And if he has not,' said the sister, 'he has a chair up stairs; and the shop is our own, I hope.'

This grossness so much disgusted me, that I took the stool, and carrying it back to Mr. Macartney myself, I returned him thanks, as civilly as I could, for his politeness, but said that I had rather stand.

He looked at me as if unaccustomed to such attention, bowed very respectfully, but neither spoke, nor yet made use of it.

I soon found that I was an object of derision to all present, except M. Du Bois, and, therefore, I begged Mr. Branghton would give me an answer for Madame Duval, as I was in haste to return.

'Well, then, Tom,—Biddy,—where have you a mind to go to-night? your Aunt and Miss want to be abroad and amongst them.'

'Why then, Papa,' said Miss Branghton, 'we'll go to Don Saltero's. Mr. Smith likes that place, so may be he'll go along with us.'

'No, no,' said the son, 'I'm for White-Conduit House,[72] so let's go there.'

'White-Conduit House, indeed?' cried his sister, 'no, Tom, that I won't.'

'Why then let it alone; nobody wants your company;—we shall do as well without you, I'll be sworn, and better too.'

'I'll tell you what Tom, if you don't hold your tongue, I'll make you repent it,—that I assure you.'

Just then, Mr. Smith came into the shop, which he seemed to intend passing through; but when he saw me, he stopped and began a most courteous enquiry after my health, protesting that, had he known I was there, he should have come down sooner. 'But, bless me, Ma'am,' added he, 'what is the reason you stand?' and then he flew to bring me the seat from which I had just parted.

'Mr. Smith, you are come in very good time,' said Mr. Branghton, 'to end a dispute between my son and daughter, about where they shall all go to-night.'

'O fie, Tom,—dispute with a lady!' cried Mr. Smith, 'Now, as for me, I'm for where you will, provided this young Lady is of the party,—one place is the same as another to me, so that it be but agreeable to the ladies,—I would go any where with you, Ma'am,' (to me) 'unless, indeed, it were to *church*;—ha, ha, ha,—you'll excuse me, Ma'am, but, really, I never could conquer my fear of a parson; ha, ha, ha,—really, ladies, I beg your pardon, for being so rude, but I can't help laughing for my life!'

'I was just saying, Mr. Smith,' said Miss Branghton, 'that I should like to go to Don Saltero's;—now pray where should *you* like to go?'

'Why really, Miss Biddy, you know I always let the ladies decide; I never fix any thing myself; but I should suppose it would be rather hot at the coffee-house,—however, pray, Ladies, settle it among yourselves,—I'm agreeable to whatever you chuse.'

It was easy for me to discover, that this man, with all his parade of *conformity*, objects to every thing that is not proposed by himself: but he is so much admired, by this family, for his *gentility*, that he thinks himself a compleat fine gentleman!

'Come,' said Mr. Branghton, 'the best way will be to put it to the vote, and then every body will speak their minds. Biddy, call Poll down stairs. We'll start fair.'

'Lord, Papa,' said Miss Branghton, 'why can't you as well send Tom?—you're always sending me of the errands.'

A dispute then ensued, but Miss Branghton was obliged to yield.

When Mr. Brown and Miss Polly made their appearance, the latter uttered many complaints of having been called, saying she did not want to come, and was very well where she was.

'Now, Ladies, your votes;' cried Mr. Smith, 'and so, Ma'am,' (to me) 'we'll begin with you. What place shall you like best?' and then, in a whisper, he added, 'I assure you, I shall say the same as you do, whether I like it or not.'

I said, that as I was ignorant what choice was in my power, I must beg to hear their decisions first. This was reluctantly assented to; and then Miss Branghton voted for Saltero's Coffee-house; her sister, for a party to *Mother Red Cap's*:[73] the brother, for White-Conduit House; Mr. Brown, for Bagnigge Wells;[74] Mr. Branghton for Saddler's Wells; and Mr. Smith for Vauxhall.

'Well now, Ma'am,' said Mr. Smith, 'we have all spoken, and so you must give the casting vote. Come, what will you fix upon?'

'Sir,' answered I, 'I was to speak *last*.'

'Well, so you will,' said Miss Branghton, 'for we've all spoke first.'

'Pardon me,' returned I, 'the voting has not yet been quite general.'

And I looked towards Mr. Macartney, to whom I wished extremely to shew that I was not of the same brutal nature with those by whom he was treated so grossly.

'Why pray,' said Mr. Branghton, 'who have we left out? would you have the cats and dogs vote?'

'No Sir,' cried I, with some spirit, 'I would have *that gentleman* vote,—if, indeed, he is not superior to joining our party.'

They all looked at me, as if they doubted whether or not they had heard me right: but, in a few moments, their surprise gave way to a rude burst of laughter.

Very much displeased, I told M. Du Bois that if he was not ready to go, I would have a coach called for myself.

O yes, he said, he was always ready to attend me.

Mr. Smith then advancing, attempted to take my hand, and begged me not to leave them till I had settled the evening's plan.

'I have nothing, Sir,' said I, 'to do with it, as it is my intention to stay at home; and therefore Mr. Branghton will be so good as to send Madame Duval word what place is fixed upon, when it is convenient to him.'

And then, making a slight courtsie, I left them.

How much does my disgust for these people increase my pity for poor Mr. Macartney! I will not see them when I can avoid so doing; but I am determined to take every opportunity in my power, to shew civility to this unhappy man, whose misfortunes, with this family, only render him an object of scorn. I was, however, very well pleased with M. Du Bois, who, far from joining in their mirth, expressed himself extremely shocked at their ill-breeding.

We had not walked ten yards before we were followed by Mr. Smith, who came to make excuses, and to assure me they were *only joking*,[75] and hoped I took nothing ill, for, if I did, he would make a quarrel of it himself with the Branghtons, rather than I should receive any offence.

I begged him not to take any trouble about so immaterial an affair, and assured him I should not myself. He was so officious, that he would not be prevailed upon to return home, till he had walked with us to Mr. Dawkins's.

Madame Duval was very much displeased that I brought her so little satisfaction. White-Conduit House was, at last, fixed upon; and, notwithstanding my great dislike of such parties and such places, I was obliged to accompany them.

Very disagreeable, and much according to my expectations, the evening proved. There were many people all smart and gaudy, and so pert and low-bred, that I could hardly endure being amongst them; but the party to which, unfortunately, I belonged, seemed all *at home*.

LETTER XV

Evelina in continuation

Holborn, June 17th

Yesterday Mr. Smith carried his point, of making a party for Vauxhall, consisting of Madame Duval, M. Du Bois, all the Branghtons, Mr. Brown, himself,—and me!—for I find all endeavours vain to escape any thing which these people desire I should not.

There were twenty disputes previous to our setting out; first, as to the *time* of our going. Mr. Branghton, his son, and young Brown, were for six o'clock; and all the ladies and Mr. Smith were for eight;—the latter, however, conquered.

Then, as to the *way* we should go; some were for a boat, others for a coach, and Mr. Branghton himself was for walking: but the boat,[76] at length, was decided upon. Indeed this was the only part of the expedition that was agreeable to me, for the Thames was delightfully pleasant.

The Garden is very pretty, but too formal; I should have been better pleased, had it consisted less of strait walks, where

Grove nods at grove, each alley has its brother.[77]

The trees, the numerous lights, and the company in the circle round the orchestra make a most brilliant and gay appearance; and, had I been with a party less disagreeable to me, I should have thought it a place formed for animation and pleasure. There was a concert, in the course of which, a hautboy[78] concerto was so charmingly played, that I could have thought myself upon enchanted ground, had I had spirits more gentle to associate with. The hautboy in the open air is heavenly.

Mr. Smith endeavoured to attach himself to me, with such officious assiduity, and impertinent freedom, that he quite sickened me. Indeed, M. Du Bois was the only man of the party to whom, voluntarily, I ever addressed myself. He is civil and respectful, and I have found nobody else so since I left Howard Grove. His English is very bad, but I prefer it to speaking French myself, which I dare not venture to do.[79] I converse with him frequently, both to disengage myself from others, and to oblige Madame Duval, who is always pleased when he is attended to.

As we were walking about the orchestra, I heard a bell ring, and, in a moment, Mr. Smith, flying up to me, caught my hand, and, with a motion too quick to be resisted, ran away with me many yards before I had breath to ask his meaning, though I struggled as well as I could to get from him. At last, however, I insisted upon stopping; 'Stopping, Ma'am!' cried he, 'why, we must run on, or we shall lose the cascade!'[80]

And then again, he hurried me away, mixing with a crowd of people, all running with so much velocity, that I could not imagine what had raised such an alarm. We were soon followed by the rest of the party; and my surprise and ignorance proved a source of diversion to them all, which was not exhausted the whole evening. Young Branghton, in particular, laughed till he could hardly stand.

The scene of the cascade I thought extremely pretty, and the general effect striking and lively.

But this was not the only surprise which was to divert them at my expence; for they led me about the garden, purposely to enjoy my first sight of various other deceptions.[81]

About ten o'clock, Mr. Smith having chosen a *box* in a very conspicuous place, we all went to supper.[82] Much fault was found with every thing that was ordered, though not a morsel of any thing was left; and the dearness of the provisions, with conjectures upon what profit was made by them, supplied discourse during the whole meal.

When wine and cyder were brought, Mr. Smith said, 'Now let's enjoy ourselves; now is the time, or never. Well, Ma'am, and how do you like Vauxhall?'

'Like it!' cried young Branghton, 'why, how can she help liking it? She has never seen such a place before, that I'll answer for.'

'For my part,' said Miss Branghton, 'I like it because it is not vulgar.'

'This must have been a fine treat for you, Miss,' said Mr. Branghton; 'why, I suppose you was never so happy in all your life before?'

I endeavoured to express my satisfaction with some pleasure, yet I believe they were much amazed at my coldness.

'Miss ought to stay in town till the last night,' said young Branghton, 'and then, it's my belief, she'd say something to it! Why, Lord, it's the best night of any; there's always a riot,[83]— and there the folks run about,—and then there's such squealing and squalling!—and there all the lamps are broke,—and the women run skimper scamper,[84]—I declare I would not take five guineas to miss the last night!'

I was very glad when they all grew tired of sitting, and called for the waiter to pay the bill. The Miss Branghtons said they would walk on, while the gentlemen settled the account, and asked me to accompany them; which, however, I declined.

'You girls may do as you please,' said Madame Duval, 'but as to me, I promise you, I sha'n't go no where without the gentlemen.'

'No more, I suppose, will my *Cousin*,' said Miss Branghton, looking reproachfully towards Mr. Smith.

This reflection, which I feared would flatter his vanity, made me, most unfortunately, request Madame Duval's permission to attend them. She granted it, and away we went, having promised to meet in the room.[85]

To the room therefore, I would immediately have gone: but the sisters agreed that they would first have a *little pleasure*, and they tittered, and talked so loud, that they attracted universal notice.

'Lord, Polly,' said the eldest, 'suppose we were to take a turn in the dark walks!'[86]

'Ay, do,' answered she, 'and then we'll hide ourselves, and then Mr. Brown will think we are lost.'

I remonstrated very warmly against this plan, telling them that it would endanger our missing the rest of the party all the evening.

'O dear,' cried Miss Branghton, 'I thought how uneasy Miss would be, without a beau!'

This impertinence I did not think worth answering; and, quite by compulsion, I followed them down a long alley, in which there was hardly any light.

By the time we came near the end, a large party of gentlemen, apparently very riotous, and who were hallowing, leaning on one another, and laughing immoderately, seemed to rush suddenly from behind some trees, and, meeting us face to face, put their arms at their sides, and formed a kind of circle, which first stopped our proceeding, and then our retreating, for we were presently entirely enclosed. The Miss Branghtons screamed aloud, and I was frightened exceedingly: our screams were answered with bursts of laughter, and, for some minutes, we were kept prisoners, till, at last, one of them, rudely, seizing hold of me, said I was a pretty little creature.

Terrified to death, I struggled with such vehemence to disengage myself from him, that I succeeded, in spite of his efforts to detain me; and immediately, and with a swiftness which fear only could have given me, I flew rather than ran up the walk, hoping to secure my safety by returning to the lights and company we had so foolishly left: but, before I could possibly accomplish my purpose, I was met by another party of men, one of whom placed himself so directly in my way, calling out, 'Whither so fast, my love?'—that I could only have proceeded, by running into his arms.

In a moment, both my hands, by different persons, were caught hold of; and one of them, in a most familiar manner, desired, when I ran next, to accompany me in a race; while the rest of the party stood still and laughed.

I was almost distracted with terror, and so breathless with running, that I could not speak, till another advancing, said, I was as handsome as an angel, and desired to be of the party. I then just articulated, 'For Heaven's sake, Gentlemen, let me pass!'

Another, then, rushing suddenly forward, exclaimed, 'Heaven and earth! what voice is that?—'

'The voice of the prettiest little actress[87] I have seen this age,' answered one of my persecutors.

'No,—no,—no,—' I *panted* out, 'I am no actress,—pray let me go,—pray let me pass—'

'By all that's sacred,' cried the same voice, which I then knew for Sir Clement Willoughby's, ''tis herself!'

'Sir Clement Willoughby!' cried I. 'O Sir, assist—assist me—or I shall die with terror!—'

'Gentlemen,' cried he, disengaging them all from me in an instant, 'pray leave this lady to me.'

Loud laughs proceeded from every mouth, and two or three said, '*Willoughby has all the luck!*' But one of them, in a passionate manner, vowed he would not give me up, for that he had the first right to me, and would support it.

'You are mistaken,' said Sir Clement, 'this lady is—I will explain myself to you another time; but, I assure you, you are all mistaken.'

And then, taking my willing hand, he led me off, amidst the loud acclamations, laughter, and gross merriment of his impertinent companions.

As soon as we had escaped from them, Sir Clement, with a voice of surprise, exclaimed, 'My dearest creature, what wonder, what strange revolution, has brought you to such a spot as this?'

Ashamed of my situation, and extremely mortified to be thus recognized by him, I was for some time silent, and when he repeated his question, only stammered out, 'I have,—I hardly know how,—lost myself from my party.—'

He caught my hand, and eagerly pressing it, in a passionate voice, said, 'O that I had sooner met with thee!'

Surprised at a freedom so unexpected, I angrily broke from him, saying, 'Is this the protection you give me, Sir Clement?'

And then I saw, what the perturbation of my mind had prevented my sooner noticing, that he had led me, though I know not how, into another of the dark alleys, instead of the place whither I meant to go.

'Good God!' I cried, 'where am I?—What way are you going?—'

'Where,' answered he, 'we shall be least observed.'

Astonished at this speech, I stopped short, and declared I would go no further.

'And why not, my angel?' again endeavouring to take my hand.

My heart beat with resentment; I pushed him away from me with all my strength, and demanded how he dared treat me with such insolence?

'Insolence!' repeated he.

'Yes, Sir Clement, *insolence*; from you, who know me, I had a claim for protection,—not to such treatment as this.'

'By heaven,' cried he with warmth, 'you distract me,—why, tell me,—why do I see you here?—Is this a place for Miss Anville?—these dark walks!—no party!—no companion!—by all that's good, I can scarce believe my senses!'

Extremely offended at this speech, I turned angrily from him, and, not deigning to make any answer, walked on towards that part of the garden whence I perceived the lights and company.

He followed me; but we were both some time silent.

'So you will not explain to me your situation?' said he, at length.

'No, Sir,' answered I, disdainfully.

'Nor yet—suffer me to make my own interpretation?—'

I could not bear this strange manner of speaking; it made my very soul shudder,—and I burst into tears.

He flew to me, and actually flung himself at my feet, as if regardless who might see him, saying, 'O Miss Anville—loveliest of women—forgive my—my—I beseech you forgive me;—if I have offended,—if I have hurt you—I could kill myself at the thought!—'

'No matter, Sir, no matter,' cried I, 'if I can but find my friends,—I will never speak to—never see you again!'

'Good God!—good Heaven!—my dearest life, what is it I have done?—what is it I have said?—'

'You best know, Sir, *what* and *why*;—but don't hold me here,—let *me* be gone; and do *you*!'

'Not till you forgive me!—I cannot part with you in anger.'

'For shame, for shame, Sir!' cried I indignantly, 'do you suppose I am to be thus compelled?—do you take advantage of the absence of my friends, to affront me?'

'No, Madam,' cried he, rising, 'I would sooner forfeit my life than act so mean a part. But you have flung me into amazement unspeakable, and you will not condescend to listen to my request of giving me some explanation.'

'The manner, Sir,' said I, 'in which you spoke that request, made, and will make me scorn to answer it.'

'Scorn!—I will own to you, I expected not such displeasure from Miss Anville.'

'Perhaps, Sir, if you had, you would less voluntarily have merited it.'

'My dearest life, surely it must be known to you, that the man does not breathe, who adores you so passionately, so fervently, so tenderly as I do!—why then will you delight in perplexing me?—in keeping me in suspence—in torturing me with doubt?—'

'I, Sir, delight in perplexing you!—You are much mistaken.— Your suspence, your doubts, your perplexities,—are of your own creating; and believe me, Sir, they may *offend*, but they can never *delight* me:—but, as you have yourself raised, you must yourself satisfy them.'

'Good God!—that such haughtiness and such sweetness can inhabit the same mansion!'

I made no answer, but quickening my pace, I walked on silently and sullenly; till this most impetuous of men, snatching my hand, which he grasped with violence, besought me to forgive him, with such earnestness of supplication, that, merely to escape his importunities, I was forced to speak, and, in some measure, to grant the pardon he requested: though it was accorded with a very ill grace: but, indeed, I knew not how to resist the humility of his entreaties: yet never shall I recollect the occasion he gave me of displeasure, without feeling it renewed.

We now soon arrived in the midst of the general crowd, and my own safety being then insured, I grew extremely uneasy for the Miss Branghtons, whose danger, however imprudently in-

curred by their own folly, I too well knew how to tremble for.
To this consideration all my pride of heart yielded, and I
determined to seek my party with the utmost speed; though not
without a sigh did I recollect the fruitless attempt I had made,
after the opera, of concealing from this man my unfortunate
connections, which I was now obliged to make known.

I hastened, therefore, to the room, with a view of sending
young Branghton to the aid of his sisters. In a very short time, I
perceived Madame Duval, and the rest, looking at one of the
paintings. I must own to you, honestly, my dear Sir, that an
involuntary repugnance seized me, at presenting such a set to Sir
Clement,—he, who had been used to see me in parties so
different!—My pace slackened as I approached them,—but they
presently perceived me.

'*Ah, Mademoiselle!*' cried M. Du Bois, '*Que je suis charmé de vous
voir!*'[88]

'Pray, Miss,' cried Mr. Brown, 'where's Miss Polly?'

'Why, Miss, you've been a long while gone,' said Mr. Branghton; 'we thought you'd been lost. But what have you done with
your cousins?'

I hesitated,—for Sir Clement regarded me with a look of
wonder.

'*Pardi,*' cried Madame Duval, 'I sha'n't let you leave me again
in a hurry. Why, here we've been in such a fright!—and, all the
while, I suppose you've been thinking nothing about the
matter.'

'Well,' said young Branghton, 'as long as Miss is come back, I
don't mind, for as to Bid and Poll, they can take care of
themselves. But the best joke is, Mr. Smith is gone all about a-
looking for you.'

These speeches were made almost all in a breath: but when, at
last, they waited for an answer, I told them, that in walking up
one of the long alleys, we had been frightened and separated.

'The long alleys!' repeated Mr. Branghton, 'and, pray, what
had you to do in the long alleys? why, to be sure, you must all of
you have had a mind to be affronted!'[89]

This speech was not more impertinent to me, than surprising

to Sir Clement, who regarded all the party with evident astonishment. However, I told young Branghton that no time ought to be lost, for that his sisters might require his immediate protection.

'But how will they get it?' cried this brutal brother; 'if they've a mind to behave in such a manner as that, they ought to protect themselves; and so they may for me.'

'Well,' said the simple Mr. Brown, 'whether you go or no, I think I may as well see after Miss Polly.'

The father, then, interfering, insisted that his son should accompany him; and away they went.

It was now that Madame Duval first perceived Sir Clement; to whom turning with a look of great displeasure, she angrily said, '*Ma foi*, so you are comed here, of all the people in the world!—I wonder, child, you would let such a—such a *person* as that keep company with you.'

'I am very sorry, Madam,' said Sir Clement, in a tone of surprise, 'if I have been so unfortunate as to offend you; but I believe you will not regret the honour I now have of attending Miss Anville, when you hear that I have been so happy as to do her some service.'

Just as Madame Duval, with her usual *Ma foi*, was beginning to reply, the attention of Sir Clement was wholly drawn from her, by the appearance of Mr. Smith, who coming suddenly behind me, and freely putting his hands on my shoulders, cried, 'O ho, my little runaway, have I found you at last? I have been scampering all over the gardens for you, for I was determined to find you, if you were above ground.—But how could you be so cruel as to leave us?'

I turned round to him, and looked with a degree of contempt that I hoped would have quieted him; but he had not the sense to understand me; and, attempting to take my hand, he added, 'Such a demure looking lady as you are, who'd have thought of your leading one such a dance?—Come, now, don't be so coy,—only think what a trouble I have had in running after you!'

'The trouble, Sir,' said I, 'was of your own choice,—not mine.' And I walked round to the other side of Madame Duval.

Perhaps I was too proud,—but I could not endure that Sir Clement, whose eyes followed him with looks of the most surprised curiosity, should witness his unwelcome familiarity.

Upon my removal, he came up to me, and, in a low voice, said, 'You are not, then, with the Mirvans?'

'No, Sir.'

'And pray—may I ask,—have you left them long?'

'No, Sir.'

'How unfortunate I am!—but yesterday I sent to acquaint the Captain I should reach the Grove by to-morrow noon! However, I shall get away as fast as possible. Shall you be long in town?'

'I believe not, Sir.'

'And then, when you leave it,—which way—will you allow me to ask, which way you shall travel?'

'Indeed,—I don't know.'

'Not know!—But do you return to the Mirvans any more?'

'I—I can't tell, Sir.'

And then, I addressed myself to Madame Duval, with such a pretended earnestness, that he was obliged to be silent.

As he cannot but observe the great change in my situation, which he knows not how to account for, there is something in all these questions, and this unrestrained curiosity, that I did not expect from a man, who when he pleases can be so well-bred, as Sir Clement Willoughby. He seems disposed to think that the alteration in my companions authorizes an alteration in his manners. It is true, he has always treated me with uncommon freedom, but never before with so disrespectful an abruptness. This observation, which he has given me cause to make, of his *changing with the tide*, has sunk him more in my opinion, than any other part of his conduct.

Yet I could almost have laughed, when I looked at Mr. Smith, who no sooner saw me addressed by Sir Clement, than, retreating aloof from the company, he seemed to lose at once all his happy self-sufficiency and conceit; looking now at the baronet, now at himself, surveying, with sorrowful eyes, his dress, struck with his air, his gestures, his easy gaiety; he gazed at him with envious admiration, and seemed himself, with conscious inferiority, to shrink into nothing.

Soon after, Mr. Brown, running up to us, called out, 'La, what, i'n't Miss Polly come yet?'

'Come!' said Mr. Branghton, 'why, I thought you went to fetch her yourself, did n't you?'

'Yes, but I could n't find her;—yet I dare say I've been over half the garden.'

'Half! but why did not you go over it all?'

'Why, so I will: but only I thought I'd just come and see if she was here first?'

'But where's Tom?'

'Why, I don't know; for he would not stay with me, all as ever I could say; for we met some young gentlemen of his acquaintance, and so he bid me go and look by myself, for he said, says he, I can divert myself better another way, says he.'

This account being given, away again went this silly young man! and Mr. Branghton, extremely incensed, said he would go and see after them himself.

'So now,' cried Madame Duval, 'he's gone too! why, at this rate we shall have to wait for one or other of them all night!'

Observing that Sir Clement seemed disposed to renew his enquiries, I turned towards one of the paintings,⁹⁰ and, pretending to be very much occupied in looking at it, asked M. Du Bois some questions concerning the figures.

'O, *Mon Dieu!*' cried Madame Duval, 'don't ask him; your best way is to ask Mr. Smith, for he's been here the oftenest. Come, Mr. Smith, I dare say you can tell us all about them.'

'Why, yes, Ma'am, yes,' said Mr. Smith, who, brightening up at this application, advanced towards us, with an air of assumed importance, which, however, sat very uneasily upon him, and begged to know what he should explain first; 'For I have attended,' said he, 'to all these paintings, and know every thing in them perfectly well; for I am rather fond of pictures, Ma'am; and, really, I must say, I think a pretty picture is a—a very—is really a very—is something very pretty.—'

'So do I too,' said Madame Duval, 'but pray now, Sir, tell us who that is meant for,' pointing to a figure of Neptune.

'That!—why that, Ma'am, is,—Lord bless me, I can't think

how I come to be so stupid, but really I have forgot his name,—
and yet, I know it as well as my own, too,—however, he's a
General, Ma'am, they are all Generals.'

I saw Sir Clement bite his lips; and, indeed, so did I mine.

'Well,' said Madame Duval, 'it's the oddest dress for a General
ever I see!'

'He seems so capital a figure,' said Sir Clement to Mr. Smith,
'that I imagine he must be *Generalissimo*[91] of the whole army.'

'Yes, Sir, yes,' answered Mr. Smith, respectfully bowing, and
highly delighted at being thus referred to, 'you are perfectly
right,—but I cannot for my life think of his name;—perhaps,
Sir, you may remember it?'

'No, really,' replied Sir Clement, 'my acquaintance among the
Generals is not so extensive.'

The ironical tone of voice in which Sir Clement spoke,
entirely disconcerted Mr. Smith; who, again retiring to an humble
distance, seemed sensibly mortified at the failure of his attempt
to recover his consequence.

Soon after, Mr. Branghton returned, with his youngest daughter, whom he had rescued from a party of insolent young men;
but he had not yet been able to find the eldest. Miss Polly was
really frightened, and declared she would never go into the dark
walks again. Her father, leaving her with us, went in quest of
her sister.

While she was relating her adventures, to which nobody
listened more attentively than Sir Clement, we saw Mr. Brown
enter the room. 'O la!' cried Miss Polly, 'let me hide myself, and
don't tell him I'm come.'

She then placed herself behind Madame Duval, in such a
manner that she could not be seen.

'So Miss Polly is not come yet!' said the simple swain;[92] 'well,
I can't think where she can be! I've been a-looking, and looking,
and looking all about, and I can't find her, all I can do.'

'Well but, Mr. Brown,' said Mr. Smith, 'sha'n't you go and
look for the lady again?'

'Yes, Sir,' said he, sitting down, 'but I must rest me a little bit
first. You can't think how tired I am.'

'O fie, Mr. Brown, fie,' cried Mr. Smith, winking at us, 'tired of looking for a lady! Go, go, for shame!'

'So I will, Sir, presently; but you'd be tired too, if you'd walked so far: besides, I think she's gone out of the garden, or else I must have seen something or other of her.'

A *he, he, he*! of the tittering Polly, now betrayed her, and so ended this ingenious little artifice.

At last appeared Mr. Branghton and Miss Biddy, who, with a face of mixed anger and confusion, addressing herself to me, said, 'So Miss, so you ran away from me! Well, see if I don't do as much by you, some day or other! But I thought how it would be, you'd no mind to leave the *gentlemen*, though you'd run away from *me*.'

I was so much surprised at this attack, that I could not answer her for very amazement; and she proceeded to tell us how ill she had been used, and that two young men had been making her walk up and down the dark walks by absolute force, and as fast as ever they could tear her along; and many other particulars, which I will not tire you with relating. In conclusion, looking at Mr. Smith, she said, 'But, to be sure, thought I, at least all the company will be looking for me; so I little expected to find you all here, talking as comfortably as ever you can. However, I know I may thank my cousin for it!'

'If you mean *me*, Madam,' said I, very much shocked, 'I am quite ignorant in what manner I can have been accessary to your distress.'

'Why, by running away so. If you'd stayed with us, I'll answer for it, Mr. Smith, and M. Du Bois would have come to look for us; but I suppose they could not leave your ladyship.'

The folly and unreasonableness of this speech would admit of no answer. But what a scene was this for Sir Clement! his surprise was evident; and, I must acknowledge, my confusion was equally great.

We had now to wait for young Branghton, who did not appear for some time; and, during this interval, it was with difficulty that I avoided Sir Clement, who was on the rack of curiosity, and dying to speak to me.

When, at last, the hopeful youth returned, a long and frightful quarrel ensued between him and his father, in which his sisters occasionally joined, concerning his neglect; and he defended himself only by a brutal mirth, which he indulged at their expence.

Every one, now, seemed inclined to depart,—when, as usual, a dispute arose, upon the *way* of our going, whether in a coach or a boat. After much debating, it was determined that we should make two parties, one by the water and the other by land; for Madame Duval declared she would not, upon any account, go into a boat at night.

Sir Clement then said, that if she had no carriage in waiting, he should be happy to see her and me safe home, as his was in readiness.

Fury started into her eyes, and passion inflamed every feature, as she answered, '*Pardi*, no—you may take care of yourself, if you please; but as to me, I promise you I shan't trust myself with no such person.'

He pretended not to comprehend her meaning, yet, to wave a discussion, acquiesced in her refusal. The coach party fixed upon consisted of Madame Duval, M. Du Bois, Miss Branghton, and myself.

I now began to rejoice, in private, that, at least, our lodgings would be neither seen nor known by Sir Clement. We soon met with a hackney coach, into which he handed me, and then took leave.

Madame Duval, having already given the coachman her direction, he mounted the box, and we were just driving off, when Sir Clement exclaimed, 'By Heaven, this is the very coach I had in waiting for myself!'[93]

'This coach, your honour!' said the man, 'no, that it i'n't.'

Sir Clement, however, swore that it was, and, presently, the man, begging his pardon, said he had really forgotten that he was engaged.

I have no doubt but that this scheme occurred to him at the moment, and that he made some sign to the coachman, which induced him to support it: for there is not the least probability that the accident really happened, as it is most likely his own chariot was in waiting.

The man then opened the coach-door, and Sir Clement advancing to it, said, 'I don't believe there is another carriage to be had, or I would not incommode you; but, as it may be disagreeable to you to wait here any longer, I beg you will not get out, for you shall be set down before I am carried home, if you will be so good as to make a little room.'

And so saying, in he jumps, and seated himself between M. Du Bois and me, while our astonishment at the whole transaction was too great for speech. He then ordered the coachman to drive on, according to the directions he had already received.

For the first ten minutes, no one uttered a word; and then, Madame Duval, no longer able to contain herself, exclaimed, '*Ma foi*, if this is n't one of the impudentest things ever I see!'

Sir Clement, regardless of this rebuke, attended only to me; however, I answered nothing he said, when I could possibly avoid so doing. Miss Branghton made several attempts to attract his notice, but in vain, for he would not take the trouble of paying her any regard.

Madame Duval, during the rest of the ride, addressed herself to M. Du Bois in French, and in that language exclaimed with great vehemence against boldness and assurance.

I was extremely glad when I thought our journey must be nearly at an end, for my situation was very uneasy to me, as Sir Clement perpetually endeavoured to take my hand. I looked out of the coach-window, to see if we were near home; Sir Clement, stooping over me did the same, and then, in a voice of infinite wonder, called out, 'Where the d—l is the man driving to?—why we are in broad St. Giles's!'[94]

'O, he's very right,' cried Madame Duval, 'so never trouble your head about that, for I sha'n't go by no directions of yours, I promise you.'

When, at last, we stopped, at *a Hosier's* in *High Holborn*[95]—Sir Clement said nothing, but his *eyes*, I saw, were very busily employed in viewing the place, and the situation of the house. The coach, he said, belonged to him, and therefore he insisted upon paying for it; and then he took leave. M. Du Bois walked home with Miss Branghton, and Madame Duval and I retired to our apartments.

How disagreeable an evening's adventure! not one of the party seemed satisfied, except Sir Clement, who was in high spirits: but Madame Duval, was enraged at meeting with him; Mr. Branghton, angry with his children; the frolic of the Miss Branghtons had exceeded their plan, and ended in their own distress; their brother was provoked that there had been no riot; Mr. Brown was tired; and Mr. Smith mortified. As to myself, I must acknowledge, nothing could be more disagreeable to me, than being seen by Sir Clement Willoughby with a party at once so vulgar in themselves, and so familiar to me.

And you, too, my dear Sir, will, I know, be sorry that I have met him; however, there is no apprehension of his visiting here, as Madame Duval is far too angry to admit him.

LETTER XVI

Evelina in continuation

Holborn, June 18th

Madame Duval rose very late this morning, and, at one o'clock, we had but just breakfasted, when Miss Branghton, her brother, Mr. Smith, and Monsieur Du Bois, called to enquire after our healths.

This civility in young Branghton, I much suspect, was merely the result of his father's commands; but his sister and Mr. Smith, I soon found, had motives of their own. Scarce had they spoken to Madame Duval, when, advancing eagerly to me, 'Pray, Ma'am,' said Mr. Smith, 'Who was that gentleman?'

'Pray, Cousin,' cried Miss Branghton, 'was not he the same gentleman you ran away with that night at the opera?'

'Goodness! that he was,' said young Branghton; 'and, I declare, as soon as ever I saw him, I thought I knew his face.'

'I'm sure I'll defy you to forget him,' answered his sister, 'if once you had seen him: he is the finest gentleman I ever saw in my life; don't you think so, Mr. Smith?'

'Why, you won't give the Lady time to speak,' said Mr. Smith.——'Pray, Ma'am, what is the gentleman's name?'

'Willoughby, Sir.'

'Willoughby! I think I have heard the name. Pray, Ma'am, is he married?'

'Lord, no, that he is not,' cried Miss Branghton; 'he looks too smart, by a great deal, for a married man. Pray, Cousin, how did you get acquainted with him?'

'Pray, Miss,' said young Branghton, in the same breath, 'what's his business?'

'Indeed I don't know,' answered I.

'Something very genteel, I dare say,' added Miss Branghton, 'because he dresses so fine.'

'It ought to be something that brings in a good income,' said Mr. Smith, 'for I'm sure he did not get that suit of cloaths he had on, under thirty or forty pounds; for I know the price of cloaths pretty well;—pray, Ma'am, can you tell me what he has a year?'

'Don't talk no more about him,' cried Madame Duval, 'for I don't like to hear his name; I believe he's one of the worst persons in the world; for though I never did him no manner of harm, nor so much as hurt a hair of his head, I know he was an accomplice with that fellow, Captain Mirvan, to take away my life.'

Every body but myself, now crowding around her for an explanation, a violent rapping at the street-door was unheard; and, without any previous notice, in the midst of her narration, Sir Clement Willoughby entered the room. They all started, and, with looks of guilty confusion, as if they feared his resentment for having listened to Madame Duval, they scrambled for chairs, and, in a moment were all formally seated.

Sir Clement, after a general bow, singling out Madame Duval, said, with his usual easiness, 'I have done myself the honour of waiting on you, Madam, to enquire if you have any commands to Howard Grove, whither I am going to-morrow morning.'

Then, seeing the storm that gathered in her eyes, before he allowed her time to answer, he addressed himself to me;—'And if you, Madam, have any with which you will honour me, I shall be happy to execute them.'

'None at all, Sir.'

'None!—not to Miss Mirvan!—no message! no letter!—'

'I wrote to Miss Mirvan yesterday by the post.'

'My application should have been earlier, had I sooner known your address.'

'*Ma foi*,' cried Madame Duval, recovering from her surprise, 'I believe never nobody saw the like of this!'

'Of what! Madam!' cried the undaunted Sir Clement, turning quick towards her. 'I hope no one has offended you!'

'You don't hope no such a thing!' cried she, half choaked with passion, and rising from her chair. This motion was followed by the rest, and, in a moment, every body stood up.

Still Sir Clement was not abashed; affecting to make a bow of *acknowledgement* to the company in general, he said, 'Pray—I beg—Ladies,—Gentlemen,—pray don't let me disturb you, pray keep your seats.'

'Pray, Sir,' said Miss Branghton, moving a chair towards him, 'won't you sit down yourself?'

'You are extremely good, Ma'am:—rather than make any disturbance—'

And so saying, this strange man seated himself, as did, in an instant, every body else, even Madame Duval herself, who, overpowered by his boldness, seemed too full for utterance.

He then, and with as much composure as if he had been an expected guest, began to discourse on the weather,—its uncertainty,—the heat of the public places in summer,—the emptiness of the town,—and other such common topics.

Nobody, however, answered him; Mr. Smith seemed afraid, young Branghton ashamed, M. Du Bois amazed, Madame Duval enraged, and myself determined not to interfere. All that he could obtain, was the notice of Miss Branghton, whose nods, smiles, and attention, had some appearance of entering into conversation with him.

At length, growing tired, I suppose, of engaging every body's eyes, and nobody's tongue; addressing himself to Madame Duval and to me, he said, 'I regard myself as peculiarly unfortunate, Ladies, in having fixed upon a time for my visit to Howard Grove, when you are absent from it.'

'So I suppose, Sir, so I suppose,' cried Madame Duval, hastily rising, and the next moment as hastily seating herself,—'you'll be a-wanting of somebody to make your game of, and so you may think to get *me* there again;—but, I promise you, Sir, you won't find it so easy a matter to make me a fool: and besides that,' raising her voice, 'I've found you out, I assure you; so if ever you go to play your tricks upon me again, I'll make no more ado, but go directly to a justice of peace; so, Sir, if you can't think of nothing but making people ride about the country, at all hours of the night, just for your diversion, why you'll find I know some justices, as well as Justice Tyrell.'[96]

Sir Clement was evidently embarrassed at this attack; yet he affected a look of surprise, and protested he did not understand her meaning.

'Well,' cried she, 'if I don't wonder where people can get such impudence! if you'll say that, you'll say any thing; however, if you swear till you're black in the face, I sha'n't believe you; for nobody sha'n't persuade me out of my senses, that I'm resolved.'

'Doubtless not, Madam,' answered he with some hesitation, 'and I hope you do not suspect I ever had such an intention; my respect for you—'

'O Sir, you're vastly polite, all of a sudden! but I know what it's all for;—it's only for what you can get!—you could treat me like nobody at Howard Grove—but now you see I've a house of my own you've a mind to wheedle yourself into it; but I sees your design, so you need n't trouble yourself to take no more trouble about that, for you shall never get nothing at my house,—not so much as a dish of tea:—so now, Sir, you see I can play you trick for trick.'

There was something so extremely gross in this speech, that it even disconcerted Sir Clement, who was too much confounded to make any answer.

It was curious to observe the effect which his embarrassment, added to the freedom with which Madame Duval addressed him, had upon the rest of the company: every one, who, before, seemed at a loss how, or if at all, to occupy a chair, now filled it with the most easy composure: and Mr. Smith, whose countenance had exhibited the most striking picture of mortified envy, now began to recover his usual expression of satisfied conceit. Young Branghton, too, who had been apparently awed by the presence of so fine a gentleman, was again himself, rude and familiar; while his mouth was wide distended into a broad grin, at hearing *his aunt give the beau such a trimming.*[97]

Madame Duval encouraged by this success, looked around her with an air of triumph, and continued her harangue: 'And so, Sir, I suppose you thought to have had it all your own way, and to have comed here as often as you pleased, and to have got me to Howard Grove again, on purpose to have served me as you did before; but you shall see I'm as cunning as you, so you may go and find somebody else to use in that manner, and to put your mask on, and to make a fool of; for as to me, if you go to tell me your stories about the Tower again, for a month together, I'll never believe 'em no more; and I'll promise you, Sir, if you think I like such jokes, you'll find I'm no such person.'

'I assure you, Ma'am,—upon my honour—I really don't comprehend—I fancy there is some misunderstanding—'

'What, I suppose you'll tell me next you don't know nothing of the matter?'

'Not a word, upon my honour.'

O Sir Clement! thought I, is it thus you prize your honour!

'*Pardi*,' cried Madame Duval, 'this is the most provokingest part of all! why you might as well tell me I don't know my own name.'

'Here is certainly some mistake; for I assure you, Ma'am—'

'Don't assure me nothing,' cried Madame Duval, raising her voice, 'I know what I'm saying, and so do you too; for did not you tell me all that about the Tower, and about M. Du Bois?—

why M. Du Bois was n't never there, nor nigh it, and so it was all your own invention.'

'May there not be two persons of the same name? the mistake was but natural.—'

'Don't tell me of no mistake, for it was all on purpose; besides, did not you come, all in a mask, to the chariot-door, and help to get me put in that ditch?—I'll promise you, I've had the greatest mind in the world to take the law of you ever since, and if ever you do as much again, so I will, I assure you!'

Here Miss Branghton tittered; Mr. Smith smiled contemptuously, and young Branghton thrust his handkerchief into his mouth to stop his laughter.

The situation of Sir Clement, who saw all that passed, became now very awkward, even to himself, and he stammered very much in saying, 'Surely, Madam—surely you—you cannot do me the—the injustice to think—that I had any share in the—the—the misfortune which—'

'*Ma foi*, Sir,' cried Madame Duval, with increasing passion, 'you'd best not stand talking to me at that rate; I know it *was* you,—and if you stay there a-provoking me in such a manner, I'll send for a constable[98] this minute.'

Young Branghton, at these words, in spite of all his efforts, burst into a loud laugh; nor could either his sister, or Mr. Smith, though with more moderation, forbear joining in his mirth.

Sir Clement darted his eyes towards them, with looks of the most angry contempt, and then told Madame Duval, that he would not now detain her to make his vindication, but would wait on her some time when she was alone.

'O *pardi*, Sir,' cried she, 'I don't desire none of your company; and if you was n't the most boldest person in the world, you would not dare look me in the face.'

The ha, ha, ha's, and he, he, he's, grew more and more uncontroulable, as if the restraint from which they had burst, had added to their violence. Sir Clement could no longer endure being the object who excited them, and, having no answer ready for Madame Duval, he hastily stalked towards Mr. Smith and young Branghton, and sternly demanded what they laughed at?

Struck by the air of importance which he assumed, and alarmed at the angry tone of his voice, their merriment ceased, as instantaneously as if it had been directed by clock work, and they stared foolishly, now at him, now at each other, without making any answer but a simple 'Nothing, Sir!'

'O pour le coup,'[99] cried Madame Duval, 'this is too much! pray, Sir, what business have you to come here, a-ordering people that comes to see me. I suppose next, nobody must laugh but yourself!'

'With me, Madam,' said Sir Clement, bowing, 'a lady may do any thing, and, consequently, there is no liberty in which I shall not be happy to indulge you:—but it has never been my custom to give the same licence to gentlemen.'

Then, advancing to me, who had sat very quietly, on a window, during this scene, he said, 'Miss Anville, I may at least acquaint our friends at Howard Grove, that I had the honour of leaving you in good health.' And then, lowering his voice, he added, 'For Heaven's sake, my dearest creature, who are these people? and how came you so strangely situated?'

'I beg my respects to all the family, Sir,' answered I, aloud, 'and I hope you will find them well.'

He looked at me reproachfully, but kissed my hand; and then, bowing to Madame Duval and Miss Branghton, passed hastily by the men, and made his exit.

I fancy he will not be very eager to repeat his visits, for I should imagine he has rarely, if ever, been before in a situation so awkward and disagreeable.

Madame Duval has been all spirits and exultation ever since he went, and only wishes Captain Mirvan would call, that she might do the same by him. Mr. Smith, upon hearing that he was a Baronet, and seeing him drive off in a very beautiful chariot, declared that he would not have laughed upon any account, had he known his rank, and regretted extremely having missed such an opportunity of making so genteel an acquaintance. Young Branghton vowed, that, if he had known as much, he would have asked for his custom:[100] and his sister has sung his praises ever since, protesting she thought, all along, he was a man of quality by his look.

LETTER XVII

Evelina in continuation

June 21

The last three evenings have passed tolerably quiet, for the Vauxhall adventures had given Madame Duval a surfeit of public places: home, however, soon growing tiresome, she determined to-night, she said, to relieve her *ennui*, by some amusement; and it was therefore settled that we should call upon the Branghtons, at their house, and thence proceed to Marybone Gardens.

But, before we reached Snow Hill, we were caught in a shower of rain: we hurried into the shop, where the first object I saw was Mr. Macartney, with a book in his hand, seated in the same corner where I saw him last; but his looks were still more wretched than before, his face yet thinner, and his eyes sunk almost hollow into his head. He lifted them up as we entered, and I even thought that they emitted a gleam of joy: involuntarily, I made to him my first courtsie; he rose and bowed, with a precipitation that manifested surprise and confusion.

In a few minutes, we were joined by all the family, except Mr. Smith, who fortunately was engaged.

Had all the future prosperity of our lives depended upon the good or bad weather of this evening, it could not have been treated as a subject of greater importance. 'Sure never any thing was so unlucky!—' 'Lord how provoking!—' 'It might rain for ever, if it would hold up now!—' These, and such expressions, with many anxious observations upon the kennels,[101] filled up all the conversation till the shower was over.

And then a very warm debate arose, whether we should pursue our plan, or defer it to some finer evening; Miss Branghtons were for the former; their father was sure it would rain again; Madame Duval, though she detested returning home, yet dreaded the dampness of the gardens.

M. Du Bois then proposed going to the top of the house, to

examine whether the clouds looked threatening or peaceable; Miss Branghton, starting at this proposal, said they might go to Mr. Macartney's room, if they would, but not to hers.[102]

This was enough for the brother; who, with a loud laugh, declared he would have some *fun*,[103] and immediately led the way, calling to us all to follow. His sisters both ran after him, but no one else moved.

In a few minutes, young Branghton, coming half-way down stairs, called out, 'Lord, why don't you all come? why here's Poll's things all about the room!'

Mr. Branghton then went, and Madame Duval, who cannot bear to be excluded from whatever is going forward, was handed up stairs by M. Du Bois.

I hesitated a few moments, whether or not to join them; but, soon perceiving that Mr. Macartney had dropped his book, and that I engrossed his whole attention, I prepared, from mere embarrassment, to follow them.

As I went, I heard him move from his chair, and walk slowly after me. Believing that he wished to speak to me, and earnestly desiring myself to know if, by your means, I could possibly be of any service to him, I first slackened my pace, and then turned back. But, though I thus met him half-way, he seemed to want courage or resolution to address me; for when he saw me returning, with a look extremely disordered, he retreated hastily from me.

Not knowing what I ought to do, I went to the street-door, where I stood some time, hoping he would be able to recover himself: but, on the contrary, his agitation increased every moment; he walked up and down the room, in a quick, but unsteady pace, seeming equally distressed and irresolute: and, at length, with a deep sigh, he flung himself into a chair.

I was so much affected by the appearance of such extreme anguish, that I could remain no longer in the room; I therefore glided by him, and went up stairs; but, ere I had gone five steps, he precipitately followed me, and, in a broken voice, called out, 'Madam!—for Heaven's sake—'

He stopped, but I instantly descended, restraining, as well as I was able, the fullness of my own concern. I waited some time, in painful expectation, for his speaking: all that I had heard of his poverty, occurring to me, I was upon the point of presenting him my purse, but the fear of mistaking or offending him, deterred me. Finding, however, that he continued silent, I ventured to say, 'Did you—Sir, wish to speak to me?'

'I did!' cried he, with quickness, 'but now—I cannot!'—

'Perhaps, Sir, another time,—perhaps if you recollect yourself—'

'Another time!' repeated he mournfully, 'alas! I look not forward but to misery and despair!'

'O Sir,' cried I, extremely shocked, 'you must not talk thus!—if you forsake *yourself*, how can you expect—'

I stopped. 'Tell me, tell me,' cried he, with eagerness, 'who you are?—whence you come?—and by what strange means you seem to be arbitress and ruler of the destiny of such a wretch as I am?'

'Would to Heaven,' cried I, 'I could serve you!'

'You can!'

'And how? pray tell me how?'

'To tell you—is death to me! yet I *will* tell you,—I have a *right* to your assistance,—you have deprived me of the only resource to which I could apply,—and therefore—'

'Pray, pray, speak;' cried I, putting my hand into my pocket, 'they will be down stairs in a moment!'

'I will, Madam.—Can you—will you—I think you will!—may I then—' he stopped and paused, 'say, will you——' then suddenly turning from me, 'Great Heaven! I cannot speak!' and he went back to the shop.

I now put my purse in my hand, and following him, said, 'If indeed, Sir, I can assist you, why should you deny me so great a satisfaction? Will you permit me to—'

I dared not go on; but with a countenance very much softened, he approached me, and said, 'Your voice, Madam, is the voice of compassion!—such a voice as these ears have long been strangers to!'

Just then, young Branghton called out vehemently to me, to

come up stairs; I seized the opportunity of hastening away: and therefore saying, 'Heaven, Sir, protect and comfort you!' I let fall my purse upon the ground, not daring to present it to him, and ran up stairs with the utmost swiftness.

Too well do I know you, my ever honoured Sir, to fear your displeasure for this action: I must, however, assure you I shall need no fresh supply during my stay in town, as I am at little expence, and hope soon to return to Howard Grove.

Soon, did I say! when not a fortnight is yet expired, of the long and tedious month I must linger out[104] here!

I had many witticisms to endure from the Branghtons, upon account of my staying so long with the *Scotch mope*, as they call him; but I attended to them very little, for my whole heart was filled with pity and concern. I was very glad to find the Marybone scheme was deferred, another shower of rain having put a stop to the dissention upon this subject; the rest of the evening was employed in most violent quarrelling between Miss Polly and her brother, on account of the discovery made by the latter, of the state of her apartment.

We came home early; and I have stolen from Madame Duval and M. Du Bois, who is here for ever, to write to my best friend.

I am most sincerely rejoiced, that this opportunity has offered for my contributing what little relief was in my power, to this unhappy man; and I hope it will be sufficient to enable him to pay his debts to this pitiless family.

LETTER XVIII

Mr. Villars to Evelina

Berry Hill

Displeasure? my Evelina!—you have but done your duty; you have but shewn that humanity without which I should blush to

own my child. It is mine, however, to see that your generosity
be not repressed by your suffering from indulging it; I remit to
you, therefore, not merely a token of my approbation, but an
acknowledgement of my desire to participate in your charity.

O my child, were my fortune equal to my confidence in thy
benevolence, with what transport should I, through thy means,
devote it to the relief of indigent virtue! yet let us not repine at
the limitation of our power, for, while our bounty is proportioned to our ability, the difference of the greater or less donation, can weigh but little in the scale of justice.

In reading your account of the misguided man, whose misery
has so largely excited your compassion, I am led to apprehend,
that his unhappy situation is less the effect of misfortune, than of
misconduct. If he is reduced to that state of poverty represented
by the Branghtons, he should endeavour by activity and industry
to retrieve his affairs; and not pass his time in idle reading in the
very shop of his creditor.

The pistol scene made me shudder: the courage with which
you pursued this desperate man, at once delighted and terrified
me. Be ever thus, my dearest Evelina, dauntless in the cause of
distress! let no weak fears, no timid doubts, deter you from the
exertion of your duty, according to the fullest sense of it that
Nature has implanted in your mind. Though gentleness and
modesty are the peculiar attributes of your sex, yet fortitude and
firmness, when occasion demands them, are virtues as noble and
as becoming in women as in men: the right line of conduct is the
same for both sexes, though the manner in which it is pursued,
may somewhat vary, and be accommodated to the strength or
weakness of the different travellers.

There is, however, something so mysterious in all you have
yet seen or heard of this wretched man, that I am unwilling to
stamp a bad impression of his character, upon so slight and
partial a knowledge of it. Where any thing is doubtful, the ties
of society, and the laws of humanity, claim a favourable interpretation; but remember, my dear child, that those of discretion have
an equal claim to your regard.

As to Sir Clement Willoughby, I know not how to express my

indignation at his conduct. Insolence so insufferable, and the implication of suspicions so shocking, irritate me to a degree of wrath, which I hardly thought my almost worn-out passions were capable of again experiencing. You must converse with him no more; he imagines, from the pliability of your temper, that he may offend you with impunity; but his behaviour justifies, nay, calls for, your avowed resentment: do not, therefore, hesitate in forbidding him your sight.

The Branghtons, Mr. Smith, and young Brown, however ill-bred and disagreeable, are objects too contemptible for serious displeasure: yet I grieve much that my Evelina should be exposed to their rudeness and impertinence.

The very day that this tedious month expires, I shall send Mrs. Clinton to town, who will accompany you to Howard Grove. Your stay there will, I hope, be short, for I feel daily an increasing impatience to fold my beloved child to my bosom!

ARTHUR VILLARS

LETTER XIX

Evelina to the Rev. Mr. Villars

Holborn, June 27th

I have just received, my dearest Sir, your kind present, and still kinder letter. Surely never had orphan so little to regret as your grateful Evelina! Though motherless, though worse than father-less, bereft from infancy of the two first and greatest blessings of life, never has she had cause to deplore their loss; never has she felt the omission of a parent's tenderness, care, or indulgence; never, but from sorrow for *them*, had reason to grieve at the separation! Most thankfully do I receive the token of your approbation, and most studiously will I endeavour so to dispose of it, as may merit your generous confidence in my conduct.

Your doubts concerning Mr. Macartney give me some uneasiness. Indeed, Sir, he has not the appearance of a man whose sorrows are the effect of guilt. But I hope, before I leave town, to be better acquainted with his situation, and enabled, with more certainty of his worth, to recommend him to your favour.

I am very willing to relinquish all acquaintance with Sir Clement Willoughby, as far as it may depend upon myself so to do; but indeed, I know not how I should be able to absolutely *forbid him my sight.*

Miss Mirvan, in her last letter, informs me that he is now at Howard Grove, where he continues in high favour with the Captain, and is the life and spirit of the house. My time, since I wrote last, has passed very quietly, Madame Duval having been kept at home by a bad cold, and the Branghtons by bad weather. The young man, indeed, has called two or three times, and his behaviour, though equally absurd, is more unaccountable than ever: he speaks very little, takes hardly any notice of Madame Duval, and never looks at me, without a broad grin. Sometimes he approaches me, as if with intention to communicate intelligence of importance, and then, suddenly stopping short, laughs rudely in my face.

O how happy shall I be, when the worthy Mrs. Clinton arrives!

June 29th

Yesterday morning, Mr. Smith called, to acquaint us that the Hampstead assembly was to be held that evening; and then he presented Madame Duval with one ticket, and brought another to me.[105] I thanked him for his intended civility, but told him I was surprised he had so soon forgotten my having already declined going to the ball.

'Lord, Ma'am,' cried he, 'how should I suppose you was in earnest? come, come, don't be cross; here's your Grand-mama ready to take care of you, so you can have no fair objection, for she'll see that I don't run away with you. Besides, Ma'am, I got the tickets on purpose.'

'If you were determined, Sir,' said I, 'in making me this offer, to allow me no choice of refusal or acceptance, I must think myself less obliged to your intention, than I was willing to do.'

'Dear Ma'am,' cried he, 'you're so smart,[106] there is no speaking to you;—indeed, you are monstrous smart, Ma'am! but come, your Grand-mama shall ask you, and then I know you'll not be so cruel.'

Madame Duval was very ready to interfere; she desired me to make no further opposition, said she should go herself, and insisted upon my accompanying her. It was in vain that I remonstrated; I only incurred her anger, and Mr. Smith, having given both the tickets to Madame Duval, with an air of triumph, said he should call early in the evening, and took leave.

I was much chagrined at being thus compelled to owe even the shadow of an obligation to so forward a young man; but I determined that nothing should prevail upon me to dance with him, however my refusal might give offence.

In the afternoon, when he returned, it was evident that he purposed to both charm and astonish me by his appearance; he was dressed in a very showy manner, but without any taste, and the inelegant smartness of his air and deportment, his visible struggle, against education,[107] to put on the fine gentleman, added to his frequent conscious glances at a dress to which he was but little accustomed, very effectually destroyed his aim of *figuring*,[108] and rendered all his efforts useless.

During tea, entered Miss Branghton and her brother. I was sorry to observe the consternation of the former, when she perceived Mr. Smith. I had intended applying to her for advice upon this occasion, but been always deterred by her disagreeable abruptness. Having cast her eyes several times from Mr. Smith to me, with manifest displeasure, she seated herself sullenly in the window, scarce answering Madame Duval's enquiries, and when I spoke to her, turning absolutely away from me.

Mr. Smith delighted at this mark of his importance, sat indolently quiet on his chair, endeavouring by his looks rather to display, than to conceal, his inward satisfaction.

'Good gracious!' cried young Branghton, 'why, you're all as fine as five-pence![109] Why, where are you going?'

'To the Hampstead ball,' answered Mr. Smith.

'To a ball!' cried he, 'Why, what, is Aunt going to a ball? Ha, ha, ha!'

'Yes, to be sure,' cried Madame Duval; 'I don't know nothing need hinder me.'

'And pray, Aunt, will you dance too?'[110]

'Perhaps I may; but I suppose, Sir, that's none of your business, whether I do or not.'

'Lord! well, I should like to go! I should like to see Aunt dance, of all things! But the joke is, I don't believe she'll get ever a partner.'

'You're the most rudest boy ever I see,' cried Madame Duval, angrily: 'but, I promise you, I'll tell your father what you say, for I've no notion of such vulgarness.'

'Why, Lord, Aunt, what are you so angry for? there's no speaking a word, but you fly into a passion: you're as bad as Biddy or Poll for that, for you're always a-scolding.'

'I desire, Tom,' cried Miss Branghton, 'you'd speak for yourself, and not make so free with my name.'

'There, now, she's up! there's nothing but quarrelling with the women: it's my belief they like it better than victuals and drink.'

'Fie, Tom,' cried Mr. Smith, 'you never remember your manners before the ladies: I'm sure you never heard *me* speak so rude to them.'

'Why, Lord, *you* are a beau; but that's nothing to me. So, if you've a mind, you may be so polite as to dance with Aunt yourself.' Then, with a loud laugh, he declared it would be *good fun* to see them.

'Let it be never so good, or never so bad,' cried Madame Duval, 'you won't see nothing of it, I promise you; so pray don't let me hear no more of such vulgar pieces of fun; for, I assure you, I don't like it. And as to my dancing with Mr. Smith, you may see wonderfuller things than that any day in the week.'

'Why, as to that, Ma'am,' said Mr. Smith, looking much surprised, 'I always thought you intended to play at cards, and so I thought to dance with the young lady.'

I gladly seized this opportunity to make my declaration, that I should not dance at all.

'Not dance at all!' repeated Miss Branghton; 'yes, that's a likely matter truly, when people go to balls.'

'I wish she may n't,' said the brother; 'cause then Mr. Smith will have nobody but Aunt for a partner. Lord, how mad he'll be!'

'O, as to that,' said Mr. Smith, 'I don't at all fear prevailing with the young lady, if once I get her to the room.'

'Indeed, Sir,' cried I, much offended by his conceit, 'you are mistaken; and therefore I beg leave to undeceive you, as you may be assured my resolution will not alter.'

'Then pray, Miss, if it is not impertinent,' cried Miss Branghton, sneeringly, 'what do you go for?'

'Merely and solely,' answered I, 'to comply with the request of Madame Duval.'

'Miss,' cried young Branghton, 'Bid only wishes it was she, for she has cast a sheep's-eye[111] at Mr. Smith this long while.'

'Tom,' cried the sister, rising, 'I've the greatest mind in the world to box your ears! How dare you say such a thing of me?'

'No, hang it, Tom, no, that's wrong,' said Mr. Smith, simpering, 'it is indeed, to tell the lady's secrets.—But never mind him, Miss Biddy, for I won't believe him.'

'Why, I know Bid would give her ears to go,' returned the brother; 'but only Mr. Smith likes Miss best,—so does every body else.'

While the sister gave him a very angry answer, Mr. Smith said to me, in a low voice, 'Why now, Ma'am, how can you be so cruel as to be so much handsomer than your cousins? Nobody can look at them when you are by.'

'Miss,' cried young Branghton, 'whatever he says to you, don't mind him, for he means no good; I'll give you my word for it, he'll never marry you, for he has told me again and again, he'll never marry as long as he lives; besides, if he'd any mind to be married, there's Bid would have had him long ago, and thanked him too.'

'Come, come, Tom, don't tell secrets; you'll make the ladies afraid of me: but, I assure you,' lowering his voice, 'if I *did* marry, it should be your cousin.'

Should be!—did you ever, my dear Sir, hear such unauthorized freedom? I looked at him with a contempt I did not wish to repress, and walked to the other end of the room.

Very soon after, Mr. Smith sent for a hackney-coach. When I would have taken leave of Miss Branghton, she turned angrily from me, without making any answer. She supposes, perhaps, that I have rather sought, than endeavoured to avoid, the notice and civilities of this conceited young man.

The ball was at the *long room* at Hampstead.[112]

This room seems very well named, for I believe it would be difficult to find any other epithet which might, with propriety, distinguish it, as it is without ornament, elegance, or any sort of singularity, and merely to be marked by its length.

I was saved from the importunities of Mr. Smith, the beginning of the evening, by Madame Duval's declaring her intention to dance the two first dances with him herself. Mr. Smith's chagrin was very evident, but as she paid no regard to it, he was necessitated to lead her out.

I was, however, by no means pleased, when she said she was determined to dance a minuet. Indeed, I was quite astonished, not having had the least idea she would have consented to, much less proposed, such an exhibition of her person. She had some trouble to make her intentions known, as Mr. Smith was rather averse to speaking to the master of the ceremonies.[113]

During this minuet, how much did I rejoice in being surrounded only with strangers! She danced in a style so uncommon; her age, her showy dress, and an unusual quantity of *rouge*, drew upon her the eyes, and, I fear, the derision of the whole company.[114] Who she danced with, I know not; but Mr. Smith was so ill-bred as to laugh at her very openly, and to speak of her with as much ridicule as was in his power. But I would neither look at, nor listen to him; nor would I suffer him to proceed with a speech which he began, expressive of his vexation at being forced to dance with her. I told him, very gravely, that complaints upon such a subject might, with less impropriety, be made to every person in the room, than to me.

When she returned to us, she distressed me very much, by asking what I thought of her minuet. I spoke as civilly as I could, but the coldness of my compliment evidently disappointed her. She then called upon Mr. Smith to secure a good place among the country-dancers;[115] and away they went, though not before he had taken the liberty to say to me in a low voice, 'I protest to you, Ma'am, I shall be quite out of countenance, if any of my acquaintance should see me dancing with the old lady!'

For a few moments I very much rejoiced at being relieved from this troublesome man; but scarce had I time to congratulate myself, before I was accosted by another, who *begged the favour of hopping a dance*[116] with me.

I told him that I should not dance at all; but he thought proper to importune me, very freely, not to be so cruel; and I was obliged to assume no little haughtiness before I could satisfy him I was serious.

After this, I was addressed, much in the same manner, by several other young men, of whom the appearance and language were equally inelegant and low-bred: so that I soon found my situation was both disagreeable and improper; since, as I was quite alone, I fear I must seem rather to invite, than to forbid, the offers and notice I received. And yet, so great was my apprehension of this interpretation, that I am sure, my dear Sir, you would have laughed had you seen how proudly grave I appeared.

I knew not whether to be glad or sorry, when Madame Duval and Mr. Smith returned. The latter instantly renewed his tiresome entreaties, and Madame Duval said she would go to the card-table: and as soon as she was accommodated, she desired us to join the dancers.

I will not trouble you with the arguments which followed. Mr. Smith teazed me till I was weary of resistance; and I should at last have been obliged to submit, had I not fortunately recollected the affair of Mr. Lovel, and told my persecutor, that it was impossible I should dance with him, even if I wished it, as I had refused several persons in his absence.

He was not contented with being extremely chagrined, but

took the liberty, openly and warmly, to expostulate with me upon not having said I was engaged.

The total disregard with which, involuntarily, I heard him, made him soon change the subject. In truth, I had no power to attend to him, for all my thoughts were occupied in re-tracing the transactions of the two former balls at which I had been present. The party—the conversation—the company—O how great the contrast!

In a short time, however, he contrived to draw my attention to himself, by his extreme impertinence; for he chose to express what he called his *admiration* of me, in terms so open and familiar, that he forced me to express my displeasure with equal plainness.

But how was I surprised, when I found he had the temerity—what else can I call it?—to impute my resentment to doubts of his honour; for he said, 'My dear Ma'am, you must be a little patient; I assure you I have no bad designs, I have not upon my word; but, really, there is no resolving upon such a thing as matrimony all at once; what with the loss of one's liberty, and what with the ridicule of all one's acquaintance,—I assure you, Ma'am, you are the first lady who ever made me even demur upon this subject;[117] for, after all, my dear Ma'am, marriage is the devil!'

'Your opinion, Sir,' answered I, 'of either the married or the single life, can be of no manner of consequence to me, and therefore I would by no means trouble you to discuss their different merits.'

'Why, really, Ma'am, as to your being a little out of sorts, I must own I can't wonder at it, for, to be sure, marriage is all in all with the ladies; but with us gentlemen it's quite another thing! Now only put yourself in my place,—suppose you had such a large acquaintance of gentlemen as I have,—and that you had always been used to appear a little—a little smart[118] among them,—why now, how should you like to let yourself down all at once into a married man?'

I could not tell what to answer; so much conceit, and so much ignorance, both astonished and silenced me.

'I assure you, Ma'am,' added he, 'there is not only Miss Biddy,—though I should have scorned to mention her, if her brother had not blabbed, for I'm quite particular in keeping ladies' secrets,—but there are a great many other ladies that have been proposed to me,—but I never thought twice of any of them,—that is, not in a *serious* way,—so you may very well be proud,' offering to take my hand, 'for I assure you, there is nobody so likely to catch me at last as yourself.'

'Sir,' cried I, drawing myself back as haughtily as I could, 'you are totally mistaken, if you imagine you have given me any pride I felt not before, by this conversation; on the contrary, you must allow me to tell you, I find it too humiliating to bear with it any longer.'

I then placed myself behind the chair of Madame Duval; who, when she heard of the partners I had refused, pitied my ignorance of the world, but no longer insisted upon my dancing.

Indeed, the extreme vanity of this man makes me exert a spirit which I did not, till now, know that I possessed: but I cannot endure that he should think me at his disposal.

The rest of the evening passed very quietly, as Mr. Smith did not again attempt speaking to me; except, indeed, after we had left the room, and while Madame Duval was seating herself in the coach, he said, in a voice of *pique*,[119] 'Next time I take the trouble to get any tickets for a young lady, I'll make a bargain beforehand that she sha'n't turn me over to her grand-mother.'

We came home very safe; and thus ended this so long projected, and most disagreeable affair.

LETTER XX

Evelina in continuation

I have just received a most affecting letter from Mr. Macartney. I will enclose it, my dear Sir, for your perusal. More than ever have I cause to rejoice that I was able to assist him.

Mr. Macartney to Miss Anville

Madam,

Impressed with the deepest, the most heart-felt sense of the exalted humanity with which you have rescued from destruction an unhappy stranger, allow me, with the humblest gratitude, to offer you my fervent acknowledgements, and to implore your pardon for the terror I have caused you.

You bid me, Madam, live: I have now, indeed, a motive for life, since I should not willingly quit the world, while I withhold from the needy and distressed any share of that charity which a disposition so noble would, otherwise, bestow upon them.

The benevolence with which you have interested yourself in my affairs, induces me to suppose you would wish to be acquainted with the cause of that desperation from which you snatched me, and the particulars of that misery of which you have, so wonderfully, been a witness. Yet, as this explanation will require that I should divulge secrets of a nature the most delicate, I must entreat you to regard them as sacred, even though I forbear to mention the names of the parties concerned.

I was brought up in Scotland, though my mother, who had the sole care of me, was an Englishwoman, and had not one relation in that country. She devoted to me her whole time. The retirement in which we lived, and the distance from our natural friends, she often told me, were the effect of an unconquerable melancholy with which she was seized, upon the sudden loss of my father, some time before I was born.

At Aberdeen, where I finished my education, I formed a friendship with a young man of fortune, which I considered as the chief happiness of my life;—but, when he quitted his studies, I considered it as my chief misfortune, for he immediately prepared, by direction of his friends, to make the tour of Europe. As I was designed for the church,[120] and had no prospect even of maintenance but from my own industry, I scarce dared permit even a wish of accompanying him. It is true, he would joyfully have borne my expences; but my affection was as free from meanness as his own, and I made a determination the most solemn, never to lessen its dignity, by submitting to pecuniary obligations.

We corresponded with great regularity, and the most unbounded confidence, for the space of two years, when he arrived at Lyons in his way home. He wrote me, thence, the most pressing invitation to meet him at Paris, where he intended to remain some time. My desire to comply with his request, and shorten our absence, was so earnest, that my mother, too indulgent to controul me, lent me what assistance was in her power, and, in an ill-fated moment, I set out for that capital.

My meeting with this dear friend was the happiest event of my life: he introduced me to all his acquaintance; and so quickly did time seem to pass at that delightful period, that the six weeks I had allotted for my stay were gone, ere I was sensible I had missed so many days. But I must now own, that the company of my friend was not the sole subject of my felicity: I became acquainted with a young lady, daughter of an Englishman of distinction, with whom I formed an attachment which I have a thousand times vowed, a thousand times sincerely thought, would be lasting as my life. She had but just quitted a convent,[121] in which she had been placed when a child, and though English by birth, she could scarcely speak her native language. Her person and disposition were equally engaging; but chiefly I adored her for the greatness of the expectations which, for my sake, she was willing to resign.

When the time for my residence in Paris expired, I was almost distracted at the idea of quitting her; yet I had not the courage to make our attachment known to her father, who might reasonably form for her such views as would make him reject, with a contempt which I could not bear to think of, such an offer as mine. Yet I had free access to the house, where she seemed to be left almost wholly to the guidance of an old servant, who was my fast friend.[122]

But, to be brief, the sudden and unexpected return of her father, one fatal afternoon, proved the beginning of the misery which has ever since devoured me. I doubt not but he had listened to our conversation, for he darted into the room with the rage of a madman. Heavens! what a scene followed!—what abusive language did the shame of a clandestine affair, and the consciousness of acting ill, induce me to brook! At length, however, his fury exceeded my patience,—he called me a beggarly, cowardly Scotchman. Fired at the words, I drew my sword; he, with equal alertness, drew his; for he was not an old man, but, on the contrary, strong and able as myself. In vain his daughter pleaded;—in vain did I, repentant of my anger, retreat;—his reproaches continued; myself, my country, were loaded with infamy, till, no longer constraining my rage—we fought,—and he fell!

At that moment I could almost have destroyed myself! The young lady fainted with terror; the old servant, drawn to us by the noise of the scuffle, entreated me to escape, and promised to bring intelligence of what should pass to my apartment. The disturbance which I heard raised in the house obliged me to comply, and, in a state of mind inconceivably wretched, I tore myself away.

My friend, who I found at home, soon discovered the whole affair. It was near midnight before the woman came. She told me that her master was living, and her young mistress restored to her senses. The absolute necessity for my leaving Paris, while any danger remained,[123] was forcibly urged by my friend: the servant promised to acquaint him of whatever passed, and he to transmit to me her information. Thus circumstanced, with the assistance of this dear friend, I effected my departure from Paris, and, not long after, I returned to Scotland. I would fain have stopped by the way, that I might have been nearer the scene of all my concerns, but the low state of my finances denied me that satisfaction.

The miserable situation of my mind was soon discovered by my mother: nor would she rest till I communicated the cause. She heard my whole story with an agitation which astonished me;—the *name* of the parties concerned, seemed to strike her with horror;—but when I said, *We fought, and he fell*;—'My son,' cried she, 'you have then murdered your father!' and she sunk breathless at my feet. Comments, Madam, upon such a scene as this, would to you be superfluous, and to me agonizing: I cannot, for both our sakes, be too concise. When she recovered, she confessed all the particulars of a tale which she had hoped never to have revealed.—Alas! the loss she had sustained of my father was not by death!—bound to her by no ties but those of honour, he had voluntarily deserted her!—Her settling in Scotland was not the effect of choice,—she was banished thither by a family but too justly incensed;—pardon, Madam, that I cannot be more explicit!

My senses, in the greatness of my misery, actually forsook me, and for more than a week I was wholly delirious. My unfortunate mother was yet more to be pitied, for she pined with unmitigated sorrow, eternally reproaching herself for the danger to which her too strict silence had exposed me. When I recovered my reason, my impatience to hear from Paris almost deprived me of it again; and though the length of time I waited for letters might justly be attributed to contrary winds, I could not bear the delay, and was twenty times upon the point of returning thither at all hazards. At length, however, several letters arrived at once, and from the most insupportable of my afflictions I was then relieved, for they acquainted me that the horrors of parricide[124] were not in reserve for me. They informed me also, that as soon as the wound was healed, a journey would be made to England, where my unhappy *sister* was to be received by an aunt with whom she was to live.

This intelligence somewhat quieted the violence of my sorrows. I instantly formed a plan of meeting them in London, and, by revealing the whole dreadful story, convincing this irritated parent that he had nothing more to apprehend from his daughter's unfortunate choice. My mother consented, and gave me a letter to prove the truth of my assertions. As I could but ill afford to make this journey, I travelled in the cheapest way that was possible. I took an obscure lodging,—I need not, Madam, tell you where,—and boarded with the people of the house.

Here I languished, week after week, vainly hoping for the arrival of my *family*; but my impetuosity had blinded me to the imprudence of which I was guilty in quitting Scotland so hastily. My wounded father, after his recovery, relapsed; and when I had waited in the most comfortless situation, for six weeks, my friend wrote me word, that the journey was yet deferred for some time longer.

My finances were then nearly exhausted, and I was obliged, though most unwillingly, to beg further assistance from my mother, that I might return to Scotland. Oh! Madam!—my answer was not from herself,—it was written by a lady who had long been her companion, and acquainted me that she had been taken suddenly ill of a fever,—and was no more!

The compassionate nature of which you have given such noble proofs, assures me I need not, if I could, paint to you the anguish of a mind overwhelmed with such accumulated sorrows.

Enclosed was a letter to a near relation, which she had, during her illness, with much difficulty, written, and in which, with the strongest maternal tenderness, she described my deplorable situation, and entreated his interest to procure me some preferment. Yet so sunk was I by misfortune, that a fortnight elapsed before I had the courage or spirit to attempt delivering this letter. I was then compelled to it by want. To make my appearance with some decency, I was necessitated, myself, to the melancholy task of changing my coloured cloaths for a suit of mourning;—and then I proceeded to seek my relation.

I was informed that he was not in town.

In this desperate situation, the pride of my heart, which hitherto had not bowed to adversity, gave way, and I determined to entreat the assistance of my friend, whose offered services I had a thousand times rejected. Yet, Madam, so hard is it to root from the mind its favourite principles, or prejudices, call them which you please, that I lingered another week ere I had the resolution to send away a letter which I regarded as the death of my independence.

At length, reduced to my last shilling, dunned insolently by the people of the house, and almost famished, I sealed this fatal letter, and, with a heavy heart, determined to take it to the post-office. But Mr. Branghton and his son suffered me not to pass through their shop with impunity; they insulted me grossly, and threatened me with imprisonment, if I did not immediately satisfy their demands. Stung to the soul, I bid them have but a day's patience, and flung from them, in a state of mind too terrible for description.

My letter, which I now found would be received too late to save me from disgrace, I tore into a thousand pieces, and scarce could I refrain from putting an instantaneous, an unlicensed period to my existence.

In this disorder of my senses, I formed the horrible plan of turning foot-pad;[125] for which purpose I returned to my lodging, and collected whatever of my apparel I could part with, which I immediately sold, and with the profits purchased a brace of pistols, powder and shot. I hope, however, you will believe me, when I most solemnly assure you, my sole intention was to *frighten* the passengers[126] I should assault with these dangerous weapons, which I had not loaded, but from a resolution,—a dreadful one, I own,—to save *myself* from an ignominious death if seized.[127] And, indeed, I thought that if I could but procure money sufficient to pay Mr. Branghton, and make a journey to Scotland, I should soon be able, by the public papers, to discover whom I had injured, and to make private retribution.[128]

But, Madam, new to every species of villainy, my perturbation was so great that I could with difficulty support myself: yet the Branghtons observed it not as I passed through the shop.

Here I stop: what followed is better known to yourself. But no time can ever efface from my memory that moment, when in the very action of preparing for my own destruction, or the lawless seizure of the property of others, you rushed into the room, and arrested my arm!—It was, indeed, an awful moment!—the hand of Providence seemed to intervene between me and eternity; I beheld you as an angel!—I thought you dropped from the clouds;—the earth, indeed, had never before presented to my view a form so celestial! What wonder, then, that a spectacle so astonishing should, to a man disordered as I was, appear too beautiful to be human?

And now, Madam, that I have performed that painful task, the more grateful one remains of rewarding, as far as is in my power, your generous goodness, by assuring you it shall not be thrown away. You have awakened me to a sense of the false pride by which I have been actuated,—a pride which, while it scorned assistance from a friend, scrupled not to compel it from a stranger, though at the hazard of reducing that stranger to a situation as destitute as my own. Yet, Oh! how violent was the struggle which tore my conflicting soul, ere I could persuade myself to profit by the benevolence which you were so evidently disposed to exert in my favour!

By means of a ring, the gift of my much-regretted mother, I have for the present satisfied Mr. Branghton; and by means of your compassion, I hope to support myself, either till I hear from my friend, to whom, at length, I have written, or till the relation of my mother returns to town.

To talk to you, Madam, of paying my debt, would be vain; I never can! the service you have done me exceeds all power of return; you have restored me to my senses, you have taught me to curb those passions which bereft me of them, and, since I cannot avoid calamity, to bear it as a man! An interposition so wonderfully circumstanced can never be recollected without benefit. Yet allow me to say, the pecuniary part of my obligation must be settled by my first ability.

I am, Madam, with the most profound respect, and heart-felt gratitude,

Your obedient,

and devoted humble servant,

J. MACARTNEY

LETTER XXI

Evelina in continuation

Holborn, July 1, 5 o'clock in the morn.

O Sir, what an adventure have I to write!—all night it has occupied my thoughts, and I am now risen thus early, to write it to you.

Yesterday it was settled that we should spend the evening in Marybone Gardens, where M. Torre,[129] a celebrated foreigner, was to exhibit some fireworks. The party consisted of Madame Duval, all the Branghtons, M. Du Bois, Mr. Smith, and Mr. Brown.

We were almost the first persons who entered the Gardens, Mr. Branghton having declared he would have *all he could get for his money*, which, at best, was only fooled away, at such silly and idle places.

We walked in parties, and very much detached from one another; Mr. Brown and Miss Polly led the way by themselves; Miss Branghton and Mr. Smith followed, and the latter seemed determined to be revenged for my behaviour at the ball, by transferring all his former attention for me, to Miss Branghton, who received it with an air of exultation: and very frequently they each of them, though from different motives, looked back, to discover whether I observed their good intelligence. Madame Duval walked with M. Du Bois; and Mr. Branghton by himself; but his son would willingly have attached himself wholly to me, saying frequently, 'Come, Miss, let's you and I have a little fun together; you see they have all left us, so now let us leave them.' But I begged to be excused, and went to the other side of Madame Duval.

This Garden, as it is called, is neither striking for magnificence nor for beauty; and we were all so dull and languid, that I was extremely glad when we were summoned to the orchestra, upon the opening of a concert; in the course of which, I had the pleasure of hearing a concerto on the violin by Mr. Barthelemon,[130] who, to me, seems a player of exquisite fancy, feeling, and variety.

When notice was given us, that the fireworks were preparing, we hurried along to secure good places for the sight; but, very soon, we were so encircled and incommoded by the crowd, that Mr. Smith proposed the *ladies* should make interest for a form[131] to stand upon; this was soon effected, and the men then left us, to accommodate themselves better, saying they would return the moment the exhibition was over.

The firework was really beautiful, and told, with wonderful ingenuity, the story of Orpheus and Eurydice;[132] but, at the moment of the fatal look, which separated them for ever, there was such an explosion of fire, and so horrible a noise, that we all as of one accord, jumped hastily from the form, and ran away some paces, fearing that we were in danger of mischief, from the innumerable sparks of fire which glittered in the air.

For a moment or two, I neither knew nor considered whither I had run; but my recollection was soon awakened by a stranger's addressing me with, 'Come along with me, my dear, and I'll take care of you.'

I started, and then, to my great terror, perceived that I had out-run all my companions, and saw not one human being I knew! with all the speed in my power, and forgetful of my first fright, I hastened back to the place I had left;—but found the form occupied by a new set of people.

In vain, from side to side, I looked for some face I knew; I found myself in the midst of a crowd, yet without party, friend, or acquaintance. I walked, in disordered haste, from place to place, without knowing which way to turn, or whither I went. Every other moment, I was spoken to, by some bold and unfeeling man, to whom my distress, which, I think, must be very apparent, only furnished a pretence for impertinent witticisms, or free gallantry.

At last, a young officer, marching fiercely up to me, said, 'You are a sweet pretty creature, and I enlist you in my service;' and then, with great violence, he seized my hand. I screamed aloud with fear, and, forcibly snatching it away, I ran hastily up to two ladies, and cried, 'For Heaven's sake, dear ladies, afford me some protection!'

They heard me with a loud laugh, but very readily said, 'Ay, let her walk between us;' and each of them took hold of an arm.

Then, in a drawling, ironical tone of voice, they asked *what had frightened my little Ladyship*? I told them my adventure very simply, and entreated they would have the goodness to assist me in finding my friends.

O yes, to be sure, they said, I should not want for friends, whilst I was with them.[133] Mine, I said, would be very grateful for any civilities with which they might favour me. But imagine, my dear Sir, how I must be confounded, when I observed, that every other word I spoke produced a loud laugh! However, I will not dwell upon a conversation, which soon, to my inexpressible horror, convinced me I had sought protection from insult, of those who were themselves most likely to offer it! You, my dearest Sir, I well know, will both feel for, and pity my terror, which I have no words to describe.

Had I been at liberty, I should have instantly run away from them, when I made the shocking discovery; but, as they held me fast, that was utterly impossible: and such was my dread of their resentment or abuse, that I did not dare make any open attempt to escape.

They asked me a thousand questions, accompanied by as many hallows,[134] of who I was, what I was, and whence I came. My answers were very incoherent,—but what, good Heaven, were my emotions, when, a few moments afterwards, I perceived advancing our way,—Lord Orville!

Never shall I forget what I felt at that instant: had I, indeed, been sunk to the guilty state, which such companions might lead him to suspect, I could scarce have had feelings more cruelly depressing.

However, to my infinite joy, he passed us without distinguishing me; though I saw that, in a careless manner, his eyes surveyed the party.

As soon as he was gone, one of these unhappy women said, 'Do you know that young fellow?'

Not thinking it possible she should mean Lord Orville by such a term, I readily answered, 'No, Madam.'

'Why then,' answered she, 'you have a monstrous good stare, for a little country Miss.'

I now found I had mistaken her, but was glad to avoid an explanation.

A few minutes after, what was my delight, to hear the voice of Mr. Brown, who called out, 'Lord, i'n't that Miss what's her name?'

'Thank God,' cried I, suddenly springing from them both, 'thank God, I have found my party.'

Mr. Brown was, however, alone, and, without knowing what I did, I took hold of his arm.

'Lord, Miss,' cried he, 'we've had such a hunt you can't think! some of them thought you was gone home; but I says, says I, I don't think, says I, that she's like to go home all alone, says I.'

'So that gentleman belongs to you, Miss, does he?' said one of the women.

'Yes, Madam,' answered I, 'and I now thank you for your civility; but, as I am safe, will not give you any further trouble.'

I courtsied slightly, and would have walked away; but, most unfortunately, Madame Duval and the two Miss Branghtons just then joined us.

They all began to make a thousand enquiries, to which I briefly answered, that I had been obliged to these two ladies for walking with me, and would tell them more another time: for, though I felt great *comparative* courage, I was yet too much intimidated by their presence, to dare be explicit.

Nevertheless, I ventured, once more, to wish them good night, and proposed seeking Mr. Branghton. These unhappy women listened to all that was said with a kind of callous curiosity, and seemed determined not to take any hint. But my vexation was terribly augmented, when, after having whispered something to each other, they very cavalierly declared, that they intended joining our party! and then, one of them very boldly took hold of my arm, while the other, going round, seized that of Mr. Brown; and thus, almost forcibly, we were moved on between them, and followed by Madame Duval and the Miss Branghtons.

It would be very difficult to say which was greatest, my fright, or Mr. Brown's consternation; who ventured not to make the least resistance, though his uneasiness made him tremble almost as much as myself. I would instantly have withdrawn my arm; but it was held so tight, I could not move it; and poor Mr. Brown was circumstanced in the same manner on the other side;

for I heard him say, 'Lord, Ma'am, there's no need to squeeze one's arm so!'

And this was our situation,—for we had not taken three steps, when,—O Sir,—we again met Lord Orville!—but not again did he pass quietly by us,—unhappily I caught his eye;—both mine, immediately, were bent to the ground; but he approached me, and we all stopped.

I then looked up. He bowed. Good God, with what expressive eyes did he regard me! Never were surprise and concern so strongly marked,—yes, my dear Sir, he looked *greatly* concerned; and that, the remembrance of that, is the only consolation I feel, for an evening the most painful of my life.

What he first said I know not; for, indeed, I seemed to have neither ears nor understanding; but I recollect that I only courtsied in silence. He paused for an instant, as if—I believe so,—as if unwilling to pass on; and then, finding the whole party detained, he again bowed, and took leave.

Indeed, my dear Sir, I thought I should have fainted, so great was my emotion from shame, vexation, and a thousand other feelings, for which I have no expressions. I absolutely tore myself from the woman's arm, and then, disengaging myself from that of Mr. Brown, I went to Madame Duval, and besought that she would not suffer me to be again parted from her.

I fancy—that Lord Orville saw what passed; for scarcely was I at liberty, ere he returned. Methought, my dear Sir, the pleasure, the surprise of that moment, recompensed me for all the chagrin I had before felt: for do you not think, that this return manifests, from a character so quiet, so reserved as Lord Orville's, something like solicitude in my concerns?—such, at least, was the interpretation I involuntarily made upon again seeing him.

With a politeness to which I have been some time very little used, he apologized for returning, and then enquired after the health of Mrs. Mirvan, and the rest of the Howard Grove family. The flattering conjecture which I have just acknowledged, had so wonderfully restored my spirits, that I believe I never answered him so readily, and with so little constraint. Very short, however, was the duration of this conversation: for we were soon most disagreeably interrupted.

The Miss Branghtons, though they saw almost immediately the characters of the women to whom I had so unfortunately applied, were, nevertheless, so weak and foolish, as merely to *titter* at their behaviour. As to Madame Duval, she was for some time so strangely imposed upon, that she thought they were two real fine ladies. Indeed it is wonderful to see how easily and how frequently she is deceived: our disturbance, however, arose from young Brown, who was now between the two women, by whom his arms were absolutely pinioned to his sides: for a few minutes, his complaints had been only murmured; but he now called out aloud, 'Goodness, Ladies, you hurt me like any thing! why I can't walk at all, if you keep pinching my arms so!'

This speech raised a loud laugh in the women, and redoubled the tittering of the Miss Branghtons. For my own part, I was most cruelly confused; while the countenance of Lord Orville manifested a sort of indignant astonishment; and, from that moment, he spoke to me no more, till he took leave.

Madame Duval, who now began to suspect her company, proposed our taking the first box we saw empty, bespeaking a supper, and waiting till Mr. Branghton should find us.

Miss Polly mentioned one she had remarked, to which we all turned; Madame Duval instantly seated herself; and the two bold women, forcing the frightened Mr. Brown to go between them, followed her example.

Lord Orville, with an air of gravity that wounded my very soul, then wished me good night. I said not a word; but my face, if it had any connection with my heart, must have looked melancholy indeed: and so, I have some reason to believe, it did; for he added, with much more softness, though not less dignity, 'Will Miss Anville allow me to ask her address, and to pay my respects to her before I leave town?'

O how I changed colour at this unexpected request!—yet what was the mortification I suffered, in answering, 'My Lord, I am—in Holborn!'

He then bowed and left us.

What, what can he think of this adventure! how strangely, how cruelly have all appearances turned against me! Had I been blessed with any presence of mind; I should instantly have explained to him the accident which occasioned my being in such terrible company;—but I have none!

As to the rest of the evening, I cannot relate the particulars of what passed; for, to you, I only write of what I think, and I can think of nothing but this unfortunate, this disgraceful meeting. These two wretched women continued to torment us all, but especially poor Mr. Brown, who seemed to afford them uncommon diversion, till we were discovered by Mr. Branghton, who very soon found means to release us from their persecutions, by frightening them away. We stayed but a short time after they left us, which was all employed in explanations.

Whatever may be the construction which Lord Orville may put upon this affair, to me it cannot fail of being unfavourable; to be seen—gracious Heaven!—to be seen in company with two women of such character! How vainly, how proudly have I wished to avoid meeting him when only with the Branghtons and Madame Duval,—but now, how joyful should I be had he seen me to no greater disadvantage!—Holborn, too! what a direction!—he who had always—but I will not torment you, my dearest Sir, with any more of my mortifying conjectures and apprehensions: perhaps he may call,—and then I shall have an opportunity of explaining to him all the most shocking part of the adventure. And yet, as I did not tell him at whose house I lived, he may not be able to discover me; I merely said *in Holborn*, and he, who I suppose saw my embarrassment, forbore to ask any other direction.

Well, I must take my chance!

Yet let me, in justice to Lord Orville, and in justice to the high opinion I have always entertained of his honour and delicacy,—let me observe the difference of his behaviour, when nearly in the same situation to that of Sir Clement Willoughby. He had at least equal cause to depreciate me in his opinion, and to mortify and sink me in my own: but far different was his conduct;—perplexed, indeed, he looked, and much surprised,—

but it was benevolently, not with insolence. I am even inclined to think, that he could not see a young creature whom he had so lately known in a higher sphere, appear so suddenly, so strangely, so disgracefully altered in her situation, without some pity and concern. But, whatever might be his doubts and suspicions, far from suffering them to influence his behaviour, he spoke, he looked, with the same politeness and attention with which he had always honoured me when countenanced by Mrs. Mirvan.

Once again, let me drop this subject.

In every mortification, every disturbance, how grateful to my heart, how sweet to my recollection, is the certainty of your never-failing tenderness, sympathy, and protection! Oh Sir, could I, upon this subject, could I write as I feel,—how animated would be the language of

Your devoted
EVELINA!

LETTER XXII

Evelina to the Rev. Mr. Villars

Holborn, July 1

Listless, uneasy, and without either spirit or courage to employ myself, from the time I had finished my last letter, I indolently seated myself at the window, where, while I waited Madame Duval's summons to breakfast, I perceived, among the carriages which passed by, a coronet coach,[135] and, in a few minutes, from the window of it, Lord Orville! I instantly retreated, but not, I believe, unseen; for the coach immediately drove up to our door.

Indeed, my dear Sir, I must own I was greatly agitated; the idea of receiving Lord Orville by myself,—the knowledge that his visit was entirely to *me*,—the wish of explaining the unfortunate adventure of yesterday,—and the mortification of my present circumstances,—all these thoughts, occurring to me nearly at the same time, occasioned me more anxiety, confusion, and perplexity, than I can possibly express.

I believe he meant to send up his name; but the maid, unused to such a ceremony, forgot it by the way,[136] and only told me, that a great Lord was below, and desired to see me: and, the next moment, he appeared himself.

If formerly, when in the circle of high life, and accustomed to its manners, I so much admired and distinguished the grace, the elegance of Lord Orville, think, Sir, how they must strike me now,—now, when, far removed from that splendid circle, I live with those to whom even civility is unknown, and decorum a stranger!

I am sure I received him very awkwardly; depressed by a situation so disagreeable, could I do otherwise? When his first enquiries were made, 'I think myself very fortunate,' he said, 'in meeting with Miss Anville at home, and still more so, in finding her disengaged.'

I only courtsied. He then talked of Mrs. Mirvan; asked how long I had been in town, and other such general questions, which, happily, gave me time to recover from my embarrassment. After which, he said, 'If Miss Anville will allow me the honour of sitting by her a few minutes' (for we were both standing) 'I will venture to tell her the motive which, next to enquiring after her health, has prompted me to wait on her thus early.'

We were then both seated, and, after a short pause, he said, 'How to apologize for so great a liberty as I am upon the point of taking, I know not;—shall I, therefore, rely wholly upon your goodness, and not apologize at all?'

I only bowed.

'I should be extremely sorry to appear impertinent,—yet hardly know how to avoid it.'

'Impertinent! O my Lord,' cried I, eagerly, 'that, I am sure, is impossible!'

'You are very good,' answered he, 'and encourage me to be ingenuous—'

Again he stopped: but my expectation was too great for speech: at last, without looking at me, in a low voice and hesitating manner, he said, 'Were those ladies with whom I saw you last night, ever in your company before?'

'No, my Lord,' cried I, rising, and colouring violently, 'nor will they ever be again.'

He rose too, and, with an air of the most condescending concern, said, 'Pardon, Madam, the abruptness of a question which I knew not how to introduce as I ought, and for which I have no excuse to offer, but my respect for Mrs. Mirvan, joined to the sincerest wishes for your happiness: yet I fear I have gone too far!'

'I am very sensible of the honour of your Lordship's attention,' said I, 'but——.'

'Permit me to assure you,' cried he, finding I hesitated, 'that officiousness is not my characteristic, and that I would by no means have risked your displeasure, had I not been fully satisfied you were too generous to be offended, without a real cause of offence.'

'Offended!' cried I, 'no, my Lord, I am only grieved,—grieved, indeed! to find myself in a situation so unfortunate, as to be obliged to make explanations which cannot but mortify and shock me.'

'It is I alone,' cried he, with some eagerness, 'who am shocked, as it is I who deserve to be mortified; I seek no explanation, for I have no doubt; but, in mistaking me, Miss Anville injures herself: allow me, therefore, frankly and openly to tell you the intention of my visit.'

I bowed, and we both returned to our seats.

'I will own myself to have been greatly surprised,' continued he, 'when I met you yesterday evening, in company with two persons who I was sensible merited not the honour of your notice; nor was it easy for me to conjecture the cause of your being so situated; yet, believe me, my incertitude did not for a moment do you injury; I was satisfied that their characters must be unknown to you, and I thought with concern of the shock you would sustain, when you discovered their unworthiness. I should not, however, upon so short an acquaintance, have usurped the privilege of intimacy, in giving my unasked sentiments upon so delicate a subject, had I not known that credulity is the sister of innocence, and therefore feared you might be deceived. A something, which I could not resist, urged me to the freedom I have taken to caution you; but I shall not easily forgive myself, if I have been so unfortunate as to give you pain.'

The pride which his first question had excited, now subsided into delight and gratitude, and I instantly related to him, as well as I could, the accident which had occasioned my joining the unhappy women with whom he had met me. He listened with an attention so flattering, seemed so much interested during the recital, and, when I had done, thanked me, in terms so polite, for what he was pleased to call my condescension, that I was almost ashamed either to look at, or hear him.

Soon after, the maid came to tell me, that Madame Duval desired to have breakfast made in her own room.

'I fear,' cried Lord Orville, instantly rising, 'that I have intruded upon your time,—yet who, so situated, could do otherwise?' Then, taking my hand, 'Will Miss Anville allow me thus to seal my peace?' He pressed it to his lips, and took leave.

Generous, noble Lord Orville! how disinterested his conduct! how delicate his whole behaviour! willing to advise, yet afraid to wound me!—Can I ever, in future, regret the adventure I met with at Marybone, since it has been productive of a visit so flattering? Had my mortifications been still more humiliating, my terrors still more alarming, such a mark of esteem—may I not call it so?—from Lord Orville, would have made me ample amends.

And indeed, my dear Sir, I require some consolation in my present very disagreeable situation; for, since he went, two incidents have happened, that, had not my spirits been particularly elated, would greatly have disconcerted me.

During breakfast, Madame Duval, very abruptly, asked if I should like to be married? and added, that Mr. Branghton had been proposing a match for me with his son. Surprised, and, I must own, provoked, I assured her that, in thinking of me, Mr. Branghton would very vainly lose his time.

'Why,' cried she, 'I have had grander views for you, myself, if once I could get you to Paris, and make you be owned; but, if I can't do that, and you can do no better, why, as you are both my relations, I think to leave my fortune between you, and then, if you marry, you never need want for nothing.'

I begged her not to pursue the subject, as, I assured her, Mr. Branghton was totally disagreeable to me: but she continued her admonitions and reflections, with her usual disregard of whatever I could answer. She charged me, very peremptorily, neither wholly to discourage, nor yet to accept Mr. Branghton's offer, till she saw what could be done for me: the young man, she added, had often intended to speak to me himself, but, not well knowing how to introduce the subject, he had desired her to pave the way for him.

I scrupled not, warmly and freely to declare my aversion[137] to this proposal; but it was to no effect; she concluded, just as she had begun, by saying, that I should not *have him*, *if I could do better*.

Nothing, however, shall persuade me to listen to any other person concerning this odious affair.

My second cause of uneasiness arises, very unexpectedly, from M. Du Bois, who, to my infinite surprise, upon Madame Duval's quitting the room after dinner, put into my hand a note, and immediately left the house.

This note contains an open declaration of an attachment to me, which, he says, he should never have presumed to have acknowledged, had he not been informed that Madame Duval destined my hand to young Branghton,——a match which he cannot endure to think of. He beseeches me, earnestly to pardon his temerity, professes the most inviolable respect, and commits his fate to time, patience, and pity.

This conduct in M. Du Bois gives me real concern, as I was disposed to think very well of him. It will not, however, be difficult to discourage him, and therefore I shall not acquaint Madame Duval of his letter, as I have reason to believe it would greatly displease her.

LETTER XXIII

Evelina in continuation

July 3

O Sir, how much uneasiness must I suffer, to counterbalance one short morning of happiness!

Yesterday, the Branghtons proposed a party to Kensington Gardens,[138] and, as usual, Madame Duval insisted upon my attendance.

We went in a hackney-coach to Piccadilly,[139] and then had a walk through Hyde Park[140] which, in any other company, would have been delightful. I was much pleased with Kensington Gardens, and think them infinitely preferable to those of Vauxhall.

Young Branghton was extremely troublesome; he insisted upon walking by my side, and talked with me almost by compulsion: however, my reserve and coldness prevented his entering upon the hateful subject which Madame Duval had prepared me to apprehend. Once, indeed, when I was, accidentally, a few yards before the rest, he said, 'I suppose, Miss, Aunt has told you about you know what?—ha'n't she, Miss?'—But I turned from him without making any answer. Neither Mr. Smith nor Mr. Brown were of the party; and poor M. Du Bois, when he found that I avoided him, looked so melancholy, that I was really sorry for him.

While we were strolling round the garden, I perceived, walking with a party of ladies at some distance, Lord Orville! I instantly retreated behind Miss Branghton, and kept out of sight till we had passed him: for I dreaded being seen by him again, in a public walk, with a party of which I was ashamed.

Happily I succeeded in my design, and saw no more of him; for a sudden and violent shower of rain made us all hasten out of the gardens. We ran till we came to a small green-shop,[141] where we begged shelter. Here we found ourselves in company with two footmen, whom the rain had driven into the shop. Their livery, I thought, I had before seen; and upon looking from the window, I perceived the same upon a coachman belonging to a carriage, which I immediately recollected to be Lord Orville's.

Fearing to be known, I whispered Miss Branghton not to speak my name. Had I considered but a moment, I should have been sensible of the inutility of such a caution, since not one of the party call me by any other appellation than that of *Cousin*, or of *Miss*; but I am perpetually involved in some distress or dilemma [142] from my own heedlessness.

This request excited very strongly her curiosity; and she attacked me with such eagerness and bluntness of enquiry, that I could not avoid telling her the reason of my making it, and, consequently, that I was known to Lord Orville: an acknowledgement which proved the most unfortunate in the world; for she would not rest till she had drawn from me the circumstances attending my first making the acquaintance. Then, calling to her sister, she said, 'Lord, Polly, only think! Miss has danced with a Lord!'

'Well,' cried Polly, 'that's a thing I should never have thought of! And pray Miss, what did he say to you?'

This question was much sooner asked than answered; and they both became so very inquisitive and earnest, that they soon drew the attention of Madame Duval and the rest of the party, to whom, in a very short time, they repeated all they had gathered from me.

'Goodness, then,' cried young Branghton, 'if I was Miss, if I would not make free with his Lordship's coach to take me to town.'

'Why ay,' said the father, 'there would be some sense in that; that would be making some use of a Lord's acquaintance, for it would save us coach-hire.'

'Lord, Miss,' cried Polly, 'I wish you would, for I should like of all things to ride in a coronet coach!'

'I promise you,' said Madame Duval, 'I'm glad you've thought of it, for I don't see no objection,—so let's have the coachman called.'

'Not for the world,' cried I, very much alarmed, 'indeed it is utterly impossible.'

'Why so?' demanded Mr. Branghton; 'pray where's the good of your knowing a Lord, if you're never the better for him?'

'*Ma foi*, child,' said Madame Duval, 'you don't know no more of the world than if you was a baby. Pray, Sir,' (to one of the footmen) 'tell that coachman to draw up, for I wants to speak to him.'

The man stared, but did not move. 'Pray, pray, Madam,' said I, 'pray, Mr. Branghton, have the goodness to give up this plan; I know but very little of his Lordship, and cannot, upon any account, take so great a liberty.'

'Don't say nothing about it,' said Madame Duval, 'for I shall have it my own way: so if *you* won't call the coachman, Sir, I'll promise you I'll call him myself.'

The footman, very impertinently, laughed and turned upon his heel. Madame Duval, extremely irritated, ran out in the rain, and beckoned the coachman, who instantly obeyed her summons. Shocked beyond all expression, I flew after her, and entreated her with the utmost earnestness, to let us return in a hackney-coach:—but oh!—she is impenetrable to persuasion! She told the man she wanted him to carry her directly to town, and that she would answer for him to Lord Orville. The man, with a sneer, thanked her, but said he should answer for himself; and was driving off, when another footman came up to him, with information that his Lord was gone into Kensington Palace,[143] and would not want him for an hour or two.

'Why then, friend,' said Mr. Branghton (for we were followed by all the party), 'where will be the great harm of your taking us to town?'

'Besides,' said the son, 'I'll promise you a pot of beer[144] for my own share.'

These speeches had no other answer from the coachman than a loud laugh, which was echoed by the insolent footmen. I rejoiced at their resistance, though I was certain that if their Lord had witnessed their impertinence, they would have been instantly dismissed his service.

'*Pardi*,' cried Madame Duval, 'if I don't think all the footmen are the most impudentest fellows in the kingdom! But I'll promise you I'll have your master told of your airs, so you'll get no good by 'em.'

'Why pray,' said the coachman, rather alarmed, 'did my Lord give you leave to use the coach?'

'It's no matter for that,' answered she; 'I'm sure if he's a gentleman, he'd let us have it sooner than we should be wet to the skin: but I'll promise you he shall know how saucy you've been, for this young lady knows him very well.'

'Ay, that she does,' said Miss Polly; 'and she's danced with him too.'

Oh how I repented my foolish mismanagement! The men bit their lips, and looked at one another in some confusion. This was perceived by our party, who, taking advantage of it, protested they would write Lord Orville word of their ill behaviour without delay. This quite startled them, and one of the footmen offered to run to the palace and ask his Lord's permission for our having the carriage.

This proposal really made me tremble; and the Branghtons all hung back upon it: but Madame Duval is never to be dissuaded from a scheme she has once formed. 'Do so,' cried she, 'and give this child's compliments to your master, and tell him, as we ha'n't no coach here, we should be glad to go just as far as Holborn in his.'

'No, no, no!' cried I; 'don't go,—I know nothing of his Lordship,—I send no message,—I have nothing to say to him!'

The men, very much perplexed, could with difficulty restrain themselves from resuming their impertinent mirth. Madame Duval scolded me very angrily, and then desired them to go directly. 'Pray, then,' said the coachman, 'what name is to be given to my Lord?'

'Anville,' answered Madame Duval, 'tell him Miss Anville wants the coach; the young lady he danced with once.'

I was really in an agony; but the winds could not have been more deaf to me, than those to whom I pleaded! and therefore the footman, urged by the repeated threats of Madame Duval, and perhaps recollecting the name himself, actually went to the palace with this strange message!

He returned in a few minutes, and bowing to me with the greatest respect, said, 'My Lord desires his compliments, and his carriage will be always at Miss Anville's service.'

I was so much affected by this politeness, and chagrined at the whole affair, that I could scarce refrain from tears. Madame Duval and the Miss Branghtons eagerly jumped into the coach, and desired me to follow. I would rather have submitted to the severest punishment;—but all resistance was vain.

During the whole ride, I said not a word; however, the rest of the party were so talkative, that my silence was very immaterial. We stopped at our lodgings; but when Madame Duval and I alighted, the Branghtons asked if they could not be carried on to Snow Hill? The servants, now all civility, made no objection. Remonstrances from me, would, I too well knew, be fruitless; and therefore, with a heavy heart, I retired to my room, and left them to their own direction.

Seldom have I passed a night in greater uneasiness:—so lately to have cleared myself in the good opinion of Lord Orville,—so soon to forfeit it!—to give him reason to suppose I presumed to boast of his acquaintance,—to publish his having danced with me!—to take with him a liberty I should have blushed to have taken with the most intimate of my friends!—to treat with such impertinent freedom one who has honoured *me* with such distinguished respect!—indeed, Sir, I could have met with no accident that would so cruelly have tormented me!

If such were, then, my feelings, imagine,—for I cannot describe, what I suffered during the scene I am now going to write.

This morning, while I was alone in the dining-room, young Branghton called. He entered with a most important air, and strutting up to me, said, 'Miss, *Lord Orville* sends his compliments to you.'

'Lord Orville!'—repeated I, much amazed.

'Yes, Miss, Lord Orville;—for *I* know his Lordship now, as well as you.—And a very civil gentleman he is, for all he's a Lord.'

'For Heaven's sake,' cried I, 'explain yourself.'

'Why you must know, Miss, after we left you, we met with a little misfortune; but I don't mind it now, for it's all turned out for the best: but, just as we were a-going up Snow Hill, plump we comes against a cart,[145] with such a jogg it almost pulled the coach-wheel off; however, that i'n't the worst, for as I went to open the door in a hurry, a-thinking the coach would be broke down, as ill-luck would have it, I never minded that the glass was up,[146] and so I poked my head fairly through it. Only see, Miss, how I've cut my forehead!'

A much worse accident to himself, would not, I believe, at that moment, have given me any concern for him: however, he proceeded with his account, for I was too much confounded to interrupt him.

'Goodness, Miss, we were in such a stew, us, and the servants, and all, as you can't think; for, besides the glass being broke, the coachman said how the coach would n't be safe to go back to Kensington. So we did n't know what to do; however, the footmen said they'd go and tell his Lordship what had happened. So then father grew quite uneasy, like, for fear of his Lordship's taking offence, and prejudicing us in our business: so he said I should go this morning and ask his pardon, 'cause of having broke the glass. So then I asked the footmen the direction, and they told me he lived in Berkeley Square;[147] so this morning I went,—and I soon found out the house.'

'You did!' cried I, quite out of breath with apprehension.

'Yes, Miss, and a very fine house it is. Did you ever see it?'

'No.'

'No!—why then, Miss, I know more of his Lordship than you do, for all you knew him first. So, when I came to the door, I was in a peck of troubles,[148] a-thinking what I should say to him; however, the servants had no mind I should see him, for they told me he was busy, but I might leave my message. So I was just a-coming away, when I bethought myself to say I come from you.'

'From *me*!—'

'Yes. Miss,—for you know why should I have such a long

walk as that for nothing? So I says to the porter,[149] says I, tell his
Lordship, says I, one wants to speak to him as comes from one
Miss Anville, says I.'

'Good God,' cried I, 'and by what authority did you take such
a liberty?'

'Goodness, Miss, don't be in such a hurry, for you'll be as
glad as me when you hear how well it all turned out. So then
they made way for me, and said his Lordship would see me
directly; and there I was led through such a heap of servants,
and so many rooms, that my heart quite misgave me; for I
thought, thinks I, he'll be so proud he'll hardly let me speak; but
he's no more proud than I am, and he was as civil as if I'd been a
lord myself. So then I said, I hoped he would n't take it amiss
about the glass, for it was quite an accident; but he bid me not
mention it, for it did n't signify. And then he said he hoped you
got safe home, and was n't frightened; and so I said yes, and I
gave your duty to him.'

'My duty to him!' exclaimed I,—'and who gave you leave?—
who desired you?'

'O, I did it of my own head, just to make him think I came
from you. But I should have told you before how the footman
said he was going out of town to-morrow evening, and that his
sister was soon to be married, and that he was a-ordering a heap
of things for that; so it come into my head, as he was so affable,
that I'd ask him for his custom. So I says, says I, my Lord, says
I, if your Lordship i'n't engaged particularly, my father is a
silver-smith, and he'd be very proud to serve you, says I; and
Miss Anville, as danced with you, is his cousin, and she's my
cousin too, and she'd be very much obligated[150] to you, I'm
sure.'

'You'll drive me wild,' I cried (starting from my seat), 'you
have done me an irreparable injury;—but I will hear no more!'—
and then I ran into my own room.

I was half frantic, I really raved; the good opinion of Lord
Orville seemed now irretrievably lost: a faint hope, which in the
morning I had vainly encouraged, that I might see him again,
and explain the transaction, wholly vanished, now I found he

was so soon to leave town: and I could not but conclude that, for the rest of my life, he would regard me as an object of utter contempt.

The very idea was a dagger to my heart!—I could not support it, and—but I blush to proceed—I fear your disapprobation, yet I should not be conscious of having merited it, but that the repugnance I feel to relate to you what I have done, makes me suspect I must have erred. Will you forgive me, if I own that I *first* wrote an account of this transaction to Miss Mirvan?—and that I even thought of *concealing* it from you?—Short-lived, however, was the ungrateful idea, and sooner will I risk the justice of your displeasure, than unworthily betray your generous confidence.

You are now probably prepared for what follows—which is a letter,—a hasty letter, that, in the height of my agitation, I wrote to Lord Orville.

My Lord,

I am so infinitely ashamed of the application made yesterday for your Lordship's carriage in my name, and so greatly shocked at hearing how much it was injured, that I cannot forbear writing a few lines, to clear myself from the imputation of an impertinence which I blush to be suspected of, and to acquaint you, that the request for your carriage was made against my consent, and the visit with which you were importuned this morning, without my knowledge.

I am inexpressibly concerned at having been the instrument, however innocently, of so much trouble to your Lordship; but I beg you to believe, that reading these lines is the only part of it which I have given voluntarily.

I am, my Lord,

Your Lordship's most humble servant,

EVELINA ANVILLE

I applied to the maid of the house to get this note conveyed to Berkeley Square; but scarce had I parted with it, before I regretted having written at all, and I was flying down stairs to recover it, when the voice of Sir Clement Willoughby stopped me. As Madame Duval had ordered we should be denied to him, I was obliged to return up stairs; and after he was gone, my application was too late, as the maid had given it to a porter.[151]

My time did not pass very serenely while he was gone; however, he brought me no answer, but that Lord Orville was not at home. Whether or not he will take the trouble to send any;—or whether he will condescend to call;—or whether the affair will rest as it is, I know not;—but, in being ignorant, am most cruelly anxious.

LETTER XXIV

Evelina in continuation

July 4

You may now, my dear Sir, send Mrs. Clinton[152] for your Evelina with as much speed as she can conveniently make the journey, for no further opposition will be made to her leaving this town: happy had it perhaps been for her had she never entered it!

This morning Madame Duval desired me to go to Snow Hill, with an invitation to the Branghtons and Mr. Smith, to spend the evening with her: and she desired M. Du Bois, who break-fasted with us, to accompany me. I was very unwilling to obey her, as I neither wished to walk with M. Du Bois, nor yet to meet young Branghton. And, indeed, another, a yet more power-ful reason, added to my reluctance,—for I thought it possible that Lord Orville might send some answer, or perhaps might call, during my absence; however, I did not dare dispute her commands.

Poor M. Du Bois spoke not a word during our walk, which was, I believe, equally unpleasant to us both. We found all

the family assembled in the shop. Mr. Smith, the moment he
perceived me, addressed himself to Miss Branghton, whom he
entertained with all the gallantry in his power. I rejoice to find
that my conduct at the Hampstead ball has had so good an
effect. But young Branghton was extremely troublesome, he
repeatedly laughed in my face, and looked so impertinently
significant, that I was obliged to give up my reserve to M. Du
Bois, and enter into conversation with him, merely to avoid such
boldness.

'Miss,' said Mr. Branghton, 'I'm sorry to hear from my son
that you was n't pleased with what we did about that Lord
Orville; but I should like to know what it was you found fault
with, for we did all for the best.'

'Goodness!' cried the son, 'why if you'd seen Miss, you'd have
been surprised—she went out of the room quite in a huff,[153]
like.'

'It is too late, now,' said I, 'to reason upon this subject; but,
for the future, I must take the liberty to request, that my name
may never be made use of without my knowledge. May I tell
Madame Duval that you will do her the favour to accept her
invitation?'

'As to me, Ma'am,' said Mr. Smith, 'I am much obliged to the
old lady, but I've no mind to be taken in by her again; you'll
excuse me, Ma'am.'

All the rest promised to come, and I then took leave: but as I
left the shop, I heard Mr. Branghton say, 'Take courage, Tom,
she's only coy.' And, before I had walked ten yards, the youth
followed.

I was so much offended that I would not look at him; but
began to converse with M. Du Bois, who was now more lively
than I had ever before seen him; for, most unfortunately, he
misinterpreted the reason of my attention to him.

The first intelligence I received when I came home, was, that
two gentlemen had called, and left cards. I eagerly enquired for
them, and read the names of Lord Orville and Sir Clement
Willoughby. I by no means regretted that I missed seeing the
latter, but perhaps I may all my life regret that I missed the former,

for probably he has now left town,—and I may see him no more!

'My goodness!' cried young Branghton, rudely looking over me, 'only think of that Lord's coming all this way! It's my belief he'd got some order ready for father, and so he'd a mind to call and ask you if I'd told him the truth.'

'Pray, Betty,' cried I, 'how long has he been gone?'

'Not two minutes, Ma'am.'

'Why then I'll lay you any wager,' said young Branghton, 'he saw you and I a-walking up Holborn Hill!'

'God forbid!' cried I, impatiently; and, too much chagrined to bear with any more of his remarks, I ran up stairs: but I heard him say to M. Du Bois, 'Miss is so *uppish*[154] this morning, that I think I had better not speak to her again.'

I wish M. Du Bois had taken the same resolution; but he chose to follow me into the dining-room, which we found empty.

'*Vous ne l' aimez donc pas, ce garçon, Mademoiselle!*'[155] cried he.

'Me!' cried I, 'no, I detest him!' for I was quite sick at heart.

'*Ah, tu me rends la vie!*'[156] cried he, and flinging himself at my feet, he had just caught my hand, as the door was opened by Madame Duval.

Hastily, and with marks of guilty confusion in his face, he arose; but the rage of that lady quite amazed me! advancing to the retreating M. Du Bois, she began, in French, an attack which her extreme wrath and wonderful volubility almost rendered unintelligible; yet I understood but too much, since her reproaches convinced me she had herself proposed being the object of his affection.

He defended himself in a weak and evasive manner, and upon her commanding him from her sight, very readily withdrew: and then, with yet greater violence, she upbraided me with having *seduced* his heart, called me an ungrateful, designing girl, and protested she would neither take me to Paris, nor any more interest herself in my affairs, unless I would instantly agree to marry young Branghton.

Frightened as I had been at her vehemence, this proposal restored all my courage; and I frankly told her that in this point I never could obey her. More irritated than ever, she ordered me to quit the room.

Such is the present situation of affairs. I shall excuse myself from seeing the Branghtons this afternoon: indeed, I never wish to see them again. I am sorry, however innocently, that I have displeased Madame Duval, yet I shall be very glad to quit this town, for I believe it does not, now, contain one person I ever wish to again meet. Had I but seen Lord Orville, I should regret nothing: I could then have more fully explained what I so hastily wrote; yet it will always be a pleasure to me to recollect that he called, since I flatter myself it was in consequence of his being satisfied with my letter.

Adieu, my dear Sir; the time now approaches when I hope once more to receive your blessing, and to owe all my joy, all my happiness, to your kindness.

LETTER XXV

Mr. Villars to Evelina

Berry Hill, July 7

Welcome, thrice welcome, my darling Evelina, to the arms of the truest, the fondest of your friends! Mrs. Clinton, who shall hasten to you with these lines, will conduct you directly hither, for I can consent no longer to be parted from the child of my bosom!——the comfort of my age!——the sweet solace of all my infirmities! Your worthy friends at Howard Grove must pardon me that I rob them of the visit you proposed to make them before your return to Berry Hill, for I find my fortitude unequal to a longer separation.

I have much to say to you, many comments to make upon your late letters, some parts of which give me no little uneasiness; but I will reserve my remarks for our future conversations. Hasten, then, to the spot of thy nativity, the abode of thy youth, where never yet care or sorrow had power to annoy thee,—O that they might ever be banished this peaceful dwelling!

Adieu, my dearest Evelina! I pray but that thy satisfaction at our approaching meeting may bear any comparison with mine!

ARTHUR VILLARS

LETTER XXVI

Evelina to Miss Mirvan

Berry Hill, July 14

My sweet Maria will be much surprised, and, I am willing to flatter myself, concerned, when, instead of her friend, she receives this letter;—this cold, this inanimate letter, which will but ill express the feelings of the heart which indites it.

When I wrote to you last Friday, I was in hourly expectation of seeing Mrs. Clinton, with whom I intended to have set out for Howard Grove; Mrs. Clinton came, but my plan was necessarily altered, for she brought me a letter,—the sweetest that ever was penned, from the best and kindest friend that ever orphan was blessed with, requiring my immediate attendance at Berry Hill.

I obeyed,—and pardon me if I own I obeyed without reluctance; after so long a separation, should I not else have been the most ungrateful of mortals?—And yet,—oh Maria! though I *wished* to leave London, the gratification of my wish afforded me no happiness! and though I felt an impatience inexpressible to return hither, no words, no language can explain the heaviness of heart with which I made the journey. I believe you would hardly have known me;—indeed, I hardly know myself. Perhaps had I first seen *you*, in your kind and sympathizing bosom I might have ventured to have reposed every secret of my soul; and then—but let me pursue my journal.

Mrs. Clinton delivered Madame Duval a letter from Mr. Villars, which requested her leave for my return, and, indeed, it was very readily accorded: yet, when she found, by my willingness to quit town, that M. Du Bois was really indifferent to me, she somewhat softened in my favour, and declared that, but for punishing his folly in thinking of such a child, she would not have consented to my being again buried in the country.

All the Branghtons called to take leave of me: but I will not write a word more about them; indeed I cannot with any patience think of that family, to whose forwardness and impertinence is owing all the uneasiness I at this moment suffer!

So great was the depression of my spirits upon the road, that it was with difficulty I could persuade the worthy Mrs. Clinton I was not ill: but alas, the situation of my mind was such as would have rendered any mere bodily pain, by comparison, even enviable!

And yet, when we arrived at Berry Hill,—when the chaise stopped at this place,—how did my heart throb with joy! And when, through the window, I beheld the dearest, the most venerable of men, with uplifted hands, returning, as I doubt not, thanks for my safe arrival,—good God! I thought it would have burst my bosom!—I opened the chaise-door myself, I flew,—for my feet did not seem to touch the ground,—into the parlour; he had risen to meet me, but the moment I appeared, he sunk into his chair, uttering with a deep sigh, though his face *beamed* with delight, 'My God, I thank thee!'

I sprung forward, and, with a pleasure that bordered upon agony, I embraced his knees, I kissed his hands, I wept over them, but could not speak: while he, now raising his eyes in thankfulness towards heaven, now bowing down his reverend head, and folding me in his arms, could scarce articulate the blessings with which his kind and benevolent heart overflowed.

O Miss Mirvan, to be so beloved by the best of men,—should I not be happy?—Should I have one wish save that of meriting his goodness?—Yet think me not ungrateful; indeed I am not, although the internal sadness of my mind unfits me, at present, for enjoying as I ought the bounties of Providence.

I cannot journalize;[157] cannot arrange my ideas into order.

How little has situation to do with happiness! I had flattered myself that, when restored to Berry Hill, I should be restored to tranquillity: far otherwise have I found it, for never yet had tranquillity and Evelina so little intercourse.

I blush for what I have written. Can you, Maria, forgive my gravity? but I restrain it so much and so painfully in the presence of Mr. Villars, that I know not how to deny myself the consolation of indulging it to you.

Adieu, my dear Miss Mirvan.

Yet one thing I must add; do not let the seriousness of this letter deceive you; do not impute to a wrong cause the melancholy I confess, by supposing that the heart of your friend mourns a too great susceptibility; no, indeed! believe me it never was, never can be, more assuredly her own than at this moment. So witness in all truth,

Your affectionate
EVELINA

You will make my excuses to the honoured Lady Howard, and to your dear mother.

LETTER XXVII

Evelina in continuation

Berry Hill, July 21

You accuse me of mystery, and charge me with reserve: I cannot doubt but I must have merited the accusation;—yet, to clear myself,—you know not how painful will be the task. But I cannot resist your kind entreaties,—indeed, I do not wish to resist them, for your friendship and affection will soothe my chagrin. Had it arisen from any other cause, not a moment would I have deferred the communication you ask;—but, as it is,

I would, were it possible, not only conceal it from all the world, but endeavour to disbelieve it myself. Yet, since I *must* tell you, why trifle with your impatience?

I know not how to come to the point; twenty times have I attempted it in vain;—but I will *force* myself to proceed.

Oh, Miss Mirvan, could you ever have believed, that one who seemed formed as a pattern for his fellow-creatures, as a model of perfection,—one whose elegance surpassed all description,— whose sweetness of manners disgraced all comparison,—Oh, Miss Mirvan, could you ever have believed that *Lord Orville* would have treated me with indignity?

Never, never again will I trust to appearances,—never confide in my own weak judgement,—never believe that person to be good, who seems to be amiable! What cruel maxims are we taught by a knowledge of the world!—But while my own reflections absorb me, I forget you are still in suspence.

I had just finished the last letter which I wrote to you from London, when the maid of the house brought me a note. It was given to her, she said, by a footman, who told her he would call the next day for an answer.

This note,—but let it speak for itself.

To Miss Anville

With transport, most charming of thy sex, did I read the letter with which you yesterday morning favoured me. I am sorry the affair of the carriage should have given you any concern, but I am highly flattered by the anxiety you express so kindly. Believe me, my lovely girl, I am truly sensible of the honour of your good opinion, and feel myself deeply penetrated with love and gratitude. The correspondence you have so sweetly commenced I shall be proud of continuing, and I hope the strong sense I have of the favour you do me, will prevent your withdrawing it. Assure yourself that I desire nothing more ardently, than to pour forth my thanks at your feet, and to offer those vows which are so justly the tribute of your charms and accomplishments. In your next, I entreat you to acquaint me how long you shall remain in town. The servant whom I shall commission to call for an answer, has orders to ride post[158] with it to me. My impatience for his arrival will be very great, though inferior to that with which I burn to tell you, in person, how much I am, my sweet girl,

> Your grateful admirer,
> ORVILLE

What a letter! how has my proud heart swelled every line I have copied! What I wrote to him you know; tell me then, my dear friend, do you think it merited such an answer?—and that I have deservedly incurred the liberty he has taken? I meant nothing but a simple apology, which I thought as much due to my own character, as to his; yet, by the construction he seems to have put upon it, should you not have imagined it contained the avowal of sentiments which might, indeed, have provoked his contempt?

The moment the letter was delivered to me, I retired to my own room to read it, and so eager was my first perusal, that,—I am ashamed to own—it gave me no sensation but of delight. Unsuspicious of any impropriety from Lord Orville, I perceived not immediately the impertinence it implied,—I only marked the expressions of his own regard; and I was so much surprised, that I was unable, for some time, to compose myself, or read it again,—I could only walk up and down the room, repeating to myself, 'Good God, is it possible?—am I, then, loved by Lord Orville?'

But this dream was soon over, and I awoke to far different feelings; upon a second reading, I thought every word changed,—it did not seem the same letter,—I could not find one sentence that I could look at without blushing: my astonishment was extreme, and it was succeeded by the utmost indignation.

If, as I am very ready to acknowledge, I erred in writing to Lord Orville, was it for *him* to punish the error? If he was offended, could he not have been silent? If he thought my letter ill-judged, should he not have pitied my ignorance? have considered my youth, and allowed for my inexperience?

Oh Maria, how have I been deceived in this man! Words have
no power to tell the high opinion I had of him; to that was
owing the unfortunate solicitude which prompted my writing,—
a solicitude I must for ever repent!

Yet perhaps I have rather reason to rejoice than to grieve,
since this affair has shewn me his real disposition, and removed
that partiality, which, covering his every imperfection, left only
his virtues and good qualities exposed to view. Had the deception
continued much longer, had my mind received any additional
prejudice in his favour, who knows whither my mistaken ideas
might have led me? Indeed I fear I was in greater danger than I
apprehended, or can now think of without trembling,—for oh,
if this weak heart of mine had been penetrated with too deep an
impression of his merit,—my peace and happiness had been lost
for ever!

I would fain encourage more chearful thoughts, fain drive
from my mind the melancholy that has taken possession of it,—
but I cannot succeed; for added to the humiliating feelings
which so powerfully oppress me, I have yet another cause of
concern;—alas, my dear Maria, I have broken the tranquillity of
the best of men!

I have never had the courage to shew him this cruel letter: I
could not bear so greatly to depreciate in his opinion, one whom
I had, with infinite anxiety, raised in it myself. Indeed, my first
determination was to confine my chagrin totally to my own
bosom; but your friendly enquiries have drawn it from me; and
now I wish I had made no concealment from the beginning,
since I know not how to account for a gravity which not all my
endeavours can entirely hide or repress.

My greatest apprehension is, lest he should imagine that my
residence in London has given me a distaste to the country.
Every body I see takes notice of my being altered, and looking
pale and ill. I should be very indifferent to all such observations,
did I not perceive that they draw upon me the eyes of Mr.
Villars, which glisten with affectionate concern.

This morning, in speaking of my London expedition, he
mentioned Lord Orville. I felt so much disturbed, that I would

instantly have changed the subject; but he would not allow me, and, very unexpectedly, he began his panegyric, extolling, in strong terms, his manly and honourable behaviour in regard to the Marybone adventure. My cheeks glowed with indignation every word he spoke;—so lately as I had myself fancied him the noblest of his sex, now that I was so well convinced of my mistake, I could not bear to hear his undeserved praises uttered by one so really good, so unsuspecting, so pure of heart!

What he thought of my silence and uneasiness I fear to know, but I hope he will mention the subject no more. I will not, however, with ungrateful indolence, give way to a sadness which I find infectious to him who merits the most chearful exertion of my spirits. I am thankful that he has forborne to probe my wound, and I will endeavour to heal it by the consciousness that I have not deserved the indignity I have received. Yet I cannot but lament to find myself in a world so deceitful, where we must suspect what we see, distrust what we hear, and doubt even what we feel!

LETTER XXVIII

Evelina in continuation

Berry Hill, July 29

I must own myself somewhat distressed how to answer your raillery: yet believe me, my dear Maria, your suggestions are those of *fancy*, not of *truth*. I am unconscious of the weakness you suspect; yet, to dispel your doubts, I will animate myself more than ever to conquer my chagrin, and to recover my spirits.

You wonder, you say, since my *heart* takes no part in this affair, why it should make me so unhappy? And can you, acquainted as you are with the high opinion I entertained of

Lord Orville, can you wonder that so great a disappointment in his character should affect me? indeed, had so strange a letter been sent to me from *any* body, it could not have failed shocking me; how much more sensibly, then, must I feel such an affront, when received from the man in the world I had imagined least capable of giving it?

You are glad I made no reply; assure yourself, my dear friend, had this letter been the most respectful that could be written, the clandestine air given to it, by his proposal of sending his servant for my answer, instead of having it directed to his house, would effectually have prevented my writing. Indeed, I have an aversion the most sincere to all mysteries, all private actions; however foolishly and blameably, in regard to this letter, I have deviated from the open path which, from my earliest infancy, I was taught to tread.

He talks of my having *commenced a correspondence* with him; and could Lord Orville indeed believe I had such a design?[159] believe me so forward, so bold, so strangely ridiculous? I know not if his man called or not, but I rejoice that I quitted London before he came, and without leaving any message for him. What, indeed, could I have said? it would have been a condescension very unmerited to have taken any, the least notice of such a letter.

Never shall I cease to wonder how he could write it. Oh, Maria, what, what could induce him so causelessly to wound and affront one who would sooner have died than wilfully offended *him*?—How mortifying a freedom of style! how cruel an implication conveyed by his *thanks*, and expressions of gratitude! Is it not astonishing, that any man can *appear* so modest, who is so vain?

Every hour I regret the secrecy I have observed with my beloved Mr. Villars; I know not what bewitched me, but I felt, at first, a repugnance to publishing this affair that I could not surmount,—and now, I am ashamed of confessing that I have any thing to confess! Yet I deserve to be punished for the false delicacy[160] which occasioned my silence; since, if Lord Orville himself was contented to forfeit his character, was it for me, almost at the expence of my own, to support it?

Yet I believe I should be very easy, now the first shock is

over, and now that I see the whole affair, with the resentment it merits, did not all my good friends in this neighbourhood, who think me extremely altered, teaze me about my gravity, and torment Mr. Villars with observations upon my dejection, and falling away.[161] The subject is no sooner started, than a deep gloom overspreads his venerable countenance, and he looks at me with a tenderness so melancholy, that I know not how to endure the consciousness of exciting it.

Mrs. Selwyn, a lady of large fortune, who lives about three miles from Berry Hill, and who has always honoured me with very distinguishing marks of regard, is going, in a short time, to Bristol, and has proposed to Mr. Villars to take me with her, for the recovery of my health. He seemed very much distressed whether to consent or refuse; but I, without any hesitation, warmly opposed the scheme, protesting my health could no where be better than in this pure air. He had the goodness to thank me for this readiness to stay with him: but he is all goodness! Oh that it were in my power to be, indeed, what in the kindness of his heart he has called me, the comfort of his age, and solace of his infirmities!

Never do I wish to be again separated from him. If here I am grave, elsewhere I should be unhappy. In his presence, with a very little exertion, all the chearfulness of my disposition seems ready to return; the benevolence of his countenance reanimates, the harmony of his temper composes, the purity of his character edifies me! I owe to him every thing; and, far from finding my debt of gratitude a weight, the first pride, first pleasure of my life is the recollection of the obligations conferred upon me by a goodness so unequalled.

Once, indeed, I thought there existed another,—who, when *time had wintered o'er his locks*,[162] would have shone forth among his fellow-creatures, with the same brightness of worth which dignifies my honoured Mr. Villars; a brightness, how superior in value to that which results from mere quickness of parts, wit, or imagination! a brightness, which, not contented with merely diffusing smiles, and gaining admiration from the sallies of the spirits, reflects a real and a glorious lustre upon all mankind! Oh how great was my error! how ill did I judge! how cruelly have I been deceived!

I will not go to Bristol, though Mrs. Selwyn is very urgent with me;—but I desire not to see any more of the world; the few months I have already passed in it have sufficed to give me a disgust even to its name.

I hope, too, I shall see Lord Orville no more; accustomed, from my first knowledge of him, to regard him as a *being superior to his race*, his presence, perhaps, might banish my resentment, and I might forget his ill conduct,—for oh, Maria—I should not know how to see *Lord Orville*—and to think of displeasure!

As a sister I loved him,—I could have entrusted him with every thought of my heart, had he deigned to wish my confidence; so steady did I think his honour, so *feminine* his delicacy, and so amiable his nature! I have a thousand times imagined that the whole study of his life, and whole purport of his reflections, tended solely to the good and happiness of others:—but I will talk,—write,—think of him no more!

Adieu, my dear friend!

LETTER XXIX

Evelina in continuation

Berry Hill, August 10

You complain of my silence, my dear Miss Mirvan,—but what have I to write? Narrative does not offer, nor does a lively imagination supply the deficiency. I have, however, at present, sufficient matter for a letter, in relating a conversation I had yesterday with Mr. Villars.

Our breakfast had been the most chearful we have had since my return hither; and, when it was over, he did not, as usual, retire to his study, but continued to converse with me while I

worked. We might, probably, have passed all the morning thus
sociably, but for the entrance of a farmer, who came to solicit
advice concerning some domestic affairs. They withdrew together into the study.

The moment I was alone, my spirits failed me; the exertion
with which I had supported them, had fatigued my mind: I flung
away my work,[163] and, leaning my arms on the table, gave way
to a train of disagreeable reflections, which, bursting from the
restraint that had smothered them, filled me with unusual sadness.

This was my situation, when, looking towards the door,
which was open, I perceived Mr. Villars, who was earnestly
regarding me. 'Is Farmer Smith gone, Sir?' cried I, hastily rising,
and snatching up my work.

'Don't let me disturb you,' said he, gravely; 'I will go again to
my study.'

'Will you, Sir?—I was in hopes you were coming to sit here.'

'In hopes!—and why, Evelina, should you hope it?'

This question was so unexpected, that I knew not how to
answer it; but, as I saw he was moving away, I followed, and
begged him to return. 'No, my dear, no,' said he, with a forced
smile, 'I only interrupt your meditations.'

Again I knew not what to say; and while I hesitated, he
retired. My heart was with him, but I had not the courage to
follow. The idea of an explanation, brought on in so serious a
manner, frightened me. I recollected the inference *you* had drawn
from my uneasiness, and I feared that he might make a similar
interpretation.

Solitary and thoughtful, I passed the rest of the morning in
my own room. At dinner I again attempted to be chearful; but
Mr. Villars himself was grave, and I had not sufficient spirits to
support a conversation merely by my own efforts. As soon as
dinner was over, he took a book, and I walked to the window. I
believe I remained near an hour in this situation. All my thoughts
were directed to considering how I might dispel the doubts
which I apprehended Mr. Villars had formed, without acknowledging a circumstance which I had suffered so much pain merely

to conceal. But, while I was thus planning for the future, I forgot the present; and so intent was I upon the subject which occupied me, that the strange appearance of my unusual inactivity and extreme thoughtfulness, never occurred to me. But when, at last, I recollected myself, and turned round, I saw that Mr. Villars, who had parted with his book, was wholly engrossed in attending to me. I started from my reverie, and, hardly knowing what I said, asked if he had been reading?

He paused a moment, and then replied, 'Yes, my child;—a book that both afflicts and perplexes me!'

He means *me*, thought I; and therefore I made no answer.

'What if we read it together?' continued he, 'will you assist me to clear its obscurity?'

I knew not what to say, but I sighed, involuntarily, from the bottom of my heart. He rose, and, approaching me, said, with emotion, 'My child, I can no longer be a silent witness of thy sorrow,—is not *thy* sorrow *my* sorrow?—and ought I to be a stranger to the cause, when I so deeply sympathize in the effect?'

'Cause, Sir!' cried I, greatly alarmed, 'what cause?—I don't know,—I can't tell—I—'

'Fear not,' said he, kindly, 'to unbosom thyself to me, my dearest Evelina; open to me thy whole heart,—it can have no feelings for which I will not make allowance. Tell me, therefore, what it is that thus afflicts us both, and who knows but I may suggest some means of relief?'

'You are too, too good,' cried I, greatly embarrassed; 'but indeed I know not what you mean.'

'I see,' said he, 'it is painful to you to speak: suppose then, I endeavour to save you by guessing?'

'Impossible! impossible!' cried I, eagerly, 'no one living could ever guess, ever suppose—' I stopped abruptly; for I then recollected I was acknowledging something *was* to be guessed: however, he noticed not my mistake.

'At least let me try,' answered he, mildly; 'perhaps I may be a better diviner than you imagine: if I guess every thing that is probable, surely I must approach near the real reason. Be honest, then, my love, and speak without reserve,—does not the country, after so much gaiety, so much variety, does it not appear insipid and tiresome?'

'No, indeed! I love it more than ever, and more than ever do I wish I had never, never quitted it!'

'Oh my child! that I had not permitted the journey! My judgement always opposed it, but my resolution was not proof against persuasion.'

'I blush, indeed,' cried I, 'to recollect my earnestness;—but I have been my own punisher!'

'It is too late, now,' answered he, 'to reflect upon this subject; let us endeavour to avoid repentance for the time to come, and we shall not have erred without reaping some instruction.' Then seating himself, and making me sit by him, he continued: 'I must now guess again; perhaps you regret the loss of those friends you knew in town,—perhaps you miss their society, and fear you may see them no more?—perhaps Lord Orville——'

I could not keep my seat, but rising hastily, said, 'Dear Sir, ask me nothing more!—for I have nothing to own,—nothing to say; my gravity has been merely accidental, and I can give no reason for it at all. Shall I fetch you another book?—or will you have this again?'

For some minutes he was totally silent, and I pretended to employ myself in looking for a book: at last, with a deep sigh, 'I see,' said he, 'I see but too plainly, that though Evelina is returned,—I have lost my child!'

'No, Sir, no,' cried I, inexpressibly shocked, 'she is more your's than ever! Without you, the world would be a desart to her, and life a burthen;—forgive her, then, and,—if you can,—condescend to be, once more, the confidant of all her thoughts.'

'How highly I value, how greatly I wish for her confidence,' returned he, 'she cannot but know;—yet to extort, to tear it from her,—my justice, my affection, both revolt at the idea. I am sorry that I was so earnest with you;—leave me, my dear, leave me and compose yourself;—we will meet again at tea.'

'Do you then refuse to hear me?'

'No, but I abhor to compel you. I have long seen that your mind has been ill at ease, and mine has largely partaken of your

concern: I forbore to question you, for I hoped that time, and
absence from whatever excited your uneasiness, might best oper-
ate in silence: but alas! your affliction seems only to augment,—
your health declines,—your look alters,—Oh Evelina, my aged
heart bleeds to see the change!—bleeds to behold the darling it
had cherished, the prop it had reared for its support, when
bowed down by years and infirmities, sinking itself under the
pressure of internal grief!—struggling to hide, what it should
seek to participate!—But go, my dear, go to your own room,—
we both want composure, and we will talk of this matter some
other time.'

'Oh Sir,' cried I, penetrated to the soul, 'bid me not leave
you!—think me not so lost to feeling, to gratitude—'

'Not a word of that,' interrupted he; 'it pains me you should
think upon that subject; pains me you should ever remember
that you have not a natural, an hereditary right to every thing
within my power. I meant not to affect you thus,—I hoped to
have soothed you!—but my anxiety betrayed me to an urgency
that has distressed you. Comfort yourself, my love, and doubt
not but that time will stand your friend, and all will end well.'

I burst into tears: with difficulty had I so long restrained
them; for my heart, while it glowed with tenderness and gratitude, was oppressed with a sense of its own unworthiness. 'You
are all, all goodness!' cried I, in a voice scarce audible, 'little as I
deserve,—unable as I am to repay, such kindness,—yet my
whole soul feels,—thanks you for it!'

'My dearest child,' cried he, 'I cannot bear to see thy tears;—
for *my* sake dry them,—such a sight is too much for me: think of
that, Evelina, and take comfort, I charge thee!'

'Say then,' cried I, kneeling at his feet, 'say then that you
forgive me! that you pardon my reserve,—that you will again
suffer me to tell you my most secret thoughts, and rely upon my
promise never more to forfeit your confidence!—father! my
protector!—my ever-honoured—ever-loved—my best and only
friend!—say you forgive your Evelina, and she will study better
to deserve your goodness!'

He raised, he embraced me; he called me his sole joy, his only earthly hope, and the child of his bosom! He folded me to his heart, and, while I wept from the fullness of mine, with words of sweetest kindness and consolation, he soothed and tranquillized me.

Dear to my remembrance will ever be that moment, when, banishing the reserve I had so foolishly planned and so painfully supported, I was restored to the confidence of the best of men!

When, at length, we were again quietly and composedly seated by each other, and Mr. Villars waited for the explanation I had begged him to hear, I found myself extremely embarrassed how to introduce the subject which must lead to it. He saw my distress, and, with a kind of benevolent pleasantry, asked me if I would let him *guess* any more? I assented in silence.

'Shall I, then, go back to where I left off?'

'If—if you please;—I believe so,—' said I, stammering.

'Well then, my love, I think I was speaking of the regret it was natural you should feel upon quitting those from whom you had received civility and kindness, with so little certainty of ever seeing them again, or being able to return their good offices? These are circumstances that afford but melancholy reflections to young minds; and the affectionate disposition of my Evelina, open to all social feelings, must be hurt more than usual by such considerations.—You are silent, my dear?—Shall I name those whom I think most worthy the regret I speak of? We shall then see if our opinions coincide.'

Still I said nothing, and he continued.

'In your London journal, nobody appears in a more amiable, a more respectable light, than Lord Orville, and perhaps——'

'I knew what you would say,' cried I, hastily, 'and I have long feared where your suspicions would fall; but indeed, Sir, you are mistaken: I hate Lord Orville,—he is the last man in the world in whose favour I should be prejudiced.'

I stopped; for Mr. Villars looked at me with such infinite surprise, that my own warmth made me blush. 'You *hate* Lord Orville!' repeated he.

I could make no answer, but took from my pocket-book the letter, and giving it to him, 'See, Sir,' said I, 'how differently the same man can *talk* and *write*!'

He read it three times before he spoke; and then said, 'I am so much astonished, that I know not what I read. When had you this letter?'

I told him. Again he read it; and after considering its contents some time, said, 'I can form but one conjecture concerning this most extraordinary performance: he must certainly have been intoxicated when he wrote it.'

'Lord Orville intoxicated!' repeated I; 'once I thought him a stranger to all intemperance,—but it is very possible, for I can believe any thing now.'

'That a man who had behaved with so strict a regard to delicacy,' continued Mr. Villars, 'and who, as far as occasion had allowed, manifested sentiments the most honourable, should thus insolently, thus wantonly insult a modest young woman, in his perfect senses, I cannot think possible. But, my dear, you should have enclosed this letter in an empty cover,[164] and have returned it to him again: such a resentment would at once have become *your* character, and have given him an opportunity, in some measure, of clearing his own. He could not well have read this letter the next morning, without being sensible of the impropriety of having written it.'

Oh Maria! why had not I this thought? I might then have received some apology; the mortification would then have been *his*, not *mine*. It is true, he could not have reinstated himself so highly in my opinion as I had once ignorantly placed him, since the conviction of such intemperance would have levelled him with the rest of his imperfect race; yet, my humbled pride might have been consoled by his acknowledgements.

But why should I allow myself to be humbled by a man who can suffer his reason to be thus abjectly debased, when I am exalted by one who knows no vice, and scarcely a failing,—but by hearsay? To think of his kindness, and reflect upon his praises, might animate and comfort me even in the midst of affliction. 'Your indignation,' said he, 'is the result of virtue; you fancied Lord Orville was without fault—he had the appearance of infinite worthiness, and you supposed his character accorded with his appearance: guileless yourself, how could you prepare against the duplicity of another? Your disappointment has but been proportioned to your expectations, and you have chiefly owed its severity to the innocence which hid its approach.'

I will bid these words dwell ever in my memory, and they shall chear, comfort, and enliven me! This conversation, though extremely affecting to me at the time it passed, has relieved my mind from much anxiety. Concealment, my dear Maria, is the foe of tranquillity: however I may err in future, I will never be disingenuous in acknowledging my errors. To you, and to Mr. Villars, I vow an unremitting confidence.

And yet, though I am more at ease, I am far from well: I have been some time writing this letter; but I hope I shall send you, soon, a more chearful one.

Adieu, my sweet friend. I entreat you not to acquaint even your dear mother with this affair; Lord Orville is a favourite with her, and why should I publish that he deserves not that honour?

LETTER XXX

Evelina in continuation

Bristol Hotwell,[165] August 28

You will be again surprised, my dear Maria, at seeing whence I date my letter: but I have been very ill, and Mr. Villars was so much alarmed, that he not only insisted upon my accompanying Mrs. Selwyn hither, but earnestly desired she would hasten her intended journey.

We travelled very slowly, and I did not find myself so much fatigued as I expected. We are situated upon a most delightful spot; the prospect is beautiful, the air pure, and the weather very favourable to invalids.[166] I am already better, and I doubt not but I shall soon be well; as well, in regard to mere health, as I wish to be.

I cannot express the reluctance with which I parted from my

revered Mr. Villars: it was not like that parting which, last April, preceded my journey to Howard Grove, when, all expectation and hope, though I wept, I rejoiced, and though I sincerely grieved to leave him, I yet wished to be gone: the sorrow I now felt was unmixed with any livelier sensation; expectation was vanished, and hope I had none! All that I held most dear upon earth, I quitted, and that upon an errand to the success of which I was totally indifferent, the re-establishment of my health. Had it been to have seen my sweet Maria, or her dear mother, I should not have repined.

Mrs. Selwyn is very kind and attentive to me. She is extremely clever; her understanding, indeed, may be called *masculine*; but, unfortunately, her manners deserve the same epithet; for, in studying to acquire the knowledge of the other sex, she has lost all the softness of her own. In regard to myself, however, as I have neither courage nor inclination to argue with her, I have never been personally hurt at her want of gentleness; a virtue which, nevertheless, seems so essential a part of the female character, that I find myself more awkward, and less at ease, with a woman who wants it, than I do with a man. She is not a favourite with Mr. Villars, who has often been disgusted at her unmerciful propensity to satire: but his anxiety that I should try the effect of the Bristol waters,[167] overcame his dislike of committing me to her care. Mrs. Clinton is also here; so that I shall be as well attended as his utmost partiality could desire.

I will continue to write to you, my dear Miss Mirvan, with as much constancy as if I had no other correspondent; though during my absence from Berry Hill, my letters may, perhaps, be shortened on account of the minuteness of the journal which I must write to my beloved Mr. Villars: but you, who know his expectations, and how many ties bind me to fulfil them, will, I am sure, rather excuse any omission to yourself, than any negligence to him.

END OF THE SECOND VOLUME

Volume Three

LETTER I

Evelina to the Rev. Mr. Villars

Bristol Hotwells, Sept. 12

The first fortnight that I passed here, was so quiet, so serene, that it gave me reason to expect a settled calm during my stay; but if I may now judge of the time to come, by the present state of my mind, the calm will be succeeded by a storm, of which I dread the violence!

This morning, in my way to the Pump-room,[1] with Mrs. Selwyn, we were both very much incommoded by three gentlemen, who were sauntering by the side of the Avon,[2] laughing, and talking very loud, and lounging so disagreeably, that we knew not how to pass them. They all three fixed their eyes very boldly upon me, alternately looking under my hat, and whispering one another. Mrs. Selwyn assumed an air of uncommon sternness, and said, 'You will please, Gentlemen, either to proceed yourselves, or to suffer us.'

'Oh! Ma'am,' cried one of them, 'we will suffer *you*, with the greatest pleasure in life.'

'You will suffer us *both*,' answered she, 'or I am much mistaken; you had better, therefore, make way quietly, for I should be sorry to give my servant the trouble of teaching you better manners.'

Her commanding air struck them, yet they all chose to laugh, and one of them wished the fellow would begin his lesson, that he might have the pleasure of rolling him into the Avon; while another advancing to me with a freedom which made me start, said, 'By my soul I did not know you!—but I am sure I cannot be mistaken;—had not I the honour of seeing you, once, at the Pantheon?'

I then recollected the nobleman who, at that place, had so

much embarrassed me. I courtsied without speaking. They all bowed, and making, though in a very easy manner, an apology to Mrs. Selwyn, they suffered us to pass on, but chose to accompany us.

'And where,' continued this Lord, 'can you so long have hid yourself? do you know I have been in search of you this age? I could neither find you out, nor hear of you: not a creature could inform me what was become of you. I cannot imagine where you could be immured. I was at two or three public places every night, in hopes of meeting you. Pray did you leave town?'

'Yes, my Lord.'

'So early in the season!—what could possibly induce you to go before the birth-day?'

'I had nothing, my Lord, to do with the birth-day.'

'By my soul, all the women who *had*, may rejoice you were away. Have you been here any time?'

'Not above a fortnight, my Lord.'

'A fortnight!—how unlucky that I did not meet you sooner! but I have had a run of ill luck ever since I came. How long shall you stay?'

'Indeed, my Lord, I don't know.'

'Six weeks, I hope; for I shall wish the place at the devil when you go.'

'Do you, then, flatter yourself, my Lord,' said Mrs. Selwyn, who had hitherto listened in silent contempt, 'that you shall see such a beautiful spot as this, when you visit the dominions of the devil?'

'Ha, ha, ha! Faith, my Lord,' said one of his companions, who still walked with us, though the other had taken leave; 'the Lady is rather hard upon you.'

'Not at all,' answered Mrs. Selwyn; 'for as I cannot doubt but his Lordship's rank and interest will secure him a place there, it would be reflecting on his understanding, to suppose he should not wish to enlarge and beautify his dwelling.'

Much as I was disgusted with this Lord, I must own Mrs. Selwyn's severity rather surprised me: but you, who have so often observed it, will not wonder she took so fair an opportunity of indulging her humour.

'As to *places*,' returned he, totally unmoved, 'I am so indifferent to them, that the devil take me if I care which way I go! *objects*, indeed, I am not so easy about; and therefore I expect that those angels with whose beauty I am so much enraptured in this world, will have the goodness to afford me some little consolation in the other.'

'What, my Lord!' cried Mrs. Selwyn, 'would you wish to degrade the habitation of your friend, by admitting into it the insipid company of the upper regions?'

'What do you do with yourself this evening?' said his Lordship, turning to me.

'I shall be at home, my Lord.'

'O, à-propos³—where are you?'

'Young ladies, my Lord,' said Mrs. Selwyn, 'are *no where*.'

'Prithee,' whispered his Lordship, 'is that queer woman your mother?'

Good Heavens, Sir, what words for such a question!

'No, my Lord.'

'Your maiden aunt, then?'

'No.'

'Whoever she is, I wish she would mind her own affairs: I don't know what the devil a woman lives for after thirty: she is only in other folks' way. Shall you be at the assembly?'⁴

'I believe not, my Lord.'

'No!—why then how in the world can you contrive to pass your time?'

'In a manner which your Lordship will think very extra-ordinary,' cried Mrs. Selwyn; 'for the young Lady *reads*.'

'Ha, ha, ha! Egad, my Lord,' cried the facetious companion, 'you are got into bad hands.'

'You had better, Madam,' answered he, 'attack Jack Coverley, here, for you will make nothing of me.'

'Of *you*, my Lord!' cried she; 'Heaven forbid I should ever entertain so idle an expectation! I only talk, like a silly woman, for the sake of talking; but I have by no means so low an opinion of your Lordship, as to suppose you vulnerable to censure.'

'Do, pray, Ma'am,' cried he, 'turn to Jack Coverley; he's the very man for you;—he'd be a wit himself if he was not too modest.'

'Prithee, my Lord, be quiet,' returned the other; 'if the Lady is contented to bestow all her favours upon *you*, why should you make such a point of my going snacks?'[5]

'Don't be apprehensive, Gentlemen,' said Mrs. Selwyn, drily, 'I am not romantic,[6]—I have not the least design of doing good to either of you.'

'Have not you been ill since I saw you?' said his Lordship again, addressing himself to me.

'Yes, my Lord.'

'I thought so; you are paler than you was, and I suppose that's the reason I did not recollect you sooner.'

'Has not your Lordship too much gallantry,' cried Mrs. Selwyn, 'to discover a young lady's illness by her looks?'

'The devil a word can I speak for that woman,' said he, in a low voice; 'do, prithee, Jack, take her in hand.'

'Excuse me, my Lord!' answered Mr. Coverley.

'When shall I see you again?' continued his Lordship; 'do you go to the Pump-room every morning?'

'No, my Lord.'

'Do you ride out?'

'No, my Lord.'

Just then we arrived at the Pump-room, and an end was put to our conversation, if it is not an abuse of words to give such a term to a string of rude questions and free compliments.

He had not opportunity to say much more to me, as Mrs. Selwyn joined a large party, and I walked home between two ladies. He had, however, the curiosity to see us to the door.

Mrs. Selwyn was very eager to know how I had made acquaintance with this nobleman, whose manners so evidently announced the character of a confirmed libertine: I could give her very little satisfaction, as I was ignorant even of his name. But, in the afternoon, Mr. Ridgeway the apothecary,[7] gave us very ample information.

As his person was easily described, for he is remarkably tall, Mr. Ridgeway told us he was Lord Merton, a nobleman who is but lately come to his title, though he has already dissipated more than half his fortune: a professed admirer of beauty, but a

man of most licentious character: that among men, his companions consisted chiefly of gamblers and jockies, and among
women, he was rarely admitted.

'Well, Miss Anville,' said Mrs. Selwyn, 'I am glad I was not more
civil to him. You may depend upon *me* for keeping him at a distance.'

'O, Madam,' said Mr. Ridgeway, 'he may now be admitted
any where, for he is going to *reform.*'

'Has he, under that notion, persuaded any fool to marry him?'

'Not yet, Madam, but a marriage is expected to take place
shortly: it has been some time in agitation, but the friends of the
Lady have obliged her to wait till she is of age: however, her
brother, who has chiefly opposed the match, now that she is near
being at her own disposal, is tolerably quiet. She is very pretty, and
will have a large fortune. We expect her at the Wells every day.'

'What is her name?' said Mrs. Selwyn.

'Larpent,' answered he, 'Lady Louisa Larpent, sister of Lord
Orville.'

'Lord Orville!' repeated I, all amazement.

'Yes, Ma'am; his Lordship is coming with her. I have had
certain information. They are to be at the honourable Mrs.
Beaumont's.[8] She is a relation of my Lord's and has a very fine
house upon Clifton Hill.'[9]

His Lordship is coming with her!—Good God, what an emotion
did those words give me! How strange, my dear Sir, that, just at
this time, he should visit Bristol! It will be impossible for me to
avoid seeing him, as Mrs. Selwyn is very well acquainted with
Mrs. Beaumont. Indeed, I have had an escape in not being under
the same roof with him, for Mrs. Beaumont invited us to her
house immediately upon our arrival; but the inconveniency of
being so distant from the Pump-room made Mrs. Selwyn decline
her civility.

Oh that the first meeting was over!—or that I could quit
Bristol without seeing him!—inexpressibly do I dread an interview: should the same impertinent freedom be expressed by his
looks, which dictated his cruel letter, I shall not know how to
endure either him or myself. Had I but returned it, I should be
easier, because my sentiments of it would then be known to him;

but now, he can only gather them from my behaviour, and I
tremble lest he should mistake my indignation for confusion!—
lest he should misconstrue my reserve into embarrassment!—for
how, my dearest Sir, how shall I be able totally to divest myself
of the respect with which I have been used to think of him?—
the pleasure with which I have been used to see him?

Surely he, as well as I, must recollect the letter at the moment
of our meeting, and he will, probably, mean to gather my
thoughts of it from my looks;—oh that they could but convey to
him my real detestation of impertinence and vanity! then would
he see how much he had mistaken my disposition when he
imagined them my due.

There was a time when the very idea that such a man as Lord
Merton should ever be connected with Lord Orville, would
have both surprised and shocked me, and even yet I am pleased
to hear of his repugnance to the marriage.

But how strange, that a man of so abandoned a character
should be the choice of a sister of Lord Orville! and how strange
that, almost at the moment of the union, he should be so
importunate in gallantry to another woman! What a world is this
we live in! how corrupt! how degenerate! well might I be
contented to see no more of it! If I find that the *eyes* of Lord
Orville agree with his *pen*,—I shall then think, that of all
mankind, the only virtuous individual resides at Berry Hill.

LETTER II

Evelina in continuation

Bristol Hotwells, Sept. 16

Oh Sir, Lord Orville is still himself! still, what from the moment
I beheld, I believed him to be—all that is amiable in man! and
your happy Evelina, restored at once to spirits and tranquillity,

is no longer sunk in her own opinion, nor discontented with the world,—no longer, with dejected eyes, sees the prospect of passing her future days in sadness, doubt, and suspicion!—with revived courage she now looks forward, and expects to meet with goodness, even among mankind:—though still she feels, as strongly as ever, the folly of hoping, in any *second* instance, to meet with *perfection*.

Your conjecture was certainly right; Lord Orville, when he wrote that letter, could not be in his senses. Oh that intemperance should have power to degrade so low, a man so noble!

This morning I accompanied Mrs. Selwyn to Clifton Hill, where, beautifully situated, is the house of Mrs. Beaumont. Most uncomfortable were my feelings during our walk, which was very slow, for the agitation of my mind made me more than usually sensible how weak I still continue. As we entered the house, I summoned all my resolution to my aid, determined rather to die than give Lord Orville reason to attribute my weakness to a wrong cause. I was happily relieved from my perturbation, when I saw Mrs. Beaumont was alone. We sat with her for, I believe, an hour without interruption, and then we saw a phaeton[10] drive up to the gate, and a lady and gentleman alight from it.

They entered the parlour with the ease of people who were at home. The gentleman, I soon saw, was Lord Merton; he came shuffling into the room with his boots on, and his whip in his hand; and, having made something like a bow to Mrs. Beaumont, he turned towards me. His surprise was very evident, but he took no manner of notice of me. He waited, I believe, to discover, first, what chance had brought me to that house, where he did not look much rejoiced at meeting me. He seated himself very quietly at the window, without speaking to any body.

Mean time, the lady, who seemed very young, hobbling rather than walking into the room, made a passing courtsie to Mrs. Beaumont, saying, 'How are you, Ma'am?' and then, without noticing any body else, with an air of languor she flung herself upon a sofa, protesting, in a most affected voice, and speaking so softly she could hardly be heard, that she was fatigued to death. 'Really, Ma'am, the roads are so monstrous dusty,—you can't imagine how troublesome the dust is to one's eyes!—and the sun, too, is monstrous disagreeable!—I dare say I shall be so tanned I sha'n't be fit to be seen this age. Indeed, my Lord, I won't go out with you any more, for you don't care where you take one.'

'Upon my honour,' said Lord Merton, 'I took you the pleasantest ride in England; the fault was in the sun, not me.'

'Your Lordship is in the right,' said Mrs. Selwyn, 'to transfer the fault to the *sun*, because it has so many excellencies to counterbalance partial inconveniences, that a *little* blame will not injure *that* in our estimation.'

Lord Merton looked by no means delighted at this attack; which I believe she would not so readily have made, but to revenge his neglect of us.

'Did you meet your brother, Lady Louisa?' said Mrs. Beaumont.

'No Ma'am. Is he rode out this morning?'

I then found, what I had before suspected, that this Lady was Lord Orville's sister: how strange, that such near relations should be so different to each other! There is, indeed, some resemblance in their features, but in their manners, not the least.

'Yes,' answered Mrs. Beaumont, 'and I believe he wished to see you.'

'My Lord drove so monstrous fast,' said Lady Louisa, 'that perhaps we passed him. He frighted me out of my senses; I declare my head is quite giddy: Do you know, Ma'am, we have done nothing but quarrel all the morning?—You can't think how I've scolded;—have not I, my Lord?' and she smiled expressively at Lord Merton.

'You have been, as you always are,' said he, twisting his whip with his fingers, 'all sweetness.'

'O fie, my Lord,' cried she, 'I know you don't think so; I know you think me very ill-natured;—don't you, my Lord?'

'No, upon my honour;—how can your Ladyship ask such a question? Pray how goes time? my watch stands.'[11]

'It is almost three,' answered Mrs. Beaumont.

'Lord, Ma'am, you frighten me!' cried Lady Louisa; and then turning to Lord Merton, 'why now, you wicked creature, you, did not you tell me it was but one?'

Mrs. Selwyn then rose to take leave; but Mrs. Beaumont asked if she would look at the shrubbery. 'I should like it much,' answered she, 'but that I fear to fatigue Miss Anville.'

Lady Louisa then, raising her head from her hand, on which it had leaned, turned round to look at me, and, having fully satisfied her curiosity, without any regard to the confusion it gave me, turned about, and, again leaning on her hand, took no further notice of me.

I declared myself very able to walk, and begged that I might accompany them. 'What say *you*, Lady Louisa,' cried Mrs. Beaumont, 'to a strole in the garden?'

'Me, Ma'am!—I declare I can't stir a step; the heat is so excessive, it would kill me. I'm half dead with it already; besides, I shall have no time to dress. Will any body be here to-day, Ma'am?'

'I believe not, unless Lord Merton will favour us with his company.'

'With great pleasure, Madam.'

'Well, I declare you don't deserve to be asked,' cried Lady Louisa, 'you wicked creature, you! I *must* tell you one thing, Ma'am,—you can't think how abominable he was! do you know we met Mr. Lovel in his new phaeton, and my Lord was so cruel as to drive against it?[12]—we really flew. I declare I could not breathe. Upon my word, my Lord, I'll never trust myself with you again,—I won't indeed!'

We then went into the garden, leaving them to discuss the point at their leisure.

Do you remember a *pretty but affected young lady*[13] I mention to have seen, in Lord Orville's party, at the Pantheon? How little did I then imagine her to be his sister! yet Lady Louisa Larpent is the very person. I can now account for the piqued manner of her speaking to Lord Merton that evening, and I can now account for the air of displeasure with which Lord Orville marked the undue attention of his future brother-in-law to me.

We had not walked long, ere, at a distance, I perceived Lord
Orville, who seemed just dismounted from his house, enter the
garden. All my perturbation returned at the sight of him!—yet I
endeavoured to repress every feeling but resentment. As he
approached us, he bowed to the whole party; but I turned away
my head, to avoid taking any share in his civility. Addressing
himself immediately to Mrs. Beaumont, he was beginning to
enquire after his sister, but upon seeing my face, he suddenly
exclaimed 'Miss Anville!—' and then he advanced, and made his
compliments to me,—not with an air of vanity or impertinence,
nor yet with a look of consciousness or shame,—but with a
countenance open, manly, and charming!—with a smile that
indicated pleasure, and eyes that sparkled with delight! on *my*
side was all the consciousness, for by him, I really believe, the
letter was, at that moment, entirely forgotten.

With what politeness did he address me! with what sweetness
did he look at me! the very tone of his voice seemed flattering!
he congratulated himself upon his good fortune in meeting with
me,—hoped I should spend some time at Bristol, and enquired,
even with anxiety enquired, if my health was the cause of my
journey, in which case his satisfaction would be converted into
apprehension.

Yet, struck as I was with his manner, and charmed to find him
such as he was wont to be, imagine not, my dear Sir, that I
forgot the resentment I owe him, or the cause he has given me
of displeasure; no, my behaviour was such as, I hope, had you
seen, you would not have disapproved: I was grave and distant,
I scarce looked at him when he spoke, or answered him when he
was silent.

As he must certainly observe this alteration in my conduct, I
think it could not fail making him both recollect and repent the
provocation he had so causelessly given me: for surely he was
not so wholly lost to reason, as to be now ignorant he had ever
offended me.

The moment that, without absolute rudeness, I was able, I
turned entirely from him, and asked Mrs. Selwyn if we should
not be late home? How Lord Orville looked I know not, for I

avoided meeting his eyes, but he did not speak another word as we proceeded to the garden-gate. Indeed I believe my abruptness surprised him, for he did not seem to expect I had so much spirit. And, to own the truth, convinced as I was of the propriety, nay, necessity of shewing my displeasure, I yet almost hated myself for receiving his politeness so ungraciously.

When we were taking leave, my eyes accidentally meeting his, I could not but observe that his gravity equalled my own, for it had entirely taken place of the smiles and good-humour with which he had met me.

'I am afraid this young Lady,' said Mrs. Beaumont, 'is too weak for another long walk till she is again rested.'

'If the Ladies will trust to my driving,' said Lord Orville, 'and are not afraid of a phaeton, mine shall be ready in a moment.'

'You are very good, my Lord,' said Mrs. Selwyn, 'but my will is yet unsigned, and I don't chuse to venture in a phaeton with a young man while that is the case.'

'O,' cried Mrs. Beaumont, 'you need not be afraid of my Lord Orville, for he is remarkably careful.'

'Well, Miss Anville,' answered she, 'what say you?'

'Indeed,' cried I, 'I had much rather walk.—' But then, looking at Lord Orville, I perceived in his face a surprise so serious at my abrupt refusal, that I could not forbear adding, 'for I should be sorry to occasion so much trouble.'

Lord Orville brightening at these words, came forward, and pressed his offer in a manner not to be denied;—so the phaeton was ordered! And indeed, my dear Sir,—I know not how it was,—but, from that moment, my coldness and reserve insensibly wore away! You must not be angry,—it was my intention, nay, my endeavour, to support them with firmness; but when I formed the plan, I thought only of the letter,—not of Lord Orville!—and how is it possible for resentment to subsist without provocation? yet, believe me, my dearest Sir, had he sustained the part he began to act when he wrote the ever-to-be-regretted letter, your Evelina would not have forfeited her title to your esteem, by contentedly submitting to be treated with indignity.

We continued in the garden till the phaeton was ready. When

we parted from Mrs. Beaumont, she repeated her invitation to Mrs. Selwyn to accept an apartment in her house, but the reason I have already mentioned made it be again declined.

Lord Orville drove very slow, and so cautiously, that, notwithstanding the height of the phaeton, fear would have been ridiculous. I supported no part in the conversation, but Mrs. Selwyn extremely well supplied the place of two. Lord Orville himself did not speak much, but the excellent sense and refined goodbreeding which accompany every word he utters, give value and weight to whatever he says.

'I suppose, my Lord,' said Mrs. Selwyn, when we stopped at our lodgings, 'you would have been extremely confused had we met any gentlemen who have the honour of knowing you.'

'If I had,' answered he, gallantly, 'it would have been from mere compassion at their envy.'

'No, my Lord,' answered she, 'it would have been from mere shame, that, in an age so daring you alone should be such a coward as to forbear to frighten women.'

'O,' cried he laughing, 'when a man is in a fright for himself, the ladies cannot but be in security; for you have not had half the apprehension for the safety of your persons, that I have for that of my heart.' He then alighted, handed us out, took leave, and again mounting the phaeton, was out of sight in a minute.

'Certainly,' said Mrs. Selwyn, when he was gone, 'there must have been some mistake in the birth of that young man; he was, undoubtedly, designed for the last age; for he is really polite!'

And now, my dear Sir, do not you think, according to the present situation of affairs, I may give up my resentment, without imprudence or impropriety? I hope you will not blame me. Indeed, had you, like me, seen his respectful behaviour, you would have been convinced of the impracticability of supporting any further indignation.

LETTER III

Evelina in continuation

Bristol Hotwells, Sept. 19th

Yesterday morning, Mrs. Selwyn received a card from Mrs. Beaumont, to ask her to dine with her to-day; and another, to the same purpose, came to me. The invitation was accepted, and we are but just arrived from Clifton Hill.

We found Mrs. Beaumont alone in the parlour. I will write you the character of that lady, in the words of our satirical friend Mrs. Selwyn. 'She is an absolute *Court Calendar bigot*;[14] for, chancing herself to be born of a noble and ancient family, she thinks proper to be of opinion, that *birth* and *virtue* are one and the same thing. She has some good qualities, but they rather originate from pride than principle, as she piques herself upon being too high born to be capable of an unworthy action, and thinks it incumbent upon her to support the dignity of her ancestry. Fortunately for the world in general, she has taken it into her head, that condescension is the most distinguishing virtue of high life; so that the same pride of family which renders others imperious, is with her the motive of affability. But her civility is too formal to be comfortable, and too mechanical to be flattering. That she does *me* the honour of so much notice, is merely owing to an accident which, I am sure, is very painful to her remembrance; for it so happened that I once did her some service, in regard to an apartment, at Southampton; and I have since been informed, that, at the time she accepted my assistance she thought I was a woman of quality;[15] and I make no doubt but she was miserable when she discovered me to be a mere country gentlewoman: however, her nice[16] notions of decorum have made her load me with favours ever since. But I am not much flattered by her civilities, as I am convinced I owe them neither to attachment nor gratitude, but solely to a desire of cancelling an obligation which she cannot brook being under, to one whose name is no where to be found in the Court Calendar.'

You well know, my dear Sir, the delight this lady takes in giving way to her satirical humour.

Mrs. Beaumont received us very graciously, though she somewhat distressed me by the question she asked concerning my family,—such as, Whether I was related to the Anvilles in the North?—Whether some of my name did not live in Lincolnshire? and many other enquiries, which much embarrassed me.

The conversation, next, turned upon the intended marriage in her family. She treated the subject with reserve, but it was evident she disapproved Lady Louisa's choice. She spoke in terms of the highest esteem of Lord Orville, calling him, in Marmontel's words, *Un jeune homme comme il y en a peu.*[17]

I did not think this conversation very agreeably interrupted by the entrance of Mr. Lovel. Indeed I am heartily sorry he is now at the Hotwells. He made his compliments with the most obsequious respect to Mrs. Beaumont, but took no sort of notice of any other person.

In a few minutes Lady Louisa Larpent made her appearance. The same manners prevailed; for courtsying, with, 'I hope you are well, Ma'am,' to Mrs. Beaumont, she passed straight forward to her seat on the sofa, where, leaning her head on her hand, she cast her languishing eyes round the room, with a vacant stare, as if determined, though she looked, not to see who was in it.

Mr. Lovel, presently approaching her, with reverence the most profound, hoped her Ladyship was not indisposed.

'Mr. Lovel!' cried she, raising her head, 'I declare I did not see you: Have you been here long?'

'By my *watch*, Madam,' said he, 'only five minutes,—but by your Ladyship's absence, as many hours.'

'O! now I think of it,' cried she, 'I am very angry with you,— so go along, do, for I sha'n't speak to you all day.'

'Heaven forbid your La'ship's displeasure should last so long! in such cruel circumstances, a day would seem an age. But in what have I been so unfortunate as to offend?'

'O, you half killed me, the other morning, with terror! I have not yet recovered from my fright. How could you be so cruel as to drive your phaeton against my Lord Merton's?'

''Pon honour, Ma'am, your La'ship does me wrong; it was all owing to the horses,—there was no curbing them. I protest I suffered more than your Ladyship from the terror of alarming you.'

Just then entered Lord Merton; stalking up to Mrs. Beaumont, to whom alone he bowed, he hoped he had not made her wait; and then advancing to Lady Louisa, said, in a careless manner, 'How is your Ladyship this morning?'

'Not well at all,' answered she; 'I have been dying with the head-ach ever since I got up.'

'Indeed!' cried he, with a countenance wholly unmoved, 'I am very unhappy to hear it. But should not your Ladyship have some advice?'

'I am quite sick of advice,' answered she; 'Mr. Ridgeway has but just left me,—but he has done me no good. Nobody here knows what is the matter with me, yet they all see how indifferent I am.'

'Your Ladyship's constitution,' said Mr. Lovel, 'is infinitely delicate.'

'Indeed it is,' cried she, in a low voice, 'I am *nerve* all over!'

'I am glad, however,' said Lord Merton, 'that you did not take the air this morning, for Coverley has been driving against me as if he was mad: he has got two of the finest spirited horses I ever saw.'

'Pray, my Lord,' cried she, 'why did not you bring Mr. Coverley with you? he's a droll creature; I like him monstrously.'

'Why, he promised to be here as soon as me. I suppose he'll come before dinner's over.'

In the midst of this trifling conversation Lord Orville made his appearance. O how different was his address! how superior did he look and move, to all about him! Having paid his respects to Mrs. Beaumont, and then to Mrs. Selwyn, he came up to me, and said, 'I hope Miss Anville has not suffered from the fatigue of Monday morning!' Then, turning to Lady Louisa, who seemed rather surprised at his speaking to me, he added 'Give me leave, Sister, to introduce Miss Anville to you.'

Lady Louisa, half-rising, said, very coldly, that she should be glad of the honour of knowing me; and then, abruptly turning to Lord Merton and Mr. Lovel, continued, in a half-whisper, her conversation.

For my part, I had risen and courtsied, and now, feeling very foolish, I seated myself again; first I blushed at the unexpected politeness of Lord Orville, and immediately afterwards, at the contemptuous failure of it in his sister. How can that young lady see her brother so universally admired for his manners and deportment, and yet be so unamiably opposite to him in hers! But while *his* mind, enlarged and noble, rises superior to the little prejudices of rank, *hers*, feeble and unsteady, sinks beneath their influence.

Lord Orville, I am sure, was hurt and displeased: he bit his lips, and turning from her, addressed himself wholly to me, till we were summoned to dinner. Do you think I was not grateful for his attention? yes, indeed, and every angry idea I had entertained, was totally obliterated.

As we were seating ourselves at the table, Mr. Coverley came into the room: he made a thousand apologies in a breath for being so late, but said he had been retarded by a little accident, for that he had overturned his phaeton, and broke it all to pieces. Lady Louisa screamed at this intelligence, and looking at Lord Merton, declared she would never go into a phaeton again.

'O,' cried he, 'never mind Jack Coverley, for he does not know how to drive.'

'My Lord,' cried Mr. Coverley, 'I'll drive against *you* for a thousand pounds.'

'Done!' returned the other; 'Name your day, and we'll each chuse a judge.'

'The sooner the better,' cried Mr. Coverley; 'to-morrow, if the carriage can be repaired.'

'These enterprizes,' said Mrs. Selwyn, 'are very proper for men of rank, since 'tis a million to one but both parties will be incapacitated for any better employment.'

'For Heaven's sake,' cried Lady Louisa, changing colour, 'don't talk so shockingly! Pray, my Lord, pray Mr. Coverley, don't alarm me in this manner.'

'Compose yourself, Lady Louisa,' said Mrs. Beaumont, 'the gentlemen will think better of the scheme, they are neither of them in earnest.'

'The very mention of such a scheme,' said Lady Louisa, taking out her salts, 'makes me tremble all over! Indeed, my Lord, you have frightened me to death! I sha'n't eat a morsel of dinner.'

'Permit me,' said Lord Orville, 'to propose some other subject for the present, and we will discuss this matter another time.'

'Pray, Brother, excuse me; my Lord must give me his word to drop this project,—for, I declare, it has made me sick as death.'

'To compromise the matter,' said Lord Orville, 'suppose, if both parties are unwilling to give up the bet, that, to make the ladies easy, we change its object to something less dangerous?'

This proposal was so strongly seconded by all the party, that both Lord Merton and Mr. Coverley were obliged to comply with it: and it was then agreed that the affair should be finally settled in the afternoon.

'I shall now be entirely out of conceit with phaetons again,' said Mrs. Selwyn, 'though Lord Orville had almost reconciled me to them.'

'My Lord Orville!' cried the witty Mr. Coverley, 'why, my Lord Orville is as careful,—egad, as careful as an old woman! Why, I'd drive a one-horse cart against my Lord's phaeton for a hundred guineas!'

This sally occasioned much laughter; for Mr. Coverley, I find, is regarded as a man of infinite humour.

'Perhaps, Sir,' said Mrs. Selwyn, 'you have not discovered the *reason* my Lord Orville is so careful?'

'Why, no, Ma'am; I must own, I never heard any particular reason for it.'

'Why then, Sir, I'll tell it you; and I believe you will confess it to be *very* particular; his Lordship's friends are not yet tired of him.'

Lord Orville laughed and bowed. Mr. Coverley, a little confused, turned to Lord Merton, and said, 'No foul play, my
Lord! I remember your Lordship recommended me to the notice of this lady the other morning, and, egad, I believe you have
been doing me the same office to-day.'

'Give you joy, Jack!' cried Lord Merton, with a loud laugh.

After this, the conversation turned wholly upon eating, a
subject which was discussed with the utmost delight; and, had I
not known they were men of rank and fashion, I should have
imagined that Lord Merton, Mr. Lovel, and Mr. Coverley, had
all been professed cooks; for they displayed so much knowledge
of sauces and made dishes, and of the various methods of
dressing the same things, that I am persuaded they must have
given much time, and much study, to make themselves such
adepts in this *art*. It would be very difficult to determine,
whether they were most to be distinguished as *gluttons*, or *epicures*;[18]
for they were, at once, dainty and voracious, understood the
right and the wrong of every dish, and alike emptied the one
and the other. I should have been quite sick of their remarks,
had I not been entertained by seeing that Lord Orville, who,
I am sure, was equally disgusted, not only read my sentiments,
but, by his countenance, communicated to me his own.

When dinner was over, Mrs. Beaumont recommended the
gentlemen to the care of Lord Orville, and then attended the
ladies to the drawing-room.

The conversation, till tea-time, was extremely insipid; Mrs.
Selwyn reserved herself for the gentlemen, Mrs. Beaumont was
grave, and Lady Louisa languid.

But, at tea, every body revived; we were joined by the
gentlemen, and gaiety took place of dullness.

Since I, as Mr. Lovel says, am *Nobody*,*[19] I seated myself
quietly on a window, and not very near to any body: Lord
Merton, Mr. Coverley, and Mr. Lovel, severally passed me
without notice, and surrounded the chair of Lady Louisa Larpent.
I must own, I was rather piqued at the behaviour of Mr. Lovel,

* Vol. I. p. 39

as he had formerly known me. It is true, I most sincerely despise his foppery, yet I should be grieved to meet with *contempt* from any body. But I was by no means sorry to find, that Lord Merton was determined not to know me before Lady Louisa, as his neglect relieved me from much embarrassment. As to Mr. Coverley, his attention or disregard were equally indifferent to me. Yet, altogether, I felt extremely uncomfortable in finding myself considered in a light very inferior to the rest of the company.

But, when Lord Orville appeared, the scene changed: he came up stairs last, and seeing me sit alone, not only spoke to me directly, but drew a chair next mine, and honoured me with his entire attention.

He enquired very particularly after my health, and hoped I had already found benefit from the Bristol air. 'How little did I imagine,' added he, 'when I had last the pleasure of seeing you in town, that ill health would, in so short a time, have brought you hither! I am ashamed of myself for the satisfaction I feel at seeing you,—yet how can I help it!'

He then enquired after the Mirvan family, and spoke of Mrs. Mirvan in terms of most just praise. 'She is gentle and amiable,' said he, 'a true feminine character.'

'Yes, indeed,' answered I, 'and her sweet daughter, to say every thing of her at once, is just the daughter such a mother deserves.'

'I am glad of it,' said he, 'for both their sakes, as such near relations must always reflect credit or disgrace on each other.'

After this, he began to speak of the beauties of Clifton; but, in a few moments, he was interrupted by a call from the company, to discuss the affair of the wager. Lord Merton and Mr. Coverley, though they had been discoursing upon the subject some time, could not fix upon any thing that satisfied them both.

When they asked the assistance of Lord Orville, he proposed that every body present should vote something, and that the two gentlemen should draw lots which, from the several votes, should decide the bet.

'We must then begin with the ladies,' said Lord Orville; and applied to Mrs. Selwyn.

'With all my heart,' answered she, with her usual readiness; 'and, since the gentlemen are not allowed to risk their *necks*, suppose we decide the bet by their *heads*?'

'By our heads?' cried Mr. Coverley; 'Egad, I don't understand you.'

'I will then explain myself more fully. As I doubt not but you are both excellent classics,[20] suppose, for the good of your own memories, and the entertainment and surprise of the company, the thousand pounds should fall to the share of him who can repeat by heart the longest ode of Horace?'[21]

Nobody could help laughing, the two gentlemen applied to excepted; who seemed, each of them, rather at a loss in what manner to receive this unexpected proposal. At length Mr. Coverley, bowing low, said, 'Will your Lordship please to begin?'

'Devil take me if I do!' answered he, turning on his heel, and stalking to the window.

'Come, Gentlemen,' said Mrs. Selwyn, 'why do you hesitate? I am sure you cannot be afraid of a weak *woman*? Besides, if you should chance to be out, Mr. Lovel, I dare say, will have the goodness to assist you.'

The laugh, now, turned against Mr. Lovel, whose change of countenance manifested no great pleasure at the transition.

'Me, Madam!' said he, colouring, 'no, really I must beg to be excused.'

'Why so, Sir?'

'Why so, Ma'am?—Why, really,—as to that,—'pon honour, Ma'am, you are rather—a little severe;—for how is it possible for a man who is in the House,[22] to study the classics? I assure you, Ma'am,' (with an affected shrug) 'I find quite business enough for *my* poor head, in studying politics.'

'But, did you study politics at school, and at the university?'[23]

'At the university!' repeated he with an embarrassed look; 'why, as to that, Ma'am—no, I can't say I did; but then, what with riding,—and—and—and so forth,—really, one has not much time, even at the university, for mere reading.'

'But, to be sure, Sir, you *have* read the classics?'

'O dear, yes, Ma'am!—very often,—but not very—not very lately.'

'Which of the odes do you recommend to these gentlemen to begin with?'

'Which of the odes!—Really, Ma'am, as to that, I have no very particular choice,—for, to own the truth, that Horace was never a very great favourite with me.'

'In truth I believe you!' said Mrs. Selwyn, very drily.

Lord Merton, again advancing into the circle, with a nod and a laugh, said, 'Give you joy, Lovel!'

Lord Orville next applied to Mrs. Beaumont for her vote.

'It would very agreeably remind me of past times,' said she, 'when *bowing* was in fashion, if the bet was to depend upon the best-made bow.'

'Egad, my Lord!' cried Mr. Coverley, 'there I should beat you hollow, for your Lordship never bows at all.'

'And, pray Sir, do *you*?' said Mrs. Selwyn.

'Do *I*, Ma'am?' cried he, 'Why, only see!'

'I protest,' cried she, 'I should have taken *that* for a *shrug*, if you had not told me 'twas a bow.'

'My Lord,' cried Mr. Coverley, 'let's practise;' and then, most ridiculously, they pranced about the room, making bows.

'We must now,' said Lord Orville, turning to me, 'call upon Miss Anville.'

'O no, my Lord,' cried I, 'indeed I have nothing to propose.' He would not, however, be refused, but urged me so much to say *something*, that at last, not to make him wait any longer, I ventured to propose an extempore couplet upon some given subject.[24]

Mr. Coverley instantly made me a bow, or, according to Mrs. Selwyn, a *shrug*, crying, 'Thank you, Ma'am; egad, that's my *fort*![25]—Why, my Lord, the Fates[26] seem against you.'

Lady Louisa was then applied to; and every body seemed eager to hear her opinion. 'I don't know what to say, I declare,' cried she, affectedly; 'can't you pass me?'

'By no means!' said Lord Merton.

'Is it possible your Ladyship can make so cruel a request?' said Mr. Lovel.

'Egad,' cried Mr. Coverley, 'if your Ladyship does not help us in this dilemma, we shall be forced to return to our phaetons.'

'Oh,' cried Lady Louisa, screaming, 'you frightful creature, you, how can you be so abominable!'

I believe this trifling lasted near half an hour; when, at length, every body being tired, it was given up, and she said she would consider against another time.

Lord Orville now called upon Mr. Lovel, who, after about ten minutes deliberation, proposed, with a most important face, to determine the wager by who should draw the longest straw!

I had much difficulty to forbear laughing at this unmeaning scheme; but saw, to my great surprise, not the least change of countenance in any other person: and, since we came home, Mrs. Selwyn has informed me, that to *draw straws* is a fashion of betting by no means uncommon! Good God! my dear Sir, does it not seem as if money were of no value or service, since those who possess, squander it away in a manner so infinitely absurd!

It now only remained for Lord Orville to speak; and the attention of the company shewed the expectations he had raised; yet, I believe, they by no means prevented his proposal from being heard with amazement; for it was no other, than that the money should be his due, who, according to the opinion of two judges, should bring the worthiest object with whom to share it!

They all stared, without speaking. Indeed, I believe every one, for a moment at least, experienced something like shame, from having either proposed or countenanced an extravagance so useless and frivolous. For my part, I was so much struck and affected by a rebuke so noble to these spendthrifts, that I felt my eyes filled with tears.

The short silence, and momentary reflection into which the company was surprised, Mr. Coverley was the first to dispel, by saying, 'Egad, my Lord, your Lordship has a most remarkable odd way of taking things.'

'Faith,' said the incorrigible Lord Merton, 'if this scheme takes, I shall fix upon my Swiss[27] to share with me; for I don't know a worthier fellow breathing.'

After a few more of these attempts at wit, the two gentlemen agreed that they would settle the affair the next morning.

The conversation then took a different turn, but I did not give it sufficient attention to write any account of it. Not long after, Lord Orville resuming his seat next mine, said, 'Why is Miss Anville so thoughtful?'

'I am sorry, my Lord,' said I, 'to consider myself among those who have so justly incurred your censure.'

'My censure!—you amaze me!'

'Indeed, my Lord, you have made me quite ashamed of myself, for having given my vote so foolishly, when an opportunity offered, if, like your Lordship, I had had the sense to use it, of shewing some humanity.'

'You treat this too seriously,' said he, smiling; 'and I hardly know if you do not now mean a rebuke to *me*.'

'To you, my Lord!'

'Nay, who are most deserving of it, those who adapt the conversation to the company, or, those who affect to be superior to it?'

'O, my Lord, who else would do you so little justice?'

'I flatter myself,' answered he, 'that, in fact, your opinion and mine, in this point, are the same, though you condescended to comply with the humour of the company. It is for me, therefore, to apologize for so unreasonable a gravity, which, but for the particular interest that I now take in the affairs of Lord Merton, I should not have been so officious to display.'

Such a compliment as this could not fail to reconcile me to myself; and with revived spirits, I entered into a conversation, which he supported with me till Mrs. Selwyn's carriage was announced, and we returned home.

During our ride, Mrs. Selwyn very much surprised me, by asking if I thought my health would now permit me to give up my morning walks to the Pump-room, for the purpose of spending a week at Clifton? 'for this poor Mrs. Beaumont,' added she, 'is so eager to have a discharge in full of her debt to me, that, out of mere compassion, I am induced to listen to her. Besides she has always a house full of people, and though they are chiefly fools and coxcombs, yet there is some pleasure in cutting them up.'[28]

I begged I might not, by any means, prevent her following her inclination, as my health was now very well established. And so, my dear Sir, to-morrow we are to be, actually, the guests of Mrs. Beaumont.

I am not much delighted at this scheme; for, greatly as I am flattered by the attention of Lord Orville, it is not very comfortable to be neglected by every body else. Besides, as I am sure I owe the particularity of his civility to a generous feeling for my situation, I cannot expect him to support it so long as a week.

How often do I wish, since I am absent from you, that I was under the protection of Mrs. Mirvan! It is true, Mrs. Selwyn is very obliging, and, in every respect, treats me as an equal; but she is contented with behaving well herself, and does not, with a distinguishing politeness, raise and support me with others. Yet I mean not to blame her, for I know she is sincerely my friend; but the fact is, she is herself so much occupied in conversation, when in company, that she has neither leisure nor thought to attend to the silent.

Well, I must take my chance! But I knew not, till now, how requisite are birth and fortune to the attainment of respect and civility.

LETTER IV

Evelina in continuation

Clifton, Sept. 20th

Here I am, my dear Sir, under the same roof; and inmate of the same house, as Lord Orville! Indeed, if this were not the case, my situation would be very disagreeable, as you will easily believe, when I tell you the light in which I am generally considered.

'My dear,' said Mrs. Selwyn, 'did you ever before meet with that egregious fop, Lovel?'

I very readily satisfied her as to my acquaintance with him.

'O then,' said she, 'I am the less surprised at his ill-nature, since he has already injured you.'

I begged her to explain herself; and then she told me, that while Lord Orville was speaking to me, Lady Louisa said to Mr. Lovel, 'do you know who that is?'

'Why, Ma'am, no, 'pon honour,' answered he, 'I can't absolutely say I do; I only know she is a kind of a toad-eater.[29] She made her first appearance in that capacity last Spring, when she attended Miss Mirvan, a young lady of Kent.'

How cruel is it, my dear Sir, to be thus exposed to the impertinent suggestions of a man who is determined to do me ill offices! Lady Louisa may well despise a *toad-eater*; but, thank Heaven, her brother has not heard, or does not credit, the mortifying appellation. Mrs. Selwyn said, she would advise me to *pay my court* to this Mr. Lovel; 'for,' said she, 'though he is malicious, he is fashionable, and may do you some harm in the great world.' But I should disdain myself as much as I do him, were I capable of such duplicity, as to flatter a man who I scorn and despise.

We were received by Mrs. Beaumont with great civility, and by Lord Orville with something more. As to Lady Louisa, she scarcely perceived that we were in the room.

There has been company here all day; part of which I have spent most happily; for after tea, when the ladies played at cards, Lord Orville, who does not, and I who cannot play, were consequently at our own disposal; and then his Lordship entered into a conversation with me, which lasted till supper-time.

Almost insensibly, I find the constraint, the reserve, I have been wont to feel in his presence, wear away; the politeness, the sweetness, with which he speaks to me, restore all my natural cheerfulness, and make me almost as easy as he is himself; and the more so, as, if I may judge by his looks, I am rather raised, than sunk, of late in his opinion.

I asked him, how the bet was, at last, to be decided? He told

me, that, to his great satisfaction, the parties had been prevailed
upon to lower the sum from one thousand to one hundred
pounds; and that they had agreed it should be determined, by a
race between two old women, one of which was to be chosen by
each side, and both were to be proved more than eighty years of
age, though, in other respects, strong and healthy as possible.

When I expressed my surprise at this extraordinary method of
spending so much money, 'I am charmed,' said he, 'at the
novelty of meeting with one so unhackneyed in the world, as
not to be yet influenced by custom to forget the use of reason:
for certain it is, that the prevalence of fashion makes the greatest
absurdities pass uncensured, and the mind naturally accommod-
ates itself, even to the most ridiculous improprieties, if they
occur frequently.'

'I should have hoped,' said I, 'that the humane proposal made
yesterday by your Lordship, would have had more effect.'

'O,' cried he, laughing, 'I was so far from expecting any
success, that I shall think myself very fortunate if I escape the
wit of Mr. Coverley in a lampoon![30] yet I spoke openly, because
I do not wish to conceal that I am no friend to gaming.'

After this, he took up the New Bath Guide,[31] and read it with
me till supper-time. In our way down stairs, Lady Louisa said, 'I
thought, Brother, you were engaged this evening?'

'Yes, Sister,' answered he, 'and I *have* been engaged.' And he
bowed to me with an air of gallantry that rather confused me.

September 23d

Almost insensibly have three days glided on since I wrote last,
and so serenely, that, but for your absence, I could not have
formed a wish. My residence here is much happier than I had
dared expect. The attention with which Lord Orville honours
me is as uniform as it is flattering, and seems to result from a
benevolence of heart that proves him as much a stranger to
caprice as to pride; for, as his particular civilities arose from a
generous resentment at seeing me neglected, so will they, I trust,
continue, as long as I shall, in any degree, deserve them. I am
now not merely easy, but even gay in his presence: such is the

effect of true politeness, that it banishes all restraint and embarrassment. When we walk out, he condescends to be my companion, and keeps by my side all the way we go. When we read, he marks the passages most worthy to be noticed, draws out my sentiments, and favours me with his own. At table, where he always sits next to me, he obliges me by a thousand nameless attentions, while the distinguishing good-breeding with which he treats me, prevents my repining at the visibly-felt superiority of the rest of the company. A thousand occasional meetings could not have brought us to that degree of social freedom, which four days spent under the same roof have, insensibly, been productive of: and, as my only friend in this house, Mrs. Selwyn, is too much engrossed in perpetual conversation to attend much to me, Lord Orville seems to regard me as a helpless stranger, and, as such, to think me entitled to his good offices and protection. Indeed, my dear Sir, I have reason to hope, that the depreciating opinion he formerly entertained of me is succeeded by one infinitely more partial.—It may be that I flatter myself, but yet his looks, his attentions, his desire of drawing me into conversation, and his solicitude to oblige me, all conspire to make me hope I do not. In short, my dearest Sir, these last four happy days would repay me for months of sorrow and pain!

LETTER V

Evelina in continuation

Clifton, Sept. 24th

This morning I came down stairs very early, and, supposing that the family would not assemble for some time, I strolled out, purposing to take a long walk, in the manner I was wont to do at Berry Hill, before breakfast. But I had scarce shut the garden-

gate, before I was met by a gentleman, who, immediately bowing
to me, I recollected to be the unhappy Mr. Macartney. Very
much surprised, I courtsied, and stopped till he came up to me.
He was still in mourning, but looked better than when I saw
him last, though he had the same air of melancholy which so
much struck me at first sight of him.

Addressing me with the utmost respect, 'I am happy, Madam,'
said he, 'to have met with you so soon. I came to Bristol but
yesterday, and have had no small difficulty in tracing you to
Clifton.'

'Did you know, then, of my being here?'

'I did, Madam; the sole motive of my journey was to see you.
I have been to Berry Hill, and there I had my intelligence, and,
at the same time, the unwelcome information of your ill health.'

'Good God! Sir,—and can you possibly have taken so much
trouble?'

'Trouble! Oh, Madam, could there be any, to return you, the
moment I had the power, my personal acknowledgements for
your goodness?'

I then enquired after Madame Duval, and the Snow Hill family.
He told me, they were all well, and that Madame Duval proposed
soon returning to Paris. When I congratulated him upon looking
better, 'It is *yourself*, Madam,' said he, 'you should congratulate,
for to your humanity alone it may now be owing that I exist at
all.' He then told me, that his affairs were now in a less desperate
situation, and that he hoped, by the assistance of time and reason,
to accommodate his mind to a more chearful submission to his
fate. 'The interest you so generously took in my affliction,' added
he, 'assures me you will not be displeased to hear of my better
fortune: I was therefore eager to acquaint you with it.' He then
told me, that his friend, the moment he had received his letter,
quitted Paris, and flew to give him his personal assistance and
consolation. With a heavy heart, he acknowledged, he accepted it;
'but yet,' he added, 'I *have* accepted it, and therefore, as bound
equally by duty and honour, my first step was to hasten to the
benefactress of my distress, and to return' (presenting me something in a paper) 'the only part of my obligations that *can* be

returned; for the rest, I have nothing but my gratitude to offer, and must always be contented to consider myself her debtor.'

I congratulated him most sincerely upon his dawning prosperity, but begged he would not deprive me of the pleasure of being his friend, and declined receiving the money, till his affairs were more settled.

While this point was in agitation, I heard Lord Orville's voice, enquiring of the gardener if he had seen me? I immediately opened the garden-gate, and his Lordship, advancing to me with quickness, said, 'Good God, Miss Anville, have you been out, alone? Breakfast has been ready some time, and I have been round the garden in search of you.'

'Your Lordship has been very good,' said I; 'but I hope you have not waited.'

'Not waited!' repeated he, smiling. 'Do you think we could sit down quietly to breakfast, with the idea that you had run away from us? But come,' (offering to hand me) 'if we do not return, they will suppose *I* am run away too; and they very naturally may, as they know the attraction of the magnet that draws me.'

'I will come, my Lord,' said I, rather embarrassed, 'in two minutes.' Then, turning to Mr. Macartney, with yet more embarrassment, I wished him good morning.

He advanced towards the garden, with the paper still in his hand.

'No, no,' cried I, 'some other time.'

'May I then, Madam, have the honour of seeing you again?'

I did not dare take the liberty of inviting any body to the house of Mrs. Beaumont, nor yet had I the presence of mind to make an excuse; and therefore, not knowing how to refuse him, I said, 'Perhaps you may be this way again to-morrow morning,—and I believe I shall walk out before breakfast.'

He bowed, and went away; while I, turning again to Lord Orville, saw his countenance so much altered, that I was frightened at what I had so hastily said. He did not again offer me his hand, but walked, silent and slow, by my side. Good Heaven! thought I, what may he not suppose from this adventure? May he not, by my desire of meeting Mr. Macartney to-morrow, imagine it was by design I walked out to meet him to-day?

Tormented by this apprehension, I determined to avail myself of
the freedom which his behaviour since I came hither has encouraged; and, since he would not ask any questions, begin an
explanation myself. I therefore slackened my pace, to gain time,
and then said, 'Was not your Lordship surprised to see me
speaking with a stranger?'

'A stranger!' repeated he; 'is it possible that gentleman can be
a stranger to you?'

'No, my Lord'—said I, stammering, 'not to *me*,—but only it
might look—he might seem—'

'No, believe me,' said he, with a forced smile, 'I could never
suppose Miss Anville would make an appointment with a stranger.'

'An appointment, my Lord!' repeated I, colouring violently.

'Pardon me, Madam,' answered he, 'but I thought I had heard
one.'

I was so much confounded, that I could not speak; yet,
finding he walked quietly on, I could not endure he should make
his own interpretation of my silence; and therefore, as soon as I
recovered from my surprise, I said, 'Indeed, my Lord, you are
much mistaken,—Mr. Macartney had particular business with
me,—and I could not,—I knew not how to refuse seeing him,—
but indeed, my Lord—I had not,—he had not,'—I stammered
so terribly that I could not go on.

'I am very sorry,' said he, gravely, 'that I have been so
unfortunate as to distress you; but I should not have followed
you, had I not imagined you were merely walked out for the
air.'

'And so I was!' cried I, eagerly, 'indeed, my Lord, I was! My
meeting with Mr. Macartney was quite accidental; and if your
Lordship thinks there is any impropriety in my seeing him to-
morrow, I am ready to give up that intention.'

'If *I* think!' said he, in a tone of surprise; 'surely Miss Anville
must best judge for herself! surely she cannot leave the arbitration
of a point so delicate, to one who is ignorant of all the circumstances which attend it?'

'If,' said I, 'it was worth your Lordship's time to hear them,—
you should *not* be ignorant of the circumstances which attend it.'

'The sweetness of Miss Anville's disposition,' said he, in a softened voice, 'I have long admired, and the offer of a communication which does me so much honour, is too grateful to me not to be eagerly caught at.'

Just then, Mrs. Selwyn opened the parlour-window, and our conversation ended. I was rallied upon my passion for solitary walking, but no questions were asked me.

When breakfast was over, I hoped to have had some opportunity of speaking with Lord Orville; but Lord Merton and Mr. Coverley came in, and insisted upon his opinion of the spot they had fixed upon for the old women's race. The ladies declared they would be of the party, and, accordingly, we all went.

The race is to be run in Mrs. Beaumont's garden; the two gentlemen are as anxious as if their joint lives depended upon it. They have, at length, fixed upon objects, but have found great difficulty in persuading them to practise running, in order to try their strength. This grand affair is to be decided next Thursday.

When we returned to the house, the entrance of more company still prevented my having any conversation with Lord Orville. I was very much chagrined, as I knew he was engaged at the Hotwells in the afternoon. Seeing, therefore, no probability of speaking to him before the time of my meeting Mr. Macartney arrived, I determined that, rather than risk his ill opinion, I would leave Mr. Macartney to his own suggestions.

Yet, when I reflected upon his peculiar situation, his poverty, his sadness, and, more than all the rest, the idea I knew he entertained of what he calls his obligations to me, I could not resolve upon a breach of promise, which might be attributed to causes of all others the most offensive to one whom misfortune has made extremely suspicious of slights and contempt.

After the most uneasy consideration, I at length determined upon writing an excuse, which would, at once, save me from either meeting or affronting him. I therefore begged Mrs. Selwyn's leave to send her man to the Hotwells, which she instantly granted; and then I wrote the following note.

To Mr. Macartney

Sir,

As it will not be in my power to walk out to-morrow morning, I would by no means give you the trouble of coming to Clifton. I hope, however, to have the pleasure of seeing you before you quit Bristol. I am,

Sir,

Your obedient servant,

EVELINA ANVILLE

I desired the servant to enquire at the Pump-room where Mr. Macartney lived, and returned to the parlour.

As soon as the company dispersed, the ladies retired to dress. I then, unexpectedly, found myself alone with Lord Orville; who, the moment I rose to follow Mrs. Selwyn, advanced to me, and said, 'Will Miss Anville pardon my impatience, if I remind her of the promise she was so good as to make me this morning?'

I stopped, and would have returned to my seat, but, before I had time, the servants came to lay the cloth. He retreated, and went towards the window; and while I was considering in what manner to begin, I could not help asking myself what *right* I had to communicate the affairs of Mr. Macartney; and I doubted whether, to clear myself from one act of imprudence, I had not committed another.

Distressed by this reflection, I thought it best to quit the room, and give myself some time for consideration before I spoke; and therefore, only saying I must hasten to dress, I ran up stairs: rather abruptly, I own, and so, I fear, Lord Orville must think; yet what could I do? unused to the situations in which I find myself, and embarrassed by the slightest difficulties, I seldom, till too late, discover how I ought to act.

Just as we were all assembled to dinner, Mrs. Selwyn's man, coming into the parlour, presented to me a letter, and said, 'I can't find out Mr. Macartney, Madam; but the post-office[32] people will let you know if they hear of him.'

I was extremely ashamed of this public message; and meeting

the eyes of Lord Orville, which were earnestly fixed on me, my confusion redoubled, and I knew not which way to look. All dinner-time, he was as silent as myself, and, the moment it was in my power, I left the table, and went to my own room. Mrs. Selwyn presently followed me, and her questions obliged me to own almost all the particulars of my acquaintance with Mr. Macartney, in order to excuse my writing to him. She said it was a most romantic[33] affair, and spoke her sentiments with great severity, declaring that she had no doubt but he was an adventurer and an impostor.

And now, my dear Sir, I am totally at a loss what I ought to do: the more I reflect, the more sensible I am of the utter impropriety, nay, treachery, of revealing the story, and publishing the misfortunes and poverty of Mr. Macartney? who has an undoubted right to my secrecy and discretion, and whose letter charges me to regard his communication as sacred.—And yet, the appearance of mystery,—perhaps something worse, which this affair must have to Lord Orville,—his seriousness,—and the promise I have made him, are inducements scarce to be resisted for trusting him, with the openness he has reason to expect from me.

I am equally distressed, too, whether or not I should see Mr. Macartney to-morrow morning.

Oh, Sir, could I now be enlightened by your counsel, from what anxiety and perplexity should I be relieved!

But no,—I ought not to betray Mr. Macartney, and I will not forfeit a confidence which would never have been reposed in me, but from a reliance upon my honour which I should blush to find myself unworthy of. Desirous as I am of the good opinion of Lord Orville, I will endeavour to act as if I was guided by your advice, and, making it my sole aim to *deserve* it, leave to time and to fate my success or disappointment.

Since I have formed this resolution, my mind is more at ease; but I will not finish my letter till the affair is decided.

Sept. 25th

I rose very early this morning, and, after a thousand different plans, not being able to resolve upon giving poor Mr. Macartney leave to suppose I neglected him, I thought it incumbent upon me to keep my word, since he had not received my letter; I therefore determined to make my own apologies, not to stay with him two minutes, and to excuse myself from meeting him any more.

Yet, uncertain whether I was wrong or right, it was with fear and trembling that I opened the garden-gate,—judge, then, of my feelings, when the first object I saw was Lord Orville!—he, too, looked extremely disconcerted, and said, in a hesitating manner, 'Pardon me, Madam,—I did not intend,—I did not imagine you would have been here so soon—or,—or I would not have come.'—And then, with a hasty bow, he passed me, and proceeded to the garden.

I was scarce able to stand, so greatly did I feel myself shocked; but, upon my saying, almost involuntarily, 'Oh my Lord!'—he turned back, and, after a short pause, said, 'Did you speak to *me*, Madam?'

I could not immediately answer; I seemed *choaked*, and was even forced to support myself by the garden-gate.

Lord Orville, soon recovering his dignity, said, 'I know not how to apologize for being, just now, at this place;—and I cannot immediately,—if *ever*,—clear myself from the imputation of impertinent curiosity, to which I fear you will attribute it: however, at present, I will only entreat your pardon, without detaining you any longer.' Again he bowed, and left me.

For some moments, I remained fixed to the same spot, and in the same position, immoveably as if I had been transformed to stone. My first impulse was to call him back, and instantly tell him the whole affair; but I checked this desire, though I would have given the world to have indulged it; something like pride aided what I thought due to Mr. Macartney, and I determined not only to keep his secret, but to delay any sort of explanation, till Lord Orville should condescend to request it.

Slowly he walked, and before, he entered the house, he looked back, but hastily withdrew his eyes, upon finding I observed him.

Indeed, my dear Sir, you cannot easily imagine a situation more uncomfortable than mine was at that time; to be suspected by Lord Orville of any clandestine actions, wounded my soul; I was too much discomposed to wait for Mr. Macartney, nor, in truth, could I endure to have the design of my staying so well known. Yet I was so extremely agitated, that I could hardly move, and, I have reason to believe, Lord Orville, from the parlour-window, saw me tottering along, for, before I had taken five steps, he came out, and hastening to meet me, said, 'I fear you are not well; pray allow me' (offering his arm) 'to assist you.'

'No, my Lord,' said I, with all the resolution I could assume; yet I was affected by an attention, at that time so little expected, and forced to turn away my head to conceal my emotion.

'You *must*,' said he, with earnestness, 'indeed you must,—I am sure you are not well;—refuse me not the honour of assisting you;' and, almost forcibly, he took my hand, and drawing it under his arm obliged me to lean upon him. That I submitted was partly the effect of surprise at an earnestness so uncommon in Lord Orville, and partly, that I did not, just then, dare trust my voice to make any objection.

When we came to the house, he led me into the parlour, and to a chair, and begged to know if I would not have a glass of water.

'No, my Lord, I thank you,' said I, 'I am perfectly recovered;' and, rising, I walked to the window, where, for some time, I pretended to be occupied in looking at the garden.

Determined as I was to act honourably by Mr. Macartney, I yet most anxiously wished to be restored to the good opinion of Lord Orville; but his silence, and the thoughtfulness of his air, discouraged me from speaking.

My situation soon grew disagreeable and embarrassing, and I resolved to return to my chamber till breakfast was ready. To remain longer, I feared, might seem *asking* for his enquiries; and I was sure it would ill become me to be more eager to speak, than he was to hear.

Just as I reached the door, turning to me hastily, he said, 'Are you going, Miss Anville?'

'I am, my Lord,' answered I, yet I stopped.

'Perhaps to return to—but I beg your pardon!' he spoke with

a degree of agitation that made me readily comprehend he meant
to *the Garden*, and I instantly said, 'To my own room, my Lord.'
And again I would have gone; but, convinced by my answer that
I understood him, I believe he was sorry for the insinuation; he
approached me with a very serious air, though, at the same time,
he forced a smile, and said, 'I know not what evil genius pursues
me this morning, but I seem destined to do or to say something
I ought not: I am so much ashamed of myself, that I can scarce
solicit your forgiveness.'

'My forgiveness! my Lord?' cried I, abashed, rather than elated
by his condescension, 'surely you cannot—you are not serious?'

'Indeed never more so; yet, if I may be my own interpreter,
Miss Anville's countenance pronounces my pardon.'

'I know not, my Lord, how any one can *pardon*, who has
never been offended.'

'You are very good; yet I could expect no less from a
sweetness of disposition which baffles all comparison: will you
not think I am an encroacher, and that I take advantage of your
goodness, should I once more remind you of the promise you
vouchsafed me yesterday?'

'No, indeed; on the contrary, I shall be very happy to acquit
myself in your Lordship's opinion.'

'Acquittal you need not,' said he, leading me again to the
window, 'yet I own my curiosity is strongly excited.'

When I was seated, I found myself much at a loss what to say;
yet, after a short silence, assuming all the courage in my power,
'Will you not, my Lord,' said I, 'think me trifling and capricious,
should I own I have repented the promise I made, and should I
entreat your Lordship not to insist upon my strict performance
of it?—'I spoke so hastily, that I did not, at the time, consider
the impropriety of what I said.

As he was entirely silent, and profoundly attentive, I continued
to speak without interruption.

'If your Lordship, by any other means, knew the circumstances
attending my acquaintance with Mr. Macartney, I am most sure
you would yourself disapprove my relating them. He is a gentleman, and has been very unfortunate,—but I am not,—I think,—

at liberty to say more; yet I am sure, if he knew your lordship wished to hear any particulars of his affairs, he would readily consent to my acknowledging them;—shall I, my Lord, ask his permission?'

'*His* affairs!' repeated Lord Orville; 'by no means, I have not the least curiosity about them.'

'I beg your Lordship's pardon,—but indeed I had understood the contrary.'

'Is it possible, Madam, you could suppose the affairs of an utter stranger can excite my curiosity?'

The gravity and coldness with which he asked this question, very much abashed me; but Lord Orville is the most delicate of men, and, presently recollecting himself, he added, 'I mean not to speak with indifference of any friend of yours,—far from it; any such will always command my good wishes: yet I own I am rather disappointed; and though I doubt not the justice of your reason, to which I implicitly submit, you must not wonder, that, when upon the point of being honoured with your confidence, I should feel the greatest regret at finding it withdrawn.'

Do you think, my dear Sir, I did not, at that moment, require all my resolution to guard me from frankly telling him whatever he wished to hear? yet I rejoice that I did not; for added to the actual wrong I should have done, Lord Orville himself, when he had heard, would, I am sure, have blamed me. Fortunately, this thought occurred to me, and I said, 'Your Lordship shall yourself be my judge; the promise I made, though voluntary, was rash and inconsiderate; yet, had it concerned myself, I would not have hesitated in fulfilling it; but the gentleman whose affairs I should be obliged to relate—'

'Pardon me,' cried he, 'for interrupting you; yet allow me to assure you, I have not the slightest desire to be acquainted with his affairs, further than what belongs to the motives which induced you yesterday morning—' He stopped; but there was no occasion to say more.

'That, my Lord,' cried I, 'I will tell you honestly. Mr. Macartney had some particular business with me,—and I could not take the liberty to ask him hither.'

'And why not?—Mrs. Beaumont, I am sure,—'

'I could not, my Lord, think of intruding upon Mrs. Beaumont's complaisance; and so, with the same hasty folly I promised your Lordship, I much *more* rashly, promised to meet him.'

'And did you?'

'No, my Lord,' said I, colouring, 'I returned before he came.'

Again, for some time, we were both silent; yet, unwilling to leave him to reflections which could not but be to my disadvantage, I summoned sufficient courage to say, 'There is no young creature, my Lord, who so greatly wants, or so earnestly wishes for, the advice and assistance of her friends, as I do; I am new to the world, and unused to acting for myself,—my intentions are never wilfully blameable, yet I err perpetually!—I have, hitherto, been blessed with the most affectionate of friends, and, indeed, the ablest of men, to guide and instruct me upon every occasion;—but he is too distant, now, to be applied to at the moment I want his aid; —and *here*,—there is not a human being whose counsel I can ask!'

'Would to Heaven,' cried he, with a countenance from which all coldness and gravity were banished, and succeeded by the mildest benevolence, 'that *I* were worthy,—and capable,—of supplying the place of such a friend to Miss Anville!'

'You do me but too much honour,' said I; 'yet I hope your Lordship's candour,—perhaps I ought to say indulgence,—will make some allowance, on account of my inexperience, for behaviour, so inconsiderate:—May I, my Lord, hope that you will?'

'May *I*,' cried he, 'hope that you will pardon the ill-grace with which I have submitted to my disappointment? and that you will permit me' (kissing my hand) 'thus to seal my peace?'

'*Our* peace, my Lord,' said I, with, revived spirits.

'This, then,' said he, again pressing it to his lips, 'for *our* peace: and now,—are we not friends?'

Just then, the door opened, and I had only time to withdraw my hand, before the ladies came in to breakfast.

I have been, all day, the happiest of human beings!—to be thus reconciled to Lord Orville, and yet to adhere to my resolution,—what could I wish for more?—he, too, has been very chearful, and more attentive, more obliging to me than ever. Yet Heaven forbid I should again be in a similar situation, for I cannot express how much uneasiness I have suffered from the fear of incurring his ill opinion.

But what will poor Mr. Macartney think of me? happy as I am, I much regret the necessity I have been under of disappointing him.

Adieu, my dearest Sir.

LETTER VI

Mr. Villars to Evelina

Berry Hill, Sept. 28

Dead to the world, and equally insensible to its pleasures or its pains, I long since bid adieu to all joy, and defiance to all sorrow, but what should spring from my Evelina,—sole source, to me, of all earthly felicity. How strange, then, is it, that the letter in which she tells me she is the *happiest of human beings*, should give me the most mortal inquietude!

Alas, my child!—that innocence, the first, best gift of Heaven, should, of all others, be the blindest to its own danger,—the most exposed to treachery,—and the least able to defend itself, in a world where it is little known, less valued, and perpetually deceived!

Would to Heaven you were here!—then, by degrees, and with gentleness, I might enter upon a subject too delicate for distant discussion. Yet is it too interesting, and the situation too critical, to allow of delay.—Oh my Evelina, your situation is critical indeed!—your peace of mind is at stake, and every chance for your future happiness may depend upon the conduct of the present moment.

Hitherto I have forborne to speak with you upon the most important of all concerns, the state of your heart:—alas, I need no information! I have been silent, indeed, but I have not been blind.

Long, and with the deepest regret, have I perceived the ascendancy which Lord Orville has gained upon your mind.— You will start at the mention of his name,—you will tremble every word you read;—I grieve to give pain to my gentle Evelina, but I dare not any longer spare her.

Your first meeting with Lord Orville was decisive. Lively, fearless, free from all other impressions, such a man as you describe him could not fail exciting your admiration, and the more dangerously, because he seemed as unconscious of his power as you of your weakness; and therefore you had no alarm, either from *his* vanity or *your own* prudence.

Young, animated, entirely off your guard, and thoughtless of consequences, *Imagination* took the reins, and *Reason*, slow-paced, though sure-footed, was unequal to a race with so eccentric and flighty a companion. How rapid was then my Evelina's progress through those regions of fancy and passion whither her new guide conducted her!—She saw Lord Orville at a ball,—and he was *the most amiable of men*!—She met him again at another,—and *he had every virtue under heaven*!

I mean not to depreciate the merit of Lord Orville, who, one mysterious instance alone excepted, seems to have deserved the idea you formed of his character; but it was not time, it was not the knowledge of his worth, obtained your regard; your new comrade had not patience to wait any trial; her glowing pencil,[34] dipped in the vivid colours of her creative ideas, painted to you, at the moment of your first acquaintance, all the excellencies, all the good and rare qualities, which a great length of time, and intimacy, could alone have really discovered.

You flattered yourself, that your partiality was the effect of esteem, founded upon a general love of merit, and a principle of justice: and your heart, which fell the sacrifice of your error, was totally gone ere you suspected it was in danger.

A thousand times have I been upon the point of shewing you the perils of your situation; but the same inexperience which occasioned your mistake, I hoped, with the assistance of time and absence, would effect a cure: I was, indeed, most unwilling to destroy your illusion, while I dared hope it might itself contribute to the restoration of your tranquility; since your ignorance of the danger and force of your attachment, might possibly prevent that despondency with which young people, in similar circumstances, are apt to persuade themselves that what is only difficult, is absolutely impossible.

But now, since you have again met, and are become more intimate than ever, all my hope from silence and seeming ignorance is at an end.

Awake, then, my dear, my deluded child, awake to the sense of your danger, and exert yourself to avoid the evils with which it threatens you,—evils which, to a mind like yours, are most to be dreaded, secret repining, and concealed, yet consuming regret! Make a noble effort for the recovery of your peace, which now, with sorrow I see it, depends wholly upon the presence of Lord Orville. This effort, may, indeed, be painful, but trust to my experience, when I assure you it is requisite.

You must quit him!—his sight is baneful to your repose, his society is death to your future tranquillity! Believe me, my beloved child, my heart aches for your suffering, while it dictates its necessity.

Could I flatter myself that Lord Orville would, indeed, be sensible of your worth, and act with a nobleness of mind which should prove it congenial to his own, then would I leave my Evelina to the unmolested enjoyment of the chearful society and increasing regard of a man she so greatly admires: but this is not an age in which we may trust to appearances, and imprudence is much sooner regretted than repaired. Your health, you tell me, is much mended,—can you then consent to leave Bristol?—not abruptly, that I do not desire, but in a few days from the time you receive this? I will write to Mrs. Selwyn, and tell her how much I wish your return; and Mrs. Clinton can take sufficient care of you.

I have meditated upon every possible expedient that might tend to your happiness, ere I fixed upon exacting from you a compliance which I am convinced will be most painful to you;— but I can satisfy myself in none. This will at least be safe, and as to success,—we must leave it to time.

I am very glad to hear of Mr. Macartney's welfare.

Adieu, my dearest child; Heaven preserve and strengthen you!

A. V.

LETTER VII

Evelina to the Rev. Mr. Villars

Clifton, Sept. 28

Sweetly, most sweetly, have two days more passed since I wrote; but I have been too much engaged to be exact in my journal.

To-day has been less tranquil. It was destined for the decision of the important bet, and has been productive of general confusion throughout the house. It was settled that the race should be run at five o'clock in the afternoon. Lord Merton breakfasted here, and stayed till noon. He wanted to engage the Ladies to *bet on his side*,[35] in the true spirit of gaming, without seeing the racers. But he could only prevail on Lady Louisa, as Mrs. Selwyn said she never laid a wager against her own wishes, and Mrs. Beaumont would not *take sides*. As for *me*, I was not applied to. It is impossible for negligence to be more pointed, than that of Lord Merton to me, in the presence of Lady Louisa.

But, just before dinner, I happened to be alone in the drawing-room, when his Lordship suddenly returned, and coming in with his usual familiarity, he was beginning, 'You see, Lady Louisa,—' but stopping short, 'Pray where's every body gone?'

'Indeed I don't know, my Lord.'

He then shut the door, and, with a great alteration in his face and manner, advanced eagerly towards me, and said, 'How glad I am, my sweet girl, to meet you, at last, alone! By my soul, I began to think there was a plot against me, for I've never been able to have you a minute to myself.' And, very freely, he seized my hand.

I was so much surprised at this address, after having been so long totally neglected, that I could make no other answer than staring at him with unfeigned astonishment.

'Why now,' continued he, 'if you was not the cruellest little angel in the world, you would have helped me to some expedient: for you see how I am watched here; Lady Louisa's eyes are never off me. She gives me a charming foretaste of the pleasures of a wife! however, it won't last long.'

Disgusted to the greatest degree, I attempted to draw away my hand, but I believe I should not have succeeded, if Mrs. Beaumont had not made her appearance. He turned from me with the greatest assurance, and said, 'How are you, Ma'am?—how is Lady Louisa?—you see I can't live a moment out of the house.'

Could you, my dearest Sir, have believed it possible for such effrontery to be in man?

Before dinner, came Mr. Coverley, and before five o'clock, Mr. Lovel and some other company. The place marked out for the race, was a gravel-walk in Mrs. Beaumont's garden, and the length of the ground twenty yards. When we were summoned to the *course*, the two poor old women made their appearance. Though they seemed very healthy for their time of life, they yet looked so weak, so infirm, so feeble, that I could feel no sensation but that of pity at the sight. However, this was not the general sense of the company, for they no sooner came forward, than they were greeted with a laugh from every beholder, Lord Orville excepted, who looked very grave during the whole transaction. Doubtless he must be greatly discontented at the dissipated conduct and extravagance, of a man with whom he is, soon, to be so nearly connected.

For some time, the scene was truly ridiculous; the agitation of the parties concerned, and the bets that were laid upon the old women, were absurd beyond measure. *Who are you for?* and *whose side are you of?* was echoed from mouth to mouth by the whole company. Lord Merton and Mr. Coverley were both so excessively gay and noisy, that I soon found they had been too free in drinking to their success. They handed, with loud shouts, the old women to the race-ground, and encouraged them, by liberal promises, to exert themselves.[36]

When the signal was given for them to set off, the poor creatures, feeble and frightened, ran against each other, and neither of them able to support the shock, they both fell on the ground.

Lord Merton and Mr. Coverley flew to their assistance. Seats were brought for them, and they each drank a glass of wine. They complained of being much bruised; for, heavy and helpless, they had not been able to save themselves, but fell, with their whole weight upon the gravel. However, as they seemed equal sufferers, both parties were too eager to have the affair deferred.

Again, therefore, they set off, and hobbled along, nearly even with each other, for some time, yet frequently, and to the inexpressible diversion of the company, they stumbled and tottered; and the confused hallowing of '*Now Coverley!*' '*Now Merton!*' rung from side to side during the whole affair.

Not long after, a foot of one of the poor women slipped, and, with great force, she came again to the ground. Involuntarily, I sprung forward to assist her, but Lord Merton, to whom she did not belong, stopped me, calling out 'No foul play! no foul play!'

Mr. Coverley, then, repeating the same words, went himself to help her, and insisted that the other should stop. A debate ensued; but the poor creature was too much hurt to move, and declared her utter inability to make another attempt. Mr. Coverley was quite brutal; he swore at her with unmanly rage, and seemed scarce able to refrain even from striking her.

Lord Merton then, in great rapture, said it was a *hollow thing*;[37] but Mr. Coverley contended that the fall was accidental, and time should be allowed for the woman to recover. However, all the company being against him, he was pronounced the loser.

We then went to the drawing-room, to tea. After which, the evening being remarkably warm we all walked in the garden. Lord Merton was quite riotous, and Lady Louisa in high spirits; but Mr. Coverley endeavoured in vain to conceal his chagrin.

As Lord Orville was thoughtful, and walked by himself, I expected that, as usual, *I* should pass unnoticed, and be left to my own meditations; but this was not the case, for Lord Merton, entirely off his guard, giddy equally from wine and success, was very troublesome to me; and, regardless of the presence of Lady Louisa, which, hitherto, has restrained him even from common civility, he attached himself to me, during the walk, with a freedom of gallantry that put me extremely out of countenance. He paid me the most high-flown compliments, and frequently and forcibly seized my hand, though I repeatedly, and with undissembled anger, drew it back. Lord Orville, I saw, watched us with earnestness, and Lady Louisa's smiles were converted into looks of disdain.

I could not bear to be thus situated, and complaining I was tired, I quickened my pace, with intention to return to the house; but Lord Merton, hastily following, caught my hand, and saying the *day was his own*, vowed he would not let me go.

'You *must*, my Lord,' cried I, extremely flurried.

'You are the most charming girl in the world,' said he, 'and never looked better than at this moment.'

'My Lord,' cried Mrs. Selwyn, advancing to us, 'you don't consider, that the better Miss Anville looks, the more striking is the contrast with your Lordship; therefore, for your own sake, I would advise you not to hold her.'

'Egad, my Lord,' cried Mr. Coverley, 'I don't see what right you have to the best *old*, and the best *young* woman too, in the same day.'

'*Best young woman!*' repeated Mr. Lovel; ''pon honour, Jack, you have made a most unfortunate speech; however, if Lady Louisa can pardon you,—and her Ladyship is all goodness,—I am sure nobody else can, for you have committed an outrageous solecism in good manners.'

'And pray, Sir,' said Mrs. Selwyn, 'under what denomination may your own speech pass?'

Mr. Lovel, turning another way, affected not to hear her: and Mr. Coverley, bowing to Lady Louisa, said, 'Her Ladyship is well acquainted with my devotion,—but egad, I don't know how it is,—I had always an unlucky turn at an epigram,[38] and never could resist a smart play upon words in my life.'

'Pray, my Lord,' cried I, 'let go my hand! pray, Mrs. Selwyn, speak for me.'

'My Lord,' said Mrs. Selwyn, 'in detaining Miss Anville any longer, you only lose time, for we are already as well convinced of your valour and your strength as if you were to hold her an age.'

'My Lord,' said Mrs. Beaumont, 'I must beg leave to interfere; I know not if Lady Louisa can pardon you, but, as this young Lady is at my house, I do not chuse to have her made uneasy.'

'*I* pardon him!' cried Lady Louisa, 'I declare I am monstrous glad to get rid of him.'

'Egad, my Lord,' cried Mr. Coverley, 'while you are grasping at a shadow, you'll lose a substance;[39] you'd best make your peace while you can.'

'Pray, Mr. Coverley, be quiet,' said Lady Louisa, peevishly, 'for I declare I won't speak to him. Brother,' (taking hold of Lord Orville's arm) 'will you walk in with me?'

'Would to Heaven,' cried I, frightened to see how much Lord Merton was in liquor, 'that I, too, had a brother!—and then I should not be exposed to such treatment!'

Lord Orville, instantly quitting Lady Louisa, said, 'Will Miss Anville allow *me* the honour of taking that title?' and then, without waiting for any answer, he disengaged me from Lord Merton, and, handing me to Lady Louisa, 'Let me,' added he, 'take equal care of *both* my sisters;' and then, desiring her to take hold of one arm, and begging me to make use of the other, we reached the house in a moment. Lord Merton, disordered as he was, attempted not to stop us.

As soon as we entered the house I withdrew my arm, and courtsied my thanks, for my heart was too full for speech. Lady Louisa, evidently hurt at her brother's condescension, and piqued extremely by Lord Merton's behaviour, silently drew away her's, and biting her lips, with a look of infinite vexation, walked sullenly up the hall.

Lord Orville asked her if she would not go into the parlour?

'No,' answered she, haughtily; 'I leave you and your new sister together;' and then she walked up stairs.

I was quite confounded at the pride and rudeness of this speech. Lord Orville himself seemed thunderstruck; I turned from him, and went into the parlour; he followed me, saying, 'Must I, now, apologize to Miss Anville for the liberty of my interference?—or ought I to apologize that I did not, as I wished, interfere sooner?'

'O my Lord,' cried I, with an emotion I could not repress, 'it is from you alone I meet with any respect,—all others treat me with impertinence or contempt!'

I am sorry I had not more command of myself, as he had reason, just then, to suppose I particularly meant his sister; which, I am sure, must very much hurt him.

'Good Heaven,' cried he, 'that so much sweetness and merit can fail to excite the love and admiration so justly their due! I cannot,—I dare not express to you half the indignation I feel at this moment!'

'I am sorry, my Lord,' said I, more calmly, 'to have raised it; but yet,—in a situation that calls for protection, to meet only with mortifications,—indeed, I am but ill formed to bear them!'

'My *dear* Miss Anville,' cried he, warmly, 'allow *me* to be your friend; think of me as if I were indeed your brother, and let me entreat you to accept my best services, if there is any thing in which I can be so happy as to shew my regard,—my respect for you!'

Before I had time to speak, the rest of the party entered the parlour, and, as I did not wish to see any thing more of Lord Merton, at least before he had slept, I determined to leave it. Lord Orville, seeing my design, said, as I passed him, 'Will you go?' 'Had not I best, my Lord?' said I. 'I am afraid,' said he, smiling, 'since I must now speak as your *brother*, I am afraid you *had*;—you see you may trust me, since I can advise against my own interest.'

I then left the room, and have been writing ever since. And methinks I can never lament the rudeness of Lord Merton, as it has more than ever confirmed to me the esteem of Lord Orville.

LETTER VIII

Evelina in continuation

Sept. 30

Oh Sir, what a strange incident have I to recite! what a field of conjecture to open!

Yesterday evening, we all went to an assembly. Lord Orville presented tickets to the whole family, and did me the honour, to the no small surprise of all here, I believe, to dance with me.[40] But every day abounds in fresh instances of his condescending politeness, and he now takes every opportunity of calling me his *friend*, and his *sister*.

Lord Merton offered a ticket to Lady Louisa; but she was so much incensed against him, that she refused it with the utmost disdain; neither could he prevail upon her to dance with him; she sat still the whole evening, and deigned not to look at, or speak to him. To me, her behaviour is almost the same, for she is cold, distant, and haughty, and her eyes express the greatest contempt. But for Lord Orville, how miserable would my residence here make me!

We were joined, in the ball-room, by Mr. Coverley, Mr. Lovel, and Lord Merton, who looked as if he was doing penance, and sat all the evening next to Lady Louisa, vainly endeavouring to appease her anger.

Lord Orville began the minuets;[41] he danced with a young Lady who seemed to engage the general attention, as she had not been seen here before. She is pretty, and looks mild and good-humoured.

'Pray, Mr. Lovel,' said Lady Louisa, 'who is that?'

'Miss Belmont,' answered he, 'the young heiress; she came to the Wells yesterday.'

Struck with the name, I involuntarily repeated it, but nobody heard me.

'What is her family?' said Mrs. Beaumont.

'Have you not heard of her, Ma'am?' cried he, 'she is only daughter and heiress of Sir John Belmont.'

Good Heaven, how did I start! the name struck my ear like a thunder-bolt. Mrs. Selwyn, who immediately looked at me, said, 'Be calm, my dear, and we will learn the truth of all this.'

Till then, I had never imagined her to be acquainted with my story; but she has since told me, that she knew my unhappy mother, and was well informed of the whole affair.

She asked Mr. Lovel a multitude of questions, and I gathered from his answers, that this young Lady was just come from abroad, with Sir John Belmont, who was now in London; that she was under the care of his sister, Mrs. Paterson; and that she would inherit a considerable estate.

I cannot express the strange feelings with which I was agitated during this recital. What, my dearest Sir, can it possibly mean? Did you ever hear of any after-marriage?[42]— or must I suppose, that, while the lawful child is rejected, another is adopted?—I know not what to think! I am bewildered with a contrariety of ideas!

When we came home, Mrs. Selwyn passed more than an hour in my room, conversing upon this subject. She says that I ought instantly to go to town, find out my father, and have the affair cleared up. She assures me I have too strong a resemblance to my dear, though unknown mother, to allow of the least hesitation in my being owned, when once I am seen. For my part, I have no wish but to act by your direction.

I cannot give any account of the evening; so disturbed, so occupied am I by this subject, that I can think of no other. I have entreated Mrs. Selwyn to observe the strictest secrecy, and she has promised that she will. Indeed, she has too much sense to be idly communicative.

Lord Orville took notice of my being absent and silent, but I ventured not to entrust him with the cause. Fortunately, he was not of the party at the time Mr. Lovel made the discovery.

Mrs. Selwyn says that if you approve my going to town, she will herself accompany me. I had a thousand times rather ask the protection of Mrs. Mirvan, but, after this offer, that will not be possible.

Adieu, my dearest Sir. I am sure you will write immediately, and I shall be all impatience till your letter arrives.

LETTER IX

Evelina in continuation

Oct. 1st

Good God, my dear Sir, what a wonderful tale have I again to relate! even yet, I am not recovered from my extreme surprise.

Yesterday morning, as soon as I had finished my hasty letter, I was summoned to attend a walking party to the Hotwells. It consisted only of Mrs. Selwyn and Lord Orville. The latter walked by my side all the way, and his conversation dissipated my uneasiness, and insensibly restored my serenity.

At the Pump-room, I saw Mr. Macartney; I courtsied to him twice ere he would speak to me. When he did, I began to apologize for having disappointed him; but I did not find it very easy to excuse myself, as Lord Orville's eyes, with an expression of anxiety that distressed me, turned from him to me, and me to him, every word I spoke. Convinced, however, that I had really trifled with Mr. Macartney, I scrupled not to beg his pardon. He was then, not merely appeased, but even grateful.

He requested me to see him to-morrow: but I had not the folly to be again guilty of an indiscretion which had, already, caused me so much uneasiness; and therefore, I told him, frankly, that it was not in my power, at present, to see him, but by accident; and, to prevent his being offended, I hinted to him the reason I could not receive him as I wished to do.

When I had satisfied both him and myself upon this subject, I turned to Lord Orville, and saw, with concern, the gravity of his countenance; I would have spoken to him, but knew not how; I believe, however, he read my thoughts, for, in a little time, with a sort of serious smile, he said, 'Does not Mr. Macartney complain of his disappointment?'

'Not much, my Lord.'

'And how have you appeased him?' Finding I hesitated what to answer, 'Am I not your brother,' continued he, 'and must I not enquire into your affairs?'

'Certainly, my Lord,' said I, laughing, 'I only wish it were better worth your Lordship's while.'

'Let me, then, make immediate use of my privilege. When shall you see Mr. Macartney again?'

'Indeed, my Lord, I can't tell.'

'But,—do you know that I shall not suffer *my sister* to make a private appointment?'

'Pray, my Lord,' cried I, earnestly, 'use that word no more! Indeed you shock me extremely.'

'That would I not do for the world,' cried he; 'yet you know not how warmly, how deeply I am interested, not only in all your concerns, but in all your actions.'

This speech,—the most particular one Lord Orville had ever made to me, ended our conversation at that time; for I was too much struck by it to make any answer.

Soon after, Mr. Macartney, in a low voice, entreated me not to deny him the gratification of returning the money. While he was speaking, the young Lady I saw yesterday at the assembly, with the large party, entered the Pump-room. Mr. Macartney turned as pale as death, his voice faltered, and he seemed not to know what he said. I was myself almost equally disturbed, by the crowd of confused ideas that occurred to me. Good Heaven, thought I, why should he be thus agitated?—is it possible this can be the young Lady he loved?—

In a few minutes, we quitted the Pump-room, and though I twice wished Mr. Macartney good morning, he was so absent he did not hear me.

We did not immediately return to Clifton, as Mrs. Selwyn had business at a pamphlet-shop.[43] While she was looking at some new poems, Lord Orville again asked me when I should see Mr. Macartney?

'Indeed, my Lord,' cried I, 'I know not, but I would give the universe for a few moments conversation with him!' I spoke this with a simple sincerity, and was not aware of the force of my own words.

'The universe!' repeated he, 'Good God, Miss Anville, do you say this to *me*?'

'I would say it,' returned I, 'to any body, my Lord.'

'I beg your pardon,' said he, in a voice that shewed him ill pleased, 'I am answered!'

'My Lord,' cried I, 'you must not judge hardly of me. I spoke inadvertently; but if you knew the painful suspense I suffer at this moment, you would not be surprised at what I have said.'

'And would a meeting with Mr. Macartney relieve you from that suspense?'

'Yes, my Lord, two words might be sufficient.'

'Would to Heaven,' cried he, after a short pause, 'that I were worthy to know their import!'

'Worthy, my Lord!—O, if that were all, your Lordship could ask nothing I should not be ready to answer! If I were but at liberty to speak, I should be *proud* of your Lordship's enquiries; but indeed I am not, I have not any right to communicate the affairs of Mr. Macartney,—your Lordship cannot suppose I have.'

'I will own to you,' answered he, 'I know not *what* to suppose; yet there seems a frankness even in your mystery,—and such an air of openness in your countenance, that I am willing to hope— ' He stopped a moment, and then added, 'This meeting, you say, is essential to your repose?'

'I did not say *that*, my Lord; but yet I have the most important reasons for wishing to speak to him.'

He paused a few minutes, and then said, with warmth, 'Yes, you *shall* speak to him!—I will myself assist you!—Miss Anville, I am sure, cannot form a wish against propriety, I will ask no questions, I will rely upon her own purity, and uninformed, blindfold as I am, I will serve her with all my power!' And then he went into the shop, leaving me so strangely affected by his generous behaviour, that I almost wished to follow him with my thanks.

When Mrs. Selwyn had transacted her affairs, we returned home.

The moment dinner was over, Lord Orville went out, and did not come back till just as we were summoned to supper. This is the longest time he has spent from the house since I have been at Clifton, and you cannot imagine, my dear Sir, how much I missed him. I scarce knew before how infinitely I am indebted to him alone for the happiness I have enjoyed since I have been at Mrs. Beaumont's.

As I generally go down stairs last, he came to me the moment the ladies had passed by, and said, 'Shall you be at home to-morrow morning?'[44]

'I believe so, my Lord.'

'And will you, then, receive a visitor for me?'

'For you, my Lord!'

'Yes;—I have made acquaintance with Mr. Macartney, and he has promised to call upon me to-morrow about three o'clock.'

And then, taking my hand, he led me down stairs.

O Sir!—was there ever such another man as Lord Orville?— Yes, *one* other now resides at Berry Hill!

This morning there has been a great deal of company here, but at the time appointed by Lord Orville, doubtless with that consideration, the parlour is almost always empty, as every body is dressing.

Mrs. Beaumont, however, was not gone up stairs, when Mr. Macartney sent in his name.

Lord Orville immediately said, 'Beg the favour of him to walk in. You see, Madam, that I consider myself as at home.'

'I hope so,' answered Mrs. Beaumont, 'or I should be very uneasy.'

Mr. Macartney then entered. I believe we both felt very conscious to whom the visit was paid: but Lord Orville received him as his own guest, and not merely entertained him as such while Mrs. Beaumont remained in the room, but for some time after she had left it: a delicacy that saved me from the embarrassment I should have felt, had he immediately quitted us.

In a few minutes, however, he gave Mr. Macartney a book,—

for I, too, by way of pretence for continuing in the room, pretended to be reading,—and begged he would be so good as to look it over, while he answered a note, which he would dispatch in a few minutes, and return to him.

When he was gone, we both parted with our books, and Mr. Macartney, again producing the paper with the money, besought me to accept it.

'Pray,' said I, still declining, it, 'did you know the young lady who came into the Pump-room yesterday morning?'

'Know her!' repeated he, changing colour, 'Oh, but too well!'

'Indeed!'

'Why, Madam, do you ask?'

'I must beseech you to satisfy me further upon this subject; pray tell me who she is.'

'Inviolably as I meant to keep my secret, I can refuse you, Madam, nothing;—that lady—is the daughter of Sir John Belmont!—of my father!'

'Gracious Heaven!' cried I, involuntarily laying my hand on his arm, 'you are then—', *my brother*, I would have said, but my voice failed me, and I burst into tears.

'Oh, Madam,' cried he, 'what does this mean?—What can thus distress you?'

I could not answer, but held out my hand to him. He seemed greatly surprised, and talked in high terms of my condescension.

'Spare yourself,' cried I, wiping my eyes, 'spare yourself this mistake,—you have a *right* to all I can do for you; the similarity of our circumstances—'

We were then interrupted by the entrance of Mrs. Selwyn; and Mr. Macartney, finding no probability of our being left alone, was obliged to take leave, though I believe, very reluctantly, while in such suspence.

Mrs. Selwyn then, by dint of interrogatories, drew from me the state of this affair. She is so penetrating, that there is no possibility of evading to give her satisfaction.

Is not this a strange event? Good Heaven, how little did I think that the visits I so unwillingly paid at Mr. Branghton's would have introduced me to so near a relation! I will never again regret the time I spent in town this summer: a circumstance so fortunate will always make me think of it with pleasure.

*   *   *   *   *

I have just received your letter,—and it has almost broken my heart!—Oh, Sir! the illusion is over indeed!—How vainly have I flattered, how miserably deceived myself! Long since, doubtful of the situation of my heart, I dreaded a scrutiny,—but now, now that I have so long escaped, I began, indeed, to think my safety insured, to hope that my fears were causeless, and to believe that my good opinion and esteem of Lord Orville might be owned without suspicion, and felt without danger:—miserably deceived, indeed!

His sight is baneful to my repose,—his society is death to my future tranquillity!—Oh, Lord Orville! could I have believed that a friendship so grateful to my heart, so soothing to my distresses,— a friendship which, in every respect, did me so much honour, would only serve to embitter all my future moments!—What a strange, what an unhappy circumstance, that my gratitude, though so justly excited, should be so fatal to my peace!

Yes, Sir, I *will* quit him;—would to Heaven I could at this moment! without seeing him again,—without trusting to my now conscious emotion!—Oh, Lord Orville, how little do you know the evils I owe to you! how little suppose that, when most dignified by your attention, I was most to be pitied,—and when most exalted by your notice, you were most my enemy!

You, Sir, relied upon my ignorance;—I, alas, upon your experience; and, whenever I doubted the weakness of my heart, the idea that *you* did not suspect it, reassured me,—restored my courage, and confirmed my error!—Yet am I most sensible of the kindness of your silence.

Oh, Sir! why have I ever quitted you! why been exposed to dangers to which I am so unequal?

But I will leave this place,—leave Lord Orville,—leave him, perhaps, for ever! no matter; your counsel, your goodness, may teach me how to recover the peace and the serenity of which my unguarded folly has beguiled me. To you alone do I trust,—in you alone confide for every future hope I may form.

The more I consider of parting with Lord Orville, the less fortitude do I feel to bear the separation;—the friendship he has shewn me,—his politeness,—his sweetness of manners,—his concern in my affairs,—his solicitude to oblige me,—all to be given up!—

No, I cannot tell him I am going,—I dare not trust myself to take leave of him,—I will run away without seeing him:— implicitly will I follow your advice, avoid his sight, and shun his society!

To-morrow morning I will set off for Berry Hill. Mrs. Selwyn and Mrs. Beaumont shall alone know my intention. And to-day,—I will spend in my own room. The readiness of my obedience is the only atonement I can offer, for the weakness which calls for its exertion.

Can you, will you, most honoured, most dear Sir! sole prop by which the poor Evelina is supported,—can you, without reproach, without displeasure, receive the child you have so carefully reared,—from whose education better fruit might have been expected, and who, blushing for her unworthiness, fears to meet the eye by which she has been cherished?—Oh yes, I am sure you will! Your Evelina's errors are those of the judgement,—and you, I well know, pardon all but those of the heart!

LETTER X

Evelina in continuation

Clifton, October 1

I have only time, my dearest Sir, for three words, to overtake my last letter, and prevent your expecting me immediately; for, when I communicated my intention to Mrs. Selwyn, she would not hear of it, and declared it would be highly ridiculous for me to go before I received an answer to my intelligence concerning the journey from Paris. She has, therefore, insisted upon my waiting till your next letter arrives. I hope you will not be displeased at my compliance, though it is rather against my own judgement; but Mrs. Selwyn quite overpowered me with the force of her arguments. I will, however, see very little of Lord Orville; I will never come down stairs before breakfast; give up all my walks in the garden;—seat myself next to Mrs. Selwyn, and not merely avoid his conversation, but shun his presence. I will exert all the prudence and all the resolution in my power, to prevent this short delay from giving you any further uneasiness.

Adieu, my dearest Sir. I shall not now leave Clifton till I have your directions.

LETTER XI

Evelina in continuation

October 2d

Yesterday, from the time I received your kind, though heart-piercing letter, I kept my room,—for I was equally unable and unwilling to see Lord Orville: but this morning, finding I seemed destined to pass a few days longer here, I endeavoured to calm my spirits, and to appear as usual; though I determined to avoid him to the utmost of my power. Indeed, as I entered the parlour, when called to breakfast, my thoughts were so much occupied with your letter, that I felt as much confusion at his sight, as if he had himself been informed of its contents.

Mrs. Beaumont made me a slight compliment upon my recovery, for I had pleaded illness to excuse keeping my room: Lady Louisa spoke not a word: but Lord Orville, little imagining himself the cause of my indisposition, enquired concerning my health with the most distinguishing politeness. I hardly made any answer, and, for the first time since I have been here, contrived to sit at some distance from him.

I could not help observing that my reserve surprised him; yet he persisted in his civilities, and seemed to wish to remove it. But I paid him very little attention; and the moment breakfast was over, instead of taking a book, or walking in the garden, I retired to my own room.

Soon after, Mrs. Selwyn came to tell me that Lord Orville had been proposing I should take an airing, and persuading her to let him drive us both in his phaeton. She delivered the message with an archness that made me blush; and added, that an airing, in *my Lord Orville's carriage*, could not fail to revive my spirits. There is no possibility of escaping her discernment; she has frequently rallied me upon his Lordship's attention,—and, alas!—upon the pleasure with which I have received it! However, I absolutely refused the offer.

'Well,' said she, laughing, 'I cannot just now indulge you with any solicitation; for, to tell you the truth, I have business to transact at the Wells, and am glad to be excused myself. I would ask you to walk with *me*,—but, since *Lord Orville* is refused, I have not the presumption to hope for success.'

'Indeed,' cried I, 'you are mistaken; I will attend you with pleasure.'

'O rare coquetry!' cried she, 'surely it must be inherent in our sex, or it could not have been imbibed at Berry Hill.'

I had not spirits to answer her, and therefore put on my hat and cloak in silence.

'I presume,' continued she, drily, 'his Lordship may walk with us?'

'If so, Madam,' said I, 'you will have a companion, and I will stay at home.'

'My dear child,' cried she, 'did you bring the certificate of your birth[45] with you?'

'Dear Madam, no!'

'Why then, we shall never be known again at Berry Hill.'

I felt too conscious to enjoy her pleasantry; but I believe she was determined to torment me; for she asked if she should inform Lord Orville that I desired him not to be of the party?

'By no means, Madam;—but, indeed, I had rather not walk myself.'

'My dear,' cried she, 'I really do not know you this morning,—you have certainly been taking a lesson of Lady Louisa.'

She then went down stairs; but presently returning, told me she had acquainted Lord Orville that I did not chuse to go out in the phaeton, but preferred a walk, *tête-à-tête* with her, by way of *variety*.

I said nothing, but was really vexed. She bid me go down stairs, and said she would follow immediately.

Lord Orville met me in the hall. 'I fear,' said he, 'Miss Anville is not yet quite well?' and he would have taken my hand, but I turned from him, and courtsying slightly, went into the parlour.

Mrs. Beaumont and Lady Louisa were at work: Lord Merton was talking with the latter, for he has now made his peace, and is again received into favour.

I seated myself, as usual, by the window. Lord Orville, in a few minutes, came to me, and said, 'Why is Miss Anville so grave?'

'Not grave, my Lord,' said I, 'only stupid;' and I took up a book.

'You will go,' said he, after a short pause, 'to the assembly to-night?'

'No, my Lord, certainly not.'

'Neither, then, will I; for I should be sorry to sully the remembrance I have of the happiness I enjoyed at the last.'

Mrs. Selwyn then coming in, general enquires were made, to all but me, of who would go to the assembly. Lord Orville instantly declared he had letters to write at home; but every one else settled to go.

I then hastened Mrs. Selwyn away, though not before she had said to Lord Orville, 'Pray, has your Lordship obtained Miss Anville's leave to favour us with your company?'

'I have not, Madam,' answered he, 'had the vanity to ask it.'

During our walk, Mrs. Selwyn tormented me unmercifully. She told me, that since I declined any addition to our party, I must, doubtless, be conscious of my own powers of entertainment; and begged me, therefore, to exert them freely. I repented a thousand times having consented to walk alone with her: for though I made the most painful efforts to appear in spirits, her raillery quite overpowered me.

We went first to the Pump-room. It was full of company! and the moment we entered, I heard a murmuring of, '*That's she!*' and, to my great confusion, I saw every eye turned towards me. I pulled my hat over my face,[46] and, by the assistance of Mrs. Selwyn, endeavoured to screen myself from observation: nevertheless, I found I was so much the object of general attention, that I entreated her to hasten away. But unfortunately, she had entered into conversation, very earnestly, with a gentleman of her acquaintance, and would not listen to me but said, that if I was tired of waiting, I might walk on to the milliner's with the Miss Watkins, two young ladies I had seen at Mrs. Beaumont's, who were going thither.

I accepted the offer very readily, and away we went. But we had not gone three yards, before we were followed by a party of young men, who took every possible opportunity of looking at us, and, as they walked behind, talked aloud, in a manner at once unintelligible and absurd. 'Yes,' cried one, ''tis certainly she!—mark but her *blushing cheek*!'

'And then her *eye*,—her *downcast eye*!' cried another.

'True, oh most true,' said a third, '*every beauty is her own*!'

'But then,' said the first, 'her *mind*,—now the difficulty is, to find out the truth of *that*, for she will not say a word.'

'She is *timid*,' answered another; 'mark but her *timid air*.'

During this conversation, we walked on silent and quick; as we knew not to whom it was particularly addressed, we were all equally ashamed, and equally desirous to avoid such unaccountable observations.

Soon after, we were caught in a shower of rain. We hurried on, and these gentlemen, following us, offered their services in the most pressing manner, begging us to make use of their arms; and while I almost ran, in order to avoid their impertinence, I was suddenly met by Sir Clement Willoughby!

We both started; 'Good God,' he exclaimed, 'Miss Anville!' and then, regarding my tormentors with an air of displeasure, he earnestly enquired, if any thing had alarmed me?

'No, no,' cried I, for I found no difficulty, now, to disengage myself from these youths, who, probably, concluding from the commanding air of Sir Clement, that he had a right to protect me, quietly gave way to him, and entirely quitted us.

With his usual impetuosity, he then began a thousand enquires, accompanied with as many compliments; and he told me, that he arrived at Bristol but this morning, which he had entirely devoted to endeavours to discover where I lodged.

'Did you know then,' said I, 'that I was at Bristol?'

'Would to Heaven,' cried he, 'that I *could* remain in ignorance of your proceedings with the same contentment you do of mine! then should I not for ever journey upon the wings of hope, to meet my own despair! *You* cannot even judge of the cruelty of my fate, for the ease and serenity of your mind, incapacitates you from feeling for the agitation of mine.'

The ease and serenity of *my* mind! alas, how little do I merit those words!

'But,' added he, 'had *accident* brought me hither, had I not known of your journey, the voice of fame would have proclaimed it to me instantly upon my arrival.'

'The voice of fame!' repeated I.

'Yes, for your's was the first name I heard at the Pump-room. But had I *not* heard your name, such a description could have painted no one else.'

'Indeed,' said I, 'I do not understand you.' But, just then arriving at the milliner's, our conversation ended; for Miss Watkins called me to look at caps and ribbons.[47]

Sir Clement, however, has the art of being always *at home*; he was very soon engaged, as busily as ourselves, in looking at lace ruffles. Yet he took an opportunity of saying to me in a low voice, 'How charmed I am to see you look so well! I was told you were ill,—but I never saw you in better health,—never more infinitely lovely!'

I turned away, to examine the ribbons, and soon after Mrs.

Selwyn made her appearance. I found that she was acquainted with Sir Clement, and her manner of speaking to him, convinced me that he was a favourite with her.

When their mutual compliments were over, she turned to me, and said, 'Pray, Miss Anville, how long can you live without nourishment?'

'Indeed, Ma'am,' said I, laughing, 'I have never tried.'

'Because so long, and no longer,' answered she, 'you may remain at Bristol.'

'Why, what is the matter, Ma'am?'

'The matter!—why, all the ladies are at open war with you,—the whole Pump-room is in confusion; and you, innocent as you pretend to look, are the cause. However, if you take my advice, you will be very careful how you eat and drink during your stay.'

I begged her to explain herself: and she then told me, that a copy of verses had been dropped in the Pump-room, and read there aloud: 'The Beauties of the Wells,' said she, 'are all mentioned, but *you* are the Venus to whom the prize is given.'[48]

'Is it then possible,' cried Sir Clement, 'that you have not seen these verses?'

'I hardly know,' answered I, 'whether *any* body has.'

'I assure you,' said Mrs. Selwyn, 'if you give *me* the invention of them, you do me an honour I by no means deserve.'

'I wrote down in my tablets,' said Sir Clement, 'the stanzas which concern Miss Anville, this morning at the Pump-room; and I will do myself the honour of copying them for her this evening.'

'But why the part that concerns *Miss Anville?*' said Mrs. Selwyn; 'Did you ever see her before this morning?'

'Oh yes,' answered he, 'I have had that happiness frequently at Captain Mirvan's. Too, too frequently!' added he, in a low voice, as Mrs. Selwyn turned to the milliner: and, as soon as she was occupied in examining some trimmings, he came to me, and, almost whether I would or not, entered into conversation with me.

'I have a thousand things,' cried he, 'to say to you. Pray where are you?'

'With Mrs. Selwyn, Sir.'

'Indeed—then, for once, Chance is my friend. And how long have you been here?'

'About three weeks.'

'Good Heaven! what an anxious search have I had, to discover your abode, since you so suddenly left town! The termagant[49] Madame Duval refused me all intelligence. Oh, Miss Anville, did you know what I have endured! the sleepless, restless state of suspence I have been tortured with, you could not, all cruel as you are, you could not have received me with such frigid indifference!'

'*Received* you, Sir!'

'Why, is not my visit to *you*? Do you think I should have made this journey, but for the happiness of again seeing you?'

'Indeed it is possible I might,—since so many others do.'

'Cruel, cruel girl! you *know* that I adore you! you *know* you are the mistress of my soul, and arbitress of my fate!'

Mrs. Selwyn then advancing to us, he assumed a more disengaged air, and asked if he should not have the pleasure of seeing her, in the evening, at the assembly?

'Oh yes,' cried she, 'we shall certainly be there; so you may bring the verses with you, if Miss Anville can wait for them so long.'

'I hope, then,' returned he, 'that you will do me the honour to dance with me?'

I thanked him, but said I should not be at the assembly.

'Not be at the assembly!' cried Mrs. Selwyn, 'Why, have *you*, too, letters to write?'

She looked at me with a significant archness that made me colour; and I hastily answered, 'No, indeed, Ma'am!'

'You have not!' cried she, yet more drily, 'then pray, my dear, do you stay at home to *help*,—or to *hinder* others?'

'To do neither, Ma'am,' answered I, in much confusion; 'so, if you please, I will *not* stay at home.'

'You allow me, then,' said Sir Clement, 'to hope for the honour of your hand?'

I only bowed,—for the dread of Mrs. Selwyn's raillery made me not dare refuse him.

Soon after this we walked home; Sir Clement accompanied us,

and the conversation that passed between Mrs. Selwyn and him was supported in so lively a manner that I should have been much entertained, had my mind been more at ease: but alas! I could think of nothing but the capricious, the unmeaning appearance which the alteration in my conduct must make in the eyes of Lord Orville? And, much as I wish to avoid him, greatly as I desire to save myself from having my weakness known to him,—yet I cannot endure to incur his ill opinion,—and, unacquainted as he is with the reasons by which I am actuated, how can he fail contemning a change to him so unaccountable?

As we entered the garden, he was the first object we saw. He advanced to meet us, and I could not help observing, that at sight of each other both he and Sir Clement changed colour.

We went into the parlour, where we found the same party we had left. Mrs. Selwyn presented Sir Clement to Mrs. Beaumont; Lady Louisa and Lord Merton he seemed well acquainted with already.

The conversation was upon the general subjects, of the weather, the company at the Wells, and the news of the day. But Sir Clement, drawing his chair next to mine, took every opportunity of addressing himself to me in particular.

I could not but remark the striking difference of *his* attention, and that of Lord Orville: the latter has such gentleness of manners, such delicacy of conduct, and an air so respectful, that, when he flatters most, he never distresses, and when he most confers honour, appears to receive it! The former *obtrudes* his attention, and *forces* mine; it is so pointed, that it always confuses me, and so public, that it attracts general notice. Indeed I have sometimes thought that he would rather *wish*, than dislike to have his partiality for me known, as he takes great care to prevent my being spoken to by any body but himself.

When, at length, he went away, Lord Orville took his seat, and said with a half-smile, 'Shall *I* call Sir Clement,—or will *you* call me an usurper, for taking this place?—You make me no answer?—Must I then suppose that Sir Clement—'

'It is little worth your Lordship's while,' said I, 'to suppose any thing upon so insignificant an occasion.'

'Pardon me,' cried he,—'to *me* nothing is insignificant in which you are concerned.'

To this I made no answer, neither did he say any thing more, till the ladies retired to dress; and then, when I would have followed them, he stopped me, saying, 'One moment, I entreat you!'

I turned back, and he went on. 'I greatly fear that I have been so unfortunate as to offend you; yet so repugnant to my very soul is the idea, that I know not how to suppose it possible I can unwittingly have done the thing in the world that, designedly, I would most wish to avoid.'

'No, indeed, my Lord, you have not!' said I.

'You sigh!' cried he, taking my hand, 'would to Heaven I were the sharer of your uneasiness whencesoever it springs! with what earnestness would I not struggle to alleviate it!—Tell me, my dear Miss Anville,—my new-adopted sister, my sweet and most amiable friend!—tell me, I beseech you, if I can afford you any assistance?'

'None, none, my Lord!' cried I, withdrawing my hand, and moving towards the door.

'Is it then impossible I can serve you?—perhaps you wish to see Mr. Macartney again?'

'No, my Lord.' And I held the door open.

'I am not, I own, sorry for that. Yet, oh, Miss Anville, there *is* a question,—there is a conjecture,—I know not how to mention, because I dread the result!—But I see you are in haste;—perhaps in the evening I may have the honour of a longer conversation.—Yet one thing will you have the goodness to allow me to ask?—Did you, this morning when you went to the Wells,—did you *know* who you should meet there?'

'Who, my Lord?'

'I beg your pardon a thousand times for a curiosity so unlicensed,—but I will say no more at present.'

He bowed, expecting me to go,—and then, with quick steps, but a heavy heart, I came to my own room. His question, I am sure, meant Sir Clement Willoughby; and, had I not imposed upon myself the severe task of avoiding, flying Lord Orville with all my power, I would instantly have satisfied him of my ignorance of Sir Clement's journey. And yet more did I long to say something of the assembly, since I found he depended upon my spending the evening at home.

I did not go down stairs again till the family was assembled to dinner. My dress, I saw, struck Lord Orville with astonishment; and I was myself so much ashamed of appearing whimsical and unsteady, that I could not look up.

'I understood,' said Mrs. Beaumont, 'that Miss Anville did not go out this evening?'

'Her intention in the morning,' said Mrs. Selwyn, 'was to stay at home; but there is a fascinating power in an *assembly*, which, upon second thoughts, is not to be resisted.'

'The assembly!' cried Lord Orville, 'are you then going to the assembly?'

I made no answer; and we all took our places at table.

It was not without difficulty that I contrived to give up my usual seat; but I was determined to adhere to the promise in my yesterday's letter, though I saw that Lord Orville seemed quite confounded at my visible endeavours to avoid him.

After dinner, we all went into the drawing-room together, as there were no gentlemen to detain his Lordship; and then, before I could place myself out of his way, he said, 'You are then really going to the assembly?——May I ask if you shall dance?'

'I believe not,—my Lord.'

'If I did not fear,' continued he, 'that you would be tired of the same partner at two following assemblies, I would give up my letter-writing till to-morrow, and solicit the honour of your hand.'

'If I *do* dance,' said I, in great confusion, 'I believe I am engaged.'

'Engaged!' cried he, with earnestness, 'May I ask to whom?'

'To—Sir Clement Willoughby, my Lord?'

He said nothing, but looked very little pleased, and did not address himself to me any more all the afternoon. Oh, Sir!—thus situated, how comfortless were the feelings of your Evelina!

Early in the evening, with his accustomed assiduity, Sir Clement came to conduct us to the assembly. He soon contrived to seat himself next me, and, in a low voice, paid me so many compliments, that I knew not which way to look.

Lord Orville hardly spoke a word, and his countenance was grave and thoughtful; yet, whenever I raised my eyes, his, I perceived, were directed towards me, though instantly, upon meeting mine, he looked another way.

In a short time, Sir Clement, taking from his pocket a folded paper, said, almost in a whisper, 'Here, loveliest of women, you will see a faint, an unsuccessful attempt to paint the object of all my adoration! yet, weak as are the lines for the purpose, I envy beyond expression the happy mortal who has dared make the effort.'

'I will look at them,' said I, 'some other time.' For, conscious that I was observed by Lord Orville, I could not bear he should see me take a written paper, so privately offered, from Sir Clement. But Sir Clement is an impracticable man, and I never yet succeeded in any attempt to frustrate whatever he had planned.

'No,' said he, still in a whisper, 'you must take them now, while Lady Louisa is away;' for she and Mrs. Selwyn were gone up stairs to finish their dress, 'as she must by no means see them.'

'Indeed,' said I, 'I have no intention to shew them.'

'But the only way,' answered he, 'to avoid suspicion, is to take them in her absence. I would have read them aloud myself, but that they are not proper to be seen by any body in this house, yourself and Mrs. Selwyn excepted.'

Then again he presented me the paper, which I now was obliged to take, as I found declining it was vain. But I was sorry that this action should be seen, and the whispering remarked, though the purport of the conversation was left to conjecture.

As I held it in my hand, Sir Clement teazed me to look at it immediately; and told me, that the reason he could not produce the lines publicly, was, that, among the ladies who were mentioned, and supposed to be rejected, was Lady Louisa Larpent. I am much concerned at this circumstance, as I cannot doubt but that it will render me more disagreeable to her than ever, if she should hear of it.

I will now copy the verses, which Sir Clement would not let me rest till I had read.

SEE last advance, with bashful grace,
Downcast eye, and blushing cheek,
Timid air, and beauteous face,
Anville,—whom the Graces[50] seek,

Though ev'ry beauty is her own,
And though her mind each virtue fills,
Anville,—to her power unknown,
Artless strikes,—unconscious kills!

I am sure, my dear Sir, you will not wonder that a panegyric such as this, should, in reading, give me the greatest confusion; and, unfortunately, before I had finished it, the ladies returned.

'What have you there, my dear?' said Mrs. Selwyn.

'Nothing, Ma'am,' said I, hastily folding, and putting it in my pocket.

'And has *nothing*,' cried she, 'the power of *rouge*?'

I made no answer; a deep sigh which escaped Lord Orville at that moment, reached my ears, and gave me sensations—which I dare not mention!

Lord Merton then handed Lady Louisa and Mrs. Beaumont to the latter's carriage. Mrs. Selwyn led the way to Sir Clement's, who handed me in after her.

During the ride, I did not once speak; but when I came to the assembly-room, Sir Clement took care that I should not preserve my silence. He asked me immediately to dance; I begged him to excuse me, and seek some other partner. But on the contrary, he told me he was very glad I would sit still, as he had a million of things to say to me.

He then began to tell me how much he had suffered from absence; how greatly he was alarmed when he heard I had left town, and how cruelly difficult he had found it to trace me; which, at last, he could only do by sacrificing another week to Captain Mirvan.

'And Howard Grove,' continued he, 'which, at my first visit, I thought the most delightful spot upon earth, now appeared to be the most dismal; the face of the country seemed altered: the walks which I had thought most pleasant, were now most stupid: Lady Howard, who had appeared a chearful and respectable old lady, now seemed in the common John Trot style[51] of other aged dames: Mrs. Mirvan, whom I had esteemed as an amiable piece of still-life,[52] now became so insipid, that I could hardly keep awake in her company: the daughter too, whom I had regarded as a good-humoured, pretty sort of girl, now seemed too insignificant for notice: and as to the Captain, I had always thought him a booby,—but now he appeared a savage!'

'Indeed, Sir Clement,' cried I, angrily, 'I will not hear you talk thus of my best friends.'

'I beg your pardon,' said he, 'but the contrast of my two visits was too striking, not to be mentioned.'

He then asked what I thought of the verses?

'Either,' said I, 'that they are written ironically, or by some madman.'

Such a profusion of compliments ensued, that I was obliged to propose dancing, in my own defence. When we stood up, 'I intended,' said he, 'to have discovered the author by his looks; but I find you so much the general loadstone[53] of attention, that my suspicions change their object every moment. Surely you must yourself have some knowledge who he is?'

I told him, no. Yet, my dear Sir, I must own to you, I have no doubt but that Mr. Macartney must be the author; no one else would speak of me so partially; and, indeed, his poetical turn puts it, with me, beyond dispute.

He asked me a thousand questions concerning Lord Orville; how long he had been at Bristol?—what time I had spent at Clifton?—whether he rode out every morning?—whether I ever trusted myself in a phaeton? and a multitude of other enquiries, all tending to discover if I was honoured with much of his Lordship's attention, and all made with his usual freedom and impetuosity.

Fortunately, as I much wished to retire early, Lady Louisa makes a point of being among the first who quit the rooms, and therefore we got home in very tolerable time.

Lord Orville's reception of us was grave and cold: far from distinguishing me, as usual, by particular civilities, Lady Louisa herself could not have seen me enter the room with more frigid unconcern, nor have more scrupulously avoided honouring me with any notice. But chiefly I was struck to see, that he suffered Sir Clement, who stayed supper,[54] to sit between us, without any effort to prevent him, though till then, he had seemed to be even tenacious of a seat next mine.

This little circumstance affected me more than I can express: yet I endeavoured to *rejoice* at it, since neglect and indifference from him may be my best friends.—But, alas!—so suddenly, so abruptly to forfeit his attention!—to lose his friendship!—Oh Sir, these thoughts pierced my soul!—scarce could I keep my seat; for not all my efforts could restrain the tears from trickling down my cheeks: however, as Lord Orville saw them not, for Sir Clement's head was constantly between us, I tried to collect my spirits, and succeeded so far as to keep my place with decency, till Sir Clement took leave: and then, not daring to trust my eyes to meet those of Lord Orville, I retired.

I have been writing ever since; for, certain that I could not sleep, I would not go to bed. Tell me, my dearest Sir, if you possibly can, tell me that you approve my change of conduct,—tell me that my altered behaviour to Lord Orville is right,—that my flying his society, and avoiding his civilities, are actions which *you* would have dictated.—Tell me this, and the sacrifices I have made will comfort me in the midst of my regret,—for never, never can I cease to regret that I have lost the friendship of Lord Orville!—Oh Sir, I have slighted, have rejected,—have thrown it away!—No matter, it was an honour I merited not to preserve, and I now see,—that my mind was unequal to sustaining it without danger.

Yet so strong is the desire you have implanted in me to act with uprightness and propriety, that, however the weakness of my heart may distress and afflict me, it will never, I humbly trust, render me wilfully culpable. The wish of doing well governs every other, as far as concerns my conduct,—for am I not *your* child?—the creature of your own forming?—Yet, Oh Sir, friend, parent of my heart!—my feelings are all at war with my duties; and, while I most struggle to acquire self-approbation, my peace, my happiness, my hopes,—are lost!

'Tis you alone can compose a mind so cruelly agitated; you, I well know, can feel pity for the weakness to which you are a stranger; and, though you blame the affliction, soothe and comfort the afflicted.

LETTER XII

Mr. Villars to Evelina

Berry Hill, Oct 3

Your last communication, my dearest child, is indeed astonishing; that an acknowledged daughter and heiress of Sir John Belmont should be at Bristol, and still my Evelina bear the name of Anville, is to me inexplicable: yet the mystery of the letter to Lady Howard prepared me to expect something extraordinary upon Sir John Belmont's return to England.

Whoever this young lady may be, it is certain she now takes a place to which you have a right indisputable. An *after-marriage* I never heard of; yet, supposing such a one to have happened, Miss Evelyn was certainly the first wife, and therefore her daughter must, at least, be entitled to the name of Belmont.

Either there are circumstances in this affair at present utterly incomprehensible, or else some strange and most atrocious fraud has been practised; which of these two is the case, it now behoves us to enquire.

My reluctance to this step, gives way to my conviction of its propriety, since the reputation of your dear and much-injured mother must now either be fully cleared from blemish, or receive its final and indelible wound.

The public appearance of a daughter of Sir John Belmont will revive the remembrance of Miss Evelyn's story in all who have heard it,—who the *mother* was, will be universally demanded,— and if any other Lady Belmont shall be named,—the birth of my

Evelina will receive a stigma, against which honour, truth, and
innocence may appeal in vain! a stigma which will eternally blast
the fair fame of her virtuous mother, and cast upon her blameless
self the odium of a title,[55] which not all her purity can rescue
from established shame and dishonour!

No, my dear child, no; I will not quietly suffer the ashes of
your mother to be treated with ignominy! Her spotless character
shall be justified to the world—her marriage shall be acknowledged, and her child shall bear the name to which she is lawfully
entitled.

It is true, that Mrs. Mirvan would conduct this affair with
more delicacy than Mrs. Selwyn; yet, perhaps, to save time is, of
all considerations, the most important, since the longer this
mystery is suffered to continue, the more difficult may be
rendered its explanation. The sooner, therefore, you can set out
for town, the less formidable will be your task.

Let not your timidity, my dear love, depress your spirits: I
shall, indeed, tremble for you at a meeting so singular, and so
affecting, yet there can be no doubt of the success of your
application: I enclose a letter from your unhappy mother, written,
and reserved purposely for this occasion: Mrs. Clinton, too, who
attended her in her last illness, must accompany you to town.—
But, without any other certificate of your birth, that which you
carry in your countenance, as it could not be effected by artifice,
so it cannot admit of a doubt.

And now, my Evelina, committed, at length, to the care of
your real parent, receive the fervent prayers, wishes, and blessings, of him who so fondly adopted you!

May'st thou, oh child of my bosom! may'st thou, in this
change of situation, experience no change of disposition! but
receive with humility, and support with meekness, the elevation
to which thou art rising! May thy manners, language, and
deportment, all evince that modest equanimity, and chearful
gratitude, which not merely deserve, but dignify prosperity!
May'st thou, to the last moments of an unblemished life, retain
thy genuine simplicity, thy singleness of heart, thy guileless
sincerity! And may'st thou, stranger to ostentation, and superior

to insolence, with true greatness of soul, shine forth conspicuous only in beneficence!

ARTHUR VILLARS

LETTER XIII

[Enclosed in the preceding Letter]

Lady Belmont to Sir John Belmont

In the firm hope that the moment of anguish which approaches will prove the period of my sufferings, once more I address myself to Sir John Belmont, in behalf of the child, who, if it survives its mother, will hereafter be the bearer of this letter.

Yet in what terms, oh most cruel of men!—can the lost Caroline address you, and not address you in vain? Oh deaf to the voice of compassion—deaf to the sting of truth,—deaf to every tie of honour—say, in what terms may the lost Caroline address you, and not address you in vain?

Shall I call you by the loved, the respected title of husband?—No, you disclaim it!—the father of my infant?—No, you doom it to infamy! the lover who rescued me from a forced marriage?—No, you have yourself betrayed me!—the friend from whom I hoped succour and protection?—No, you have consigned me to misery and destruction!

Oh hardened against every plea of justice, remorse, or pity! how, and in what manner, may I hope to move thee? Is there one method I have left untried? remains there one resource unessayed? No! I have exhausted all the bitterness of reproach, and drained every sluice of compassion!

Hopeless, and almost desperate, twenty times have I flung away my pen;—but the feelings of a mother, a mother agonizing for the fate of her child, again animating my courage, as often I have resumed it.

Perhaps when I am no more, when the measure of my woes is compleated, and the still, silent, unreproaching dust has received my sad remains,—then, perhaps when accusation is no longer to be feared, nor detection to be dreaded, the voice of equity, and the cry of nature may be heard.

Listen, oh Belmont, to their dictates! reprobate[56] not your child, though you have reprobated its mother. The evils that are past, perhaps, when too late, you may wish to recall; the young creature you have persecuted, perhaps, when too late, you may regret that you have destroyed;—you may think with horror of the deceptions you have practised, and the pangs of remorse may follow me to the tomb:—oh Belmont, all my resentment softens into pity at the thought! what will become of thee, good Heaven, when with the eye of penitence, thou reviewest thy past conduct!

Hear, then, the solemn, the last address with which the unhappy Caroline will importune thee.

If, when the time of thy contrition arrives,—for arrive it must!—when the sense of thy treachery shall rob thee of almost every other, if then thy tortured heart shall sigh to expiate thy guilt,—mark the conditions upon which I leave thee my forgiveness.

Thou know'st I am thy wife!—clear, then, to the world the reputation thou hast sullied, and receive as thy lawful successor the child who will present thee this my dying request!

The worthiest, the most benevolent, the best of men, to whose consoling kindness I owe the little tranquillity I have been able to preserve, has plighted me his faith that, upon no other conditions, he will part with his helpless charge.

Should'st thou, in the features of this deserted innocent, trace the resemblance of the wretched Caroline,—should its face bear the marks of its birth, and revive in thy memory the image of its mother, wilt thou not, Belmont, wilt thou not therefore renounce it?—Oh babe of my fondest affection! for whom already I experience all the tenderness of maternal pity!—look not like thy unfortunate mother,—lest the parent whom the hand of death may spare, shall be snatched from thee by the more cruel means of unnatural antipathy!

I can write no more. The small share of serenity I have painfully acquired, will not bear the shock of the dreadful ideas that crowd upon me.

Adieu,—for ever!—

Yet oh!—shall I not, in this last farewell, which thou wilt not read till every stormy passion is extinct,—and the kind grave has embosomed all my sorrows,—shall I not offer to the man once so dear to me, a ray of consolation to those afflictions he has in reserve? Suffer me, then, to tell thee, that my pity far exceeds my indignation,—that I will pray for thee in my last moments,—and that the recollection of the love I once bore thee, shall swallow up every other!

Once more, adieu!

CAROLINE BELMONT

LETTER XIV

Evelina to the Rev. Mr. Villars

Clifton, Oct. 3d

This morning I saw from my window, that Lord Orville was walking in the garden; but I would not go down stairs till breakfast was ready: and then, he paid me his compliments almost as coldly as Lady Louisa paid hers.

I took my usual place, and Mrs. Beaumont, Lady Louisa, and Mrs. Selwyn, entered into their usual conversation.—Not so your Evelina: disregarded, silent, and melancholy, she sat like a cypher,[57] whom to nobody belonging, by nobody was noticed.

Ill brooking such a situation, and unable to support the neglect of Lord Orville, the moment breakfast was over, I left the room; and was going up stairs, when, very unpleasantly, I was stopped by Sir Clement Willoughby, who, flying into the hall, prevented my proceeding.

He enquired very particularly after my health, and entreated
me to return into the parlour. Unwillingly I consented, but
thought any thing preferable to continuing alone with him; and
he would neither leave me, nor suffer me to pass on. Yet, in
returning, I felt not a little ashamed of appearing thus to take the
visit of Sir Clement to myself. And, indeed, he endeavoured, by
his manner of addressing me, to give it that air.

He stayed, I believe, an hour; nor would he, perhaps, even
then have gone, had not Mrs. Beaumont broken up the party, by
proposing an airing in her coach. Lady Louisa consented to
accompany her: but Mrs. Selwyn, when applied to, said, 'If my
Lord, or Sir Clement, will join us, I shall be happy to make
one;—but really, a trio of females will be nervous to the last
degree.'[58]

Sir Clement readily agreed to attend them; indeed, he makes it
his evident study to court the favour of Mrs. Beaumont. Lord
Orville excused himself from going out; and I retired to my own
room. What he did with himself I know not, for I would not go
down stairs till dinner was ready: his coldness, though my own
change of behaviour has occasioned it, so cruelly depresses my
spirits, that I know not how to support myself in his presence.

At dinner, I found Sir Clement again of the party. Indeed he
manages every thing his own way; for Mrs. Beaumont, though
by no means easy to please, seems quite at his disposal.

The dinner, the afternoon, and the evening, were to me the
most irksome imaginable: I was tormented by the assiduity of Sir
Clement, who not only *took*, but *made* opportunities of speaking
to me,—and I was hurt,—oh how inexpressibly hurt!—that
Lord Orville not only forbore, as hitherto, *seeking*, he even
neglected all occasions of talking with me!

I begin to think, my dear Sir, that the sudden alteration in my
behaviour was ill-judged and improper; for, as I had received no
offence, as the cause of the change was upon *my* account, not *his*,
I should not have assumed, so abruptly, a reserve for which I
dared assign no reason,—not have shunned his presence so
obviously, without considering the strange appearance of such a
conduct.

Alas, my dearest Sir, that my reflections should always be too late to serve me! dearly, indeed, do I purchase experience! and much I fear I shall suffer yet more severely, from the needless indiscretion of my temper, ere I attain that prudence and consideration, which, by foreseeing distant consequences, may rule and direct in present exigencies.

Oct. 4th

Yesterday morning, every body rode out, except Mrs. Selwyn and myself: and we two sat for some time together in her room; but, as soon as I could, I quitted her, to saunter in the garden; for she diverts herself so unmercifully with rallying me, either upon my gravity,—or concerning Lord Orville,—that I dread having any conversation with her.

Here I believe I spent an hour by myself; when, hearing the garden-gate open, I went into an arbour at the end of a long walk, where ruminating, very unpleasantly, upon my future prospects, I remained quietly seated but a few minutes, before I was interrupted by the appearance of Sir Clement Willoughby.

I started, and would have left the arbour, but he prevented me. Indeed I am almost certain he had heard in the house where I was, as it is not, otherwise, probable he would have strolled down the garden alone.

'Stop, stop,' cried he, 'loveliest and most beloved of women, stop and hear me!'

Then, making me keep my place, he sat down by me, and would have taken my hand; but I drew it back, and said I could not stay.

'Can you, then,' cried he, 'refuse me even the smallest gratification, though, but yesterday, I almost suffered martyrdom for the pleasure of seeing you?'

'Martyrdom! Sir Clement.'

'Yes, beauteous insensible! *martyrdom*: for did I not compel myself to be immured in a carriage, the tedious length of a whole morning, with the three most fatiguing women in England?'

'Upon my word the Ladies are extremely obliged to you.'

'O,' returned he, 'they have, every one of them, so copious a share of their own personal esteem, that they have no right to repine at the failure of it in the world; and, indeed, they will themselves be the last to discover it.'

'How little,' cried I, 'are those Ladies aware of such severity from *you*!'

'They are guarded,' answered he, 'so happily and so securely by their own conceit, that they are not aware of it from any body. Oh Miss Anville, to be torn away from *you*, in order to be shut up with *them*,—is there a human being, except your cruel self, could forbear to pity me?'

'I believe, Sir Clement, however hardly you may chuse to judge of them, your situation, by the world in general, would rather have been envied, than pitied.'

'The world in general,' answered he, 'has the same opinion of them that I have myself: Mrs. Beaumont is every where laughed at, Lady Louisa ridiculed, and Mrs. Selwyn hated.'

'Good God, Sir Clement, what cruel strength of words do you use!'

'It is you, my angel, are to blame, since your perfections have rendered their faults so glaring. I protest to you, during our whole ride, I thought the carriage drawn by snails. The absurd pride of Mrs. Beaumont, and the respect she exacts, are at once insufferable and stupifying; had I never before been in her company, I should have concluded that this had been her first airing from the herald's-office,[59]—and wished her nothing worse than that it might also be the last. I assure you, that but for gaining the freedom of her house, I would fly her as I would plague, pestilence, and famine.[60] Mrs. Selwyn, indeed, afforded some relief from this formality, but the unbounded licence of her tongue—'

'O Sir Clement, do *you* object to that?'

'Yes, my sweet reproacher, in a *woman*, I do; in a *woman* I think it intolerable. She has wit, I acknowledge, and more understanding than half her sex put together; but she keeps alive a perpetual expectation of satire, that spreads a general uneasiness among all who are in her presence; and she talks so much, that even the best things she says, weary the attention. As to the little Louisa, 'tis such a pretty piece of langour, that 'tis almost cruel to speak rationally about her,—else I should say, she is a mere compound of affectation, impertinence, and airs.'

'I am quite amazed,' said I, 'that, with such opinions, you can behave to them all with so much attention and civility.'

'Civility! my angel,—why I could worship, could adore them, only to procure myself a moment of your conversation? Have you not seen me pay my court to the gross Captain Mirvan, and the virago[61] Madame Duval? Were it possible that a creature so horrid could be formed, as to partake of the worst qualities of all these characters,—a creature who should have the haughtiness of Mrs. Beaumont, the brutality of Captain Mirvan, the self-conceit of Mrs. Selwyn, the affectation of Lady Louisa, and the vulgarity of Madame Duval,—even to such a monster as that, I would pay homage, and pour forth adulation, only to obtain one word, one look from my adored Miss Anville!'

'Sir Clement,' said I, 'you are greatly mistaken if you suppose such duplicity of character recommends you to my good opinion. But I must take this opportunity of begging you never more to talk to me in this strain.'

'Oh Miss Anville, your reproofs, your coldness, pierce me to the soul! look upon me with less rigour, and make me what you please;—you shall govern and direct all my actions,—you shall new-form, new-model me:—I will not have even a wish but of your suggestion;—only deign to look upon me with pity, if not with favour!'

'Suffer me, Sir,' said I very gravely, 'to make use of this occasion to put a final conclusion to such expressions. I entreat you never again to address me in a language so flighty, and so unwelcome. You have already given me great uneasiness; and I must frankly assure you, that if you do not desire to banish me from wherever you are, you will adopt a very different style and conduct in future.'

I then rose, and was going, but he flung himself at my feet to prevent me, exclaiming, in a most passionate manner, 'Good God! Miss Anville, what do you say?—is it, can it be possible, that so unmoved, that with such petrifying indifference, you can tear from me even the remotest hope!'

'I know not, Sir,' said I, endeavouring to disengage myself from him, 'what hope you mean, but I am sure that I never intended to give you any.'

'You distract me!' cried he, 'I cannot endure such scorn;—I beseech you to have some moderation in your cruelty, lest you make me desperate:—say, then, that you pity me—O fairest inexorable! loveliest tyrant!—say, tell me, at least, that you pity me!'

Just then, who should come in sight, as if intending to pass by the arbour, but Lord Orville! Good Heaven, how did I start! and he the moment he saw me, turned pale, and was hastily retiring;—but I called out, 'Lord Orville!—Sir Clement, release me,—let go my hand!'

Sir Clement, in some confusion, suddenly rose, but still grasped my hand. Lord Orville, who had turned back, was again walking away; but, still struggling to disengage myself, I called out, 'Pray, pray, my Lord, don't go!—Sir Clement, I *insist* upon your releasing me!'

Lord Orville then, hastily approaching us, said, with great spirit, 'Sir Clement, you cannot wish to detain Miss Anville by force!'

'Neither, my Lord,' cried Sir Clement, proudly, 'do I request the honour of your Lordship's interference.'

However, he let go my hand, and I immediately ran into the house.

I was now frightened to death lest Sir Clement's mortified pride should provoke him to affront Lord Orville: I therefore ran hastily to Mrs. Selwyn, and entreated her, in a manner hardly to be understood, to walk towards the arbour. She asked no questions, for she is quick as lightning in taking a hint, but instantly hastened into the garden.

Imagine, my dear Sir, how wretched I must be till I saw her return! scarce could I restrain myself from running back: however, I checked my impatience, and waited, though in agonies, till she came.

And, now, my dear Sir, I have a conversation to write, the most interesting to me, that I ever heard. The comments and questions with which Mrs. Selwyn interrupted her account, I shall not mention; for they are such as you may very easily suppose.

Lord Orville and Sir Clement were both seated very quietly in the arbour: and Mrs. Selwyn, standing still, as soon as she was within a few yards of them, heard Sir Clement say, 'Your question, my Lord, alarms me, and I can by no means answer it, unless you will allow me to propose another?'

'Undoubtedly, Sir.'

'You ask me, my Lord, what are my intentions?—I should be very happy to be satisfied as to your Lordship's.'

'I have never, Sir, professed *any*.'

Here they were both, for a few moments, silent; and then Sir Clement said, 'To what, my Lord, must I, then, impute your desire of knowing mine?'

'To an unaffected interest in Miss Anville's welfare.'

'Such an interest,' said Sir Clement, drily, 'is, indeed, very generous: but, except in a father,—a brother,—or a lover—'

'Sir Clement,' interrupted his Lordship, 'I know your inference: and I acknowledge I have not the right of enquiry which any of those three titles bestow, and yet I confess the warmest wishes to serve her, and to see her happy. Will you, then, excuse me, if I take the liberty to repeat my question?'

'Yes, if your Lordship will excuse my repeating that I think it a rather extraordinary one.'

'It may be so,' said Lord Orville; 'but this young lady seems to be peculiarly situated; she is very young, very inexperienced, yet appears to be left totally to her own direction. She does not, I believe, see the dangers to which she is exposed, and I will own to you, I feel a strong desire to point them out.'

'I don't rightly understand your Lordship,—but I think you cannot mean to prejudice her against me?'

'Her sentiments of *you*, Sir, are as much unknown to me as your intentions towards *her*. Perhaps, were I acquainted with either, my officiousness might be at an end: but I presume not to ask upon what terms—'

Here he stopped; and Sir Clement said, 'You know, my Lord, I am not given to despair; I am by no means such a puppy as to tell you I am upon *sure ground*,[62] however, perseverance—'

'You are, then, determined to persevere?'

'I am, my Lord.'

'Pardon me, then, Sir Clement, if I speak to you with freedom. This young lady, though she seems alone, and, in some measure, unprotected, is not entirely without friends; she has been extremely well educated, and accustomed to good company; she has a natural love of virtue, and a mind that might adorn *any* station, however exalted: is such a young lady, Sir Clement, a proper object to trifle with?—for your principles, excuse me, Sir, are well known.'

'As to that, my Lord, let Miss Anville look to herself; she has an excellent understanding, and needs no counsellor.'

'Her understanding is, indeed, excellent; but she is too young for suspicion, and has an artlessness of disposition that I never saw equalled.'

'My Lord,' cried Sir Clement, warmly, 'your praises make me doubt your disinterestedness, and there exists not the man who I would so unwillingly have for a rival as yourself. But you must give me leave to say, you have greatly deceived me in regard to this affair.'

'How so, Sir,' cried Lord Orville, with equal warmth.

'You were pleased, my Lord,' answered Sir Clement, 'upon our first conversation concerning this young lady, to speak of her in terms by no means suited to your present encomiums; you said she was a *poor*, *weak*, ignorant girl, and I had great reason to believe you had a most contemptuous opinion of her.'

'It is very true,' said Lord Orville, 'that I did not, at our first acquaintance, do justice to the merit of Miss Anville; but I knew not, then, how new she was to the world; at present, however, I am convinced, that whatever might appear strange in her behaviour, was simply the effect of inexperience, timidity, and a retired education, for I find her informed, sensible, and intelligent. She is not, indeed, like most modern young ladies; to be known in half an hour; her modest worth, and fearful excellence, require both time and encouragement to shew themselves. She does not, beautiful as she is, seize the soul by surprise, but, with more dangerous fascination, she steals it almost imperceptibly.'

'Enough, my Lord,' cried Sir Clement, 'your solicitude for her welfare is now sufficiently explained.'

'My friendship and esteem,' returned Lord Orville, 'I do not wish to disguise; but assure yourself, Sir Clement, I should not have troubled *you* upon this subject, had Miss Anville and I ever conversed but as friends. However, since you do not chuse to avow your intentions, we must drop the subject.'

'My intentions,' cried he, 'I will frankly own, are hardly known to myself. I think Miss Anville the loveliest of her sex, and, were I a *marrying man*, she, of all the women I have seen, I would fix upon for a wife: but I believe that not even the philosophy of your Lordship would recommend to me a connection of that sort, with a girl of obscure birth, whose only dowry is her beauty, and who is evidently in a state of dependency.'

'Sir Clement,' cried Lord Orville, with some heat, 'we will discuss this point no further; we are both free agents, and must act for ourselves.'

Here Mrs. Selwyn, fearing a surprise, and finding my apprehensions of danger were groundless, retired hastily into another walk, and soon after came to give me this account.

Good Heaven, what a man is this Sir Clement! so designing, though so easy; so deliberately artful, though so flighty! Greatly, however, is he mistaken, all confident as he seems; for the girl, obscure, poor, dependent as she is, far from wishing the honour of his alliance, would not only *now*, but *always* have rejected it.

As to Lord Orville,—but I will not trust my pen to mention him,—tell me, my dear Sir, what *you* think of him?—tell me if he is not the noblest of men?—and if you can either wonder at, or blame my admiration?

The idea of being seen by either party, immediately after so singular a conversation, was both awkward and distressing to me; but I was obliged to appear at dinner. Sir Clement, I saw, was absent and uneasy; he watched me, he watched Lord Orville, and was evidently disturbed in his mind. Whenever he spoke to me, I turned from him with undisguised disdain, for I am too much irritated against him, to bear with his ill-meant assiduities any longer.

But, not once,—not a moment did I dare meet the eyes of Lord Orville! All consciousness myself, I dreaded his penetration, and directed mine every way—but towards his. The rest of the day I never quitted Mrs. Selwyn.

Adieu, my dear Sir: to-morrow I expect your directions whether I am to return to Berry Hill, or once more to visit London.

LETTER XV

Evelina in continuation

Oct, 6th

And now, my dearest Sir, if the perturbation of my spirits will allow me, I will finish my last letter from Clifton Hill.

This morning, though I did not go down stairs early, Lord Orville was the only person in the parlour when I entered it. I felt no small confusion at seeing him alone, after having so long and successfully avoided such a meeting. As soon as the usual compliments were over, I would have left the room, but he stopped me by saying, 'If I disturb you, Miss Anville, I am gone.'

'My Lord,' said I, rather embarrassed, 'I did not mean to stay.'

'I flattered myself,' cried he, 'I should have had a moment's conversation with you.'

I then turned back; and he seemed himself in some perplexity: but after a short pause, 'You are very good,' said he, 'to indulge my request; I have, indeed, for some time past, most ardently desired an opportunity of speaking to you.'

Again he paused; but I said nothing, so he went on.

'You allowed me, Madam, a few days since, you allowed me to lay claim to your friendship,—to interest myself in your affairs,—to call you by the affectionate title of sister;—and the honour you did me, no man could have been more sensible of; I am ignorant, therefore, how I have been so unfortunate as to forfeit it:—but, at present, all is changed! you fly me,—your averted eye shuns to meet mine, and you sedulously avoid my conversation.'

I was extremely disconcerted at this grave, and but too just accusation, and I am sure I must look very simple;—but I made no answer.

'You will not, I hope,' continued he, 'condemn me unheard; if there is any thing I have done,—or any thing I have neglected, tell me, I beseech you, *what*, and it shall be the whole study of my thoughts how to deserve your pardon.'

'Oh my Lord,' cried I, penetrated at once with shame and gratitude, 'your too, too great politeness oppresses me!—you have done nothing,—I have never dreamt of offence,—if there is any pardon to be asked, it is rather for *me*, than for *you*, to ask it.'

'You are all sweetness and condescension!' cried he, ' and I flatter myself you will again allow me to claim those titles which I find myself so unable to forego. Yet, occupied as I am with an idea which gives me the severest uneasiness, I hope you will not think me impertinent, if I still solicit, still entreat, nay implore you to tell me, to what cause your late sudden, and to me most painful, reserve was owing?'

'Indeed, my Lord,' said I, stammering, 'I don't,—I can't,—indeed, my Lord,—'

'I am sorry to distress you,' said he, 'and ashamed to be so urgent,—yet I know not how to be satisfied while in ignorance,—and the *time* when the change happened, makes me apprehend—may I, Miss Anville, tell you *what* it makes me apprehend?'

'Certainly, my Lord.'

'Tell me, then,—and pardon a question most essentially important to me;—Had, or had not, Sir Clement Willoughby, any share in causing your inquietude?'

'No, my Lord,' answered I, with firmness, 'none in the world.'

'A thousand, thousand thanks!' cried he: 'you have relieved me from a weight of conjecture which I supported very painfully. But one thing more; is it, in any measure, to Sir Clement that I may attribute the alteration in your behaviour to myself, which I could not but observe, began the very day of his arrival at the Hotwells?'

'To Sir Clement, my Lord,' said I, 'attribute nothing. He is the last man in the world who would have any influence over my conduct.'

'And will you, then, restore to me that share of confidence and favour with which you honoured me before he came?'

Just then, to my great relief,—for I knew not what to say,— Mrs. Beaumont opened the door, and in a few minutes, we went to breakfast.

Lord Orville was all gaiety; never did I see him more lively or more agreeable. Very soon after, Sir Clement Willoughby called, to pay his respects, he said, to Mrs. Beaumont. I then came to my own room, where, indulging my reflections, which now soothed, and now alarmed me, I remained very quietly, till I received your most kind letter.

Oh Sir, how sweet are the prayers you offer for your Evelina! how grateful to her are the blessings you pour upon her head!— You *commit me to my real parent*,—Ah, Guardian, Friend, Protector of my youth!—by whom my helpless infancy was cherished, my mind formed, my very life preserved,—*you* are the Parent my heart acknowledges, and to you do I vow eternal duty, gratitude, and affection!

I look forward to the approaching interview with more fear than hope; but important as is this subject, I am just now, wholly engrossed with another, which I must hasten to communicate.

I immediately acquainted Mrs. Selwyn with the purport of your letter. She was charmed to find your opinion agreed with her own, and settled that we should go to town to-morrow morning. And a chaise is actually ordered to be here by one o'clock

She then desired me to pack up my cloaths; and said she must go, herself, to *make speeches*, and *tell lies* to Mrs. Beaumont.

When I went down stairs to dinner, Lord Orville, who was still in excellent spirits, reproached me for secluding myself so much from the company. He sat next me,—he *would* sit next me,—at table; and he might, I am sure, repeat what he once said of me before, *that he almost exhausted himself in fruitless endeavours to entertain me*;[63]—for, indeed, I was not to be entertained: I was totally spiritless and dejected; the idea of the approaching meeting,—and oh Sir, the idea of the approaching parting,—gave a heaviness to my heart, that I could neither conquer nor repress. I even regretted the half explanation that had passed, and wished Lord Orville had supported his own reserve, and suffered me to support mine.

However, when, during dinner, Mrs. Beaumont spoke of our journey, my gravity was no longer singular; a cloud instantly overspread the countenance of Lord Orville, and he became nearly as thoughtful and as silent as myself.

We all went together to the drawing-room. After a short and unentertaining conversation, Mrs. Selwyn said she must prepare for her journey, and begged me to see for some books she had left in the parlour.

And here, while I was looking for them, I was followed by Lord Orville. He shut the door after he came in, and approaching me with a look of great anxiety, said, 'Is this true, Miss Anville, are you going?'

'I believe so, my Lord,' said I, still looking for the books.

'So suddenly, so unexpectedly, must I lose you?'

'No great loss, my Lord,' cried I, endeavouring to speak chearfully.

'Is it possible,' said he, gravely, 'Miss Anville can doubt my sincerity?'

'I can't imagine,' cried I, 'what Mrs. Selwyn has done with these books.'

'Would to Heaven,' continued he, 'I might flatter myself you would allow me to prove it!'

'I must run up stairs,' cried I, greatly confused, 'and ask what she has done with them.'

'You are going, then,' cried he, taking my hand, 'and you give me not the smallest hope of your return!—will you not, then, my too lovely friend!—will you not, at least, teach me, with fortitude like your own, to support your absence?'

'My Lord,' cried I, endeavouring to disengage my hand, 'pray let me go!'

'I will;' cried he, to my inexpressible confusion, dropping on one knee, 'if you wish to leave me!'

'Oh, my Lord,' exclaimed I, 'rise, I beseech you, rise!—such a posture to me!—surely your Lordship is not so cruel as to mock me!'

'Mock you!' repeated he earnestly, 'no, I revere you! I esteem and I admire you above all human beings! you are the friend to whom my soul is attached as to its better half! you are the most amiable, the most perfect of women! and you are dearer to me than language has the power of telling!'

I attempt not to describe my sensations at that moment; I scarce breathed; I doubted if I existed,—the blood forsook my cheeks, and my feet refused to sustain me: Lord Orville, hastily rising, supported me to a chair, upon which I sunk, almost lifeless.

For a few minutes, we neither of us spoke; and then, seeing me recover, Lord Orville, though in terms hardly articulate, entreated my pardon for his abruptness. The moment my strength returned, I attempted to rise, but he would not permit me.

I cannot write the scene that followed, though every word is engraven on my heart: but his protestations, his expressions, were too flattering for repetition: nor would he, in spite of my repeated efforts to leave him, suffer me to escape;—in short, my dear Sir, I was not proof against his solicitations—and he drew from me the most sacred secret of my heart!

I know not how long we were together, but Lord Orville was upon his knees, when the door was opened by Mrs. Selwyn!— To tell you, Sir, the shame with which I was overwhelmed, would be impossible;—I snatched my hand from Lord Orville,—he, too, started and rose, and Mrs. Selwyn, for some instants, stood facing us both in silence.

At last, 'My Lord,' said she, sarcastically, 'have you been so good as to help Miss Anville to look for my books?'

'Yes, Madam,' answered he, attempting to rally, 'and I hope we shall soon be able to find them.'

'Your Lordship is extremely kind,' said she, drily, 'but I can by no means consent to take up any more of your time.' Then, looking on the window-seat, she presently found the books, and added, 'Come, here are just three and so, like the servants in the Drummer,[64] this important affair may give employment to us all.' She then presented one of them to Lord Orville, another to me, and taking a third herself, with a most provoking look, she left the room.

I would instantly have followed her; but Lord Orville, who could not help laughing, begged me to stay a minute, as he had many important matters to discuss.

'No, indeed, my Lord, I cannot,—perhaps I have already stayed too long.'

'Does Miss Anville so soon repent her goodness?'

'I scarce know what I do, my Lord,—I am quite bewildered!'

'One hour's conversation,' cried he, 'will I hope compose your spirits, and confirm my happiness. When, then, may I hope to see you alone?—shall you walk in the garden to-morrow before breakfast?'

'No, no, my Lord; you must not, a second time, reproach me with making an *appointment*.'

'Do you then,' said he, laughing, 'reserve that honour only for Mr. Macartney?'

'Mr. Macartney,' said I, 'is poor, and thinks himself obliged to me; otherwise—'

'Poverty,' cried he, 'I will not plead; but if being *obliged* to you has any weight, who shall dispute *my* title to an appointment?'

'My Lord, I can stay no longer,—Mrs. Selwyn will lose all patience.'

'Deprive her not of the pleasure of her *conjectures*;—but, tell me, are you under Mrs. Selwyn's care?'

'Only for the present, my Lord.'

'Not a few are the questions I have to ask Miss Anville:

among them, the most important is, whether she depends wholly on herself, or whether there is any other person for whose interest I must solicit?'

'I hardly know, my Lord, I hardly know myself to whom I most belong.'

'Suffer, suffer me, then,' cried he, with warmth, 'to hasten the time when that shall no longer admit a doubt!—when your grateful Orville may call you all his own!'

At length, but with difficulty, I broke from him. I went, however, to my own room, for I was too much agitated to follow Mrs. Selwyn. Good God, my dear Sir, what a scene! surely the meeting for which I shall prepare to-morrow, cannot so greatly affect me! To be loved by Lord Orville,—to be the honoured choice of his noble heart,—my happiness seemed too infinite to be borne, and I wept, even bitterly I wept, from the excess of joy which overpowered me.

In this state of almost painful felicity, I continued, till I was summoned to tea. When I re-entered the drawing-room, I re-joiced much to find it full of company, as the confusion with which I met Lord Orville was rendered the less observable.

Immediately after tea, most of the company played at cards,— and then,—and till supper-time, Lord Orville devoted himself wholly to me.

He saw that my eyes were red, and would not let me rest till he had made me confess the cause; and when, though most reluctantly, I had acknowledged my weakness, I could with difficulty refrain from weeping again at the gratitude he ex-pressed.

He earnestly desired to know if my journey could not be postponed; and when I said no, entreated permission to attend me to town.

'Oh, my Lord,' cried I, 'what a request!'

'The sooner,' answered he, 'I make my devotion to you public, the sooner I may expect, from your delicacy, you will convince the world you encourage no mere *danglers*.'[65]

'You teach me, then, my Lord, the inference I might expect, if I complied.'

'And can you wonder I should seek to hasten the happy time, when no scruples, no discretion will demand our separation? and when the most punctilious delicacy will rather promote, than oppose, my happiness in attending you?'

To this I was silent, and he re-urged his request.

'My Lord,' said I, 'you ask what I have no power to grant. This journey will deprive me of all right to act for myself.'

'What does Miss Anville mean?'

'I cannot now explain myself; indeed, if I could, the task would be both painful and tedious.'

'O Miss Anville,' cried he, 'when may I hope to date the period of this mystery? when flatter myself that my promised friend will indeed honour me with her confidence?'

'My Lord,' said I, 'I mean not to affect any mystery,—but my affairs are so circumstanced, that a long and most unhappy story, can alone explain them. However, if a short suspense will give your Lordship any uneasiness,—'

'My beloved Miss Anville,' cried he, eagerly, 'pardon my impatience!—You shall tell me nothing you would wish to conceal,—I will wait your own time for information, and trust to your goodness for its speed.'

'There is *nothing*, my Lord, I wish to conceal,—to *postpone* an explanation is all I desire.'

He then requested, that, since I would not allow him to accompany me to town, I would permit him to write to me, and promise to answer his letters.[66]

A sudden recollection of the two letters which had already passed between us occurring to me, I hastily answered, 'No indeed, my Lord!—'

'I am extremely sorry,' said he, gravely, 'that you think me too presumptuous. I must own I had flattered myself that to soften the inquietude of an absence which seems attended by so many inexplicable circumstances, would not have been to incur your displeasure.'

This seriousness hurt me; and I could not forbear saying, 'Can you indeed desire, my Lord, that I should, a second time, expose myself, by an unguarded readiness to write to you?'

'A *second time! unguarded readiness!*' repeated he; 'you amaze me!'

'Has your Lordship then quite forgot the foolish letter I was so imprudent as to send you when in town?'

'I have not the least idea,' cried he, 'of what you mean.'

'Why then, my Lord,' said I, 'we had better let the subject drop.'

'Impossible!' cried he, 'I cannot rest without an explanation!'

And then, he obliged me to speak very openly of both the letters; but, my dear Sir, imagine my surprise, when he assured me, in the most solemn manner, that far from having ever written me a single line, he had never received, seen, or heard of my letter!

This subject, which caused mutual astonishment and perplexity to us both, entirely engrossed us for the rest of the evening; and he made me promise to shew him the letter I had received in his name to-morrow morning, that he might endeavour to discover the author.

After supper, the conversation became general.

And now, my dearest Sir, may I not call for your congratulations upon the events of this day? a day never to be recollected by me but with the most grateful joy! I know how much you are inclined to think well of Lord Orville, I cannot, therefore, apprehend that my frankness to him will displease you. Perhaps the time is not very distant when your Evelina's choice may receive the sanction of her best friend's judgement and approbation,—which seems now all she has to wish!

In regard to the change in my situation which must first take place, surely I cannot be blamed for what has passed! the partiality of Lord Orville must not only reflect honour upon me, but upon all to whom I do, or may belong.

Adieu, most dear sir. I will write again when I arrive in London.

LETTER XVI

Evelina in continuation

Clifton, Oct. 7th

You will see, my dear Sir, that I was mistaken in supposing I should write no more from this place, where my residence, now, seems more uncertain than ever.

This morning, during breakfast, Lord Orville took an opportunity to beg me, in a low voice, to allow him a moment's conversation before I left Clifton; 'May I hope,' added he, 'that you will strole into the garden after breakfast?'

I made no answer, but I believe my looks gave no denial; for, indeed I much wished to be satisfied concerning the letter. The moment, therefore, that I could quit the parlour I ran up stairs for my calash;[67] but before I reached my room, Mrs. Selwyn called after me, 'If you are going to walk, Miss Anville, be so good as to bid Jenny bring down my hat, and I'll accompany you.'

Very much disconcerted, I turned into the drawing-room, without making any answer, and there I hoped to wait unseen, till she had otherwise disposed of herself. But, in a few minutes the door opened, and Sir Clement Willoughby entered.

Starting at the sight of him, in rising hastily, I let drop the letter which I had brought for Lord Orville's inspection, and, before I could recover it, Sir Clement, springing forward, had it in his hand. He was just presenting it to me, and, at the same time, enquiring after my health, when the signature caught his eye, and he read aloud 'Orville.'

I endeavoured, eagerly, to snatch it from him, but he would not permit me, and, holding it fast, in a passionate manner exclaimed, 'Good God, Miss Anville, is it possible you can value such a letter as this?'

The question surprised and confounded me, and I was too much ashamed to answer him; but finding he made an attempt to secure it, I prevented him, and vehemently demanded him to return it.

'Tell me first,' said he, holding it above my reach, 'tell me if you have, since, received any more letters from the same person?'

'No, indeed,' cried I, 'never!'

'And will you, also, sweetest of women, promise that you never *will* receive any more? Say that, and you will make me the happiest of men.'

'Sir Clement,' cried I, greatly confused, 'pray give me the letter.'

'And will you not first satisfy my doubts?—will you not relieve me from the torture of the most distracting suspence?— tell me but that the detested Orville has written to you no more!'

'Sir Clement,' cried I, angrily, 'you have no right to make any conditions,—so pray give me the letter directly.'

'Why such solicitude about this hateful letter? can it possibly deserve your eagerness? tell me, with truth, with sincerity tell me; Does it really merit the least anxiety?'

'No matter, Sir,' cried I, in great perplexity, 'the letter is mine, and therefore—'

'I must conclude, then,' said he, 'that the letter deserves your utmost contempt,—but that the name of Orville is sufficient to make you prize it.'

'Sir Clement,' cried I, colouring, 'you are quite—you are very much—the letter is not—'

'O Miss Anville,' cried he, 'you blush!—you stammer!—Great Heaven! it is then all as I feared!'

'I know not,' cried I, half frightened, 'what you mean; but I beseech you to give me the letter, and to compose yourself.'

'The letter,' cried he, gnashing his teeth, 'you shall never see more! You ought to have burnt it the moment you had read it!' And in an instant, he tore it into a thousand pieces.

Alarmed at a fury so indecently outrageous, I would have run out of the room; but he caught hold of my gown, and cried, 'Not yet, not yet must you go! I am but half-mad yet, and you must stay to finish your work. Tell me, therefore, does Orville know your fatal partiality?—Say *yes*,' added he, trembling with passion, 'and I will fly you for ever!'

'For Heaven's sake, Sir Clement,' cried I, 'release me!—if you do not, you will force me to call for help.'

'Call then,' cried he, 'inexorable and most unfeeling girl; call, if you please, and bid all the world witness your triumph;—but could ten worlds obey your call, I would not part from you till you had answered me. Tell me, then, does Orville know you love him?'

At any other time, an enquiry so gross would have given me inexpressible confusion; but now, the wildness of his manner terrified me, and I only said, 'Whatever you wish to know, Sir Clement, I will tell you another time; but for the present, I entreat you to let me go!'

'Enough,' cried he, 'I understand you!—the art of Orville has prevailed;—cold, inanimate, phlegmatic as he is, you have rendered him the most envied of men!—One thing more, and I have done:—Will he marry you?'

What a question! my cheeks glowed with indignation, and I felt too proud to make any answer.

'I see, I see how it is,' cried he, after a short pause, 'and I find I am undone for ever!' Then, letting loose my gown, he put his hand to his forehead, and walked up and down the room in a hasty and agitated manner.

Though now at liberty to go, I had not the courage to leave him: for his evident distress excited all my compassion. And this was our situation, when Lady Louisa, Mr. Coverley, and Mrs. Beaumont entered the room.

'Sir Clement Willoughby,' said the latter, 'I beg pardon for making you wait so long, but—'

She had not time for another word; Sir Clement, too much disordered to know or care what he did, snatched up his hat, and, brushing hastily past her, flew down stairs, and out of the house.

And with him went my sincerest pity, though I earnestly hope I shall see him no more. But what, my dear Sir, am I to conclude from his strange speeches concerning the letter? does it not seem as if he was himself the author of it? How else should he be so well acquainted with the contempt it merits? Neither do I know another human being who could serve any interest by such a deception. I remember, too, that just as I had given my own letter to the maid, Sir Clement came into the shop; probably he prevailed upon her, by some bribery, to give it to him, and afterwards, by the same means, to deliver to me an answer of his own writing. Indeed I can in no other manner account for this affair. Oh, Sir Clement, were you not yourself unhappy, I know not how I could pardon an artifice that has caused me so much uneasiness!

His abrupt departure occasioned a kind of general consternation.

'Very extraordinary behaviour this!' cried Mrs Beaumont.

'Egad,' said Mr. Coverley, 'the Baronet has a mind to tip us a touch of the heroicks this morning!'[68]

'I declare,' cried Lady Louisa, 'I never saw any thing so monstrous in my life! it's quite abominable,—I fancy the man's mad;—I'm sure he has given me a shocking fright!'

Soon after, Mrs. Selwyn came up stairs, with Lord Merton. The former, advancing hastily to me, said, 'Miss Anville, have you an almanack?'[69]

'Me!—no, Madam.'

'Who has one, then?'

'Egad,' cried Mr. Coverley, 'I never bought one in my life; it would make me quite melancholy to have such a time-keeper in my pocket. I would as soon walk all day before an hour-glass.'

'You are in the right,' said Mrs. Selwyn, 'not to *watch time*, lest you should be betrayed, unawares, into reflecting how you employ it.'

'Egad, Ma'am,' cried he, 'if Time thought no more of me, than I do of Time, I believe I should bid defiance, for one while, to old age and wrinkles,—for deuce take me if ever I think about it at all.'

'Pray, Mr. Coverley,' said Mrs. Selwyn, 'why do you think it necessary to tell me this so often?'

'Often!' repeated he, 'Egad, Madam, I don't know why I said it now,—but I'm sure I can't recollect that ever I owned as much before.'

'Owned it before!' cried she, 'why, my dear Sir, you own it all day long; for every word, every look, every action proclaims it.'

I know not if he understood the full severity of her satire, but he only turned off with a laugh: and she then applied to Mr. Lovel, and asked if *he* had an almanack?

Mr. Lovel, who always looks alarmed when she addresses him, with some hesitation answered, 'I assure you, Ma'am, I have no manner of antipathy to an almanack,—none in the least,—I assure you;—I dare say I have four or five.'

'Four or five!—pray may I ask what use you make of so many?'

'Use!—really, Ma'am, as to that,—I don't make any particular use of them,—but one must have them, to tell one the day of the month,—I'm sure, else, I should never keep it in my head.'

'And does your time pass so smoothly unmarked, that, without an almanack, you could not distinguish one day from another?'

'Really, Ma'am,' cried he, colouring, 'I don't see any thing so very particular in having a few almanacks; other people have them, I believe, as well as me.'

'Don't be offended,' cried she, 'I have but made a little digression. All I want to know, is the state of the moon,—for if it is at the *full* I shall be saved a world of conjectures, and know at once to what cause to attribute the inconsistencies I have witnessed this morning.[70] In the first place, I heard Lord Orville excuse himself from going out, because he had business of importance to transact at home,—yet have I seen him sauntering alone in the garden this half-hour. Miss Anville, on the other hand, I invited to walk out with me; and, after seeking her every where round the house, I find her quietly seated in the drawing-room. And but a few minutes since, Sir Clement Willoughby, with even more than his usual politeness, told me he was come to spend the morning here,—when, just now, I met him flying down stairs, as if pursued by the Furies;[71] and, far from repeating his compliments, or making any excuse, he did not even answer a question I asked him, but rushed past me, with the rapidity of a thief from a bailiff!'

'I protest,' said Mrs. Beaumont, 'I can't think what he meant; such rudeness from a man of any family is quite incomprehensible.'

'My Lord,' cried Lady Louisa to Lord Merton, 'Do you know he did the same by *me*?—I was just going to ask him what was the matter, but he ran past me so quick, that I declare he quite dazzled my eyes. You can't think, my Lord, how he frighted me; I dare say I look as pale—don't I look very pale, my Lord?'

'Your Ladyship,' said Mr. Lovel, 'so well becomes the lilies, that the roses might blush to see themselves so excelled.'

'Pray, Mr. Lovel,' said Mrs. Selwyn, 'if the roses should blush, how would you find it out?'

'Egad,' cried Mr. Coverley, 'I suppose they must blush, as the saying is, like a blue dog,[72]—for they are *red* already.'

'Prithee, Jack,' said Lord Merton, 'don't you pretend to talk about blushes, that never knew what they were in your life.'

'My Lord,' said Mrs. Selwyn, 'if experience alone can justify mentioning them, what an admirable treatise upon the subject may we not expect from your Lordship!'

'O, pray, Ma'am,' answered he, 'stick to Jack Coverley,—he's your only man; for my part, I confess I have a mortal aversion to arguments.'

'O fie, my Lord,' cried Mrs. Selwyn, 'a senator[73] of the nation! a member of the noblest parliament in the world!—and yet neglect the art of oratory?'

'Why, faith, my Lord,' said Mr. Lovel, 'I think, in general, your House is not much addicted to study; we of the lower House[74] have indubitably most application; and, if I did not speak before a superior power,' bowing low to Lord Merton, 'I should presume to add, we have likewise the most able speakers.'

'Mr. Lovel,' said Mrs. Selwyn, 'you deserve immortality for that discovery! But for this observation, and the confession of Lord Merton, I protest I should have supposed that a peer of the realm, and an able logician, were synonymous terms.'

Lord Merton, turning upon his heel, asked Lady Louisa if she should *take the air* before dinner?

'Really,' answered she, 'I don't know;—I'm afraid it's monstrous hot; besides,' (putting her hand to her forehead) 'I a'n't half well; it's quite horrid to have such weak nerves!—the least thing in the world discomposes me: I declare, that man's oddness has given me such a shock,—I don't know when I shall recover from it. But I'm a sad weak creature,—don't you think I am, my Lord?'

'O, by no means,' answered he, 'your Ladyship is merely delicate,—and devil take me if ever I had the least passion for an Amazon.'[75]

'I have the honour to be quite of your Lordship's opinion,' said Mr. Lovel, looking maliciously at Mrs. Selwyn, 'for I have an insuperable aversion to strength, either of body or mind, in a female.'

'Faith, and so have I,' said Mr. Coverley; 'for egad I'd as soon see a woman chop wood, as hear her chop logic.'[76]

'So would every man in his senses,' said Lord Merton; 'for a woman wants nothing to recommend her but beauty and good-nature; in every thing else she is either impertinent or unnatural. For my part, deuce take me if ever I wish to hear a word of sense from a woman as long as I live!'

'It has always been agreed,' said Mrs. Selwyn, looking round her with the utmost contempt, 'that no man ought to be connected with a woman whose understanding is superior to his own. Now I very much fear, that to accommodate all this good company, according to such a rule, would be utterly impracticable, unless we should chuse subjects from Swift's hospital of ideots.'[77]

How many enemies, my dear Sir, does this unbounded severity excite! Lord Merton, however, only whistled; Mr. Coverley sang; and Mr. Lovel, after biting his lips some time, said, ''Pon honour, that lady—if she was *not* a lady,—I should be half tempted to observe,—that there is something,—in such severity,—that is rather, I must say,—rather—*oddish*.'[78]

Just then, a servant brought Lady Louisa a note, upon a

waiter,[79] which is a ceremony always used to her Ladyship; and I took the opportunity of this interruption to the conversation, to steal out of the room.

I went immediately to the parlour, which I found quite empty; for I did not dare walk in the garden after what Mrs. Selwyn had said.

In a few minutes, a servant announced Mr. Macartney, saying, as he entered the room, that he would acquaint Lord Orville he was there.

Mr. Macartney rejoiced much at finding me alone. He told me he had taken the liberty to enquire for Lord Orville, by way of pretext for coming to the house.

I then very eagerly enquired if he had seen his father.

'I have, Madam,' said he; 'and the generous compassion you have shewn made me hasten to acquaint you, that upon reading my unhappy mother's letter, he did not hesitate to acknowledge me.'[80]

'Good God,' cried I, with no little emotion, 'how similar are our circumstances! And did he receive you kindly?'

'I could not, Madam, expect that he would: the cruel transaction which obliged me to fly Paris, was too recent in his memory.'

'And,—have you seen the young lady?'

'No, Madam,' said he mournfully, 'I was forbid her sight.'

'Forbid her sight!—and why?'

'Partly, perhaps, from prudence,—and partly from the remains of a resentment which will not easily subside. I only requested leave to acquaint her with my relationship, and be allowed to call her sister;—but it was denied me!—*You have no sister*, said Sir John, *you must forget her existence*. Hard, and vain command!'

'You have, you have a sister!' cried I, from an impulse of pity which I could not repress, 'a sister who is most warmly interested in your welfare, and who only wants opportunity to manifest her friendship and regard.'

'Gracious Heaven!' cried he, 'what does Miss Anville mean?'

'Anville,' said I, 'is not my real name; Sir John Belmont is my father,—he is your's,—and I am your sister!—You see, therefore, the claim we mutually have to each other's regard; we are not merely bound by the ties of friendship, but by those of blood. I feel for you, already, all the affection of a sister,—I felt it, indeed, before I knew I was one.—Why, my dear brother, do you not speak?—do you hesitate to acknowledge me?'

'I am so lost in astonishment,' cried he, 'that I know not if I hear right!'—

'I have then found a brother,' cried I, holding out my hand, 'and he will not own me!'

'Own you!—Oh, Madam,' cried he, accepting my offered hand, 'is it, indeed, possible *you* can own *me*?—a poor, wretched adventurer! who so lately had no support but from your generosity?—whom your benevolence snatched from utter destruction?—Can *you*,—Oh Madam, can you indeed, and without a blush, condescend to own such an outcast for a brother?'

'Oh, forbear, forbear,' cried I, 'is this language proper for a sister? are we not reciprocally bound to each other? —Will you not suffer me to expect from *you* all the good offices in your power?—But tell me, where is our father at present?'

'At the Hotwell, Madam; he arrived there yesterday morning.'

I would have proceeded with further questions, but the entrance of Lord Orville prevented me. The moment he saw us, he started, and would have retreated; but, drawing my hand from Mr. Macartney's, I begged him to come in.

For a few moments we were all silent, and, I believe, all in equal confusion. Mr. Macartney, however, recollecting himself, said, 'I hope your Lordship will forgive the liberty I have taken in making use of your name?'

Lord Orville, rather coldly, bowed, but, said nothing.

Again we were all silent, and then Mr. Macartney took leave.

'I fancy,' said Lord Orville, when he was gone, 'I have shortened Mr. Macartney's visit?'

'No, my Lord, not at all.'

'I had presumed,' said he, with some hesitation, 'I should have seen Miss Anville in the garden;—but I knew not she was so much better engaged.'

Before I could answer, a servant came to tell me the chaise was ready, and that Mrs. Selwyn was enquiring for me.

'I will wait on her immediately,' cried I, and away I was running; but Lord Orville, stopping me, said, with great emotion, 'Is it thus, Miss Anville, you leave me?'

'My Lord,' cried I, 'how can I help it?—perhaps, soon, some better opportunity may offer—'

'Good Heaven!' cried he, 'do you indeed take me for a Stoic?[81] What better opportunity may I hope for?—is not the chaise come?—are you not going? have you even deigned to tell me whither?'

'My journey, my Lord, will now be deferred. Mr. Macartney has brought me intelligence which renders it, at present, unnecessary.'

'Mr. Macartney,' said he, gravely, 'seems to have great influence,—yet he is a very young counsellor.'

'Is it possible, my Lord, Mr. Macartney can give you the least uneasiness?'

'My dearest Miss Anville,' said he, taking my hand, 'I see, and I adore the purity of your mind, superior as it is to all little arts, and all apprehensions of suspicion; and I should do myself, as well as you, injustice, if I were capable of harbouring the smallest doubts of that goodness which makes you mine for ever: nevertheless, pardon me, if I own myself surprised,—nay, alarmed, at these frequent meetings with so young a man as Mr. Macartney.'

'My Lord,' cried I, eager to clear myself, 'Mr. Macartney is my brother!'

'Your brother! you amaze me!—What strange mystery, then, makes his relationship a secret?'

Just then, Mrs. Selwyn opened the door. 'O, you are here!' cried she; 'Pray is my Lord so kind as to assist you in *preparing* for your journey,—or in *retarding* it?'

'I should be most happy,' said Lord Orville, smiling, 'if it were in my power to do the *latter*.'

I then acquainted her with Mr. Macartney's communication.

She immediately ordered the chaise away, and then took me into her own room, to consider what should be done.

A few minutes sufficed to determine her, and she wrote the following note.

To Sir John Belmont, Bart.

Mrs. Selwyn presents her compliments to Sir John Belmont, and, if he is at leisure, will be glad to wait on him this morning, upon business of importance.

She then ordered her man to enquire at the Pump-room for a direction; and went herself to Mrs. Beaumont to apologize for deferring her journey.

An answer was presently returned, that he would be glad to see her.

She would have had me immediately accompany her to the Hotwells; but I entreated her to spare me the distress of so abrupt an introduction, and to pave the way for my reception. She consented rather reluctantly, and, attended only by her servant, walked to the Wells.

She was not absent two hours, yet so miserably did time seem to linger, that I thought a thousand accidents had happened, and feared she would never return. I passed the whole time in my own room, for I was too much agitated even to converse with Lord Orville.

The instant that, from my window, I saw her returning, I flew down stairs, and met her in the garden.

We both walked to the arbour.

Her looks, in which disappointment and anger were expressed, presently announced to me the failure of her embassy. Finding that she did not speak, I asked her, in a faultering voice, Whether or not I had a father?

'You have *not*, my dear!' said she, abruptly.

'Very well, Madam,' said I, with tolerable calmness, 'let the chaise, then, be ordered again,—I will go to Berry Hill,—and there, I trust, I shall still find one!'

It was some time ere she could give, or I could hear, the account of her visit; and then she related it in a hasty manner; yet I believe I can recollect every word.

'I found Sir John alone. He received me with the utmost politeness. I did not keep him a moment in suspense as to the purport of my visit. But I had no sooner made it known, than, with a supercilious smile, he said, "And have you, Madam, been prevailed upon to revive that ridiculous old story?" Ridiculous, I told him, was a term which he would find no one else do him the favour to make use of, in speaking of the horrible actions belonging to the *old story* he made so light of; "actions," continued I, "which would dye still deeper the black annals of Nero or Caligula."[82] He attempted in vain to rally, for I pursued him with all the severity in my power, and ceased not painting the enormity of his crime, till I stung him to the quick, and in a voice of passion and impatience, he said, "No more, Madam,— this is not a subject upon which I need a monitor." "Make then," cried I, "the only reparation in your power.—Your daughter is now at Clifton; send for her hither, and, in the face of the world, proclaim the legitimacy of her birth, and clear the reputation of your injured wife." "Madam," said he, "you are much mistaken, if you suppose I waited for the honour of this visit, before I did what little justice now depends upon me, to the memory of that unfortunate woman: her daughter has been my care from her infancy; I have taken her into my house; she bears my name, and she will be my sole heiress." For some time this assertion appeared so absurd, that I only laughed at it; but at last, he assured me, I had myself been imposed upon, for that the very woman who attended Lady Belmont in her last illness, conveyed the child to him while he was in London, before she was a year old. "Unwilling," he added, "at that time to confirm the rumour of my being married, I sent the woman with the child to France; as soon as she was old enough, I put her into a convent, where she has been properly educated; and now I have taken her home. I have acknowledged her for my lawful child, and paid, at length, to the memory of her unhappy mother, a tribute of fame,[83] which has made me wish to hide myself hereafter from all the world." This whole story sounded so improbable, that I did not scruple to tell him I discredited every word. He then rung his bell, and enquiring if his hair-dresser[84] was come, said he was sorry to leave me, but that, if I would favour him with my company to-morrow, he would do himself the honour of introducing Miss Belmont to *me*, instead of troubling me to introduce her to *him*. I rose in great indignation, and assuring him I would make his conduct as public as it was infamous, I left the house.'

Good Heaven, how strange the recital! how incomprehensible an affair! The Miss Belmont, then, who is actually at Bristol, passes for the daughter of my unhappy mother!—passes, in short, for your Evelina! Who she can be, or what this tale can mean, I have not any idea.

Mrs. Selwyn soon after left me to my own reflections. Indeed they were not very pleasant. Quietly as I had borne her relation, the moment I was alone I felt most bitterly both the disgrace and the sorrow of a rejection so cruelly inexplicable.

I know not how long I might have continued in this situation, had I not been awakened from my melancholy reverie by the voice of Lord Orville. 'May I come in,' cried he, 'or shall I interrupt you?'

I was silent, and he seated himself next me.

'I fear,' he continued, 'Miss Anville will think I persecute her; yet so much as I have to say, and so much as I wish to hear, with so few opportunities for either, she cannot wonder,—and I hope she will not be offended,—that I seize with such avidity every moment in my power to converse with her. You are grave,' added he, taking my hand; 'I hope you do not regret the delay of your journey?—I hope the pleasure it gives to *me*, will not be a subject of pain to *you*?—You are silent?—Something, I am sure, has afflicted you:—Would to Heaven I were able to console you!—Would to Heaven I were worthy to participate in your sorrows!'

My heart was too full to bear this kindness, and I could only answer by my tears. 'Good Heaven,' cried he, 'how you alarm me!—My love, my sweet Miss Anville, deny me no longer to be the sharer of your griefs!—tell me, at least, that you have not withdrawn your esteem!—that you do not repent the goodness you have shewn me!—that you still think me the same grateful Orville whose heart you have deigned to accept!'

'Oh, my Lord,' cried I, 'your generosity overpowers me!' And

I wept like an infant. For now that all my hopes of being acknowledged seemed finally crushed, I felt the nobleness of his disinterested regard so forcibly, that I could scarce breathe under the weight of gratitude which oppressed me.

He seemed greatly shocked, and in terms the most flattering, the most respectfully tender, he at once soothed my distress, and urged me to tell him its cause.

'My Lord,' said I, when I was able to speak, 'you little know what an outcast you have honoured with your choice!—a child of bounty,—an orphan from infancy,—dependent, even for subsistence dependent, upon the kindness of compassion!—Rejected by my natural friends,[85]—disowned for ever by my nearest relation,—Oh, my Lord, so circumstanced, can I deserve the distinction with which you honour me? No, no, I feel the inequality too painfully;—you must leave me, my Lord, you must suffer me to return to obscurity,—and there, in the bosom of my first, best, my only friend,—I will pour forth all the grief of my heart!—while you, my Lord, must seek elsewhere—'

I could not proceed; my whole soul recoiled against the charge I would have given, and my voice refused to utter it.

'Never!' cried he, warmly; 'my heart is yours, and I swear to you an attachment eternal!—You prepare me, indeed, for a tale of horror, and I am almost breathless with expectation,—but so firm is my conviction, that, whatever are your misfortunes, to have merited them is not of the number, that I feel myself more strongly, more invincibly devoted to you than ever!—Tell me but where I may find this noble friend, whose virtues you have already taught me to reverence,—and I will fly to obtain his consent and intercession, that henceforward our fates may be indissolubly united,—and then shall it be the sole study of my life to endeavour to soften your past,—and guard you from future misfortunes!'

I had just raised my eyes, to answer this most generous of men, when the first object they met was Mrs. Selwyn!

'So, my dear,' cried she, 'what, still courting the rural shades![86]—I thought ere now you would have been satiated with this retired seat, and I have been seeking you all over the house.

But I find the only way to meet with *you*,—is to enquire for *Lord Orville*. However, don't let me disturb your meditations; you are possibly planning some pastoral dialogue.'

And, with this provoking speech, she walked on.

In the greatest confusion, I was quitting the arbour, when Lord Orville said, 'Permit *me* to follow Mrs. Selwyn,—it is time to put an end to all impertinent conjectures; will you allow me to speak to her openly?'

I assented in silence, and he left me.

I then went to my own room, where I continued till I was summoned to dinner; after which, Mrs. Selwyn invited me to hers.

The moment she had shut the door, 'Your Ladyship,' said she, 'will, I hope, be seated.'.

'Ma'am!' cried I, staring.

'O the sweet innocent! So you don't know what I mean?—but, my dear, my sole view is to accustom you a little to your dignity elect, lest, when you are addressed by your title, you should look another way, from an apprehension of listening to a discourse not meant for you to hear.'

Having, in this manner, diverted herself with my confusion, till her raillery was almost exhausted, she congratulated me very seriously upon the partiality of Lord Orville, and painted to me, in the strongest terms, his disinterested desire of being married to me immediately. She had told him, she said, my whole story; and yet he was willing, nay eager, that our union should take place of any further application to my family. 'Now, my dear,' continued she, 'I advise you by all means to marry him directly; nothing can be more precarious than our success with Sir John; and the young men of this age are not to be trusted with too much time for deliberation, where their interests are concerned.'

'Good God, Madam,' cried I, 'do, you think I would *hurry* Lord Orville?'

'Well, do as you will,' said she; 'luckily you have an excellent subject for Quixotism;[87]—otherwise, this delay might prove your ruin; but Lord Orville is almost as romantic as if he had been born and bred at Berry Hill.'

She then proposed, as no better expedient seemed likely to be suggested, that I should accompany her at once in her visit to the Hotwells to-morrow morning.

The very idea made me tremble; yet she represented so strongly the necessity of pursuing this unhappy affair with spirit, or giving it totally up, that, wanting her force of argument, I was almost obliged to yield to her proposal.

In the evening, we all walked in the garden: and Lord Orville, who never quitted my side, told me he had been listening to a tale, which, though it had removed the perplexities that had so long tormented him, had penetrated him with sorrow and compassion. I acquainted him with Mrs. Selwyn's plan for to-morrow, and confessed the extreme terror it gave me. He then, in a manner almost unanswerable, besought me to leave to him the conduct of the affair, by consenting to be his before an interview took place.

I could not but acknowledge my sense of his generosity; but I told him I was wholly dependent upon you, and that I was certain your opinion would be the same as mine, which was, that it would be highly improper I should dispose of myself for ever, so very near the time which must finally decide by whose authority I ought to be guided. The subject of this dreaded meeting, with the thousand conjectures and apprehensions to which it gives birth, employed all our conversation then, as it has all my thoughts since.

Heaven only knows how I shall support myself, when the long-expected,—the wished,—yet terrible moment arrives, that will prostrate me at the feet of the nearest, the most reverenced of all relations, whom my heart yearns to know, and longs to love!

LETTER XVII

Evelina in continuation

Oct. 9

I could not write yesterday, so violent was the agitation of my mind,—but I will not, now, lose a moment till I have hastened to my best friend an account of the transactions of a day I can never recollect without emotion.

Mrs. Selwyn determined upon sending no message, 'Lest,' said she, 'Sir John, fatigued with the very idea of my reproaches, should endeavour to avoid a meeting: all we have to do, is to take him by surprise. He cannot but see who you are, whether he will do you justice or not.'

We went early, and in Mrs. Beaumont's chariot; into which, Lord Orville, uttering words of the kindest encouragement, handed us both.

My uneasiness, during the ride, was excessive, but, when we stopped at the door, I was almost senseless with terror! the meeting, at last, was not so dreadful as that moment! I believe I was carried into the house;[88] but I scarce recollect what was done with me: however, I know we remained some time in the parlour, before Mrs. Selwyn could send any message up stairs.

When I was somewhat recovered, I entreated her to let me return home, assuring her I felt myself quite unequal to supporting the interview.

'No,' said she, 'you must stay now; your fears will but gain strength by delay, and we must not have such a shock as this repeated.' Then, turning to the servant, she sent up her name.

An answer was brought, that he was going out in great haste, but would attend her immediately. I turned so sick, that Mrs. Selwyn was apprehensive I should have fainted; and opening a door which led to an inner apartment, she begged me to wait there till I was somewhat composed, and till she had prepared for my reception.

Glad of every moment's reprieve, I willingly agreed to the proposal, and Mrs. Selwyn had but just time to shut me in, before her presence was necessary.

The voice of a *father*—Oh dear and revered name!—which then, for the first time, struck my ears, affected me in a manner I cannot describe, though it was only employed in giving orders to a servant as he came down stairs.

Then, entering the parlour, I heard him say, 'I am sorry, Madam, I made you wait, but I have an engagement which now calls me away: however, if you have any commands for me, I shall be glad of the honour of your company some other time.'

'I am come, Sir,' said Mrs. Selwyn, 'to introduce your daughter to you.'

'I am infinitely obliged to you,' answered he, 'but I have just had the satisfaction of breakfasting with her. Ma'am, your most obedient.'

'You refuse, then, to see her?'

'I am much indebted to you, Madam, for this desire of encreasing my family, but you must excuse me if I decline taking advantage of it. I have already a daughter, to whom I owe every thing; and it is not three days since, that I had the pleasure of discovering a son; how many more sons and daughters may be brought to me, I am yet to learn, but I am, already, perfectly satisfied with the size of my family.'

'Had you a thousand children, Sir John,' said Mrs. Selwyn, warmly, 'this only one, of which Lady Belmont was the mother, ought to be most distinguished; and, far from avoiding her sight, you should thank your stars, in humble gratitude, that there yet remains in your power the smallest opportunity of doing the injured wife you have destroyed, the poor justice of acknowledging her child!'

'I am very unwilling, Madam,' answered he, 'to enter into any discussion of this point; but you are determined to compel me to speak. There lives not, at this time, the human being who should talk to *me* of the regret due to the memory of that ill-fated woman; no one can feel it so severely as myself: but let me, nevertheless, assure you I have already done all that remained in my power to prove the respect she merited from me; her child I have educated and owned for my lawful heiress; if, Madam, you can suggest to me any other means by which I may more fully do her justice, and more clearly manifest her innocence, name them to me, and though they should wound my character still deeper, I will perform them readily.'

'All this sounds vastly well,' returned Mrs. Selwyn, 'but I must own it is rather too enigmatical for *my* faculties of comprehension. You can, however, have no objection to seeing this young lady?'

'None in the world.'

'Come forth, then, my dear,' cried she, opening the door, 'come forth, and see your father!' Then, taking my trembling hand, she led me forward. I would have withdrawn it, and retreated, but as he advanced instantly towards me, I found myself already before him.

What a moment for your Evelina!—an involuntary scream escaped me, and covering my face with my hands, I sunk on the floor.

He had, however, seen me first; for in a voice scarce articulate he exclaimed, 'My God! does Caroline Evelyn still live!'

Mrs. Selwyn said something, but I could not listen to her; and, in a few minutes, he added, 'Lift up thy head,—if my sight has not blasted thee,—lift up thy head, thou image of my long-lost Caroline!'

Affected beyond measure, I half arose, and embraced his knees, while yet on my own.

'Yes, yes,' cried he, looking earnestly in my face, 'I see, I see thou art her child! she lives—she breathes—she is present to my view!—Oh God, that she indeed lived!—Go, child, go,' added he, wildly starting, and pushing me from him, 'take her away, Madam,—I cannot bear to look at her!' And then, breaking hastily from me, he rushed out of the room.

Speechless, motionless myself, I attempted not to stop him: but Mrs. Selwyn, hastening after him, caught hold of his arm. 'Leave me, Madam,' cried he, with quickness, 'and take care of the poor child;—bid her not think me unkind, tell her I would at this moment plunge a dagger in my heart to serve her,—but she has set my brain on fire, and I can see her no more!'[89] Then, with a violence almost frantic, he ran up stairs.

Oh Sir, had I not indeed cause to dread this interview?—an interview so unspeakably painful and afflicting to us both! Mrs. Selwyn would have immediately returned to Clifton; but I entreated her to wait some time, in the hope that my unhappy father, when his first emotion was over would again bear me in his sight. However, he soon after sent his servant to enquire how I did, and to tell Mrs. Selwyn he was much indisposed, but would hope for the honour of seeing her to-morrow, at any time she would please to appoint.

She fixed upon ten o'clock in the morning; and then, with a heavy heart, I got into the chariot. Those afflicting words, *I can see her no more*, were never a moment absent from my mind.

Yet the sight of Lord Orville, who handed us from the carriage, gave some relief to the sadness of my thoughts. I could not, however, enter upon the painful subject, but begging Mrs. Selwyn to satisfy him, I went to my own room.

As soon as I communicated to the good Mrs. Clinton the present situation of my affairs, an idea occurred to her, which seemed to clear up all the mystery of my having been so long disowned.

The woman, she says, who attended my ever-to-be-regretted mother in her last illness, and who nursed me the first four months of my life, soon after being discharged from your house, left Berry Hill entirely, with her baby, who was but six weeks older than myself. Mrs. Clinton remembers, that her quitting the place appeared, at the time, very extraordinary to the neighbours, but, as she was never heard of afterwards, she was, by degrees, quite forgotten.

The moment this was mentioned, it struck Mrs. Selwyn, as well as Mrs. Clinton herself, that my father had been imposed upon, and that the nurse who said she had brought his child to him, had, in fact, carried her own.

The name by which I was known, the secrecy observed in regard to my family, and the retirement in which I lived, all conspired to render this scheme, however daring and fraudulent, by no means impracticable, and, in short, the idea was no sooner started, than conviction seemed to follow it.

Mrs. Selwyn determined immediately to discover the truth or mistake of this conjecture; therefore, the moment she had dined, she walked to the Hotwells, attended by Mrs. Clinton.

I waited in my room till her return, and then heard the following account of her visit:

She found my poor father in great agitation. She immediately informed him of the occasion of her so speedy return, and of her suspicions of the woman who had pretended to convey to him his child. Interrupting her with quickness, he said he had just sent her from his presence: that the certainty I carried in my countenance, of my real birth, made him, the moment he had recovered from a surprise which had almost deprived him of reason, suspect, himself, the imposition she mentioned. He had, therefore, sent for the woman, and questioned her with the utmost austerity: she turned pale, and was extremely embarrassed, but still she persisted in affirming, that she had really brought him the daughter of Lady Belmont. His perplexity, he said, almost distracted him; he had *always* observed that his daughter bore no resemblance to either of her parents, but, as he had never doubted the veracity of the nurse, this circumstance did not give birth to any suspicion.

At Mrs. Selwyn's desire, the woman was again called, and interrogated with equal art and severity; her confusion was evident, and her answers often contradictory, yet she still declared she was no imposter. 'We will see that in a minute,' said Mrs. Selwyn, and then desired Mrs. Clinton might be called up stairs. The poor wretch, changing colour, would have escaped out of the room, but, being prevented, dropped on her knees, and implored forgiveness. A confession of the whole affair was then extorted from her.

Doubtless, my dear Sir, you must remember *Dame Green*,[90] who was my first nurse. The deceit she has practised, was suggested, she says, by a conversation she overheard, in which my unhappy mother besought you, that, if her child survived her, you would take the sole care of its education; and, in particular, if it should be a female, you would by no means part with her early in life. You not only consented, she says, but assured her you would even retire abroad with me yourself, if my father should importunately demand me. Her own child, she said, was then in her arms, and she could not forbear wishing it were possible to give *her* the fortune which seemed so little valued for me. This wish once raised, was not easily suppressed; on the contrary, what at first appeared a mere idle desire, in a short time seemed a feasible scheme. Her husband was dead, and she had little regard for any body but her child; and, in short, having saved money for the journey, she contrived to enquire a direction to my father, and telling her neighbours she was going to settle in Devonshire, she set out on her expedition.

When Mrs. Selwyn asked her, how she dared perpetrate such a fraud,[91] she protested she had no ill designs, but that, as *Miss* would be never the worse for it, she thought it pity *nobody* should be the better.

Her success we are already acquainted with. Indeed everything seemed to contribute towards it: my father had no correspondent at Berry Hill, the child was instantly sent to France, where being brought up in as much retirement as myself, nothing but accident could discover the fraud.

And here, let me indulge myself in observing, and rejoicing to observe, that the total neglect I thought I met with, was not the effect of insensibility or unkindness, but of imposition and error; and that at the very time, we concluded I was unnaturally rejected, my deluded father meant to shew me most favour and protection.

He acknowledges that Lady Howard's letter flung him into some perplexity; he immediately communicated it to Dame Green, who confessed it was the greatest shock she had ever received in her life; yet she had the art and boldness to assert, that Lady Howard must herself have been deceived: and as she had, from the beginning of her enterprise, declared she had stolen away the child without your knowledge, he concluded that some deceit was *then* intended him; and this thought occasioned his abrupt answer.

Dame Green owned, that from the moment the journey to England was settled, she gave herself up for lost. All her hope was to have had her daughter married before it took place, for which reason she had so much promoted Mr. Macartney's addresses: for though such a match was inadequate to the pretensions of *Miss Belmont*, she well knew it was far superior to those *her daughter* could form, after the discovery of her birth.

My first enquiry was, if this innocent daughter was yet acquainted with the affair? No, Mrs. Selwyn said, nor was any plan settled how to divulge it to her. Poor unfortunate girl! how hard is her fate! She is entitled to my kindest offices, and I shall always consider her as my sister.

I then asked whether my father would again allow me to see him?

'Why no, my dear, not yet,' answered she; 'he declares the sight of you is too much for him: however, we are to settle everything concerning you to-morrow, for this woman took up all our time to-day.'

This morning, therefore, she is again gone to the Hotwell. I am waiting in all impatience for her return; but as I know you will be anxious for the account this letter contains, I will not delay sending it.

LETTER XVIII

Evelina in continuation

Oct. 9

How agitated, my dear Sir, is the present life of your Evelina! every day seems important, and one event only a prelude to another.

Mrs. Selwyn, upon her return this morning from the Hotwell, entering my room very abruptly, said, 'Oh my dear, I have terrible news for you!'

'For me, Ma'am!—Good God! what now?'

'Arm yourself,' cried she, 'with all your Berry Hill philosophy;—con over every lesson of fortitude or resignation you ever learned in your life,—for know,—you are next week to be married to Lord Orville!'

Doubt, astonishment, and a kind of perturbation I cannot describe, made this abrupt communication alarm me extremely, and, almost breathless, I could only exclaim, 'Good God, Madam, what do you tell me?'

'You may well be frightened, my dear,' said she, ironically, 'for really there is something mighty terrific, in becoming, at once, the wife of the man you adore,—and a Countess!'⁹²

I entreated her to spare her raillery, and tell me her real meaning. She could not prevail with herself to grant the *first* request, though she readily complied with the second.

My poor father, she said, was still in the utmost uneasiness. He entered upon his affairs with great openness, and told her he was equally disturbed how to dispose either of the daughter he had discovered, or the daughter he was now to give up; the former he dreaded to trust himself with again beholding, and the latter he knew not how to shock with the intelligence of her disgrace. Mrs. Selwyn then acquainted him with my situation in regard to Lord Orville; this delighted him extremely, and, when he heard of his Lordship's eagerness, he said he was himself of opinion, the sooner the union took place the better: and, in return, he informed her of the affair of Mr. Macartney. 'And, after a very long conversation,' continued Mrs. Selwyn, 'we agreed, that the most eligible scheme for all parties would be to have both the real and the fictitious daughter married without delay. Therefore, if either of you have any inclination to pull caps for the title of Miss Belmont, you must do it with all speed, as next week will take from both of you all pretensions to it.'

'Next week!—dear Madam, what a strange plan!—without my being consulted—without applying to Mr. Villars,—without even the concurrence of Lord Orville!'

'As to consulting *you*, my dear, it was out of all question, because, you know, young ladies' hearts and hands are always to be given with reluctance;—as to Mr. Villars, it is sufficient we know him for your friend;—and as for Lord Orville, he is a party concerned.'

'A party concerned!—you amaze me!'

'Why, yes; for as I found our consultation likely to redound to his advantage, I persuaded Sir John to send for him.'

'Send for him!—Good God!'

'Yes, and Sir John agreed. I told the servant, that if he could not hear of his Lordship in the house, he might be pretty certain of encountering him in the arbour.—Why do you colour, my dear?—Well, he was with us in a moment; I introduced him to Sir John, and we proceeded to business.'

'I am very, very sorry for it!—Lord Orville must, himself, think this conduct strangely precipitate.'

'No, my dear, you are mistaken, Lord Orville has too much good sense. Every thing was then discussed in a rational manner. You are to be married privately, though not secretly, and then go to one of his Lordship's country seats:[93] and poor little Miss Green and your brother, who have no house of their own, must go to one of Sir John's.'

'But why, my dear Madam, why all this haste? why may we not be allowed a little longer time.'

'I could give you a thousand reasons,' answered she, 'but that I am tolerably certain *two* or *three* will be more than you can controvert, even with all the logic of genuine coquetry. In the first place, you doubtless wish to quit the house of Mrs. Beaumont,—to whose, then, can you with such propriety remove, as to Lord Orville's?'

'Surely, Madam,' cried I, 'I am not more destitute now, than when I thought myself an orphan?'

'Your father, my dear,' answered she, 'is willing to save the little impostor as much of the mortification of her disgrace as is in his power: now if you immediately take her place, according to your right, as Miss Belmont, why not all that either of you can do for her, will prevent her being eternally stigmatized, as the Bantling of Dame Green,[94] wash-woman and wet nurse of Berry Hill, Dorsetshire. Now such a genealogy will not be very flattering, even to Mr. Macartney, who, all-dismal as he is, you will find by no means wanting in pride and self-consequence.'

'For the universe,' interrupted I, 'I would not be accessary to the degradation you mention; but, surely, Madam, I may return to Berry Hill?'

'By no means,' said she; 'for though compassion may make us wish to save the poor girl the confusion of an immediate and public fall, yet justice demands you should appear, henceforward, in no other light than that of Sir John Belmont's daughter. Besides, between friends, I, who know the world, can see that half this prodigious delicacy for the little usurper, is the mere result of self-interest; for while *her* affairs are hushed up, Sir John's, you know, are kept from being brought further to light. Now the double marriage we have projected, obviates all rational objections. Sir John will give you, immediately, £30,000; all settlements, and so forth, will be made for you in the name of Evelina Belmont;—Mr. Macartney will, at the same time, take poor Polly Green,—and yet, at first, it will only be generally known, that *a daughter of Sir John Belmont's* is married.'

In this manner, though she did not convince me, yet the quickness of her arguments silenced and perplexed me. I enquired, however, if I might not be permitted to again see my father, or whether I must regard myself as banished his presence for ever?

'My dear,' said she, 'he does not know you; he concludes that you have been brought up to detest him, and therefore he is rather prepared to dread, than to love you.'

This answer made me very unhappy; I wished, most impatiently, to remove his prejudice, and endeavour, by dutiful assiduity, to engage his kindness, yet knew not how to propose seeing him, while conscious he wished to avoid me.

This evening, as soon as the company was engaged with cards, Lord Orville exerted his utmost eloquence to reconcile me to this hasty plan: but how was I startled, when he told me that next *Tuesday* was the day appointed by my father to be the most important of my life!

'Next Tuesday!' repeated I, quite out of breath, 'Oh my Lord!—'

'My sweet Evelina,' said he, 'the day which will make me the happiest of mortals, would probably appear awful to you, were it to be deferred a twelvemonth: Mrs. Selwyn has, doubtless, acquainted you with the many motives which, independent of my eagerness, require it to be speedy; suffer, therefore, its acceleration, and generously complete my felicity, by endeavouring to suffer it without repugnance.'

'Indeed, my Lord, I would not wilfully raise objections, nor do I desire to appear insensible of the honour of your good opinion;—but there is something in this plan, so very hasty,—so unreasonably precipitate,—besides, I shall have no time to hear from Berry Hill,—and believe me, my Lord, I should be for ever miserable, were I in an affair so important, to act without the sanction of Mr. Villars' advice.'

He offered to wait on you himself; but I told him I had rather write to you. And then he proposed, that, instead of my immediately accompanying him to Lincolnshire, we should, first, pass a month *at my native Berry Hill.*

This was, indeed, a grateful proposal to me, and I listened to it with undisguised pleasure. And, in short I was obliged to consent to a compromise, in merely deferring the day till Thursday![95] He readily undertook to engage my father's concurrence in this little delay, and I besought him, at the same time, to make use of his influence to obtain me a second interview, and to represent the deep concern I felt in being thus banished his sight.

He would then have spoken of *settlements,*[96] but I assured him, I was almost ignorant even of the word.

And now, my dearest Sir, what is your opinion of these hasty proceedings? believe me, I half regret the simple facility with which I have suffered myself to be hurried into compliance, and, should you start but the smallest objection, I will yet insist upon being allowed more time.

I must now write a concise account of the state of my affairs to Howard Grove, and to Madame Duval.

Adieu, dearest and most honoured Sir! everything, at present, depends upon your single decision, to which, though I yield in trembling, I yield implicitly.

LETTER XIX

Evelina in continuation

Oct. 11

Yesterday morning, as soon as breakfast was over, Lord Orville went to the Hotwells, to wait upon my father with my double petition.

Mrs. Beaumont then, in general terms, proposed a walk in the garden. Mrs. Selwyn said she had letters to write, but Lady Louisa arose to accompany her.

I had had some reason to imagine, from the notice with which her Ladyship had honoured me during breakfast, that her brother had acquainted her with my present situation: and her behaviour now confirmed my conjecture; for, when I would have gone up stairs, instead of suffering me, as usual, to pass disregarded, she called after me with an affected surprise, 'Miss Anville, don't you walk with us?'

There seemed something so little-minded in this sudden change of conduct, that, from an involuntary motion of contempt, I thanked her, with a coldness like her own, and declined her offer. Yet, observing that she blushed extremely at my refusal, and recollecting she was sister to Lord Orville, my indignation subsided, and upon Mrs. Beaumont's repeating the invitation, I accepted it.

Our walk proved extremely dull; Mrs. Beaumont, who never says much, was more silent than usual; Lady Louisa strove in vain to lay aside the restraint and distance she has hitherto preserved; and as to me, I was too conscious of the circumstances to which I owed their attention, to feel either pride or pleasure from receiving it.

Lord Orville was not long absent; he joined us in the garden with a look of gaiety and good-humour that revived us all. 'You are just the party,' said he, 'I wished to see together. Will you, Madam,' taking my hand, 'allow me the honour of introducing you, by your real name, to two of my nearest relations? Mrs. Beaumont, give me leave to present to you the daughter of Sir John Belmont; a young lady who, I am sure, must long since have engaged your esteem and admiration, though you were a stranger to her birth.'

'My Lord,' said Mrs. Beaumont, graciously saluting me, 'the young lady's rank in life,—your Lordship's recommendation,— or her own merit, would any one of them have been sufficient to have entitled her to my regard; and I hope she has always met with that respect in my house which is so much her due; though, had I been sooner made acquainted with her family, I should, doubtless, have better known how to have secured it.'

'Miss Belmont,' said Lord Orville, 'can receive no lustre from family, whatever she may give to it. Louisa, you will, I am sure, be happy to make yourself an interest in the friendship of Miss Belmont, whom I hope shortly,' kissing my hand, and joining it with her Ladyship's, 'to have the happiness of presenting to you by yet another name, and by the most endearing of all titles.'

I believe it would be difficult to say whose cheeks were, at that moment, of the deepest dye, Lady Louisa's or my own; for the conscious pride with which she has hitherto slighted me, gave to her an embarrassment which equalled the confusion that an introduction so unexpected gave to me. She saluted me, however, and, with a faint smile, said, 'I shall esteem myself very happy to profit by the honour of Miss Belmont's acquaintance.'

I only courtsied, and we walked on; but it was evident, from the little surprise they expressed, that they had been already informed of the state of the affair.

We were, soon after, joined by more company: and Lord Orville then, in a low voice, took an opportunity to tell me the success of his visit. In the first place, Thursday was agreed to; and, in the second, my father, he said, was much concerned to hear of my uneasiness, sent me his blessing, and complied with my request of seeing him, with the same readiness he should agree to any other I could make. Lord Orville, therefore, settled that I should wait upon him in the evening, and, at his particular request, unaccompanied by Mrs. Selwyn.

This kind message, and the prospect of so soon seeing him, gave me sensations of mixed pleasure and pain, which wholly occupied my mind till the time of my going to the Hotwell.

Mrs. Beaumont lent me her chariot, and Lord Orville absolutely insisted upon attending me. 'If you go alone,' said he, 'Mrs. Selwyn will certainly be offended; but, if you allow me to conduct you, though she may give the freer scope to her raillery, she cannot possibly be affronted: and we had much better suffer her laughter, than provoke her satire.'

Indeed, I must own I had no reason to regret being so accompanied; for his conversation supported my spirits from drooping, and made the ride seem so short, that we actually stopped at my father's door, before I knew we had proceeded ten yards.

He handed me from the carriage, and conducted me to the parlour, at the door of which I was met by Mr. Macartney. 'Ah, my dear brother,' cried I, 'how happy am I to see you here!'

He bowed and thanked me. Lord Orville, then, holding out his hand, said, 'Mr. Macartney, I hope we shall be better acquainted; I promise myself much pleasure from cultivating your friendship.'

'Your Lordship does me but too much honour,' answered Mr. Macartney.

'But where,' cried I, 'is my sister? for so I must already call, and always consider her:—I am afraid she avoids me;—you must endeavour, my dear brother, to prepossess her in my favour, and reconcile her to owning me.'

'Oh Madam,' cried he, 'you are all goodness and benevolence! but at present, I hope you will excuse her, for I fear she has hardly fortitude sufficient to see you: in a short time, perhaps—'

'In a *very* short time, then,' said Lord Orville, 'I hope you will yourself introduce her, and that we shall have the pleasure of wishing you both joy: allow me, my Evelina, to say *we*, and permit me, in your name as well as my own, to entreat that the first guests we shall have the happiness of receiving, may be Mr. and Mrs. Macartney.'

A servant then came to beg I would walk up stairs.

I besought Lord Orville to accompany me; but he feared the displeasure of Sir John, who had desired to see me alone. He led me, however, to the foot of the stairs, and made the kindest efforts to give me courage, but indeed he did not succeed, for the interview appeared to me in all its terrors, and left me no feeling but apprehension.

The moment I reached the landing place, the drawing-room door was opened, and my father, with a voice of kindness, called out, 'My child, is it you?'

'Yes, Sir,' cried I, springing forward, and kneeling at his feet, 'it is your child, if you will own her!'

He knelt by my side, and folding me in his arms, 'Own thee,' repeated he, 'yes, my poor girl, and Heaven knows with what bitter contrition!' Then raising both himself and me, he brought me into the drawing-room, shut the door, and took me to the window, where, looking at me with great earnestness, 'Poor unhappy Caroline!' cried he, and, to my inexpressible concern, he burst into tears. Need I tell you, my dear Sir, how mine flowed at the sight?

I would again have embraced his knees; but, hurrying from me, he flung himself upon a sofa, and leaning his face on his arms, seemed, for some time, absorbed in bitterness of grief.

I ventured not to interrupt a sorrow I so much respected, but waited in silence, and at a distance, till he recovered from his violence. But then it seemed, in a moment, to give way to a kind of frantic fury; for, starting suddenly, with a sternness which at once surprised and frightened me. 'Child,' cried he, 'hast thou yet sufficiently humbled thy father?—if thou hast, be contented with this proof of my weakness, and no longer force thyself into my presence!'

Thunderstruck by a command so unexpected, I stood still and speechless, and doubted whether my own ears did not deceive me.

'Oh, go, go!' cried he, passionately, 'in pity—in compassion,—if thou valuest my senses, leave me,—and for ever!'

'I will, I will,' cried I, greatly terrified; and I moved hastily towards the door: yet stopping when I reached it, and, almost involuntarily, dropping on my knees, 'Vouchsafe,' cried I, 'oh, Sir, vouchsafe but once to bless your daughter, and her sight shall never more offend you!'

'Alas,' cried he, in a softened voice, 'I am not worthy to bless thee!—I am not worthy to call thee daughter!—I am not worthy that the fair light of heaven should visit my eyes!—Oh God! that I could but call back the time ere thou wast born,—or else bury its remembrance in eternal oblivion!'

'Would to Heaven,' cried I, 'that the sight of me were less terrible to you! that, instead of irritating, I could soothe your sorrows!—Oh Sir, how thankfully would I then prove my duty, even at the hazard of my life!'

'Are you so kind?' cried he, gently; 'come hither, child,—rise, Evelina;—alas, it is for *me* to kneel, not you—and I *would* kneel,—I would crawl upon the earth;—I would kiss the dust,—could I, by such submission, obtain the forgiveness of the representative of the most injured of women!'

'Oh, Sir,' exclaimed I, 'that you could but read my heart!—that you could but see the filial tenderness and concern with which it overflows!—you would not then talk thus,—you would not then banish me your presence, and exclude me from your affection!'

'Good God,' cried he, 'is it then possible that you do not hate me?—Can the child of the wronged Caroline look at,—and not execrate me? Wast thou not born to abhor, and bred to curse me? did not thy mother bequeath thee her blessing, on condition that thou shouldst detest and avoid me?'

'Oh no, no, no!' cried I, 'think not so unkindly of her, nor so hardly of me.' I then took from my pocket-book her last letter, and, pressing it to my lips, with a trembling hand, and still upon my knees, I held it out to him.

Hastily snatching it from me, 'Great Heaven!' cried he, ''tis her writing—Whence comes this?—who gave it you?—why had I it not sooner?'

I made no answer; his vehemence intimidated me, and I ventured

not to move from the suppliant posture in which I had put
myself.

He went from me to the window, where his eyes were for
some time rivetted upon the direction of the letter, though his
hand shook so violently he could hardly hold it. Then, bringing
it to me, 'Open it,' cried he,—'for I cannot!'

I had, myself, hardly strength to obey him; but, when I had,
he took it back, and walked hastily up and down the room, as if
dreading to read it. At length, turning to me, 'Do you know,'
cried he, 'its contents?'

'No, Sir,' answered I, 'it has never been unsealed.'

He then again went to the window, and began reading.
Having hastily run it over, he cast up his eyes with a look of
desperation; the letter fell from his hand, and he exclaimed, 'Yes!
thou art sainted!—thou art blessed!—and I am cursed for ever!'
He continued some time fixed in this melancholy position; after
which, casting himself with violence upon the ground, 'Oh
wretch,' cried he, 'unworthy life and light, in what dungeon
canst thou hide thy head?'

I could restrain myself no longer; I rose and went to him; I
did not dare speak, but with pity and concern unutterable, I
wept and hung over him.

Soon after, starting up, he again seized the letter, exclaiming,
'Acknowledge thee, Caroline!—yes, with my heart's best blood
would I acknowledge thee!—Oh that thou couldst witness the
agony of my soul!—Ten thousand daggers could not have
wounded me like this letter!'

Then, after again reading it, 'Evelina,' he cried, 'she charges
me to receive thee;—wilt thou, in obedience to her will, own for
thy father the destroyer of thy mother?'

What a dreadful question! I shuddered, but could not speak.

'To clear her fame, and receive her child,' continued he,
looking stedfastly at the letter, 'are the conditions upon which
she leaves me her forgiveness: her fame, I have already
cleared;—and oh how willingly would I take her child to my
bosom,—fold her to my heart,—call upon her to mitigate my
anguish, and pour the balm of comfort on my wounds, were I

not conscious I deserve not to receive it, and that all my affliction is the result of my own guilt!'

It was in vain I attempted to speak; horror and grief took from me all power of utterance.

He then read aloud from the letter, '*Look not like thy unfortunate mother!*—Sweet soul, with what bitterness of spirit hast thou written?—Come hither, Evelina: Gracious Heaven!' looking earnestly at me, 'never was likeness more striking!—the eye,—the face,—the form,—Oh my child, my child!' Imagine, Sir,—for I can never describe my feelings, when I saw him sink upon his knees before me! 'Oh dear resemblance of thy murdered mother!—Oh all that remains of the most-injured of women! behold thy father at thy feet!—bending thus lowly to implore you would not hate him;—Oh then, thou representative of my departed wife, speak to me in her name, and say that the remorse which tears my soul, tortures me not in vain!'

'Oh rise, rise, my beloved father,' cried I, attempting to assist him, 'I cannot bear to see you thus;—reverse not the law of nature, rise yourself, and bless your kneeling daughter!'

'May Heaven bless thee, my child!—' cried he, 'for *I* dare not.' He then rose, and embracing me most affectionately, added, 'I see, I see that thou art all kindness, softness, and tenderness; I need not have feared thee, thou art all the fondest father could wish, and I will try to frame my mind to less painful sensations at thy sight. Perhaps the time may come when I may know the comfort of such a daughter,—at present, I am only fit to be alone: dreadful as are my reflections, they ought merely to torment myself.—Adieu, my child;—be not angry,—I cannot stay with thee,—oh Evelina! thy countenance is a dagger to my heart!—just so, thy mother looked,—just, so—'

Tears and sighs seemed to choak him!—and waving his hand, he would have left me,—but, clinging to him, 'Oh, Sir,' cried I, 'will you so soon abandon me?—am I again an orphan?—oh my dear, my long-lost father, leave me not, I beseech you! take pity on your child, and rob her not of the parent she so fondly hoped would cherish her!'

'You know not what you ask,' cried he; 'the emotions which

now rend my soul are more than my reason can endure: suffer me, then, to leave you,—impute it not to unkindness, but think of me as well as thou canst—Lord Orville has behaved nobly;— I believe he will make thee happy.' Then, again embracing me, 'God bless thee, my Evelina!—endeavour to love,—at least not to hate me,—and to make me an interest in thy filial bosom by thinking of me as thy father.'

I could not speak; I kissed his hands on my knees; and then, with yet more emotion, he again blessed me, and hurried out of the room,—leaving me almost drowned in tears.

Oh Sir, all goodness as you are, how much will you feel for your Evelina, during a scene of such agitation! I pray Heaven to accept the tribute of his remorse, and restore him to tranquillity!

When I was sufficiently composed to return to the parlour, I found Lord Orville waiting for me with the utmost anxiety: and then, a new scene of emotion, though of a far different nature, awaited me; for I learned, by Mr. Macartney, that this noblest of men had insisted the so-long-supposed Miss Belmont should be considered *indeed* as my sister, and as the co-heiress of my father! though not in *law*, in *justice*, he says, she ought ever to be treated as the daughter of Sir John Belmont.

Oh Lord Orville!—it shall be the sole study of my happy life, to express, better than by words, the sense I have of your exalted benevolence, and greatness of mind!

LETTER XX

Evelina in continuation

Clifton, Oct. 12

This morning, early, I received the following letter from Sir Clement Willoughby.

To Miss Anville

I have this moment received intelligence that preparations are actually making for your marriage with Lord Orville.

Imagine not that I write with the imbecile idea of rendering those preparations abortive. No, I am not so mad. My sole view is to explain the motive of my conduct in a particular instance, and to obviate the accusation of treachery which may be laid to my charge.

My unguarded behaviour when I last saw you, has, probably, already acquainted you, that the letter I then saw you reading was written by myself. For your further satisfaction, let me have the honour of informing you, that the letter you had designed for Lord Orville, had fallen into my hands.

However I may have been urged on by a passion the most violent that ever warmed the heart of man, I can by no means calmly submit to be stigmatized for an action seemingly so dishonourable; and it is for this reason that I trouble you with my justification.

Lord Orville,—the happy Orville, whom you are so ready to bless,—had made me believe he loved you not,—nay, that he held you in contempt.

Such were my thoughts of his sentiments of you, when I got possession of the letter you meant to send him; I pretend not to vindicate either the means I used to obtain it, or the action of breaking the seal;—but I was impelled by an impetuous curiosity to discover the terms upon which you wrote to him.

The letter, however, was wholly unintelligible to me, and the perusal of it only added to my perplexity.

A tame suspense I was not born to endure, and I determined to clear my doubts at all hazards and events.

I answered it, therefore, in Orville's name.

The views which I am now going to acknowledge, must, infallibly, incur your displeasure,—yet I scorn all palliation.

Briefly, then,—I concealed your letter to prevent a discovery of your capacity,—and I wrote you an answer which I hoped would prevent your wishing for any other.

I am well aware of every thing which can be said upon this subject. Lord Orville will, possibly, think himself ill used;—but I am extremely indifferent as to his opinion, nor do I now write by way of offering any apology to him, but merely to make known to yourself the reasons by which I have been governed.

I intend to set off next week for the Continent. Should his Lordship have any commands for me in the mean time, I shall be glad to receive them. I say not this by way of defiance,—I should blush to be suspected of so doing through an indirect channel,[97]—but simply that, if you shew him this letter, he may know I dare defend, as well as excuse my conduct.

CLEMENT WILLOUGHBY

What a strange letter! how proud and how piqued does its writer appear! To what alternate *meanness* and *rashness* do the passions lead, when reason and self-denial do not oppose them! Sir Clement is conscious he has acted dishonourably, yet the same unbridled vehemence which urged him to gratify a blameable curiosity, will sooner prompt him to risk his life, than confess his misconduct. The rudeness of his manner of writing to me springs from the same cause: the proof he has received of my indifference to him, has stung him to the soul, and he has neither the delicacy nor forbearance to disguise his displeasure.

I determined not to shew this letter to Lord Orville, and thought it most prudent to let Sir Clement know I should not. I therefore wrote the following note.

To Sir Clement Willoughby

Sir,

The letter you have been pleased to address to me, is so little calculated to afford Lord Orville any satisfaction, that you may depend upon my carefully keeping it from his sight. I will bear you no resentment for what is past; but I most earnestly entreat, nay implore, that you will not write again, while in your present frame of mind, by *any* channel, direct or indirect.

I hope you will have much pleasure in your purposed expedition, and I beg leave to assure you of my good wishes.

Not knowing by what name to sign, I was obliged to send it without any.

The *preparations* which Sir Clement mentions, go on just as if your consent were arrived: it is in vain that I expostulate; Lord Orville says, should any objections be raised, all shall be given up, but that, as his hopes forbid him to expect any, he must proceed as if already assured of your concurrence.

We have had, this afternoon, a most interesting conversation, in which we have traced our sentiments of each other from our first acquaintance. I have made him confess how ill he thought of me, upon my foolish giddiness at Mrs. Stanley's ball; but he flatters me with assurances, that every succeeding time he saw me, I appeared to something less and less disadvantage.

When I expressed my amazement that he could honour with his choice a girl who seemed so infinitely, in *every* respect, beneath his alliance, he frankly owned, that he had fully intended making more minute enquiries into my family and connections, and particularly concerning *those people* he saw me with at Marybone,[98] before he acknowledged his prepossession in my favour: but the suddenness of my intended journey, and the uncertainty of seeing me again, put him quite off his guard, and 'divesting him of prudence, left him nothing but love'. These were his words; and yet, he has repeatedly assured me, that his partiality has known no bounds from the time of my residing at Clifton.

*   *   *   *   *

Mr. Macartney has just been with me, on an embassy from my father. He has sent me his kindest love, and assurances of favour, and desired to know if I am happy in the prospect of changing my situation, and if there is any thing I can name which he can do for me. And, at the same time, Mr. Macartney delivered to me a draught[99] on my father's banker for a thousand pounds, which he insisted that I should receive entirely for my own use, and expend in equipping myself properly for the new rank of life to which I seem destined.

I am sure I need not say how much I was penetrated by this goodness; I wrote my thanks, and acknowledged, frankly, that if I could see *him* restored to tranquillity, my heart would be without a wish.

LETTER XXI

Evelina in continuation

Clifton, October 13

The time approaches now, when I hope we shall meet,—yet I cannot sleep,—great joy is as restless as sorrow,—and therefore I will continue my journal.

As I had never had an opportunity of seeing Bath,[100] a party was formed last night for shewing me that celebrated city; and this morning, after breakfast, we set out in three phaetons. Lady Louisa and Mrs. Beaumont with Lord Merton; Mr. Coverley with Mr. Lovel; and Mrs. Selwyn and myself with Lord Orville.

We had hardly proceeded half a mile, when a gentleman from a post-chaise, which came galloping after us, called out to the servants, 'Holla, my Lads,—pray is one Miss Anville in any of them *thing-em-bobs?*'

I immediately recollected the voice of Captain Mirvan, and Lord Orville stopped the phaeton. He was out of the chaise, and with us in a moment. 'So, Miss Anville,' cried he, 'how do you do? so I hear you're Miss Belmont now;—pray how does old Madame French do?'

'Madame Duval,' said I, 'is, I believe, very well.'

'I hope she's in *good case*,'[101] said he, winking significantly, 'and won't flinch at seeing service: she has laid by long enough to refit and be made tight.[102] And pray how does poor *Monseer* Doleful do? is he as lank-jawed as ever?'

'They are neither of them,' said I, 'in Bristol.'

'No!' cried he, with a look of disappointment, 'but surely the old dowager intends coming to the wedding! 'twill be a most excellent opportunity to shew off her best Lyons silk. Besides, I purpose to dance a new-fashioned jig[103] with her. Don't you know when she'll come?'

'I have no reason to expect her at all.'

'No!—'Fore George, this here's the worst news I'd wish to hear!—why I've thought of nothing all the way but what trick I should serve her!'

'You have been very obliging!' said I, laughing.

'O, I promise you,' cried he, 'our Moll would never have wheedled me into this jaunt, if I'd known she was not here; for, to let you into the secret, I fully intended to have treated the old buck with another frolic.'

'Did Miss Mirvan, then, persuade you to this journey?'

'Yes, and we've been travelling all night.'

'*We!*' cried I: 'Is Miss Mirvan, then, with you?'

'What, Molly?—yes, she's in that there chaise.'

'Good God, Sir, why did not you tell me sooner?' cried I; and immediately, with Lord Orville's assistance, I jumped out of the phaeton, and ran to the dear girl. Lord Orville opened the chaise-door, and I am sure I need not tell you what unfeigned joy accompanied our meeting.

We both begged we might not be parted during the ride, and Lord Orville was so good as to invite Captain Mirvan into his phaeton.

I think I was hardly ever more rejoiced than at this so seasonable visit from my dear Maria; who had no sooner heard the situation of my affairs, than with the assistance of Lady Howard and her kind mother, she besought her father with such earnestness to consent to the journey, that he had not been able to withstand their united entreaties; though she owned that, had he not expected to have met with Madame Duval, she believes he would not so readily have yielded. They arrived at Mrs. Beaumont's but a few minutes after we were out of sight, and overtook us without much difficulty.

I say nothing of our conversation, because you may so well

suppose both the subjects we chose, and our manner of discuss-
ing them.

We all stopped at a great hotel, where we were obliged to
enquire for a room, as Lady Louisa, *fatigued to death*, desired to
take something[104] before we began our rambles.[105]

As soon as the party was assembled, the Captain, abruptly
saluting me, said, 'So, Miss Belmont, I wish you joy; so I hear
you've quarrelled with your new name already?'

'Me!—no, indeed, Sir.'

'Then please for to tell me the reason you're in such a hurry
to change it.'

'Miss Belmont!' cried Mr. Lovel, looking around him with
the utmost astonishment, 'I beg pardon,—but, if it is not
impertinent,—I must beg leave to say, I always understood that
Lady's name was Anville.'

''Fore George,' cried the Captain, 'it runs in my head, I've seen
you somewhere before! and now I think on't, pray a'n't you the
person I saw at the play one night, and who did n't know, all the
time, whether it was a tragedy or a comedy, or a conceit of
fiddlers?'[106]

'I believe, Sir,' said Mr. Lovel, stammering, 'I had once,—I
think—the pleasure of seeing you last spring.'

'Ay, and if I live an hundred springs,' answered he, 'I shall
never forget it; by Jingo,[107] it has served me for a most excellent
good joke ever since. Well, howsomever, I'm glad to see you
still in the land of the living,' shaking him roughly by the hand;
'pray, if a body may be so bold, how much a night may you give
at present to keep the undertakers aloof?'

'Me, Sir!' said Mr. Lovel, very much discomposed; 'I protest I
never thought myself in such imminent danger as to—really, Sir,
I don't understand you.'

'O, you don't!—why then I'll make free for to explain myself.
Gentlemen and Ladies, I'll tell you what; do you know this here
gentleman, simple as he sits there, pays five shillings a night to
let his friends know he's alive!'

'And very cheap too,' said Mrs. Selwyn, 'if we consider the
value of the intelligence.'

Lady Louisa, being now refreshed, we proceeded upon our expedition.

The charming city of Bath answered all my expectations. The Crescent,[108] the prospect from it, and the elegant symmetry of the Circus,[109] delighted me. The Parades,[110] I own, rather disappointed me; one of them is scarce preferable to some of the best paved streets in London; and the other, though it affords a beautiful prospect, a charming view of Prior Park[111] and of the Avon, yet wanted something in *itself* of more striking elegance than a mere broad pavement, to satisfy the ideas I had formed of it.

At the Pump-room, I was amazed at the public exhibition of the ladies in the bath:[112] it is true, their heads are covered with bonnets, but the very idea of being seen, in such a situation, by whoever pleases to look, is indelicate.

"Fore George,' said the Captain, looking into the bath, 'this would be a most excellent place for old Madame French to dance a fandango[113] in! By Jingo, I would n't wish for better sport than to swing her round this here pond!'

'She would be very much obliged to you,' said Lord Orville, 'for so extraordinary a mark of your favour.'

'Why, to let you know,' answered the Captain, 'she hit my fancy mightily: I never took so much to an old tabby[114] before.'

'Really, now,' cried Mr. Lovel, looking also into the bath, 'I must confess it is, to me, very incomprehensible why the ladies chuse that frightful unbecoming dress to bathe in![115] I have often pondered very seriously upon the subject, but could never hit upon the reason.'

'Well, I declare,' said Lady Louisa, 'I should like of all things to set something new a-going; I always hated bathing, because one can get no pretty dress for it; now do, there's a good creature, try to help me to something.'

'Who? me!—O dear Ma'am,' said he, simpering, 'I can't pretend to assist a person of your Ladyship's taste; besides, I have not the least head for fashions.—I really don't think I ever invented above three in my life!—but I never had the least turn for dress,—never any notion of fancy or elegance.'

'O fie, Mr. Lovel! how can you talk so?—don't we all know that you lead the *ton* in the *beau monde*?[116] I declare, I think you dress better than any body.'

'O dear Ma'am, you confuse me to the last degree! *I* dress well!—I protest I don't think I'm ever fit to be seen!—I'm often shocked to death to think what a figure I go. If your Ladyship will believe me, I was full half an hour this morning thinking what I should put on!'

'Odds my life,' cried the Captain, 'I wish I'd been near you! I warrant I'd have quickened your motions a little! Half an hour thinking what you'd put on? and who the deuce do you think cares the snuff of a candle[117] whether you've any thing on or not?'

'O pray, Captain,' cried Mrs. Selwyn, 'don't be angry with the gentleman for *thinking*, whatever be the cause, for I assure you he makes no common practice of offending in that way.'

'Really, Ma'am, you're prodigiously kind!' said Mr. Lovel, angrily.

'Pray, now,' said the Captain, 'did you ever get a ducking in that there place yourself?'

'A ducking, Sir!' repeated Mr. Lovel, 'I protest I think that's rather an odd term!—but if you mean a *bathing*, it is an honour I have had many times.'

'And pray, if a body may be so bold, what do you do with that frizle-frize top[118] of your own? Why I'll lay you what you will, there is fat and grease enough on your crown,[119] to buoy you up, if you were to go in head downwards.'

'And I don't know,' cried Mrs. Selwyn, 'but that might be the easiest way, for I'm sure it would be the lightest.'

'For the matter of that there,' said the Captain, 'you must make him a soldier, before you can tell which is lightest, head or heels. Howsomever, I'd lay ten pounds to a shilling, I could whisk him so dexterously over into the pool, that he should light plump upon his foretop, and turn round like a tetotum.'[120]

'Done!' cried Lord Merton; 'I take your odds!'

'Will you?' returned he; 'why then, 'fore George, I'd do it as soon as say Jack Robinson.'

'He, he!' faintly laughed Mr. Lovel, as he moved abruptly

from the window, ' 'pon honour, this is pleasant enough, but I don't see what right any body has to lay wagers about one, without one's consent.'

'There, Lovel, you are out;' cried Mr. Coverley; 'any man may lay what wager about you he will; your consent is nothing to the purpose: he may lay that your nose is a sky-blue, if he pleases.'

'Ay,' said Mrs. Selwyn, 'or that your mind is more adorned than your person;—or any absurdity whatsoever.'

'I protest,' said Mr. Lovel, 'I think it's a very disagreeable privilege, and I must beg that nobody may take such a liberty with *me*.'

'Like enough you may,' cried the Captain; 'but what's that to the purpose? suppose I've a mind to lay that you've never a tooth in your head?—pray, how will you hinder me?'

'You'll allow me, at least, Sir, to take the liberty of asking how you'll *prove* it?'

'How?—why, by knocking them all down your throat.'

'Knocking them all down my throat, Sir!' repeated Mr. Lovel, with a look of horror, 'I protest I never heard any thing so shocking in my life; and I must beg leave to observe, that no wager, in my opinion, could justify such a barbarous action.'

Here Lord Orville interfered, and hurried us to our carriages.

We returned in the same order we came. Mrs. Beaumont invited all the party to dinner, and has been so obliging as to beg Miss Mirvan may continue at her house during her stay. The Captain will lodge at the Wells.

The first half-hour after our return, was devoted to hearing Mr. Lovel's apologies for dining in his riding-dress.[121]

Mrs. Beaumont then, addressing herself to Miss Mirvan and me, enquired how we liked Bath?

'I hope,' said Mr. Lovel, 'the Ladies do not call this seeing Bath.'

'No?—what should ail 'em?' cried the Captain; 'do you suppose they put their eyes in their pockets?'

'No, Sir; but I fancy you will find no person,—that is, no person of any condition,[122]—call going about a few places in a morning *seeing Bath*.'

'Mayhap, then,' said the literal Captain, 'you think we should see it better by going about at midnight?'

'No, Sir, no,' said Mr. Lovel, with a supercilious smile, 'I perceive you don't understand me,—*we* should never call it *seeing Bath*, without going at the right season.'[123]

'Why, what a plague, then,' demanded he, 'can you only see at one season of the year?'

Mr. Lovel again smiled; but seemed superior to making any answer.

'The Bath amusements,' said Lord Orville, 'have a sameness in them, which, after a short time, renders them rather insipid: but the greatest objection that can be made to the place, is the encouragement it gives to gamesters.'

'Why I hope, my Lord, you would not think of abolishing *gaming*,' cried Lord Merton; ''tis the very *zest*[124] of life! Devil take me if I could live without it!'

'I am sorry for it,' said Lord Orville, gravely, and looking at Lady Louisa.

'Your Lordship is no judge of this subject,' continued the other;—'but if once we could get you to a gaming-table, you'd never be happy away from it.'

'I hope, my Lord,' cried Lady Louisa, 'that nobody *here* ever occasions your quitting it.'

'Your Ladyship,' said Lord Merton, recollecting himself, 'has power to make me quit any thing.'

'Except *herself*,' said Mr. Coverley. 'Egad, my Lord, I think I've helped you out there.'

'You men of wit, Jack,' answered his Lordship, 'are always ready;—for my part, I don't pretend to any talents that way.'

'Really, my Lord?' asked the sarcastic Mrs. Selwyn; 'well, that is wonderful, considering success would be so much in your power.'

'Pray, Ma'am,' said Mr. Lovel to Lady Louisa, 'has your Ladyship heard the news?'

'News!—what news?'

'Why the report circulating at the Wells concerning a certain person?'

'O Lord, no; pray tell me what it is!'

'O no, Ma'am, I beg your La'ship will excuse me; 'tis a profound secret, and I would not have mentioned it, if I had not thought you knew it.'

'Lord, now, how can you be so monstrous?—I declare, now, you're a provoking creature! But come, I know you'll tell me;—won't you, now?'

'Your La'ship knows I am but too happy to obey you; but 'pon honour, I can't speak a word, if you won't all promise me the most inviolable secrecy.'

'I wish you'd wait for that from me,' said the Captain, 'and I'll give you my word you'd be dumb for one while. Secrecy, quoth a!—'Fore George, I wonder you a'n't ashamed to mention such a word, when you talk of telling it to a woman. Though for the matter of that, I'd as lieve blab it to the whole sex at once, as to go for to tell it to such a thing as you.'

'Such a thing as me, Sir!' said Mr. Lovel, letting fall his knife and fork, and looking very important: 'I really have not the honour to understand your expression.'

'It's all one for that,' said the Captain; 'you may have it explained whenever you like it.'

''Pon honour, Sir,' returned Mr. Lovel, 'I must take the liberty to tell you, that I should be extremely offended, but that I suppose it to be some sea-phrase and therefore I'll let it pass without further notice.'

Lord Orville, then, to change the discourse, asked Miss Mirvan if she should spend the ensuing winter in London?

'No, to be sure,' said the Captain, 'what should she for? she saw all that was to be seen before.'

'Is London, then,' said Mr. Lovel, smiling at Lady Louisa, 'only to be regarded as a *sight*?'

'Why pray, Mr. Wiseacre, how are you pleased for to regard it yourself?—Answer me to that?'

'O Sir, *my* opinion I fancy you would hardly find intelligible. I don't understand *sea-phrases* enough to define it to your comprehension. Does n't your La'ship think the task would be rather difficult?'

'O Lard, yes,' cried Lady Louisa, 'I declare I'd as soon teach my parrot to talk Welch.'

'Ha! ha! ha! admirable!—'Pon honour your La'ship's quite in luck to-day;—but that, indeed, your La'ship is every day. Though to be sure, it is but candid[125] to acknowledge, that the gentlemen of the ocean have a set of ideas, as well as a dialect, so opposite to *ours*, that it is by no means surprising *they* should regard London as a mere *shew*, that may be seen by being *looked at*. Ha! ha! ha!'

'Ha! ha!' echoed Lady Louisa: 'Well, I declare you are the drollest creature!'

'He! he! 'pon honour I can't help laughing at the conceit of *seeing London* in a few weeks!'

'And what a plague should hinder you?' cried the Captain; 'do you want to spend a day in every street?'

Here again Lady Louisa and Mr. Lovel interchanged smiles.

'Why, I warrant you, if I had the shewing it, I'd haul you from St. James's to Wapping[126] the very first morning.'

The smiles were now, with added contempt, repeated; which the Captain observing, looked very fiercely at Mr. Lovel, and said, 'Hark'ee, my spark, none of your grinning!—'tis a lingo I don't understand; and if you give me any more of it, I shall go near to lend you a box o' the ear.'[127]

'I protest, Sir,' said Mr. Lovel, turning extremely pale, 'I think it's taking a very particular liberty with a person, to talk to one in such a style as this!'

'It's like you may,' returned the Captain; 'but give a good gulp and I warrant you'll swallow it.' Then, calling for a glass of ale, with a very provoking and significant nod, he drank to his easy digestion.

Mr. Lovel made no answer, but looked extremely sullen: and soon after, we left the gentlemen to themselves.

I had then two letters delivered to me; one from Lady Howard and Mrs. Mirvan, which contained the kindest congratulations; and the other from Madame Duval,—but not a word from *you*,—to my no small surprise and concern.

Madame Duval seems greatly rejoiced at my late intelligence: a violent cold, she says, prevents her coming to Bristol. The

Branghtons she tells me, are all well; Miss Polly is soon to be married to Mr. Brown, but Mr. Smith has changed his lodgings, 'which,' she adds, 'has made the house extremely dull. However, that's not the worst news; *pardi*, I wish it was! but I've been used like nobody,—for Monsieur Du Bois has had the baseness to go back to France without me.' In conclusion, she assures me as you prognosticated she would, that I shall be sole heiress of all she is worth, when Lady Orville.

At tea-time, we were joined by all the gentlemen but Captain Mirvan, who went to the hotel where he was to sleep, and made his daughter accompany him, to separate her *trumpery*, as he called it, from his cloaths.

As soon as they were gone, Mr. Lovel, who still appeared extremely sulky, said, 'I protest, I never saw such a vulgar, abusive fellow in my life, as that Captain: 'pon honour, I believe he came here for no purpose in the world but to pick a quarrel; however, for my part, I vow I won't humour him.'

'I declare,' cried Lady Louisa, 'he put me in a monstrous fright,—I never heard any body talk so shocking in my life!'

'I think,' said Mrs. Selwyn, with great solemnity, 'he threatened to box your ears, Mr. Lovel,—did not he?'

'Really, Ma'am,' said Mr. Lovel, colouring, 'if one was to mind every thing those low kind of people say,—one should never be at rest for one impertinence or other,—so I think the best way is to be above taking any notice of them.'

'What,' said Mrs. Selwyn, with the same gravity, 'and so receive the blow in silence!'

During this discourse, I heard the Captain's chaise stop at the door, and ran down stairs to meet Maria. She was alone, and told me that her father, who, she was sure, had some scheme in agitation against Mr. Lovel, had sent her on before him. We continued in the parlour till his return, and were joined by Lord Orville, who begged me not to insist on a patience so unnatural, as submitting to be excluded our society. And let me, my dear Sir, with a grateful heart let me own, I never before passed half an hour in such perfect felicity.

I believe we were all sorry when the Captain returned; yet his inward satisfaction, from however different a cause, did not seem inferior to what ours had been. He chucked Maria under the chin, rubbed his hands, and was scarce able to contain the fullness of his glee. We all attended him to the drawing-room, where, having composed his countenance, without any previous attention to Mrs. Beaumont, he marched up to Mr. Lovel, and abruptly said, 'Pray have you e'er a brother in these here parts!'

'Me, Sir?—no, thank Heaven, I'm free from all incumbrances of that sort.'

'Well,' cried the Captain, 'I met a person just now, so like you, I could have sworn he had been your twin-brother.'

'It would have been a most singular pleasure to me,' said Mr. Lovel, 'if I also could have seen him; for, really, I have not the least notion what sort of a person I am, and I have a prodigious curiosity to know.'

Just then, the Captain's servant opening the door, said, 'A little gentleman below desires to see one Mr. Lovel.'

'Beg him to walk up stairs,' said Mrs. Beaumont. 'But pray what is the reason William is out of the way?'

The man shut the door without any answer.

'I can't imagine who it is,' said Mr. Lovel; 'I recollect no little gentleman of my acquaintance now at Bristol,—except, indeed, the Marquis of Charlton,—but I don't much fancy it can be him. Let me see, who else is there so very little?'—

A confused noise among the servants now drew all eyes towards the door; the impatient Captain hastened to open it, and then, clapping his hands, called out, ''Fore George, 'tis the same person I took for your relation!'

And then, to the utter astonishment of every body but himself, he hauled into the room a monkey! full dressed, and extravagantly *à-la-mode*!

The dismay of the company was almost general. Poor Mr. Lovel seemed thunderstruck with indignation and surprise; Lady Louisa began a scream, which for some time was incessant; Miss Mirvan and I jumped involuntarily upon the seats of our chairs; Mrs. Beaumont herself followed our example; Lord Orville placed himself before me as a guard; and Mrs. Selwyn, Lord Merton, and Mr. Coverley, burst into a loud, immoderate, ungovernable fit of laughter, in which they were joined by the Captain, till, unable to support himself, he rolled on the floor.

The first voice which made its way through this general noise, was that of Lady Louisa, which her fright and screaming rendered extremely shrill. 'Take it away!' cried she, 'take the monster away,—I shall faint, I shall faint if you don't!'

Mr. Lovel, irritated beyond endurance, angrily demanded of the Captain what he meant?

'Mean?' cried the Captain, as soon as he was able to speak, 'why only to shew you in your proper colours.' Then rising, and pointing to the monkey, 'Why now, Ladies and Gentlemen, I'll be judged by you all!—Did you ever see any thing more like? Odds my life, if it was n't for this here tail, you would n't know one from t'other.'

'Sir,' cried Mr. Lovel, stamping, 'I shall take a time to make you feel my wrath.'

'Come, now,' continued the regardless Captain, 'just for the fun's sake, duff your coat and waistcoat, and swop with Monsieur *Grinagain* here, and I'll warrant you'll not know yourself which is which.'

'Not know myself from a monkey?—I assure you, Sir, I'm not to be used in this manner, and I won't bear it,—curse me if I will!'

'Why hey-day,' cried the Captain, 'what, is Master in a passion?—well, don't be angry,—come, he sha'n't hurt you;—here, shake a paw with him,—why he'll do you no harm, man!—come, kiss and friends!'[128]—

'Who I?' cried Mr. Lovel, almost mad with vexation, 'as I'm a living creature, I would not touch him for a thousand worlds!'

'Send him a challenge,' cried Mr. Coverley, 'and I'll be your second.'

'Ay, do,' said the Captain, 'and I'll be second to my friend Monsieur Clapperclaw[129] here. Come, to it at once!—tooth and nail!'

'God forbid!' cried Mr. Lovel, retreating, 'I would sooner trust my person with a mad bull!'

'I don't like the looks of him myself,' said Lord Merton, 'for he grins most horribly.'

'Oh I'm frightened out of my senses!' cried Lady Louisa, 'take him away, or I shall die!'

'Captain,' said Lord Orville, 'the ladies are alarmed, and I must beg you would send the monkey away.'

'Why, where can be the mighty harm of one monkey more than another?' answered the Captain; 'howsomever, if it's agreeable to the ladies, suppose we turn them out together?'

'What do you mean by that, Sir?' cried Mr. Lovel, lifting up his cane.

'What do *you* mean?' cried the Captain, fiercely: 'be so good as to down with your cane.'

Poor Mr. Lovel, too much intimidated to stand his ground, yet too much enraged to submit, turned hastily round, and, forgetful of consequences, vented his passion by giving a furious blow to the monkey.

The creature darting forwards, sprung instantly upon him, and clinging round his neck, fastened his teeth to one of his ears.

I was really sorry for the poor man, who, though an egregious fop, had committed no offence that merited such chastisement.

It was impossible, now, to distinguish whose screams were loudest, those of Mr. Lovel, or of the terrified Lady Louisa, who, I believe thought her own turn was approaching: but the unrelenting Captain roared with joy.

Not so Lord Orville: ever humane, generous, and benevolent, he quitted his charge, who he saw was wholly out of danger, and seizing the monkey by the collar, made him loosen the ear, and then, with a sudden swing, flung him out of the room, and shut the door.

Poor Mr. Lovel, almost fainting with terror, sunk upon the floor, crying out, 'Oh I shall die, I shall die!—Oh I'm bit to death!'

'Captain Mirvan,' said Mrs. Beaumont, with no little indignation, 'I must own I don't perceive the wit of this action; and I am sorry to have such cruelty practised in my house.'

'Why, Lord, Ma'am,' said the Captain, when his rapture abated sufficiently for speech, 'how could I tell they'd fall out so?—by Jingo, I brought him to be a messmate[130] for t'other.'

446 EVELINA

'Egad,' said Mr. Coverley, 'I would not have been served so for a thousand pounds!'

'Why then there's the odds of it,' said the Captain, 'for you see he is served so for nothing. But come,' (turning to Mr. Lovel) 'be of good heart, all may end well yet, and you and *Monseer* Longtail be as good friends as ever.'

'I'm surprised, Mrs. Beaumont,' cried Mr. Lovel, starting up, 'that you can suffer a person under your roof to be treated so inhumanly.'

'What argufies so many words?' said the unfeeling Captain, 'it is but a slit of the ear; it only looks as if you had been in the pillory.'[131]

'Very true,' added Mrs. Selwyn, 'and who knows but it may acquire you the credit of being an anti-ministerial writer?'[132]

'I protest,' cried Mr. Lovel, looking ruefully at his dress, 'my new riding-suit's[133] all over blood!'

'Ha, ha, ha!' cried the Captain; 'see what comes of studying for an hour what you shall put on.'

Mr. Lovel then walked to the glass, and looking at the place, exclaimed, 'Oh Heaven, what a monstrous wound! my ear will never be fit to be seen again!'

'Why then,' said the Captain, 'you must hide it;—'tis but wearing a wig.'[134]

'A wig!' repeated the affrighted Mr. Lovel, '*I* wear a wig?— no, not if you would give me a thousand pounds an hour!'

'I declare,' said Lady Louisa, 'I never heard such a shocking proposal in my life!'

Lord Orville then, seeing no prospect that the altercation would cease, proposed to the Captain to walk. He assented; and having given Mr. Lovel a nod of exultation, accompanied his Lordship down stairs.

''Pon honour,' said Mr. Lovel, the moment the door was shut, 'that fellow is the greatest brute in nature! he ought not to be admitted into a civilized society.'

'Lovel,' said Mr. Coverley, affecting to whisper, 'you must certainly pink him:[135] you must not put up with such an affront.'[136]

'Sir,' said Mr. Lovel, 'with any common person, I should not deliberate an instant; but, really, with a fellow who has done nothing but fight all his life, 'pon honour, Sir, I can't think of it!'

'Lovel,' said Lord Merton, in the same voice, 'you *must* call him to account.'

'Every man,' said he, pettishly, 'is the best judge of his own affairs, and I don't ask the honour of any person's advice.'

'Egad, Lovel,' said Mr. Coverley, 'you're in for it!—you can't possibly be off!'

'Sir,' cried he, very impatiently, 'upon any proper occasion, I should be as ready to shew my courage as any body;—but as to fighting for such a trifle as this,—I protest I should blush to think of it!'

'A trifle!' cried Mrs. Selwyn; 'good Heaven! and have you made this astonishing riot about a *trifle?*'

'Ma'am,' answered the poor wretch, in great confusion, 'I did not know at first but that my cheek might have been bit: but as 'tis no worse, why it does not a great deal signify. Mrs. Beaumont, I have the honour to wish you good evening; I'm sure my carriage must be waiting.' And then, very abruptly, he left the room.

What a commotion has this mischief-loving Captain raised! Were I to remain here long, even the society of my dear Maria could scarce compensate for the disturbances which he excites.

When he returned, and heard of the quiet exit of Mr. Lovel, his triumph was intolerable. 'I think, I think,' cried he, 'I have peppered him well! I'll warrant he won't give an hour to-morrow morning to settling what he shall put on; why his coat,' turning to me, 'would be a most excellent match for old Madame Furbelow's[137] best Lyons silk! 'Fore George, I'd desire no better sport, than to have that there old cat here, to go her snacks!'[138]

All the company then, Lord Orville, Miss Mirvan, and myself excepted, played at cards, and *we*—oh how much better did we pass our time!

While we were engaged in a most delightful conversation, a servant brought me a letter, which he told me had, by some accident, been mislaid. Judge of my feelings, when I saw, my dearest Sir, your revered hand-writing! My emotions soon betrayed to Lord Orville whom the letter was from; the importance of the contents he well knew, and, assuring me I should not be seen by the card-players, he besought me to open it without delay.

Open it, indeed I did,—but read it I could not;—the willing, yet aweful consent you have granted,—the tenderness of your expressions,—the certainty that no obstacle remained to my eternal union with the loved owner of my heart, gave me sensations too various, and though joyful, too little placid for observation. Finding myself unable to proceed, and blinded by the tears of gratitude and delight, which started into my eyes, I gave over the attempt of reading, till I retired to my own room: and, having no voice to answer the enquiries of Lord Orville, I put the letter into his hands, and left it to speak both for me and itself.

Lord Orville was himself affected by your kindness; he kissed the letter as he returned it, and, pressing my hand affectionately to his heart, 'You are now,' (said he, in a low voice) 'all my own! Oh my Evelina, how will my soul find room for its happiness?—it seems already bursting!' I could make no reply; indeed I hardly spoke another word the rest of the evening; so little talkative is the fullness of contentment.

O my dearest Sir, the thankfulness of my heart I must pour forth at our meeting, when, at your feet, my happiness receives its confirmation from your blessing, and when my noble-minded, my beloved Lord Orville, presents to you the highly-honoured and thrice-happy Evelina.

A few lines I will endeavour to write on Thursday, which shall be sent off express, to give you, should nothing intervene, yet more certain assurance of our meeting.

Now then, therefore, for the first—and probably the last time I shall ever own the name, permit me to sign myself,

Most dear Sir,

Your gratefully affectionate,

EVELINA BELMONT

Lady Louisa, at her own particular desire, will be present at the ceremony, as well as Miss Mirvan and Mrs. Selwyn: Mr. Macartney will, the same morning, be united to my foster-sister, and my father himself will give us both away.

LETTER XXII

Mr. Villars to Evelina

Every wish of my soul is now fulfilled—for the felicity of my Evelina is equal to her worthiness!

Yes, my child, thy happiness is engraved, in golden characters, upon the tablets of my heart! and their impression is indelible; for, should the rude and deep-searching hand of Misfortune attempt to pluck them from their repository, the fleeting fabric of life would give way, and in tearing from my vitals the nourishment by which they are supported, she would but grasp at a shadow insensible to her touch.

Give thee my consent?—Oh thou joy, comfort, and pride of my life, how cold is that word to express the fervency of my approbation! yes, I do indeed give thee my consent, and so thankfully, that, with the humblest gratitude to Providence, I would seal it with the remnant of my days.

Hasten, then, my love, to bless me with thy presence, and to receive the blessings with which my fond heart overflows!— And, oh my Evelina, hear and assist in one only, humble, but ardent prayer which yet animates my devotions: that the height of bliss to which thou art rising may not render thee giddy; but that the purity of thy mind may form the brightest splendor of thy prosperity!—and that the weak and aged frame of thy almost idolizing parent, nearly worn out by time, past afflictions, and infirmities, may yet be able to sustain a meeting with all its better part holds dear; and then, that all the wounds which the former severity of fortune inflicted, may be healed and purified by the ultimate consolation of pouring forth my dying words in blessings on my child!—closing these joy-streaming eyes in her presence, and breathing my last faint sighs in her loved arms!

Grieve not, oh child of my care, grieve not at the inevitable moment; but may thy own end be equally propitious! Oh may'st thou, when full of days, and full of honour, sink down as gently to rest,—be loved as kindly, watched as tenderly as thy happy father! And may'st thou, when thy glass is run, be sweetly but not bitterly mourned, by some remaining darling of thy affections,—some yet surviving Evelina!

ARTHUR VILLARS

LETTER XXIII

Evelina to the Rev. Mr. Villars

All is over, my dearest Sir, and the fate of your Evelina is decided! This morning, with fearful joy, and trembling gratitude, she united herself for ever with the object of her dearest, her eternal affection.

I have time for no more; the chaise now waits which is to conduct me to dear Berry Hill, and to the arms of the best of men.

EVELINA

FINIS

NOTES

1. *To* —— ——: The hidden dedicatee is Frances Burney's father, Dr. Charles Burney, who was kept in ignorance of the writing and publication of *Evelina*. The opening line was originally 'Friend of my Soul, & Parent of my Heart', according to what seems a first draft now in the British Library. On the back of the MS of this Ode Frances Burney pencilled '4 in the Morn^g'; apparently she was inspired to write this prefatory piece after a night of writing or revision, probably when publication was imminent.
2. *Hygieia*: Correct spelling of the name of Greek goddess of health, now customarily spelled Hygeia; her 'blessings' would be health and vitality.
3. *niggard*: Niggardly, stingy.
4. *The Monthly and Critical Reviews*: The *Monthly Review*, founded in 1749 by Ralph Griffiths who remained its editor, published its own extended reviews of books, including fiction. So too did the *Critical Review*, a Tory review founded in 1756 to counteract the *Monthly Review*; it had been edited by Smollett and was supported by Samuel Johnson.

   Frances Burney had reason to know about dealing with *Reviews* and reviewers. Her father, Charles Burney, went to great lengths to ensure that his books were reviewed by his friends, William Bewley at the *Monthly* and Samuel Crisp at the *Critical* (see Roger Lonsdale, *Dr. Charles Burney* (Oxford, 1965), pp. 106–11; 120–23; 153–7; 209–19). As she was publishing anonymously, Frances Burney knew that her book must take its chance without this kind of behind-the-scenes support.
5. *annotations*: Comments, thus criticism, in unfavourable sense.
6. *Censors*: In Roman sense of magistrates responsible for conduct, for maintaining standards and moulding public opinion.

7. *integrity ... impartiality*: As Charles Burney's amanuensis and research assistant, Frances Burney was most probably aware of the efforts that her father made to ensure favourable reviews; we may suspect her of irony here.

8. *perfumes of Arabia*: A recollection of Lady Macbeth: 'All the perfumes of Arabia will not sweeten this little hand.' (*Macbeth*, V, i, 48–9)

9. *It droppeth ... beneath*: Portia in *The Merchant of Venice* (IV, i, 182–3); 'like' should be 'as'.

10. *The penalty and forfeit of your bond*: Deliberate misquotation of Shylock in same scene (*The Merchant of Venice*) claiming 'The penalty and forfeit of my bond' (IV, i, 207).

11. *garretteer*: Frances Burney's coinage for one who lives in a garret, as poor hack writers were frequently represented as doing.

12. *Oblig'd by hunger—and request of friends*: Pope, *Epistle to Dr. Arbuthnot*, I, 44.

13. *EGOTISM*: A relatively new word (*OED* gives 1714) which Johnson had defined as a tendency to talk about oneself. This is the meaning here, but Frances Burney uses the word elsewhere with the more modern shades of meaning indicating self-devotion, talkative or not.

14. *a monster*: Reminiscent of Pope: 'Vice is a monster of so frightful mien,/As, to be hated, needs but to be seen;/Yet seen too oft, familiar with her face,/We first endure, then pity, then embrace' (*An Essay on Man*, Ep. II, 217–20).

15. *Rousseau*: Jean-Jacques Rousseau (1712–78), an acquaintance of Dr. Burney, a Swiss-French musician and philosopher who wrote (as well as a number of philosophical works) a novel, *La Nouvelle Héloïse* (1761); some would have thought the subject matter and the story (dealing with premarital sex and temptations to adultery) too risqué for a young lady to read.

16. *Johnson*: Samuel Johnson (1709–84), essayist, poet, lexicographer, considered here as the author of the moral Oriental tale, *The History of Rasselas, Prince of Abyssinia* (1759). Charles Burney and Johnson were already acquainted, but Frances Burney did not get to know Johnson until after the success of *Evelina*.

17. *Marivaux*: Pierre Carlet de Chamblain de Marivaux (1688–1763), dramatist and novelist, author of *La Vie de Marianne* (1731–41) and *Le Paysan parvenu* (1735–6).

18. *Fielding*: Henry Fielding (1707–54), dramatist, magistrate and novel-

ist, best known for *The History of the Adventures of Joseph Andrews and his Friend, Mr. Abraham Adams* (1742), *The History of Tom Jones, a Foundling* (1749) and *Amelia* (1751). Frances Burney later claimed that *Amelia* was the only novel in her father's library. The references to Continental authors here, and the theoretical programme invoked in the next paragraph may be influenced by a recollection of the first chapter of Bk. III in Fielding's *Joseph Andrews*.

19. *Richardson*: Samuel Richardson (1689–1761), author of *Pamela, or Virtue Rewarded* (1740–41); *Clarissa, or the History of a Young Lady* (1747–8); and *The History of Sir Charles Grandison* (1753–4). All of these novels are epistolary; the epistolary mode of *Evelina* is directly influenced by Richardson (and by some of his successors).

20. *Smollet*: Properly 'Smollett', Tobias Smollett (1721–71), surgeon, historian and novelist, author of *The Adventures of Roderick Random* (1748); *The Adventures of Peregrine Pickle* (1751); *The Adventures of Ferdinand Count Fathom* (1753); *The Life and Adventures of Sir Launcelot Greaves* (1760–61); and *The Expedition of Humphry Clinker* (1771). Some of the violent or farcical scenes in Burney's novels are comparable to scenes in Smollett's novels.

21. *To draw . . . manners of the times*: A succinct summary of neo-classical principles as these had been applied to the novel; among the most immediate sources for this statement are Smollett's mock-Dedication to *Ferdinand Count Fathom* (an influence on Burney's entire mock-dedication of *Evelina* here) and Fielding's introductory chapters to books of his novels, especially Bk. III of *Joseph Andrews*: 'I describe not men but manners, not an individual but a species' (III, ch. i, p.185).

22. *No faultless Monster, that the world ne'er saw*: Allusion to poetic advice by John Sheffield (1648–1721) on writing drama:

> Reject that vulgar errour (which appears
> So fair) of making perfect characters;
> There's no such thing in nature, and you'll draw
> A faultless monster, which the world ne'er saw.
> Some faults must be, that his misfortunes drew,
> But such as may deserve compassion too.

John Sheffield, Duke of Buckingham, *An Essay on Poetry*, 230–35 in *Minor English Poets 1660–1780*, ed. David P. French, 10 vols. [reprint of selections from Alexander Chalmers' 21-volume *The*

English Poets, 1810], (New York: Benjamin Blom Inc., 1967), II, p. 649.

Richardson was similarly concerned about his hero, Sir Charles, 'lest I should draw a faultless monster' (to Hester Mulso, 11 July 1751, *Selected Letters of Samuel Richardson* ed. John Carroll (Oxford, 1964), p. 185).

23. *Madame Duval*: Evelina's grandmother, was an important character in the precedent novel, 'The History of Caroline Evelyn'. The central story of 'Caroline Evelyn' is given in the first four letters of *Evelina*.

24. *tutor*: It was customary for some worthy and well-educated but poor man, preferably one in holy orders, like the Revd. Mr. Villars, to accompany young gentlemen of quality when they made the Grand Tour.

25. *certificate of their marriage*: Burney is thinking of the customs in England since Lord Hardwicke's Marriage Act of 1753, which regularized the legalities of marriage and controlled the parties concerned, but in order to make the marriage more difficult to prove, she sets the wedding (apparently) in France. Hardwicke's Act was designed to prevent runaway matches by heiresses, and also false marriages.

26. *Anville*: Anville, a made-up name, is almost an anagram of 'Evelina'; for the girl to go by her mother's name, 'Evelyn', would declare her what the world thinks she is, a bastard.

27. *rustic*: A country person, unpolished.

28. *Dorchester*: Central market town of the county of Dorset, a beautifully rural county in the West of England.

29. *no intelligence . . . common report*: No information save by rumour or gossip.

30. *caps*: Ladies were expected to wear something on the head at all times; most caps were little confections of muslin, lace or ribbon; Maria wants to have some very good ones as she is to be seen in London.

31. *Two Play-houses are open*: Since the Restoration only two playhouses had found constant favour with governments who were anxious to limit the number; these two main theatres were Drury Lane and Covent Garden. It is apparently after Easter that the party goes to town, during the height of the London season, which lasted until the celebration of the King's birthday, on 4 June.

32. *Opera-House*: The King's Theatre in the Haymarket, forbidden to produce plays after the Licensing Act of 1737, became the Opera House, with seating capacity of about 3000 persons. Frances Brooke, the dramatist, and the actress Mary Ann Yates managed the Opera House from 1773–8. In November 1774 Frances Burney, with her stepmother and sister Susanna, was invited to accompany Mrs. Brooke to the London opening night of *Armida*, the first opera of the season. (*Early Journals and Letters*, ed. L. E. Troide (Oxford, 1988; 1990) [hereafter cited as *EJL*], II, pp. 54–7.)

33. *Ranelagh*: The Ranelagh Pleasure Grounds in Chelsea (opened in 1742) were designed to out-do Vauxhall; admission was half a crown per head, or five shillings on firework nights. Visitors could look at gardens, paintings, sculpture, or take light refreshment in the rotunda, while listening to an orchestra. Frances Burney went to Ranelagh with her stepmother and stepsister on 19 April 1771: 'The Room was extremely Crowded & very brilliant ... I saw few People there that I knew, & none that I cared for' (*EJL*, I. p. 146).

34. *Pantheon*: The Pantheon, a large building in Oxford Street, equivalent to Ranelagh, opened in 1772 as a winter site of concerts, masquerades and dances; on ordinary evenings visitors could take supper and play cards in rooms off the central rotunda. Music was a constant feature of the entertainment; in, or about, 1776 Dr. Charles Burney was given a salary of about one hundred pounds by the proprietors of the Pantheon and in 1777 he himself bought a fiftieth share of the Pantheon for seven hundred (L. E. Troide, n. to *EJL*, II, p. 210 and R. Lonsdale, pp. 227–8). See also the scene in the Pantheon in *Cecilia, or Memories of an Heiress*, ed. Margaret Anne Doody and Peter Sabor (Oxford, 1988), II, pp. 274–89.

35. *urgent*: Being a strong advocate for something, urging an action, and pressing for an immediate response.

36. *I cannot ... claim?*: Evelina's last name is a fiction, as Villars knows, and she cannot claim her father's name while her father both disowns her and denies her legitimacy. The plot answers the question there is another name that she can eventually claim.

37. *Queen-Ann-Street*: Street in West End, on the Portland estate, near Wimpole Street and Harley Street. Edmund Burke lodged there 1764–5.

38. *Drury-Lane Theatre. . . Mr. Garrick*: Drury-Lane Theatre, remodelled by Garrick who became manager in 1747, redecorated in 1775 by

the Adams brothers; its seating capacity was about 2000. David Garrick (1717–79) was England's leading actor, also a dramatist and theatre manager (producer); manager of Drury Lane Theatre until his retirement in 1776. By the time *Evelina* was published, Garrick performed no more at Drury Lane, but Frances Burney kept the complimentary reference to the great actor who was also a family friend. For accounts of visits from Garrick and his jokes with the Burney children, see *EJL*, I, pp. 183–4; II, pp. 95–7.

39. *Ranger*: Rake-hero in Benjamin Hoadly's *The Suspicious Husband* (1747), a play 'which succeeded ... partly because of Garrick's inimitable acting of the part of Ranger' according to Allardyce Nicoll (*A History of English Drama 1660–1900* (Cambridge, 1925), II, p. 207).

40. *Londonize*: Frances Burney's own coinage; *OED* gives date of *Evelina* as date of first use.

41. *Clarinda*: Heroine of *The Suspicious Husband*. See above, n. 39.

42. *Portland Chapel*: St Paul's in Great Portland Street.

43. *the Mall of St. James's Park*: Pall Mall, named after a game related to croquet because it was the site of the seventeenth-century alley where the game was played; it became the most fashionable walk in London after the Restoration, as it was near the Palace of St. James. People of quality walked there, to see and be seen, in the late eighteenth century as in the Restoration, although the fact that it was accessible to all disgusted some.

44. *Kensington Gardens*: Queen Caroline, displeased at the vulgar use of St. James's Park, had Kensington Gardens extended and laid out according to the principles of the new landscape gardening of Bridgman and Kent. The alterations (1730–33) produced the Round Pond and the Serpentine. From this new park 'the rabble' were excluded by royal servants. See below, II, n. 138.

45. *a-shopping*: A relatively new activity (in effect dating from the Restoration) with an even newer name; the *OED* gives first use of 'shopping' as 1764.

46. *gauzes*: 'Gauze' is 'a very thin, transparent fabric of silk, linen or cotton' (*OED*).

47. *mercers*: Dealers in textiles, especially costly fabrics, such as silk.

48. *milliners*: In her next work, the unacted and unpublished play 'The Witlings', Burney sets her first act in a milliner's shop, and presents us with the shoppers who don't mean to purchase.

49. *more frequently . . . than by women*: In 1799, Mary Ann Radcliffe (not the Gothic novelist) was to make much of this point, emphasizing the lack of jobs for female workers, and what she saw as the usurpation of women's work by 'effeminate tradesmen' serving in dry-goods shops. See *The Female Advocate; or, An Attempt to Recover the Rights of Women from Male Usurpation* (London, 1799).

50. *compleat suit of linen*: Either a complete set of underclothing made to measure, or (more probably) a linen gown with underskirt and apron.

51. *hair dressed*: The late 1770s saw the craze for towering hairdos; a woman's hair was raised to a height on top of her head, with the help of false hair and padding. The hair itself was anointed with pomade (a scented grease), and then powdered. A 'dressed head' took time to complete, and London fashion demanded the service of a professional hairdresser. After the hair was dressed, it was not taken down or cleaned for days, perhaps weeks; Evelina might well wonder when she could comb it again.

52. *at school*: Evelina could not have attended a day school in the country so she must have attended a girls' boarding-school for a while; the girls would dance with each other.

53. *private ball*: A private ball given by a private family in a private house to invited guests, as distinct from a subscription ball to which regular subscribers came, or a public ball in which anyone who paid an admission fee might participate.

54. *cards . . . elderly ladies*: Older people were expected not to dance, and card tables were provided for them in separate rooms. Age was calculated very strictly and, except on the most informal of occasions (usually in the country), a lady of years beyond twenty-five or thirty was not supposed to wish to dance but to join the 'elderly'.

55. *foppish*: In the manner of a fop, or affected dandy, a man who pays too much attention to his attire.

56. *words of course*: Habitual or customary expressions, thus largely meaningless. Evelina realizes that socially she has no 'honour' to bestow, as she is young, without birth or high quality (at least these are not acknowledged) and lacking in compensating entitlement to status, such as money.

57. *difficult dance*: Evidently a 'country dance' with complex figures, like Scottish dances or American square dances today. Evelina would have known how to deal with the formal minuet, but the

minuets are over and more complicated and lively dances take up the later part of the evening. Not until the era of the waltz did a couple perform exclusively with each other during the whole of one melodic dance.

58. *nice*: 'Nice' in the sense of exact, discerning; see Henry Tilney's lecture on the correct use of this word in *Northanger Abbey*, ch. 14, pp. 122–3.

59. *rally*: To speak with good-humoured ridicule, to speak jestingly, as in 'raillery,' but here Evelina (if she could speak as she would wish) would not engage in raillery *of* Lord Orville, but would rally *with* him upon some other person or topic. A talent for raillery was prized in eighteenth-century conversation, and the essence of raillery is that it presents compliments or gratification in a teasing form. Mrs. Selwyn believes Evelina must enjoy being teased about Lord Orville's attentions to her.

60. *beau*: A well-dressed single gentleman with a good opinion of himself, as the Baron is a beau in Pope's *The Rape of the Lock*; a less denigrating word than fop or dandy.

61. *assembly*: Not just a gathering of persons, but a social gathering, a large party of persons met for an occasion of polite entertainment (cf. French *assemblée*); also the occasion itself.

62. *coxcomb*: From 'cockscomb', a conceited and dressy young man.

63. *Helen*: Helen of Troy, the most beautiful woman in the world, hence a paragon of female beauty. Frances Burney was reading Pope's translation of *The Iliad* in 1768 and took offence 'for the honour of the sex' at Homer's presentation of Helen: 'Thus has Homer proved his opinion of our poor sex—that the Love of Beauty is our most prevailing passion . . . But I don't in fact *believe* it . . .' (*EJL*, I, p. 37).

64. *Lovel*: Name was probably suggested by the name of Richard III's henchman, given by Shakespeare in *King Richard III*, and perhaps too by the anti-Richard propaganda distich 'A cat, a rat, and Lovel our dog,/Rule all England under a hog.'

65. *Lord Orville . . . without troubling himself to call*: It was customary for gentlemen to call next day upon young ladies with whom they had danced, and to make enquiries after their health; a gentleman was particularly supposed to call upon a young lady to whom he had paid any marked attention. Lord Orville did distinguish Evelina with marked attention, but she is not, after all, someone to whom he has been introduced otherwise than on the dance-

floor, and there is nothing in her social position to invite his call. Sending servants with a card was also becoming a fashionable mode of 'calling', and unannounced personal calls were passing out of style, as Maria suggests. By sending only his servant, Lord Orville is free to drop the acquaintance. On another occasion Sir Clement calls in person, to try to ingratiate himself with Evelina (see p. 73).

66. *serious opera*: A translation of the Italian nomenclature, *opera seria*, as distinct from *opera buffa*. *Opera buffa* is comic, but *opera seria* is not necessarily tragic, for, despite dangers and melancholy characters, events can end happily.

67. *seeing sights*: Italics indicate a new expression – a new concept; sightseeing is a relatively new occupation, including not only the old-fashioned sights like the lions in the Tower (with which country bumpkins used to entertain themselves in the previous two centuries), but also new sights belonging to a highly urban, sophisticated and commercial London.

68. *auctions*: The most common cause of an auction is the bankruptcy of some wealthy individual or family, whose goods may be seized and sold at auction by creditors. Miss Larolles in *Cecilia* is a dedicated follower of auctions. In 1773 the Adams brothers, steeped in debt, offered a valuable collection of antiquities and *objects de vertu* in a sale, and Frances Burney, with many others, went to view the display (*EJL*, I, pp. 242–3).

69. *King Lear . . . sad*: Evelina saw Garrick's *King Lear*. Shakespeare's tragedy was usually produced in the revision by Nahum Tate, which made Edgar into Cordelia's suitor and provided a happy ending as well as much pseudo-Shakespearian verse. Garrick restored much, though not all, of Shakespeare's play. Frances Burney remarks on a performance of Garrick in the role, 'he was exquisitely Great,' though she objects to the feeble modern lines that still intrude on Shakespeare's verse (*EJL*, I, p. 242). Garrick's acting is effective enough to make Evelina feel sad despite these literary drawbacks. As *King Lear* deals with a daughter denied by her father, Evelina has personal reasons for emotional response.

70. *pit*: The 'pit' is the area near the stage at ground level, as distinct from the balconies and boxes; in modern British usage 'stalls'; in modern American, 'orchestra'. Fashionable people sat in the pit at the Opera, but at the playhouses gentlefolk (especially ladies) sat in the boxes, and the pit was the province of writers, Bohemians,

law students, and gentlemen not accompanied by ladies (see p. 100).

71. *chat*: 'Chat' is a verb here, italicized to indicate slang.

72. *ridotto*: An entertainment consisting chiefly of music and dancing (as distinct from one in which the guests are substantially fed). Charles Burney's *History of Music* is the major source of definition of 'ridotto'; he dates its advent in 1722.

73. *smoked with filth*: Reference to the well-known smoke of London, where air pollution (arising from numerous coal and wood fires) was already a threat.

74. *smoked with a burning sun*: I.e., sun-tanned, cured like meat that has been smoked.

75. *fair-weather chap*: A sailor's term of insult – who cannot bear bad weather and is really a landsman; 'chap', meaning 'fellow', is a usage arising in the eighteenth century. Italics emphasize Evelina's direct quotation of phrases distinctly characteristic of other speakers, and here also point to low slang elements in the Captain's speech.

76. *party*: 'Party' here, as elsewhere, a noun referring to a group of people and not to the occasion in the abstract. Evelina objects first to being one of the party or group that goes to the ridotto.

77. *already engaged*: I.e., already claimed as a partner for this one dance.

78. *like patience on a monument*: From the account given by Shakespeare's Viola of the (imaginary) lady who died from suppressed passion: 'She never told her love,/. . ./She sat like Patience on a monument, /Smiling at grief' (*Twelfth Night*, II, iv, 109–14).

79. *booby*: A dull or stupid person, term usually used of country folk of limited education and experience.

80. *bastinado*: To cudgel with a stick or *bâton*.

81. *done our duty of walking up the dance*: The couple cannot just take their turn and go down the chain formed by the two rows facing each other; they must return to their places and continue to participate as the next couple in the country dance dances down the line. Evelina took her partner's remark that she must 'go down one dance' with him (see p. 48) to mean that she would be free after that.

82. *educated*: 'Educated', here, means 'bred'. Sir Clement Willoughby is not interested in Evelina's knowledge of foreign languages etc., but is struck with her lack of female politeness and docility, and scornfully wonders where she could have been brought up.

83. *Fantocini*: Fantocini are 'little puppets', a puppet-show brought from Italy, or based on the Italian model.

84. *Ma foi, Monsieur*: Faith, Sir.

85. *Mon Dieu . . . Je suis au désespoir!:* My God (or Heavens) . . . I am in despair!

86. *woman of the town*: A prostitute, especially a streetwalker.

87. *golden rule*: The Golden Rule is generally rendered as 'Do unto others as ye would they should do unto you,' a misquotation based on Matt. 7:12 and Luke 6:31.

88. *hackney-coach*: A two-horse four-wheeled vehicle kept solely for hire, and licensed.

89. *Pardi*: A short form of *par dieu*, meaning 'by God'.

90. *enough . . . pick our pockets already*: Mirvan reflects common chauvinism and suspicion of other countries; many Britons believed that other nations had gained and had made England suffer during the wars past and present, a suspicion that included allies such as Prussia, Hanover and Austria, as well as enemies like France.

91. *the quality*: The gentry and aristocracy.

92. *wash-woman*: A washerwoman, one of the most humble of women employed in one of the most menial and physically taxing jobs.

93. *Mrs. Frog*: The common explanation for the English calling the French 'Frogs' was that the French ate frogs (or frogs' legs), a practice the English viewed as bizarre, and a symptom of the universal poverty of France.

94. *Justice Fielding*: Sir John Fielding (d. 1780), blind half-brother of Henry Fielding, who succeeded Henry as Magistrate for Middlesex in 1754 and carried on the work of crime control and crime fighting in London, including the organization of the 'Bow Street Runners', London's first police force. If Madame Duval wished to lay a complaint against Mirvan for common assault, or assault and battery, she would have had to go to Fielding's office (also site of the Magistrate's Court) in Bow Street.

95. *Madame Duval came to tea . . . day is almost over*: Working people took their main meal at noon, and people in the country dined in the early afternoon: Frances Burney in King's Lynn in 1768 records that 'we Dine precisely at 2' (*EJL*,I, p. 14). But the dinner hour of the fashionable in London was later, and Evelina, fresh from the country, is surprised that they are dining in the late afternoon, evidently at three-thirty or four o'clock, although even more fashionable people had already pushed the dinner hour

towards six o'clock. Tea was taken after the main meal, at the end of the afternoon, in much the same manner as our after-dinner coffee. Tea was already showing signs of becoming a meal on its own account, and in the next century remained an event of the late afternoon, while the dinner hour went forward to seven or eight o'clock.

96. *desert*: Now spelled 'dessert', not pudding or pie, but nuts, raisins, dried or crystallized fruit etc.

97. *spark*: A young beau, also a suitor or admirer.

98. *Monseer*: I.e., Monsieur (with derisively English pronunciation).

99. *take a round*: Walk about the place once.

100. *with hats on*: English ladies never went into public places without hats or bonnets, and a bare-headed woman was considered totally immodest; the same custom did not apply in France, and in any case Madame Duval's English origins are too low for her to care about the correct thing.

101. *old Nick*: The devil.

102. *flummering*: Offering meaningless flattery, from verb 'to flummer' based on noun 'flummery', nonsense, empty compliments.

103. *comprehensive*: Italics indicate quotation; Evelina alludes to Sir Clement's remark, 'A very comprehensive question,' (see p. 66).

104. *palaver*: Idle or flattering talk, originally nautical slang (according to the *OED*) and first commonly used of conversation with native peoples regarded as inferior.

105. *hair-pinchers and shoe-blacks*: Mirvan transforms Madame Duval's 'hairdressers' to the contemptuous 'hair-pinchers' (Frances Burney's own nonce word?), since they pinch the hair with curling tongs, as he turns her 'shoe-makers' into 'shoe-blacks', the poor urchins in the streets who offer to polish gentlemen's shoes with 'blacking', a black paste to make boots shiny.

106. *Beldame*: An aged woman, a hag, a witch.

107. *negligee*: Not the modern sense of négligé, which implies boudoir attire, but a loose gown worn on informal or semi-formal occasions.

108. *Lyons silk*: French silk from Lyons, a city near Grenoble in East France, was of high quality, and very expensive; the English, in trying to set up their own silk industry, taxed French material very heavily at entry ports, so Madame Duval would have found it difficult and costly to replace her gown with one of similar quality.

109. *chariot*: A light four-wheeled vehicle.

110. *very mad*: Unusual use of the word 'mad' for angry, now a common meaning.

111. *birth*: Usually 'berth', a nautical term, a room where any number of the officers or ship's company mess and reside.

112. *beat up your quarters*: Visit you unceremoniously, disturb your habitation (slang from nautical – and military – use).

113. *trumpery*: Rubbish, trifles of no value (here referring to the women's clothing).

114. *nastiness*: Something 'nasty', something extremely filthy and offensive – an expressive word reminding us that the 'mud' of London's horse-travelled and lived-in streets, in an age of totally inadequate sewers or rubbish disposal, contained material other than wet earth.

115. *touched English Ground*: Comic use of a legal and political phrase that had recently been in the news; Lord Mansfield's judgment in the Somerset case (1772) validated the idea that a slave was free as soon as he touched English soil. Foreigners were supposed to be grateful to touch the earth of the land of liberty; Monsieur Du Bois has certainly had contact with English ground.

116. *foreign customs*: French ladies received guests of both sexes in the bedchamber, a custom which grew in the French literary coteries of *précieuses* in the seventeenth century; to offer such hospitality was to hold a *ruelle* (named after space between bed and wall). Very few English ladies of reputation found it appropriate to receive parties while abed, though visitors of all sorts were invited into the boudoir as the lady was in the last stages of getting dressed (see Hogarth's *Marriage à la Mode*, Plate IV).

117. *weeds*: Widow's weeds, garments of mourning in black, appropriate to a widow; there were several stages of mourning for a widow, but it was generally considered appropriate for any widow in middle age to wear mourning for the rest of her life; Madame Duval seems to have thrown it off as soon as possible.

118. *chandler's-shop woman*: A woman who worked in the shop of a maker and seller of candles, as the wife of the proprietor, or as the owner. Chandlers' shops often dealt in common provisions or groceries in a small way, like the modern corner shop.

119. *the city*: The City of London (as customarily written) refers to a definite geographical and political entity with its own government (the Lord Mayor and Alderman); the City was the abode of the

mercantile classes, including artisans, merchants, bankers and great traders. The City of London was distinct from the 'town' where the fashionable lived, west of the City, and the high born and elegant looked down on mere citizens of London from the Restoration through the era of Jane Austen. Miss Branghton has learned the snobbery of those above her, and is ashamed of her home.

120. *Snow Hill*: Street in east central London, between Holborn and Cock Lane, just west of St. Bartholemew's Hospital.

121. *cast*: Cast out, i.e., defeated.

122. *apron*: Not protective wear for the kitchen, but a piece of fashionable attire, made of delicate material, and often embroidered; Evelina has evidently made or embroidered the one she wears ('your own work').

123. *sprigs*: Designs imitating small shoots or sprays of plants, implying numbers rather than two or three.

124. *lutestring*: A glossy fabric of fine silk.

125. *Tower*: The Tower of London, built by William the Conqueror, and in former times a palace, and prison; then, as now, one of the best-known sights in the City of London.

126. *St. Paul's Church*: St. Paul's Cathedral, also in the City; built according to a design by Sir Christopher Wren to replace the Gothic building lost in the Great Fire.

127. *tête-à-tête*: French (literally, 'head-to-head') meaning alone together, in a confidential party of two.

128. *warm room ... cold bath*: The Captain pretends to treat the events of the Ranelagh evening as if they were a sequence of treatments taken at a spa, such as Bath, where those taking the cure went from hot baths, or hot steam rooms, to cold baths and back.

129. *soused*: Drenched by an act of immersion.

130. *hallowing*: Hallooing, shouting out loud with laughter.

131. *draggle-tailed*: Having skirts or other clothes that have trailed in mud and wet; an insulting term usually used of a woman, with suggestion of sexually slatternly behaviour.

132. *Cox's Museum*: Museum set up by James Cox, jeweller, in 1772 in the Great Room, Spring Gardens, near present Admiralty Arch; the display of jewels, gold and jewel-encrusted *automata* showed off Western ingenuity as well as riches (the clockwork curios were originally made to sell to China). Admission price was an amazing ten shillings and sixpence. See Richard D. Altick, *The Shows of London* (Cambridge, MA and London; Belknap Press, 1978), pp. 69–72.

133. *kickshaw*: A kickshaw is a trifle, something unsubstantial, first used of dishes in cookery (from French *quelque chose*). Use of this noun as an adjective seems Frances Burney's own.

134. *conjurer*: A conjurer or magician; used negatively ('he's no conjurer') of someone who is far from being very clever.

135. *Coronation Anthem*: Handel's, for the Coronation of George II (1727), used again for Coronation of George III (1760).

136. *salts*: Smelling-salts (carbonate of ammonia), used in faintness; ladies carried small bottles or phials of smelling-salts, usually ornamental.

137. *places . . . side-box*: Places in the boxes could be secured in advance from an office near the stage door (hence the term box-office). In 1783 the managers of Drury Lane explained in the *Public Advertiser* how places in a box could be reserved: 'Half the Price to be paid at the Time of taking the Place, and the rest at Admission . . . It is not required that Ladies taking Side Boxes should have Tickets for the whole Number the Box contains. Plans of the Boxes . . . will be left in the Lobby' (Charles Beecher Hogan, *The London Stage 1776–1800: A Critical Introduction* (Carbondale, IL, 1968), p. xxv). Mrs. Mirvan did not have to rent the whole box, but merely seats in one of the side-boxes extending along the sides of the auditorium. A box-seat cost five shillings (see p. 99).

138. *stage-box*: The stage-boxes, the most desirable and expensive seating in the theatre, were on the forestage in front of the proscenium arch.

139. *Love for Love*: Comedy by William Congreve (1670–1729), first produced at Lincoln's Inn Fields Theatre in 1695.

140. *stay the Farce*: Stay for the farce; the full-length play (tragedy or comedy) was followed by an afterpiece, a farce.

141. *les etiquettes de nous autres*: Our etiquette, with emphasis on the difference between country-bred Evelina and those who are other (*autres*).

142. *mauvaise honte*: Bashfulness.

143. *Jezabel*: Usually spelled 'Jezebel', wicked wife of King Ahab. Jezebel, on hearing of the advent of Jehu the messenger, 'painted her face, and tied her head' (II Kgs. 9:30 [*KJV*]); hence she has long served for the archetype of the painted hussy.

144. *enthusiast*: One who is carried away by supposed inspiration, one who rhapsodizes in irrational rapture. 'Enthusiasm' had a negative connotation for most of the eighteenth century, being associated

in the rationalist and Anglican mind with the charismatic practices of certain dissenting sects who were also revolutionaries in the seventeenth century.

145. *play-bills*: Not only bills posted up outside the theatre as advertisement, but also the equivalent of the modern programme, sold by the 'orange-women' who sold fruit as refreshment in the theatre (Hogan, *The London Stage*, p. xlii).

146. *the house*: Usually 'the House', i.e., House of Commons. Lovel is an MP; see III, n. 74.

147. *Mr. Tattle*: The insinuating town fop and noted gossip in *Love for Love*.

148. *Mr. Ben*: Another character in *Love for Love*, a rough-mannered, honest young sailor newly arrived from sea.

149. *Miss Prue*: An ignorant rustic young hoyden, seduced by Tattle in *Love for Love*.

150. *mais . . . façon de parler?*: But obviously it's only a matter of speaking?

151. *Angelica*: The heroine of *Love for Love*, who marries her lover Valentine Legend at the end of the play.

152. *The Deuce is in him*: A farce by George Colman the Elder (1732–94), *The Deuce is in Him* was first produced at Drury Lane in 1763.

153. *à-la-mode*: In the mode, in fashion, in present use among people of quality.

154. *evening . . . six o'clock*: See above, n. 95.

155. *Haymarket*: Not the little Theatre in the Haymarket but the King's Opera House, across the street.

156. *their dress . . . impracticable*: At the musical drama a seat in the pit (modern stalls or orchestra) was (as not at the play) among the most desirable and expensive places, and fashionable folk dressed up for attending the opera, as they do now. The Branghton girls do not realize that they are not finely enough attired to join Mrs. Mirvan's party.

157. *Goody*: An insulting address by the Captain to his wife; 'Goody' was used as a condescending title for a married woman of very humble rank (the correct form for the Captain to use to his wife would, of course, be 'Madam').

158. *a wipe*: A cutting remark; a sarcastic reproof or rebuff; a jeer (*OED*).

159. *ma foi*: Literally, 'my faith' or 'by my faith', but by now a vague intensifier standing for 'indeed' or 'really'.

160. *hat or bonnet*: Evelina's hair is evidently elaborately dressed off the face, to suit her highly formal rich attire, and she is wearing only a token head covering. She would like to be more appropriately attired for the new situation, but Madame Duval pays no attention to the English convention that demands that women wear a substantial piece of modest headgear on almost all occasions. The door-keeper notes that the Branghton girls have hats (instead of lace headdress) signifying that they are not wearing the formal attire suitable for the boxes (see p. 100).

161. *door-keeper's bars*: There were different entrances and different posts of ticket-selling for various parts of the auditorium. 'Bar' here probably signifies not an iron bar that stops the way but a counter.

162. *half a guinea*: Half a guinea is ten shillings and sixpence, a guinea being twenty-one shillings (one shilling more than a pound).

163. *gallery*: Much cheaper site of seats, where audience members do not themselves form part of the show. The door-keeper indicates his opinion of the Branghtons' rank and appropriate place.

164. *people's abating*: Italics emphasize commercial turn of the Branghtons' speech, as they speculate on reductions and discounts.

165. *books of the Opera*: Copies of the libretto of the night's performance.

166. *pit price*. Mr. Branghton is thinking of the price of a place in the pit at the playhouse, not at the Opera, where, as we have seen, the cost of an individual place was ten shillings and sixpence.

167. *one-shilling gallery*: The cheapest area of the auditorium in the standard playhouse; the gallery at the very top. As the Branghtons have been going upstairs, we can see that they have been sent to the cheaper part of the house, but they are not prepared to realize that the cheapest seats at the King's Theatre cost as much as very good seats at Drury Lane or Covent Garden. A letter to the *Public Advertiser* of 1775 describes the Opera House's gallery as 'neat and commodious' with a good view (quoted in George Winchester Stone (ed.), *The London Stage 1747–1776* (Princeton, 1968), p. xlii). But the Branghtons go to the one-shilling gallery. Costs were high because expenses were 'enormous' as Stone notes, 'production costs running to over 14,000 pounds annually' (ibid., p. lx).

168. *crinkum-crankum*: 'Anything full of twists and turns, or intricately elaborated' (*OED*); a jocular expression for something elaborately nonsensical.

169. *language of another country*: Operas at the King's Theatre were

performed in Italian; the opera was generally referred to as 'the Italian opera'.

170. *Signor Millico*: Giuseppe Millico (1737–1802), like all the other celebrated Italian male stars of opera, was a castrato soprano. Millico, like many other musicians, became a friend of the Burney family during his stay in England. Frances Burney first heard him in May 1772: 'We then heard Millico, the new singer ... While He sang—I forgot everything but himself—He is, indeed, a delightful Performer' (*EJL*, I, p. 221). She heard him again in February 1773 at the opera and records, 'Millico sung like an Angel' (ibid., p. 238). This visit to the opera with her stepmother and sister Susanna was attended with the sort of contretemps we find in *Evelina*; the party of women arrived late, the house was very crowded, and on leaving:

[W]e got with difficulty to our Coach; but, after the usual perils and dangers we were drove out of the Haymarket, & into Suffolk Street. Here we concluded we were safe,—but as we afterwards found, there had been left a load of Gravel in the street ... presently the Coach was entirely overturned, & we came side ways on the Ground. (Ibid., p. 239)

Frances was saved from damage by flying glass because she 'had a Beaver Hat on'.

171. *the dance*: The *entr'acte*; cf. *Cecilia*, I, pp. 134–5.

172. *symphony*: The instrumental passage played between sung sections of a composition chiefly for the voice.

173. *Bedlam*: Bethlehem Hospital in Moorfields, the hospital for lunatics. Visitors could buy a ticket to watch the lunatics.

174. *riot in the house*: Tom Branghton recollects some important riots at the playhouses, especially the 'half price' riots of 1763; having forced Garrick at Drury Lane to give way to their claims, after breaking the chandeliers and ruining the theatre, the rioters attacked Covent Garden, where they did even greater damage. Thaddeus Fitzpatrick and his followers wanted the managers to maintain the old custom of letting the audience in for half price after the third act of the main piece. Young Branghton may also have heard of the production of the ballet *The Chinese Festival*, in November 1755, when the Drury Lane audience rioted against foreigners, both the Chinese represented and the French dancers performing. There was to be a major riot (led by young noblemen) at the King's Opera House in 1789.

175. *go . . . pit yourself*: Evelina is not properly dressed for the pit and ladies were not supposed to stroll about the theatre without proper escort (as prostitutes might do). Neither should she be left standing alone without escort. A young lady should not be at the theatre without a respectable female companion.

176. *chair*: Sedan chair.

177. *strange chairmen*: The porters who carried sedan chairs were among the poorest of the London working poor, as well as among the strongest; largely Irish, they were thought rough-and-ready types. In Richardson's *Sir Charles Grandison* the heroine suffers abduction as a consequence of entering a sedan chair carried by porters she does not know, even though the chair had been 'engaged for the night' (see *Sir Charles Grandison*, ed. Jocelyn Harris, 3 vols. (Oxford, 1972), I, p. 116).

178. *called aloud to the man to stop*: This sequence, the abortive abduction of Evelina by Sir Clement Willoughby, looks back to Richardson's novels. There are echoes of *Clarissa*, when the heroine tries to command the chariot not to stop at Mrs. Sinclair's (see *Clarissa*, ed. Angus Ross (Penguin Books, 1985), pp. 1006–7), and of *Grandison*, when Harriet Byron is abducted by Sir Hargrave Pollexfen; Harriet too does not realize for a time that she has been carried in the wrong direction (see *Sir Charles Grandison*, I, pp. 124–5). Evelina is more timely, and her threats and outcry more efficacious.

179. *upper end of Piccadilly*: I.e., going east instead of west, continuing up the Haymarket to Piccadilly by what is now (but *not* then) Piccadilly Circus.

180. *concerted scheme*: A joint plan, got up by both Evelina and Sir Clement.

181. *waited upon*: Called upon, but the formula here intimates that Orville called upon Lovel with a challenge to a duel, unless Lovel would apologize and promise to make no more trouble (which he evidently did with cowardly alacrity).

182. *how cool . . . is true courage*: Similar praise is showered upon Richardson's Sir Charles Grandison, but Grandison, unlike Lord Orville, has forsworn duelling and can overcome armed men without drawing his sword; refusing to fight, he still subdues Sir Hargrave Pollexfen and makes him apologize. Like Sir Charles, Lord Orville manages to chastise the heroine's insulter without a duel taking place.

183. *go to law . . . relationship*: Although the court might give preference
to Evelina's male guardian, Villars' legal status as a guardian is
unclear; if Evelina's mother left no written will naming Villars as
the guardian, the girl's grandmother would have a very strong
case if she chose to pursue it legally. Any such lawsuit would be
fought on the basis of Evelina's illegitimacy, causing public disgrace. The authority of a legal father would of course override all
other claims; if Sir John were to own Evelina as a legitimate
child, the grandmother would have no claim at all.

184. *easiness*: Being easy in the sense of 'free and easy', ignoring
formal constraints and taking liberties with etiquette.

185. *no gods . . . built for them*: The word 'pantheon' means 'all of the
gods', and the building was designed to reduplicate the Pantheon
in Rome, a temple to all the gods, rebuilt in the second century
AD.

186. *dead stand*: A total standstill; a 'stand' can mean 'a state of
perplexity or nonplus' (*OED*).

187. *cat o' nine tails*: Whip with nine knotted lashes, used to discipline
sailors in the Navy, and not employed in schools.

188. *making puddings and pies*: A familiar phrase, indicating the proper
scope of woman's knowledge, and her knowing her place in the
domestic sphere. Cf. Frances Burney's misogynist character Old
Waverley in her unacted play *The Woman Hater* (*c.* 1800): Old
Waverley asks (rhetorically) regarding women: 'What do they
know? And what ought they to know? Except to sew a Gown,
& make a Pudding?' See Margaret Anne Doody, *Frances Burney*:
The Life in the Works (New Brunswick, NJ and Cambridge, 1988),
p. 309.

189. *megrims*: The word basically means migraine but the 'megrim',
thought to be caused by 'spleen', was related to fantasy (particularly feminine fantasy) and came to signify a whimsy or fancy.

190. *It is a shame . . . for suffering them*: Captain Mirvan participates in
the anti-operatic prejudice in its most vulgar and nationalistic
form, but hostility to the opera was often expressed by satirists
and dramatists throughout the century, and the contrast between
good, moral and *English* drama and bad, meaningless and *foreign*
opera is very common. Magistrates could 'put down' unlicensed
theatrical performance, but the magistrates couldn't possibly have
wished to offend the wealthy and fashionable by making any
attempt at suppressing opera.

191. *comedians*: 'Comedians' are actors, whether performing tragedy or comedy.

192. *canaille*: Rabble, riff-raff; *canaille* is a French colloquial word meaning 'pack of dogs', naturalized into English (*OED* gives 1676 as date of first use).

193. *jem cracks*: Gimcracks; a gimcrack is 'a trumpery article, a knick-knack' from 1676 and also 'a mechanical contrivance' from 1712 (*OED*).

194. *price is plebeian*: Admission to Ranelagh (half a crown) was cheaper than that to the Pantheon and some other places of fashionable resort, but was not really suited to the income of the true plebeian, or lower orders.

195. *d'un vrai goût*: Of a true taste; *les gens comme il faut*: genteel folk; *ennui*: boredom.

196. *patriarch*: According to the Bible, the first fathers of the people, or 'patriarchs', from Adam through the twelve sons of Jacob, were all long-lived, particularly Methuselah, who lived for 969 years. If this Lord had such a life expectancy, he could endure a conversational pause of seven years.

197. *Black-hole in Calcutta*: More commonly referred to as the Black Hole of Calcutta, 'black hole' being a traditional phrase for a punishment cell in a barracks. In 1756 the Nawab of Bengal, Suraj-ud-daulah, took Calcutta and stuffed 146 Europeans (mostly members of the East India Company) into the small cell at Fort William, Calcutta; only twenty-three were alive the next morning. The English considered this an outrage, and it was avenged by Robert Clive in the Battle of Plassey.

198. *swabber*: One who swabs the decks, a common seaman; *bag and a sword*: bag-wig, the back hair tied back in a bag, and sword, the sign of a gentleman.

199. *conscious quality*: Awareness of his own rank and social position.

200. *thorny paths*: Reversal of the conceit in Ophelia's speech in *Hamlet*: 'Do not, as some ungracious pastors do, / Show me the steep and thorny way to heaven/ Whiles like a puffed and reckless libertine / Himself the primrose path of dalliance treads' (I, iii, 47–50), perhaps suggested to Frances Burney by association with 'libertine' in Villars' previous paragraph; Villars is a gracious pastor, but his advice is like that of Laertes to Ophelia in *Hamlet* (I, iii, 10–44).

201. *Eh, laissez-le, mon ami, ne le corrigez pas; c'est un vilain bête qui n'en*

vaut pas la peine: Oh, let him alone, my friend, do not correct him; he is a nasty beast who is not worth the trouble.

202. *Monsieur le Capitaine . . . voulez-vous bien me demander pardon?:* Mr. Captain, do you really wish to ask my pardon?

203. *Plaît-il, Monsieur?:* 'Please, Sir?' in the sense of 'I beg your pardon?', meaning 'I don't understand what you are saying.'

204. *nor dish me*: Captain Mirvan's pun on *plaît*, which he hears as 'plate'; to 'dish' someone is to do the person in: to 'do for; cheat, circumvent' (*OED* gives first use date as 1798).

205. *I can see as far into a mill-stone as another man*: Common saying, meaning I have an ordinary amount of intelligence.

206. *in a hobble*: In an awkward situation, unable to proceed (highly colloquial).

207. *as soon . . . the nature of colours with the blind*: Examples consistently used by John Locke (and his successors) in proving that there are no innate ideas, and that sensations are necessary to thought and to language: 'Those [words] which are not intelligible at all, such as names standing for any simple ideas which another has not organs or faculties to attain, as the names of colours to a blind man or sounds to a deaf man, need not here be mentioned' (*An Essay Concerning Human Understanding*, Bk. III, ch. ix).

208. *blazon*: To represent according to the rules of heraldry, which set forth the proper heraldic shield of a knight or nobleman, hence to publish in a boastful manner. Villars' somewhat archaic word captures both the claim of gentle status and the publicity involved in claiming Caroline Belmont's status as a married woman and that of her child as legitimate.

209. *with a shilling*: Not 'without a shilling' because it was legally safer to disinherit someone specifically by mentioning that person by name in the will and bequeathing the lowest sum legally convenient, a token shilling; an individual not named in a will could claim that a natural or inevitable claim had been overlooked.

210. *The die is thrown*: Traditional, from Julius Caesar's remark on crossing the Rubicon (according to Suetonius), '*iacta alea est*', 'the die is cast'.

211. *forwarded in the ambassador's packet*: Lady Howard is of sufficiently high station to be able to command the use of the ambassadorial post, or private bag; her letter will arrive in Paris with the greatest promptitude possible, with the dispatches from the government in England to the English ambassador to France.

VOLUME TWO

1. *the birth-day*: The King's birthday, 4 June, which marked the climax and the end of the London season.

2. *to play the old Dowager off*: to 'play off' is to pit one person or thing against another; as Captain Mirvan pits himself against Madame Duval; he ironically honours the woman with the title of 'Dowager' which is usually used for propertied widows of high rank, although as a widow who has inherited property from her husband Madame Duval might claim such a status for herself.

3. *Tower*: See above, I, n. 67. A normal site for tourists, here made fun of by Sir Clement; only country visitors or foreigners would want to see the Tower of London.

4. *taken up . . . treasonable practices against the government*: The war with the American colonies involved a war with France, and the government was very suspicious of foreigners and French spies.

5. *read his commission to his ship's company*: Once a ship was out to sea, the captain would read his orders to the company (officers and men), telling them the nature and purpose of the voyage and remarking the discipline to be observed. Mirvan treats everyone present as his crew.

6. *crazy vessel*: A 'crazy vessel' in nautical terms is an impaired, leaky, unsound ship (here with a sexual pun in 'vessel').

7. *Mutinying . . . adrift*: To mutiny is to revolt against authority, especially in military and naval services; a sea captain could set mutineers ashore on a desert island or make them go to sea in a small boat ('set adrift'), but the legal penalty for mutiny was hanging.

8. *Mon Dieu! quel avanture! que ferai-je?*: My God! What a misfortune! What shall I do?

9. *sousing single or double*: Being immersed in company with another person (double) in the mud puddle (see above, I, p. 72) or being all alone when immersed in the horse-pond by the mob (single).

10. *ninny*: Simpleton (perhaps an abbreviation of 'innocent'); a fool.

11. *country . . . punishment without proof*: A common boast about the British law, in contrast to the customs pertaining in France with its *lettres de cachet*; as we see, however, Mirvan reserves to himself the authority to inflict punishment without any respect whatsoever for the law.

12. *a country justice of peace*: A magistrate appointed as a Justice of the

Peace, to preserve the peace in a country town. There were urban magistrates in London. No Frenchman taken up in London on suspicion of spying or treason would be sent to a country magistrate for examination.

13. *impertinent people ... my best friends*: By 'impertinent' Sir Clement means irrelevant to his purpose and thus intrusive, rather than saucy; Evelina defends them as her 'best friends', because they are people who have befriended her and take on some of the attributes of the more extended meaning of 'friends' which includes parents, relatives and teachers (see below, III, n. 85).

14. *old buck*: An unusual epithet for a woman, as 'buck' was usually used of a man (i.e., 'buck' for male deer) and an old buck is an old rake; Captain Mirvan is probably thinking of the other 'buck', a washing-tub, which fits in with his allusions to washerwomen and to 'vessel'.

15. *sheer off ... all aground*: Nautical jargon; 'to sheer off' is to alter course, swerving at the order of the helmsman, in order, for instance, not to run aground or bring the ship against rocks, a reef or sands where she or her cargo might be lost.

16. *pomatum and powder from her head*: Pomatum, or pomade, was a scented ointment used in dressing the hair, especially in order to make the hair powder stick; the powder was supposed to be made of grain flour: 'The powder had by law to contain starch though this was often omitted' (C. Willett and P. Cunnington, *Handbook of English Costume in the Eighteenth Century* (London, 1957), p. 95). Hair powder was expensive at two shillings a pound. The fashions of the 1770s called for ridiculously high towering hair (see above, I, n. 51 and p. 30).

17. *curls*: The curled wig that Madame Duval wears to eke out her own hair; the 'curls' are combined into one piece, as we see when the 'curls' are referred to as 'it'.

18. *quartered alive*: His body cut into four pieces while he was still conscious; Madame Duval is thinking of the penalty for treason, which is to be hanged, drawn and quartered.

19. *mummy*: 'A pulpy substance or mass' (*OED*).

20. *dowdies*: Strange use of the noun 'dowdy', usually used of an unattractively and unfashionably dressed woman, but here used to refer to the dowdy clothes and accessories themselves.

21. *campaign*: Troops were allowed to rest after battles or long marches, or after an elaborate series of military actions (a cam-

paign), in order to get ready for a new series of military operations, or fresh campaign.

22. *sacque*: A loose-fitting gown, with a train in the back, or a piece of material making a train when attached to the shoulders of a loose gown. In Madame Duval's usage it probably means the same thing as 'negligee'.

23. *lonesome*: This is a somewhat vulgar or rural use of the word 'lonesome' for this period. Madame Duval shows her unfitness for high society by not appreciating the values of the country and rural retirement.

24. *dish-clout*: Dishcloth.

25. *pocket tamely*: To 'pocket' an affront or insult is to submit to it; Madame Duval does not want to put up meekly with such an injury.

26. *competency*: Sufficient means to live upon, an adequate but not handsome income, including the idea of the assurance of regular income.

27. *the die is cast*: Repetition of Caesar's line; see above, I, n. 210.

28. *reputation of a woman ... the most beautiful and most brittle of all human things*: This is a sentiment repeated in many conduct books of the period. To Pope and others writing earlier in the century (as in the Restoration) the brittleness of female *chastity* is a subject, but the conduct books emphasize the difficulty of even a virtuous woman keeping her *reputation* for chastity intact – something even more necessary for wordly success than chastity itself. Mary Bennet in Jane Austen's *Pride and Prejudice* (1813) seems to have this passage in *Evelina* in mind: 'Loss of virtue in a female is irretrievable—... her reputation is no less brittle than it is beautiful,—... she cannot be too much guarded in her behaviour towards the undeserving of the other sex' (III, ch. 5).

29. *lubber*: A stupid, low-class oaf, a lout; Mirvan may also mean a landlubber; a person unfamiliar with the sea or sailing.

30. *Bishopsgate-Street*: Although they travel in a private carriage, a chaise, Evelina and Madame Duval stop at an inn, as if they were passengers in a stage-coach, which always terminated its route at an inn. Bishopsgate-Street runs through the heart of the City of London connecting Shoreditch and Eastcheap; her arrival here marks Evelina's crossing a social boundary and departing from the fashionable world.

31. *Justice Fielding*: See above, I, n. 94.

32. *rush upon her mind*: Italics indicate a probable quotation.

33. *two pair of stairs*: Two flights of stairs, to the second storey (in America, the third).

34. *Ah, mon Dieu! ... voilà Mademoiselle!*: Oh, Good heavens!... here's Miss!

35. *grumpy*: Italics indicate that this (new) word is low and slangy.

36. *O ciel! quel barbare!*: O Heaven! what a barbarian!

37. *funny*: 'Fun' (an eighteenth-century slang word) could involve not only boisterous drollery but also hoaxing or abusing someone; the adjective is italicized to indicate the word's low status.

38. *actionable*: A wrong done capable of being pursued at civil law, by a legal action against the perpetrator.

39. *Dieu merci*: Thank God.

40. *owes me a great grudge*: Bears great ill will or resentment towards me, a resentment which Madame Duval thinks should have a reciprocal cause in something she did.

41. *haberdasher*: Originally a hatter, the haberdasher of the eighteenth century was a dealer in thread, tape, ribbons and other small dry goods, such as handkerchiefs.

42. *Holborn*: Long street in east central London; one of the central business arteries from medieval times. Holborn in the eighteenth century was the site of many businesses, including a distillery, though its connection with the nearby Inns of Court gave it some picturesque qualities. Evelina's lodgings are slightly west of Snow Hill.

43. *hosier*: Presumably not just a seller of stockings but a manufacturer of hose.

44. *quality hours*: 'Quality hours' would be the late times for rising and taking meals preferred by the fashionable folk, the 'quality'. See above, I, n. 95.

45. *Had they been without pretensions ... succeeded*: Compare Oliver Goldsmith's moral in *The Citizen of the World* (1762), in which we meet Beau Tibbs and observe his ridiculous pretensions to gentility in his garret lodging (n. 55).

46. *catch a Scotchman ... what they can get*: Resentment against the Scots, already sharpened by what was seen as their ungrateful rebellion in 1745, was refreshed by George III's confidence in the Scottish John Stuart, Lord Bute, to whom he gave important ministerial posts, to the fury of the long-entrenched Whigs. Bute retired from public life in 1765, but suspicion of Scottish intrigue continued, and the poverty-stricken Scots who streamed into

England looking for employment (a group that had included Smollett and Boswell as well as many poorer men) aroused automatic ridicule throughout the century. Samuel Johnson's jokes against the Scots are famous (although it was Bute who got him his pension), but many of Johnson's friends were Scots, among whom should be counted Charles Burney (originally Macburney). Herself both Scottish and French by descent, Frances Burney is perceptive about the slurs cast on both groups.

47. *genteel message*: This is not a 'genteel message' but a most ungracious one, although both Smith and the Branghtons are too underbred to know this; Smith indicates he has no interest in or intention of entertaining the party, so they are not on the footing of guests.

48. *dullness . . . described by Pope*: Pope's *Dunciad* (1728; 1743) describes the Goddess of Dulness [*sic*], the presiding deity of the poem, who appears to Cibber on the night after the Lord Mayor's procession: 'Her ample presence fills up all the place; / A veil of fogs dilates her awful face; / Great in her charms! as when on Shrieves and May'rs / She looks, and breathes herself into their airs' (I, 260–64). Pope's Goddess of Dulness is associated with city manners and tastes, and has pert followers as well as heavy, so Mr. Smith could certainly come under her aegis.

49. *Hampstead assembly*: Hampstead, a region north-west of London, famous for its Heath and country air, had set up as a small spa. At the very beginning of the century 'Hampstead Wells' acquired a Great Room for dances, as well as other amenities; although that building was converted into a chapel in 1733, another room for public dances was constructed, and concerts and other events were also held. The company was somewhat mixed and occasionally raffish.

50. *tell him my reasons*: Evelina's main reason for refusal is that the Hampstead assemblies are for vulgar people, not for those of her own class; another reason (apart from the fact that she finds Smith himself objectionable in every way (see below, n. 105) is that a girl should not take gifts from young men. Mr. Smith does not even know that he should make sure Evelina is provided with a chaperone, for in his circles such rules do not apply.

51. *something . . . small leather bag*: Presumably gunpowder and shot; see p. 257.

52. *He looked a bloodless image of despair!*: Part of a contemptuous

description of the 'pale coward' given by Idomeneus in the *Iliad*, Bk. XIII, 280–83; Pope's *Iliad* (translated 1715–20) gives us 'With chattering teeth he stands, and stiffning hair,/ And looks a bloodless image of despair' (XIII, 364–5). Frances Burney read Pope's *Iliad* in the autumn of 1768; after finishing it she notes in her Journal 'I never was so charmed with a poem in my life—I've Read the Odyssey since . . .' (*EJL*, I, p. 40).

53. *put him in prison . . . get by that*: Mr. Branghton, as his lodger's creditor, could have the young man arrested for debt, and sent to a debtors' prison (such as the Marshalsea) but a prisoner could not earn money to repay the debt; this remedy at law was more valuable to the creditor when the prisoner had friends to pay for him.

54. *over-reached*: To 'over-reach' is to get the better of someone in a bargain; thus, to cheat.

55. *I shall . . . my right to it all one*: Loose and colloquial speech, meaning 'I shall be able to prove that I have a good (legal) right to it, so it's all one to me.'

56. *such a fuss*: Colloquial speech; 'fuss' is a relatively new low word for (comic) anxiety and ado.

57. *George's at Hampstead*: Possibly the tea garden called New Georgia in Hampstead, Edward Bloom suggests in a note to Oxford Novels edition of *Evelina* (1968), p. 429; but New Georgia flourished earlier in the century. More probably a tavern or hotel in Hampstead, taking advantage of the celebrated prospects of the place.

58. *Don Saltero's at Chelsea*: James Salter, a former servant, owned a combined barber's shop and coffee shop which he moved to Cheyne Walk, Chelsea in 1715; Salter was nicknamed 'Don Saltero' by Vice-Admiral Munden. 'Saltero' dropped the barbering business, but added to his coffee shop the attraction of a museum of curiosities; the business was taken over by his daughter after his death in 1728, and continued until 1799. See Christopher Hibbert and Ben Weinreb, *The London Encyclopedia* (London, 1983), p. 233.

59. *Sadler's Wells*: The Wells in East London became a small spa which flourished briefly in the late seventeenth century; Thomas Sadler put up the first theatre there in 1683 to entertain visitors to the spa. When the Wells declined, the theatre was used by rope-dancers, jugglers and other strolling entertainers, and the audience was of the lower classes and thought of as rough. In 1746 the theatre was restored, and in 1753 acquired a regular company. In 1772 Tom King, former manager of Drury Lane, took over the

business and succeeded in raising the social tone and reputation of the theatre; during this decade, however, its former reputation hung about it, and the audiences were considered mixed.

60. *Monument*: Obelisk designed by Christopher Wren and Robert Hooke to commemorate the Great Fire of London. The column, erected in 1672, is 202 feet high, the tallest free-standing column in the world; the summit can be reached by a spiral staircase of 311 steps. Pope notes with disfavour the attribution of the Great Fire to the Roman Catholics (in lines added to the original inscription in 1681 and removed in 1830): 'Where London's column, pointing at the skies,/ Like a tall bully, lifts the head and lies' (Epistle to Bathurst, ll. 339–40). Fashionable people, especially ladies, were not likely to ascend the column (though the summit offered a superb view of London); the Monument was associated with the pride and Protestantism of London middle-class citizens. See *London Encyclopedia*, pp. 525–6.

61. *Paul's Church*: St. Paul's Cathedral, designed by Wren and put up after the Great Fire, the pride of the City, with a dome to rival St. Peter's in Rome.

62. *Vauxhall*: Vauxhall Gardens, originally known as the New Spring Garden, were pleasure grounds opened just before the Restoration; after 1732 they became fashionable, and a shilling admission was charged. The gardens were decorated with sculpture, fine music was played and supper could be taken in the supper-boxes.

63. *Marybone*: Vulgar pronunciation of 'Marylebone' for Marylebone Gardens, pleasure gardens first opened in 1650 as a site for bear-baiting, cock-fighting, etc. These gardens became the resort of such celebrities as famous highwaymen; in 1738, however, they were enlarged, and an entrance fee of sixpence was charged (or a season ticket which cost half a guinea). In the 1760s Samuel Arnold, composer, leased the gardens and made them a musical centre (with some of the best fireworks ever seen in London). See also pp. 259–66

64. *Foote's*: Samuel Foote (1721–77), actor, comedian and dramatist, procured a patent and built the new Theatre in the Haymarket in 1767. The entertainments put on there were usually, graced by Foote's famous mimicry of celebrated contemporaries and by his inimitable use of his artificial leg as a prop. Frances Burney was always fond of Foote's unorthodox satiric farces.

65. *the Minor*: *The Minor*, a play first produced in Dublin in 1760,

succeeded better in the longer version put on in London. The hero is the son of a mercantile family who is trying to forget his low origins, a false genteel climber who here reflects on Mr. Smith.

66. *the Commissary*: Foote's *The Commissary* (1765) has as its central character and satiric butt a war profiteer. Both of these plays exhibit a raddled old bawd as a major character; these were among Foote's favourite roles. Many years later Frances Burney comments upon seeing a performance of *The Commissary* at Weymouth, that the play is 'comic to convulsion' (*Diary and Letters of Madame D'Arblay*, ed. Charlotte Barrett, 7 vols. (London, 1842–6), V, p. 31).

67. *supper*: Late meal, not necessarily taken daily, serving as a last substantial meal or snack before bedtime. Frances Burney notes in her Journal for 1768 that in King's Lynn 'we Dine precisely at 2 Drink Tea about 6—& sup exactly at 9' (*EJL*, I, p. 14).

68. *vapours*: malady supposedly resulting from noxious vapours arising from some organ, such as the spleen, hence hypochondria, depression.

69. *North Briton*: The favourable liberal term for a Scot, with a reminder that all are members of one British nation.

70. *fond*: 'Fond' here means not only 'foolishly loving' but also sexually demonstrative in fondling.

71. *the chair . . . to receive her*: Evelina politely rises for her hostess, but Miss Branghton has not been bred even to understand such nice social signals.

72. *White-Conduit House*: Tavern beside the White Conduit at Islington. It had become a sort of rural tea garden, famous for its hot loaves, and boasting a maze and fishpond, and a cricket ground nearby.

73. *Mother Red Cap's*: A public house at the crossroads of the Kentish Town Road and Hampstead Road, the sign of which was a high hat.

74. *Bagnigge Wells*: A small spa in King's Cross Road, owned by a tobacconist, Thomas Hughes, who opened the gardens in 1758, charging threepence for drinking the waters; the Wells grew elaborate with tea gardens, bowling green, formal walks and concerts. The fashionable came there, and so did highwaymen as well as honest citizens. See *London Encyclopedia*, p. 32.

75. *only joking*: Italics indicate low slang.

76. *walking . . . boat*: The traditional way to go to Vauxhall was by

water, but since the construction of Westminister Bridge in 1750 it was possible to go by land.

77. *Grove nods at grove, each alley has its brother*: Pope, *Epistle to Burlington*, l. 117: 'Grove nods at grove, each Alley has a brother.'

78. *hautboy*: Literally 'high wood'; oboe.

79. *speaking French myself, which I dare not venture to do*: Frances Burney herself was shy of speaking French, perhaps because her two sisters had had some education in Paris while she had been left at home; her maternal grandmother was a Frenchwoman, but Frances may have feared that the French spoken at home was vulgar and incorrect. She records in her Journal for 1770 that she has been reading French, 'having taught myself that charming language for the sake of its bewitching authors—for I shall never want to speak it' (*EJL*, I, p. 139). The Journals bear witness, however, that she could understand and record conversational French.

Evelina has other reasons for not speaking French to M. Du Bois, as the two might be suspected of carrying on an intrigue.

80. *we shall lose the cascade*: The waterworks, which included an artificial waterfall played at nine o'clock. Jonathan Tyers, who managed the gardens from 1728 and owned them outright after 1758, had the cascade installed. (Cf. Oliver Goldsmith, *The Citizen of the World*, n. 61.)

81. *other deceptions*: The ornaments of Vauxhall Gardens, especially those put in when Tyers became the owner, included many decorative effects of artificial ruins and fake classical arches, as well as statues.

82. *box . . . we all went to supper*: Jonathan Tyers had special supper-boxes made, decorated with paintings by Francis Hayman. Here parties who were willing to spend their money on the famously thin Vauxhall ham and other high-priced eatables could watch the people and the lights and be entertained by music in the background. Cf. *Cecilia*, III, pp. 398–423.

83. *always a riot*: There was a big riot on the night of 4 September 1774, when a mob of young bucks broke many of the lamps and pulled the orchestra door off its hinges; the last night of the season was customarily uproarious, but not usually so riotous.

84. *skimper scamper*: Frances Burney was fond of noting the use of rhyming words in absurd phrases like 'bang wang', 'whisky frisky', which have the effect of turning an activity into nonsense.

85. *the room*: The large Picture Room east of the Rotunda.

86. *the dark walks!:* Vauxhall was noted for its unlighted winding alleyways, in contrast to the main routes that were illuminated by hundreds of lamps. The dark walks allowed easy assignations. In 1764 they were fenced off, but the fences were broken down. By going into the dark walks, the Branghton girls risk being mistaken for prostitutes, who found Vauxhall a profitable place in which to ply their trade.

87. *actress:* 'Actress' is used here as a euphemism for 'whore', as actresses were traditionally thought of as women of easy virtue.

88. *Ah, Mademoiselle! . . . Que je suis charmé de vous voir!:* Ah Miss! . . . How charmed I am to see you!

89. *a mind to be affronted:* An intention to be sexually accosted.

90. *one of the paintings:* The Picture Room east of the Rotunda had paintings commissioned by Jonathan Tyers. Austin Dobson, in his edition of *Evelina* (1903), identifies the painting here under discussion: 'It must have been Hayman's allegorical representation of Admiral Hawke's defeat at Quiberon Bay' (p. xvii) – i.e., Hawke's defeat of the French navy in November 1759, for which he was given the thanks of the House of Parliament and a large pension.

91. *Generalissimo:* Italian for commander-in-chief, supreme commander.

92. *simple swain:* A mocking phrase from the pastoral tradition. A swain is a man of low degree, a rustic; in pastorals, the swain is a rustic lover, a shepherd in love, and hence swain comes to signify wooer or lover. Mr. Brown is a 'simple swain' in that he is a simple-minded suitor of Polly Branghton.

93. *the very coach I had in waiting for myself:* Sir Clement suddenly and not very credibly claims that he had reserved this very hackney-coach for his own use. It is likely he really came in his own coach. Hackney cabs could be identified by number.

94. *broad St. Giles's:* 'Broad' is not here a measure of the width of the street, but an intensifier; the meaning is 'we are clearly and undeniably in St. Giles!' The parish of St. Giles-in-the-Fields, where the plague originally began in 1665, was a very disreputable area. Before the New Oxford Street was built in 1849, it was the site of the 'rookery of St. Giles', a famous slum; the main thoroughfare went via St. Giles High Street to High Holborn.

95. *High Holborn:* Frances Burney seems uncertain whether to place Evelina in Holborn or High Holborn.

96. *Justice Tyrell*: The country justice before whom M. Du Bois was brought according to fiction concocted by Willoughby and Mirvan. See above, pp. 153; 69.

97. *his aunt give the beau such a trimming*: Italics indicate the language of young Branghton as Evelina imagines him to word his thoughts. A 'trimming' originally meant a beating or drubbing – here, a tongue-lashing.

98. *constable*: Parish officer of the peace; the police force had not yet been formed.

99. *pour le coup*: For the moment, on this occasion.

100. *asked for his custom*: Solicited his business, i.e., as a customer at the silversmith's shop.

101. *kennels*: Channels in the streets to provide for run-off; after a heavy rain these would be full to overflowing and choked with garbage and sewage, as Swift records in his comic poem 'Description of a City Shower'.

102. *Miss Branghton ... not to hers*: The Miss Branghtons' bedroom is evidently in the attic storey of the house, as is the room let to Macartney.

103. *fun*: 'Fun' is italicized to indicate slang nature of the word; see above, n. 37.

104. *linger out*: 'Linger' is here a quasi-transitive verb, with the object 'month'; cf. Falstaff, 'borrowing only lingers and lingers it out' (*2 Henry IV*, I, ii, 267).

105. *Hampstead assembly ... ticket ... another to me*: See above, n. 49. Public balls required subscription tickets purchased in advance. It is not polite of Smith to give the ticket to Evelina, as young ladies were not supposed to accept direct gifts of any kind from male acquaintances; he should give both tickets to Madame Duval – as indeed he is forced to do, though it is extremely ungallant of him to insist on Evelina's going against her will.

106. *smart*: Slangy and vulgar use of the word, in what is now its most common sense: intelligent, clever and quick with the tongue.

107. *education*: 'Education' here has little to do with Smith's knowledge of books and the sciences; his education is his breeding (or rather the lack of it); he has not been trained in any of the ways of a real gentleman.

108. *figuring*: Making a fine figure; italics indicate slang or colloquial usage.

109. *as fine as five-pence*: An accepted cliché of low origin; presumably

five shining individual pennies is the image that furnishes this alliterative phrase; sixpence was a coin but fivepence was not.

110. *will you dance too?*: The Branghtons are ignorant enough of manners to be surprised that Madame Duval is going to accompany Evelina and Mr. Smith, as her dress indicates; in the upper classes young ladies going to balls were always accompanied by mother or chaperone, but in the Branghtons' class, young men and young women go out together unsupervised. Madame Duval, however, does not cast herself as a chaperone; she insists upon defying English custom, which dictates that an older woman should not dance. Chaperones were expected to look on, or to play cards, as Mr. Smith indicates below: a woman of thirty or even twenty-five might be considered as too old to dance. Hence, the young Branghton's question is a jeer, but he could hardly believe his aunt would behave in such an extraordinary fashion.

111. *cast a sheep's-eye*: Throw amorous glances at someone.

112. *long room at Hampstead*: Assembly room built to replace the Great Room at the old Hampstead spa, which was converted into a chapel in 1733. The Long Room was on the opposite side of Well Walk.

113. *speaking to the master of the ceremonies*: As at Bath assemblies, parties are to be introduced to the Master of Ceremonies, who then may himself perform introductions; this personage was also responsible for the keeping of order. Mr. Smith is reluctant to introduce Madame Duval as a would-be dancer so that the Master might find a set of dancers for them to join, and partners for her.

114. *During this minuet . . . derision of the whole company*: The minuet was the most stately and formal of dances (see below, III, n. 41). Madame Duval turns the minuet into farce by her participation, and Frances Burney emphasizes the grotesque elements in the occasion. Madame Duval appears like a female character rendered by a male impersonator. Susanna Burney records a moment of spontaneous theatre when the Burneys' friend Mr. Crisp donned a woman's cap, cloak, apron and ruffles and 'in this ridiculous trim he danced a Minuet with Hetty, personifying *Mad^e Duval*, while she acted Mr Smith at the Long Room Hampstead!' (letter of 25 August 1779; see Doody, *Frances Burney: The Life in the Works*, pp. 50–51.

115. *country-dancers*: People dancing 'country dances'; a 'country dance'

(supposedly derived from French *contre-dance*) is a dance with folk origins in which two long lines of people face each other, as in the 'Sir Roger de Coverley'. Country dances, like the square dances and Scottish reels that have survived to our own time, were more lively and less formal than the minuet.

116. *begged the favour of hopping a dance*: Italics indicate slangy colloquialism, and also call attention to the mixture of registers. Note that this vulgar dancer does not, like the gentlemen at Evelina's first ball, ask for the *honour*; the language is more commercial. The word 'hop' was a colloquialism for 'a dance' as early as 1731, according to the *OED*.

117. *demur upon this subject*: To 'demur' in this sense is to hesitate, to pause in uncertainty (this particular meaning seems earlier than the date of first use given in *OED*); Smith means that he has never even paused to think of the possibility of marriage before, but the word 'demur' emphasizes his state of hesitation.

118. *smart*: Here 'smart' has the sense of well-dressed, stylish, fashionable.

119. *pique*: From French *piquer*, to prick and *se piquer*, to take offence; 'pique' for resentment had existed in English since the sixteenth century, but Frances Burney's italics indicate that she thinks it a word not yet fully naturalized into English.

120. *designed for the church*: Macartney was to take clerical orders and become a clergyman after finishing his education.

121. *convent*: English young ladies, including those of Protestant families, were sometimes sent to French convents for their education; the nuns ran what were in effect boarding-schools for girls of good birth.

122. *free access to the house … fast friend*: Frances Burney's stepsister, Elizabeth Allen, seems to have been in a somewhat similar situation. Sent to Paris to perfect her French and her manners, she took up with an adventurer, Samuel Meeke; unlike the girl in the novel, 'Bessy' Allen eloped with her lover to Ypres, where they were married (October 1777). The 'shame of a clandestine affair' did not extend so far in the case of Macartney and his beloved.

123. *necessity for my leaving … danger remained*: Macartney could be arrested, tried and executed for murder if the young lady's father were to die as a result of this encounter.

124. *parricide*: The murder of one's father; 'parricide' sometimes refers to the murder of any close relative.

125. *foot-pad*: Robber on street or highway, differing from a highway-man in not being mounted; in modern terms, 'a mugger'.

126. *passengers*: 'Passengers' in the sense of foot-passengers, passers-by, people on the streets, not in a conveyance.

127. *ignominious death if seized*: A street robber who stole more than one shilling's worth was subject to the death penalty, and the fact that the robber was armed would deter juries and judges from any motions of clemency, so he would be hanged.

128. *public papers . . . private retribution*: Thieves and their victims did use the newspapers, particularly the *Daily Advertiser*; robbery victims would advertise for their stolen property in the hopes of retrieving it, and since the time of Jonathan Wild thieves had been notoriously ready to return personal effects for payment, but there is no record of a thief using newspapers, as Macartney claims he would have done, for repaying the injured party. In Burney's next novel the heroine is advertised in the *Daily Advertiser* as if she were a found object (*Cecilia*, V, p. 901).

129. *M. Torre*: Giovanni Battista Torré of Italy (d. 1780), who in 1772 became director of fireworks at Marylebone Gardens. Frances Burney notes in her Journal of 1773 that her family went on 11 June 'to Marybone [*sic*] Gardens intending to see the Fire Works of the celebrated Signor Torre. But a violent Rain came on . . .' (*EJL*, I, pp. 267–8). 'Signor' is correct, but in *Evelina* Frances Burney uses M. for Monsieur, perhaps as a general term for a foreign gentleman.

130. *Mr. Barthelemon*: François-Hippolyte Barthélemon (d. 1808), violin-ist and composer; he had moved to London in 1764. In her Journal for 1773 Frances Burney notes 'We were . . . at a Concert at Mr. Barthelemon's [*sic*], at which he performed his part very delightfully' (*EJL*, I, p. 230). She also refers to Barthélemon's playing at Vauxhall (*EJL*, II, p. 37).

131. *a form*: A backless bench.

132. *Orpheus and Eurydice*: Orpheus (whose story is most notably told by Ovid) went to Hades to bring his wife Eurydice back from the dead. The power of his music persuaded Pluto to allow Eurydice to return, on condition that she should follow her husband and that Orpheus should not look back during their journey through the underworld up to the world of the living. Orpheus looked back at the last moment, 'the fatal look', and the two lovers were separated, Eurydice mournfully returning to Hades.

133. *should not want for friends, whilst I was with them*: The two 'ladies' are ironic; their 'friends' are the prostitutes' would-be customers who accost and pay them.

134. *hallows*: Pronounced 'halloos', loud outbursts or cries of laughter.

135. *a coronet coach*: Coach with a coronet upon the side panel, denoting its ownership by a member of the nobility. A Lord (who may be Marquis, Earl or Viscount) is entitled to wear the coronet or 'little crown' upon ultra-formal dress occasions in the presence of royalty (at coronations and royal weddings, for instance).

136. *to send up his name . . . forgot it by the way*: Lord Orville intended to give his name to the servant who would announce his visit, but of course Orville is used to a different sort of household with knowledgeable staff; the maid of the hosier's house, unused to such formality and quite flustered, forgets the great man's name on her way upstairs.

137. *aversion*: 'Aversion' is a word with almost technical specificity in such an instance; parents and guardians were repeatedly advised not to force an arranged marriage upon either a young man or a young woman who declared 'an invincible aversion' to the party proposed.

138. *Kensington Gardens*: Extensive grounds in Kensington, west of London, first turned into gardens under Queen Mary, after Nottingham House was converted into Kensington Palace in 1690. In 1726 Henry Wise and Charles Bridgman redesigned the gardens as an ambitious modern example of urban landscape gardening in the new open style. 'George II opened the gardens on Saturdays to "respectably dressed people" when the court was at Richmond' (*London Encyclopedia*, p. 424). The grounds were beautified with a small temple, the Round Pond, and a revolving summer house. See above, I, n. 44.

139. *Piccadilly*: An ancient highway leading west out of London; it became built up in the seventeenth century, by such entrepreneurs as the Strand tailor who made his fortune out of selling 'picadils', the collar then in fashion. Piccadilly developed rapidly after the Restoration and in the 1770s was the site of many new town houses overlooking Hyde Park and Green Park.

140. *Hyde Park*: Hyde Park, largest of the London parks, merges with Kensington Gardens at its western end. The Park was once a monastery manor, retained by Henry VIII and Elizabeth as a hunting ground. In the early seventeenth century it was opened to

the public. During the Restoration the Park was a resort of fashionable people and their fine carriages. William III had the *route du roi* (Rotten Row) hung with lamps; it was the first road to be lit at night. Queen Caroline oversaw extensive landscaping from 1730, her chief contribution being the artificial lake, the Serpentine.

141. *green-shop*: Greengrocer.

142. *dilemma*: Strictly speaking, dilemma means a choice of two disagreeable alternatives, but popularly the word was used to indicate any perplexing or difficult situation.

143. *Kensington Palace*: Once a country manor house, redesigned by Christopher Wren and Hawksmoor as a palace for William III and Queen Mary, Kensington Palace, a building of considerable charm, was the principal residence of George II and Queen Caroline. George III preferred Buckingham House (which became known as the Palace), and Kensington Palace fell into disuse. We may wonder what business Lord Orville had at the Palace; Edward A. Bloom suggests that as the building 'housed an impressive collection of paintings,' these pictures 'might have been the attraction which drew Lord Orville into the palace' (*Evelina* (Oxford, 1968), p. 433).

144. *pot of beer*: A pot of beer would be the amount filling a pewter or leathern pot used instead of glasses in public houses for individual drinks. The coachman and footman laugh disdainfully as the servants of aristocrats were accustomed to much more munificent tips than a literal pot of beer.

145. *plump we comes against a cart*: To come 'plump' at, upon, or against something is to meet it entirely and abruptly 'with full or direct impact' (*OED*).

146. *the glass was up*: The window glass was up (as in the modern car). Glass was at first so rare in vehicles that one possessing them was called 'a glass coach'; cheaper hired vehicles often used cheaper materials for keeping out draughts and closing the window holes – young Branghton isn't used to this luxury.

147. *Berkeley-Square*: Berkeley Square was a new square, a very high-class building development on lands purchased from Lord Berkeley by the Duke of Devonshire, who built Devonshire House there. Berkeley Square was not really a square but two rows of large houses. Clive of India lived in Berkeley Square (and died there 1774), and Horace Walpole and the Prince of Wales visited friends there.

148. *peck of troubles*: OED gives date of first use of this phrase as 1535; it seems to have been a rural figure, surviving in low speech. A 'peck' is literally a quarter of a bushel or two gallons, but here merely means 'a lot'.

149. *porter*: The 'porter' is the servant who waits at the door, as in modern 'hall porter' or medieval 'porter's lodge'; the use of 'butler' for this functionary comes later.

150. *obligated*: OED describes the use of 'obligated' as dialect or colloquial use meaning 'obliged'. Young Branghton perhaps thinks the longer word adds to the graciousness of the sentiment, but instead he adds to its vulgarity, and implicates Evelina in his illiteracy.

151. *a porter*: The word 'porter' here has a different sense from that above; 'porters' plied for trade as carriers of messages and goods from one part of town to another.

152. *Mrs. Clinton*: Mrs. Clinton is described in the fourth letter by Villars as 'a most worthy woman, formerly her [Evelina's] nurse, and now my housekeeper'(see p. 20).

153. *in a huff*: 'A fit of petulance or offended dignity caused by an affront' (OED, which gives date of first use as 1757, but cites this instance).

154. *uppish*: Irritable (with probable suggestion of same meaning as American 'uppity' and likewise vulgar); OED uses this instance.

155. *Vous ne l'aimez donc pas, ce garçon*, Mademoiselle!: So you don't love him, that boy, Miss!

156. *Ah, tu me rends la vie!*: Ah, you restore me to life!

157. *journalize*: OED gives 1774 as date of first use of word meaning 'to make entries in or to keep a journal'.

158. *ride post*: to ride with the greatest swiftness; the letter has *not* been sent through the public post.

159. *commenced a correspondence . . . such a design?*: Young ladies of quality and reputation did not write to young men to whom they were not engaged; a correspondence would indicate (and facilitate) a sexual liaison.

160. *false delicacy*: Phrase in vogue since the production in 1768 of the play, *False Delicacy*, by Hugh Kelly and David Garrick; 'false delicacy' is a misplaced reluctance to bring out facts that need to be known.

161. *falling away*: Growing thinner.

162. *time had wintered o'er his locks*: Not identified.

163. *work*: A lady's 'work' is always her sewing unless some other occupation is specified.

164. *empty cover*: Blank sheet of paper; there were no ready-made envelopes in the eighteenth century.

165. *Bristol Hotwell*: Also termed 'the Hotwells', one and a half miles from Bristol city, in the parish of Clifton on the Gloucestershire side of the river Avon; a pumping system had been built in 1695 and the Hotwell became a place of resort in the eighteenth century. Bath's season was in the autumn and winter, but the Bristol Hotwell was a summer resort: 'strangers who come either for health or pleasure, commonly arrive about the beginning of May, from which time to the end of September, there is generally a great resort of company, therefore that is termed the season' (E. Shiercliff, *The Bristol and Hotwell Guide*, (Bristol: Bulgin and Rosser, 1793), p. 73).

166. *We are situated . . . favourable to invalids*: The area was known for its fine view and good air:

> [I]magination could not form any thing more enchanting and beautiful than the views about the *Hotwell*, whether seen from below, or from the summit of the clifts . . . in some places the rocks rise venerably majestic . . . craggy, and bare; in others clothed with the most luxuriant shrubs and stately trees . . . accompanied with every hue, and elegance of colour, that Nature could bestow on her most favourite productions . . . the ground also . . . abounds with a variety of rare flowers, aromatic plants . . . and the air being perfumed with their refreshing fragrance, the valetudinarian seems to breathe new life, and to enjoy again the blessings that await returning health and cheerfulness. (Ibid., p. 66)

167. *try the effect of the Bristol waters*: The waters of the Bristol Hotwell were warm and sparkling, not sulphurous, but 'milky', impregnated with magnesia and 'calcareous earth' (carbonate of lime); these waters were prescribed particularly for persons suffering from diabetes, tuberculosis, and other consumptive maladies. Frances Burney's own mother had been sent to the Hotwells in Bristol, in a last desperate effort to re-establish her health, shortly before her death (supposedly from tubercular consumption) in 1762.

VOLUME THREE

1. *Pump-room*: The centre of daytime activity at the spa: 'The usual method of drinking the water is to go to the Pump-room in the morning and drink a glass of it, which contains a full half pint, and then to sit down with the company in the room half an hour; a band of music plays every morning during the season' (*Bristol and Hotwell Guide*, p. 72).

2. *by the side of the Avon*: The path was actually some distance above the Avon, but followed its course and took in a river view:

   For those who prefer exercise to sitting still, there is a colonade [*sic*] with shops erected under the rocks, and a gravel walk shaded with trees by the side of the river, which has been considerably extended, so that the invalid has an opportunity of a pleasant and dry walk in the wettest weather, or of a cool and shady one in the warmest season; add to which, if it be at the time of the tide's coming in or going out, they will be agreeably entertained with seeing the variety of vessels that are continually passing by. (Ibid., p. 72)

3. *à-propos*: 'To the point' or 'pertinently'; Frances Burney does not italicize this French phrase as foreign, indicating that it has been naturalized through use by writers such as Addison.

4. *assembly*: Most probably the subscription ball held every Tuesday evening at the Hotwells.

5. *going snacks*: 'Going snacks' is slang (probably originally thieves' cant) for dividing something into equal shares, in this case 'going halves'.

6. *romantic*: 'Romantic' in the sense of being quixotically idealistic, harbouring unrealistic expectations.

7. *apothecary*: A medical practitioner licensed by the Apothecaries' Company, but looked down upon by physicians and surgeons, who were better educated and charged more, but whose treatments were often more violent. Mr. Ridgeway (the name may be that of a real person) is presumably Evelina's medical man and is seeing her regularly on a professional basis.

8. *honourable Mrs. Beaumont's*: 'Honourable' (now written with a capital H) is a courtesy title usually given to sons and daughters of peers below the rank of Marquess; Mrs. Beaumont is an aristocrat.

9. *fine house upon Clifton Hill*: As the guidebook says:

> Clifton . . . is situated on the South and West of a cliff or hill
> (whence its name) one mile westward of the city of *Bristol* . . . The
> delightful situation of *Clifton*, has long since tempted several
> persons of large fortune to make it their principal residence, and
> others continuing to follow the example, has occasioned the hill
> to be almost every where covered with respectable mansions,
> most of them built with freestone in a very elegant stile . . . (Ibid.,
> pp. 76–8)

10. *phaeton*: A light, four-wheeled carriage with two seats facing
    forward. This carriage had a high centre of gravity and was easily
    overturned; hence, its name, after the mythological character who
    overturned the chariot of the sun.

11. *my watch stands*: My watch has stopped.

12. *drive against it*: To race with it.

13. *pretty but affected young lady*: Evelina quotes herself; see I, L. xxiii,
    p. 123.

14. *Court Calendar bigot*: The Court Calendar (or Court Almanac) was
    'an annual handbook of royal families and their courts' (*OED*).
    Mrs. Beaumont is a 'bigot' in her irrational prejudice in favour of
    royalty and the nobility, and in her prejudice against all who have
    no claim to attend a court.

15. *woman of quality*: A woman of noble or gentle family.

16. *nice*: 'Nice' in the sense of exact, precise or fastidious.

17. *Marmontel's words, Un jeune homme comme il y en a peu*: Not quite the
    words of Jean-François Marmontel (1723–99), whose *Contes moraux*
    (collected in 1761) include a story with the title 'La Femme
    comme il y en a peu' [literally, 'The Woman like (whom) there are
    few']. There are too few like Lord Orville.

18. *gluttons, or epicures*: Gluttons are merely greedy and eat everything
    they can stuff in; epicures are fastidious, searching for novel foods
    and new taste sensations, while being very willing to criticize and
    dismiss dishes that do not meet their standards.

19. *Nobody*: A significant word in FB's writings. Compare the begin-
    ning of Frances Burney's Journal, 27 March 1768:

> To Nobody, then, will I write my Journal! since To Nobody can I
> be wholly unreserved . . . The love, the esteem, I entertain for
> Nobody, No-body's self has not power to destroy . . . I will

suppose you, then, to be my best friend ... my dearest companion—& a romantic Girl ... From this moment, then my dear Girl—but why, permit me to ask, must a *female* be made Nobody? (*EJL*, I, p. 2)

20. *classics*: 'Classic' here in the sense of 'classical scholar', though *OED* gives date of first use of this sense as 1805.

21. *the longest ode of Horace*: Quintus Horatius Flaccus (65–8 BC) wrote four books of *carmina* or songs. The Horatian ode is customarily short, graceful and pithy; some are only eight lines long. The longest ode would be the 'Carmen Saeculare' (seventy-six lines) though that is not one of the four books of *carmina*.

22. *in the House*: The House of Commons; Lovel is an MP.

23. *at the university*: There were only two Universities in England – Oxford and Cambridge.

24. *an extempore couplet upon some given subject*: In Frances Burney's next work, the unacted and unpublished play 'The Witlings', the would-be wit Dabler is disgraced by his inability to produce a poem extempore (i.e., made up on the spot) on any one of a succession of subjects proposed by Censor, who suggests as topics self-sufficiency, war and, finally, the use of time (see Doody, *Frances Burney: The Life in the Works*, p. 85).

25. *fort*: 'Fort' for *forte*, strong point; Frances Burney evidently considers this a mis-pronunciation by Coverley, although correct pronunciation varies, depending on whether one derives the word from French or Italian.

26. *Fates*: A classical allusion; in Greek and Roman mythology the three Fates are Clotho, Lachesis and Atropos.

27. *my Swiss*: The 'Swiss' here is Lord Merton's Swiss servant; he rejoices in a Continental valet.

28. *cutting them up*: Making fun of them by cutting wit.

29. *a kind of a toad-eater*: A 'toad-eater' or 'toady' is a hanger-on who flatters another in return for benefits, including subsistence, like the female 'humble companion' of a rich lady. The term is supposedly derived from the activity of the assistant to a mountebank, who would eat toads in order to show how he could be cured of the effects of the toad's supposed venom by the quack's elixir. Frances Burney is very sensitive to the ways in which women are put into the position of 'toad-eater'; cf. the discussion in *The Wanderer* in which the shocked Giles Arbe learns 'what is

meant ... by a toad-eater' and concludes that a 'toad-eater-maker'
is still worse. (*The Wanderer*, ed. Margaret Anne Doody, Robert L.
Mack and Peter Sabor (Oxford, 1991), III, pp. 520–24)

30. *lampoon*: A personal satire against an individual; in 'The Witlings'
only the fear of Censor's lampoon makes Lady Smatter agree to
her nephew's marriage to the heroine.

31. *the New Bath Guide*: *The New Bath Guide: Or Memoirs of the B–N–
R–D Family. In a Series of Poetical Epistles* (1766), a comic work in
verse by Christopher Anstey (1724–1805). The light-hearted verses
(in varying metres) give satirical pictures of type characters in the
typical activities of a watering place. Gambling is among the
subjects, as in the epistle by the simple Mr. Simkin B–N–R–D to
his mother:

> A sum my dear mother, far heavier yet,
> Captain CORMORANT won when I learn'd lansquenet;
> Two hundred I paid him, and five am in debt.
> For the five I had nothing to do but to *write*,
> For the Captain was very well bred and polite,
> And took, as he saw my expences were great,
> My bond, to be paid on the *Clodpole* estate;

(edn. 10, 1776, p. 136)

32. *post-office*: The servant failed to find out Macartney's address at
the Pump-room (where the fashionable registered themselves) and,
evidently, went on his own initiative to enquire at the post office,
where the penny post was officially handled. According to the
Bristol and Hotwell Guide of 1793, the post office for Clifton was
at the Clifton Hotel; inns and hotels were customarily central post
offices because the post carriages could stop there for fresh horses.
The principal post office for Bristol was next to the Exchange.

33. *romantic*: 'Romantic' not in the erotic sense but meaning irrational,
foolishly unpractical and ill-considered.

34. *pencil*: This 'pencil' is a slender, fine paintbrush, not the writing
implement, hence 'dipped in vivid colours'; Evelina's 'new comrade', her imagination, has acted like a colourful painter.

35. *bet on his side*: Italics indicate quotation (transposed to third
person); Frances Burney evidently considers this and 'take sides'
below as a kind of sporting slang, although the expressions were
established.

36. *They handed ... to exert themselves*: The foot-race (including its set-

ting and arrangements) is not incredible given the rage of the time for staging races and other events on which wagers could be laid; see Earl R. Anderson, 'Footnotes more Pedestrian than Sublime: A Historical Background for the Foot-races in *Evelina* and *Humphry Clinker*', *Eighteenth-century Studies*, 14 (Fall, 1980), pp. 56–68.

37. *hollow thing*: Colloquialism for complete affair, an unquestionable victory; *OED* gives 1750 as date of first use of 'hollow' for 'complete, thorough, out-and-out'.

38. *unlucky turn at an epigram*: An unfortunate talent or aptitude for uttering a pointed and witty expression.

39. *grasping at a shadow you'll lose a substance*: Proverbial expression arising from Aesop's fable about a dog with meat in his mouth who snaps at his reflection.

40. *Lord Orville presented tickets to the whole family ... dance with me*: Contrast the conduct of Mr. Smith in II, pp. 244–5.

41. *Lord Orville began the minuets*: The minuet, the most formal of dances, began the evening; in 1791 the 'Established Rules' of the assemblies held at the Assembly Room in Princes Street, the Hotwell, required '*That the minuets begin at half past six o'clock, and end at eight, when country dances are to commence*' (*Bristol and Hotwell Guide*, p. 50). The persons of highest rank present were supposed to dance the first minuet; the Master of Ceremonies evidently introduced Lord Orville, the gentleman of highest rank, to Miss Belmont as a lady of high rank and an heiress worthy of his attention. Lord Merton and Lady Louisa, who would also have the claim of rank, are in no humour to dance.

42. *after-marriage*: A second marriage, i.e., of Sir John Belmont to a second wife after the death of Evelina's mother.

43. *pamphlet-shop*: Shop selling unbound pamphlets (and probably newspapers); humbler and more specialized than the more elegant booksellers' shops or libraries, which were established places for ladies to while away the time (cf. *Camilla, or A Picture of Youth*, ed. Edward A. Bloom and Lillian D. Bloom (Oxford, 1972), I, pp. 99–104). Mrs. Selwyn is a serious reader who keeps up with current literature, and displays her masculine taste also in her interest in pamphlets which were largely on politics and current affairs (cf. Jane Austen's *Northanger Abbey*, ed. Anne Ehrenpreis (Penguin Books, 1972), pp. 190–91).

44. *to-morrow morning*: By 'morning' Lord Orville means, not the time before noon, but the fashionable morning, used for making morn-

ing calls, a time which extended to the dinner hour, which was now four or five o'clock. Lord Orville can thus invite Macartney to pay a brief call at three o'clock in the afternoon (still 'morning') when people will be dressing for dinner and thus not likely to intrude on Macartney and Evelina.

45. *certificate of your birth*: There was not the modern official apparatus for supplying these forms (or the demand for them), but such a certificate could be had from the parish clergyman where one had been baptized, and could be carried for identification. It seems highly indelicate of Mrs. Selwyn to mention such a document to Evelina, whose birth is under a cloud.

46. *I pulled my hat over my face*: The fashionable straw hats with a wide front brim would allow Evelina to shield her face thus; she is, of course, wearing a hat, see I, p. 100.

47. *milliner's ... caps and ribbons*: Milliners sold not only hats and bonnets but also ribbons and other accessories. In Frances Burney's unpublished work, 'The Witlings', the first act is set in a milliner's shop: 'A Counter is spread with Caps, Ribbons, Fans & Band Boxes.' Shoppers and time-wasters, including men, come in, look over Mrs. Wheedle's 'little tasty things' and disarrange the goods ('The Witlings', I). In her last novel, *The Wanderer*, the heroine herself works in a milliner's shop (chs. 45-7).

48. *the Venus to whom the prize is given*: Reference to the contest between three goddesses, Hera, Athena and Aphrodite (or Venus) which Paris was called upon to decide; he gave the prize for beauty to the goddess of love, who rewarded him with Helen, the most beautiful woman.

49. *termagant*: Originally the name for a violent deity who, medieval Christians imagined, was worshipped by Muslims, hence any loud, violent personage, particularly a scolding woman.

50. *the Graces*: Aglaia, Thalia and Euphrosyne, sister goddesses who bestow grace and charm; they 'seek' Miss Anville as a model, instead of the mortal seeking their aid, as is usually the case.

51. *John Trot style*: Limited, ordinary, going through life at a jogtrot.

52. *still-life*: 'Still-life' is a term from painting, referring to representations of flowers, game, fruit, dishes, etc. in the style made popular by Dutch painters of the seventeenth century; the term, however, is used jocularly with a wide reference in eighteenth-century English, referring to persons, places and manners that are lacking in animation, or merely dull.

53. *loadstone*: 'Loadstone' (or 'lodestone') is 'magnetic oxide of iron;

a piece of this used as a magnet' (*OED*). Used metaphorically for anything that attracts. A 'general loadstone' attracts all.

54. *stayed supper*: We would say 'stayed to supper'; the party takes this last late meal (probably around ten o'clock) at home, and not at the Assembly.

55. *odium of a title ... dishonour*: The 'title' here is the unwanted 'title' (or name) of bastard.

56. *reprobate*: To reprobate something or someone is to reject it (her) utterly, to cast out.

57. *like a cypher*: Like a nonentity, literally like a zero.

58. *nervous to the last degree*: The party of females will be characterized by excessive disorder of the nerves – or does Mrs. Selwyn mean that she does not want to go in an all-female party because the superlative femininity will get on her nerves?

59. *first airing from the herald's-office*: Her first trip away from the office of the Herald's College, 'a royal corporation ... consisting of the Earl Marshal, kings-of-arms, heralds and pursuivants ... recording proved pedigrees and granting armorial bearings' (*OED*). Mrs. Beaumont is as proud as someone who has just been granted inclusion in the ranks of the nobility or gentry.

60. *plague, pestilence, and famine*: Recollection of Rev. 6.

61. *virago*: A man like woman, loud and overbearing, cf. 'termagant', n. 49 above.

62. *sure ground*: Safe and certain ground, like terrain taken from an enemy; Sir Clement is not going to assert that he is certain of Evelina's affection, but believes that if he perseveres she will give in.

63. *he almost exhausted himself ... to entertain me*: See I, p. 39.

64. *like the servants in the Drummer*: *The Drummer; or, The Haunted House*, Joseph Addison's only stage comedy, was first produced at Drury Lane in March 1716; it had been revived in the 1770s. The Burney children, their stepsisters and some friends, put on *The Drummer* in their own amateur performance in October 1771, when inspired by the forthcoming revival for a royal command performance. Frances played Lady Truman (see *EJL*, I, pp. 171–2). The allusion here refers to the opening of Act V.

65. *danglers*: The followers of a lady, not attached to her by any firm commitment. Charlotte Grandison says, 'One wants now-and-then a *dangling* fellow or two after one in public' (*Sir Charles Grandison*, III, p. 86).

66. *to write to me ... answer his letters*: This, to Lord Orville, is (as it

should be) a serious sign of their engagement to marry; young ladies were not supposed to correspond with gentlemen to whom they were not related except in the circumstances of engagement. Evelina formerly broke that rule, and feels that Lord Orville punished her for her ignorant forwardness.

67. *calash*: A large hood supported by hoops, popular in the period.

68. *to tip us a touch of the heroicks this morning*: Mr. Coverley speaks in comic slang; 'to tip' in this sense (from thieves' slang) means to represent or impersonate: Sir Clement is offering a sample of what he can do in the heroic style, like a stage tragedian.

69. *almanack*: Now spelled 'almanac': a calendar giving not only the days of the month and week, but other important information such as times of the moon and tides. There were pocket diaries and almanacs, which explains Mr. Coverley's reference to keeping 'such a time-keeper in my pocket'.

70. *state of the moon . . . this morning*: Mrs. Selwyn indicates jokingly that the odd behaviour of various members of the party could be explained if the moon was full – as the full moon was thought to affect the mind and bring on fits of insanity (a belief still current).

71. *pursued by the Furies*: The Furies, euphemistically known as the Eumenides, are traditionally three female deities (Tisiphone, Megaera, Alecto) who come from the nether world to punish human crimes.

72. *blush, as the saying is, like a blue dog*: The traditional saying is actually 'To blush like a black dog,' but Swift, in *A Complete Collection of Polite and Ingenious Conversation* (1738), has 'Blush! ay, blush like a blue dog' (Tilley, *Dictionary of Proverbs*, p. 167). Frances Burney evidently got her version of the saying from Swift's *Polite Conversation*, a work she knew very well (see *The Life in the Works*, pp. 48–9).

73. *senator*: Lord Merton is a 'senator' in the sense that he is a member of the governing body, Parliament, because of his noble rank.

74. *your House . . . we of the lower House*: By 'your House' Lovel means the House of Lords, to which Lord Merton belongs; the 'lower House' is the House of Commons, to which Lovel has been elected. The two Houses together compose Parliament.

75. *Amazon*: Female warrior of Greek myth and story; 'Amazon' is a derogatory name for a strong woman, like 'termagant' and 'virago'. See above, ns. 49; 61.

76. *chop logic*: Coverley puns on two different meanings of the verb

'to chop'. 'Chop' in 'chop logic' has the sense of 'barter' or 'bandy', and not of 'cut'. One who 'chops logic' is one who is able to participate in an exchange of argument about subtleties; traditionally, logic-choppers are over-subtle, or pedantic.

77. *Swift's hospital of ideots*: Mrs. Selwyn may be thinking of the hospital for the imbecilic and insane that Swift founded in his will, and to which he caustically refers in 'Verses on the Death of Dr. Swift': 'He gave the little Wealth he had, / To build a House for Fools and Mad:' (*Poetical Works: Jonathan Swift*, ed. Herbert Davis (Oxford, 1967), p. 512). But it is more likely that Mrs. Selwyn is alluding to the madhouse described in Swift's *A Tale of a Tub* (1704).

78. *oddish*: The word 'oddish', which fits in with the slovenly inaccuracy and the hesitancy of Lovel's speech, seems to be a nonce-word.

79. *waiter*: 'A salver, small tray, 1738' (*OED*).

80. *hesitate to acknowledge me*: In third edition, 'hesitate acknowledge'. ·

81. *Stoic*: In general popular sense, a 'Stoic' is one who is impervious to human passion; the philosophic Stoics emphasized control of the passions and their transcendence in the name of true virtue and a higher sense of the good.

82. *black annals of Nero or Caligula*: Mrs. Selwyn resorts with pardonable hyperbole to horrific accounts of the worst excesses of the worst of the Roman emperors; Caligula (AD 12–41) possibly caused the death of his predecessor Tiberius and, upon his accession to empire, amazed the Roman world by his extravagance and conceit. Nero (AD 37–68) was even more bloodthirsty, killing not only Britannicus, his rival, but also his own mother Agrippina, and later his wife Poppea. Many attributed to him the great fire of Rome (AD 64) for which Nero himself blamed the Christians, whom he persecuted ruthlessly.

83. *a tribute of fame*: The 'tribute of fame' is here the owed offering of good fame, good reputation; Sir John has done justice to his first wife's memory at last by restoring her reputation.

84. *hair-dresser*: The hair-dresser visits Sir John in his own chamber to powder and possibly curl his hair, or, more likely to shave his head and arrange and curl his wig.

85. *natural friends*: The term 'natural friends' may seem to us like a contradiction, but in eighteenth-century usage one's 'friends' were not primarily chosen companions of sympathetic personality but those persons who were bound to one in a particular benevolent

relationship. Hence, the primary 'friends' of any person are close relatives; Evelina has been rejected by those who stood in a relationship of benevolence to her by right of birth, that is, by all of her father's family.

86. *courting the rural shades*: Mrs. Selwyn teases Evelina with mock-poetic language; noting that Evelina and Lord Orville look like the conventional lovers in a pastoral poem, she rallies Evelina with seeking the retirement of a natural nook (Mrs. Beaumont's arbour) as if she were a shepherdess courting under the shade of a pastoral tree.

87. *Quixotism*: 'Quixotism' (from Cervantes' *Don Quixote*) had come to signify unpractical idealism and generosity.

88. *carried into the house*: 'Carried' here does not mean that Evelina was lifted bodily up by someone else, but merely that she was led or conducted into the house.

89. *but she has set my brain on fire, and I can see her no more!*: Compare the breakdown of Mrs. Delvile 'who, striking her hand upon her forehead, cried "My brain is on fire!" and rushed out of the room' (*Cecilia*, IV, p. 680).

90. *Dame Green*: 'Dame' is a courtesy title given to respectable working women of the lowest class, most particularly those who possess some little property and set up in a line of work on their own account (hence 'dame school').

91. *such a fraud*: Dame Green would be subject to the penalties of the law (presumably culminating in transportation) for perpetrating such a fraud upon property and inheritance, but the injured party (Sir John) could not bear to inflict the pain upon his family that the necessary trial would cause, so there is no real attempt to punish the nurse.

92. *Countess*: At last we find out Orville's exact rank. If his wife will be a 'Countess' he is evidently an Earl; the word 'Count' is used in English only for male holders of foreign titles, an exception which applies even to the term 'Count Palatine'. Ironically, Frances Burney herself was to become, late in life, a 'Countess' or rather a *Comtesse*, by the title conferred on her husband by Louis XVIII.

93. *country seats*: Lord Orville is indeed wealthy if he has more than one grand estate in the country; the term 'seat', however, is normally used only of the principal and most ancient holding, and a family, however greatly propertied, should have only one seat.

94. *Bantling of Dame Green*: A 'bantling' is a brat, with the primary meaning of 'bastard'. We know nothing of the impostor's father.

In a later unacted and unpublished play, 'The Woman Hater', Frances Burney uses a similar story, basing the interest of the drama on the reactions of the young impostor, Joyce, who discovers she is the daughter of her old nurse and a shoemaker.

95. *Thursday*: Frances Burney apparently recalls the novels of Samuel Richardson, whose heroines Pamela and Harriet both marry on a Thursday; Harriet Byron is pushed into a wedding on 'Thursday, next week' with almost as little time for adjustment as Evelina (see Richardson, *Sir Charles Grandison*, III, p. 191).

96. *settlements*: The sums to be settled on the wife and her children should the wife outlive her husband; settlements were arranged in a pre-nuptial contract, but the making of that contract was the business of the bride's male relatives and their agents, not of the bride herself, and Evelina exhibits due modesty in refusing to deal with the financial side of her marriage. Only women whose families had property could expect money to be settled on them.

97. *not ... defiance ... indirect channel*: Sir Clement means that the remarks he sends to Lord Orville through Evelina are not to be construed as a challenge; he would not send a challenge to a duel through a third party, but he is able to explain his conduct to Lord Orville's face, if his rival will see him. (As Evelina realizes, such an explanation could still lead to a duel.)

98. *those people he saw me with at Marybone*: The term *those people* seems to refer to the prostitutes (with whom Lord Orville first saw Evelina at Marylebone Gardens) rather than to the odd party made up by Mr. Brown, the prostitutes, Madame Duval and the Miss Branghtons (II, pp. 259–66). See Lord Orville's question, II, p. 267.

99. *draught*: More commonly 'draft'.

100. *Bath*: Bath, about twelve miles from Bristol, the largest and most fashionable spa, in the autumn, at the very beginning of its season. Frances Burney had not yet seen Bath: her sister and brother-in-law invited her to stay with them in Bath in 1773, but she could not go (*EJL*, I, p. 230–31). She was to visit it with the Thrales in the spring of 1780.

101. *good case*: In good physical condition.

102. *won't flinch ... made tight*: Captain Mirvan's rude speech treats Madame Duval as an old vessel that has been refitted in port, has had planking repaired, and been caulked, etc. so as to keep out water ('made tight') and can now be called upon again, like a warship, to see some more 'service'.

103. *new-fashioned jig*: A new kind of dance; Captain Mirvan draws on the idea of dancing at Evelina's wedding to indicate that he has invented some new torture for the girl's grandmother.

104. *take something*: Have some refreshment; said by a man, this would indicate a desire for alcoholic refreshment, but we may believe Lady Louisa is only thinking of a little luncheon.

105. *rambles*: Excursions made purely for pleasure, without any seriously-defined objective; rambling can be said to be an eighteenth-century invention in the era's attention to travelling for amusement.

106. *a'n't you the person . . . at the play . . . concert of fiddlers?*: See I, pp. 89–90.

107. *by Jingo*: Euphemism for blasphemous expression, supposedly derived from a conjuror's expression (like 'hey presto'); Urquhart and Motteux popularized an expression more Scottish than English by translating Rabelais' 'par Dieu' as 'by Jingo'.

108. *the Crescent*: The Royal Crescent, designed by John Wood the Younger; this magnificent semi-circle or ellipse (over 600 feet long) of town houses took about eight years to complete (it was begun in 1767), and is commonly thought one of the triumphs of European domestic architecture. Houses in the Royal Crescent commanded a fine view.

109. *The Circus*: The King's Circus, designed by John Wood the Elder, begun in 1754; a beautiful pattern of town houses, built in a circle.

110. *The Parades*: North Parade and South Parade. Frances Burney stayed in South Parade during her visit with the Thrales. She was later to live in Bath (in Gay Street) and is buried in Wolcot Churchyard in Bath, with her husband and son.

111. *Prior Park*: Prior Park, about one mile south-east of Bath, the estate of Ralph Allen, with a Palladian house designed for him by John Wood the Elder in 1743. Ralph Allen (d. 1764), the original for Mr. Allworthy in Fielding's *Tom Jones*, had entertained eminent gentlemen such as Pope and Fielding, so his house and grounds had – and have – literary associations.

112. *public exhibition of the ladies in the bath*: Ladies and gentlemen entered the bath together, and walked about in it in a manner some thought shameful, even though the ladies wore special clothes for the occasion and kept headgear on, as Evelina notices. For another description, see Smollett's *Humphry Clinker*, as his character Lydia Melford depicts the scene:

Right under the Pump-room windows is the King's Bath; a huge cistern, where you see the patients up to their necks in hot water. The ladies wear jackets and petticoats of brown linen, with chip hats . . . but truly . . . they look so flushed, and so frightful, that I always turn my eyes another way—My aunt, who says every person of fashion should make her appearance in the bath, as well as in the abbey church, contrived a cap with cherry-coloured ribbons to suit her complexion, and obliged Win to attend her yesterday morning in the water. (*Humphry Clinker* (Penguin Books, 1967), pp. 68–9)

113. *fandango*: Spanish word for 'a lively dance in 3/4 time' (*OED*), perhaps ultimately of African origin; here, any wild fantastic dance.

114. *tabby*: Richardson, or his Lovelace in *Clarissa*, seems to be the originator of 'tabby' in this sense i.e., old maid or elderly female: 'The two antiques only bowed their tabby heads' (*Clarissa* (Penguin Books, 1985), p. 1026). 'Hadst thou seen how the two tabbies, and the young grimalkins, looked at one another?' (Ibid., p. 1032)

115. *frightful . . . dress to bathe in*: The 'jackets and petticoats of brown linen' described by Smollett in the Bath scenes in *Humphry Clinker*; see above, n. 112.

116. *ton*: French word frequently used in English to mean fashion or style, also the people of fashion, wealthy and well-bred persons of taste who set the social tone; *beau monde*: Literally 'beautiful world', *beau monde* means 'the fashionable world'.

117. *snuff of a candle*: The burnt-out wick of a candle, something most worthless.

118. *frizle-frize top*: Evidently Frances Burney's coinage, an emphatic way of saying that Lovel's hair has been frizzed, or put into curls by the hairdresser, whose repeated efforts have raised Lovel's hair most artificially.

119. *fat and grease enough on your crown*: Fashions in hair for both sexes required a high build-up of hair (see above, I, n. 51; II, n. 16). Artificial hair could be woven in with real hair, the whole stuck together with grease (goose grease, lard or even bear's grease), which also served to fix the powder, made of grain flour, scented (e.g. with orris root) and available in several colours (white, grey, yellow and blue were common). See C. Willett and P. Cunnington, *Handbook*, p. 95.

120. *tetotum*: Usually 'teetotum' (originally 'T totum'); a small four-sided die, each face with a letter upon it, and a spindle passing through the cube so it could be spun. The teetotum was used in word games and in fortune-telling games; the word came to mean any whirligig of the kind.

121. *dining in his riding-dress*: Mr. Lovel belongs to the upper classes who dress for dinner; in accepting the unexpected invitation to dine, he cannot change his apparel, but he breaches true good manners by calling attention at length to the fact.

122. *person of any condition*: Person of an important rank or status.

123. *right season*: The best season for going to Bath would be in the winter.

124. *zest*: A term taken from cookery, where it means orange and lemon peel used for flavour, hence anything giving spice or savour; Lord Merton's use seems to add the extra meaning of that which supplies keen relish or enthusiasm, 'gusto', a significance *OED* dates as first appearing in 1791.

125. *candid*: Being fair in judgement, making disinterested allowance for all, without prejudice; candour was a prized quality in the eighteenth century.

126. *St James's to Wapping*: From St. James's Palace, the ancient centre of courtly life in London and the heart of the West End, to Wapping, the dockyard area in the East End. Captain Mirvan is probably very well acquainted with Wapping, the site of warehouses and ships' stores and shops (including brothels) catering to sailors, as well as Execution Dock where pirates were hanged. Wapping is not an area to which Evelina ever ventures.

127. *lend you a box o' the ear*: Give you a blow on the ear; Fielding records a similar use of 'lend' in threats of blows, in West Country dialect of Squire Western in *Tom Jones*.

128. *kiss and friends*: A common formula used after a quarrel of any kind, more commonly rendered as 'kiss and be friends,' here used sarcastically.

129. *Monsieur Clapperclaw*: To 'clapperclaw' is to strike with open hand and nails, 'to revile' (*OED*).

130. *messmate*: From seaman's use, someone who eats with one at the ship's meal, or mess.

131. *slit of the ear . . . pillory*: The pillory, an apparatus which imprisoned head and hands, immobilizing the prisoner in a public place, was still a criminal penalty used as a means of degradation for offenders

against decency, including homosexuals (although the penalty for sodomy itself was hanging) and writers who had offended the government – most notably Defoe in 1703. The old penalties that ordered the ears of seditious persons to be slit were rarely enforced although, as William Blackstone noted in 1769, such penalties still remained on the books: 'Some [punishments] though rarely, occasion a mutilation or dismembring [sic], by cutting off the hand or ears; others fix a lasting stigma on the offender, by slitting the nostrils, or branding on the hand or face' (Blackstone, *Commentaries on the Laws of England*, fac. of 1st edn., 4 vols. (Chicago: University of Chicago Press, 1979), IV, p. 370).

132. *anti-ministerial writer*: The war with the colonies, begun in 1776, had renewed the government's interest in penalties for anything it could call 'seditious libel', any written expression of hostility to government measures. The ministry in 1778 was led by Lord North, whose indecisiveness was frequently faulted; the great Pitt, Lord Chatham, died in the spring of 1778, and a lack of present leadership was remarked on. The cabinet were distracted by resignations and problems with Ireland, as well as the war with America and France.

133. *my new riding-suit*: A man's suit consisted of breeches, coat and waistcoat; it was the fashion in the 1770s and 1790s for these to be made of different materials, in different colours. The 'riding-suit' would include a pair of long breeches to be worn with top boots, and a 'riding frock', a frock coat, short and divided, the skirts already caught back or able easily to be flung back out of the rider's way (see C. Willett and P. Cunnington, *Handbook*, p. 217; pp. 226-7).

134. *wearing a wig*: Wigs were going out of style, and the newer styles involved the torturing and plastering of one's own hair, as Lovel exhibits with his 'frizle-frize top' (see p. 437).

135. *pink him*: To 'pink' someone is to stab him with a poniard or sword, punch a hole in him.

136. *put up with such an affront*: Coverley means that Lovel is bound to fight a duel with Mirvan.

137. *Furbelow's*: A 'furbelow' is originally a flounce, it became synonymous with any kind of trimming.

138. *go her snacks*: To 'go her snacks' is a slangy way of saying 'come in for her share'.

CHRONOLOGY

1747–8	Courtship of Charles Burney, musician (companion and officially apprentice of Fulke Greville), and Esther Sleepe, daughter of James Sleepe of Foster Lane, London, and his wife, née Dubois.
1749	*May*: Birth of Esther (Hester) Burney, first child of CB and Esther Sleepe.
	25 June: Marriage of Charles Burney and Esther Sleepe.
1750	Birth of FB's brother James (eventually to be Captain, later Rear-Admiral, Burney).
1751	CB goes to King's Lynn, Norfolk, (in part to ward off suspected consumption in a better air); takes post as organist at St Margaret's Church.
1752	*13 June*: Frances Burney born, King's Lynn, Norfolk.
1755	Birth of Susanna Elizabeth Burney, FB's sister and closest confidante.
1757	Birth of FB's favourite brother Charles.
1760	Burney family removes to Poland Street, London; James sent to sea, on man of war *Princess Amelia*.
1761	Birth of FB's youngest full sister, Charlotte.
1761/62	Esther Sleepe Burney visits Bristol Hotwells for health.
1762	*27 September*: Death of Esther Sleepe Burney; James transferred to the *Boston*.
1764	FB's sisters Esther (Hester) and Susanna sent to France for education; FB partly in care of grandmother Dubois.
1766	*Summer*: Hester Burney returns from France. Susanna returns slightly later.
1767	*13 June*: FB and her sister Susanna burn all her early works, including 'History of Caroline Evelyn'.
	2 October: Secret marriage of CB and widow Elizabeth Allen, mother of three children: Maria, Stephen and Elizabeth (Bessy).
1768	*27 March*: FB begins writing new journal.
	20 November: Birth of half-brother Richard.

1769   *23 June*: CB receives degree of Doctor of Music at Oxford.

1770   *September*: Marriage of sister Hester and cousin Charles Rousseau Burney, musician.

1772   *May*: Secret marriage of stepsister Maria Allen to Martin Rishton, in Ypres.

    July: Brother James departs on Captain James Cooke's second expedition as a sailor.

    29 August: Birth of FB's half-sister Sarah Harriet.

    November: James made second lieutenant of the *Adventure*.

1774   CB moves family to house in St Martin's Street, Leicester Square (formerly Isaac Newton's home; FB works as CB's amanuensis and research assistant.

1775   FB badgered by unwanted marriage proposals from Thomas Barlow.

1776   FB's stepmother Elizabeth Allen Burney goes to Bristol Hotwells for her health, with husband CB and his daughter Charlotte.

    August: James joins Captain Cook's expedition for three-year voyage to Pacific.

    Negotiations with booksellers, with help of brother Charles and cousin Edward Francesco, for sale of 'a MS novel'. Dodsley rejects.

1777   *January*: Thomas Lowndes expresses interest in novel; refuses to publish until third volume completed.

    October: FB's stepsister Elizabeth (Bessy) Allen, in Paris for education, elopes with Mr Meeke. Brother Charles expelled from Caius College, Cambridge, for stealing books from library.

    FB completes third volume of *Evelina*, revises, and copies the whole in 'feigned hand', as FB's own handwriting too well known to printers. FB deals with Lowndes under the pseudonym 'Mr Grafton'.

1778   *29 January: Evelina* published, without CB's knowledge. Author paid 20 guineas. Favourable reviews in *London Review* (February) and *Monthly Review* (April).

    June: FB confesses to CB that she is author of the novel. Four editions by end of 1779.

1778–84   Friendship with Dr Samuel Johnson and the Thrales. FB encouraged by dramatists Arthur Murphy and Richard

Brinsley Sheridan to write a play; FB works on *The Witlings*.

1779   *May*: *The Witlings* completed.

August: CB and Samuel Crisp decry, and decree suppression.

1782   *January*: Marriage of Susanna Burney to Molesworth Phillips.

12 July: Publication of *Cecilia, or Memoirs of an Heiress*.

1784   *July*: Estrangement from Hester Lynch Salusbury Thrale over her marriage to Gabriel Piozzi.

20 December: Death of Samuel Johnson.

1785   FB's half-brother Richard considered disgraced, sent to India.

1786   *July*: FB reluctantly enters court service as Assistant Keeper of the Robes to Queen Charlotte.

1788   King George III's first serous bout of madness. Courtiers confined. FB begins *Edwy and Elgiva*.

1790   Completes *Edwy and Elgiva*, begins *Hubert de Vere* and *The Siege of Pevensey*.

1791   Begins writing *Elberta*.

7 July: Escapes from court under plea of ill health; Queen grants her a pension of 100*l*. p.a.

1793   *28 July*: Marries Alexandre d'Arblay, émigré, exiled Adjutant-General of the Marquis de Lafayette. Kemble accepts *Hubert de Vere* for Drury Lane (later withdrawn and *Edwy and Elgiva* substituted).

November: Charitable appeal in pamphlet *Brief Reflections Relative to the Emigrant French Clergy*.

1794   *18 December*: Birth of son and only child, Alexander.

1795   *21 March*: Failed production of *Edwy and Elgiva* at Drury Lane Theatre, with Mrs Siddons and John Philip Kemble in title roles.

1796   *12 July*: Publication of *Camilla, or a Picture of Youth*, by subscription. Molesworth Phillips removes himself and Susanna to Ireland, against her wishes.

October: Elizabeth Allen Burney, stepmother, dies.

1798   *1 March*: Charlotte marries Ralph Broome, against family's wishes. FB writing comedy *Love and Fashion*.

2 September: Brother James and half-sister Sarah Harriet elope together.

1799	Thomas Harris, manager of Covent Garden theatre, offers 400*l.* for *Love and Fashion*, intending production in March 1800.
1800	*6 January*: Death of beloved sister Susanna. Play withdrawn.
1800–1802	Writing of late comedies *The Woman-Hater* and *A Busy Day*.
1802	Husband General d'Arblay returns to France during Peace of Amiens.
	April: FB follows with child. Renewal of hostilities of Napoleonic wars entails prolonged sojourn in France
1811	*30 September*: FB undergoes a mastectomy.
1812	Return to England, with son and unfinished MS of *The Wanderer*.
1814	*28 March*: Publication of *The Wanderer*.
	12 April: Death of father.
	Son Alexander enters Cambridge.
1815	FB crosses Channel to Belgium.
	June: Husband fighting in allied army against Napoleon; FB in town of Waterloo during battle.
	October: D'Arblays return to England.
	Removal to Bath.
1817	*December*: Death of brother Charles Burney.
1818	*3 May*: Death of husband Alexandre, in Bath.
	Burial in Walcot Churchyard. FB returns to London.
	October: FB takes house at 11 Bolton Street, Piccadilly.
	Preparation of *Memoirs of Dr Burney*.
1819	Son Alexander ordained priest in the Church of England.
1821	*November*: Death of brother James.
1832	*February*: Death of sister Esther Burney Burney.
	November: *Memoirs of Doctor Burney* (3 volumes) published.
1837	*19 January*: Death of son Alexander.
1838	*12 September*: Death of sister Charlotte Broome.
1840	*6 January*: Death of Frances née Burney, comtesse d'Arblay; buried in Walcot Churchyard, Bath, beside husband and son.

READ MORE IN PENGUIN

In every corner of the world, on every subject under the sun, Penguin represents quality and variety – the very best in publishing today.

For complete information about books available from Penguin – including Puffins, Penguin Classics and Arkana – and how to order them, write to us at the appropriate address below. Please note that for copyright reasons the selection of books varies from country to country.

In the United Kingdom: Please write to *Dept. EP, Penguin Books Ltd, Bath Road, Harmondsworth, West Drayton, Middlesex UB7 0DA*

In the United States: Please write to *Consumer Services, Penguin Putnam Inc., 405 Murray Hill Parkway, East Rutherford, New Jersey 07073-2136.* VISA and MasterCard holders call 1-800-631-8571 to order Penguin titles

In Canada: Please write to *Penguin Books Canada Ltd, 10 Alcorn Avenue, Suite 300, Toronto, Ontario M4V 3B2*

In Australia: Please write to *Penguin Books Australia Ltd, 487 Maroondah Highway, Ringwood, Victoria 3134*

In New Zealand: Please write to *Penguin Books (NZ) Ltd, Private Bag 102902, North Shore Mail Centre, Auckland 10*

In India: Please write to *Penguin Books India Pvt Ltd, 11 Community Centre, Panchsheel Park, New Delhi 110017*

In the Netherlands: Please write to *Penguin Books Netherlands bv, Postbus 3507, NL-1001 AH Amsterdam*

In Germany: Please write to *Penguin Books Deutschland GmbH, Metzlerstrasse 26, 60594 Frankfurt am Main*

In Spain: Please write to *Penguin Books S. A., Bravo Murillo 19, 1°B, 28015 Madrid*

In Italy: Please write to *Penguin Italia s.r.l., Via Vittorio Emanuele 45/a, 20094 Corsico, Milano*

In France: Please write to *Penguin France, 12, Rue Prosper Ferradou, 31700 Blagnac*

In Japan: Please write to *Penguin Books Japan Ltd, Iidabashi KM-Bldg, 2-23-9 Koraku, Bunkyo-Ku, Tokyo 112-0004*

In South Africa: Please write to *Penguin Books South Africa (Pty) Ltd, P.O. Box 751093, Gardenview, 2047 Johannesburg*